RUNEFROST

BOOK TWO OF THE SILVERLINE CHRONICLES

SANAN KOLVA

ISBN: 978-1-7325872-9-8 (ebook)

ISBN: 979-8-9868952-0-8 (paperback)

Cover design: damonza.com

https://sanankolva.com

In memory of Joseph
With special thanks to Krystal, Luke, and Chelsey. You're awesome.

CHAPTER 1

When the first hints of fresh ocean air reached him, Alistar threw open the carriage windows and leaned out, drawing a deep breath. His mouth curled in a grin at the familiar smell of home as the spring wind teased at his black hair and beard.

On the bench facing Alistar, his wife, Saskia laughed, her slanted brown eyes dancing. She shook her head, making her strawberry blonde curls bob. "Every time we visit your family, I wonder how you survive living in Lewarden without an ocean in sight."

Alistar chuckled. When he'd first moved to Lewarden, capital city of Calarand, five years ago, he'd wondered the same thing many times. Some days, even passion for his work hadn't seemed like enough, and only pride and a refusal to admit defeat had stopped him from returning home. Now, though, Lewarden was as much his home as Rillwater.

"Well, the capital has certain advantages, such as my career. I do miss the ocean, though. Just smell the air!"

Much as he enjoyed sailing and the life of a privateer, Alistar had, against his mother's objections, pursued a vocation far from ships and plunder when he chose to become a magic power engineer with Silverline Power Cooperative. Founded and owned by Prince Cero Feyblade, the Silver Prince, younger brother to His Majesty, King Suelton Feyblade, Silverline Power produced and distributed the magic that fueled all of Lewarden, from factories to homes. Although rumors rose on occasion about Silverline Power expanding beyond the limits of Lewarden, for now, Alistar's career required that he remain in the capital.

And after events two winters ago, when Alistar thwarted saboteurs' attempts to not only subvert the magic for their own purposes, but also stage a coup, that career had, unofficially, gained the favor of the Crown. Alistar rarely interacted directly with Prince Cero now, but he knew the prime assignments frequently given to him rather than to engineers with greater seniority marked him as being in the Silver Prince's favor. It was a mixed blessing, especially considering the snarls that plagued his most recent assignment.

The carriage drew into the port city of Rillwater, home to the infamous privateering fleet that safeguarded the waters of Calarand. Throughout the land, the name of Admiral As'enel struck fear and awe in nobles and commoners alike. Often enough, Alistar had heard retellings of the wildly inflated tales from two-chip novels. Aside from the admiral, few knew any of Rillwater's other figures of note. Even members of the Lewarden nobility would be hard-pressed to name another noble family of Rillwater. All reasons why Alistar chose to use his matronym, De'seneth, in his engineering career rather than the infamous admiral's surname.

The streets always bustled with activity. People paused to study the unfamiliar carriage, exchanging whispers. Alistar leaned out the window and waved, calling out to people he recognized. Their faces brightened when they saw him. Those he greeted returned the welcome warmly, and the people who didn't recognize him took their cues from the rest.

Their driver, a native of Rillwater himself, deftly guided the team of horses through the crowd and onto the drive leading up to the largest estate in the city. No matter how many times Alistar told himself to relax, lean back, not to worry, tension still crept up his spine and across his shoulders when he faced the house where he had been raised and he would one day inherit.

Saskia gave him a warm, confident smile. "I'm looking forward to seeing your parents."

"They always enjoy seeing you." Alistar smiled back. They enjoyed seeing him too, of course, but his mother rarely passed up an opportunity to ask whether he was done playing at being an engineer and ready to come home for good.

The carriage drew to a halt outside the manor doors. No footman jumped out to open the door or lower the steps for them, as they would have in Lewarden. Alistar smiled again. It was good to be home. He hopped out of the carriage, then offered Saskia a hand down to the cobblestone walk.

The front door opened, and Admiral As'enel strode out to greet his eldest son. He only sailed infrequently anymore, but he'd not lost his barrel chest or thick, muscled arms. His beard and hair, once as black as Alistar's, were more salt than pepper. A booming voice that could cut through a monsoon echoed from his chest.

"Alistar! Saskia! Welcome, welcome! How was the trip? Come in."

Alistar's mother, Captain As'enel, followed her husband outside. Her silvering hair hung in a braid down her back. Her green eyes were stern, but they warmed when they fell on her son and daughter-in-law. "I'm glad you could come home now."

Alistar smiled at his parents. "For our first anniversary, we could hardly do less." He kissed his mother on the cheek.

They entered the house, and Father waved everyone into the drawing room, exchanging the usual pleasantries. Though enchanted communication stones allowed for conversation over vast distances, they were no substitute for face-to-face. The family sipped chilled citrus tea and exchanged tales of life on sea and land, as if this was a social visit, and just the first-year anniversary celebration Alistar had claimed when he requested the holiday from Silverline Power.

"How's your father, Saskia?" Father asked. "Still running the clinic?"

Saskia smiled. "He is, and he's doing very well. Coiled Dragon Clinic gained prestige as one of the few clinics in the Lower City that successfully treated cases of Rat's Disease. We even have a number of elven patients, though we still don't have a healer on staff."

Elven taboos frowned greatly on the unnecessary exposure of bare skin below the neck. Staunch traditionalists wore gloves even while eating. Before the arrival of humans in Calarand, medical treatment had been exclusively the purview of healers. The idea of a doctor, before whom a patient had to disrobe to receive diagnosis and treatment, horrified most elves.

"Nasty business, Rat's Disease," the admiral agreed with a shudder. "Glad you put an end to it."

Saskia nodded. "So am I." Her hand sought Alistar's, and he gave it a reassuring squeeze. The outbreak had proven to be a poison rather than a disease, but the name had stuck. Even now rare, isolated incidents would come up as someone discovered a cache of the poisoned drug and took their chances. "But the clinic does well and has a strong, loyal base. And since my marriage to Alistar, it's also attracted a number of more wealthy donors. Nothing extravagant, but enough to help. There's an elven boy from the Lower City who's fascinated with the idea of becoming a doctor. His family supports the idea. They have pretty much nothing, so any chance at their child getting a trade, even a trade that goes against tradition, is an opportunity in their eyes."

"Now there's a thought," Father chuckled. "Glad you're finding ways of stirring up things in that hornet's nest of Lewarden tradition."

"They certainly need shaken up more often than not," Alistar's mother added. "And what about you, Alistar? Still preparing for the Grand Exhibition?"

Alistar nodded. "I'm glad I could get this time off—the schedule is getting tighter every day. Crown Prince Filipp has been throwing his all into preparing the Exhibition, and his demands for resources continue to mount."

"Channeling his grief over his wife and daughter?" his mother asked.

"Rumors around Silverline Power suggest a combination of that and a drive to prove to whoever sent the assassins that he won't be broken," Alistar told her.

The assassination attempt on the crown prince last summer hadn't been connected to the coup Alistar foiled. From everything he'd heard, the assassins had been foreign, but no country claimed responsibility, but speculations ran wild in Silverline Power. Prince Filipp had escaped the attack uninjured, but his wife and daughter had fallen to the assassins' blades.

Finally, Admiral As'enel set aside his teacup. "Well, let's get to business."

Alistar finished his tea and straightened in his chair. "Your message indicated a need to discuss something in person, but if you included any reasons why, you coded them a little too well."

Father chuckled. "No, you didn't miss any deeply coded message, Alistar. I didn't want any hints of this matter to reach anyone else's eyes, especially given the staff around your place."

Alistar's Lewarden manor was part of his reward for stopping the coup and saving Prince Cero's life. His staff was an interesting mix of his spies. His father's, put in place to maintain the Admiral's web of information on the capital, spies from various noble families of Lewarden who hoped to learn about Rillwater and about anything Alistar might be doing for the Silver Prince, and Prince Cero's, who worked as much to prevent the other spies from learning anything of value as they did to spy on Alistar. A few servants were just there to do their official job, but almost anyone qualified to serve in a noble's manor had some connection to someone important.

"From what I heard, at least, the staff accepted the message at face value," Saskia said. "An invitation for us to celebrate our first anniversary with family."

"Oh, we will certainly do that as well, Saskia," Mother promised, smiling. "We'd not pass up such an opportunity to celebrate here, especially since we couldn't do so at the wedding."

Alistar let that small barb pass without comment. "What did you want to tell us about?"

"We've been seeing an increasing number of ships without colors," Father said, growing serious. "Fast ships. More often than not, unless we really get the jump on them, they're able to cut and outrun us, but those we've caught have been carrying interesting cargo."

"Smugglers? What sorts of goods?" Alistar asked. Smugglers sometimes tried to slip ships through, though knowing the reputation of the Rillwater privateers, many decided it wasn't worth the risk, and sought other routes to move their illicit goods. An increase in activity was troubling.

Father grimaced. "I don't exactly know what to make of the things we've found, but anyone's best guess is they have something to do with the work you do. That's one of the reasons I wanted you to come in person."

Alistar frowned. "Are they coming into Calarand, or leaving?" If someone was attempting to smuggle out equipment to control or monitor the mahiy lines that transported magic around the city, Prince Cero needed to know immediately.

"Into the country," Mother clarified. "My *Escapade* intercepted the first ship. The crew refused to answer any questions about their cargo and carried no manifest, but some of the items resembled components of the devices you showed us in the Lewarden generators." Unlike her husband, Captain As'enel continued to maintain a strong presence on the waters.

Father smiled proudly at his wife. "We thought it might be an isolated incident, but other smuggling ships we've caught have carried similar cargo. Right now, we're storing it in the West Warehouse. You can take a look when you have a chance."

Alistar frowned as he considered the implications. "If someone's smuggling *in* devices to control a mahiy line network, they're probably taking them somewhere other than Lewarden. It would be foolish to challenge the Silver Prince in his own territory."

"Before you speculate too far, Alistar, wait until Roddek arrives," Mother said. "The *Conquest* is due in today, and he took another of the smuggler ships. He reported that he'd found some information on the ship. The smugglers were careless and didn't successfully divest themselves of all incriminating documentation."

Saskia had mostly been listening and sipping her tea, but she smiled at that. "Will Cheska be coming as well?" Alistar's younger siblings, Cheska and Roddek, both captained ships in the fleet.

"Unfortunately, she's still several weeks out," Captain As'enel said. "So, unless you can stay for longer than I expect, we'll have to catch her up once she makes port."

The two captains had a long-standing friendly rivalry, so Cheska was probably furious that Roddek would be getting the details of this matter before her.

"You're right about how long we can stay. Especially if this smuggling does relate to Silverline Power. His Highness will want to know immediately," Alistar said.

"Before any of that, though, we should let the two of you get settled!" Father declared. "Your luggage is already up in your suite. We'll gather for the family meeting after dinner. Go stretch your legs and relax for a bit."

Accepting the dismissal, Alistar and Saskia headed outside for a stroll through the grounds. Alistar pointed out trees that had been his favorites to climb in his youth, spots where he and his siblings had built forts and staged mock combats. Saskia had seen some of them on previous visits, but she enjoyed hearing about his childhood escapades. Alistar thought he succeeded in keeping his thoughts from dwelling on the smuggling and its implications until Saskia broached the subject.

"Alistar, what if this smuggling of components is a continuation of one of Cemar's plans?" she asked suddenly, interrupting his story about the time he and Cheska tried, much to their parents' amusement, to dig a moat.

Alistar stopped. The half-elf Cemar had been one of the three masterminds behind the attempted coup, the theft of the magic, and the attempt on Prince Cero's life. "You mean, what if Sunward is trying to continue his work?"

"Exactly," Saskia said. "We don't know what long-term plots they might have set in motion well in advance. I know it's been nearly a year and a half since Cemar died, but all things considered, that wouldn't be an unreasonable length of time for someone to start copying and manufacturing equipment for the mahiy lines, would it?"

Cemar was dead, officially crushed by the collapse of the ballroom ceiling in the Silver Prince's mansion. More accurately, he'd been crushed between two barriers created by Rykka Onyxflame, the elven criminal Alistar had pressed into service. One of the other leaders of the coup, the human Baron Sok'lof, had been arrested and executed for treason. The third member, Lady Celyn Sunward, had escaped, using the resources of her family to elude capture and vanish. Her parents claimed not to know where she'd gone, and she'd not been seen since, so far as Alistar knew.

"It would be a shockingly short time to go from prototype to functioning model, if these components do actually function," Alistar said. "If it is connected to Cemar's plots, their source has probably been working on it for even longer." He gazed into the distance. "I wonder who and where their source is. Maybe we'll be lucky enough to find a crafter's stamp tucked away on a piece somewhere."

"Alistar! Saskia!" Roddek vaulted over the fence separating the grounds from the horse pasture and bounded to them like a spring storm, vibrant, energetic, and chaotic. His chestnut hair was bleached golden brown by the sun and his skin bore a deep tan. He was five years younger than Alistar, with powerful arms and hands coarse from hauling ropes.

Alistar embraced him. "Welcome home, little brother. How goes the plundering?"

"Never better! Cheska's still a galley ahead of me by last count, but I'll catch up in no time. I didn't know you were going to be home, though. It's good to see both of you!" He turned to Saskia and wrapped her in a bear hug.

She laughed. "Alistar requested the time off to celebrate our anniversary, and your parents asked us to come."

"Blood and sand, has it been a year already?" Roddek asked. "And you're still putting up with him?"

Saskia laughed again. "So far. Even despite his siblings!"

Roddek put a hand to his chest as if wounded, but grinned. "You know, I worried when I heard Alistar was marrying a woman he'd met in Lewarden. Wasn't sure if a city girl would be able to handle the rough and tumble of this family. I'm glad you proved me wrong, Saskia!"

"Have you talked to Father yet, Roddek?" Alistar asked.

"Yep. He told me you two were out here. I assume he told you what's going on?" Roddek immediately grew serious.

Alistar nodded. "He said you had more to add."

Roddek ignored the gentle prompt to expound. "We're meeting tonight, so I'll explain what my *Conquest* recovered then. I'll be bringing a member of my crew to the meeting, too. She's got an eye for this sort of thing."

"Anyone I know?" Alistar asked.

Roddek shook his head. "Doubt it. She's a newer recruit, not a Rillwater native."

Alistar nodded. "I'm interested to hear what you found."

Roddek looked to the sky and sighed. "I better get back to the *Conquest* to finish unloading and get everything in order. See you both after dinner!"

Dinner was a simple affair, just Alistar, Saskia, and his parents. After they finished, Alistar and Saskia went to their suite to change clothes for the evening. When the clock chimed seven, Alistar linked arms with his wife. They climbed the stairs to Admiral As'enel's study, long ago dubbed the "War Room" by Alistar and his siblings. The door was just starting to swing closed behind Roddek and his crew member. Alistar caught it in time to hear Roddek making introductions.

"Admiral, Captain, this is Darkwood. She's been with the *Conquest* for nine months now and has been an exemplary member of my crew. Her search of the captain's cabin on the smuggler's ship turned up documents in places I'd never have thought to look."

"Is that so?" Captain As'enel asked. "Where do you hail from, Darkwood?"

"Lewarden, Captain," Darkwood answered.

Alistar's brow creased in a frown. Not because of Darkwood's answer—many people with nothing to lose made their way to Rillwater and signed on with the fleet, enamored with the idealistic privateer life portrayed in two-chip novels. His moment of disquiet came instead from a feeling that he recognized her voice. From her surname, she was an elf, and from her accent, she was probably from one of the slum districts, but that unfortunately did little to narrow down her identity.

He opened the study door the rest of the way and entered with Saskia. She closed the door behind them, shutting out sounds from the rest of the house. Roddek and Darkwood stood with their backs toward the door, facing Alistar's parents. Darkwood wore the long-sleeved blue shirt and sturdy brown trousers that were as close to the uniform of Rillwater privateers as anything was. She was a little shorter than the average elf, about five foot nine. Her brown hair was pulled back in a tail. She stood straight, undaunted by the impressive personages before her.

Admiral As'enel looked past Roddek and Darkwood. "Ah, good. You're here. Come join us."

"Thank you. Roddek, this must be the crew member you mentioned," Alistar said.

Darkwood stiffened sharply, sucking in a sharp breath that sounded suspiciously like a curse.

Roddek turned toward his brother, one eyebrow rising as he glanced to Darkwood. "Yes. Alistar, Saskia, this is Darkwood. Darkwood, my elder brother Alistar and his wife Saskia."

"Hematic perdition, the gods hate me." Darkwood drew a deep breath and turned to face Alistar. Forcing her expression into a devil-may-care smile that Alistar recognized in an instant, she said, "Hello, De'seneth."

Alistar stared at her for long seconds before finally speaking. "Hello, Onyxflame."

CHAPTER 2

Roddek's eyebrows shot for the ceiling, but Alistar's parents retained their composure. Both of them rested hands on the hilts of their sabers, however, as Father calmly asked, "You know this elf, Alistar?"

Onyxflame looked like she was assessing her chances of bolting, either past Alistar for the door, or out one of the windows.

Alistar's eyes never left her as he answered his father. "Yes. This is Rykka Onyxflame, formerly my conscripted assistant in the business with Cemar, Rat's Disease, and that little mess back in Lewarden. You helped me flesh out Lord Aspendark's persona for Onyxflame, Admiral."

"Hmm. As I recall, Alistar, *Lord* Aspendark was a man. As was the notorious thief Onyxflame." Father gazed at Alistar.

"Rykka's brother Tiyron," Alistar said. "He was murdered by Cemar, and Rykka assumed his identity, which I didn't learn until quite late in the investigation."

Onyxflame's mouth twitched in a tight, nervous smile. "Yeah, sorry about that."

"And the report of Onyxflame's death?" Mother asked.

Onyxflame cleared her throat. "I, uh, collapsed the Silver Prince's ballroom on Cemar and myself. I intended that it appear I'd died there."

Mother looked to Alistar, one eyebrow raised in question. Alistar nodded. "At the time I wrote my report, I wasn't certain whether Onyxflame had survived or not. However, after the aid she'd given me, I owed it to her to ensure the Crown didn't search for her. Promises or not, I wasn't confident His Highness would respect the terms I negotiated with Onyxflame at the start of the investigation. If nothing else, he could claim they were made falsely because I believed I was negotiating with Tiyron, not Rykka."

Roddek glowered at Onyxflame, eyes narrow. "You've been hiding this from me the entire time you've been on my ship."

Onyxflame flinched. "Yes, Captain."

Roddek folded his arms across his chest and continued to gaze at her in a passable imitation of the admiral's fierce glare, capable of driving seasoned privateers to their knees.

Onyxflame massaged the back of her neck. "I learned something of Rillwater and sailing in my role of Lord Aspendark. Once I had the freedom to travel where I wished, I thought I'd try the privateer life for myself. But by the Reyker's sense of humor, I was assigned to your ship. A nasty shock when I realized my captain was an As'enel. I thought it best to keep my previous history with De'seneth and Silverline Power private."

Aside from Admiral and Captain As'enel, Rillwater captains went by their given names. Primarily, the tradition avoided the confusion sure to come from having multiple captains with the same patronym, but it also reduced the chance that a new sailor would attempt to get on a ship captained by a particularly famous or infamous family. More often than not, a new sailor didn't know the pedigree of their captain until well into the first voyage.

"You thought it best to keep *this* a secret?" Roddek said.

"There are a great many ships, and a great many sailors in the fleet, Captain. I thought the odds of avoiding an accidental encounter with De'seneth were in my favor." Onyxflame smiled wryly. "The Reyker clearly had other ideas."

Onyxflame was one of the few elves of Alistar's acquaintance who worshiped the human pantheon, known as the Reyker, rather than the more strictly stratified and caste-bound elven faith, the Tenants and the Path. The Reyker, at least, encouraged adherents to improve their station in life.

"Well, given her background, I understand how Onyxflame knew all the odd nooks where someone might hide information and documents they didn't want found, but didn't want to destroy," Saskia said.

Her words reminded everyone of the original reason for the family meeting. Roddek still scowled at Onyxflame, but Admiral and Captain As'enel both nodded to Saskia for the attempt to steer them back on course. Mother asked, "Roddek, before now, have you had any complaints with Darkwood's service aboard the *Conquest?*"

Roddek sighed, but admitted, "No, Captain. Darkwood learned quickly, didn't make the same mistake twice, and acted exemplarily when on shore leave. No brawls, no skipping out on the bill, no lewd behavior in public."

Onyxflame cleared her throat. "You did tell me those were the rules regarding shore leave, with a strong implication that anyone tossed in the local jail would be staying there, Captain."

"Yes, but you've actually followed those rules," Roddek said. "Any number of new recruits thinks such things don't apply to them. In fact, sometimes seasoned sailors need the reminder as well."

"I learned that the captain's word is law before I arrived in Rillwater." Onyxflame cast a glance at Alistar.

"In short, Captain, no, I've had no complaints about her before now." Roddek acknowledged.

"I'm slightly alarmed to hear you are following the rules, all things considered," Alistar said quietly.

"I can follow the rules when the alternative is less appealing, De'seneth," Onyxflame said. "And I do not swim nearly well enough to reach shore from a ship at sea."

Alistar's parents looked at each other, conveying silent and unreadable messages by glance alone. Father nodded. "Report on your findings on the smugglers' ship, Darkwood."

Onyxflame blinked, collected herself, and faced him. "Captain Roddek has the documents we recovered, Admiral. The ship's captain hid the most important papers in a compartment concealed in the frame of the bed. His map indicated the point of collection for the goods was Tarish Island."

Alistar wasn't surprised, but slightly disappointed to hear that the last known location of the smuggled goods had been the infamous black market and pirate den. The privateers of Rillwater knew its location but didn't venture near except in rare situations. Even if they came under neutral colors, they were far from welcome in such company. They'd have better luck stopping a storm than convincing the inhabitants of Tarish to reveal the origins of the goods.

Onyxflame continued. "The ship's captain wrote the manifest in code, and I haven't had a chance to decipher it yet. From what little I can tell so far, he didn't describe the goods in any detail, and may not have known himself what they were or their purpose. I also found a short message with coordinates indicating where the goods were to be delivered and how full payment would be rendered. It appears the recipient paid part in advance, with the rest due on delivery. The only signature on the message was the letter 'C'."

Cemar? Alistar glanced sidelong at Saskia, wondering if she was thinking the same thing. "What was the intended destination?"

"A small port town a day and a half from Lewarden," Roddek

answered. "I planned to ask the Admiral's leave to pay a visit there."

Father nodded curtly. "We'll discuss it. Darkwood, your opinion on the goods themselves?"

Onyxflame shifted her weight from one foot to the other. "I haven't had the chance to examine them in depth, Admiral, but I think they might be components used to regulate and direct magic. Maybe someone intends to use them to divert power from the mahiy lines? Or wants to establish their own network to break the Silver Prince's monopoly. I would need to see more of the components to make a more definitive conclusion."

Mother raised an eyebrow. "You are familiar enough with such devices to reach conclusions about their purpose?"

Alistar still wasn't certain what to think of finding Onyxflame here, in his family home, but he could speak to this matter. "She's a self-taught artificer, and she designed and built the original machine Cemar stole and altered."

Onyxflame's expression tightened at Cemar's name, but she nodded. "I've had opportunities in the past to study the mahiy lines and the devices used to manipulate them, Captain As'enel."

The admiral stood. "Roddek, your cargo has been moved to the West Warehouse?"

"Yes sir," Roddek answered.

"Good. Let's have a look, now that our experts are here."

The West Warehouse held plunder that should not or could not be distributed to the crew that captured it, for whatever reason. Father led the way to the massive wood and stone structure and produced an iron key to open the heavy lock. Inside, he began lighting lanterns along the hall. Alistar missed the ghost-lights of Lewarden that automatically illuminated when someone approached.

Wooden shelves reinforced with iron rose to the catwalks. The admiral waved them on to a large open area, where stacks of crates waited. At his father's gesture of permission, Alistar pried the lid off a crate and scooped aside the packing straw. He lifted out a heavy metal framework and set it atop another crate, frowning. The piece didn't look like any component he recognized. He carefully searched in the straw again, and his second attempt produced something more familiar.

"This looks like some type of energy regulator, though it's smaller than those we use in Lewarden. Much smaller. If the recipient intends to set up their own mahiy network, they'll need dozens of these for each line if they want it to be at all stable."

Onyxflame edged closer for a look. "It could be meant for use on a device, if one needed to operate on a different frequency than that produced by Silverline Power. I had to cobble together something similar a few times when I couldn't make mine work otherwise. Although mine didn't look nearly that nice."

Alistar frowned. He'd been thinking on a larger scale: competition or sabotage to Silverline Power rather than contraband devices being adjusted to work with the available magic. "That's a thought. Admiral, can I take some of these components back to Lewarden and analyze them on my equipment there?"

"Take whatever you need, Alistar," Father answered.

Alistar continued to examine components. Now that Onyxflame had said it, they did seem more like pieces of a device. Or maybe several devices, though he had no idea as to their purpose. "Darkwood, do you know what this might be?"

"Not from just these pieces. It might not even be a device; that was just a guess."

Roddek looked through another crate. From his expression, he had no idea what to make of the contents. "Is this stuff actually worth anything, Alistar?"

"It was worth enough for someone to smuggle it to Calarand," Alistar said. He turned to his parents and Saskia. "I'm afraid this will make our visit shorter than I'd like."

"Much as I would love to get you aboard a ship and chasing the smugglers for yourself, I'm afraid you're right," Mother said, a rare concession to her eldest son's choice of a career outside the family business. "We don't know how many shipments like this have slipped past us."

Once Alistar selected an assortment of components to bring back to Lewarden, they all left the warehouse. Roddek and Onyxflame headed back to Roddek's ship and the rest of the family returned to the manor.

"Do you trust Darkwood, Alistar?" Mother asked.

He gave the question long, serious thought. "I don't know. On my assignment, she worked with me because she had to, and eventually because it meant getting revenge on Cemar. After our partnership ended, I assumed she would vanish and I'd never see her again."

"Aside from attending our wedding," Saskia put in. Both Alistar's parents looked at her questioningly. She smiled. "Do you remember the absolutely hideously wrapped gift no one would claim? Onyxflame brought it. Apparently, she was fulfilling a promise she made to Alistar."

"If there is one thing I can say for her, she keeps her word," Alistar admitted. "What I don't understand yet is why she came to Rillwater and signed on with the fleet rather than leaving the country and starting over somewhere new."

"Yes, the reason she gave was rather uninformative." Father considered. "I plan to send Roddek to investigate the port where these goods were bound. However, Darkwood might do more good in Lewarden."

"You want to send her with us?" Saskia asked.

Father nodded. "Roddek needs time to cool off. Darkwood needs to be moved, at least temporarily, out of his command. We could send her to another ship, but this is a better use of her skills. It should be simple enough to explain a new member of your staff."

"We can make a place for Darkwood," Saskia said. She smiled warmly at Alistar's parents. "It's been a long day, though. Alistar and I should retire for the night."

"Of course. We'll see you in the morning," Mother said.

~

Alistar and Saskia sat together on their balcony, looking toward the sea. He wrapped an arm around her, and she leaned her head against his shoulder.

"I forgot how dark it is at night in Rillwater," Saskia murmured.

Alistar smiled. "I miss seeing the stars. This is nice."

In Lewarden, not even night was truly dark. Even without the ghostlights that lit the streets, the mahiy lines that carried magic throughout the city shed soft violet light. Silverline Power existed to create and maintain those lifelines of magic that fed the capital's voracious appetite.

After a moment, Saskia said, "I have a thought about Onyxflame and bringing her into the house."

"Oh? An objection, or…"

"Not an objection. An idea. Before we left Lewarden, we talked about asking Soluthos for recommendations as to a new lady's maid for me."

Alistar nodded. His footman, Soluthos Windshadow, was a former soldier, now one of Prince Cero's spies. He and Alistar had reached an agreement early in his employment as to what information from Alistar's house would or would not reach the ears of the Silver Prince, and so far the arrangement had worked well. Saskia, however, had not had good luck with her lady's maid. "I hadn't brought it up with him before we left. I didn't want rumors to start around the house in our absence."

"I need to dismiss Merris regardless, once we return. She can find a lady more suited to her view of 'proper' conduct." Saskia made a sour face. "I need someone who won't turn up her nose at the notion of a lady being a doctor."

"How does that relate to…" Alistar stopped. "Saskia, are you suggesting bringing in *Onyxflame* as your lady's maid?"

She laughed at his shocked tone. "Temporarily, I promise. And only if she's agreeable to the idea. I don't *need* a lady's maid any more than you *need* a footman. But it will give her a legitimate reason to be in the house and working closely with us."

"It's also a position of a lot of trust, and gives her access to the rest of the house," Alistar said cautiously. "Knowing that even I don't know all the secrets of our manor yet, I'm not sure what to think about that."

She snuggled closer against him. "Think about it. Sleep on it tonight. We can talk about it tomorrow."

He kissed her. "That I can do."

As night fell, they retired to bed. Alistar slept deep, his wife in his arms and the sea in his dreams.

CHAPTER 3

"You want me to do *what?*" Onyxflame stared at Saskia in disbelief.

"Introducing you under the guise of my new lady's maid will establish your standing in the household and avoid quite a few questions," Saskia said patiently.

"You want *me* to be your *lady's maid?* That's... that's..."

"Are you saying you think such a role beneath you, Darkwood?" Captain As'enel asked coolly.

Onyxflame's mouth snapped shut and her back straightened. "No, Captain. It is, however, outside my normal skill set."

"This wouldn't be a permanent assignment," Saskia promised. "At the end of the mission, you can return to sailing, with the Admiral and Captain's permission." She nodded to Captain As'enel.

"Assuming my son is satisfied with your work, and you wish to return to the sea, we will ensure there is a place for you in the fleet," Captain As'enel agreed, her gaze fixed on Onyxflame like a stalking cat on its prey.

Alistar had offered to speak to Onyxflame with Saskia, but she'd declined, thinking his presence more likely to be a distraction than a help. All things considered, though, Saskia suspected that at the moment, Onyxflame would much prefer to have Alistar in the sitting room than Captain As'enel.

The elf shifted uncomfortably. "Of course, Captain." She looked to Saskia again. "Lady De'seneth, it seems I must accept your gracious offer."

Not an enthusiastic acceptance, but it was an acceptance. "Thank you. I wonder whether it would be better to present you as coming from Rillwater, or being hired in Lewarden?"

"In my experience playing Lord Aspendark, claiming to be a native of Rillwater excuses one from a great many expectations among the nobility," Onyxflame offered. "I swear some people questioned whether Aspendark knew how to use a privy, or if he would relieve himself in the bushes."

Saskia was sure that was an exaggeration. "Perhaps, but at the same time, staff from Rillwater are automatically assumed to be in the service of the As'enels—accurately so, admittedly. But if people believe you a local, you'll have much more opportunity to gather information with less suspicion."

Onyxflame stood and paced around the sitting room. "Will I, though? Unless you have some minor noble family ready to claim me, anyone with a bit of skill will know I'm no noblewoman."

Saskia made a face. "My last three lady's maids have been young noblewomen. None of them have been able to accept the idea that I am a doctor, that I will continue to work in my father's practice, and that I *do not care* whether they think it a proper profession for a lady of rank."

Captain As'enel's eyebrows rose. "Pompous twits, from the sound of it."

"And each of them came well recommended, too," Saskia sighed. She was tired of justifying her reasons for not only her work as a doctor, but the very existence of her father's clinic and its mission to serve the poor of Lewarden. Too many nobles of the capital, elven and human alike, viewed the populace of the city's slums as lesser creatures who somehow deserved their wretched lot. "But I am more than ready to explain to anyone who asks that after my difficulties, I decided to look outside the lower nobility. Instead, a reasonably wealthy but common-born patron offered a donation to the clinic with the stipulation that I also take in his daughter. Or perhaps his niece, if you'd like a little more distance from this fictional patron."

Onyxflame blinked. "I don't have to play a noble?"

"No. You'd be a well-to-do commoner, but still a commoner."

"What are my responsibilities? Do I have to go to the clinic with you?" Onyxflame shifted uncomfortably.

Saskia remembered the elf's phobia of doctors and smiled reassuringly. "Not in the normal course of your day. Officially, you'll be responsible for assisting me in preparing for the day or any events I'm going to attend. Sometimes you might need to attend with me, though I don't expect that to be required often. Unofficially, you'll be working with Alistar on this smuggling situation. And if you have free time you would like to use to pursue other interests or studies, we can discuss arranging that."

Onyxflame frowned. "Lady De'seneth, I'm aware of how rumors can spread in Lewarden, especially among servants and staff. Won't it cause… talk if your new lady's maid is spending more time with your husband than in her duties to you?"

Saskia started to answer, but before she could, Captain As'enel said, "I would hope you could find methods to mitigate any such potential damage to my family's reputation, Darkwood."

"Easily," Onyxflame said with a hint of indignation. "The simplest would be for me to dress as a man again while working with De'seneth. But if that's not acceptable, I need to know."

"Do you *want* to take that role again?" Saskia asked.

Onyxflame gave her a puzzled look. "It's just a role."

"But is it one you want to play?" Saskia persisted. "Adding a second role for you is an extra complication, and it's not necessary. While I understand your concern, and appreciate it, we have an advantage that many nobles don't have."

Onyxflame's brow pinched in confusion. "What would that be?"

"A Rillwater nobleman in the employ of Silverline Power and his wife, who is a female doctor. We can already be assumed to act outside the norms. We're *eccentric*."

"But how does that connect to my role?" Onyxflame asked, cautious.

"I've already shown that I don't *need* a lady's maid. So why not hire one who has other useful skills, maybe even has aspirations to earn enough to further her education. Perhaps you hope to join Silverline Power yourself, and want Alistar to mentor you in the field."

Onyxflame grimaced slightly at that. "Maybe not *that*, but… all right."

"We can figure that role out when we need to. My point is you don't have to add a second persona just to work with Alistar if we present your role correctly from the start."

Onyxflame nodded slowly. "Possible, I suppose. Well, if I'm a local hire, I won't be traveling back to Lewarden with you and your husband."

"Will that be a problem?" Saskia asked. "Do you still maintain a residence in the capital?"

The question startled a laugh from Onyxflame. "Nothing worthy of such a lofty name, no. I don't know if anyone's moved into my old bolt holes. Can't say I left much in any of them that would be worthy of a lady's maid."

"We'll get you proper attire for the post," Saskia told her.

"We will see to it you have appropriate transportation to Lewarden and funds to establish an identity," Captain As'enel said. "You are dismissed, Darkwood."

"Yes, Captain." Onyxflame withdrew hastily.

Saskia turned to her mother-in-law. "I think she would have agreed without the threats."

Captain As'enel raised one eyebrow. "I didn't threaten, Saskia. Darkwood needs to clearly understand the consequences of failing this assignment." She nodded in the direction Onyxflame had gone. "That's a woman whose heart has been taken by the sea. It's rare to find in someone not native-born to Rillwater, and it would be a waste to condemn her to serving on merchant skiffs for the rest of her days. But she's broken trust with my sons, and unless she can earn it back and prove herself worthy, she'll not set foot on another of our ships."

Saskia nodded slowly. She didn't always understand the mindset of Rillwater privateers, but she respected her formidable mother-in-law, and trusted that she had good reason for her decisions. "I don't know that Alistar distrusts her so much as he was not expecting to see her again, and certainly not here."

Captain As'enel made a noncommittal noise. "Whether he trusts her or not, I'd keep a close eye on her if I were you."

"I will."

"Of course, if Alistar had his own ship and an official crew, it would be a simple matter to transfer Darkwood under his command," Captain As'enel added.

"Maybe, but that wouldn't put either of them in the place they need to track these smuggled goods in Lewarden," Saskia said.

The captain sighed. "I suppose not. Still, it would simplify matters."

Saskia just smiled and shook her head, certain neither Alistar nor Onyxflame would agree with that assessment.

∼

Saskia found Alistar walking along the beach, his shoes in his hands and his trousers rolled up to his knees. He greeted her with a warm smile. "How did it go?"

"Onyxflame agreed. She's not thrilled with the idea, but she did agree." She slipped off her shoes and stockings and joined him. The sun-warmed sand squished under her toes.

Alistar nodded. "I didn't expect her to like it. Hopefully she'll decide the reward is worth the effort."

"Your mother thinks Onyxflame's found her place at sea and believes that should be a strong incentive for her to earn her place back on Ruddek's ship." Saskia slipped off her shoes and walked beside her husband. The wet sand squished between her toes and the waves lapped at her feet. The water was chill and a gentle but steady breeze blew across the beach.

Alistar looked over the water, then turned his gaze to her with a wry smile. "This isn't how I expected to celebrate our first anniversary."

She took his hand in hers. "Alistar, my love, I knew I was marrying the heir to the Rillwater fleets. I didn't marry you because I expected our life together to be dull, quiet, and peaceful. The last year has been wonderful and relatively uneventful for us, but I never expected that to last forever. Not when I married into *this* family. If I can't handle a bit of family business on our anniversary, we both chose our life partner very unwisely."

He wrapped his arm around her shoulder. "That's one worry I will never have."

She leaned against him. "Nor will I." They walked together across the beach for a time. "Will you tell His Highness about the smuggled goods when we return to Lewarden?"

Alistar's expression grew pensive. "I should at some point, but I want to have an idea what we're dealing with first. Is someone building illegal devices? Are they trying to sabotage the mahiy lines? Could all this be a ruse to distract us from something else? Before I bring this news to the Silver Prince, I want to have an idea exactly what news I have."

"You have an idea where to start in figuring that out?" Saskia asked.

"First step on my end will be determining the purpose of the components. That will give me an idea what the device could be used for. Hopefully Onyxflame can help there."

"I thought about that. She brought up concern about the appearances of my new lady's maid spending her time around my husband, but I have an idea to address that.

"I didn't consider that." Alistar's mouth twitched in a small smile. "I suppose I'd been thinking of her in her Aspendark role. What do you have in mind?"

"I thought we could present her as someone hired to fill multiple roles. She wasn't keen on the idea of coming in pretending to want to become an engineer for Silverline Power, but I'm sure there are other options."

Alistar laughed. "Slee's Beard, no, she'd hate that. She loathes Prince Cero." He stepped over a hunk of driftwood. "An artificer, on the other hand, suits her. She's self-taught, but she has a knack for it."

"You know her skills better than I do. It sounds reasonable to me." A particularly cold wave washed over Saskia's ankles, and she yelped in surprise, then laughed. "All right, I need to warm up before my toes turn blue."

They walked back to Rillwater proper. Saskia slipped her shoes back on after brushing as much sand as possible off her feet, though she knew she'd still be finding it for weeks to come. They passed crews of workers unloading a ship, and another set loading cargo from one of the warehouses into a ship's hold. Alistar made for Roddek's *Conquest*.

Though her husband could describe the features of any ship of the fleet in detail, Saskia had yet to learn all the finer points of sailing or ship craft. Still, she knew the *Conquest* was built for speed, to overtake other ships and cut off their route of retreat. She also knew Roddek was fiercely proud of his ship and his promotion to captain two years ago.

They saw Roddek and Onyxflame on the dock. Roddek turned when they approached. "Afternoon Alistar, Saskia. Getting Darkwood her official traveling documents." He gestured with the bundle of paper in his hand.

"I'll be curious to see how official Rillwater travel documents compare to those forged by palace scribes," Onyxflame said.

"Rillwater documents forged by palace scribes?" Saskia asked.

"From when she was playing the role of Lord Aspendark in my assignment," Alistar explained. "One difference I know is that court forgeries of such documents are legible."

Onyxflame's eyebrows rose. "I thought being able to read the document was part of its purpose."

"In theory, sure. But most Rillwater captains have the penmanship of a drunken octopus," Alistar said, grinning at his brother.

Roddek straightened indignantly. "Alistar! Comparing my writing to that is an insult to drunken octopuses everywhere!"

Saskia laughed at the banter and looked to Onyxflame. "You're leaving soon, I take it?"

"Yes. I'm supposed to arrive in Lewarden before you so I have a little time to 'get settled' and take care of anything I need to do."

"While we're on the topic, do you need anything to get settled back in the capital, Darkwood?" Alistar asked.

"I haven't had much reason to spend my pay so far. It shouldn't be too long between my arrival and your return to the city," Onyxflame said. "So, what's my role to be?"

"In addition to being my lady's maid, we're hiring you for your artificing skills," Saskia said. "Unless you object?"

Roddek looked between them, puzzled, but Onyxflame

considered it. "That could work. I'll need to pick up some gear before I show up." She smiled slightly. "An artificer. Well, that's a title I never thought I'd claim."

"I suspect the coming months will involve many things none of us thought we'd never see or do," Saskia said. *Like inviting Onyxflame into our home, or Alistar working with her again.*

CHAPTER 4

"Lord De'seneth, Lady De'seneth, welcome home." Alistar's butler, Dorne, bowed as they entered the manor. As the son of Admiral As'enel's Master of the House, Dorne took great pleasure in finally having a place to make his own domain.

"Thank you. It's good to be back," Alistar said. "Any news around the house in our absence?"

Dorne grimaced as he collected their travel bags. "With apologies for not asking your leave first, Lady De'seneth, I had to dismiss Merris."

"What happened?" Saskia asked. "If you thought it demanded immediate dismissal, the matter must have been serious."

He headed through the entry gallery and up the sweeping staircase that curved around the foyer. "We caught her attempting to access the restricted area of the manor. She got as far as the second door, where she discovered that even her house key didn't open it."

"Merris did?" Saskia repeated, stopping short on the stairs. "She never expressed interest or even curiosity about that area of the manor. Whose orders did she act under?"

"She insisted she was acting on her own, Lady De'seneth," Dorne answered. "I don't believe her, but she stuck to that lie."

The manor house Alistar and Saskia called home had once served as the headquarters for Cemar's cabal. Here, Cemar had employed his powerful charisma to convince his followers that he sought to reforge the country into a place without the divisions of class and race that strangled so many of its citizens.

Prince Cero had bestowed the manor on Alistar with the understanding that he would delve into its secrets. Of primary interest to the Silver Prince was that the manor drew power from a source other than the mahiy lines. Alistar's attempts to locate the power source, however, revealed that the mysteries ran far deeper.

At some point, the basement had been expanded well beyond the original blueprints. Not only were some doors locked, with no keys to be found, other rooms were designed as elaborate puzzles. Alistar believed the puzzles were intended to be solvable only by the rare "internal" channelers who Cemar and Sunward had recruited. The skill remained a powerful mystery that remained unsolved despite the work of a dedicated team of Silverline researchers.

Few people could draw magic directly from the mahiy lines. Those who could were called channelers, and their skills focused into a particular area—healing, manipulation of a particular element, occasionally even into shaping the energy into barriers or weapons.

Cemar's work with condensing magic into a solid form and employing it as a drug revealed that some people could, given an infusion of magic, draw that power out from within themselves rather than from the mahiy lines. The discovery flew in the face of conventional magic theory. Some dismissed it entirely, citing a lack of scientific verification that the ability even existed.

"Thank you for keeping the house in our absence, Dorne," Alistar said.

"Of course, sir." Dorne bowed. "Lady De'seneth, Windshadow told me that when you are ready to interview a new lady to take Merris's place, he can offer several suggestions."

"While I appreciate the offer, I already have that in hand," Saskia assured him.

Dorne's eyebrows rose in surprise, but he nodded. "I see." He opened the door to their suite. "In that case, I'll take my leave."

Saskia kissed Alistar on the cheek and headed to her chamber to unpack. Normally that would have been the responsibility of her lady's maid, but Saskia preferred to handle it herself even before Merris's dismissal. Alistar entered his chamber, where his footman was already at work.

"Good afternoon, Soluthos."

Soluthos Windshadow saluted Alistar with crisp, military poise. A red leather patch covered his right eye, and he was missing the tip of his right ear, both courtesy of a Narnan sniper. His blond hair hung in a neat braid, and he wore a red and gold uniform. "Good afternoon, sir. Welcome home. I trust that Dorne already informed you of the situation with Merris?"

"He did," Alistar said. "Any other news I should be aware of?"

"Lady Syri wishes to speak with you once you have returned to work. Aside from that, I don't believe so." Soluthos brushed off Alistar's suits and hung them in the wardrobe. "Although if the Lady De'seneth wishes any proposals as to candidates to take Merris's place…"

"She already has someone in mind," Alistar said. "Although if it doesn't work out, I'll let you know."

"Already?" Soluthos asked.

"She'd decided to dismiss Merris upon our return even prior to this incident," Alistar said. While it wasn't news he would normally share with his staff, the change in situation made it easier to offer the explanation now.

"Will her new lady's maid be from Rillwater, then?" Soluthos asked.

Alistar shook his head. The news would travel to Prince Cero as soon as Soluthos had the opportunity, and that would go far in establishing Onyxflame's new identity. "The niece of an elven businessman. Many of the humans working in his factory have received care at the Coiled Dragon Clinic. He's offered his support to the clinic, but requested that Saskia assist his niece, as he sees her as lacking prospects at the moment."

Soluthos nodded understanding. The proposal was a standard business arrangement, unlikely to rouse suspicion. "I hope she proves more adaptable than Merris."

"I think she will," Alistar said with confidence. One thing he could never accuse Onyxflame of was an inability to adapt. And he suspected her period of employment in his household would only prove that all the more true. "She's also an artificer, and part of our agreement to employ her was that she also assist me with some projects."

Soluthos's eyebrows rose in surprise. "I'll be sure to mention that around the house. When is she due to arrive?"

"Tomorrow." Onyxflame had left three days ahead of Alistar and Saskia, and she'd assured them it was enough time to collect what she needed. It seemed a tight timeline to Alistar, but the elf knew her work better than he did. "Her name is Rykka Darkwood."

"And her uncle?" Soluthos asked.

"Prefers to remain anonymous. He's concerned his rivals might twist his support of human doctors against him."

Another nod from Soluthos. He'd had to ask; Prince Cero would expect nothing less from his spy. The Silver Prince did not, however, expect his spy to jeopardize his position by pressing for answers that wouldn't be given, and that benefitted Alistar as well as the prince.

I must tell Onyxflame who she can and cannot trust in the house.

He considered. *No, I just need to tell her who she can trust. Unless she's changed far more than I imagine, she won't need any reminders to be suspicious of everyone.*

After a day at home to rest from the journey, Alistar returned to work. He started the morning reading and updating himself on the current status, and trying not to wonder whether the smuggled components taken by Rillwater were intended to create chaos and catastrophe at the Grand Exhibition.

Those thoughts were shortly interrupted by Sasha Lightsky, the elven engineer he'd left in charge of the Exhibition project in his absence. Lightsky knocked and entered Alistar's office. He was a few years over sixty, tall, and always wore a silkweave tail coat in amber that complemented his black hair. This morning he looked nervous, though none of the reports Alistar had read seemed to warrant concern.

"Welcome back, Senior Engineer De'seneth."

"Thank you. I'm catching up still. How has the project been while I was gone? Anything I need to know?"

Lightsky shifted uncomfortably. "The work has been fine for the most part."

Alistar's eyebrows rose. "And the parts that aren't fine?"

Lightsky swallowed and offered him a missive on heavy vellum. "I received this two days ago, sir. I've run the calculations and we can manage the requested additions, but they will consume most of the remaining margin. Another change like this will certainly exceed the estimated magic available for the Exhibition. I haven't reallocated any resources yet—not without your approval."

Alistar knew what he would find before he opened the document. Another addition to the Exhibition. He drew a deep breath and didn't curse out loud. *If Prince Filipp continues to make changes, we won't need an outside force to sabotage the Exhibition.*

"I'll take a look. Have you looked at whether there are excesses we can trim from other areas? Cut out a few spotlights?"

"Not yet, sir. Though… perhaps we wouldn't need to remove any of the lights if we just reduced their brightness," Lightsky offered. "I'll run the estimates."

"Good. Let me know what you find."

Lightsky departed with less anxiety. He was a good engineer, but still young and very intimidated to be working on the crown prince's personal project.

An hour after Lightsky left, Alistar heard another knock. An elven woman just over forty with pale blonde hair waited for him to acknowledge her, then entered his office. Lady Syri Feyblade, daughter of Prince Cero, still ranked as a technician in the Silverline hierarchy, working her way through the ranks of the organization she would one day inherit. Many in Silverline Power struggled to treat her as a technician rather than as her father's daughter, but Alistar had observed her enough to know she wanted to earn respect and deference rather than have them handed to her.

"Good morning, Technician Feyblade," he greeted. "I understand you wanted to speak to me. I'm available now." Though he wasn't her direct superior, one of Lady Syri's main projects related to his work as well, and she provided regular progress reports. Although more often than not, such updates were "lack of progress" reports.

"Good morning, Senior Engineer De'seneth. I do." She closed his office door behind her and settled in the chair across the desk from him. "I have two matters I need to discuss, in fact, though one is less directly related to work than the other."

Alistar raised an eyebrow and gestured for her to continue. "Go ahead."

"To begin with the work matter, you may not have had a chance to review the latest report from my team, but I can tell you it's as bland and unremarkable as those before it. Our instruments pick up no changes in the radiant magic emanating from the crystal, while our efforts to analyze the structure remain unsuccessful."

"But?" Alistar prompted.

Lady Syri shifted in her chair. "I've always been skeptical of the Successors' claims that Rechmal gifted the crystal to their leader. However, the more I work with it, the more I find myself questioning my skepticism. The internal structure of the crystal doesn't match that found in naturally occurring formations of crystalized magic. Nor does it match the structure of Cemar's drugs and his method of artificially forcing magic into a solid state."

The crystal in the shape of a blooming flower with eight jagged petals, similar to the frost's breath flower, was another mystery from Cemar's cabal. Baron Sok'lof, one of the three leaders of the cabal, claimed it was a gift from Rechmal, the god of magic in the human pantheon, when he used the crystal in his guise as a spiritual leader of a sect of religious fanatics known as the Successors of Heiset. Alistar had dramatically stolen it out of Sok'lof's grasp, denying the other whatever powers it possessed. He'd entrusted the crystal to Lady Syri for study. She and a team had been working on it for the last year and a half. They'd made some discoveries early on, but much of its purpose remained a mystery, and they had yet to reproduce any of the "miracles" Sok'lof had generated.

Alistar frowned slightly as he listened to Lady Syri. "You've studied the crystal more extensively than I have. Are you saying you think it could, in fact, have been given to Sok'lof by the gods?"

"I would hope the gods wouldn't have such poor judgment as to entrust such an item into his hands. But I do question its origins and have begun to wonder if there is some element of the supernatural within it. At times, I have sensed, even witnessed reactions from the crystal that our equipment did not register."

He sat straight. "What sort of reactions? Has anyone else witnessed this phenomenon?"

"Shifts in the crystal's color, flickering of lights inside it. On several occasions, it radiated light even when the room was dark, yet that light remained confined within the crystal itself rather than illuminating the rest of the room. I couldn't even see the table on which it sat.

"Several other technicians have observed the phenomenon as well. Those of us who work in closest proximity experience the effects most often. However, in the last month and a half, the frequency has increased noticeably, occurring nearly every other day. Also, individuals outside of our initial group have also experienced the effects."

"And this is the first you're reporting it?" Alistar looked at her sternly.

"At my father's instructions, we reported these events only to him until now. Also at his instructions, I must ask that you treat this information as highly confidential, Senior Engineer."

"I... see." He was deeply uncomfortable with the idea of exposing anyone to unknown, potentially harmful magical energy, and even more so with the thought of requiring those so exposed to conceal the information. "What measures have been put in place to ensure the safety of you and your team?"

"First, anyone who expressed discomfort with continuing the study of the crystal can immediately transfer to another group without repercussions. We all track instances we have experienced and undergo weekly examinations by my father's team of personal physicians. So far, several members of our team have shown slightly elevated levels of magic buildup in the blood, but otherwise, the healers have found nothing of concern."

Alistar's lips pressed in a thin line. "That doesn't make me like the circumstances more. You and your team might be under constant exposure to unknown influences, with evidence that they are affecting you, and we don't know what the cumulative effects might be. Also, the increased frequency of incidents with no discernable source is concerning."

"While I don't know the exact cause or the purpose of the increased activity, I do have a theory as to the catalyst," Lady Syri said. "The second matter I wanted to bring to your attention."

Alistar straightened, a spike of concern running down his spine. "What is it?"

"Lady Celyn Sunward has been seen in Lewarden."

"*What?*" His hands slammed against the desk as he jerked to his feet.

Sunward, a human woman adopted into a noble elven family, had been Cemar's lover, as well as one of the three leaders of the cabal. She had, at one point, both drugged and attempted to seduce Alistar. After Cemar's death, she'd slipped away and vanished. For the last year and a half, Alistar had heard not even a whisper about her. He could gladly have gone the rest of his life without hearing her name again.

"I first heard the rumor two weeks ago. Not the first time I'd heard such a rumor, but I looked into it further until I could confirm the accuracy. She's made several appearances at minor events, mostly those hosted by wealthy commoner business owners. However, she might also have attended Lord Oremeld's masquerade ball two days ago."

"You think her appearance is connected to the crystal." Alistar sank back into his chair.

"Her reason for returning to the capital remains a mystery, but the timing seems less than coincidental. We know her connection to the sabotage of the mahiy lines, the creation of Ambrosia, and the attempt to overthrow the Crown, and knowing the crystal was an artifact used by her cohorts."

Alistar considered the implications. *What about those smuggled goods? Is Sunward responsible for those as well? And if we can determine their use, will we understand her plans?* "Thank you, Technician Feyblade. I'll keep this information in confidence, but you *must* inform me of any changes, either with the crystal, your team, or the reports of Lady Sunward."

"Of course, Senior Engineer De'seneth." She curtsied and took her leave.

CHAPTER 5

Once home from work, Alistar considered the crates of components he'd brought from Rillwater. The manor outbuildings included a space that could be used as a workshop, but it wasn't designed with artificing in mind, and he didn't trust that he could keep it secure from snooping eyes or worse, light fingers.

"Dorne, I want these crates moved into the basement," he said. "The workroom, if you would."

"Of course, sir." Dorne called in several other members of the Rillwater staff to haul the heavy crates down to their new home. He glanced at Alistar as the work began and spoke in a low voice. "Sir, can I ask what they contain?"

"An interesting assortment of items acquired by Captain As'enel that she thought might be relevant to my work," Alistar answered. "I'll work on them this evening."

Dorne just nodded and resumed supervision of the transportation of the crates. Alistar headed into the library. Saskia was still at the clinic and wasn't likely to be home until dinner. He settled into one of the leather chairs to read and to not think about the implications of Sunward reappearing in Lewarden.

Half an hour later, Dorne knocked on the library door. "Sir, the crates have all been moved, though we didn't unpack them. Additionally, Miss Darkwood just arrived."

"Thank you." Alistar closed his book and rose.

In the foyer, Onyxflame waited. Her dark brown hair was pulled back and pinned up in a tight, severe bun. She wore thick, practical leather trousers and boots with a long-sleeved shirt and a vest with dozens of pockets large and small. Tools hung from her belt. The twin holdalls by her feet looked small for someone taking residence in a new house, but a lady's maid could expect that much of her wardrobe would be provided by her employer.

"Rykka, welcome. I see you've come ready to work."

Onyxflame bowed. "Yes, Lord De'seneth. I understand that Lady De'seneth is still at the clinic, but also that you have some tasks I can assist with?"

"Indeed. Come with me and I'll show you. Dorne, please ensure Rykka's bags get to her room." Alistar led the way through the manor toward the back stairs.

As they passed through the ballroom, Onyxflame paused. First checking that no one was listening, she said, "De'seneth, I can't believe you live *here*." She gestured at the massive room and the stained-glass doors onto the balcony.

Alistar waited for her. "I'm somewhat obligated to do so. The manor was part of my reward from the Silver Prince. Also, regardless of whatever memories I have associated with certain rooms, this is a location of interest to Silverline Power, so it's convenient for everyone to have me living here."

She frowned at him. "A location of interest?"

Alistar gestured for her to follow, and she obliged. He unlocked an inconspicuous door at the far end of the ballroom. Onyxflame entered, and Alistar stepped in after her, locking the door behind them.

Ghostlights glowed on the walls, casting pale blue light on

the descending stairs. The air was still and dry. The steps showed the wear of frequent use.

Alistar slipped past Onyxflame and took the lead again. Keeping his voice low, he said, "No one else should be down here. Only a handful of people in the house have a key. This staircase leads down to the rooms Cemar, Sunward, and Sok'lof used for the rites and rituals they conducted with their devotees."

Onyxflame shuddered. "Remind me not to touch anything."

"Everything's been cleaned thoroughly," Alistar promised. The cabal's gatherings had devolved into orgies on a regular basis, from what he'd heard. "Regardless, that's not the only thing down here. The investigation of the manor revealed an extensive series of hidden passages. Presumably, the tunnels run all over beneath the grounds."

"Presumably? You haven't mapped them all out yet?" Onyxflame asked.

"We've mapped the ones we can get into." Alistar opened the door at the bottom of the stairs and entered a spacious room set up like a lecture hall, with chairs facing a podium at the front of the room. "Unfortunately, we can't open some of the doors." He made himself say it as if the problem didn't constantly aggravate him.

Onyxflame's eyebrows rose. "Can't open them? Could I have a look?"

He almost agreed, then caught himself, remembering who he was speaking to. "Not right now. We have work to do."

"Ah, of course." Onyxflame's tone sounded light, but he didn't trust it.

The lights in the workroom illuminated as Alistar entered. Half a dozen crates rested against the walls, still packed and shut. The workroom's three tables lay empty, awaiting projects. Alistar grabbed a crowbar and pried open the nearest crate.

"All right, let's see what we have and what sense we can make of it." He glanced at Onyxflame. *Can I trust her?*

Onyxflame helped him unpack the components and arrange them on the table. She studied each piece curiously. "I'm surprised you don't have Silverline people here to look all this over."

Alistar raised an eyebrow. "Do you *want* Silverline 'lackeys' coming around here to help?"

"Well, no, but given all this, I'd imagine the Silver Prince would want his own people involved rather than someone outside his influence."

Alistar moved another crate over to the table. "I prefer to have a working hypothesis before bringing others in. Right now, there are too many unknown elements for additional people to offer much help."

Onyxflame stopped, then slowly set down the component she studied, eyeing him incredulously. "De'seneth, are you implying that you haven't informed your employer of all... this?"

"If these components could be used to construct something of interest or a threat to Silverline Power, Lewarden, or the Crown, I'll bring the matter to the attention of the appropriate people. Until then, however, this is a Family matter."

Onyxflame blinked. "So there's a possibility that the Silver Prince will never see any of this?"

"A possibility," Alistar agreed. "Why? Anything particular you don't want him to see?"

"Not yet," Onyxflame allowed. "I just... blight, I sometimes forget you're the As'enel heir as well as a Silverline engineer, De'seneth."

Alistar considered that a moment, then chuckled. "Good to know I'm not the only one who has trouble separating our present roles from those we played last time we worked together."

"It does feel odd, I admit," she said.

Last time, she was working for her freedom, but this time, I don't have that sort of a hold over her. What does she really want?

Onyxflame arranged sealed metal tubes by size on the table. She paused to shake one gently. "I wonder what role these serve in the device. Or devices. I see enough duplication that whoever wanted these intends to build more than one."

"Which also means our ships capturing some of the cargo doesn't necessarily mean the crafters won't be able to construct some, even if not as many as they want," Alistar said.

"Unfortunately, no. But it also means that, depending on how they configured the shipments, we might have enough components to figure out what in hematic perdition they're making. And why. Or maybe even 'why now?'"

"Why now?" Alistar repeated softly. *Is this connected to Sunward? Or am I making wild leaps, seeing connections that don't exist?* He leaned against a crate, looking over the items on the table. "That message you found on the ship—what was the signature on it?"

"Not a signature, just the letter 'C'. Why?"

"One thing living in this house does for me: it keeps Cemar and his schemes close to my thoughts."

She tensed at the name. She'd killed the half-elf, but from her expression, she wasn't thinking about that, but rather about the work she and her brother Tiyron had done with him, and Cemar's betrayal and murder of Tiyron. "Cemar did not pen that letter. Even if he wasn't dead, it wasn't his signature. And I *would* know. I forged it enough."

"But the plans Cemar started could still be in motion. Or someone else could be putting them into motion."

Onyxflame shook her head. "Who? His followers scattered or were executed."

Alistar considered how to respond. In the stillness, he heard a heavy clunk, like a door bolt changing positions.

Onyxflame's head snapped toward the open workroom doorway.

"What was that?" she hissed.

Alistar strode out the door and scanned the hall. At a glance, nothing had changed, but when he stepped out and looked more closely, he saw that the third door down on the left side stood slightly ajar. He strode to it, frowning. Steps approached behind him, then Onyxflame asked, "Is this one of those doors that wouldn't open?"

Alistar pushed the door open. "No, but there wasn't anything of interest in the room—no other doors or features."

Onyxflame stepped inside. "Ah, so that wall wasn't open before?"

"What?" Alistar followed her in.

A dark doorway gaped in a space that had previously been an unremarkable section of stone wall. Both Alistar and Onyxflame listened intently, but no sounds emerged from the darkness. Alistar approached and looked cautiously inside. Ghostlights sprang to life automatically, illuminating a new corridor.

"No, this was definitely not open before," Alistar said slowly.

"Did something we say trigger it? Or something in those components in the workroom?" she asked.

Did we? Was it? "I don't know," Alistar admitted.

He checked the wall around the doorway, seeking a latch or level. He found a concealed handhold and pulled. The section of stone wall slid from a slit, moving effortlessly on a track hidden on the inside of the passage, over the doorway. He didn't close it completely. Running his hand down the side of the movable section of wall, Alistar found notches where bolts had held it in place. Checking the side of the doorway, he located the bolts.

"No release I can find on this side of the wall," Onyxflame said. "Maybe something on the other side? I don't see any trigger mechanism."

Alistar slid the stone panel open again. "It moves without catching, despite the weight." He reached up to touch the rail. "I don't feel any cables or mechanisms for moving the panel. But it does open a little more easily than it closes, so when the bolts released, the weight of the stone could have caused it to slide open."

"Why did the bolts release, though?" Onyxflame asked. "Was there someone on the other side?"

They both looked at the passage floor. A layer of fine dust coated the smooth stones, undisturbed. "Not unless they didn't touch the ground," Alistar said finally. He stared down the passage as if he could pry out its secrets by will alone.

"Are we going in?" Onyxflame asked, one eyebrow raised and a smile tugging at the corners of her mouth.

Alistar checked his pocket watch. Saskia should be home any time, and dinner should be served shortly after. She would worry if he wasn't there. But this mysterious door might close as suddenly as it opened, and tomorrow, there might be no sign of it again. "Get something to block the door so it doesn't close on us."

Onyxflame hurried back to the workroom and returned with several chunks of metal. She arranged them to prevent the slab from sliding back into place. "That should do the trick. Now can we look into this mysteriously opening secret passage?" She studied Alistar's scowling expression. "De'seneth, I would have thought you'd be more enthusiastic about uncovering these mysteries."

"Normally, I would be," Alistar said. "The timing, however..." He shook his head.

"What, the passage opening when I'm here, and not before?" Onyxflame asked.

"Not even that. The larger timing, in relation to the other strange things that have been happening."

"Oh? I heard a few rumors down in the slums about ghosts

rising to haunt Crown Prince Filipp's Great Exhibition, but I didn't get any details."

"I haven't heard that one," Alistar said. "I'll have to ask Saskia if anyone at the clinic has been talking about it."

"So, what other strange things are happening? And why do you think they're connected to your house?" Onyxflame asked.

"Whether these strange things are connected to my house, or my house is connected to the other strange things is open for debate. But the situations just keep pointing back to Cemar's schemes." He started down the passage, his feet stirring the dust in small pale clouds.

"You were saying something about him before all the noise began. Something about his... legacy, I suppose?" Onyxflame brushed her fingers over the wall as she walked with him.

"His legacy. That's as good a term as any, I guess. Do you know anything about the crystal Sok'lof attached to his staff in his role as Zhrets Von? It resembles one formed by natural condensation of magical energy into a solid form." He knew his superiors at Silverline Power would not approve of him discussing this topic with anyone outside the company, but Onyxflame had a unique viewpoint, and he wanted her perspective.

She frowned. "I never saw it. Tiyron might have. He mentioned seeing a crystal flower a couple times."

"It's being studied by a team at Silverline Power. Sok'lof had a way of activating it that we haven't been able to duplicate yet. However, something in the crystal is still active, or intermittently active, and the team has observed some strange phenomenon when it becomes active."

Onyxflame snorted derisively. "And what poor lowborn souls did the Silver Prince consign to be exposed to an unknown artifact?"

"His daughter," Alistar said. "Lady Syri has been working with the crystal for the last year and a half."

"Oh." Onyxflame digested that for a moment. "What sorts of phenomenon?"

"That's still confidential information. But the frequency of the incidents has increased recently," Alistar said.

Onyxflame's brow furrowed. "Do you think the 'incidents' are affecting your manor? Is the crystal even close enough to affect a private residence? I know you Silverline people have all sorts of formulas for calculating the range of disruptions and the potential power of them. Could the crystal be injecting some energy into the mahiy lines that moves on a different frequency than the standard? Something in the manor could be calibrated to respond to that frequency."

For someone without formal training in magical theory, Onyxflame had a knack for the underlying concepts. Her musings spawned half a dozen theories in Alistar's mind. He seized on the one that felt most plausible.

"Energy pulses on a different frequency could theoretically travel the mahiy lines. If they were in the correct range, they'd only cause minimal degradation in line output, within the margin of error. I'll pull some reports for analysis tomorrow. But I question whether the crystal is the source of the pulses. I should have seen other phenomenon before now if that was the point of origin. However, if an external source is projecting the alternate frequency magic, both this and the crystal's behavior could be responses to those signals."

"Who or what is causing them, though?" Onyxflame asked.

"I don't know for certain, but I have a suspicion." Alistar turned to Onyxflame. He'd been uncertain about telling her about Sunward, but the more they talked, the less coincidental her arrival seemed. "Not all members of Cemar's cabal were eliminated. Lady Sunward eluded capture. And now, she's been seen in Lewarden."

Onyxflame sucked in a sharp breath. "Cemar's *lover* not only got away, but has come *back*?"

Alistar nodded, jaw tight.

The passage opened into a small room lit by ghostlights. In each corner, a smoky crystal, dark and inert, rested in a stand. The center of the room held a bare ink-stained marble table.

Onyxflame started to say something, then stopped, looking around the room. She walked to the nearest crystal and tapped it with a fingernail. A gentle chime sounded from it. She moved clockwise around the room, tapping the other crystals. Two produced a higher, sharper tone, and the other a lower one. The elf frowned.

"What is it?" Alistar asked.

"Something Tiyron told me." She shook her head. "I don't remember enough. I need to check his notes."

"Tiyron was here?"

"I know he paid visits to Cemar's hideout, or lair, or whatever you want to call it. And he mentioned a series of crystals, but I don't recall the details. I'll see what I can find tonight. Maybe the notes will tell me something."

Alistar looked around the empty room and wondered what other secrets still lay hidden. "I hope so."

CHAPTER 6

Alistar took a seat at his usual table in one of his favorite eateries near Silverline Power. Blackberry Hollow was one of a dozen small dining spots that had sprung up around the company headquarters as enterprising cooks recognized the location's potential. Some places were open for both breakfast and lunch, others, like this one, just for lunches.

The owner's daughter brought him a pot of fresh tea. "Good afternoon, Lord De'seneth. Would you like the usual?"

"The house special today, whatever's on," he told her. "And a second mug for the tea."

"Of course, sir." She set another mug at the seat across from him and vanished into the back.

Several minutes later, an elf entered Blackberry Hollow. He looked around quickly and made his way to Alistar's table. His brown hair was pulled back in a short braid. He stood several inches taller than Alistar's six feet. His build was naturally slim, but even accounting for that, he was thin. His clothes were clean and pressed, but the cuffs were a little frayed and the cloth worn, its once rich blue hue faded.

"Good to see you, Lamorage," Alistar greeted.

"Thank you." Lamorage settled into the open chair. "I've seen more of your wife in the last few months than I have you."

Alistar smiled wryly. "Entirely my fault, I know. I've been working on things for the Exhibition."

"Oh, I know." Lamorage waved that aside. "Saskia told me." The elf made himself available on call at the Coiled Dragon Clinic, employing his ability to channel healing. He'd grown more comfortable with it in the last year and had mostly come to terms with the idea that his use of the drug Ambrosia had permanently enhanced his previously weak ability.

"Well, to make up for it, lunch is on me," Alistar told him.

"You don't need to--"

"It's on me," Alistar repeated firmly. "How have you been?"

The owner's daughter arrived to take Lamorage's order. He waited until she'd returned to the kitchen before answering. "I've done some work here and there. The Admiral often sends a few things my way. His message from a few days ago indicated I should be available to assist you if needed. Though he didn't specify the reason or the sort of assistance."

Alistar chuckled softly. "That sounds about right. They received some goods that appear related to our area of expertise. I don't have anything for you yet, but I might soon." Lamorage had left Silverline in disgrace following the discovery that he'd been Cemar's unwilling pawn, trapped by debt and blackmail. His skill as an engineer had never been in question, though, and Alistar knew he could rely on his friend's advice.

Lamorage nodded. "I have a couple other small projects to keep me occupied, but if you need anything, I'll be there."

"Thank you."

Their food came out—rice bowls with soft-cooked egg, crisp vegetables, and slices of venison. Both men applied themselves to their meals while the food was still hot. Alistar pretended not to notice how quickly Lamorage devoured his. His friend deserved to keep his dignity and not to be peppered with questions like, "Can you afford food?"

"So, what's new from Botany?" Lamorage asked, scraping the last rice from his bowl. "Have they bred the kurowa flowers into a secret plant army to overrun Lewarden yet?"

"Not yet, though I'm sure they're trying."

Silverline Power was divided into two main groups: Engineering and Botany. Botany bred the kurowa flowers that produced the magical energy. Engineering directed that magic through the mahiy lines, guiding it around the city, determining the locations for new generation facilities. Neither group could effectively function without the other, but that didn't prevent rivalries between them.

Alistar shared Silverline gossip with Lamorage—what he could that was not confidential—and caught him up on the latest news until he had to return to work. He paid for both meals, giving Lamorage no opportunity to object again.

"You didn't have to," the elf told him once more. "But thank you."

"It's my apology for neglecting our lunch get-togethers," Alistar said, knowing it would assuage some of Lamorage's guilt and cover over any hints of concern about whether his friend could afford such expenses. "I'll be better about staying in contact. And if anything comes up with regard to the Admiral's message, I'll tell you."

"Whatever you need, Alistar." Lamorage raised a hand in farewell and walked down the street toward the taxi carriages.

When Alistar arrived home after work, before he reached his room to change, Onyxflame, in her Darkwood persona, caught him in the hall. Glancing around quickly to check for spying eyes or listening ears, she said, "Lord De'seneth, I need to talk to you when you have a moment."

The unease in her voice worried him. "Let me change for the evening, then we can speak in my study."

Alistar's personal study was a well-lit room with two large windows overlooking the manor grounds. Four armchairs rested in a loose semicircle around the fireplace. Tall bookshelves on either side of the fireplace held Alistar's engineering tomes and other books from his studied, as well as a leatherbound collection of nautical texts. The other bookshelves held novels and other less technical books. Alistar settled at his desk and tucked some documents into a drawer.

At a knock on the study door, he rose and opened it. Onyxflame stood in the hall holding a tray with a pot of tea. As an excuse for her to come to his study, it was clever. He let her in and closed the door behind her.

"You wanted to talk to me?" Alistar asked.

She nodded and set the tea service on a side table. "I found my brother's notes. But they aren't what I need to understand those crystals."

"Oh? What do you need?" He poured himself a cup of tea and sipped the steaming liquid.

She paced around the room, picking up trinkets and turning them over in her hands. "Tiyron never cared for reading or writing. He recognized its uses, and learned because I wanted to learn, but he wrote notes to serve as mental cues—a few words or phrases that, if he read them later, would call that memory back in detail." She shook her head. "That was a trick I couldn't master. It also means his notes aren't meant for anyone else, even me."

"So you can't decipher the meaning of those stones," Alistar said, trying to keep the disappointment out of his voice. It'd felt like he was on the verge of finding answers about the house, and now that hope slid through his fingers like water.

"I can't, no," she admitted. Her voice dropped lower. "The only person who can interpret Tiyron's notes is Tiyron."

Alistar's eyes narrowed. "Onyxflame, if you are implying a venture into necromancy, or otherwise calling up the souls of the dead..." With Onyxflame, he was willing to stretch the laws, but that was a line he wouldn't cross.

"Hematic perdition, no! No necromancy!"

"You told me your brother was dead." Alistar gazed at her without blinking.

She shifted uncomfortably. "Actually, I told you he was dying when I found him, and that I buried him." She sat on the edge of a table. "Many years back, when we were first starting out, Tiyron insisted we invest some of our first take in a pair of trinkets called 'timestops'. The claim was that they could put any object or person into stasis, though they could only do so one time. Tiyron had used his long ago, but I saved mine until... then."

Understanding slammed into Alistar. He sank into the nearest chair, reeling. "He's not dead."

"He's frozen in time heartbeats short of death." She swallowed hard. "Assuming the stasis has held and that Cemar's thefts from the mahiy lines didn't cause a disruption. The trinket requires reliable access to the mahiy lines."

"You haven't checked?" He frowned at her, focusing on that rather than pondering the implications of this revelation.

"I had to ensure he was somewhere he wouldn't be found, De'seneth. Not by Cemar, not by the Silver Prince, not by any would-be crime lord. I wasn't going to disturb that until I had a way to bring him back."

Alistar said nothing for several long minutes. *Tiyron Onyxflame isn't dead.*

Onyxflame broke the silence finally. "Cemar shared details with him. He knows things even Sunward might not. Without his help, it could take years to figure out how to navigate this maze."

Alistar held up a hand to stop her. "Saskia should be part of this conversation. Your brother needs a healer, and he needs a safe place to recover. This house isn't the place for that."

Onyxflame blinked. "You're not..." She shook herself. "I expected you to require more convincing, De'seneth."

"I'm not saying anything about this is ideal. But if this needs to happen, it needs to happen somewhere safer than here. Someplace where a severely injured man won't draw notice."

Onyxflame let out a slow breath. "All right. I'll wait in Lady Saskia's rooms until she returns from the clinic."

She took her leave. Alistar headed downstairs to tell Dorne to inform him when Saskia arrived home. Unexpectedly, she was walking through the door when he got there.

"Welcome home." He kissed her. "You're back early."

She laughed. "Meeting me at the door? What's the occasion? We didn't have many patients this afternoon, so Father sent me out early."

"Onyxflame needs to discuss something with both of us. In my study," he breathed in her ear. A little louder, he said, "I couldn't miss the opportunity to greet the most beautiful woman I know."

"Flatterer." She winked. "I'll change and be there shortly."

Alistar returned to his study and paced in thought. *Tiyron Onyxflame is still alive and might be the key I need to unlock this manor. Assuming he's willing to help. If he's anything like the persona Onyxflame portrayed during the investigation, he doesn't harbor any love for the Crown or for Silverline Power.*

Ten minutes later, Saskia entered the study with Onyxflame in tow. Saskia closed the door firmly and looked between her husband and her lady's maid. "Have you discovered something? Did new doors open?"

Onyxflame collected herself. "Not yet, but I know who might be able to open them: my brother."

Saskia looked at the elf sharply. "How?"

"He's not dead," Onyxflame said in answer to the implied question. "My brother has been in stasis for the last two years. I'm sure he knows more about this house and Cemar's plans, if we can revive and heal him."

"He's alive? And in stasis? And you've left him there?" Saskia demanded.

"My options were limited." Onyxflame's voice was tight. "He was dying."

"Why didn't you tell us? Long-term stasis on a living being can cause complications—sometimes very serious ones."

"Limited options," Onyxflame repeated. "And I hoped… that I could find a way to restore him more completely than a healer could. Cemar's tortures were intended to destroy him."

She looked at Alistar. "That's one reason I signed on with the fleet. It made chasing rumors of wondrous artifacts of healing and restoration easier. But so far, that's all they've been: rumors, legends, and fanciful tales. Time isn't with us any longer."

Saskia let out a long breath. "I'm sure you wouldn't propose trying this unless you thought it necessary. And the longer he remains in stasis, the greater the risk for complications. Can he be moved?"

Onyxflame nodded. "He can be moved without disrupting the stasis, as long as there are mahiy lines for the trinket to draw on. Where to, though?"

"The clinic," Saskia said without hesitation. "I assume you thought the same, Alistar?"

"Yes. As long as you and your father agree."

"I'll talk to him about it, but I doubt he'll object. We have private rooms for long-term care."

"He might not be a very good patient," Onyxflame warned.

"Elves in the care of a human doctor rarely are," Saskia said evenly, looking at her.

"Ah. Well, yes, there is that too. He might be more understanding of that than I was," Onyxflame said. "But he's never been patient with physical weakness. And I don't know how he'll react to being in an unfamiliar location."

"You'll be able to stay with him, if you wish to," Saskia told her.

"What about my responsibilities here?"

"I'm not so heartless that I would deny my new lady's maid time off to deal with a family emergency," Saskia told her. "The timing is unfortunate, but such things are not events one can plan for."

Onyxflame nodded slowly. "All right. What about a healer?"

"I'll talk to Lamorage tomorrow," Alistar said. "We had lunch together today, and it seems the Admiral has already alerted him I might need his assistance, although I don't think any of us thought that assistance would take this form."

"Your friend from the western mountains, who Cemar blackmailed?" Onyxflame asked. She unconsciously rubbed her shoulder, where Cemar's crossbow bolt had struck. Lamorage had healed the wound while still in a drugged haze.

"Won't Lamorage notice the similarities between your brother and 'Lord Aspendark'?" Saskia asked, referring to the persona Onyxflame had used while working with Alistar previously.

Onyxflame hesitated. "That is… unlikely," she said quietly. "After what Cemar did, no one will mistake one of us for the other again."

"Ah. I'm sorry."

For several minutes, Onyxflame said nothing. Finally, she spoke. "Just tell me when to bring him to the clinic. The rest… the rest I'll worry about later."

Lamorage still lived in the rented townhome he'd occupied while working at Silverline Power. It wasn't a bad neighborhood—better than the one Alistar had lived in prior to being granted the mansion. This morning, the streets were quiet except for a handful of children bent intently over a game of stick stack on a small patch of grass. Alistar knocked on the door and waited several minutes.

Footsteps approached in a rapid staccato and the door opened. "Can I help… De'seneth!" Lamorage's expression brightened. "Come in." He stepped aside and closed the door behind Alistar.

Lamorage's house served as his office for the odds and ends of his freelance work as well. Alistar noted the surprising order and organization of the space—more than he'd ever seen his friend display during his time as an engineer.

"I hope I'm not interrupting anything," Alistar said. "I'm sorry for not sending word before coming calling this early."

Lamorage waved the apology aside. "You're welcome any time. I'm not working on anything that can't wait. I told you that yesterday." He led Alistar through the foyer into the sitting room. "Would you care for a drink? I know it's early, but my father sent a bottle of icewine."

Alistar accepted the offered glass of pale blue wine. "Thank you. How is your father?"

"Same as ever," Lamorage answered with a vague gesture. "Although he's hinted a few times that he might like me to come home long-term." He swirled the wine in his glass and sipped. "I'm not ready to consider that yet, though. So, is this a social call, or business?"

"Business," Alistar told him. "But off the record."

Lamorage's eyebrows rose. "Off Lewarden's record, or off the Admiral's record?"

Alistar smiled slightly. "Off the Crown's record. I need a healer."

Lamorage froze a moment, then gulped a deep swallow of wine. "For who?"

Alistar sipped his wine. "A man who may have knowledge I need. He worked with Cemar, and Cemar betrayed him."

Color drained from Lamorage's face, but he gestured for Alistar to continue.

"He was tortured to the point of death. When he was dying, Cemar dumped him in a ditch somewhere. His sister found him and was able to engage a stasis trinket. She came to me about the matter last night. She's kept him in stasis in secret. Given his close involvement with Cemar before the betrayal, he may know quite a lot that no one else could."

"Demons' frozen halls," Lamorage whispered. "That's... further off the Crown's record than I expected. If the Silver Prince or the Royal Guard knew..."

"I know. And I need a healer who I can trust not to turn him over to the authorities." *Or to anyone else.*

Lamorage nodded. "I understand, De'seneth. Where is this man?"

"His sister will bring him to the Coiled Dragon Clinic tonight, after hours. I don't know what condition he's in, but I know it won't be good," Alistar warned.

Lamorage's jaw tightened. "Nothing Cemar did to people was good. Not even to his supposed allies." He drew a deep breath. "I'll help."

"Thank you, Lamorage."

"Whoever this man is, he was a victim of Cemar. That's enough for me to know. I'll be there tonight."

CHAPTER 7

Thank the Reyker I can leave my office early without being questioned as to what I'm doing or why. Twinges of guilt prodded Alistar about implying he was conducting field work related to the mahiy line project for the Exhibition, but he pushed them aside. Explaining how a trip to the Coiled Dragon Clinic applied to his work would raise far more questions than he cared to answer. Not the least of which was the identity of the expected patient.

Tiyron Onyxflame is alive, and now I have a responsibility to keep him that way.

Alistar ran a hand through his hair as the weight of that thought once again settled on his shoulders. Tiyron Onyxflame, one of the most notorious criminals in Lewarden, known for his scorn of authority and his loathing of Silverline Power. Tiyron Onyxflame, who would not know or trust Alistar the way Rykka did. Tiyron Onyxflame, who Alistar had told Prince Cero was dead, and who could destroy Alistar's career simply by revealing himself to be alive.

Saskia's father, Doctor Tan'shyo, handled the normal clinic patients, and had asked remarkably few questions as to why his daughter and son-in-law needed to reserve a private patient room for an indeterminate time. He simply waved Alistar to the back of the clinic.

"The patient and his sister arrived a little while ago. I settled in their room."

"Thank you." Alistar gave his gray-haired father-in-law a respectful bow and walked down to the end of the corridor, along another short hall, and knocked on the closed door.

"Come in." Onyxflame's voice was tight and strained even through the wood.

Alistar opened the door and stepped inside. Onyxflame sat beside the bed, hands folded tightly in her lap. A long wooden coffin lay on the floor beside her, top ajar. The boards were weathered and warped, and several nails jutted out at odd angles. A figure lay on the bed, shrouded by covers that hid even the face.

Onyxflame gave him a tight smile. "De'seneth."

"Onyxflame." It occurred to him to wonder how he would address her and her brother once Tiyron was conscious. He looked from the coffin to the bed. "I neglected to ask if you needed help transporting him."

Her lips curled in a genuine smile. "You'd be surprised how few questions a woman gets when she's walking down the street carting a coffin."

Alistar blinked, then chuckled in spite of himself. Onyxflame laughed with him, tension easing from her shoulders. They both sobered after a moment, humor fading. Before the silence grew awkward, another knock sounded on the door. Saskia didn't wait for a response, opening the door and stepping inside followed by Lamorage.

Lamorage bowed to Onyxflame. "Good evening, madam. I'm Veril Lamorage, a healer and a friend of the De'seneths."

She stood and nodded in return. "My name is Rykka. Thanks for being willing to help under the circumstances."

"It's my honor to help someone who fell victim to Cemar." Lamorage took off his coat and hung it beside the door. He glanced from the coffin to the figure on the bed.

Onyxflame pushed the coffin under the bed and out of immediate sight, then gave the others a small, somewhat apologetic shrug. "It was the least conspicuous way to move him without disrupting the stasis charm."

Saskia stepped to the bed and reached for the cover. "If I may?"

Onyxflame's head jerked in a nod. "With apologies. My brother is... not exactly decent."

Lamorage swallowed hard and nodded. Alistar wondered if he remembered how he'd been half-stripped when Cemar imprisoned him in a dark room, leaving Lamorage at the mercy of his fears and memories. Alistar stepped aside to allow Lamorage closer.

Saskia drew back the sheet, revealing a male elf. He lay on his back, limbs drawn up close against his body. From the position, Alistar guessed he'd been bound when the stasis was activated. The restraints had been removed, but his body remained frozen in the exact position it had been in when the stasis took hold.

Dried blood flecked his skin, though much had either been cleaned off or washed away by time and weather. Filth, blood, and worse permeated his shredded clothing. What cloth remained verged on indecent even by human standards, much less elven ones. His face was twisted in agony. Around his neck, a clay talisman hung from a slender cord. Alistar's stomach twisted as he took in what he saw. The elf's right eye was an empty socket, the lacerated skin around it mapped in blue and purple. Unnatural twists in his limbs told of shattered bones. At least two fingers were missing on his left hand. Brands were seared across his body and lash marks lacerated his back and chest.

Lamorage slowly sucked in a breath. "My first priority will be keeping him alive. I'll heal what else I can, but a body can only accept so much magic without… negative consequences."

"I know." Onyxflame's voice was quiet. "I'll end the stasis spell on your mark."

Lamorage reached into his pocket and withdrew a small vial containing a sliver of azure crystal. Alistar stiffened, but it was Onyxflame who asked sharply, "Is that Ambrosia?"

Lamorage showed no surprise that she recognized the drug. "I have a few slivers of it. I save them for moments when I need more magic than I can draw naturally."

"How many is 'a few'?" Alistar asked, wary.

"Two more slivers, no larger than this one." Lamorage didn't flinch from Alistar's gaze. "I know my limits. To save this man's life, I need Ambrosia."

Alistar's stomach twisted. *I can't ask him to risk becoming addicted again.* "Lamorage."

"I'll be fine, De'seneth. I know what I'm doing, and I know my limits." Lamorage opened the vial and tilted the shard into his mouth. His eyes sank shut and he crouched beside the bed. Tendrils of purple light began to stream through the ceiling into him as he drew from the mahiy lines.

"Release the stasis… now," he breathed.

Onyxflame drew a deep breath and cut the cord on the talisman around Tiyron's neck. Tiyron gasped, curling tighter in on himself. His mouth opened in what might have been a scream, but only produced wheezing, choked sounds. Blood flowed from his wounds. Saskia grabbed bandages and shoved them to Alistar. Lamorage set his hands on the writhing elf and healing poured through him.

"Do what you can to slow the bleeding, Lamorage," Saskia said. "I'm going to sedate him."

Lamorage's head jerked in a nod. "Do it lightly. I'm fighting enough to keep his heart from stopping."

Onyxflame crouched by her brother's head, speaking softly into his ear and trying to sooth him. Alistar bandaged a long gash on Tiyron's leg, a task made more difficult by the elf's struggles. He tried not to inflict more damage to broken bones.

Saskia carefully raised Tiyron's head, trickling water into his mouth a little at a time. It felt like an eternity before the bleeding visibly slowed. Tiyron's ragged gasps eased. The violet glow around Lamorage dimmed, then faded. Lamorage slumped, sweat running down his face and soaking his shirt.

"Stable," he panted. "He's... stable." He pushed to his feet and staggered. Alistar jumped to his feet and steadied him. Lamorage wiped his hands on his shirt as if something clung to them. "Excuse me. I need..."

"Need what?" Alistar asked.

"Going to be sick," Lamorage whispered.

Alistar guided him to the privy, then closed the door and gave his friend space and the illusion of privacy. When Lamorage emerged, he was pale and shaky.

"Are you all right?" Alistar asked in concern.

"Can I sleep here tonight? That will help. Maybe." Lamorage wavered and braced himself against the wall.

"Of course. We assumed you would need to. Doctor Tan'shyo prepared a room for you," Alistar assured him, though the answer didn't ease any of his concerns.

Lamorage closed his eyes. "De'seneth, the things Cemar did to that man... I... I knew he was cruel, but not that he had such depth of sadistic perversion."

Alistar had no response to offer. He helped Lamorage to the promised room. Once his friend was settled, Alistar lit the lamp by the bed and slipped out. He returned to Tiyron's room.

Saskia had put Onyxflame to work rolling bandages, a repetitive task Onyxflame performed like an automaton while Saskia assessed their patient.

"Lamorage is resting," Alistar said. "What can I do?"

"I need your help setting some bones. Onyxflame, you should step outside for this part," Saskia said firmly.

Onyxflame wordlessly shook her head.

Alistar gently took her arm. "Just into the hallway for a little while."

She didn't resist being led out and didn't try to go back inside when Alistar released her arm.

"I'll let you know when we're done," Alistar promised.

Her head moved in a tight nod.

When he returned to Tiyron's room, Saskia gave him a small smile. "Thank you. I'd rather she not have to watch this part."

Alistar closed the door behind him and moved to his wife's side. "It's bad, isn't it?"

"It's bad," she agreed softly. "Lamorage stabilized him and honestly did amazing work at reassembling pulverized bones. But we still need to set and stabilize them." She leaned against Alistar. "I've seen men crushed by collapsed walls, people trampled by horses and run over by carriages. I've seen victims of Rat's Disease. This is worse than any of them, Alistar. This was a deliberate, prolonged effort to break a man."

Alistar swallowed hard and wrapped his arms around her. "Cemar didn't succeed. If he had, he would have known about Onyxflame... Rykka."

"That doesn't make what he did any less horrible," Saskia said quietly.

"I know. But he won't win, even in this," Alistar promised. *Even if it means healing and protecting one of the most infamous criminals in Lewarden.*

Rykka paced restlessly around the room. Saskia let her. She'd offered the elf some busywork, but Rykka couldn't even focus on those tasks at the moment.

The clinic was quiet. Both Lamorage and Alistar had retired to sleep, and aside from Tiyron, they had no patients in residence.

Rykka abruptly spun and rushed to Tiyron's bed. A moment later, Saskia heard Tiyron's breathing hitch, and he moaned softly. She moved opposite Rykka and filled a mug halfway with water. She added a dose of painkiller to the water. Tiyron must be in intense pain—there was no way he couldn't be, unless he'd suffered nerve damage they weren't aware of.

"Tiyron?" Rykka asked softly. "Are you aware?"

His ragged breathing eased slightly. Tiyron's head turned toward Rykka, though his eye remained closed. He shuddered and tried to raise his arm, then gave a thin, breathless gasp of pain. Casts encased and immobilized his arms and legs. Saskia heard his breath grow sharp and panicked when he couldn't move.

Rykka caught his hand in hers. "Don't try to move. Your arms are in casts. You're safe."

"Whe…" Tiyron croaked weakly.

"You're in a clinic run by a human doctor. I used my timestop to get you here."

Saskia hated to disturb Tiyron further, but he needed both water and something to ease the pain. "I'm going to sit him up a little. I need you to tuck the cushions around him to support him," she told Rykka.

Tiyron flinched when she spoke, and again when she touched him, but he had no strength to resist. Saskia gently eased him up. The elf made a choked sound of pain. Rykka set the cushions to prop him up, and Saskia let him sink into them. Sweat streaked Tiyron's colorless face. Saskia held the mug to his cracked lips. He gulped the water as fast as she let him.

"Easy, easy," Rykka murmured to him. "We'll get you more, but you have to drink slowly."

"Mor…" His fingers twitched as if to grasp the mug.

Saskia gave him more water and wondered how long it had been since the gaunt elf last ate or drank. It appeared the stasis charm had worked properly in that regard, at least. She'd heard of animals placed under such effects where the stasis hadn't quite taken proper hold, and the creature under the spell wasted away. Far too many other things could have gone awry that they wouldn't know for certain until later, but Saskia kept those concerns to herself. Onyxflame had enough to worry about at the moment. She moved away from the bed, giving the siblings a little space.

"The pain should ease soon, Tiyron. You're safe. Rest," Rykka murmured.

His eyelid fluttered but didn't open. Rykka held his hand until he began to relax. When his breathing smoothed into something closer to sleep, Rykka untwined her fingers from his and stepped back to Saskia.

"I can't tell if he heard me or not, or if he has any idea what I'm saying."

"I'm sure he hears you," Saskia told her. "He might not understand the words yet, but he knows your voice."

"How can you be sure?" Rykka asked in a voice that desperately wanted to believe.

"The difference between how he reacts when you speak and how he reacts when I do," Saskia said gently. "He knows your voice. He tenses when I speak and relaxes when you do."

"I want to tell him Cemar is dead," Rykka whispered, pacing. "I want him to know he's safe!" She swallowed hard. "I don't want him to lie there in fear that he's going to be tortured again."

Saskia rested her hand on Rykka's shoulder. "You'll be able to tell him soon. He knows your voice, and it reassures him. He'll feel safer hearing it."

Rykka ran a hand through her hair. "This isn't how I wanted to bring him back." She cast a look at Tiyron. "I wanted to find a way to make him whole. To wake him without pain, everything restored, healed, as good as new. I wanted a miracle."

The fact Tiyron survived at all was a miracle, but it wasn't the miracle Rykka wanted, and telling her that wouldn't help. Rykka could have chased rumors and legends for the rest of her life without finding what she sought. And Tiyron could have wasted away in stasis, so that even if she found some means of restoring his broken body, she would have been too late to save him. Saskia said none of that.

"He needs you more than he needs that miracle." She guided Rykka to a chair beside the bed. "Talk to him. Let your voice guide him when he wakes."

The elf relented and sank wearily into the chair. She leaned over Tiyron and spoke to him quietly. Saskia checked his temperature and breathing, then settled near the bed to monitor him through the night.

CHAPTER 8

Through a haze of agony, Tiyron recognized he was both awake and alive.

No. No! Panic clawed into his gut. *They came back!* Mocking words still echoed in his mind, calling him weak, broken, no more use. He was sure he'd been bound and tossed into a ditch to finally die. *What's left for him to do to me?*

That question sent a fresh wave of terror through him. Would they take his feet next? Hands?

When will he let it end?

"Tiyron?" A female voice spoke softly. "Do you hear me?"

He knew her voice, and some of the panic relented. *Rykka. The priests say when you're dying, you see and hear those you love. I'm hallucinating. Or... they drugged me again. Did they really dump me in that ditch?* He shuddered.

"Tiyron, you're safe. Cemar is dead. I killed him." Rykka's voice was gentle and soothing.

I must be hallucinating. He turned toward her voice. His fingers twitched as he tried to reach toward her. Pain tore through his immobilized arms.

"Just lie still," Rykka said quickly. Warm hands rested atop his.

"Whe…" His throat was raw from screaming, and the attempt to speak nearly choked him.

"We're in a clinic in the Lower City. You're safe here."

Her words didn't quite make sense, but the sound of her voice soothed him. *At least it's pleasant, for a dying man's hallucinations.*

An arm gently raised his head, and pain flared in white-hot spikes. He gasped. Cushions were tucked around him to prop him up. A mug touched his dry, cracked lips. He opened them and gulped cool liquid. It might have been water, it might not; he didn't care.

"Easy, easy," Rykka murmured. "I'll get you more, but you have to drink slowly."

"Mo…" *More, please, give me more. I'll beg if you want me to, just give me something to drink.*

He heard liquid being poured, then the mug returned to his lips. He drank as fast as the one holding it allowed. It tasted like clean water.

"You're safe, Tiyron. Rest."

Safe. Yes, that was a good dream. He could sink into the darkness in peace with that dream.

For a time, the darkness swallowed everything: sound, sensation, and especially pain, as if he sank into a deep, black pool.

Pain sank claws into his chest and ripped down his ribs. Tiyron jerked with a choked scream that dissolved into a gasping sob. Awake. Still alive. Still not free. He panted for breath and tensed for the scornful laughter to mock him.

"He's bleeding again!" The voice was Rykka's, sharp with alarm.

"Calm him as much as you can." The other woman's voice was steady. "I need to change this dressing."

Rykka? I can't still be in the same hallucination, can I? He sucked in gulps of air and peeled his eye open a slit.

The light shone brighter than it had in his prison, painfully sharp. Shapes moved around him, floating forms without details. One lowered beside him and spoke with Rykka's voice.

"Tiyron, do you hear me? You're all right. You're safe. I know it hurts right now. The doctor has to change the bandages. Don't struggle. It won't take long."

He lifted his hand toward the shape. She moved, and warm fingers wrapped around his.

This can't be real. A drug... something. She can't be here. They can't know about her. Maybe I've gone mad, and this is how my mind escapes. The pain is... more bearable with Rykka here.

His captors had taken two of the fingers on the hand she held, removed joint by joint while he screamed. His remaining digits clung to Rykka's hand as pain assaulted his chest again. His hold tightened and he moaned, throat raw. The agony ended sooner than he expected, and in a strange mercy, he was given water afterward.

"This will ease the pain a little," promised the unknown woman. "Later, we'll try giving you a little broth."

"Why?" The question rasped from his lips.

"Too much now will make you sick. We must do this one step at a time, and you're quite weak. We'll help you regain your strength, but it must happen one step at a time."

It didn't answer the question he was trying to ask. *Why are you feeding me? Why are you trying to lessen the pain? Don't you know what Cemar will do to me?* Yet she sounded sincere, and he couldn't hear scornful laughter anywhere. It made no sense.

As the woman promised, his pain began to dull. Rykka continued to hold his hand, and her voice was a comforting murmur. He floated back into the darkness.

Coarse ropes cut into his wrists and ankles as he struggled. Cemar loomed over him, a dark smirk on the half-breed's face. "Tell me where you hid the schematics, Tiyron."

"Rot in the Plagueborn's Pits."

Hot irons pressed against his bare skin. He screamed, thrashing against his bonds. Long needles, heated white hot, pierced his flesh. He screamed again as Cemar twisted them.

He rose from the darkness with a gasp, desperately searching for something to anchor him against the mockery of Cemar's taunts.

Rykka's voice, quiet though it was, drowned out the sounds ringing through his mind. He focused, trying to understand. After several long, confused minutes, he realized she was reading to him, as she'd done when they were both far younger and he wanted to know what the news rags said about their exploits. His exploits.

She's real. This is real.

"Following the conquest of the western mountains, King Dari marched—"

"History?" he croaked in weak protest. "Reading me *history*?"

"It's what I had on hand," Rykka said indignantly. "And it's not as if you've been listening anyway, if you only just noticed."

He sank deeper into the cushions. "Wake me when we get to… human invasion." He slowly opened his eye. The light stung, but not as fiercely as the last time. The shapes gained clarity. He blinked several times and turned toward Rykka's voice.

She sat beside his bed, a book in her lap. He expected to see her dressed in his clothes with a casually carefree expression on her face, like she always did. Instead, exhaustion and worry lined her face. Instead of his practical trousers and shirt, she wore a dress. He couldn't remember the last time he'd seen her wear a dress, much less a dress that flattered her, and it was disconcerting.

Rykka scowled slightly in response to his words. "I'm skipping the arrival of the humans. This book is sickening in its bias regarding them."

"For or against?" Words stung his throat, but he desperately wanted to speak without fear and torture driving his voice. And he feared what either of them might say if he broke the established pattern of their banter. This was safe. This didn't require either of them to acknowledge why he was lying on this bed, in this place, broken and in pain.

"Against, of course. And I'm not going to insult the doctors tending to you with such outrageous lies, rumors, and exaggerations," Rykka said.

Doctors? I'm in the care of humans? He vaguely remembered Rykka saying something about doctors and a clinic. The reminder moved dangerously close to the topic of how and why he was here. "Sure they've heard worse."

"I know they have; this isn't my book. I borrowed it from Doctor Tan'shyo."

Definitely a human name. Why did you take me to human doctors, Rykka? I hate doctors. "Who... why?"

"Doctor Tan'shyo and his daughter operate the Coiled Dragon Clinic in the Lower City. They're trustworthy," Rykka said.

"Don't trust human doctors." *How could you even have had time to establish how much they can be trusted? I don't know this place. Are you certain you properly vetted it and them? Not that I don't trust you, Rykka, but how can you be sure?*

"We can trust them, Tiyron," she repeated firmly. "I know them both through Doctor De'seneth's husband, Alistar De'seneth."

"Don't know him either." Tiyron eyed her with warning. How reckless had she been?

"He's the man who helped me kill Cemar."

His head jerked up, despite the stabbing pain the movement sent through his body. He stared at Rykka. "Dead? Cemar?"

"He's dead," she repeated.

"You're sure?" *Please, whatever gods might be listening, let that be true. Let this be real.*

"I crushed him between two barriers. I saw his guts splatter across the Silver Prince's ballroom, and I ground his skull to paste. I am very, *very* sure Cemar is dead, Tiyron." Her eyes were hard and her voice grim.

He slowly closed his eye, and his head sank back, chest tight. *He's dead. Gone. He can't torture me any longer.* The panic that had sustained him faded. "How... am I... alive?"

"After you told me to destroy the schematics, you and Cemar both vanished. Evidence suggested you'd both been captured by someone. I followed the leads I could find, but there were too many dead ends and false trails. Finally, I..." Her voice dropped low, and he strained to hear. "I found you in a ditch, left to die and barely breathing."

He shuddered. "That's last I remember." He remembered the rough hands binding his broken limbs. He didn't know why they'd bothered; he couldn't have escaped even without the restraints.

"I used my timestop, Tiyron," Rykka said.

Her timestop. She'd objected when he'd proposed they acquire the trinkets, calling them stupid novelties and a waste of marks. When he eventually used his, he'd admitted she was right. But he'd never considered using the trinket on a person. He hadn't even thought about the possibility. "How long?"

Her gaze slid away from him, falling to the book in her lap. "Two years."

He stared at her without comprehension. Weeks, he'd expected. Months, even, but not... "Years?" he croaked. "*Years?* What did you do, stick me in a box and forget? Decide you didn't need me? Just hope that cut-rate trinket didn't fail on me?*

"I was looking for a miracle, Tiyron!" she hissed, eyes flashing as she leaned forward. "Do you think I *wanted* you to wake like this? Do you think I would pass up any hope that I could restore you whole? Oh, and do you think I could just call up any healer in the city and trust them not to turn you and me both over to someone?" She swiped at the tears running down her cheeks with quick, angry motions. "At least I knew you were safe."

His gaze finally lowered to the bed. A blanket was carefully tucked around him, covering most of his chest in a modicum of decorum. His arms rested atop it, immobilized in plaster casts. Bandages wrapped his hands, covering the stumps of his missing fingers. His upper body was moderately elevated, and some device held his raw back off the bed, keeping pressure off his wounds. It was like lying on air or floating in a pool. Everything was clean, the room well-lit, and he smelled chemicals rather than the stink of infection and decay.

This is no Dockside patch-up clinic. Who has Rykka gotten herself in an alliance with? What do they want from us?

"How much… was… this miracle?"

"I didn't find a miracle, Tiyron," she said.

"Still alive. Close enough to one." By all rights, he should be dead, timestop or not.

"I suppose so," Rykka allowed. "The cost… a couple of favors, a few secrets." She shook her head. "Not that I don't owe De'seneth enough of both already. The healer who saved you is another friend of De'seneth, and doesn't know your identity, just that you were a victim of Cemar. He had his own encounters with Cemar."

Who is this De'seneth, and how has he gotten such a hold on Rykka? Is he an underlord who's risen while I've been… gone? Someone high up in one of the criminal syndicates? Rykka knows how dangerous it is to be in debt to them.

The door opened. A human woman with strawberry blonde hair entered carrying a tray. She wore the green dress of a doctor, though he'd rarely seen one so clean. It didn't even have patches. "How is he, Rykka?"

"Awake," Rykka answered. She rested her hand atop Tiyron's. "Tiyron, this is Doctor Saskia De'seneth."

"Recognize the voice," he said, finally having a face to associate with the voice he'd heard in previous wakings.

The doctor smiled pleasantly. "Are you up for trying some warm broth? I don't know how long it's been since you ate anything solid, so we're going to ease you into it."

"Yes." He didn't know when he'd last been given food. The things his torturers had forced him to eat had been worse than starving. Now that he smelled the broth, hunger growled and clawed at his stomach.

"Rykka, help him sit." Doctor De'seneth pulled a wheeled table to the side of the bed and sat across from Rykka. "Stasis enchantments can have unpredictable effects on digestion, so if you start to feel at all ill, tell me immediately." She spoke with confident authority, as if attending to a patient who'd been tortured, broken, then put into stasis occurred every day.

The bed of air cushioning his back gently tilted him up. Tiyron's breath caught as pain spiked through his chest and back.

"Easy, Rykka. Slowly. As gradual as possible," Doctor De'seneth said.

"Just sit me up," Tiyron countered through clenched teeth. What was a little more pain now?

Rykka ignored him, following the doctor's instructions. The slower movement hurt less but delayed his first taste of food in... too long. He tried to raise his arm and reach for the tray, but only his hand rose slightly from the bed.

He didn't think the movement was much, but Doctor De'seneth smiled sympathetically. "Your bones haven't healed enough yet for you to be able to feed yourself. Would you prefer that Rykka do so?"

"You can." Either was humiliating, but if the doctor did it, he could pretend the choice had never been offered.

She stirred the broth. He inhaled as deeply as his battered body allowed. Chicken broth had never smelled so good. He couldn't repress a cringe when the doctor moved the spoon toward his face, but she moved smoothly, no sudden jerks, staying within his limited field of vision. He slurped the broth from the spoon. For the first few sips, his stomach was unsure how to react to the warm, lightly spiced liquid. Then his body recognized it as actual nourishment. His stomach rumbled a growl.

"How's it settling?" Doctor De'seneth asked.

"Hungry." The word was insufficient to describe the devouring emptiness in his gut. He longed to snatch the bowl from her and gulp it down rather than be fed like an invalid.

I am an invalid. Anyone could walk into this room and do whatever they wanted to me, and I'd be helpless to stop them.

He couldn't push the thought away. Panic tainted the next few spoonfuls of broth. Rykka took his bandaged hand in hers, and the terror relented. He squeezed her hand.

Doctor De'seneth set the empty bowl on the tray. "We'll see how that settles, and if it doesn't give you any trouble for a couple hours, I'll bring more."

"Still hungry," Tiyron protested.

"I would imagine so," she said with sympathy. "But until your body has adjusted and recovered further, you're best with small, frequent meals."

His mouth twisted. "Like an infant." *As if I need another reminder just how helpless I am.*

"Like a man who's suffered life-threatening injuries and is recovering," Doctor De'seneth replied. She stood. "Call me if you need anything or suffer any major changes or discomforts."

There were a great many things he needed that he already

knew she wouldn't grant him. Rather than attempt to convince her, he said, "A better book."

She raised an eyebrow at him as she picked up the tray. "Better than what?"

"I borrowed a history book from your father and was reading it aloud," Rykka told her.

"I know; I heard you when I passed earlier." Doctor De'seneth gazed at Tiyron. "What would you prefer?"

"My brother prefers books with less accurate descriptions of events," Rykka muttered.

He hadn't expected the doctor to take his request seriously. He still wasn't sure she did.

"New Masked Thief books?" Even if he hadn't been in a position to commit exploits for the last... two years... the writers of the two-chip novels rarely confined themselves to the truth anyway.

Rykka sighed and rolled her eyes, but she didn't comment further on his preferred reading material.

"We don't have any copies here at the clinic," Doctor De'seneth answered. "However, if you prefer adventure stories, we do have several collected high-seas serials." Her lips quirked in amusement. "As long as you don't mind reading around my husband's commentary, Rykka. He annotated them rather liberally the first time he read them."

"Now I'm curious," Rykka said. "Tiyron will probably enjoy those. Thanks."

Tiyron stiffened. Once the doctor left and the door closed, he said, "You used my name."

"She already knows who you are, Tiyron. So does her husband." Rykka set her book aside. "I came to them because I trust them. They know who you are, and they know who I am. They've had ample opportunity to expose or blackmail me long before now if they wanted to."

His jaw tightened. *What right do you have to decide who does and doesn't know my... our secrets? This is* my *legend. I say who we can trust with the truth. What have these humans done to earn any such rights?*

He couldn't muster the energy to put his thoughts into words or to push through the argument they would start. He closed his eye and seethed in silence.

A knock on the door jerked him back to awareness. Rykka rose and opened the door, then straightened in surprise. "De'seneth."

Tiyron expected the doctor, only to stiffen in alarm when an unfamiliar human man entered. His black hair and beard were neatly groomed. His clothes were too rich even for a rising criminal lord—more suited to a wealthy businessman or a noble.

"Mind if I come in?" the man asked pleasantly. "Saskia said you wanted reading material more lively and far more fictional than the rise of the empire." He handed Rykka three half-chip novels.

"Well, *he* wants them." Rykka nodded toward Tiyron. "I was happy enough with the official fiction we call history." She walked back to her chair.

The human followed, stopping beside the bed. Tiyron's gaze followed his every move warily. "It's good to see you awake, sir."

"Who are you?" Tiyron rasped.

"Alistar De'seneth of Rillwater," the human answered.

Tiyron sucked in a sharp breath and shot a glare at Rykka. "You're working with *pirates*?"

"Privateers." Rykka and De'seneth said the word at the same time.

"Same difference." He didn't like how quick Rykka was to defend the human.

"Not at all," De'seneth said. "Pirates rob *our* ships. Privateers are authorized by the Crown to patrol our waters, protect our allies, and repel invaders, pirates, and enemies."

Tiyron recalled his own stint on a sailing ship—an unpleasant time, but necessary to acquire certain items Rykka needed for the device she was building. "Narnan ship called you pirates."

De'seneth smiled pleasantly. "Well, the Narnans aren't exactly our allies, are they?"

Tiyron shifted uneasily. His gaze shifted to Rykka. *Just who have you gotten us tangled with?*

"In any case, there are the books. They're entertaining enough, but they bear about as much resemblance to actual sailing as the Masked Thief books do to what you actually did." De'seneth still smiled pleasantly, but Tiyron sensed the warning in his words. This man knew who he was and knew he could crush Tiyron and Rykka both with a few words to the right people.

Tiyron watched the human leave in tight-lipped silence. Only once the sound of footsteps outside had faded did he glare at Rykka. "Working with *pirates?*"

"Not now, Tiyron," Rykka said.

"Yes, now!" he snapped. "Who is he?"

Rykka slapped the books down on the table and stood. "I need some air."

"Rykka!"

She ignored his call, striding out of the room and leaving him alone.

Tiyron spat curses at the door, but she didn't return. Panting for breath, he fell back into the cushions. *How dare she? Doesn't she realize that this is what protected her from Cemar? That Cemar would have done all this to her if I hadn't held our secret? How can she bind our lives to this human and think I shouldn't have a say? How dare she?*

Rykka didn't return, and finally darkness pulled him back into its embrace.

CHAPTER 9

Alistar stared at the reports on his desk, but his weary mind refused to make sense of them. He'd barely slept the previous night, and only caught a catnap before coming to work in the morning. He scanned the papers, hoping for something to catch his attention.

Instead, a knock on his office door furthered his distraction. Stifling a sigh, Alistar called, "Come in."

A page opened the door and poked her head in. "Pardon me, Senior Engineer. Technician Feyblade sent me to ask you to come to her laboratory at your earliest convenience."

Alistar sat up straight. *The lab? What's wrong? Has the artifact caused some new phenomena?* "Thank you. I'll be sure to do so."

She bobbed in a quick bow and scurried off as if afraid of what Alistar might ask about the message. As her footfalls faded, Alistar stood, shut the reports in a desk drawer, and pulled on his suit coat. He made his way down to the secure laboratory where Lady Syri and her team conducted experiments on the crystal flower.

Four members of the Royal Guard stood watch at the door—

two more than usual. A sneaking suspicion grew in Alistar's gut. The guards waved him through the door into the laboratory.

Alistar stepped inside. The door closed behind him. He strode down the short hall to the workroom. His gaze found two elves awaiting him, and his suspicion was confirmed. He bowed. "Your Highness. Technician Feyblade."

"Very prompt, De'seneth." Prince Cero, the Silver Prince, stood even with Alistar at nearly six feet tall. His hair, source of his sobriquet, had turned white in childhood. His age now matched the color; he'd celebrated his one hundred and fortieth birthday late last winter. He wore an emerald green silkweave shirt and a silver overjacket with black pearl buttons.

"After the previous report I received about the phenomenon the technicians have observed recently, I didn't think I should delay, Your Highness," Alistar's gaze moved to the flower-shaped crystal resting in a reinforced glass case on a pedestal in the middle of the room.

He hadn't seen it since he claimed it from Baron Sok'lof. Looking at it with fresh eyes, he was struck by its resemblance to a frost's breath flower with its eight jagged petals. Frost's breath was sacred to Rechmal, the human god of magic, and was one of the few plants to naturally produce magic, though kurowa's output drastically overshadowed it.

Lady Syri checked one of the devices monitoring the crystal, her brow furrowing in thought. "Yes, thank you for coming, Senior Engineer De'seneth. I've requested that the rest of my team be temporarily reassigned to other projects while I test several theories."

One of Alistar's eyebrows rose. "What theories would those be?" he asked. Her comment did nothing to address his largest unspoken question. *Why is the Silver Prince here?* He pushed back a sudden unease that Prince Cero somehow knew about Tiyron.

Twinkles of light glowed within the crystal, but they cast no shadows on the pedestal. Lady Syri wrote a quick note on her pad before she turned to him.

"I want to first test if and how the crystal interacts with other artifacts. Those most easily available to me are, unfortunately, quite powerful—thus the precaution of sending the rest of the team to other projects. The other idea I wish to test, however, affects you more directly."

"Oh?" Alistar asked cautiously.

"We want to bring the crystal to your manor to test whether its energies will interact with the energies that maintain the seals on various doors," Prince Cero told him.

Alistar stopped, thinking about the boxes of components currently in the manor basement. The theory, however, held sound. He slowly said, "I will need time to prepare for such an experiment."

"Of course." The Silver Prince waved a hand impatiently. "There is great potential risk in moving the crystal out of this location. Any experiments conducted with the crystal in your manor must be done under strictest confidence."

"Of course, Your Highness," Alistar said, though his thoughts raced with the question of how he could enforce that requirement with Onyxflame in the house.

Does Tiyron know I work for Silverline Power? Has Onyxflame told him yet? Has she told him anything about what she's done since putting him in stasis?

Someone knocked on the door. All heads turned toward it. A young man in the uniform of the lobby staff cleared his throat. "Your Highness, Prince Pietro is requesting a meeting with you."

Prince Cero's eyes narrowed. "Is he, in fact, *requesting* an audience?"

The young man shifted his weight from one foot to the other. "Not... exactly, Your Highness."

"I thought not." Prince Cero turned back to the crystal.

Alistar tried not to wince in sympathy for the attendant.

Prince Pietro, youngest of King Suelton's children, was widely regarded as self-centered and spoiled. He was said to have little patience for delays, regardless of whose attention he demanded. Alistar personally thought the prince, a good sixty years younger than Crown Prince Filipp, would have been far better off had he been sent into the military like Princess Yulina. Sadly, military service had led the princess to an early grave, and the king had forbidden any suggestion that his youngest child follow the same path. Instead, Pietro had been coddled, his sense of entitlement encouraged and indulged.

Prince Cero reviewed Lady Syri's readings from the crystal, compared them with the previous set, and gave her several cryptic instructions. The lobby attendant waited patiently, his presence a damper on any further discussion of experiments or Alistar's manor.

Finally, the Silver Prince turned to the attendant. "Very well, I shall see if my nephew has grasped the subtle art of courtesy just yet." He nodded to his daughter and Alistar, then strode from the laboratory, attendant following in his wake.

Once the door closed and the sound of steps faded, Lady Syri sighed heavily. "Pietro has been pestering him for a good ten days now. All of a sudden, he's developed a deep interest in the company, the mahiy lines, and everything associated with them. But he wants to know everything without having to take the time to actually *learn* anything. He doesn't care the least bit about the underlying principles or theory of mahiy lines and their management."

Alistar frowned. "Then what *does* he want?"

"Oh, I think he expects the Silver Prince will be so impressed and awed by his interest that Pietro will be able to just step in and take charge of things." Lady Syri shook her head. "Even though he has no idea how anything works. Because that couldn't possibly be a problem when taking responsibility for

the system that keeps the entire city and all its industry operational."

Alistar raised an eyebrow at her. "I hope he wouldn't be
quite that overconfident."

"Only someone who's never spent any significant time with
Pietro would say that." She sighed and shook her head again. "I
apologize, Senior Engineer. I'm sure you don't want to hear the
foibles of my family."

"Considering who your family is, Technician, I'm rather sure
I *shouldn't* hear about their foibles, regardless of whether or not
I might want to."

She snorted an unladylike laugh. "At least you don't act
shocked to hear they do, in fact, have just as many problems, if
not more, than any other family."

"It would be quite hypocritical of me to be surprised by such
a thing," Alistar said with a small smile. "Now, what manner of
experiments did you have in mind, if you were to bring the
crystal to my manor?"

"Ah. Well, we already know your manor is attuned to a
different wavelength than the one produced by the mahiy lines,
and so far we've been unable to isolate exactly what level it
works at or where it draws its energy from. My theory is that
the crystal may emit energy in that wavelength. Exposing the
sealed doors to a direct source of that energy might trigger the
doors to unseal." Lady Syri studied the crystal as if hoping it
would provide insight into the validity of her theory.

"I don't know whether the crystal was frequently at the
manor. I know Sok'lof presented it as a sacred relic to the
Successors, and I'm not sure Cemar or Sunward would tie
access to their secrets to an object that might be regularly
unavailable." He thought about the door that opened while he
and Onyxflame were working with the components. "That
doesn't mean it won't work, though. It might not have been

their primary means of opening doors and accessing rooms, but we don't have that key, assuming it was an object."

"Assuming it was an object." Lady Syri considered that. "If not an object, what would you suggest?"

"A channeler. One of their 'internal' channelers," Alistar said. Conventional magic theory held that a rare few people could draw magic directly from the mahiy lines and shape it according to their talent, as Lamorage could when healing. However, even channelers required an external source from which to draw magic. Cemar had discovered some people could harness magic differently, drawing the power from within themselves. Unlike traditional channelers, they could infuse their magic into other objects. Perhaps, under the right circumstances, they could even create tools like the artifacts of the past.

Lady Syri grimaced. "Of course. A phenomenon we have no means of tracking, assessing, or studying, which none of Cemar's lackeys have been able to explain."

"Nevertheless, it *is* a real phenomenon," Alistar said stiffly.

"Your pardon, Senior Engineer—I didn't mean to imply otherwise. I know the talent exists; we simply have no methods yet for identifying individuals who have it. Which makes studying and documenting it frustrating."

"The fact that Cemar's drug seemed to play a part in awakening the talent certainly adds to the challenge," Alistar said. "Not many want to admit they used Ambrosia, to say nothing of the challenge of tracking who might have used the toxic dross he sold in the slums." At least she didn't openly scoff and dismiss the idea of internal channeling, like some people did.

"It's unfortunate that you had to destroy the core of the device Cemar built to drain the mahiy lines and condense magic." Lady Syri sighed. "I understand why it was necessary, but we could have learned so much from the device."

Alistar just nodded. He hadn't shared the secret of the

device's power source even with his family. He'd never admitted to Prince Cero or anyone else in Silverline Power that he knew anything more about the device than he'd documented in his report. And only Saskia knew how he'd gained possession the power source or where he'd hidden it.

Lady Syri continued thoughtfully. "We haven't really considered the possibility that Cemar's device served as the key to accessing the sealed areas."

"I doubt it," Alistar said. "Cemar didn't build the device himself. Onyxflame claimed responsibility for that. At least for the core device, though he also claimed he didn't intend for it to be used the way Cemar employed it. However, the evidence I've found so far indicates Cemar and his cabal used the manor as their base well before they acquired the device from Onyxflame." *And if the power source was the key to opening the doors, they should have opened long before now.* "One of the doors did open two days ago, unprompted, as far as I could determine."

"Did it?" Lady Syri straightened in surprise. "I hadn't heard."

"The room I gained access to holds a puzzle of some sort, which I'm still working on," Alistar told her. "However, between it and the discussion we had regarding this crystal, I've been forming a theory."

Lady Syri perched on a stool and settled her notepad in her lap. "Yes?"

"We might be doing ourselves a disservice by not taking Lady Sunward into account. We don't know what her goal is as of yet, but she's back in Lewarden, potentially attempting to continue Cemar's plots. I assume she wants access to my manor and that she has ways of opening the doors. While I never had the opportunity to discuss magic theory with her, we should assume she has some level of knowledge in that area. She might know how to produce the wavelengths that resonate with the crystal and the manor."

Syri nodded thoughtfully. "That theory has merit. So, this new door opening might be a response to a signal she produced."

"Possibly," Alistar agreed. "As might the intermittent reactions from this crystal. I don't know how close she would need to be to either to do so, though."

She frowned. "The laboratory is shielded against all the known wave spectra, Senior Engineer, both to prevent outside contamination of our work and to safeguard against harmful emissions from the crystal. If your theory is correct, we have been unsuccessful in both regards, and the crystal emits on a spectrum we haven't considered." She rapidly scribed notes on her pad.

"There is another possibility," Alistar warned.

"There often is," she allowed. "But I would be pleased to hear yours."

"Previously, Cemar and his people successfully subverted employees of Silverline Power, whether through promises, bribes, or blackmail. We shouldn't ignore the possibility that some of those people remain or that Sunward has found indirect access through similar means." Alistar looked around the laboratory, cursing himself for not considering the possibility sooner.

"My team is extremely loyal to the Crown, Senior Engineer," she said stiffly. "I am extremely confident of that."

"Your team, yes." Alistar had no doubt the Silver Prince had ensured they were. "What about the people responsible for shielding the laboratory? Or those responsible for maintenance on it? Or even the occasional visitor—a page, an attendant, anyone who could slip some small object inside and conceal it out of sight?" He thought of the attendant who had brought the message to Prince Cero. How easily could that man have dropped something on a table or to the floor and slid it out of sight?

She stopped writing and blinked at him. "That… oh." She looked around the laboratory. "I… see. I will ensure the laboratory and the shields are thoroughly reviewed by someone trusted. Thank you, De'seneth. I didn't consider the risk of sabotage in this situation."

"I hope this theory is incorrect," Alistar said. "Even if it does mean that the crystal has been virtually unshielded instead. While that is certainly a problem, treachery within Silverline Power is a possibility I like even less."

"With that, De'seneth, I am in complete agreement."

CHAPTER 10

When Onyxflame warned them Tiyron would "not be a good patient," Saskia hadn't realized just how much she was understating the matter. The night terrors, of course, Saskia didn't blame him for, no matter how disturbing his screams were. She'd have been more surprised if he didn't have them.

The strings of vile insults and abuse he hurled while awake, on the other hand, were less tolerable. He had no hesitation declaring his objection to medical care regardless of how necessary it was.

Partway through changing the dressings on his wounds, Saskia interrupted his hissed litany.

"Do you *want* to recover? Or would you rather die of an infection after all the work your sister did to keep you alive?"

His lips curled back in anger. "Do you always threaten your patients?"

"No, but I'm not above returning threats when they're issued. Or is 'If I could move, I'd break every bone in your arm' only acceptable when you say it?"

He opened his mouth, on the verge of denying that he'd said anything, but finally he settled on a sullen, "It's not like I *can*."

"Not at the moment, no." Saskia folded her arms and held his gaze. "But if you actually *want* to receive the care you need to be *able* to move on your own power again, I'd recommend you not insult and threaten the people caring for you."

He glanced away from her, jaw tight. "What difference is it to you? We're trapped in debt whether I curse you or lie here and meekly submit to whatever you do."

Saskia stopped. "Excuse me?"

Tiyron glowered. "I'm not stupid. You, or your husband, or someone else, wants something from me, and will call that debt due. None of this is for *my* sake."

"We're not Lower City crime lords who will break your knees to prove a point, Tiyron. But regarding debts and what is owed to whom, you'll need to talk with your sister."

He looked at her, eyes narrow. "My sister who hasn't been here the last three times I woke? Where is Rykka?"

"She's working. I believe she intends to come to the clinic this evening," Saskia said.

"Working? What's that supposed to mean?" Tiyron tried to sit up further and tried to intimidate her with his glare. He failed in both attempts.

"It means she's working. She has a job, and she gets paid to do it. What else would it mean?"

"Working where? Doing what?" Tiyron demanded.

"Ask her yourself when she comes over." Saskia fixed a stern look on him. "And try *asking*, not demanding."

"I don't need a *human* telling me how to talk to my own sister."

Then why aren't you asking yourself why she hasn't returned since the two of you argued? Or are you? Are you lashing out at me because I'm an easier target, because I'm here and she's not? "Are you going to let me finish changing those dressings or not?" Saskia asked.

He scowled. "I can't stop you, can I?"

"Are you going to keep threatening me?" Saskia asked.

"No." His unbandaged hand clenched.

"Thank you." Saskia resumed her ministrations.

Tiyron remained silent until she finished, though by his tight jaw, he worked hard to do so. He drank the water Saskia offered him without complaint, though he had to know by now that it contained a painkiller and sedative.

"I'll let you rest. Call if you need anything," she told him.

He muttered something but kept it quiet enough she couldn't hear him clearly. Saskia left the room and made her way to the clinic waiting room.

"Good afternoon, Doctor De'seneth!" Kir Featherdew greeted her from the front desk. At sixteen, he was quite young for an elf, and his scrawny build made him look even younger. A mop of brown hair trailed into his eyes. He wore a shirt a little too large for him, found in the donation box they kept at the clinic to assist the city's poor.

"Good afternoon, Kir. Are there any patients still waiting to be seen?" Saskia scanned the waiting room. Only one figure slouched in a chair, wrapped in a tattered full-length cloak, the hood up to shade his face. A pair of leather gloves worn thin covered his hands.

Kir pointed at the other. "Nitan came." Nitan was Kir's older brother.

Nitan raised his head and nodded to Saskia. He spoke slowly, enunciating each word carefully. "Kir said I should come by sometime."

"It's always good to see you," Saskia told him. "I can see you now, if you're ready."

Nitan rose and nodded. Knowing his discomfort with being in public, she led him to an examination room toward the back of the clinic, where he was less likely to encounter other patients. Nitan removed cloak and gloves without prompting.

But his desire for concealment stemmed less from elven taboo, and more from what the clothing concealed.

Kir's older brother was one of a handful of survivors of Rat's Disease. The sickness had rampaged through the slums and Lower City. Its victims died in agony, their internal organs decaying in a matter of hours, in most cases. Many victims experienced hallucinations, thinking themselves heroes of legend or avatars of the gods.

Despite the name given the sickness, its source was eventually revealed to not be a disease, but a drug—the toxic dregs of the drug Cemar and his followers crafted and sold to the upper classes. The pure version was known as Ambrosia, while the tainted street version was known by several names, most commonly "Elixir" or just "'Lixir." Not that those who partook in Elixir knew they courted death with each dose. The fear of Rat's Disease had done much to push Lewarden toward the civil war Cemar sought.

For a man who gathered his followers with calls for equality between races and classes, Cemar was far too willing to sacrifice those who need such help the most.

Nitan's hands were scarred, the right twisted like a claw. Under the cloak, the scarring was far worse, and his skin was blotchy and discolored. Saskia waited until he'd settled as comfortably as possible on the examination bed.

"Have you had any recent changes, Nitan? Aches, new sores or abrasions?"

"No, Doctor. The sores on my legs have been weeping the last few days, though. I keep them washed."

"Good. Keep doing that and let me know if it continues more than five days. Has anything else changed?" Saskia asked.

He shifted uncomfortably. "Kir wanted me to come because he doesn't want me taking 'Lixir again."

Saskia stopped. "Is someone claiming to have it for sale?" *Is Sunward trying to start a new outbreak of Rat's Disease? The chaos*

that would cause in the Lower City, on the eve of the Grand Exhibi-
tion, would be unthinkable.

"Someone always claims to have it, but most are liars. Kir heard a friend of mine talking about finding something even better, and he's scared I might try it."

"Have you tried it, Nitan? I won't say anything to Kir if you have," Saskia said.

Nitan shook his head. "My friend offered to get me some, but I haven't seen him since we talked."

"Oh? When was that?" Saskia brought a jar of salve and applied it to the oozing sores on the elf's legs.

Nitan raised four fingers. "This many days ago."

Saskia met his gaze, her eyes serious. "Nitan, I told you that Elixir was the source of Rat's Disease."

"Yes, doctor."

"It's possible this drug your friend talked about won't have damaging effects like that, but it might be just as dangerous." And his friend's absence could indicate just that. "If your friend does bring you some, I would appreciate if you bring a sample to the clinic."

Nitan had braced for a lecture against partaking in drugs. Saskia knew Kir scolded him about it. "Will you be angry if I do?"

"No, Nitan. If you bring us some, we can test it and find out if it's safe. I'll tell you whether or not it is."

The elf nodded slowly. "Thank you, Doctor."

She patted him on the shoulder. "I know Kir worries. I want to help you be safe."

He nodded again. Saskia helped him pull on the cloak and gloves, then walked him back to the waiting room. If any more patients had arrived while she was with Nitan, her father was already attending them. Almost all the clinic's patients were human. However, even elves came to the Coiled Dragon for some injuries. Saskia and her father had set many bones for elves and humans alike.

She returned to the examination room and began to clean it for the next patient. As she carried the soiled linens to the bin, she heard shifts of small, restless movements in Tiyron's room. After depositing the linens, she opened his door and looked inside. "Do you need anything? Another glass of water?"

Tiyron opened his eyes. "I heard you talking. What's Rat's Disease? Some plague that lingers around this 'clinic'?"

The question made her realize just how little Tiyron knew of events after Onyxflame put him into stasis. She closed the door and settled into the chair beside his bed. "No. It's not a true disease, even, though that's the name that became popular while it was at its peak. It wasn't transmittable between people; the source was quite different."

"Well that's just vague enough to say absolutely nothing."

"Most elves, I've found, don't care enough about human medicine to make sense of the ongoing research into disease transmission," Saskia said. "And the theory is mostly outside the scope of your question. I know you and your sister worked with Cemar for a time, and the two of you built a device that played a part in his plans."

Tiyron tensed. "Yes." His voice was tight.

"I don't know whether you know what he intended to use it for," Saskia began.

"Stealing magic from the Silver Prick," Tiyron cut in.

"And what he intended to *do* with that magic," Saskia continued as if he hadn't interrupted. "The short version, though, is that Cemar condensed the magic he stole into a solid form, then used that to craft a drug."

"He… what… a drug?" Tiyron sputtered.

"A drug. Very powerful, quite popular, as I understand it," she said. "Among the upper class, it was known as Ambrosia."

"So he fleeced a bunch of nobles by claiming he had a fancy new drug for them," Tiyron scoffed. "So?"

"He didn't claim he had a drug to sell them. He *did* have a drug to sell them, and it was quite popular. Quite strong, as well. To gather the magic to produce it, he caused blackouts in the Middle and Lower City during the middle of winter. As Ambrosia grew more popular, he also had another problem. The refinement process produced waste, and he certainly couldn't sell that to the rich people."

Tiyron shifted uneasily, listening.

"A new drug showed up in the slums," Saskia continued. "It gained the name 'Elixir,' and those who took it claimed it gave them strength, made them feel more alive, able to sense more than they ever had before. All the qualities of Ambrosia at a fraction of the price."

"What was it?" Tiyron asked.

"Toxic dross from the production of Ambrosia," she told him. "Those who took it tossed dice with the Starbinder every time. Most doses weren't immediately deadly, though some rose to that level. But it built up in their bodies, and even though most never knew, the question always remained, would this be the dose that would liquefy their internal organs? Or would it be the next one?"

Tiyron paled. "Do… what?"

"That was Rat's Disease. The waste from Cemar's drug, sold to the people he pretended to champion." Saskia gazed at him without blinking. "The young man who you overheard is one of the sixteen survivors from our clinic, out of over a hundred victims of Rat's Disease. We had the highest survival rate in the Lower City."

"That's the *highest*?" he demanded.

She nodded. "Not for lack of trying. The decay didn't respond to magical healing—no doubt because the patients' bodies were already oversaturated with magic. And Rat's

Disease wasn't the only destruction caused by Elixir. I heard reports of channelers losing control of their abilities in violent, destructive manners. Also people who didn't know they were channelers experiencing sudden onset of the talent."

"That last doesn't sound as bad, unless someone reported them," Tiyron said.

"It's bad when a six-year-old girl suddenly channels fire."

He blinked, then shook his head. "No one that young can channel."

"No one that young *should* be able to," Saskia corrected. "But the shining men gave her candy, and it burned inside, and she had to get the fire out. So… she did. That's what Cemar did with your device. That's some of the destruction he unleashed here."

Tiyron digested that in silence. Finally, he asked, "What do Rillwater pirates have with to do any of this?"

"First, privateers, not pirates. My husband might tolerate ignorant people making that mistake once or twice, but not everyone in the fleet is so generous." And she wasn't sure where Onyxflame fell on that scale. "Second…"

She paused, hearing quick steps in the hall. Tiyron tensed, hearing them as well. Saskia reached the door just as someone knocked twice.

"Doctor De'seneth?" Kir asked.

"I'm here. What is it?"

"Doctor Tan'shyo needs to consult with you about a patient."

"I'll be right there." Saskia turned to Tiyron. "I'm sorry. You'll have to excuse me. I'll be back later."

Tiyron said nothing, his jaw tight and his eyes narrow as she left.

Kir led Saskia to an examination room, then scurried back to the front desk. Inside, Saskia saw her father and a young human woman cradling a clearly broken arm.

Doctor Tan'shyo nodded to Saskia. "Apologies for calling

you away from your patient, but Miss Las'mun requested a word with you."

"Of course," Saskia agreed, though she wondered just what the young woman needed to speak to her about. It couldn't be the arm—there was no doubt it was broken, and her father had laid out everything to set and splint it.

"How can I help you, Miss Las'mun?" She cast a glance to her father for any additional hints.

He only shook his head in a brief toss of white hair and adjusted his spectacles. "I leave you in my daughter's capable hands."

Once he'd stepped out, Miss Las'mun finally spoke. "I'm sorry to be takin' you 'way from another patient, doctor."

"My other patient can wait a little while," Saskia told her. "You wanted to speak to me?"

Las'mun nodded quickly. "I know you done good for us down here. You and your father and your husband too. My sister usta work for the Silver Prince in onna the generation plants, until she died of Rat's Disease. She met your husband; said he was a good man who'd see justice done. And I know he did. My sister's husband told me."

Saskia remembered Alistar telling her about Technician Bar'rege, a Silverline employee who had been blackmailed into serving Cemar's schemes. After she spoke to Alistar about her situation, she'd been intentionally given a particularly toxic dose of Elixir. Though the healer initially called in to treat her had ruled the death as natural causes, the autopsy performed by Doctor Tan'shyo told a different story. "I didn't know you were her sister. I'm very sorry."

Las'mun shook her head. "She did what she hadta do, and it saved a lotta folk, if I heard right."

"It did," Saskia agreed, wondering what this had to do with the woman's wish to speak to her in private.

"I work in onna Lady Ravencrest's factories. The Lady

doesn't usually spend much time with the likes of us, but two days ago, she came in with another lady. I didn't see the other lady's face—she was wearing a hood and such, but I think she was human. Lady Ravencrest called a handful of folks from the floor into a meeting. All hush-hush like, too."

"Supervisors?" Saskia asked. "Or workers?"

"Normal folks," Las'mun said. "They went in and met with the ladies. I saw a couple come back out and get to working again, but the other four didn't. And I haven't seen them at the factory since, either."

Are factory workers being abducted? By their employer in the middle of the day? There must be another explanation. "Has anyone said anything about them or where they've gone? Asked questions?"

"Aye, a few folk asked after them. Got told they were recruited to work in a new factory the lady's starting, and she's only picking a select few for it," Las'mun said. "And anyone who asked more than that found themselves booted out to the street and told not to come back."

"Do you know anything about the ones who were chosen?" Saskia asked. "Things that might set them apart from others there?"

"Pretty sure all of them came from the slums. I know one of them had a scare she thought might be Rat's Disease back when 'Lixir was around and swore off the drugs since then."

"Why did you want me to know about this, Las'mun?" Saskia asked.

Las'mun lowered her voice. "One of the two who wasn't picked went crazy two days ago—ran around the factory raving about metal monsters that swallow people whole and how they were going to attack the Exhibition. The supervisors got him out pretty quick, not much fuss, and most everyone ignored it. I woulda too, except yesterday, he turned up dead."

"Dead? An accident, or...?"

"Not an accident. Got his throat cut. And anyone who tried to say anything about it at work got hushed up right fast. I got this feeling someone was afraid he'd say something they didn't want anyone knowing, and they shut him up. And if they're willing to do that, they're willing to shut other folk up too. But I know you and your husband don't stand for that, so I had to tell you."

"If you're correct, you're taking a grave risk," Saskia said. "If they discover that you've passed this on, your life is also in danger."

Las'mun shook her head. "Me? Nah, I came here to the clinic because I broke my arm, doctor."

Saskia drew a sharp breath. "You didn't..." *You didn't intentionally break your arm to give yourself a reason to come to the clinic, did you?*

Las'mun chuckled. "Now who would do a crazy thing like that? I'm just sharing a bit 'o gossip while you set it."

"Of course you are." Saskia splinted the woman's arm and helped her with a sling. "And if you have any need, come back to the clinic right away. Or if you have additional gossip to share."

"I will. Thank you, doctor."

CHAPTER 11

*I*f *I could just get out of this bed...* Tiyron fell back into the cushions in frustration. He couldn't even lift his arms, much less maneuver himself out of the sickbed. Even thinking about trying sent a wave of pain through his battered body.

Why did you bring me here, Rykka? You couldn't have found another healer somewhere? Some Dockside chop-doc who would toss me back out as soon as I was stable? I want to be back in the lair, not trapped here.

He eyed the door. It could have been a mile away, for all he could do to reach it. Worse, he couldn't stop anyone from coming in, whatever their intent might be.

Steps approached, a cadence that didn't match either Rykka or Doctor De'seneth. His pulse spiked. His breath came in ragged gulps. Sweat beaded his brow.

A light knock sounded on the door. Tiyron swallowed hard, throat dry. "Come in."

He didn't recognize the elven man who entered. He had a lanky build, a little too thin. His silkweave clothes were well made and clean, but just a little too worn and slightly thread-bare. His dark hair was cut short.

"Good afternoon, sir. I'm Veril Lamorage, a friend of De'seneth. I periodically assist the clinic as a healer."

"Which De'seneth?" Tiyron cut in.

"Both, although I've known Alistar longer."

Damn. Another pirate? Tiyron slumped back on the cushions, but his eye never left Lamorage. "So, you're Rillwater?"

Lamorage shook his head with a chuckle. "Never set foot on a ship in my life. I'm from the western mountains."

His surname gave that away, but rumors claimed Rillwater would take anyone aboard.

Lamorage continued. "I came by to see if enough residual magic had dissipated to make it safe to heal you again."

"Again?" Tiyron asked, brows pinching in a frown. *You mean you, or some other healer, chose to leave me immobile and helpless?*

"Yes. I healed you when your sister brought you out of stasis. At that point, we were fighting for your life. You came very close to slipping away several times. I healed you as much as possible but couldn't risk my healing overwhelming your body and killing you in a different way."

Tiyron shifted uncomfortably. All he remembered was endless waves of pain tearing through his body and mind, stealing every other sense. Rather than let his thoughts follow that path further, he said, "You know who I am, then."

"No. I don't, and you don't have to tell me. I know you were a victim of Cemar, and that's all I need to know."

The mix of fear and hate when Lamorage said Cemar's name resonated with him. He swallowed and nodded. "Enemy of my enemy, then."

Lamorage flinched. "More like fellow victim of your torturer," he said softly.

"My version sounds better. So, you're a healer."

"Yes. Not as a profession, but I can heal." Lamorage crossed the room to him. Tiyron couldn't help but tense. "I can check if it's safe to heal you a little further, if you're willing."

"Why wouldn't I be?" Tiyron asked warily.

Lamorage sank into the chair beside the bed with a weary sigh. "Because healing tells me everything he did to you."

"Ev—" Tiyron stiffened, breath catching. *Everything. Everything he and his minions did.* His voice was tight. "You already know what happened, then. No more secrets to find there."

"That isn't what I meant," Lamorage said quietly. "I mean are you willing to allow a stranger to place their hands on you?"

He hadn't been thinking about that requirement of healing. He'd very deliberately not been thinking about that. His throat tightened, but he said, "I'll manage."

"All right. Are you ready now?"

"Yes." If the man was going to do this, he needed to do it now, before Tiyron could think about it any longer.

"If you tell me to stop, I will," Lamorage promised.

He didn't believe him but answered with a curt nod. "You're from the mountains?" A distraction, something to think about instead.

"Yes." Lamorage rested his hand on Tiyron's chest. Violet threads of magic flowed through the ceiling into him. "I came to the capital to find my fortune and leave behind some memories."

Tiyron flinched at the touch. Warmth spread across his ribs and gradually worked its way toward his arms. The tightness in his chest from his broken ribs eased. The tightness from fear did not.

"Did it work?"

Lamorage laughed faintly. "For a while. Until I fell in with the wrong crowd. Until I was introduced to a drug called Ambrosia."

"Heard about it," Tiyron said.

"I got into debt. Badly in debt. Had to start paying in favors when I couldn't pay in marks, until I was drawn in far enough that going to the authorities would have implicated myself as much as the others. I wouldn't have survived without De'seneth's help." He lifted his hand and stepped back. His voice shifted to a more professional tone. "I'm not able to heal as much as I would like, but this is what I can do today."

He could almost breathe easily. "Feels a little better."

"Good. I'll try to come by every few days, unless you'd prefer a longer break between? I'd be able to heal more in a visit that way, but you'd be waiting longer."

He started to say that he didn't care either way, but his skin crawled from the healer's touch. Tiyron swallowed hard. "Longer gaps."

Lamorage nodded. "Of course. Can I bring you anything before I go? Or ask one of the doctors to get anything for you?"

Tiyron shook his head.

The healer stood. "Then I should bid you good day and let you rest."

He watched Lamorage leave, then finally let out his breath. Shivers ran down his spine. He squeezed his eye shut, sucking in deep gulps of air.

He didn't know how long passed before he heard light steps move down the hall. A soft knock sounded on his door. His eye snapped open and moved to the door. *That's Rykka. It must be Rykka.* "I'm awake."

Rykka slipped inside, closing the door carefully behind her. She wore a dress again, this one suited to an upper-class woman. Her hair hung in a braid.

"The doctor said you have a job."

"Good evening to you too, Tiyron," she said.

"Like I'd know what time it is," he countered. His sickroom lacked clocks and windows alike. It occurred to him that he didn't even know what season it was. So much he didn't know. He hated it.

"And yes, I have a job."

"Why?"

She raised a dubious eyebrow at him. "I like eating. Why do most people work?"

"You're not most people." *Tell me you're scamming some noble. You're carrying on our legacy.*

"True," she agreed without elaborating.

"Then what are you doing?" he demanded.

Rykka's jaw tightened. "I'm trying to unravel Cemar's work."

Tiyron stiffened. "He's dead. You said so."

"He's dead. So's Sok'lof."

A tremor ran through him, though he tried not to show it. "Yes. You killed him?"

"He was executed for treason. He rallied the Successors of Heiset in an unsuccessful coup."

His brow pinched. "Didn't think he'd split with Cemar."

"He didn't. That was part of their plan."

"Cemar talked equality." Even with all Cemar had done to him, he'd thought the half-elf believed that. Cemar had always been eager to talk about his vision of a future without the divisions of class or race and without faiths like the Tenets and the Path that demanded such barriers.

"Cemar talked a lot," Rykka said coldly. "Most of it was lies."

"And he's dead." He needed to hear her say it again.

"He's dead. Sok'lof is dead. Sunward is not."

His brow furrowed in confusion. The name was elven, and he didn't remember any elves in Cemar's inner circle.

Other than me.

"Lady Celyn Sunward," Rykka said.

Celyn... Sun... "Cemar's *lover* got out?" The question burst out as the name finally slid into place.

"She used her connections to slip away and vanish until the fuss died down."

His mind spun, trying to make sense of everything she told him. He shook his head. "Doctor told me about Rat's Disease."

"And Ambrosia?" Rykka asked. "Elixir? And who was responsible?"

He nodded.

"I couldn't have gotten to Cemar on my own. When he started to make his move, I didn't even think it could be him; too much evidence of noble involvement, and like you, I thought he actually meant all that garbage about equality."

"The drugs?" Tiyron frowned.

"No. That wasn't the part I knew about first. When he took you, Cemar also took the device we were building for him. It wasn't finished, so he got someone else to cobble it into something resembling working order. Rather than the quiet, imperceptible draw I intended it to have, the device drained mahiy lines dry. Caused blackouts all through the poor sectors of the city. In the dead of winter, no less."

"Winter?" he repeated. It had been late spring, edging toward summer, when Cemar betrayed him.

"Winter," she confirmed. "Two winters ago."

She'd told him he'd spent two years in stasis, but he struggled to wrap his mind around it. *A handful of days ago, Cemar and his underlings were torturing me. I was just there. That wasn't... two years...*

Rykka continued. "It wasn't what the device was supposed to do, and evidence pointed toward noble involvement. I didn't suspect Cemar at first, and even when indications began to support his involvement, I dismissed them. Didn't believe it until I saw him with my own eyes trying to ensnare De'seneth."

"Why pira... privateers?"

"De'seneth recruited me for my skills with the mahiy lines. He thought I was you at the time, of course."

"Why agree?" he pressed, not satisfied with her answer.

"I was in a bad spot, Tiyron, and I wasn't going to get out of it without help. He was the only one offering." She sighed and ran a hand through her hair. "The only way I could get back into a place where I could find someone to heal you was to accept his deal. And he held up his end of it. Don't ever doubt he did. He's an honorable man."

Tiyron snorted. "I'm sure."

"Judge for yourself," she told him.

"How did he even happen to come along when you needed help?" Tiyron demanded. "Convenient happenstance? We've never had dealings with Rillwater."

"*You* have never had dealings with Rillwater," she corrected. "Which is unfortunate, because it probably would have worked out better than your jaunt with the Narnans did. How many hired thugs did that captain send after you when you deserted his ship?"

He glowered at her. "They weren't all after *me*."

She rolled her eyes. "Of course not. But you want to know why De'seneth came looking for me. He knew I was in a bad position because he knew I was in Chirrod Prison, waiting to get shipped off to the Skelocs Mines. And he knew he could get me out because Alistar De'seneth was the Silverline Power engineer assigned by the Silver Prince personally to investigate the blackouts around Lewarden."

He drew a sharp breath at her mention of prison, but the rest of her answer flung those thoughts out of his mind. If he could have burst out of the bed, he would have. "He's a *Silverline* lackey?!"

Rykka didn't blink. "He is. And without him, I'd still be in prison, you'd still be in stasis, and Cemar might well be sitting on the throne and beheading anyone he didn't like."

Tiyron's lips curled back. "You think the Silver Prince is any *better*?"

"Than Cemar? Slee's Balls, Tiyron, *yes*. The royal family might collectively have their heads so far up their asses that they think their turds smell like roses, but they are better than Cemar would be. Hematic perdition, the Silver Prince's pet wyverns would be better rulers than Cemar and his followers." Her eyes narrowed as she held his gaze. "How can *you*, of anyone, think that the man who tortured and nearly killed you should have held *any* power?"

He flinched. Cemar, the radical revolutionary idealist, and Cemar, the sadistic torturer felt like two different people. He believed, and he wanted, the vision Cemar had described.

How could you give up on that, Rykka? How could you turn to the very thing we fought to destroy? He wanted to demand those answers from her, but those weren't the words that came out.

"So instead, you sold yourself to this *human*. Suppose all the shine and glow of Silverline Power made you forget our purpose. Or maybe it was De'seneth himself, hmm? Good-looking sort, for a human, I suppose."

Rykka stiffened. Her eyes flashed and her mouth pressed into a thin, tight line. "You should rethink your accusations, Tiyron."

"You should have rethought making an *alliance* with a bootlicking Silverline sheep," he snapped.

She leaned forward. Her voice was hard and cold. "I thought hard about it. I questioned the wisdom and the necessity both. And I decided I'd rather die than remain trapped in that cell. But if I died, you would as well. And the gods only know why, I wanted you to live. I accepted De'seneth's deal. Not because I wanted to help the Silver Prince." Her mouth twisted in anger. "Not because I entertained any idea of seducing De'seneth or whatever else you want to imply. Because I wanted to hold onto some hope of saving your life. So you're *welcome*, Tiyron."

"And what does this Silverline lackey, who you're *certainly* not close with, want with me?" He glowered at her.

"As part of his reward for stopping Cemar, De'seneth was given the manor Cemar used as a base. The one in the Venture District. He's been trying to uncover the secrets they hid in there. I was never there, but I know you were, and your notes indicate you had access to areas of the manor De'seneth hasn't been able to access."

He sneered. "That must grate, being unable to pry into someone else's secrets. He thinks I'll open the doors for one of his kind? De'seneth can go rot before I'll tell him anything."

"De'seneth didn't suggest consulting with you on this, Tiyron. As far as he knew, you were dead. As far as *anyone* knows, you're dead. I'm the one who said you might know more. I have your notes, but I don't know what they mean."

"So, you *did* bind me to an… agreement," he spat the word, "with Silverline. And now you expect me to keep a deal I had no say in."

"Leaving you in stasis was a bad option. I'm amazed that cut-rate trinket actually held out this long, and I had no assurance it was going to keep working. I spent a year chasing every rumor of every healing and restoration artifact or fey grove I could reach, and I found nothing. I don't know any healers I could trust with your life. I turned to the people who helped me before. The people who could have turned me in to the Crown, could have revealed me, could have told them Tiyron Onyxflame didn't die in the Silver Prince's ballroom while killing Cemar. Yes, I turned to De'seneth, and yes, I made a deal to restore you, because I had *no other options*, Tiyron!"

"Tell yourself whatever makes you feel better about it, Rykka," he snapped.

She stood. "Then next time, bring yourself back from the dead. Since apparently, I can't do that right." Rykka spun on her heels and stormed out of the room, slamming the door hard enough he felt it through the bedframe.

"Rykka! Don't walk away from me! Rykka!"

She did not return.

CHAPTER 12

She didn't slam the back door. Rykka closed it quietly behind her and leaned against it, eyes shut. She drew slow, deep breaths until her clenched fists relaxed.

Dammit, why are you like this, Tiyron? Why is anything I do differently from you automatically wrong? Why can't you see that I did what I had to do? And why do I always feel like I'm the one at fault?

Twilight hung over Lewarden. She moved down the alley, listening to carriages rumbling along the street ahead.

What am I doing? I have to convince Tiyron to help De'seneth. He's the only person I know who might know enough about Cemar's lair to get us further in before Sunward finds an access point. For all we know, she knows a dozen secret entrances and is already inside. The thought sent a chill down her spine. *How would we know if she'd gotten in?*

She left the alley and walked down the street away from the clinic with no destination in mind. The spring air still held ghostly hints of winter's chill when the sun set, and she regretted not grabbing her coat before leaving the clinic. Her steps paused as she considered going back for it, but she didn't turn around. She needed to collect herself, settle her thoughts, and remember that for Tiyron, it had been less than a month since the two of them were building their legend as the greatest, most notorious thief in Lewarden.

She brushed past a clump of drunks staggering home and paid no attention to their lewd comments. She knew how to navigate the depths of Lewarden after dark. Not that it was ever truly *dark* in Lewarden, even at night. The network of mahiy lines across the sky shed enough purple light to illuminate the alleys where the ghostlights didn't reach.

It felt like home, though this dress still felt strange and cumbersome. Much like her work at De'seneths' manor did, even if Saskia didn't expect her to play the role of lady's maid more than necessary.

I'm going to do this, and I'm going to do it right! I'm not giving Tiyron any opportunities to claim he's right and I'm wrong.

"Hey, pretty lady."

She didn't pay attention to the call at first.

"Too pretty a lady to look so sad. I can make you smile, pretty lady."

Rykka glanced toward the voice. A young elven man stood beside one of the ghostlight posts that lit the street. The light made his blond hair look specter white. He didn't quite have the build to pull off the seductive pose he attempted. His clothes were too thin for the cool night, and she could tell he was suppressing shivers. When she met his gaze, a feeble spark of hope lit his dull eyes.

"Not looking for company tonight," she said, though she stepped closer to him.

His shoulders slumped and his head drooped. Rykka sighed and fished in her purse for a few marks. Adopting a Lower City accent, she said, "Chill night to be out like this. Get yourself a hot meal and a drink to warm up, eh?"

He glanced at the marks in her hand, swallowed hard, and

shook his head. "Canna. Whitetooth don't let us keep charity marks. He'll take 'em from me soon as you gone."

These are the people Tiyron and I wanted to help. The half-starved street-side whores. The beggars. The people no one looks at, no one sees, no one cares about. Even his pimp doesn't care if he gets a meal. She glanced up the street. Another block up, she saw cheerfully lit windows and a sign proclaiming "The Beggar's Crown Tavern."

Slipping the marks back into her purse, she said, "Haven't eaten yet myself. Maybe a little dinner company would be welcome after all. How's Beggar's Crown? Any good?"

He blinked. "I... dunno. Never been there." His tone suggested she might as well have asked if he'd dined in the Silver Prince's mansion.

"We'll find out, then. Come on." Rykka motioned for him to follow her. He hesitated, clearly unsure if she was serious, then trailed after her.

The Beggar's Crown proved moderately busy this time of the evening, and as clean as could be expected in this part of the city. She found an open table and motioned for the other elf to sit across from her. The server, a muscled human man who undoubtedly also served as bouncer, looked askance at both of them.

"Whatcha havin?" His gruff tone expressed a willingness to remove them both if they didn't intend to lay down marks.

"Two meals, whatever's hot," Rykka told him. "A couple house beers." She maintained a Lower City accent.

The server considered her, judged her likely to pay, and nodded. "Aye, have it right out for ya."

Once the server headed to the kitchen, she turned to her new companion. "What's your name?"

"My... name?" He hesitated. "Seva."

She nodded. "Seva. A pleasure. I'm Rykka. When's last time you got a decent meal?"

"Yesterday?" He paused, thinking. "Day before yesterday."

"And you work for Whitetooth?" she asked. He nodded. "He feed you? Give you a safe place to sleep?"

Seva nodded quickly, glancing around nervously as if at any moment, the pimp or one of his enforcers might burst in and demand to know what he was doing here rather than working the street corner.

Their food arrived—some sort of meat stew with chunks of carrots and potatoes and thick slices of brown bread. The server set down a mug of beer by either bowl. Rykka handed him two marks, and his eyebrows flickered up in momentary surprise. She knew she was overpaying, but not by so much as to seem excessive.

Seva waited until she began eating to dive into his own meal, but once he started, he devoured the stew, barely taking a breath between bites. The food was, to Rykka's tastes, tolerable, though the meat was almost certainly mutton, and the cook took a heavy hand on the garlic and onions with not enough consideration to other spices. The bread was good, especially when drizzled with honey, and the beer was about what she expected.

Seva finally slowed enough to say, "Whitetooth won't accept this as pay." He didn't meet her eyes when he said it.

"I know. I'll pay for your time," Rykka told him. When he frowned in confusion, she said, "I hired you to have dinner with me. I'll pay you, and you give Whitetooth his cut." She paused, looking at him closely. "You *do* get to keep some of what you earn, don't you?"

His hesitation answered the question before his words did. "Gotta pay my debt." He spoke quietly. "Fer shelter and food and clothes. I'm not as good as some of the others. They get to keep a little, sometimes. Whitetooth says we'd spend it on drugs anyway, so he might as well keep it an' give us the drugs instead."

"He's a dealer too?" Rykka asked. "What's his choice for 'round here?"

"Used to be 'Lixir," Seva said. "But there's no more 'Lixir, and now he deals Lumination."

"'Lixir killed folk," Rykka said.

Seva shrugged. "Heard that, but it made things… better. And a buddy taught me how to burn out the bad parts." He toyed with the wooden spoon. "Sometimes that didn't leave much after, but it was better than nothin'."

Burn out the bad parts? Her ears perked slightly. "How'd you tell the bad from the good?"

"You have to take it, then look inside. Gotta use some of the good bits to burn out the bad ones, so if there was too much bad, you didn't get much lift from it. Lumination's better. Don't have to burn out much at all."

Her brow pinched briefly in a frown. She'd never taken Elixir, and had only had one experience with Ambrosia, but she couldn't envision how one could look in at the drug after consuming it. Unless he meant that somehow, he could look in at the magical energy and see its flow within his body?

He's not describing traditional channeling. Is this the "internal" channeling Cemar claimed to have discovered?

She focused on Seva again. "And Whitetooth deals in Lumination?"

"Does now. Used to be other drugs, but now it's just Lumination." He glanced around and spoke quietly. "I saw his supplier once. It was a nobleman. Spoke real fancy, didn't fit in at all. Whitetooth bowed and scraped all over the place, too. Never seen him bow to nobody before. He'd more likely spit in your face than make nice."

"A nobleman?" Rykka spoke as quietly, leaning toward him. "You see anything about him?"

Seva shook his head quickly. "Kept his face covered and all. Wore this mask like they wear on the stage, except his weren't painted with any expression, just blank." He shivered. "He were an elf, though. And he wore really nice gloves. Black satin with amethyst trim. He shouldn't have been wearing his rings under them—stretches the cloth where it's not supposed to."

I shouldn't be surprised a whore can assess the quality of someone's gloves at a look. "I suppose the rest of his clothes were nice too."

Seva shook his head. "Nah, the rest fit pretty well for talking business with Whitetooth. Couldn't see most anyway under his cloak. The gloves were real nice, though. An' he was rich enough to not care 'bout them. I dinna follow 'im, of course. That woulda been stupid. But I found those gloves tossed inna alley when I went out later. They even smell rich and fancy, like those oils the nobles use so they don't have to smell the rest of us."

He instantly fell silent when the server approached their table again. Rykka ordered another beer for each of them and a basket of bread. The server brought both, and she nudged the bread more to Seva's side of the table as she took a slice.

He shouldn't be telling me all this. He's got to realize that. This isn't something you should tell someone you just met. He's desperate for anyone to talk to. I wonder how long it's been since anyone treated him like a person? She watched him devour the bread. *You think I've abandoned what we stood for, Tiyron? You're wrong. Our mistake was thinking we could do this on our own. We need people like De'seneth, people who can get into places we can't go and acquire things we can't get.*

A thought occurred to her. "Do you know who Whitetooth's other suppliers were? The ones who he's not using now that he's just dealing Lumination?"

Seva hesitated. "Why...?" He swallowed hard. "Whitetooth don't like competition."

She shook her head quickly. "I'm not dealing. But the other suppliers must be upset about losing the steady cuts."

"Only know 'bout one who came to Whitetooth wantin' to

know why she were on the outs. Called herself Lady of Night-bane, and I never seen nobody mess with her. But Whitetooth just laughed and told her to leave. When she didn't, he got his heavies to toss her out and rough her up. I thought for sure we were all gonna get it from her people, but..." He swallowed hard again. "But I didn't hear nothing more. None of her people retaliated, none of them came after any of us... It's like he scared her. Like he scared them all. I don't know what they know that no one told me, but somehow... Whitetooth scared all his suppliers into line, and they aren't making a peep about him dropping them."

What in blight could make the druggers that scared of this White-tooth? Hematic perdition. I need to talk with Tiyron.

"Sounds like I don't want to get on Whitetooth's bad side," she said.

Seva shook his head quickly. "Nobody wants to get on his bad side."

She held his gaze. "If you need somewhere to lie low for a while, or a place to get care if you're hurt, do you know the Coiled Dragon Clinic?"

"Yeah. The human doctors. The ones who kept taking in Rat's Disease victims when no one else would. Whitetooth says human medicine is a bunch of smoke and mirrors, but folk claim they survived Rat's Disease because of them."

"I don't care for human medicine, but they aren't fakes," Rykka told him. "Clinic is just a little way down the street. If you need help, go there. Tell 'em Rykka sent you. They'll take care of you."

"Why?"

"It's what they do. They wanna help the folk who don't get a second look from most."

Seva shook his head. "No, I mean... why would you...?"

"Because I'm not waiting for the Avatar of Tanish to descend from on high to bless the slums again. You need a place to stay away from Whitetooth, you can go to the clinic. They'll keep you safe, I promise." Rykka took two marks from her pocket and handed them to him. "And here's the payment for your time and company."

He stared at the marks, then accepted them. "I... thanks." The marks vanished into his pocket. "I'm... usually around where I was most nights. If... you want company again."

She nodded and rose. "Thanks. Probably see you around, then."

Leaving Beggar's Crown, she made her way back to the clinic. Night was fully settled over the slums now, but the back door was still unlocked. Rykka slipped inside and locked it behind her. She followed the faint glow of light to Doctor Tan'shyo's office.

The white-haired human looked up when he heard her steps. "Good evening, Rykka. Saskia mentioned you might be around this evening. I trust you found the back door open?"

"I did. It's locked now," she answered. "How's Tiyron?"

"He appeared to be resting when last I checked."

"I'm sorry he's been difficult."

"I understand enough of the circumstances to know he has reason to be suspicious. You're welcome to check on him anytime." Doctor Tan'shyo gave her a smile.

Rykka didn't know the doctor well, but he had an air of patience that would rival the gods. She'd seen him concerned, but never angry. If anyone could tolerate Tiyron during his recovery, it would be this human.

"Thanks."

"I'll be here if you need anything." He nodded at the documents on his desk.

She nodded and made her way to Tiyron's room. She knocked once, softly, on the door and opened it.

"It's me."

A single ghostlight cast dim illumination around the room, faint enough that a patient should be able to sleep. Rykka crossed the room to the chair by the bed. As she sat, the slight glint of light on Tiyron's eye told her he was awake and watching her.

"Didn't think you were coming back," he said.

"I considered leaving and catching a ride back to the place I'm staying but decided not to."

"Our hideout?"

She snorted softly. "Our hideouts were compromised a long time ago, Tiyron. No, I have lodgings included with my job."

"Still haven't told me what job."

"You still haven't asked," she countered.

He started to say something, then stopped and let out a long breath. "What's your job, Rykka?"

The answer in her mind was "Lady De'seneth's lady's maid," but the one that actually left her lips was "Privateer."

Tiyron sputtered. "What?"

"After Cemar was dead and I'd secured my freedom, I made my way to Rillwater and signed on with the fleet. At first it was an excuse to travel to places and follow up on legends and stories about miraculous healings, but... I actually like it."

"So De'seneth is what, captain of your ship as well as a Silverline lackey?"

"No, De'seneth doesn't have time to do both. He lives here in Lewarden and works as an engineer. I serve under Captain Roddek on the *Conquest*."

"What kind of name is...?"

"Given name. Rillwater captains go by their given names. Too many large families to go by family name—you'd have a dozen ships with a 'Captain Shoalbreaker'."

Tiyron digested that for a few minutes. "Then why're you here?"

"Someone's been smuggling in components to make some so far unidentified devices. I got temporarily reassigned to assist De'seneth in determining what they're for and figuring out who the pieces are going to, because we suspect it connects to Cemar. Or more likely to Sunward."

"Why does the Pirate King or whatever he's called care?"

"Admiral. Admiral As'enel, Tiyron. First, he cared because we're talking about smuggling running through the waters we patrol."

Tiyron's expression was somewhere between a sneer and a grimace. "Didn't pay their protection money, huh?"

"As I understand it, the admiral's picky about who he accepts bribes from. And the second reason he cares about this situation is because of De'seneth and how disruptions to Silverline Power will affect him."

Tiyron snorted. "Why would *that* matter to the… admiral?"

She wasn't ready to explain that Alistar De'seneth was actually Alistar As'enel, heir to the fleet. Instead, she chose a factual but misleading answer. "The admiral's wife is a De'seneth."

Tiyron stiffened with a sharp breath. He glanced around the room uneasily, as if expecting to find Rillwater privateers watching from the shadows.

"The admiral doesn't know about you, Tiyron. Right now, only Alistar, Saskia, and Saskia's father, Doctor Tan'shyo know you're alive. As far as I know, not even the healer who saved your life knows your actual identity."

"He doesn't. He was here earlier. Healed a little more. Said all he needed to know was that I was a victim of Cemar."

She nodded. "There aren't many people I'd trust your life to, Tiyron. You know that."

He glanced away and didn't respond.

She waited in silence for several minutes. When he didn't say anything, she said, "Enough about privateers or Silverline. How about a little mystery straight from the slums?"

He glanced back to her. "What sort of mystery?"

"Ever heard of a fellow called Whitetooth? Drug dealer and pimp."

His brow wrinkled. After a moment, he slowly nodded. "Small-timer with delusions of grandeur. About half my height, face like a weasel."

"Apparently he's not so small time now. He's dealing a new drug called Lumination, and his supplier is a nobleman. He's dropped all his old suppliers like week-old rotten fish, and the only one who complained paid for it, with no evident retaliation. Even with a noble patron, what would give Weaselface that sort of clout?"

"Would have to know more," he told her. "About his patron, about his resources, his thugs..."

"I can find out some of that, but learning more about his patron will be hard. My source only saw the nobleman once, and wisely chose not to reveal to Whitetooth that he'd done so."

Tiyron's eyebrow rose. "Why'd he tell you?"

"Because he's young and scared and desperate enough to pour out his soul to the first person to give him a hot meal and talk to him like an intelligent person."

"You bought a whore dinner?"

"I bought a whore dinner. Not like you haven't done that when you wanted information." She scowled at him.

"Not scolding you, Rykka." He let out a weary breath.

"I haven't forgotten where we came from, Tiyron, and I haven't forgotten the people who are still there. But I can do more to help them by working with De'seneth and other 'Silverline lackeys' or nobles than we ever could by fighting blindly against them. I don't expect you to believe me. It doesn't matter if you don't. You'll figure it out eventually. But don't ever accuse me of turning my back on them." She fixed a hard gaze on him.

His jaw tightened, but Tiyron looked away first. "Fine. But I'm not helping your Silverline lackey."

"Then help me and call it a chance to piss on Cemar's grave."

His hands clenched, but he finally nodded. She knew he didn't like it, but for now, it would have to be enough.

CHAPTER 13

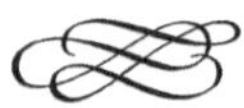

The taxi carriage dropped Rykka off at the manor gate. As the driver and his team set off in search of other late-night travelers, she walked up to the gate, but didn't open it.

Why do we persist in this pretense? Doctor De'seneth doesn't need an attendant.

She sighed and opened the gate. Moonlight bathed the cobblestone drive to the house. Owls hooted in the trees and small creatures scampered through the grounds.

A tall figure stood near the front door, backlit by the ghost-light lamps. Rykka frowned. Dorne wouldn't have reason to be staying up to talk to her, at least not outside, and the figure's build was wrong for the butler. Rykka slowed and approached cautiously. As she came closer, she identified him as Windshadow, De'seneth's footman. No one else in the house wore his red and gold eyepatch, nor did anyone else carry themselves like a soldier. He watched her but waited until she'd reached the front steps to speak.

"You're out late, Darkwood. Lady De'seneth returned home hours ago."

"And you're up late, Windshadow," she said, coming up the

two steps to the landing. "Or are you just here to scold me for staying out past my curfew?"

His eye narrowed. "I don't think you take your responsibilities to this house seriously, Darkwood."

"Quite the contrary, Windshadow. I take all my responsibilities seriously. And not that I think it your business, but I was down in the Lower City at the Coiled Dragon Clinic. As Lady De'seneth knows already." Her voice was as cool as her gaze. *She* might question the purpose of her temporary role in this house, but she wouldn't stand silent while someone else did so.

Windshadow scowled. "And does she also know you were patronizing street-corner whores while you were there?"

Rykka's eyes narrowed. "Are you spying on me?"

"Word comes to me of untoward behavior of others in the employ of this house, Darkwood. And you have not answered my question. What would Lady De'seneth think of such activities?"

Rykka snorted. "Considering that I bought that boy a meal, then strongly suggested that if he needed help, he should go to the clinic, I think Lady De'seneth would approve of me working in the spirit of the Coiled Dragon Clinic to aid the people most in need. And in case your spies didn't tell you, dinner company was the only thing I hired him for. I don't even know if the Beggar's Crown *has* rooms for rent."

"Oh yes, I'm sure nothing *questionable* could occur in such an upstanding, reputable establishment. I don't know what you think you're going to get out of this, Darkwood, but I won't tolerate you doing harm to this house or this family."

"Did you greet all Lady De'seneth's lady's maids this warmly, Windshadow? No wonder none of them lasted."

He stiffened. "I knew whose marks lined the others' purses."

"But not mine, is that it?" Rykka laughed softly. "And you think this is the way to find out? So sorry to frustrate you. And do you really expect me to believe you're motivated simply by loyalty to De'seneth and his house?"

He drew a slow, deep breath. "If you think you can—"

Rykka's hand shot up, interrupting him. Her eyes focused on the shadows just beyond the glow of the ghostlights along the drive. She strained to hear. "Someone's out there," she said in a low voice.

"Where?" Windshadow's hand fell to the hilt of his long knife —a weapon Rykka was certain was more functional than ceremonial, but his gaze remained on her.

"Moving between the trees on the west side of the drive. Wrong build to be the groundskeeper. Also too short." She tried to pick out the figure again. "Blight, lost track of them."

Windshadow took a step back and turned to scan the night. "What could you tell about them?"

"Not much," she admitted. "Slender, between five and a half to five and three-quarters feet tall, wearing dark clothes. Nothing so overdramatic as a billowing cloak or anything of that sort, but their head was covered."

Windshadow glanced back at her. "Your 'not much' is more than most people can pick up in a glance in the night."

"Try asking me what was on the second paragraph of the ninth page of a book I read two months ago sometime." She continued to search the darkness. "There, near the taller apple tree. They're holding still for the moment… and now heading toward the side of the house." She stepped off the landing, trying to keep the figure in sight.

"I see them." Windshadow vaulted over the banister and sprinted after the intruder, drawing his blade.

Rykka cursed. Not seeing any of the privateers who should have been keeping watch, she dashed back up to the door, jerked it open, and snapped at the nearest servant, "Tell Dorne there's an intruder on the grounds!"

Giving the servant no chance to respond, she ran after

Windshadow. Coming around the side of the manor, she saw the intruder spring back as Windshadow grabbed for them. Rykka pulled back into the shadows.

"Who are you? Why are you here?" Windshadow demanded.

A soft, feminine laugh answered him. "Fortune smiles. The Silver Prince's lackey comes to me." She moved light on her feet, eluding his grasp.

Windshadow stopped cold. "Merris?"

The intruder lunged at him, moonlight glinting off the long, slim blade in her hand as she took advantage of his surprise.

Rykka instinctively snatched power from the mahiy lines and flung it in a shield in front of Windshadow. The woman's blade struck the barrier and scraped across it harmlessly. Rykka's barrier shimmered briefly. Windshadow jerked back, belatedly raising his knife to block the attack.

Merris's moment of hesitation betrayed her confusion. "You're no channeler, Windshadow."

"Shouldn't be so confident you know all my secrets, Merris," Windshadow countered.

Rykka glimpsed him tensing in time to drop the barrier before he attacked Merris. Windshadow seized hold of the woman's wrist and twisted the blade from her grasp.

Merris's free hand flashed out, releasing a burst of powder. Windshadow staggered back, coughing. Rykka rushed toward them, ready to create another barrier. Behind her, more footsteps rushed out of the house.

Merris looked from Windshadow to Rykka and those behind her. The woman spat an angry curse, spun on her heels, and fled into the darkness. Windshadow staggered several steps after her, fighting for breath. "Stop her."

Rykka caught him as he stumbled. She gestured the direction Merris had fled. "She bolted that way."

While the Rillwater staff spread in pursuit, Dorne joined them. "Did either of you see enough to identify the intruder?"

"Merris," Windshadow coughed.

Dorne's expression hardened. "You're sure?"

"Yes."

"She tried to stab Windshadow, and I don't know what was in that powder she threw in his face," Rykka said. "He might need a healer."

"Not poison," Windshadow managed. He seemed to be shaking off the effects. "Don't need a healer."

"Help him into the house, Darkwood," Dorne ordered. "We'll secure the grounds."

Windshadow didn't protest. Rykka helped him inside and into the sitting room. He sank into one of the plush chairs with a groan. When Rykka moved to leave, he caught her arm.

"Wait."

She raised an eyebrow at him.

"Thank you. Without your intervention, Merris could have done a great deal of harm."

"You're welcome. And since you're probably thinking it, yes, I'm registered." Not that she liked that much, but Rillwater provided a blanket registration for channelers associated with the fleet.

He grimaced. "I wasn't going to ask, Darkwood. Though I would hope Lord and Lady De'seneth wouldn't neglect to ensure you had the proper documentation. Assuming they are aware of your talent."

Rykka's eyes narrowed. "Windshadow, based on that woman referring to you as Prince Cero's lackey, I assume you know who De'seneth is, and the role he played in stopping the attempted coup of two winters ago."

"I am." His cautious tone asked just how *she* knew of such matters.

"I hope, then, that you're also aware of recent reported sightings of a certain lady known to be involved in those plots."

Windshadow nodded slowly, cautiously.

This was the point where she had to play her hand just right. "I should think it obvious, then, that Lady De'seneth would be a choice target. And I'm sure you can see there are certain benefits to protection that comes from someone who is not identifiably an agent of the Crown."

Windshadow drew a sharp breath but collected himself. "Who *are* you associated with, then?"

She knew De'seneth wanted to keep her connections to the fleet concealed, and she wasn't inclined to share that information with the Silver Prince's spy in any case. "I'm independent. My involvement is personal, as someone directly impacted by the events that De'seneth prevented. So, who's Merris?"

Windshadow shifted uncomfortably. "She was… your predecessor as Lady De'seneth's maid. She was dismissed when she was caught attempting to enter an area of the manor she didn't have access to."

Rykka stiffened. "The woman who just tried to murder you used to be Lady De'seneth's personal attendant?" Suddenly, the tale she'd spun from implication and shadows about Saskia being in danger seemed far more plausible. "Who is *she* associated with?"

"We believed her connected to the Goldrain family. They've shown little public involvement in politics outside of lobbying in favor of fewer restrictions and regulations on their factories." Windshadow let out a heavy breath. "I wouldn't have thought Merris to be a killer." He held up the long, thin blade he'd wrestled from Merris. "Are you familiar with this style, Darkwood?"

Rykka looked the blade over. The narrow blade was made for piercing rather than slashing. "I've seen similar types in the past."

"It's meant for getting between the gaps in armor, especially those where two pieces join. It takes a keen eye and a precise hand to use effectively."

"Did she have reason to think you might be wearing armor?"

Rykka asked, looking over the footman in his striking, but hardly defensive, red and gold uniform.

Windshadow considered before speaking. Finally, he said, "I often am, and tonight was no exception. There are certain materials that are not made available to the population as a whole, but that provide protection akin to more traditional armor."

Her eyebrows rose for a moment. "I didn't think working for Lord De'seneth would require such measures. Although… given tonight, maybe it does."

He smiled tightly. "Maybe so. Regardless, if you are here at least in part to protect Lady De'seneth, you seem to spend a great deal of time engaged elsewhere, Darkwood."

"If you haven't seen me, then I'm doing my job right. Besides, physical safety is not the extent of my responsibilities, Windshadow." She fixed her gaze on him, not blinking, not looking away. "I find it easier to protect against threats if I know what they are."

"And what 'information' did you gain by dining with a whore?" he asked dubiously.

"Oh, nothing of significance. I'm sure there's no potential threat in a nobleman clandestinely funneling drugs into the slums and raising some petty wanna-be pimp into a new crime syndicate."

"What? Who?"

"The pimp? Fellow by the name of Whitetooth. If you're asking about the nobleman, my contact didn't know." Might as well elevate Seva's status a bit while she was at it.

"Can he find out?"

"Spying on his boss isn't exactly the safest pastime for him, Windshadow, nor is finding ways to pass that information on. Especially not if I am also being spied on." She gave him a dark look. He hadn't said anything about Tiyron yet, so hopefully his spies either didn't know about Tiyron, or hadn't identified him.

Windshadow had the grace to look embarrassed. He glanced away from her. "It seems my suspicions pointed the wrong direction. I… apologize, Darkwood."

Footsteps hurrying down the stairs silenced both of them. The door opened and De'seneth entered, a dressing robe hastily pulled over his nightclothes. "What happened? Who attacked you?"

Windshadow sprang to his feet. "Lord De'seneth."

De'seneth waved off further formalities. "You were attacked. What happened?"

"Darkwood and I were discussing some business outside when she spotted someone skulking about the grounds, sir. I pursued and identified the intruder as Merris. She attempted to stab me, but Darkwood…" He paused, as if trying to figure out a way to describe what happened without saying she'd channeled.

"I threw a barrier up," Rykka said. "I'm not sure whether she saw me do it, or if she thinks Windshadow pulled that trick himself."

De'seneth's shoulders relaxed. "Thanks, Rykka. Soluthos, you're sure it was Merris? Why did she attack you? Do you think she was just attempting to eliminate a witness?"

Windshadow paced. "I'm certain it was Merris. She attacked me because of my connection to His Highness." He caught De'seneth's raised eyebrow and glance at Rykka. "Merris said it plainly, sir. Darkwood heard her."

"Her words implied that while killing Windshadow might not have been her primary goal, it was somewhere on the list," Rykka said. "But we don't know what her actual purpose for coming here was."

"Blood and sand." De'seneth ran a hand through his black hair. "Merris, of all people." He looked back to Windshadow. "Report this, of course. And if you can dig up anything new on her…"

"I know the person to ask, sir," Windshadow said.

"I assumed you would," De'seneth said. "Rykka, good work tonight. Thank you."

"After all the trouble Lady De'seneth has evidently had finding a suitable lady's maid, I'd hate for you to have to suddenly need to find yourself a new footman as well, sir," Rykka said.

De'seneth smiled wryly. "Thanks. Appreciate your concern, as always."

Windshadow opened his mouth to protest her lack of proper respect, but wisely held his tongue when he recognized that De'seneth was amused rather than offended. She almost felt sympathy for him. Almost, but not quite.

Rykka stood. "Better make sure the rest of the house knows about Merris's attack. If she had any friends here, you don't want her convincing anyone to let her slip back in to 'pick up something she left' or some other excuse."

Both men grimaced and nodded.

She left the sitting room and climbed the stairs to her chambers. Shucking her clothes into the hamper, she washed and dressed for sleep. Lying in bed, she stared up at the ceiling.

New drugs in the slums and a new would-be crime lord. Now a lady's maid turned assassin. What in hematic perdition is happening in this city?

CHAPTER 14

Shortly after breakfast, Dorne announced, "Investigator Lady Ilithela Dawncloud has arrived, sir."

"Excellent." Alistar rose from the sitting room chair he'd sunk into. "Let Soluthos and Rykka know."

"Of course, sir." Dorne withdrew.

Several minutes later, another member of the staff escorted the investigator into the sitting room. Investigator Dawncloud was a tall, muscular elven woman with auburn hair tied back in a tail. Her expression was serious, and she carried herself with a stern, professional air, further enhanced by her crisp, pressed uniform.

"Lord De'seneth. The Ministry of Investigation appreciates your cooperation in this matter."

"Of course, Investigator Dawncloud." Alistar paused. "I beg your pardon, is it proper to address you as 'Investigator', as 'Lady', or both?"

"I prefer Investigator, Lord De'seneth. Thank you." He sensed a slight hint of approval in her tone.

"Very well, Investigator Dawncloud. I assume you will need

to interview the witnesses to the incident. What can I provide you in addition?"

"Did you witness the events, Lord De'seneth?"

He shook his head. "No. My footman, Soluthos Windshadow, and my wife's lady's maid, Rykka Darkwood, were the only witnesses to the intrusion and attack that took place."

Her expression shifted with recognition and concern and she straightened slightly at Soluthos's name. Investigator Dawncloud schooled her expression quickly. "Was either witness injured? Or anyone else?"

"Soluthos inhaled some powder the intruder used to mask her escape, but we've confirmed that he suffered no sustained harm from it beyond the initial coughing fit. We collected a sample of the powder. My butler can provide you with it and detail the collection methods used to avoid contaminating the sample."

One of her eyebrows rose. "Your butler is familiar with imperial evidence collection procedures?"

"He's well-trained in Rillwater evidence and sample collection procedures, which I understand follows a similar process." Alistar politely refrained from mentioning that the Ministry of Investigation had copied their procedures from those of Rillwater rather than the other way around.

Investigator Dawncloud's expression told him she knew that particular detail. "Very well. Thank you for taking such measures."

Someone knocked. At Alistar's invitation, the door opened and Soluthos entered. He bowed deeply. "Lord De'seneth, Investigator." His voice was polite, but Alistar caught a small smile on Soluthos's mouth when he looked at Investigator Dawncloud.

"Thank you for coming, Soluthos. May I present Investigator Ilithela Dawncloud?" Alistar indicated Dawncloud, pretending not to notice the indications that the two were already acquainted. He slipped a speaking stone from his pocket, activated it, and slid it into the cushions of his chair as he rose. "Investigator, you are welcome to use this room for your interviews. Unless you need anything else from me, I will leave you to your work."

"Thank you, Lord De'seneth. If I need anything further, I will let you know at once."

He left the sitting room and climbed stairs to his study, where the paired speaking stone awaited. Alistar hung a loop of gold cord on the door handle as a signal that he was not to be disturbed, closed the door, and settled at his desk. He activated the speaking stone.

Investigator Dawncloud's voice came through, slightly muffled but audible enough to understand. "What happened, Sol? You were going to confront Darkwood. What went wrong?" Her tone was deeply concerned. "Was this an ally of hers?"

"I did confront her, Ilith," Soluthos said. "We were in the midst of it when Darkwood saw the intruder. I don't believe the two worked together. If they had, Darkwood could easily have 'forgotten' to alert the rest of the house—Starbinder only knows I didn't think to do so. The intruder was Merris Teabloom— Lady De'seneth's former lady's maid."

"Darkwood alerting the rest of the house doesn't prove anything about her involvement or lack thereof," Investigator Dawncloud said.

"No, but her protecting me when Merris tried to kill me does."

Alistar raised an eyebrow at the familiar names the pair used when they thought themselves alone. And evidently, Soluthos had already spoken with Dawncloud regarding his suspicions of Onyxflame.

"Merris tried to kill you?" Dawncloud demanded.

"She did. Darkwood revealed herself to be a channeler—she can create barriers. I was careless, let myself be distracted by the surprise of learning the intruder's identity. Merris called me a lackey of His Highness and attacked. She had an assassin's blade, the sort that slips through the gaps in armor like it was water. Darkwood's shield saved my life."

Someone paced around the room. "A channeler. Is she registered?"

"She is; I checked. Her talent isn't identified in the registration, but she does have the paperwork. I'm not sure she was registered before she entered the De'seneths' service. The registration does have that particular minimalistic style typical of Rillwater," Soluthos said.

Dawncloud sighed. "Of course it does. But that means the De'seneths know of her talent?"

"Lord De'seneth does, certainly. I've not asked Lady De'seneth. However, during our discussion, Darkwood indicated that her talent is one reason she was hired for her current role. She knows of the threat posed by Sunward and reminded me that Lady De'seneth could easily become a target, especially given the lady's profession as a doctor and the location of her work."

"Hematic perdition," Dawncloud sighed. "What about connections to the Lower City criminal elements? Did she say anything about that?"

"Darkwood claims to be an independent agent, and said she was speaking with one of her contacts," Soluthos answered.

"A contact? I want to know how she managed to find anyone willing to double-time on Whitetooth. I've been trying to get an in there for months. And she says she's independent?" More pacing. "All right. Well, you'd better give me your formal statement about what happened last night so I have something for the official records."

"Right, of course."

Alistar deactivated his stone so no sounds would carry

downstairs to the speaking stone hidden in the sitting room. He let out a long breath.

Blood and sand. But if Soluthos and Dawncloud keep digging into Rykka's cover story, they may uncover things I don't want the Crown to know. I need their attention focused elsewhere.

Perhaps, ironically enough, Merris's attack will be just what we need.

CHAPTER 15

Once Investigator Dawncloud concluded her interviews, she began an examination of the manor grounds. Soluthos volunteered to accompany her, and Alistar sent Dorne with them as well. While they were occupied, Alistar took the opportunity to convene with Saskia and Onyxflame in his study.

Onyxflame flopped into a chair with a complete lack of ladylike grace. "Blackened shoals, glad that's done."

Alistar hadn't listened in on Dawncloud's interview of Onyxflame. "Problems?"

"Oh, no, I get interrogated by the Crown's investigators all the time," she countered sharply.

"Did she accuse you of anything?" Saskia settled beside Alistar.

"Not directly. Just a lot of pointed questions about what I'd been doing that night and where, and some veiled implications. But no outright accusations, and my actions to save Windshadow from getting stabbed by Merris counted in my favor."

"I suspect he's been calling in professional contacts to spy on you, Rykka," Alistar said.

"Not sure I'd call Windshadow's connection with Dawncloud purely 'professional' but yes, he's definitely had people following me. They've been good at avoiding notice, too, although admittedly, I haven't been watching for a tail. Careless on my part." Onyxflame shook her head, chagrined.

Saskia's brow furrowed. "Why would he want you followed? Did we leave some obvious flaw in your cover story?"

"Not really," Onyxflame answered. "At least, not unless you're the sort of person who thinks everyone in the Lower City are a criminal and a crime lord's underling."

"What? That's ridiculous!" Saskia protested.

That gave more context to Soluthos's statement that Onyxflame claimed to be an independent agent. "It's not that outrageous a thing to be concerned about, love. We know there are criminal factions that would be delighted to get their own people established in the clinic. Obviously Darkwood isn't one of them, but the actual concern is valid."

"Other than having no basis in fact?" Onyxflame cut in.

"Such concerns about *you* have no basis in fact. Concerns about criminals trying to get into the clinic do," Alistar said.

"Unfortunately true," Saskia admitted. "If they aren't trying to convince Father or me to hire one of their people to 'help' around the clinic, they're attempting to extort protection payments." She shook her head.

"I know your father has his own protections in place against criminals and extortionists, Saskia. Regardless, I'm more concerned with making certain Soluthos doesn't learn about Tiyron," Alistar said before they went too far off the charted course.

Onyxflame's jaw tightened. "I don't know how long Windshadow's had people following me, but they haven't found a way so far to see what I'm doing inside the clinic, as far as I can tell."

Saskia's expression grew thoughtful. "Do we need to hide Tiyron, though?"

Both Alistar and Onyxflame looked at her in disbelief.

She continued. "You're both thinking that you need to conceal him and keep this a secret. I think allowing Soluthos to know a portion of the truth would give him context that could put his concerns to rest. Yes, Rykka began working for me under somewhat mysterious circumstances. And then, not long after, her brother became a patient at the clinic."

Onyxflame blinked. "You mean, imply that I accepted this position so I could get my brother the care he needs."

Alistar leaned back in his chair. "It makes sense. Might not allay all suspicions, but it makes sense."

"And then once he's healed enough to be moved out of the clinic, he can come here without creating too much additional suspicion," Saskia said.

Alistar straightened. "Do what?"

"He'll need somewhere to stay while he continues to recuperate. And if he is willing to share his knowledge of the depths of this house, it's more convenient if he's already here."

Alistar tried to imagine having the sullen, angry elf living under his roof. "I... suppose that's true."

Onyxflame grimaced but nodded. "We don't have any secure bolt holes in Lewarden anymore, and I don't trust anyone in the Lower City enough to leave him with them."

"Do you still have contacts in the Lower City?" Saskia asked.

"Not many. Those I had know of Tiyron's reported death. They'd be immediately suspicious of any claims of his return. I'm working to establish a new network, but that takes time. I have to establish a whole new reputation without having Tiyron's name to build on, so I have to start from the bottom."

"If your contacts need a safe way to reach you, or just find themselves in need, send them to the clinic," Saskia said.

Onyxflame nodded. "I will. I did tell a new one that he could find help there if he needed it. He was hesitant, though. Apparently, the crime lord he works under claims you're fakes."

"It wouldn't be the first time," Saskia said with a thin smile. "The leaders don't want to lose control of their underlings. Who does he work for?"

"A pimp and dealer named Whitetooth," Onyxflame answered.

Saskia sighed. "Ah. Well, Whitetooth has disliked the clinic ever since my father started publicizing that Elixir was the source of Rat's Disease. He was one of the main dealers in our area. I'm sorry to hear he's still around."

"Not just still around; he's on the rise," Onyxflame said. "Dealing in a new drug now, something called Lumination."

Alistar straightened. "A new drug? How new? Where is it coming from?"

"I've only just heard about it, but so far, I know Whitetooth is the dealer, and he has a powerful backer in the nobility, who might also be his supplier. My contact saw a meeting between Whitetooth and a nobleman." Onyxflame eyed Alistar. "You think Sunward would try the same tactic twice?"

"She might. It worked well for them the first time." Alistar frowned. "I haven't heard about new drugs among the upper class, but that doesn't mean they aren't out there."

"I've heard of Lumination," Saskia said. "Kir's brother told me of it at his last checkup. He hadn't tried it, and I asked him to bring me a sample if his friend gave him a dose. We can test it for toxicity at the clinic, and also get a sense of the components. It could turn out to be just another new street drug with no direct connection to Sunward."

"I know," Alistar admitted. "But the timing..."

"The timing is suspicious, and reason enough to look into the matter further," Saskia agreed. "Rykka, anything more you can learn from your contact would be welcome."

"Sure. I'll let you know. I don't know how much more I'll be able to learn about the supplier. My contact took a big risk to learn as much as he did, but 'elven nobleman who wore rings under his gloves' isn't a lot to go on."

"Under his gloves? Interesting quirk, but you're right, not much to go on." Alistar considered. "Maybe we could point Dawncloud toward Whitetooth and his activities."

"I'd rather have her following Merris," Saskia said. "Rykka has her contact on Whitetooth and can possibly expand that. We don't know what Merris is planning or who she might be working for."

A knock on the door silenced the conversation. Alistar rose and opened the door. "Yes?"

Dorne gave him a polite bow. "Sir, Investigator Dawncloud has concluded her examination of the manor grounds and the site of the attack. She and Windshadow are downstairs in the sitting room."

"Thank you. Does she need to speak to anyone else in the house?"

"She didn't say specifically, but now that she's seen the site of the incident, she might have some more questions or clarifications to ask Darkwood."

"Of course she will," Onyxflame sighed, standing. "All right, once more into the storm."

Dorne chuckled and led the way downstairs and back to the sitting room. Investigator Dawncloud sat in one of the high-backed chairs, an expression of concentration on her face as she wrote on a notepad. Soluthos stood at parade rest near her. He nodded to Alistar, Saskia, and Onyxflame as they entered.

Dawncloud scribbled several last notes and looked up. "Lord De'seneth, Lady De'seneth. Darkwood."

"Is there anything else you need, Investigator?" Alistar asked. "Additional questions we can answer for you?"

"I understand that Merris was dismissed for misconduct while you were on holiday," Dawncloud said.

"Yes. Are you familiar with the history of this manor, Investigator?" Alistar asked.

"I know the original owners defaulted on their loan when their primary business venture failed," she said. "After that, it became a base of operations for an insurrectionist group. Upon their defeat, the property came into your possession, Lord De'seneth."

Alistar nodded. "The insurrectionists added a number of concealed chambers to the house. Merris was dismissed when she was caught attempting to access some of those chambers."

Dawncloud nodded slowly. "From the descriptions given by the witnesses, she appeared to have a destination in mind when she intruded on the grounds. Are you aware of any access points to those concealed chambers from the south-east side of the manor?"

"I'm not," Alistar said.

"Are you aware of anyone who might have that knowledge, who might have shared it with Merris?"

"I can think of several who might," Alistar said slowly. "Anyone from the higher ranks among the insurrectionists could possibly know ways into those areas, and I know that not all of them were captured, despite the work of the Royal Guard and the Royal Investigators. One of the leaders eluded arrest."

Dawncloud's mouth thinned to a line. "I have heard rumors to that effect." She turned to Onyxflame. "Darkwood, did you have any contact with Merris prior to this encounter?"

"Nope. Didn't even know who she was until Windshadow told me after the attack."

"And do you have any knowledge of these concealed areas of the manor house?"

Onyxflame raised an eyebrow. "Pretty much everyone in the house knows the manor has secrets and hidden rooms. I don't know how to get into these places, but I'd have to be deaf not to have heard stories."

Dawncloud nodded slowly, though she didn't look satisfied.

"I assume you will be following up on Merris's contacts," Saskia said. "She was originally brought to my attention by Lady Briarmark, who contacted me on behalf of her cousin's brother-in-law. I believe I still have the letter in my files, if you would find that useful."

"It could be," Dawncloud said. "If you are able to find it, please send a copy to my office." She slid a calling card out of her breast pocket. Soluthos took it and brought it to Saskia. Dawncloud rose. "I shouldn't take more of your time. Thank you for your cooperation in this investigation. As additional information becomes available, I will certainly share as much as I am able."

If you look into whatever files the Crown keeps on me, I think you'll discover you can share far more information about this case with me than you realize. Alistar schooled his expression to hide his thoughts. "Thank you, Investigator. We appreciate all your work on this matter."

After Investigator Dawncloud took her leave, Alistar made his way back into the basement. He considered the rooms, frowning thoughtfully.

Merris had a destination, and murdering Soluthos wasn't her primary goal. So where was she going?

He climbed back upstairs, and found Saskia in the ballroom looking out the windows. "Care to take a walk with me around the grounds, Love?" Alistar asked.

She took his arm. "It would be my pleasure."

Outside, they began a stroll around the manor. Alistar paused as they neared the place where Soluthos confronted Merris. Alistar's gaze moved up to the ballroom balcony that overlooked the area.

"This is where Onyxflame and I escaped from Cemar's party," he murmured. He vividly remembered bursting through the unlatched balcony doors, hurtling over the railing, and falling down into the snow below. If he tried, he could recall every sensation of those moments. Sunward and Cemar had drugged him with Ambrosia, though he hadn't realized it at the time, and the drug heightened both sensations and memories.

"I can't see what Merris might have gained by trying to get up to the balcony," Saskia mused. "But Cemar and the others spent a lot of time in that area. Maybe there's something else nearby?"

"I feel like we've searched every nook, cranny, and shadow already, but maybe we missed something." Alistar continued walking slowly. "What could she have been looking for?"

His gaze kept moving back to the manor as they proceeded —not just at the ground level, but further up the side of the house. Something nagged at his thoughts, roused by his memory of the escape off the balcony.

Did I see something? Hear something? What am I missing?

His eye fell on a window. Alistar paused. He remembered seeing lights in that window, glimpsed from the corner of his eye, and someone moving within. "Saskia, what room would that window be in?"

She cocked her head at him curiously and followed his gaze. "By the position, it should be just off the ballroom." Then she paused as well. "But none of the rooms on that end of the ballroom have windows. I can't think of anything but the privy there." She looked to Alistar and spoke in a low voice. "You think the basement might not be the only place with secret rooms."

"I think Merris knew something we don't. I need a ladder."

CHAPTER 16

To Alistar's surprise, the window opened with only a little resistance. He climbed into the room and offered Saskia a hand off the ladder.

"How did we miss this?" Saskia murmured, looking around slowly.

"I must admit, I never thought to compare the count of windows we can see from outside the manor with those we can find inside," Alistar said with a slight laugh. "Although now that I've said that, I absolutely intend to do just that."

He turned his attention to the room itself. At first glance, he saw little that would justify concealment. It looked like a private study, the bookshelves filled with tomes with innocuous titles. He began taking them down and flipping through them, checking that each was what it claimed to be. Saskia checked the desk and drawers, then tried to open the door.

"It's not locked, but something's blocking it," she said. "It could have been intentionally walled in." She turned to him. "Anything in the books?"

"Not yet. So far, the titles and contents match." He closed the book and set it in the growing pile on the side table.

Saskia paused, looking at the pile he was making, then at the shelf he was gradually emptying. "Not going to put them back when you're done?"

"The shelf is worn and the books are cleaner than the rest." Alistar gestured to the shelf above the one he was examining as a comparison.

"You think someone has been here recently?" Saskia paused, concerned.

Alistar shook his head. "Not necessarily. This looks more like a pattern of continuous, long-term wear. And with no one coming in here to clean, this room's only had the house's internal system to keep the dust down. And while that's good, it's not perfect."

"As we all know," Saskia sighed. "But you think that shelf deserves a closer look." She moved to the opposite end of the shelf and began checking the books as well. "Huh. 'Advanced Studies in Artificing and Automation' sounds like something Rykka might find useful."

"You're welcome to offer it to her, if you want," Alistar said absently.

Saskia set the tome to one side. "Maybe she can find something in it that will help the two of you figure out the purpose behind those smuggled components."

"Probably more than 'The Feyblade Ascension' will." Alistar eyed the book in his hands, an exhaustive history of the Feyblade family line's rise to the throne of Calarand. Given that it had been commissioned by the Crown, the likelihood of it containing more than five unbiased facts in its four hundred pages was slim.

"Oh blight, I've heard of that one." Saskia rolled her eyes. "No, I wouldn't inflict that on Rykka. I wouldn't even inflict it on her brother."

She picked up another book, and the entire shelf shifted. Alistar grabbed the shelf as the remaining books spilled to the floor. He felt vibration through the wood, like gears turning, as the entire bookcase turned slightly. He pushed gently, and it continued to move as if on hinges.

Saskia looked past him at the staircase descending into shadows, then she looked back to Alistar, eyebrow raised in silent question. He nodded and stepped through the opening.

Ghostlights immediately sprang to life, illuminating a long, narrow, steep staircase. He kept one hand on the wall for balance as he descended.

"Why would Merris have waited until after she was dismissed to attempt to get in this way?" Saskia murmured. "If she could have gotten into the basement through this path, why risk getting caught by taking the other route?"

Alistar considered. "Maybe she didn't know about this route at the time. Assuming she's associated with Sunward now, she might not have been part of the cabal from the beginning. She certainly wasn't in attendance at the gathering I attended. I'm positive I would recognize anyone who had been there."

"Are you sure?" Saskia asked. "By the time you escaped and made it to the clinic, you were exhausted and not at your best."

"I'm sure." Alistar let out a long breath. "Ambrosia preserved my memories of that evening in sharp clarity. I remember the face of every attendee of that gathering. Merris wasn't among them. So, she might have known our manor was the former headquarters of Cemar and the others but didn't have access to anyone with more intimate knowledge of the inner secrets. At least, not until Sunward returned to Lewarden. Perhaps she didn't even know of Sunward's return until after she was caught and dismissed."

"And she decided, or was instructed, to attempt to get back inside," Saskia finished. "To get into… wherever this goes."

They reached a door at the bottom of the stairs. The knob turned easily and the door swung open on silent hinges. As he entered the still, silent hall, Alistar heard a soft thump behind him. He spun in alarm.

"Sorry." Saskia picked up the book she'd dropped and wedged it against the door frame.

Alistar blinked. "What?"

"Since we don't know what's down here or what protection might have been set in place, I thought it better to be safe and ensure no doors close on us. I set a book at the top of the stairs as well."

"Thank you for protecting me from my own overconfidence."

Saskia smiled. "Admittedly, if I were to be trapped within my home with anyone, I'd prefer it be with you, but, you're welcome. Also, it was the best use of 'The Feyblade Ascension' I could think of."

"Don't let Soluthos hear you say that," Alistar chuckled.

"What? I would think he'd be pleased to know the great contribution the history of the Crown has made to our safety and to the further understanding of these passages." Saskia smiled sweetly. Alistar smothered a laugh. She looped her arm through his.

Ghostlights winked on as they walked down the hall. While it was wide enough for them to walk side by side, the ceiling hung uncomfortably close to Alistar's head. The sound of their steps disturbed the otherwise silent passage. Dust and dirt collected where the floor met the walls. Alistar tried to guess where they were in relation to the house above, but the passage offered no context.

It felt like an eternity, but realistically couldn't have been more than five minutes, before they reached a chamber. The ceiling was higher than it had been in the passage, but it still felt close and claustrophobic. To the left, a narrow staircase ascended, and across from it stood a closed door. Alistar turned to Saskia.

"The stairs or the door?"

"If the stairs lead us back to the manor proper, I want to know where they come out." Saskia looked up the tight staircase. "This looks like it might have been designed for servant access when the manor was built."

Alistar paused, frowning. "You know, I've been assuming these passages under the house were added by Cemar and his people. I never considered that some, or all, might predate him."

"I hadn't thought about it either until just now, but adding an underground this extensive would be a huge amount of work. But if some of it was already in place, that leaves the question of why the original owners did so." Saskia twisted a ringlet of hair around her finger.

"Smuggling, perhaps. I never looked into what business they ran or why it failed."

"Maybe what we should really do is look into whether they had any connection to Cemar." She continued to gaze up the staircase, then turned back to Alistar. "Shall we?"

He followed her up the steep stairs. It didn't feel as long as the descent had been, and he wondered if they might come out somewhere on the first floor.

A narrow landing at the top of the stairs ended in a heavy iron door. Both Alistar and Saskia eyed it uncertainly. The landing offered just enough room for Alistar to slip by his wife. He tested the latch, and it released. The door swung open on silent hinges.

The room on the other side wasn't familiar, and the walls were made of the same gray stone as other rooms in the basement. Alistar entered cautiously, frowning. "It looks like storage space."

"There's another door." Saskia pointed.

Alistar nodded. "There's probably another way back up into the house somewhere around. Let's see where this door takes us."

The second door opened into a wide hallway. They passed a few open alcoves small enough that Alistar guessed them to be intended for temporary storage of items in transit. The hall ended in a heavy iron door, barred shut from inside.

Alistar and Saskia looked at each other, then at the door. Together, they swung the bar up on its pivot and hooked the catch to hold it in place. The door resisted when Alistar pushed against it, but slowly yielded, scraping across the ground. Dirt and bits of dry grass fell from above through the opening and fresh air wafted into the hall. Rays of afternoon sun shone through the gap.

He stepped back rather than attempt to open it further and leave more evidence of his efforts. Saskia frowned. "Shouldn't we see where it opens to?"

"Eventually, yes. But I don't want to make it more obvious than necessary that we've found this passage." He tried to look through the gap, but it was too narrow to reveal more than a glimpse of dirt and grass. "If this was Merris's intended goal, someone sent her to open this door."

"Which would mean the purpose wasn't just for her to get into the manor, it was to open a path for someone else to get inside." Saskia considered that for a long minute. Then she stepped up beside Alistar, grasped the handle, and pulled the door closed.

They set the bar back in place, both studying the door pensively. "Blood and sand, I wish I knew our location relative to the manor," Alistar said finally. "I didn't think we'd walked all that far, but now I'm not sure." He gave Saskia a thin smile. "Some navigator I'd be."

Her mouth twitched in amusement. "Even an experienced navigator needs a compass, love. Let's find a way back to the manor and put Dorne to the task of mapping out these passages."

Alistar eyed the iron door one more time, then nodded.

They retraced their path back to the narrow stairs, then down again into the low-ceilinged room.

"We haven't gone through this door yet," Alistar said.

Saskia hesitated a minute, then nodded. "Let's look."

The door opened on a study not unlike the one they'd entered through. The ghostlights rested in sconces of amber tinted glass, casting illumination that imitated the hue of sunlight. Bookshelves flanked a desk of polished maple. Unlike the study upstairs in the manor, books were shelved haphazardly, stacked atop each other and jammed into whatever spaces they might fit.

Alistar checked the desk. The drawers stuck, and he worked carefully to ease them open before recognizing that they were locked. "Blackened shoals, you were a paranoid bastard, Cemar," he muttered. "Do you see a desk key anywhere, Saskia?"

"No, but if it's on one of the bookshelves, it could take hours, if not days, to find," she said, frowning at the shelves. "I don't suppose anyone from our Rillwater staff has ambitions to become an archivist?"

"Onyxflame might enjoy it," Alistar said. He considered. "Actually, Lamorage might be willing to take on the task." He eased several books off the shelf and flipped them open. "Some of these are engineering texts. Although this one seems more focused toward manufacturing methods."

Saskia sat in the desk chair. A moment later, her brow furrowed slightly. She shifted positions a little, then rose. "Alistar, sit at the desk for a minute."

He set the books down, puzzled, and sat. The shape of the seat, as well as the height, felt slightly awkward to his frame, and he looked to his wife. "What am I looking for here?"

"Is that chair comfortable for you?"

"Not particularly. I wouldn't want to spend hours sitting here, certainly. Why?"

She shooed him out of the chair and settled onto it again.

"Because it fits me very nicely. It was built for a woman's proportions. I think this was Sunward's study, not Cemar's. And the Reyker only know what she might have left here that she desperately wants back."

Alistar looked around the study again, nodding slowly. "Whatever is here, we need to find it first."

Evening was near by the time Alistar and Saskia finally climbed back down the ladder from the hidden study. Three Rillwater servants guarded the base of the ladder. Once Alistar and Saskia stood safely on the ground, one of them whisked it away. The other two maintained their guard, though they moved so they no longer stood directly at the window.

"Keep an eye on things," Alistar told them.

Both nodded. "Yes sir."

Dorne met them at the front door. Speaking quietly, he said, "You've been gone nearly three and a half hours. You found something?"

"We did, and we didn't come close to plumbing the full depths," Alistar told him. "Keep a guard on that window and don't let anyone enter without my permission."

"Understood, sir. Now, if you would like a late dinner, I'll let Miallyn know."

"Yes, thank you," Saskia answered. "Have it sent to the upstairs sitting room."

Dorne nodded and strode toward the kitchen. Alistar and Saskia climbed the stairs and washed away the dust and cobwebs that even strong dust-repellent automated cleaners couldn't completely eliminate. Soluthos assisted Alistar in dressing down for the evening, and though he clearly wanted to ask what Alistar and Saskia found, he held his questions in check. He did, however, look askance at the layer of dust and grime on Alistar's clothes.

"Yes, we determined Merri's probable goal," Alistar said.

"If there's anything I can do to assist, sir…" Soluthos said.

"Get me more information about the original owners of this manor," Alistar told him. "I especially want to know if they still reside in Lewarden."

"Certainly, sir. I'll request a copy of the report on the Zel'en family. As far as I know, they still maintain a residence in Lewarden." Soluthos collected Alistar's dusty clothes, bowed, and left.

After dinner, Alistar and Saskia retired to the study. Saskia flipped through one of the books she'd taken from the newly discovered rooms. Alistar opened the box that held the speaking stones attuned to his family. He selected the amber stone and activated it.

Several minutes passed before the stone's light glow brightened. "Sorry! Had to take care of a couple things before I could talk." Roddek's voice came through clearly, with the distant sound of wind in the background.

"Is this a bad time?" Alistar asked. "I can catch you later."

"No, this is as good a time as any," Roddek answered. "I'm well enough for the moment. You?"

"Saskia and I are well enough," Alistar said in return, the exchange of code phrases to indicate who could hear their conversation. "Have you learned anything of note yet?"

"If you'd contacted me three hours ago, I'd have said 'Not much.' But then this gods-touched storm blew in."

"How bad is it?" Alistar asked in concern.

"Mostly a lot of bluster and noise. Except that the wind and the rain have cleared away a lot more than just sand. We've got some very interesting caves to look through now." Roddek's eager grin carried through his voice. "And blackened shoals, I'm glad to finally find *something* around here. For a port town, Unen is one of the most boring places I've ever been."

"Because they hid all the interesting things in these caves you found?" Alistar asked.

"No, I'm pretty sure the locals actually *are* completely boring and lacking any imagination." Roddek sighed. "I miss having Darkwood with the crew. She has a knack for sniffing out secrets. But don't tell her I said that."

"She's been extremely helpful here," Alistar told his brother. "So as much as I'm sure she'd be a benefit to you over there, I'm selfishly glad she's here. But what about these caves? Have you gotten into them yet?"

"Oh, I'm sitting in one of them right now," Roddek answered. "Plenty of tracks and scrapes on the stone. Someone definitely moved a lot of heavy crates through here. I'm hoping they only moved them in and haven't come back to collect yet. No one in the village admitted to seeing unexpected ships or strangers around, so I suspect the smugglers wait until they have cover before making any moves."

"You mean, like a massive storm?" Alistar said.

"Reyker guide us, I hope so." Sounds of movement, then a soft thump, as if Roddek had jumped down to the ground from a rock. "Don't worry. I've got eyes on the paths into the caves, and we're not announcing ourselves. I'll let you know what we find. If you don't hear from me by this time tomorrow, assume it went bad. Otherwise, I'll talk to you as soon as I have more news."

"Be careful," Alistar said, knowing his brother would ignore it.

"Of course! You do the same."

The speaking stone dulled to a dim glow until Alistar deactivated it and nestled it back into the case. He rose and walked to the window, gazing south toward the coast, and wondering if he only imagined storm clouds on the horizon.

CHAPTER 17

A steady spring rain pattered against the windows of Alistar's office. The trees outside swayed with the wind, though the storm had lost much of its fury during its journey from the coast. The sound helped Alistar focus on his work. Despite concerns about his manor, Lady Sunward, Tiyron, and everything else tangled in that web, he still had a project to complete. And if the mahiy network was not reinforced and stable by the time of Crown Prince Filipp's planned Grand Exhibition, with all its energy demands, Alistar didn't care to consider the consequences.

He studied the most recent alterations to the projected power needs and groaned silently. His initial proposal had included a generous twenty-five percent margin, on the theory that it should be sufficient to absorb the energy needs of exhibitors whose requirements they didn't have, as well as the inevitable underestimation of needs for the Exhibition itself. Alterations and expansions to the facility and a massive reworking of several major exhibits had consumed his planned margin within the first two months of the project. He'd adjusted the plans, working with his team to ensure the mahiy network could sustainably support the needs of the Exhibition while still providing the necessary energy to the rest of the city.

The next major increase in power demand for the Exhibition came a month later. Accommodating it required Alistar to completely rewrite his plans and work through the intensive process of ensuring he didn't create new conflicts between mahiy lines and that the system would remain stable. With the blessings of Director Strey'mend, Alistar had sent a polite but pointed message to the planners of the Exhibition outlining the challenges they were inflicting on the mahiy network with their constant changes and increasing demands and recommending that they stop making any more blighted changes.

He'd worked very, very hard not to respond to the message he receive in return, which suggested, not at all subtly, that providing power to the slums and the Lower City was a waste of resource. As long as the flow of magic to sections of Lewarden that visitors would see remained stable, the problem would only affect poor people, who didn't matter anyway. And who might or might not actually count as "people."

After that exchange, though, updates to the power requirements had been relatively minor. Small increases that he could adjust for or allow to be absorbed by the calculated margin. Still, they kept gnawing into the margin like rats, always hungry to snatch a little more. And the document on his desk was just one more example.

"*Why* in the Reyker's names do you need to add a dozen dancing automatons to the center ring of the Royal Pavilion?" He ran a hand through his hair. "The thirty already there aren't enough? Blackened shoals, have you even planned enough maintenance people to handle the inevitable breakdowns?" He quickly calculated the additional cost in magic. At least most automatons had internal power sources, but when the Exhibition was going to run for a full year, those power sources would need to be recharged or replaced along the way, not even considering the other maintenance requirements.

A quick knock on his door drew Alistar from his calculations. "Yes?"

A young elf in the silver tunic of a Silverline Power page bowed. "Senior Engineer, your pardon for interrupting, but there's a messenger in the lobby needing to speak to you."

"Send them up," Alistar said.

"I tried, sir, but he said his instructions were to speak to you in the lobby. He's wearing the coat of a runner for the Ministry of the Treasury."

Alistar frowned. "Odd. All right." He stood and followed the page.

Employees and a few visitors milled in the lobby, the beginnings of the lunch gatherings. As the page told him, an elf wearing the coat of an official runner of the Ministry of the Treasury stood in the middle of the lobby on the edge of the mosaic tiles depicting a bolt of lightning striking a sword wreathed in silver fire. The runner could hardly have chosen a more disruptive spot, forcing everyone who came through the lobby to move around him.

Alistar strode up to the runner. "You have a message for me, so I'm told."

"Mister De'seneth—" the runner began.

"That's 'Senior Engineer De'seneth' or 'Lord De'seneth,'" Alistar interrupted coolly.

The other blinked once, surprised to be cut off. With no apology, he collected himself and started again. "Lord De'seneth, I have been sent on behalf of the Ministry of the Treasury regarding the matter of the debt you owe to the Crown."

"The debt I owe?" Alistar repeated dubiously. He looked the man up and down with the gaze his mother might give a green deckhand who claimed to have a wonderful idea. "And what is this debt you claim I owe?"

The elf indignantly pulled himself taller. He opened the missive in his hands—conveniently left unsealed for this purpose. "A review of the records in the Ministry of the Treasury has found you, as the owner of the Tanglewood Manor, remiss in paying the full due total of the taxes upon such estate. Given the value of the manor, the back taxes, and the fines for failure to pay such, the Ministry of the Treasury finds you, Lord De'seneth, to owe the Crown a sum of 156,000 marks."

Others in the lobby had been listening to the conversation the entire time, but now they grew less subtle about staring. Alistar felt gazes on him, searching for a reaction. *This is why you wouldn't come up to my office, isn't it? You're trying to make a public spectacle of this. Why, though? And why don't you, or whoever is responsible, know how grandly this will explode in your face?*

Pushing down the anger clawing into his thoughts, Alistar refused to give the runner the response he sought. "And how precisely did the Ministry of the Treasury come to that number?"

The runner waited a moment, as if hoping that if he just held silent a little longer, Alistar would erupt in a screaming frenzy. When Alistar simply gazed at him, silent, the elf finally spoke.

"The calculations of all fees and taxes can be found within this official statement, sir… milord, but I can assure you they have all been checked and double-checked to ensure every mark is accurately calculated and accounted for."

"Is that so?" Alistar said dryly. He held out his hand. "And that official statement is, of course, properly validated and remains sealed, being a private matter between the presumed debtor and the ministry, as required by Section 38 of the tax codes of Lewarden?"

The runner stopped cold. To one side, one of Alistar's fellow engineers leaned to another and asked, "Is that true? Hematic perdition, I need to read through the codes and find out."

The runner cleared his throat. "I… do not have such a copy on me, I am afraid. Few formally request the sealed document. I shall have to return and retrieve it, if you are, in fact, formally requesting this document."

"I am." Alistar held out his hand still. "While you do so, however, the current unsealed copy you brought will have to suffice."

"This is—" The runner paused. He couldn't claim the document he held was the official copy, given its lack of seal and validation, but he clearly didn't want to relinquish it to Alistar. But now the watching eyes of the gathered audience worked against him. Reluctantly, he set the document in Alistar's outstretched hand.

"Officially, the countdown until the deadline for payment does not begin until you receive the validated statement, but regardless, the Ministry of the Treasury has informed you of the requirement that you pay this debt in full by the due date."

Alistar tucked the documents into his coat. "Are you done, or is there someone else you still need to harass?"

"Lord De'seneth, the Ministry of the Treasury performs functions vital to the operation of Calarand."

"As does Silverline Power. And you have interrupted me in the middle of a critical project to spew this nonsense. So, are you done? If so, I believe you have some documents to fetch."

The runner glowered stiffly at Alistar, spun on his heels, and strode out the entry doors.

When he was gone, a cluster of engineers hurried over to Alistar. "De'seneth, is everything all right? What was that guy's problem? And who *does* something like that in the middle of a busy lobby?" one asked in concern.

Another snorted scornfully. "Someone who thinks his fancy coat and post give him the right to bully and push people around, even when he can't be assed to bring the right documents. If they even exist."

Alistar looked at both with surprise. They were certainly right—the runner's setup had been intended to humiliate Alistar in front of his peers. But he hadn't expected others to see the ploy for what it was.

"I'm all right. That was… unexpected. As well as ludicrous." Not that he was going to explain exactly how ludicrous the accusation was.

The others shook their heads. "I can't imagine how anyone thought that would go well. But I must say, De'seneth, I'm impressed. You kept your cool the whole time. I don't think I could have done the same, especially when he kept trying to goad you."

"He wanted a reaction," Alistar said. "It's like facing pirates— you can't show them that anything they say or do is getting to you. They see weakness and they press harder, but if you give them nothing, they get more and more frustrated."

A snort from one side, and someone dryly said, "I doubt the Ministry of the Treasury would appreciate the comparison to pirates."

"Well, let's see. No one likes to see them coming. They take your marks and goods with implicit or explicit threats of violence. They operate under their own code, which no one but them seems to understand." Alistar shrugged. "There are certain similarities."

A chorus of chuckles answered him.

"Regardless, though, I wasn't joking about him interrupting me in the middle of a project, and I need to return to it." Alistar nodded to his fellow engineers. "Thank you."

The first one who'd spoken shrugged. "If someone else had been the target, I might feel different, but everyone here knows you saved Silverline Power during the uprising. You're not going to fall victim to some idiot taxman's lackey."

Alistar nodded and slipped out of the circle. Several other people hailed him as he crossed the lobby and climbed the stairs. He acknowledged them but didn't stop. Once back in his office, he closed the door and pulled the documents out of his coat. Looking through them, the sums were staggering. He scanned through for any notations indicating the auditor found something out of the ordinary, but there was no mention of any third party responsible for paying the taxes. The auditor's signature, however, was a flourishing, illegible swoop on the line. Following it was Crown Prince Filipp's signature and stamp. Probably one of hundreds of documents the crown prince signed in a day with little more than a glance.

Folding the documents again, Alistar left his office, tucking the documents back into his coat. He strode down the hall to the executive offices. Two sets of Royal Guards stood watch outside Prince Cero's door, a strong indication that the Silver Prince was in. When Alistar approached, one of them hailed him.

"Your identification and your business, sir."

"Senior Engineer De'seneth, Fifth Class. If His Highness is available, I need to speak with him on a matter of some importance about an incident that just took place."

The Royal Guard nodded curtly and ducked into the office. She emerged a moment later. "His Highness will see you, Senior Engineer De'seneth."

"Thank you." He followed her inside.

The Silver Prince's office could have served as a drawing room in a noble house. Artwork hung on the walls, abstract patterns that held great significance to elves, who found meanings in the colors and shapes. Climbing vines lay artfully draped around lattices, small white blooms perfuming the room with gentle fragrance. A window faced the prince's manor, overlooking the vast garden. Alistar glimpsed scaffolding running up one wall of the manor. He couldn't imagine repairs still continued well over a year since the destruction of the prince's ballroom, so assumed some other renovation was underway.

Prince Cero sat at a desk nearly large enough to serve as a banquet table, reviewing a document. Setting it aside, he looked up, blue-gray eyes fixing on Alistar. He wore an emerald silk-weave shirt, the collar rising to rest against his neck. His silver-trimmed black overjacket bore the familiar lightning bolt and sword insignia.

"De'seneth. Come in."

Alistar bowed. "Thank you, Your Highness." He waited until the Royal Guard closed the door again. "I have a question, if I might ask."

One silver eyebrow rose. "By all means, ask."

"Am I correct in assuming, Your Highness, that if some alteration had taken place with regard to my manor house, especially in regard to the matter of the taxes on the property, you would have informed me?"

Now both eyebrows rose. "Your assumption is correct, De'seneth, and I have made no changes to that arrangement. It remains exactly as it was originally promised to you."

Alistar approached the desk and offered the folded documents to the Silver Prince. "A runner from the Ministry of the Treasury brought these and insisted on presenting them to me in the Silverline Power lobby."

Prince Cero frowned deeply. "The Ministry of the Treasury?" He read the first page, and his expression darkened to thunderous. "What is this idiocy?"

"I wondered that myself," Alistar told him.

"The Tanglewood Manor shouldn't even be directly linked to you by name." The Silver Prince fumed. He drew a slow, deep breath, then let it out. "De'seneth, unless you object, I will make a copy of these documents and put some of my people to investigating this matter."

"By all means, Your Highness."

Prince Cero collected the documents, rose, and lay them out on the scribing table. At his command, a translucent film spread over the table surface. A dozen quills rose from their inkwells to reproduce copies of each document on the film, darting across the surface like overexuberant hummingbirds. As they finished, the film grew opaque until it resembled parchment in both color and thickness. Prince Cero studied the reproduction, then the originals, shaking his head again.

"I'm tempted to speak to my nephew about signing his name to documents without verifying their accuracy, as well."

Thoughts of Crown Prince Filipp reminded Alistar of his project and the constantly shifting port. "I just hope this isn't someone's attempt at retaliation for me telling the Exhibition to stop changing the scope of the project every month."

Prince Cero frowned at him. "Those plans were finalized seven months ago. I signed off on them myself. Any changes taking place now should be trivial."

Alistar stopped. "Then you have neither seen nor approved the adjustments sent two months after that? And another major revision took place a month later."

"By whose approval?" Prince Cero demanded.

"Each document bore Crown Prince Filipp's seal, Your Highness, and arrived through the proper channels. So far, I've managed to accommodate the changes, but we are nearing the limits of what I can confidently complete in the time remaining."

"I see." The Silver Prince's voice was tight. "Yes, I very much need to have a word with my nephew. Thank you, De'seneth." He handed the tax documents back to Alistar. "If any additional complications arise, inform me at once. I will inform the front desk that if the Ministry of the Treasury's runner returns, any inquiries are to be directed to me."

"If he does return, I would like to be informed as well, Your

Highness. I would hate for him to decide that if he's not able to reach me, he should attempt to reach my wife instead."

"Very well. You may return to your project, De'seneth."

Alistar bowed and left, the documents safely in his coat once more. Back in his office, he tried to focus once again on the task at hand, but it was hard to pull his thoughts away from the questions.

Is this retaliation? Who's stupid enough to think that attacking the senior engineer on the Exhibition is going to make things run more smoothly? Blood and sand, I loathe politics.

He hadn't quite pulled his mind fully back to his project when a quiet chime drew his attention. He fished Roddek's speaking stone from his pocket and activated it.

"I'm at work. What news?"

Roddek spoke in a hushed voice. "I wish you could see this, Alistar. We followed the smugglers when they came in—they had a larger group than I wanted to ambush, and I'm glad for it. We didn't just find a smuggler's cache. This is a full base of operations. The caves led into a cove. I'd say this group's been here for years. It's a second village. Must be some overland routes other than the caves because I've seen people coming and going. Definitely some locals moving around very freely. Three ships in dock at the moment, and I'm guessing a couple more out at sea right now, unless they're the ones we already took down."

"Are you safe, Roddek?" Alistar asked in a low voice. *We were expecting smugglers, not a full encampment.*

"Oh, probably not, but we haven't been spotted, and we haven't had to silence any sentries. This nest will take more than just the *Conquest* to clear out. I'm hoping they'll move goods soon, and we can follow to see where those get delivered."

This smuggler den must be extensive, or Roddek wouldn't hesitate to commit the Conquest and her crew to clearing them out. "I don't like the sounds of this. Have you contacted Father and Mother yet?"

"Not yet, but they're next," Roddek promised. "We're being careful. These guys are professionals. I'm not putting my crew in danger by rushing in at half-mast and no idea which way the wind's blowing."

"It wouldn't be the first time you've done so," Alistar reminded him.

"Not this time, I promise. Not against these. We'll be careful." Alistar heard the grimace in Roddek's voice. Then, with a hint of his usual carefree air, Roddek added, "After all, if I die, Cheska wins."

"And don't you forget it, little brother," Alistar told him. "Check in when you can."

"Aye cap'n," Roddek responded. "Will do."

CHAPTER 18

S tep. Step. Step.

Pain stabbed through Tiyron's body with each movement. He gritted his teeth and forced his left leg forward again. Casts still immobilized his broken arms and he couldn't grip anything for support. Sweat ran down his face. He leaned against the foot of his bed. The door seemed so far away. Even if he reached it, he knew he couldn't open it without more painful contortions.

He pushed away from the bed and tried to move his legs in time with his forward momentum. It worked for the first five steps, then his right leg buckled. He fell, biting hard into his lip to stop a scream. He lay on the wood floor, panting, eyes watering.

At any moment, he expected the door to open. Rough hands would drag him to his feet whether or not those feet could support him. Cemar's thugs would tie him to the bedframe again, laughing and mocking his attempts to escape. Maybe they would beat him again, though they left the worst of that to Cemar.

Tiyron squeezed his eye shut and drew deep breaths, taking

in the smells of chemicals and sterilizers. This room didn't stink of blood and pain, of feces and unwashed bodies. It wasn't Cemar's torture chambers. It wasn't a cell. He didn't have to beg to be given a gulp of water.

He still flinched when steps came down the hall and paused at his door. He recognized Doctor De'seneth's gait, but part of his mind remained convinced that the next time the door opened, he would be back there.

She knocked, staccato taps on the wood. "I'm coming in."

Tiyron felt her eyes on him when she entered. He gritted his teeth and pushed up on his elbows but couldn't get further. His arms trembled, but he was resting his weight on his elbows and upper arms, where no bones had been broken. He didn't look up, but Doctor De'seneth crouched beside him.

"Would you like assistance getting up?"

"Like isn't the word I'd use," he hissed between his teeth. "Don't *want* your help." He drew several trembling breaths before finally conceding. "But do *need* it."

"All right." Doctor De'seneth was stronger than she looked. She lifted him upright, supporting his weight when his legs refused to do so. She maneuvered him to the bed and guided him to sit on the mattress.

Tiyron looked away, not meeting her eyes as he muttered a grudging "Thanks."

"I know you don't want to remain bedridden, but you'll put excessive strain on your body if you force it beyond the point where you've healed. Doing so will slow your progress, not speed it."

"Yeah, I should just lie here like a good patient," he muttered sourly.

The doctor shook her head. "We both know you're too restless for that. Perhaps we can reach a compromise, though."

Tiyron finally looked directly at her, eye narrowing suspiciously. "What do you mean?"

"Can you agree to confine yourself to the clinic and not attempt to go outside unaccompanied?"

He didn't even know how large this place was, or where exactly it was in the city. "If I must..."

"An experimental mobility device was donated to the clinic a little while back. Until your arrival, though, we hadn't had any patients who might make full use of it, so haven't been able to provide meaningful feedback to the designer. However, if you're willing to try it, you would be able to navigate yourself around the clinic."

"An experimental device." Tiyron frowned warily.

"I'll bring it in so you can see." Doctor De'seneth left the room.

Is this a trick? She didn't make any threats. No warning that she'd strap me down to the bed like a back-alley chop-doc would. Of course, they're usually threatening so their patients will pay rather than to keep their patients from leaving.

A soft sound like a small cart rolled down the hall to his door. Doctor De'seneth returned with a wheeled chair. He'd seen variants of the design before to help the lame and crippled get around, though this chair was certainly better put together than those used by beggars. Thick cushions padded the seat and back. Treaded wheels of metal and an unfamiliar material looked capable of navigating most terrain, even in the slums.

"A wheeled chair is an experimental device?" He raised an eyebrow at Doctor De'seneth. "Are the nobles that far behind the commoners?"

She laughed. "The experimental portion lies in how it moves, Tiyron. At the moment, your arms aren't healed enough to propel a wheeled chair. Fortunately, you do have nearly full mobility in your fingers and hands." She maneuvered the chair beside him and opened a panel in the left armrest.

Inside rested a long, narrow crystal. A shiver ran down Tiyron's spine as he remembered other crystals and the uses to which Cemar had put them. Doctor De'seneth set the tip of the crystal into a small indent on the chair arm, near where someone's hand would rest.

"The crystal can be placed on either the left or the right, depending on the preferences of the user. Tilting it allows you to move the chair." She sat and tilted the crystal backwards slightly. The chair, with her in it, rolled slowly backwards. "How far you tilt it determines the speed. It takes some practice to master, and trying to turn rapidly does come with the risk of tipping over." She guided the chair back beside his bed and stood. "You are welcome to test it."

"How fast can it go?" he asked.

"Faster than you can safely go inside the clinic," she told him. "And if you run over other patients, I'm afraid I'll have to revoke your access to it."

"Ah, no, I meant..." He shook his head, stopping the words. "Understood."

Still cautious, he tried to stand. Pain stole his breath before he got far. Doctor De'seneth guided him into the chair. The cushions embraced him and molded around his body. He let out a startled breath. Moving his arms hurt more than he imagined, but he got them onto the armrests. His fingers closed around the crystal.

The chair vibrated faintly. Immediately, he released the crystal. The vibrations ceased. He rested a finger lightly on it, and felt no change. Tentatively, he wrapped his hand around the crystal again. The vibrations began again. He glanced at Doctor De'seneth. "Why is it doing that?"

"Doing what?"

"I'm not moving it. Why does it react when I grip the crystal?"

She looked carefully at him, then at the chair. Her voice was gentle. "Your hand's shaking. The crystal interprets that as movement."

"I don't like it."

"I see how it could be unsettling," Doctor De'seneth agreed. "I'll pass that on to the designer as a point for improvement."

She seemed to be serious. Tiyron bit back an immediately sarcastic response, but couldn't entirely suppress a bitter, "I'm sure whatever fine noble eventually acquires one will appreciate that."

Doctor De'seneth smiled slightly. "No doubt. And hopefully the commoners who receive them without charge will appreciate it as well."

"What?"

"The inventor intends to sell them to nobles and provide them without cost to those who are unable to afford them. I don't know how well that will work out in the long term, but I support the effort."

He snorted. "Better make sure it looks different, then. No noble wants to see a beggar using 'their' chair."

"Also a good point," she agreed. "Thank you, Tiyron. Now, take as much time as you wish to learn to navigate. You're welcome to move about the clinic."

At first, the chair lurched and jerked when he moved the crystal. Doctor De'seneth stood out of the way, allowing him to get the feel of how the control and the device interacted. Once she deemed him capable of controlling the chair, she opened the door and granted him access to the rest of the clinic.

Despite the amenities he'd seen, Tiyron had envisioned the clinic as small and cramped, a slightly larger version of a chopdoc's back-alley practice. Instead, the hall was wide enough for him to maneuver the chair without crowding anyone out unless he chose to. His room stood near the back door. He guided the chair over to it and found a thick wood door that locked by means of a sliding iron bar and a pair of sturdy hooks and latches. No keyholes. If someone wanted to get in from outside and it was locked, they'd have to break down the door, while someone inside could get it open relatively easily. An escape route.

Additional doors presumably led into other patient rooms like his. He passed a linen room, and another used for storage of supplies—surprising they didn't lock that door as well. Medicine fetched a good price on the streets.

The lobby was comfortable, spacious, and as clean as the rest of the clinic. The elf boy seated at the desk looked over when Tiyron entered. Tiyron eyed him. The boy had the underfed look of a slums child—Tiyron knew it well.

"Can I help you?" the boy asked when Tiyron didn't say anything. He made an effort to mimic a Lower city accent, but the slums undertones still gave him away.

"Whatcha doing here, kid?" Tiyron asked.

"Working." The boy eyed him.

"Working? For human doctors?"

"They saved my brother's life. Is the least I can do. An' the doctors are teaching me."

Tiyron raised an eyebrow. "Teaching you what? Your letters and your numbers?"

The boy glanced at the ledger book open on the desk in front of him, then back at Tiyron. "Yeah. What of it?" His voice had a note of defensive challenge. He probably got questioned a lot.

"Learn 'em well. Plenty more opportunities for smart kids who know how to count their own wages."

"I got opportunities right here," the boy said.

Tiyron chuckled softly. "I'm sure you do, sprout. Use 'em well."

He turned the chair around and moved back up the hall to listen at a few doors, determine which were occupied and which might hold something worth exploring later, when everyone slept.

He heard the front door open, then slam shut. The boy at the front desk asked, "Hey, you okay?"

Tiyron turned, but he couldn't see who had entered. He did, however, hear someone gasping for breath. "Sorry, don't tell them I'm here! Please!"

"Don't tell who? The doctors?"

"No, no, thems who're looking for me!" The other sounded male. He stumbled to the desk, and Tiyron saw a slim elf with pale blond hair dressed in clothes that just barely covered enough not to be completely indecent. The newcomer glanced anxiously toward the door, then back to the front desk. "Rykka told me to come here if I were in need."

Tiyron straightened. The chair lurched when he jammed the crystal forward. "Rykka told you that?"

Both elves in the lobby started and looked at him. The newcomer's head bobbed in an anxious nod.

Tiyron looked to the boy at the front desk. "Tell the doctors that this fellow's hiding in my room." He gestured for the newcomer to follow him.

After a moment's hesitation, the other scrambled after Tiyron. They entered Tiyron's room bare seconds before the clinic door slammed open, and the boy in the lobby raised his voice in sharp protest.

Saskia swept into the lobby in response to Kir's shout. Two humans, a man and a woman, loomed in the lobby. Both had the look of enforcers, but neither was familiar to her. Saskia planted herself in the doorway leading into the heart of the clinic and folded her arms across her chest.

"What's your business here?" Her tone was cool but professional. "Is one of you in need of medical care?"

Saskia's gaze moved to Kir and he nodded, assuring her that he had triggered the alarm. In this part of the city, anyone who expected to operate a business should expect to pay some form of "protection" money to the local gang. Saskia's father, however, had negotiated with the gang leaders to ensure the clinic's payment didn't just keep them safe from those extracting the fee, but that it offered the clinic protection from those who might otherwise cause trouble.

The thugs barely glanced at her. "Lookin' fer a thief," the woman grunted. "'Erd he mighta scuttled in 'ere. Jest ya move outta the way an' let us 'ave a look."

"While you bumble about and disturb my patients? Absolutely not."

Both thugs straightened. "An' who you think you are?" the man demanded.

"You are out of your jurisdiction." Saskia looked them up and down. "You should leave."

"Told you, we's lookin' fer a thief," the woman said.

"And I said you have no authority here," Saskia told her.

The front door opened again, and half a dozen local thugs stomped inside. "Hey! You botherin' the doctor?"

The enforcers turned, on the verge of telling the newcomers to mind their own business. Realizing they were outnumbered, and perhaps finally recognizing that they were not in their own territory, they held their tongues.

The leader of the thugs looked past them to Saskia. "They botherin' you, doctor?"

"They were, but I believe they've decided their business here is done, and they're leaving now. Aren't you?" She looked pointedly at the enforcers.

The woman's eyes narrowed as her expression darkened, but the man jabbed her with an elbow and spoke first. "Yeah."

"Real glad to hear it," the thug leader said. "Rook, make sure the doctor don't need anything else. We'll make sure these fine visitors don't get lost on their way out, seeing as how they don't know the lay of the land and all."

A squat human man with a crooked nose nodded and stepped out of the pack. Once everyone else finally left, Rook grunted. "You want as I watch in here or out there, Doc?"

"Outside, if you would, Rook. Thank you."

Rook nodded and left the lobby to take a post on the street.

"Well done, Kir," Saskia told the younger elf.

Kir let out a long breath and swallowed hard. "Thanks, Doctor De'seneth." He paused a moment, then added, "Someone came just before those guys burst in. Said that Rykka told him to come here if he needed help. I don't know if he was a thief or not, but he was scared. The elf in the chair took him to hide."

"Thanks." She turned and walked down to Tiyron's room. She knocked once, then opened the door.

"That's Doctor De'seneth," Tiyron said, facing the bed. "Stop cowering."

She didn't immediately see who he was speaking to, though she was surprised he would speak at all positively about her. "I understand we have a new patient? The enforcers are gone."

Tiyron looked back at her, one eyebrow raised. "You ran off enforcers?"

"The local keepers of order did." Saskia closed the door. She scanned the room but saw only Tiyron. "Kir said the visitor went with you, and that the visitor said Rykka told him to come here."

Someone unfolded from the shadows. She'd seen him a few times lingering on the street corners in the area, a young blond elven man. His green eyes darted nervously around the room, to her, and quickly away. "She… she did tell me that, m'lady."

"Come out and sit down," she invited.

With obvious misgivings, he obeyed, perching on the edge of the bed. Saskia looked him over and didn't see any obvious bleeding or unexpectedly large fresh bruises. "What sort of help do you need?"

"I need…" he swallowed hard, "a place to hide."

"The enforcers called you a thief. Did you steal something?"

"Only myself." He kept his eyes on the floor.

"What's your name?"

"Seva."

"All right, Seva. You can stay in the clinic as a patient as long as you need to," Saskia told him. "No one forces a patient to leave until Doctor Tan'shyo or I discharge you, though you're free to leave on your own at any time, should you choose to."

"I have no marks," Seva said quietly.

Of course he didn't. Debt had undoubtedly forced him into becoming a whore in the first place.

"Rykka already covered that, don't worry. You'll be safe, whatever drove you to come here, Seva."

He swallowed hard. "I shouldn't stay long. It's gonna make trouble for you. Whitetooth sold my debt to a noble an' said I hafta work inna factory now, but I know that peoples who get sent there don't come back."

Indentured servitude toed the line into outright slavery, especially on the streets, and the sale of a debt from one person to another often swept straight over the line without a backward glance.

"A factory where people disappear, is it?" Tiyron cut in. "Whitetooth got mad at you for something?"

Seva shook his head quickly. "Yesterday, Whitetooth called everyone in. Gave all o' us Lumination an' his thugs made sure everyone took it and didn't hide it away for later. Then they made everyone try and finish this weird puzzle... test... thing. I don't know what it was for, but I finished it."

"Did the others finish as well?" Saskia asked.

"A couple, I think. Most folk had trouble, though."

"And the others who finished, were their debts sold to the noble too?"

"I... I don't know," Seva admitted. "Didn't see 'em again."

"You don't have to worry about the noble taking you away

from here," she told him. "You'll be safe, I promise. And if need be, we'll take you somewhere else, a place they won't be able to find you."

"Thank you." Seva looked to the floor again, biting his lip.

Tiyron looked at Seva, then turned his gaze to Saskia, studying her with what might have been a hint of respect.

"Come with me, Seva. We'll get you settled in a room of your own." *And find out what else I can about this mysterious noble.*

CHAPTER 19

When Alistar returned home, Soluthos awaited him with a portfolio. "Good evening, sir. I collected what information I could on the Zel'en family today. I intended to pull the tax records as well, but there was some sort of row in the tax offices this afternoon, and everything was shut down."

"Oh? Did the Silver Prince pay a visit?" Alistar asked with a small smile.

"The Silver Prince? Not to my knowledge, sir. I did hear Crown Prince Filipp's voice. Unfortunately, I wasn't close enough to hear what was said."

Alistar's eyebrows rose. "Crown Prince Filipp? I see." *Well, his signature was on the document. Perhaps Prince Cero had some pointed words with him about the matter.* "Try to get back there tomorrow. And Soluthos, while you're in the tax offices, I would be extremely interested in whatever rumors and conversations you might overhear."

"Is there something of particular interest to you, sir?" Soluthos frowned slightly.

"I received a visitor from the Ministry of the Treasury today who claimed I owed thousands of marks in back taxes on this manor."

"That should be impossible," Soluthos said immediately.

"Yes," Alistar agreed. "It certainly should be." He took the portfolio from Soluthos and headed into his study.

Settling into his chair, Alistar looked through the documents. He'd made a cursory study of the previous owners of the mansion in the wake of Cemar's fall, but only enough to confirm that they were not obviously linked to the coup attempt or Cemar. Soluthos, on the other hand, had been thorough, starting with the initial registration of their business venture. Rather than husband and wife, the records indicated the two Zel'ens were twins—the registrar had made special note of that, perhaps an adherent to the belief that twins were specially blessed with fortune.

Like many commoners in the explosion of industry that had seized Lewarden in the last decade, the Zel'en twins had initially shown great success, producing a variety of tools to improve communication and record-keeping. Reports shortly before the collapse of their business indicated they were developing a device that could be linked to multiple speaking stones, allowing the user to only have to carry one device rather than multiple cases of individual speaking stones. Unfortunately, it didn't appear the device existed outside of a few prototypes.

Alistar was surprised to discover the Zel'en twins still resided in Lewarden. Their current address was in the Middle City, probably their original family home. Soluthos's information didn't indicate what they did now, and the details of how they went bankrupt were also missing, probably information he'd intended to gather from the tax records. Alistar found no connections between them and Cemar or Sunward.

He grabbed a quill and parchment and penned a letter, addressing it to the Zel'en family home. For all the polite wording, he was certain no one, noble or common, would misunderstand his expectation that they should invite him to come calling.

Saskia joined him as he was sealing the letter. "You're looking serious, love. What happened today?"

He turned and gave her a thin smile. "Oh, some pompous twit got worked up over my refusal to continue making unapproved changes to the Exhibition's power lines and thought they would get revenge by trying to set the taxmen on me. It didn't work out as they expected, but it's still deeply aggravating. How was your day?"

"Tax collectors? Oh dear." She sat in the overstuffed chair beside his desk. "I had to actually call in the protection Father pays for." She described the encounter.

"What made Rykka's contact run? Did he tell you?" Alistar's brow pinched in a frown.

"Whitetooth sold Seva's debt to a noble, apparently. And given that Seva saw Whitetooth making deals with a nobleman, a certain level of fear on his part seems prudent."

"Especially if the noble decided he needed more test subjects for his drugs," Alistar said darkly.

"Seva is safely ensconced at the clinic for now. Tiyron was surprisingly helpful in handling him."

"Rykka was always good at dealing with the street kids and others during my investigation. I'm not surprised Tiyron would be as well."

Saskia laughed softly. "I'm not surprised Tiyron *can* be helpful in dealing with them. I'm surprised he *chose* to do so."

"Ah, well, yes, that is a different matter, isn't it?" Alistar leaned back in his chair. "Roddek checked in this afternoon. The smuggler den is far more extensive than we thought. He's keeping a watch on them and intended to contact Rillwater once he made his report to me. If it's as organized and large as Roddek indicated, the fleet might mobilize to clear them out. We haven't had to do that in at least a decade. If it comes to battle, it's going to be ugly and bloody. The smugglers probably have families, homes, everything they want to protect."

"You said if it comes to battle," Saskia said. "There's a chance it won't?"

"The admiral will offer them a chance to surrender or negotiate. Sometimes the leaders of a group like that can be convinced to swear under the Rillwater banner. They'd lose some independence, and they'd be under close watch until they proved themselves, but some decide that sacrifice is more tolerable than losing everything."

"How often is that sort of invitation accepted?" Saskia asked.

"Not often," Alistar admitted. "But I can hope." He closed his eyes, and for a moment, he smelled acrid smoke and saw the billowing black plumes as flames crackled and leapt between buildings while he peered at the destruction over the deck railing. "I can hope."

Alistar's letter went out first thing in the morning. Before noon, he received an invitation to call on the Zel'en twins at his pleasure. He reviewed the status of his project and decided it was in a place where the engineers and junior engineers could proceed without his immediate direction. He decided to take a long lunch, with the implicit understanding that he might not return to his office until tomorrow.

As Alistar entered the lobby, Assistant Tempest called him over to the front desk. The administrative sprite sat cross-legged atop the desk, an inkpot to one side, a quill nearly as tall as her on the other. "If you would, please, Senior Engineer, wait a few moments before you leave. The runner from the Ministry of the Treasury has been seen on his way to Silverline Power. I've informed His Highness, but based on the runner's previous behavior, I assume he hopes to make another scene by demanding your presence at a time when a reasonable person would expect you to be gone for a meal."

Alistar had always appreciated the work of Silverline Power's team of administrative sprites, but the moments when they revealed their political cunning made him admire them all the more.

"Thank you, Assistant Tempest. I'd be happy to delay my departure a little while for a good cause. And while I'm here, my project has unfortunately limited my opportunities to stay abreast of the news around Silverline Power. Have I missed anything of recent interest?"

She filled him in on the latest gossip—the administrative sprites heard almost everything, especially given how many people didn't think about who might be listening as they talked in the lobby.

A familiar elf in the Ministry of the Treasury colors entered the lobby. He strode toward the front desk. His steps stumbled a moment when he realized Alistar stood there as well, but he collected himself and tried to act like he was pleased to find his target readily available.

"Senior Engineer De'seneth." He spoke the title with tight, curt formality. "As you requested, an officially sealed copy of the statement of the Ministry's findings regarding your outstanding tax debts. And I remind you, the deadline for payment has now been set. The Ministry expects your prompt compliance in this matter."

Alistar looked the runner over closely, bothered by a nagging sense of something out of place. A faint discoloration showed through the elf's fashionable application of makeup, around his left eye. *Did someone hit him? I was tempted, certainly, but if he wanted to imply I'd done so, he wouldn't make an effort to conceal it.*

When Alistar didn't speak, the elf scowled fiercely, then finally produced the documents in a wax-sealed roll. Alistar accepted the roll and set it on Assistant Torrent's desk. "Thank you. These documents will receive all the necessary and appropriate reviews of their validity."

The runner glowered, stiff. "You will find the records in order, senior engineer."

Deliberate, measured steps descended into the lobby. Prince Cero spoke, voice chill as a winter wind. "I certainly hope so. I will be very interested to learn just who in the Ministry of the Treasury has initiated this farce."

The runner spun, an outraged retort forming on his lips. The words died with a sputter when he realized he faced the Silver Prince.

"Your… Highness."

"You are welcome to be about your business, De'seneth. I will see to it this matter is properly settled." Prince Cero's eyes never left the runner.

"Wait, but--" the runner sputtered.

Alistar picked up the documents and handed them to the prince. "Your Highness." He bowed and strode for the front door.

Behind him, he heard Prince Cero speaking in a low, clear, cold voice. "I will not stand for this infantile meddling, especially when it interferes with the work of one of my senior engineers amidst of one of the most critical projects in Lewarden's history."

Despite the temptation to linger at the doorway and listen further, Alistar kept walking. His carriage waited in the courtyard. As Alistar approached, his driver put away a book and straightened. "Where to, sir?"

"This residence." Alistar handed him the address and climbed into the carriage, settling comfortably into the cushioned seat.

Twenty minutes later, they came to a stop at a pleasant three-story house shaded by a tall oak. Flowering vines climbed trellises against the front side of the house, the buds just beginning to open. Alistar straightened his coat, collected his portfolio case, and strode from the carriage to the front door.

It opened at his knock. An elven girl in a plain navy blue dress looked up at him. "'Ello, sir. Can I help you?"

"Lord Alistar De'seneth, come to call on the Zel'en family."

"Oh! So sorry, milord. The missus and the mister said you might come, but we didn't expect you today. Please come in."

Alistar pretended not to notice that he'd interrupted a rushed cleaning of the house. The girl led him into the sitting room and cleared her throat. "Um, begging your pardon, but Lord De'seneth is here."

Both occupants of the room stood quickly, but they recovered their composures. The man stepped forward to greet Alistar. "Lord De'seneth, welcome. Please make yourself comfortable. Olive, bring refreshments. What can I offer you to drink?"

"Tea would be welcome," Alistar said with a nod. "My thanks."

The woman joined her brother. Seeing them side by side, it was obvious they were siblings, with matching round faces, short noses, and curly black hair.

"Please pardon our surprise, Lord De'seneth. Welcome to our home." She held out a hand. "I am Elena Zel'en, and this is my brother, Yuriy."

Alistar took her hand. "Lord Alistar De'seneth, Senior Engineer of Silverline Power Cooperative. It's a pleasure to meet you both."

Yuriy smiled warmly. "I understand that you now reside in our former estate. I certainly hope the place is treating you better than it did us."

Alistar settled into one of the padded leather chairs and looked at him curiously. "You had troubles with the manor?"

Elena sat and smoothed her skirts. "Where to start?

Construction was supposed to take three months and stretched to almost seven. And then the cost of materials was nearly twice the original quote. It's a beautiful mansion, certainly, but I'm still not sure it was *that* fine, and I didn't think the price of stone ran as high as our architect claimed."

Yuriy smiled wryly. "My apologies, Lord De'seneth. As you can tell, the matter does still bring up some strong feelings."

"Sometimes I feel like it was at that point when everything began to come apart," Elena sighed. "Like the gods decided that in building the manor, we'd crossed the line and moved beyond our station. All the delays, then we started losing contracts…" She shook her head. "I beg your pardon, Lord De'seneth. I'm sure this isn't why you came calling on us today."

"Actually, I do have questions about the manor," Alistar admitted. Elena's complaints felt genuine. Perhaps frequently repeated, but they didn't have the practiced air of someone intending to deflect. Either she was very skilled in deceit, or she was genuine. "Do you know if copies of the plans were filed with the proper departments?" He'd already found the copies in the archives, but those showed nothing of the extensive underground.

Elena and Yuriy looked at each other and shrugged slightly.

"As far as we know, they were, unless our architect failed in that task as well."

The servant girl returned with a cart and served tea, tarts, and fresh berries. Alistar sipped his tea. "Your architect? Who did you hire for the task?"

"A gentleman named Lorne Ashfall. He came highly recommended by several of our investors," Yuriy answered. "He probably decided that since we weren't nobility, he could get away with the delays and the increased expenses. Sadly, he was right. I never thought to follow up on whether he filed the plans. Perhaps it was too much to assume he would do at least that much right."

"If you'd like, Lord De'seneth, we have the copy of the house plans he gave us," Elena offered. Before he answered, she'd sent the servant girl scurrying off to fetch the documents.

"If I may be so bold as to ask, what inspired you to come to us about the manor?" Yuriy asked.

"I've noticed some oddities about the structure," Alistar answered, watching both of them. "Especially in the basement."

Elena frowned thoughtfully. "I always felt it was too small compared to the rest of the house. Ashfall repeatedly assured us it matched the design we agreed to, but I didn't entirely believe him. Probably because he'd already proved unreliable in terms of the expense and the schedule. What sort of oddities?"

Alistar considered how much to say. "Doors that won't open or seem to lead to nowhere. Some might have been the doing of the people who occupied the manor while it was supposedly empty."

The servant brought a bundle of oversized rolled papers and laid them out on a table. With the Zel'ens' invitation, Alistar examined the blueprints of his manor. They were similar to those he'd found on file in the archives, but he felt sure there were differences, and wished he could compare them side-by-side.

He set aside the basement and first floor blueprints and found that the next page in the stack was not a diagram of the manor, but a schematic for what appeared to be some sort of speaking stone. He frowned at it curiously.

"Oh, apologies, Lord De'seneth. I didn't realize some of our developmental schematics were still in that bundle," Yuriy apologized.

"I heard you were working on a new design of speaking stone—one that would allow multiple stones to link to one..." He searched for a word.

"One receiver, yes," Yuriy said. "We got a lot of interest in it, but to be honest, I'm not certain we could have moved it all the way into production."

Alistar raised a quizzical eyebrow at him.

"The two main families who produce speaking stones had already been in the process of acquiring and absorbing the smaller producers to solidify their holds on the market. Both old noble families, and neither would have appreciated some new commoner upstarts." Yuriy smiled tightly. "We received a few carefully worded missives with implied deeply threatening messages after we first announced the development."

"Is that when you had investors pull out?" Alistar asked. "Were they also subjected to such intimidation tactics?"

They both shook their heads. "To our knowledge, none received threats, and that wasn't when they started backing out," Elena said.

"That project would have been nice if it had succeeded, but there were others we hadn't released information about that I regret not completing far more." Yuriy sighed. "I'm particularly sad that the mining suits never progressed."

"Mining suits?" Alistar asked, curious.

"Yes!" Yuriy unrolled another schematic from the stack. "Some of our cousins and their families are miners, and it's always been dangerous work. Mine shafts collapse, workers hit pockets of dangerous gasses, equipment fails. There are too many variables in a mine for an automaton—it's been tried before without success. But we were working on a way to give a miner the strength and protection of an automaton while still retaining the instincts and reflexes of a skilled miner."

Alistar looked at sketches of a suit of armor with a miner inside. "How would you power it?"

"That was our biggest challenge. Unfortunately, we hadn't found a way around that problem when we were forced to… end our business ventures."

"Did you get as far as building a prototype?" Alistar asked.

"We did, but we don't have it anymore. It was sold with the rest of our assets. I still play with the design sometimes, though," Elena told him.

"If I might ask, what circumstances forced the liquidation of your assets and business? You seem to have many practical and useful ideas."

From the glances the two gave each other, Alistar sensed shame. After a long moment, Yuriy answered. "Taxes."

"Taxes? You… weren't paying them?"

"We were!" Elena said indignantly. "And we had a skilled accountant who ensured we paid everything we owed to the Crown. But somehow, she missed something, and we suddenly found ourselves owing thousands of marks in fees because someone in the Ministry of the Treasury claimed we weren't paying the correct window tax and gave us a ridiculously short period in which to pay it."

Alistar stopped. "You were forced to sell your assets because of taxes levied on the manor house?"

"We could have managed, barely, if several major backers had not chosen then to withdraw their support and demand the returns of their investments," Elena said.

"For a while, I was pretty sure that baron got in trouble for making investments without his family's approval." Yuriy stacked the blueprints and schematics neatly again. "Of course, then he got executed for treason, so I'm less confident of that now."

Alistar almost spoke, but the words wouldn't form. *Baron Sok'lof was one of their investors?* "Do you… would you happen to have… a list of your investors that I could see?"

Both frowned. "It's highly irregular to share such information, Lord De'seneth."

"I realize that, yes. Perhaps you could at least share those who withdrew their funds at the same time as the tax issues came to your attention?"

They still frowned, but Yuriy finally unlocked a desk drawer.

"I must ask why you want to know, Lord De'seneth, and I mean that with no disrespect."

"In the light of some other knowledge I'm privy to in my position, I'm beginning to suspect that certain people actively worked to drive you into bankruptcy. Knowing who withdrew their support may confirm this suspicion." *Was someone in the Ministry of the Treasury involved in Cemar's schemes?*

The twins looked at each other, then back to him.

"All right. For that, I'm willing to share this information with you, Lord De'seneth." Yuriy reached into the desk drawer again and took out an oblong stone that looked like a mineral similar to that used to make speaking stones. He pressed his thumb and index finger against the narrow ends and held it over the parchment in his other hand. Two runes briefly lit up on the stone, and Yuriy nodded, satisfied.

"This is another prototype. Similar to a speaking stone but designed to capture and preserve images instead. This stone can hold up to twenty images, and you can project them from the stone onto another surface to view the images." Yuriy offered it to Alistar. "I would appreciate you returning it at some point, sir, but you're welcome to borrow it."

Alistar turned the stone over in his hand. "How do I activate it?"

"Press thumb and forefinger here to capture an image, or press here to display images." Yuriy demonstrated, projecting an image of the list of investors on the desk.

"Fascinating," Alistar murmured. "Might I also capture images of the manor blueprints?"

"Of course."

There was a trick to capturing images just right, and Yuriy also showed him how to purge unwanted images. Eventually Alistar had complete and legible captures of the documents.

"Out of curiosity, do you know what happened to your factories and the prototypes like the mining suit?" he asked.

"The majority were purchased by the Ravencrest family," Elena told him. "Most of the workers were able to remain with the factories, at least. I was dreading the thought that they would all be dumped back on the streets."

Alistar frowned. *That name seems to keep coming up. Are they connected, or is it coincidence?* "Have the Ravencrests continued work on any of your projects, to your knowledge?"

"Not that we've heard. They would have needed to reconstruct any project from whatever prototypes they have; all the schematics stayed in our keeping." Elena looked particularly proud of that. Alistar understood the sentiment—often in cases of bankruptcy, especially for commoners, the debt collectors seized everything but the clothes on the debtors' backs.

"Thank you both for your time and your help." Alistar shook hands with both Yuriy and Elena. "It's been more helpful than you may realize."

"If we can do anything further to help, Lord De'seneth, don't hesitate to contact us," Elena said. "And I hope you find better fortune in that house than we did."

With a nod of thanks, he returned to his carriage and departed.

CHAPTER 20

Seva was ensconced in the upstairs apartment. Doctor Tan'shyo had checked him over and given him a relatively clean bill of health, aside from being bruised and undernourished. Seva stayed quiet and had only ventured down into the clinic once since his arrival the previous day.

Saskia was about to check on Tiyron when she heard the front door open. Kir started to speak, but a cool female voice cut him off.

"Silence, rat. Fetch someone capable."

Saskia seethed with cold fury. She strode into the lobby. "There is no reason to speak to my staff in such a manner."

An elven woman with glossy black hair hanging to her waist cast a dismissive glance in Saskia's direction.

"Rats will always be rats, and there's no reason to pretend otherwise." She wore a silkweave dress in a rich, deep shade of turquoise, the long skirts shimmering when she moved. A collar of black lace circled her neck, accented by the silver necklaces that cascaded down her chest. She looked around the clinic as if she couldn't believe someone of her station had deigned to enter such a place.

"If you find our clinic so distasteful, you are of course welcome to leave," Saskia said, voice flat and cold.

"It would be my *great* pleasure to do so, as soon as my wayward employee is returned."

"If one of your employees has come here in need of treatment, they'll be released from our care as soon as they are fit to resume their duties." Saskia schooled her voice to be professionally unemotional.

The elven woman puffed up indignantly. "I did not ask your opinion on my worker's health, *doctor*." She sneered the title. "I *told* you to return him."

"Oh?" Saskia raised an eyebrow. "And where did *you* study medicine, that I should entrust you with the care of a patient who you have not yet even identified?"

"I have no need for such base studies. Move aside. I'll find the rat myself."

Saskia folded her arms and didn't move out of the doorway. "You will do no such thing."

"I said step aside. Do you know who I am?"

The elven woman was doing everything short of stamping her feet like an angry toddler in her attempt to intimidate. Saskia almost laughed. Instead, she answered with an indifferent "Should I?"

The other drew herself up to her full height, only a few inches taller than Saskia. "I am Lady Ravencrest, Second House of the line of Shade."

"Ravencrest..." Saskia repeated the name thoughtfully. "I believe I've heard it before. Ah, yes, you requested an invitation to my wedding last spring. So sorry we couldn't include you, but my husband and I decided to limit the guests to only people we actually knew."

An expression of confusion passed briefly across Lady Ravencrest's face. "I cannot imagine why I would want attend the marriage of a Lower City doctor."

"I can't either, though I imagine the presence of the Silver Prince at the ceremony might have influenced your desire slightly," Saskia told her.

The elven woman froze. Her dark eyes grew wide in disbelief and understanding. "What?"

Saskia gave her a smile. "It's a pity you weren't able to attend His Highness's Ice Blossom Festival Ball this last winter, but I'm sure you had some unavoidable conflict."

Lady Ravencrest paled, sputtering for some response other than to admit that as a member of the lower nobility, she could never dream of being invited to the Silver Prince's exclusive private celebration. "It was... uh... with great regret that I was unable to attend."

"A shame you missed it," Saskia agreed sympathetically. "His Highness presented quite the breathtaking tribute to Crown Prince Filipp's late wife and child. However, you were *requesting* information about an employee who you believe came here for treatment. If you tell me their name, I'll check the clinic's records to determine whether they're a patient here. If so, I can offer an estimate as to when they might be fit to return to work."

"Name?" Lady Ravencrest looked genuinely surprised, as if she'd never considered that she might need to know the identity of the person she sought. She tried to recover her composure. "Surely there cannot be *that* many male elves who seek treatment from a *doctor*."

"We have a healer on staff as well." That stretched the truth a little, but she didn't think Lamorage would mind in this case. "And we treat both humans and elves here as they have need."

"The rat's name is San... Sav... Sev something."

Saskia motioned for Kir to bring her the ledger, not willing to risk moving out of the doorway. She flipped through the book, examining the records, then shook her head. "I don't see any elven patients currently checked in at the clinic under that name. Perhaps you were mistaken, and he found treatment at some other location."

Lady Ravencrest's jaw tightened. "That seems… unlikely. Are you certain?"

"Quite certain." Saskia didn't bother looking at the ledger again. "Thank you, Kir. You can return this to the front desk." She handed the book back to him.

"Yes, Doctor De'seneth." Kir scrambled back to the front desk.

Saskia caught the momentary hitch in Lady Ravencrest's breathing. "De'seneth? You?"

"I beg your pardon?" Saskia gave her a questioning look.

Lady Ravencrest shook her head. "It was nothing. It seems my business here is concluded, though. I'll take my leave."

"I hope your missing employee turns up safe and whole, Lady Ravencrest. Good day." Saskia walked her to the door and closed it firmly behind her.

Kir gazed at her in awe, but quickly turned back to his tasks. "Thank you, Doctor De'seneth. I wasn't sure what I should do when she came in."

"You did fine, Kir. If someone like that comes into the clinic, call for me or Doctor Tan'shyo at once. You shouldn't attempt to navigate that sort of situation."

He smiled gratefully. Saskia started down the hall and saw Tiyron in the wheeled chair, studying her with a frown. She raised a questioning eyebrow at him. "Yes?"

"Since when does a human doctor get to tell off an elven noble?"

"Any time, when the human doctor outranks the elven noble," Saskia told him. "I am a noble, by right of marriage."

"Not a Lewarden noble, though." Tiyron's frown grew deeper.

"True," she agreed. "However, the Silver Prince's favor more than compensates for that, and all things considered, counts for as much as rank, if not more."

The twist of Tiyron's lips expressed his feelings about Prince Cero. "I'm sure."

She studied him for a long minute. Casts held his limbs. A patch covered his ruined eye. Scars marred once-handsome features. Even so, he radiated defiance against the forces that constrained him.

"Why do you loath the nobility so much, Tiyron?"

"Why? Might as well ask why they demand fealty they've done nothing to deserve. Why should I bow down to someone who claims I deserve to starve on the street for the sin of being born in the slums? We aren't even *people* to them, just vermin feeding on their scraps."

"And that's why Cemar's promises of equality were so appealing."

He flinched at Cemar's name. "He's not the only one who wanted change. Change the nobles don't want. Change a two-hundred-year-old king won't accept."

"Change is happening whether they like it or not. But what would you have change look like, Tiyron? Violent revolution, like Cemar? Rapid change is almost always bloody. Peaceful change takes time. Which do you hope for?"

"Change in whatever form it must take," he snapped. "It's better than this."

"Is it?" Saskia held his gaze, then nodded at the chair. "That is what peaceful change looks like: people choosing to improve the lives of others, even those who have little to offer in return. As for violent change... well, the slums might have an advantage in numbers, but not in resources. You would either have a long, terrible civil war with countless deaths on both sides, or you would have a very short one, with the majority of the deaths coming from the poor, and the nobles entrenching themselves deeper into traditions."

His eye narrowed. "What would you know of such things?"

"When we humans came through the portal, leaving behind our homeland, we left our history with it. We did not, however, leave our philosophers. Their writings reveal a great deal, chiefly that we too went through cycles of change and turmoil—some of it peaceful, much of it decidedly not peaceful. So again, what manner of change do you want, Tiyron?"

"I want a change that doesn't leave a doddering old fool on the throne."

She was glad the clinic didn't have any patients in the nearby rooms to hear the elf's words. "That's a dangerous sentiment to express, even in the Lower City."

"Even if they don't say it, others are thinking it. And the crown prince is no better. He's been waiting more than half his life for his father to be out of the way of his plans."

"That's enough, Tiyron." Her voice was quiet but firm. "You can and will believe what you want, but don't express such sentiments openly here."

He snorted in derision but didn't continue his tirade against the Crown. "Change will come one way or another, though."

"Certainly, it will. Some of those changes began when the humans arrived in Calarand. Others are still to come. Just keep in mind what I asked you before. Do you want change to be peaceful or violent? And if it comes by violence, who is going to take control when it's all said and done? Can you be sure they'll be better than what they replace? What if Cemar had taken power?"

"If Cemar had taken power, he'd have been a martyr in less than a year," Tiyron muttered.

Saskia raised an eyebrow. "You don't think he'd have protected himself from assassins?"

"I think he'd have looked the wrong direction for the knife that stabbed him in the back." Tiyron's lips pressed in a thin line, as if he'd said more than he intended. He quickly navigated the chair back toward his room.

"Would Sok'lof have tried to remove him?" Saskia asked before he could reach the room. "Or Sunward?"

The chair stopped but Tiyron didn't turn. "I think Sok'lof would have taken the fall. Sunward didn't much like to share."

The chair rolled into his room and the door closed. Saskia gazed after him for a long minute, then climbed the stairs to check on Seva.

It took the better part of an hour to calm the runaway and reassure him that he wouldn't be removed from the clinic against his will. He couldn't tell Saskia anything about Lady Ravencrest aside from confirming that she had some association with Whitetooth, but he was certain she wasn't Whitetooth's contact for Lumination. He had no guesses about why she wanted him.

When Saskia got home, Alistar met her at the door, greeting her with a kiss on the cheek. Leaning close, he whispered, "Come up to my study after dinner. I have some things to show you."

"Looking forward to it." She climbed the stairs to her room to change for dinner.

Onyxflame was hanging up dresses in Saskia's closet when she came in. "Good evening, Lady De'seneth."

"Good evening Rykka. How are you?"

Onyxflame shrugged. "The day was reasonably productive, but nothing earth-shattering." She gazed at Saskia, then sighed. "What did Tiyron do today?"

"Openly expressed extremely seditious sentiments. Though fortunately not in one of the public areas of the clinic."

"Oh. Well, not surprising. We didn't build our reputation on our great love of the Crown." Onyxflame's gaze remained on the dresses. "I don't exactly support the monarchy either."

"Would you hand me that green dress?" Saskia asked. As Onyxflame lifted it from the hanger, she said, "I know the way things are has flaws—some of them terrible. But even so, I'm neither as eager for King Suelton's death nor as cynical about Crown Prince Filipp as your brother is."

Onyxflame helped her change clothes, fastening the row of pearl buttons up her back. "I'll admit that King Suelton appears to have more of his faculties than most men of his age, but as long as he keeps the throne, there are a lot of changes that aren't going to happen. He spent too long courting the nobles and building the connections to stay on the throne for him to undermine their power now. And everyone in the slums knows it."

"Cemar's rhetoric was all about equality and balancing the power between the nobles and the commoners. I wonder if Sunward is keeping the same propaganda, or if she's taking a different tactic."

Onyxflame tensed, but only said, "I haven't heard anything. I'll keep an ear out."

"Thank you."

After dinner, Alistar and Saskia retired to Alistar's study. He recounted his visit to the Zel'en twins and his findings. When he told her the details of their bankruptcy, though, Saskia stopped him. "The Ravencrest family bought their assets?"

"The majority of them, at least," Alistar said. "Why?"

"I met Lady Ravencrest today. She came to the clinic demanding the return of one of her workers. From the context, I'm certain she meant Seva, though she didn't know his name. I sent her off empty-handed; she wasn't expecting a mere human doctor to outrank her. But I also received a warning about her from another patient—rumors that she pulls employees off to work on secret projects, and those workers aren't seen again." Saskia met her husband's gaze. "She's involved in something shady, and she has connections to Whitetooth."

Alistar nodded slowly. "Her name keeps coming up in places and ways I don't expect. I can't tell if she's involved in whatever Sunward's up to, if she has any connection to the smuggling, or if she's working on her own."

Saskia frowned thoughtfully. "To use those components, the recipient would benefit from access to a manufacturing facility, I would think. Especially if the owner already had a supply of workers to shift around into the new location. Though I wonder what criteria she's using to decide who goes there. From what Seva said, there's some sort of test, but he wasn't certain what was being tested."

"I wonder..." Alistar's gaze grew thoughtful. "Could she be looking for Cemar's internal channelers? I don't know what she would want with them, or why pick them for a project, but she and Cemar had ways of discovering the ability."

Saskia's brow wrinkled. "I wonder if there's a connection between this ability and the drugs. Do the drugs trigger the manifestation of the ability? Do they strengthen it? Remove whatever instinctual barriers people put in place? If Seva is an internal channeler, that could be why he was chosen. I need a sample of Lumination so I can compare it with Ambrosia."

"Without Cemar's machine, they would have a hard time extracting magic to concentrate into drug form," Alistar argued.

"The magic might not be the catalyst that triggers the ability. If I can compare common components between the drugs, I'll have a better theory about the catalyst."

"I haven't heard of any new drugs in the upper class," Alistar said. "The supplier might be confining their distribution to the Lower City. Especially if they have reasons to make internal channelers disappear for their own ends."

"You have the locations of the facilities that the Ravencrests acquired from the Zel'ens, don't you?" Saskia asked. "Someone could investigate them, check for unusual activity or indications that the workers aren't permitted to leave. It might distract Investigator Dawncloud from digging for more information on Rykka and Tiyron once she's done following leads on Merris."

"I'm not sure we should wait." Alistar gazed out the window into the night. "We don't know the timeline we're working against. It's unfortunate that Rykka doesn't have more of a network yet."

Saskia considered who else might have contacts in the lowest classes and would be willing to use them to assist her and Alistar. "I doubt Tiyron has anyone he could reach out to now, given that he's officially dead. I don't want to involve Kir or his family if I can avoid it, nor do I want to put Seva back in danger."

"Perhaps your father would know someone?" Alistar suggested.

"Maybe." She frowned thoughtfully. "I'll talk to him about it tomorrow."

Before she said more, footsteps raced down the hall. A rapid knock sounded against the door.

"Enter." Alistar quickly tucked several documents in a drawer.

Soluthos rushed into the study, short of breath. In one hand he clutched a speaking stone. "Beg your pardon, sir. I must take my leave immediately."

"What happened?" Alistar demanded. "How long of an absence?"

"I don't know how long." Soluthos steadied himself and straightened. "His Highness Prince Cero has been attacked by assassins."

Saskia's eyes went wide and icy fingers ran down her spine. She was on her feet. "Is he alive? Is he injured?"

"Alive, as of the last report, but two of the assassins eluded the guards. I'm sorry. I must go."

"Go," Alistar told him. "Do what you need to."

Without another word, Soluthos spun on his heels and raced from the room.

CHAPTER 21

"Silver Prince Defies Assassination Attempt!"

Every news rag in Lewarden ran some version of the headline. Alistar purchased several on his way to work, but the reports were scant on details except that Prince Cero lived, with vague mention that he'd been injured and that the assassins were dead. The assassins' origins were implied to be foreign, but the articles offered no insight about who had sent them or what country they came from.

He rubbed weary eyes and ran a hand through his hair. He'd hoped to receive some sort of news during the night, and sleep had been a fitful companion. By dawn, Soluthos still hadn't returned, further fueling Alistar's suspicions that far more had been left out of the official story than had been included. He desperately wanted to know more, and the only place where he might find answers was Silverline Power.

Pandemonium ruled the lobby when he arrived. Engineers, botanists, and technicians alike urgently exchanged information, rumors, and conjectures. Alistar worked his way up to the front desk, but a look told him the administrative sprites knew little more about the situation than the rest of the company, or if they did know more, they didn't intend to offer that information for further speculation. Both Assistant Goldleaf and Assistant Torrent fluttered about the desk, organizing the piles of paper scattered around them.

Assistant Goldleaf glanced up and nodded to Alistar. "Senior Engineer De'seneth. I beg your pardon; the morning has been chaotic. Torrent, did we receive any messages for Lord De'seneth?"

"If we did, I haven't found them yet," Assistant Tempest snapped, running a hand through her frazzled shock of blue hair. "If I do, I'll send someone to your office."

"Thank you. I won't take more of your time." Alistar desperately wanted to know more, but made himself turn and walk to the stairs. A cluster of engineers congregated at the top of the stairs, their voices drifting down to him.

"Do you think there will be an announcement? Something official?"

"I haven't seen Lady Syri yet. Have you?"

"No, but I swear I saw Prince Pietro marching up the stairs when I got here."

Alistar cast a look at them as he reached the top of the stairs. "Prince Pietro is here?"

The young elven man who'd mentioned that tidbit shifted uncertainly. "Maybe? I thought I saw him, but I didn't see any Royal Guards with him. He would have had guards with him, right? Especially after an attack?"

"One would certainly hope so," Alistar said. "How long ago was this? Did you see anyone with him at all?"

The elf shook his head. "He was going around a corner. Maybe there were others with him and I didn't see them. This was... um... a quarter hour ago, I think."

"And you're sure this person you saw wasn't an engineer or technician?" Alistar asked.

"I'm... not sure, Senior Engineer," the elf admitted. "I didn't think to question him. I... I can barely think straight after the news about the Silver Prince."

Alistar nodded. "We're all struggling right now. Do what you can."

He waited until he was around the corner and out of their sight before hastening his stride. Whether the individual the young engineer saw had been Prince Pietro or not, Alistar couldn't think of any good reason for an unknown, unescorted non-employee to be roaming the depths of Silverline Power.

He didn't see Prince Pietro, but as he neared his office, a cluster of five Royal Guards converged on Alistar, with Lady Syri in their protective midst. Rather than the uniform of a technician, she wore a finely tailored suit of emerald green silk-weave trimmed with silver. Her pale blonde hair was pulled back in a braid, and she looked at least a decade older than her forty-two years.

"Senior Engineer De'seneth, I was hoping to find you. Come with me please."

"Of course, Lady Syri. How may I be of service?"

She sensed the questions he left unspoken. She spoke quietly. "The Silver Prince is injured and in the care of healers. He's expected to make a full recovery, but it might not be a quick one. We deemed it necessary to temporarily transfer leadership of Silverline to me."

Alistar nodded as they strode down the hall surrounded by Royal Guards. "And you were looking for me...?"

"As a witness." She offered no further explanation as they approached Prince Cero's office.

A single Royal Guard stood at the door, shifting uneasily. Alistar didn't recognize the man as one who regularly stood watch here. He was a younger elf, and the approaching retinue didn't put him any more at ease.

"Open the door," Lady Syri ordered, her gaze boring into him.

He swallowed hard. "Um, Lady Syri, I was told…"

"If you were told to deny me access to *my* office, you were misinformed." Her eyes narrowed.

He blinked. "Your office, my lady? I'm sorry, I thought this was…" He trailed off uncertainly, looking at the stern faces of Lady Syri's guards. "Of course, Lady Syri." He opened the office door and stepped inside, holding it for her.

A tall elven man only a few years older than Lady Syri sat at Prince Cero's desk. His brown hair hung in short ringlets. His clothes were styled in the fashion of a cavalry commander, though the colors clearly marked it as not being an actual uniform. He looked up and smiled pleasantly.

"Oh, hello Syri. I was going to send for you in a little bit. What can you tell me about—."

"Get out."

Prince Pietro blinked, head tilting to one side questioningly. "What?"

"Get out." Lady Syri marched to the desk, her voice as cold as her eyes. "My father may have tolerated you and your inept attempts to meddle. I will not. Get out of my chair. Get out of my office. Get out of my business."

The prince straightened indignantly. "That's no way to speak to your superior!"

"Then it's a good thing I don't have one in this office. Valence, remove Prince Pietro from Silverline Power property."

One of Lady Syri's guards stepped forward and rested a firm hand on Prince Pietro's shoulder. "Your Highness, it's time you departed."

The prince's guard took a step, mouth opening to protest, but restrained himself under the quelling gazes of the other Royal Guards.

Prince Pietro's jaw tightened. "You don't have that authority, cousin."

"Pietro, if you read any further than the second paragraph of the document at the very top of those papers on the desk, you would know that, as His Highness Prince Cero is temporarily unable to serve in his role as owner of Silverline Power Cooperative, those responsibilities and the authority to fulfill those responsibilities falls to his heir, Lady Syri Feyblade. And I am exercising that authority at this moment."

Prince Pietro's eyes dropped to the documents on the desk. "Syri, I know you don't *want* to be in charge here. You want to keep doing all the engineering. This works out perfectly. You keep doing what you enjoy. I'll rely on your advice for all decisions related to all of that. And you don't have to worry about annoying meetings, endless paperwork, and all the parts you don't want to deal with."

"*All* the responsibilities and *all* the authority, Pietro. It's not about what I want. It's about what *is*. Get out of my office." She nodded to the Royal Guard.

Valence shifted his grip on the prince's arm, lifting Prince Pietro out of the chair. The prince stumbled, caught himself, and cast a fierce glare at his solitary Royal Guard. When the guard made no move to aid him, the prince straightened, jerked his arm free of Valence, and stormed out of the office without another word. His guard rushed after him, and Valence followed them both.

Once the sound of their footsteps had faded, Lady Syri settled at the desk and began reorganizing the documents there. "I hoped he wouldn't be so brazen, but clearly I gave him too much credit."

Alistar glanced to the office door, now closed, then back to her. "I wouldn't presume to speak ill of the royal family, but I would have expected him to be a little more circumspect. But you said you wanted me to accompany you as a witness? To this?"

"In part." Lady Syri signaled her guards and they withdrew to take posts outside the office. "Please sit."

He settled in the chair facing the desk. Seeing Lady Syri in the tall leather chair rather than her father sent an unsettling chill down his spine. She leaned forward. "Lord As'enel, what I'm going to say must not leave this room."

"If it spreads, it won't be by any indiscretion of mine," Alistar said.

"That will have to suffice, I suppose. Do you know anything more about the attack on my father beyond what has been released to the news?"

"Not yet, Lady Syri. How seriously was he injured?"

"A few inches higher, and the assassin's strike would have been fatal. As it was, the blades were poisoned. He'll recover, but it'll take time. I know he'll try to push himself more than he should, regardless of how it will slow his healing."

"Where did the assassins come from? Who sent them?"

"They were a crew known as the Masks," she answered.

"The Masks?" Alistar straightened. "I've heard of them. A band of hired killers thought to be connected to the Wastewind Pirates."

"While none of the assassins who attacked my father originally hailed from Calarand, I have reason to suspect the marks that paid them did."

"Sunward?"

She shook her head. "She would gain little from killing the Silver Prince. If she were to go after anyone, you would be the better target. Pardon my saying so."

Alistar shook his head. "That's true enough, if she learned Alistar De'seneth and Alistar As'enel are the same man. Do you have another suspect in mind?"

"Yes." Lady Syri fell quiet for long moments. "I have a suspicion, and I wish I didn't."

Alistar waited for her to continue. A chill of unease crept down his spine.

"The individual who I suspect the most was the last person you saw sitting at this desk, Lord As'enel."

"What?" He stared at her in shock. "Prince Pietro? Why? What reason would he have to attack the Silver Prince?"

She let out a long breath. "I don't have any proof, just suspicions. Things he's said. Times he's subtly attempted to gauge my interest in the succession within Silverline Power. In a few more recent conversations, attempts to determine whether I'd be agreeable to removing obstacles that prevent me from taking charge of the company." Her voice was flat and chilly. "I didn't think he'd interpret my lack of interest in removing my father from his role as a lack of interest in my inheritance."

Alistar shook his head. "I'm sorry, Lady Syri, but that's not a lot on which to base such an accusation."

"I know. And it's not an accusation I can put forward to my father, much less to His Majesty. Not even to my guards."

"Then why tell me?" Alistar asked warily. He didn't think he would like the answer.

"When my father suspected sabotage to the mahiy lines, he trusted you to look into the rest of the noble houses of Lewarden with equal suspicion."

"That's not the same as looking for treason within the royal house, Lady Syri."

"It's not really that different," she said. "Just less politically or socially acceptable. But I don't find someone trying to kill my father to be socially acceptable either."

"I don't have access to the sorts of places where Prince Pietro might work even if he is engaged in such activities," Alistar said. "And I don't think you have the authority to grant me that access."

Her jaw tightened.

Alistar continued. "I'm not dismissing your suspicions, lady. But if you require someone who can search for treason in the royal house, I am not the person for such a task. Nor is it a task that should be linked to Rillwater or my family."

"Not even for the safety of the nation." Her voice was flat.

"For the safety of the nation, if your suspicion is correct, then the proof must come from a source beyond reproach. Even with unquestionable evidence, if His Majesty is faced with a choice between one of his own children or an outsider, who do you truly think he's more likely to side with?"

"There is… some merit to that concern," she allowed finally. Her eyes narrowed on Alistar. "Would you speak to my father so bluntly, were he to assign you to this?"

"Lady Syri, if your father were to attempt to give me this as an assignment, I would remind him of my family's firm stance of no direct interference in Lewarden's politics. If necessary, I would also remind him of the strained relations between himself and Admiral As'enel that resulted from the previous investigation he assigned me." It wasn't a point he'd wanted to bring up, but her question made it difficult to ignore.

"I'm not aware of any strained relations between…" Lady Syri trailed off. She didn't finish the thought, a concerned frown tugging at the corners of her mouth.

"They aren't in open conflict. But the admiral had strong opinions about some of Prince Cero's actions and how he used some of the information he received. In this situation, my family connections are not an asset."

"I don't have many I can trust with my suspicions, Lord As'enel."

He had no doubt of that. After a pause, Alistar offered her what he could.

"If I discover any indications of his involvement with Lady Sunward or the other matters I'm looking into, I will pursue it as much as I can, and will inform you immediately. Beyond that, though…"

Lady Syri was silent for a long moment, then finally nodded.

"If that is all you can offer, that is what I must accept. You may take your leave."

Alistar bowed and left the office.

Outside, Lady Syri's guards stood at attention. One of them nodded to him, and Alistar nodded back. He made his way to his own office and sank heavily into the desk chair.

Rumors sometimes whisper about tensions in the royal house, but treason? Assassination? Has it really gone so far? Would Prince Pietro actually attempt to have his uncle murdered? Why? What could he possibly gain from doing so?

The question stuck with him no matter how many times he tried to push it away. What could Prince Pietro gain from Prince Cero's death? What would anyone else gain from it? Who would gain the most? The Masks came from outside Calarand, but Prince Cero wasn't in the line of succession. A foreign power could find far more tempting targets.

He shuffled the papers on his desk, looking at them without seeing them. Prince Cero had plenty who disliked him, but who would take it so far as to try to have him killed?

Alistar groaned and ran a hand through his hair. "I'm not responsible for fixing this. The Crown has plenty of skilled people whose job it is to untangle royal messes. They can handle this."

He wasn't sure he believed himself.

He'd finally started to pull his mind back to his work when one of Lady Syri's guards knocked and entered his office. "Senior engineer, Lady Syri requests your presence at once."

"Of course." He rose and followed the man back to Prince Cero's office. *If this is another attempt to convince me to spy on Prince Pietro...*

Lady Syri stood laying out documents across a table when he entered. She glanced up, made sure the door closed behind him, and said, "Among the reports awaiting review, I found one that may be of interest to you, and perhaps more relevant to tasks already assigned to you."

Alistar raised an eyebrow but nodded. "I'd be glad to hear it if the information is something you can share."

She gave him a sidelong look. "No, I asked you to come back so I could tell you I have important information that I'm *not* going to tell you." She rolled her eyes. Lady Syri picked up one of the documents and offered it to him. "We've had Crown agents following Lady Sunward and tracking her activities. In the last two days, one was knifed in an apparent mugging turned violent, another stumbled off the docks in a drunken stupor and drowned, and the third vanished entirely."

Alistar accepted the document, frowning as she spoke. "Were there only the three following her? And has she been frequenting Dockside and other Lower City districts? If not, what would draw the agents into those areas?" A quick scan of the document showed that the mugging also occurred in a Lower City district.

"The last report from the agent on duty indicated that Sunward was meeting someone in the lower Middle City, possibly into the Lower City. That agent was working to discover the identity of the other party or parties when she disappeared. The other two were off duty at the time of their… accidents, and I don't yet know what drew them into that area of the city. The three agents were the only ones assigned to Sunward. I've informed my father, and he provided a list of alternates who may need to be pulled from their current assignments." She looked over the document still in her hand and paused.

Alistar raised an eyebrow. "Is there a problem? Beyond the one we already face, that is."

She cleared her throat. "Ah, no, just realizing that some of these agents could be more awkward than others to pull from their current stations." She studiously didn't meet his gaze.

Alistar frowned for a moment, then realized what that probably meant. "Am I to guess that my footman, Soluthos, is on the list?"

A thin smile answered him. "You could certainly guess that, senior engineer."

"If you need his skills, by all means, recall Soluthos. I'll miss his service in my house, and would like him to return when he's done, so I would appreciate if you could avoid causing him unnecessary harm or death."

She considered Alistar for a long minute. "I would ask how long you've known he was in the Crown's service, but I don't think I want to know."

"Let's just leave it at 'I've known for a while', then. I should, however, point out that Merris knew he was a Crown agent. I don't know for certain that she works with Sunward, but she was trying to access the hidden rooms in my manor."

"Blight!" Lady Syri hissed under her breath. "I don't know how the agents were identified, or by who. If Soluthos is already known, the risk spikes considerably for him. He's one of the best of those on the list, but that assumed he wasn't already compromised. I don't suppose you have any eyes of your own on Sunward?"

"At this point, no," Alistar told her. "The more tails on a person of interest, the more opportunities for them to get in each other's way, when they aren't coming from the same source. However, my people would have the advantage of not being known. And I have some who Merris won't recognize."

Lady Syri looked at her list once more, then back to Alistar. "Consider permission to tail Lady Sunward given to you and your people, on the condition that you share their findings with me."

I gave my explanation as an excuse, not as a veiled request. But now I have to follow through, whether I meant it or not. "Agreed, Lady Syri. This I can and will do."

CHAPTER 22

Rykka gazed at the components spread across the tables. It felt like she was trying to assemble a child's puzzle, but with random pieces missing, possibly some extras mixed in, and no clear idea of what the finished creation looked like.

Whatever devices these components belonged to, they had to be large. The sections she'd managed to cobble together implied a much larger framework in which they were intended to operate.

No clear indication as to the power source, though. No converters for drawing from the mahiy lines. I'm missing something here, but what?

She paced around the basement room, tracing her fingers over the stone walls. She'd retreated down here for relief from the constant talk about the assassination attempt. Windshadow had finally returned but was closed-lipped about anything related to the attack on the Silver Prince. Rykka had hoped that getting away from all the discussion and speculation would help, but her thoughts kept returning to the matter.

Tiyron used to talk about ideas he and Cemar had for targeting members of the Royal Family. I had doubts about some of them, but he loved the thought of it. Now he's awake, and this attack has happened. He couldn't be involved, could he? How would he? He's bedridden without a half-chip to his name and no contacts. Tiyron couldn't have had a hand in this attempt.

Despite her efforts to reassure herself, the thought lingered. *Hematic perdition, why should it even matter to me if Tiyron was involved? The Silver Prick's done nothing for us but make our lives harder. I should be regretting that the assassins failed, not worrying my brother might have somehow instigated the attack.*

She tried to push aside the uncomfortable thought that perhaps she didn't want the Silver Prince dead. It probably stemmed from the awareness that his death would make things more difficult for Alistar and Saskia.

It would also make trouble for them if Tiyron was involved and the wrong people found out. I need to talk to him to find out once and for all.

She locked the workroom door behind her and returned to the upper floors. She hoped to slip out unnoticed, but Dorne stopped her as she headed for the kitchen door.

"Darkwood, Lady De'seneth's mail is still waiting to be delivered to her sitting room."

"I'll get it later," she promised.

The butler gave her a silent, disapproving look.

"Dorne, I need to go to the clinic," she told him, glancing around to confirm that they were alone.

Dorne folded his arms across his broad chest. "Darkwood, of all the lady's maids Lady De'seneth has employed so far, you're by far the least suited to the job."

Rykka smiled faintly. "I couldn't agree with you more. But Captain As'enel made it extremely clear that my options were to take this post or take a trip halfway to the next port."

Dorne's eyebrows arched, then narrowed. His voice grew low, flavored with suspicion. "What does Captain As'enel have to do with your employment here?"

Everything she'd observed about Dorne told her he was impeccably loyal to the As'enels. Having him on her side could smooth many obstacles in the manor. Having his continuing suspicion could make things infinitely more difficult. "I'm sure you were told the same tale as everyone else about me being hired locally as a favor to some wealthy investor. The truth is that I was crew on Captain Roddick's *Conquest*, but some elements from my past came to light and caused him to lose faith in me. This option was presented as my last chance to regain the trust of the Family. So, while I'm a blighted terrible lady's maid, I *am* good at the things I do."

"Such as?" Dorne remained suspicious.

"You know what I did when Merris attacked Windshadow. Also, I'm a decent artificer, and I've been assisting Lord De'seneth with identifying the goods being stored in the basement. And I've been getting information from the sorts of people who won't talk to nobles."

"Blood and sand." Dorne shook his head. "I'm getting a guess about what sort of elements of your past Captain Roddick might have objected to."

"He didn't object to my past itself so much as he didn't like getting surprised. Now, can I go? I really do need to get to the clinic."

Dorne finally nodded slowly. "You can go, Darkwood. And if necessary, I'll have someone else take care of those letters."

"I expect to be back before Lady De'seneth is. I should be able to do that much."

"Very well. Be careful."

"Always." She was halfway out the door before she realized she'd responded to Dorne with the farewell she and Tiyron had always used when one of them went out on a mission.

Once free of the manor, she caught a carriage to the compact collection of rooms in the Southforest District she'd rented upon her return to Lewarden. A change of clothes and a little dirtying up later, she could reasonably head into the Lower City without immediately standing out. With generous smears of dirt on her face, a shapeless brown tunic, and trousers, she could pass as a man at a casual glance, and if she tried a bit, she could fool a more careful inspection. Another carriage ride brought her within a couple blocks of the Coiled Dragon Clinic. Years of habit had ingrained the idea of not taking transportation directly to her destination in the Lower City or its fringes.

This time, her route took her past several sleazy taverns. Casting a glance down the poorly lit, narrow alley between the taverns, she saw three figures leaning close together, conversing quietly. Clandestine gatherings in the shadows were common enough in this part of town, but something about the trio bothered her. Rykka continued past, then circled back, keeping to the shadows and moving on silent feet until she was close enough to hear their voices.

"Of course, milady. I've confirmed that everything is ready."

The woman's voice was familiar, but she couldn't place it, just a nagging feeling of recognition.

"Good. We can't afford many more delays. Has there been any word on the missing shipments?" The second woman spoke with an air of authority.

"Not yet. At this point, it's possible they were intercepted."

A sound of annoyance answered that. Rykka stilled, breath catching. She hadn't been able to identify the voice, but that noise of dismissive frustration called to mind a human woman with golden brown hair coifed in a bun, an expression of exasperation on her high-boned face as she turned toward her lover, Cemar.

Sunward? Here, in this part of the city? Could she know that Tiyron is alive and close?

Sunward turned to the third figure. "I suppose you've had no success either."

"No, not yet. The doors are still locked from inside, and

everyone at the manor is alert for me now." This voice she recognized as Merris. "Unless there's another entry point, we need to find some other way of getting someone inside or removing the current residents."

"A stubborn lot all around." Sunward made another sound of irritation. "Fine. Do what you can. I don't have time for this right now. Has my guest arrived?"

The young woman Rykka hadn't identified yet tilted her head to one side and raised a hand, palm up. Soft light glowed within, a small orb cupped in her hand. "Your guest has just arrived, my lady."

In the glow, Rykka finally glimpsed her face. A young human woman, a little too thin, with mouse brown hair and a round face. Her eyes were closed, and she swayed while drawing the magic from within, her expression one of rapture.

"Larisa," Sunward said firmly.

The young woman roused, and the light vanished. "I beg your pardon, my lady."

"I'm counting on you today. Remember that when the temptation grows strong."

"I won't fail you," Larisa promised.

"I know you won't. You both know what to do. I must see to my guest before a new batch of imperial spies come sniffing at my heels."

"If they do, we'll deal with them," Merris said confidently.

The trio split. Rykka pulled deeper into the shadows, cursing silently. None of the trio passed her hiding place. As soon as she dared, she tailed Sunward. Her senses were alert for any hint that she'd been spotted. Merris's declaration about dealing with Crown agents put her on edge.

Sunward navigated the alleys with confidence that belied her station. Rykka was glad her target moved further from the clinic, heading into a neighborhood primarily home to factories. The air smelled of the grease and oil that kept the machines working, and the sweat of all the laborers who operated and maintained those machines. Workers milled about outside eateries and tea stands that offered a welcome relief from the odors of industry or walked in clusters of animated conversation. Sunward's simple brown dress blended easily with the crowds, much as Rykka's comfortable laborer's pants and shirt did.

Rykka paused to check the menu board at a tea cart, keeping one eye on Sunward. The human woman running the cart was missing an eye, and a burn scar puckered the left side of her face. She ran her cart with a pleasant but curt air. "Getcha somethin' hot, scrub?"

Rykka smiled at the mild insult. "Lookin' a long day ta go. Wouldn't mind a spot o' yer—"

Sunward turned into an alley as an ear-piercing whistle shrieked from one of the factories. Rykka jumped and cursed, looking around sharply.

The tea seller made a quick shooing motion. "Get on wit' ya afore ya miss yer shift."

Rykka nodded and joined the mass of grumbling, resigned workers as they ambled back to work. She slipped free of them and ducked into the alley Sunward had chosen.

She didn't see the noblewoman immediately. For a moment, fear spiked that she'd either lost her quarry or been lured into an ambush. Rykka pulled close to the side of one building, searching for any other people, hidden or not. Seeing none, she slunk further down the grimy, shadowed alley.

At the intersection, she glimpsed movement to her right. Getting closer, she saw Sunward step through a door. It closed behind her, and Rykka hurried over in time to hear keys jangle and a bolt slide into place. A scan of the wall revealed no windows. She bit her lip to stop a curse, drew a deep breath, and waited for the sound of footsteps to fade.

Once silence enveloped the alley once again, she fished lockpicks from her belt and set to work. Tiyron had claimed there wasn't a lock in the city that could stop either of them, but he'd never seen those within Chirrod Prison.

This lock, at least, wasn't up to the standards of the prison. Tumblers shifted, turned, and finally settled. Rykka listened again for hints that a guard might be waiting on the other side, but she couldn't afford to wait too long. Not when Sunward could slip away.

The door opened into a dimly lit hall. She didn't see or hear anyone standing guard. Rykka closed the door behind her but didn't relock it. If she was discovered, she needed a clear escape route. Preferably more than one, but she'd have to take what she could. She wasn't certain where this factory stood in relation to the others, and she didn't hear any sounds of machines in operation, though the distant hum of voices indicated the presence of people in the building.

Hematic perdition, I don't even have a speaking stone to tell someone where I am or what I'm doing. Of course, it would be stupid to use one here and now, even if I did. Reyker protect me.

She moved up the hall and the sounds of voices grew louder. Tense and fearing discovery at any moment, she started when a man spoke immediately to her left.

"How long will this take?" His aristocratic accent contrasted sharply with their surroundings.

"Several hours," Sunward answered. "You won't have to stay the whole time, though."

Rykka saw a door just ahead on the left. It was closed, but the sounds of voices came from within. She softly released the breath she'd held, then remembered that lurking outside a door in an open hallway with nowhere to hide was stupid.

"Not that I object to seeing you, why do we have to meet... *here?*" He said it in much the same tone he might have used to indicate excrement.

"Because this is where we'll find the people we need,"

Sunward answered. "Besides, I know you come down to the slums sometimes, even without me."

"Not because I *want* to."

Rykka listened as much as she could while quietly passing the door and approaching the next one on the same side of the hall. She heard no one within, and it wasn't locked. She slipped inside and found herself in a storage room. Rodent droppings littered the corners and cobwebs hung from the rafters, but some effort had been made to clean it within the last month, and the dust on the floor wasn't thick enough for her to leave tracks. She pressed her ear to the wall to listen again to the couple.

"I still think you could present this to the court yourself," he said.

Sunward laughed. "I could explain it better, probably. But my reputation in the court won't win me any friends. Yours, on the other hand, remains untarnished. That's why you must present my work to the court. You can convince them of the necessity and settle any concerns people have about the process."

A chair creaked, then someone moved around the room. Rykka heard liquid being poured into goblets, then the chair creaked again. "They cannot see me here, can they?"

Sunward laughed again. "No, not even with Lumination. Even if they could, what would they see? A masked, hooded figure gazing at them. Everything will be fine; you'll see."

Rykka's room didn't have any windows, but the one Sunward and the man occupied must. Looking over the factory floor? That would mean they were in the overseer's office.

And what's going on here that she wants this man to observe? Why does she need him to explain it to others in the nobility?

Chairs shifted in the other room. "How long until it starts?" the man asked, voice low and husky.

"We have time," Sunward told him.

The sounds that followed strongly implied no meaningful conversation would be happening for a while. Rykka backed away from the wall and rocked on her heels, debating.

If I stay here, I can spy on Sunward and her lover, but if I can see what's happening below...

It wasn't a hard decision. The sounds from the other room covered her movements and the opening and closing of the storeroom door. She followed the hall until it ended in another door. Easing it open a crack, she glimpsed the factory floor. Before she opened the door any further, she heard someone on the other side mutter impatiently and shift their weight, making the floor creak. She held still. When the guard gave no indications of knowing she was there, she took in what she could see without opening the door farther.

What equipment she could see stood silent and dusty. People milled around, talking in low voices. Those she saw wore clothes too often patched, stained and filthy enough to look shabby even in this area of the city.

What brings a bunch of people from the slums to an abandoned factory?

An argument turned into a scuffle. The guard stepped away from the door to break it up. Rykka slipped onto the factory floor, closing the door behind her. She ducked behind a cold forge and took a moment to get her bearings.

Close to thirty people lingered on the factory floor, and now she could see they were a mix of people from the Lower City, not just the slums. Humans and elves alike looked around, waiting for whatever was coming. Thugs stood guard at all the doors, scowling at anyone who came too close. Some people were having second thoughts about being here, from the looks they gave the guards.

A stack of wooden boxes lined a long table. Rykka moved around the forge, hoping to get a better look.

She almost walked into Larisa.

The young human woman stopped in time to avoid a collision. She cocked her head to one side, looking at Rykka.

Panic raced through Rykka's blood. Her instincts screamed at her to run, make a break for the door and the hall, but she stood frozen.

Larisa gave her a friendly smile. "Did you get turned around? We're gathering over here."

Rykka didn't sense any recognition in the woman's gaze. She glanced to one side as if embarrassed and pitched her voice lower into a masculine range. "Sorry 'bought tha', miss. M'eyes t'aint what they useda be." A Dockside slums accent was challenging to imitate because she wasn't missing teeth, but it fit the cadences she heard all across the floor.

"No harm. Come with me." Larisa held out a hand.

Rykka grasped the young woman's hand in her own. Time aboard the *Conquest* had given her callouses fit to match any a factory worker might bear. Larisa led her to one of the clusters of people and released her.

"Here you are, friend. Don't worry. I know you're struggling, but we'll begin soon, and things will be better. You'll see."

Better? Better than what?

She allowed herself to be absorbed into the cluster, listening to their anxious murmurs before turning to a young human woman with one eye and a gap where two of her lower teeth were missing. "So, why'd you come 'ere today?"

The young woman shifted from one foot to the other. "Same as anyone. Lumination." She nodded toward the boxes on the table. Rykka followed her gaze and saw that a dozen thugs stood guard around the table. The woman shrugged again. "Sure, they say summa us gonna get payin' work that ain't whorin', but tha's not why any o' us is here. We can't get 'Lixir no more, so we come when they offer Lumination. You, me, all'a the rest."

"Hey! Listen up!" one of the thugs yelled.

The murmur of conversation trailed into silence and all eyes turned to the table and the boxes.

"All right, rats. Get yerselves inna line. I know summa ya done this before. Line up, shut up, and wait yer turn. When ya got yer dose, ya head into the back, and ya get the test." He gestured toward a section of the factory floor partitioned from the rest by walls built of crates. At a glance, Rykka couldn't see any quick way out of it. No easy escape from this part either. Her pulse raced as the thugs herded and bullied her cluster of desperate and destitute into the forming line.

Larisa appeared again, at the front of the line this time. The thugs broke open the first box, opened one of the smaller packages inside, and put something in Larisa's mouth. Sunward's lackey beamed at the thug, a tall male elf who Rykka dubbed Fleabag, and proceeded into the back area.

Seeing her go first put some of those near the front of the line more at ease. The thugs moved the line efficiently, but Rykka noticed they also took great care in their work, obviously following a practiced sequence. She wondered if they always followed their procedure to the letter, or if they were being more careful knowing Sunward and her noble lover watched them.

As she got closer, she got a better view of the procedure. The recipient allowed Fleabag to put a round capsule in their mouth. They swallowed, then Fleabag checked again to be sure they hadn't hidden the capsule in a cheek or under their tongue.

She didn't have to wait long to find out what happened if someone attempted to conceal the capsule rather than ingest it. Two thugs standing to the sides seized the recipient and shoved him to his knees. One of them gripped the man's jaw and forced it open. Fleabag plucked the capsule out of the man's mouth. The man struggled and voiced unintelligible sounds of protest and pain.

Fleabag looked over the line. "Some o' ya got an idea in yer head tha' ya can piss on the rules and we isn't gonna notice. Yer wrong, rats. Rules say ya come 'ere and we give ya whatcha want, an' all ya gotta do in return is take yer Lumination the way we give it to ya, then ya go in the back an' get tested." The thug looked down at the squirming man. "But if ya isn't gonna take it the way we give it the first time, we get less friendly."

Rykka shifted uneasily. *What are they doing? Are they going to kill this man as an example? I can't stop them even if they do. If I tried, I'd end up right there beside him.*

Fleabag forced a tube into the man's mouth, drawing half-choked sounds from the man. Rykka watched Fleabag drop the capsule into a cup, though she didn't want to guess what the liquid within was. He poured the contents into the tube and sneered at the man. The thugs holding the man dragged him to his feet and into the back. Another pair stepped up to take their place. Fleabag smirked again and waited for the next person in line.

After a moment of uncertainty, the line advanced once more. Rykka's mind raced. She couldn't slip away now; there was nowhere to hide and no way to escape unseen. Ingesting an unknown drug of questionable quality and effect wasn't an acceptable option. That left her only one alternative. It wouldn't be comfortable, but better than being drugged and susceptible to whatever "testing" took place in the back.

She reached out to the nearest mahiy line and pulled the faintest, thinnest thread of magic she could from it. The factory was fairly well lit. Hopefully it was lit well enough that no one would see the tiny strand of violet light curling down to her.

No one gave her suspicious looks or otherwise indicated an awareness of her actions. Her tension only increased the closer she came to the table. Fleabag smirked, enjoying the anxious compliance of those in line.

The young woman ahead of Rykka accepted her capsule and continued to the back. The magic Rykka drew from the mahiy line burned in her chest, meant to be used immediately, not held in reserve, and she steeled herself. This could go wrong in so many ways.

She stepped forward and let Fleabag drop the capsule into her dry mouth. She closed her lips and wrapped the capsule inside a tight ball of magic. She swallowed and presented her empty mouth to Fleabag, who grunted and waved her through.

The barrier she'd wrapped around the capsule shouldn't have added any noticeable thickness to it, but she felt the lump all the way down her throat and into her stomach. She had no chance to get it back out, either. The back area was as carefully monitored and guarded as the line had been. The people, though, were calmer, relaxed, their anxieties melting away. Larisa stood near another table, talking to those nearest her with an air of reassurance. The space was growing crowded, and Rykka wasn't sure how they expected to fit the remaining people in.

Several others trickled in after Rykka, then she heard Fleabag say, "All right, the rest o' ya gotta wait a bit. And don't get no ideas about tryin' ta cut in line."

Larisa turned her attention to all of them. Her eyes were bright and wide as she beamed at them. "So many new faces among us. Welcome, all of you. You've waited so patiently. Thank you. You understand our need for secrecy, of course. It falls on all of us to protect this precious gift from those who would steal it from us, and with it, our joy and peace."

The drug's numbing effects didn't stop her audience from raising their voices in protest. This would be a dangerous place to be revealed as an outsider. Rykka followed the lead of the others, adopting a similar slightly vacant expression as she voiced objections to the idea of anyone denying them access to this drug.

Larisa raised a slender hand, and the crowd gradually grew silent.

"I have a challenge for you today. If you can complete it, you'll be invited to a special gathering."

The words were vague enough to tell nothing about the challenge or the reward, but murmurs of excitement rose from the crowd. Larisa spread what looked like five divination cards on the table. She raised one, and a glow of amber light emanated from the image imprinted on the card.

"To succeed, you must make each card light. Whether you make each light individually, or all at once, is up to you." She set the card down, and all five began to glow. She spread her hands, and the glow faded.

Murmurs of awe ran through the crowd. The first man stepped forward eagerly and stared intently at the cards. Seconds passed, but nothing happened.

Larisa smiled kindly at the man and guided him away from the table into the keeping of a couple guards who led him through a door. Three more people made attempts without success. Each was sent through the same door.

An elven woman with a pronounced limp approached and frowned at the cards. She raised a trembling hand. Rykka's breath caught when she saw light glow on the woman's skin. The light moved from the woman to the cards.

Larisa's smile widened. "Well done!" She walked the woman to another guard, who took her out a different door than the others. Rustles of excitement ran through the crowd.

The next person approached eagerly. He too succeeded in lighting the cards. Among the next ten people, three succeeded. Each of them looked astonished by their success, almost enraptured, like the expression Rykka had seen on Larisa's face in the alley.

Is this the drug, or the act of tapping into the power that causes their response? I've never felt anything like that when I channel.

She also noticed that Larisa watched each person closely and seemed able to predict who would succeed before they did. The woman's focus made her nervous. This partition was less well-lit than the open factory floor, with deeper shadows. Her gaze swept in search of a place where she could conceal herself.

A firm hand closed on her shoulder. She froze.

A thug smirked at her, then shoved her toward the front. "Yer turn, rat."

CHAPTER 23

"Don' hafta shove," Rykka protested as the thug firmly propelled her to the front. Her mind raced as fast as her pulse. *Larisa must have realized I didn't belong here. What will they do? I have to get out of here.*

The thug released her at the table and stepped back. Larisa gazed steadily at Rykka, leaned forward, and spoke in a voice just above a whisper. "I knew you couldn't be dead, Tiyron." Her smile was hesitant. "I'm glad to see you."

Rykka sucked in a slow breath. *You had a fling, and you never told me, Tiyron? Hematic perdition, what were you thinking?*

She met Larisa's eyes and summoned all her years of acting as her brother. "Are you, though? After all, *Cemar* imprisoned, tortured, and nearly killed me. And here you are, still the loyal lackey. Yeah, I'm sure you're *so* glad to see me."

Larisa's mouth opened and her eyes gleamed with distress. "No, that's not..."

Rykka's eyes narrowed on her. "Don't pretend you didn't hear him when I crashed the party."

"He couldn't... he wouldn't..." Larisa swallowed hard, collected herself, and pasted on a smile that might have been convincing to those further from her. "I'm sorry, friend. Perhaps you'll succeed next time." As a thug stepped forward to escort Rykka out, Larisa whispered, "Don't leave, please?"

Rykka's lips pressed in a thin line. She said nothing.

The thug led her through the door the rest of the unsuccessfuls had taken. A short walk brought them to a storage room made slightly more comfortable with chairs and tattered rugs. A table held water jugs and trays of breads. Men and women slouched in the chairs or leaned against walls, faces slack and eyes glazed in a drugged haze. The thug released Rykka and closed the door. His footsteps moved back toward the partition.

The door wasn't locked, and no one stood guard.

I can get out of here right now. I have the drug and I don't want to keep holding it where it is longer than I have to.

Larisa's plea echoed in her thoughts. If she stayed, she could try to get more from the young woman.

No. Tiyron wouldn't. Not when she's still in league with the people who betrayed him. He wouldn't trust her. If she knows him at all, she'd know that. Assuming she even wants to talk and isn't planning to turn me over to Sunward at the first chance.

She cast a look over the other people in the room. The light was dim here, befitting the sleepy air of the drugged inhabitants. No one paid her much attention. She briefly examined the table of food and water but didn't trust the offerings. Still, no one watched her.

She opened the door and slipped out. No alarm rose. The passage was empty. She heard the muffled sounds of the people still on the factory floor. Turning away, she searched for an exit that would take her back out to the relative safety of the streets.

A short walk brought her to a heavy door. She popped the lock quickly and eased it open. The stink of an alley hit her nose, and sunlight filled her eyes. She could go right now, slip off and escape before they knew where to look for her.

Leaving Sunward to continue her schemes. I don't even know what she wants with these people! Especially not with the ones who succeeded in that... test.

That thought stopped her, hand wrapped around the knob. She just wanted to get this drug to the clinic, but the question remained. She thought of Seva and his desperate escape. These people didn't have anyone to help them. They didn't even know they needed help.

Cemar and Sunward deceived us. They tortured and mutilated Tiyron. Whatever Sunward is planning, whatever her reasons for collecting these people, I won't allow her to succeed. Not because she's a threat to the city. Not because she's using these people. This is personal.

Cursing silently, Rykka stepped into the alley, blocking the door open a crack behind her. Before she did anything else, she had to deal with the capsule, and she couldn't risk anyone inside the factory coming to investigate sounds of someone vomiting.

Why couldn't there be an easy way to do this?

She focused on the ball of magic in her stomach and moved it back up.

There was no helping the gagging and coughing. She doubled over, finally coughing the capsule into her hand. Her throat burned. She sucked in a deep breath, released her magic, and pocketed the capsule.

Blight, I wish I had a speaking stone to contact someone. Or even tell Dorne I'm not going to be back when I expected to.

She patted her pockets as if one might have appeared without her notice. Absent any means of sending word to others, she listened at the door for movement inside, then slipped back in and closed the door behind her.

Sunward would regret the day she made an enemy of Rykka Onyxflame.

She heard a fading sound of steps, probably a thug returning to the factory floor. She didn't hear any urgency to the stride, but wasn't sure whether that meant her departure had gone unnoticed or the thug wasn't concerned about it. Once she couldn't hear movement, she followed the hall past the exit, looking for doors or other passages to the successful candidates.

She found her way to the shipping room, stopping where she could see inside, but without exposing herself to view. The massive outer doors could accommodate vehicles of all sizes. At the moment, they stood closed, and a cluster of people sat on the bare wood floor, eyes closed and expressions euphoric. Unlike the unsuccessfuls, they were under guard, though none looked to have any inclination to attempt to escape.

Maybe someone's slipped away before and they don't want to take the risk of it happening again. Or they're worried someone like me will attempt to steal their prizes. But what in hematic perdition does Sunward want with these people? Why this elaborate setup, and why only from the Lower City?

The answer to that last question was obvious with a little thought. These were the people who would readily accept a bribe of drugs, and they were the people who could disappear without anyone "important" noticing or caring.

Larisa said those who succeeded would be invited to a special event. Doesn't look like attendance is optional. The room's been stripped—no convenient piles of crates or anything to hide behind. I can't get in there without being seen, but if they're moving these people, I might not have to. Shouldn't be hard to find these doors from the outside.

She retraced her path to the exterior doors. Nose wrinkling again at the rancid odor, Rykka followed the outer wall until the alley opened into a narrow street that ran behind several factories.

Near the shipping doors of the factory she'd been in, three unmarked and unremarkable enclosed wagons awaited cargo. The drivers tended to the teams, but also kept a cautious watch on their vehicles. Two drivers noticed Rykka and nodded in silent greeting. She nodded in return and walked past them, glancing over the wagons.

"Picking up or delivering?" she asked one of those who'd greeted her.

"Picking up," the woman grunted. "Shipment for a noble." Her tone firmly implied that this grubby stranger had no need to know more.

Rykka nodded again and continued up the street until she could turn into another alley. She hunched down in the shadows and listened for sounds of doors opening or wagons moving.

An eternity later, she heard the rumble of large doors opening. Moments after, heavy wagons creaked and groaned. Draft horses stamped impatiently. She cautiously peered around the corner and confirmed that the wagons entered Sunward's factory. They didn't post any visible sentries outside, but the level of secrecy in everything so far warned her not to trust the apparent absence.

No obvious sounds of distress or protest rose from inside the factory. Eventually, the wagons returned to the street and rolled at a steady, unhurried pace past her alley hiding place. It was impossible to see what cargo they carried. As the last one passed, she darted out, ducking low to get underneath. The back wheel grazed her leg, a sharp flash of pain. She sucked in a breath between her teeth and grabbed for a handhold on the underside.

Splinters bit her fingers. Wincing, she kicked up from the ground to brace her feet against a strut. Her hands ached as she hung on while the wagon rattled and jolted over the rough street. A particularly rough bounce threatened to unseat her. She barely managed to hook her arm over one of the beams of the wagon undercarriage. Gritting her teeth, she hung on and tried to pull further into the undercarriage, such as it was. The base of the wagon was wide enough that she wasn't immediately visible to passers-by, as long as she clung as close to the underside of the wagon bed as possible.

If I fall off, there's no hiding it. I can't fall. I can hang on. I have to hang on. How long of a trip could it be, after all?

The answer to that was far longer than she wanted it to be. She closed her eyes and clung to the wagon, focusing only to holding on as the vehicle jostled and bounced along the street. She couldn't hear anything from inside the wagon. For all she knew, it could be empty, or loaded with legitimate cargo.

Finally, when she was certain her strained limbs couldn't take any more, the wagon slowed. With a rumble, doors opened, then the wagon rolled forward slowly over a threshold. The cobbled street became a single sheet of stone. She could tell little else about the surroundings from her position, but she heard other wagons. When they stopped, the lights in the space dimmed. Rykka caught odd flickers of blues, reds, and yellows dancing across the floor.

The drivers came around and opened the back doors of the wagon. It shifted as people moved inside, then stepped out.

Larisa spoke. "Welcome. We have prepared a feast in your honor, and the festival awaits you. Let my friends show you the way."

As people murmured and moved, Rykka released her death grip on the wagon's undercarriage and lowered herself to the floor, hoping the shadows would obscure her movements. She ducked against one of the back wheels and watched through the struts.

The ghostlights that would normally illuminate the room glowed dim, casting more shadows than light. Rykka's confidence in her concealment grew. Flickers of colored light darted around the ceiling, painting the room in colors and making an ordinary warehouse into a dreamscape. The effect on the drugged guests was unmistakable. Eyes alight with wonder, they followed their guides without question. The drivers jumped down from their perches and headed through another door.

Larisa hung back. Rykka watched her warily.

Did she see me grab onto the wagon? Is she waiting for me to step out of hiding and confront her?

"You should see to our guests, Larisa." Sunward strode to her from a carriage Rykka hadn't noticed. "I have my own to attend."

"I know, my lady," Larisa answered, looking at her hands. She raised her head to meet Sunward's eyes, and her voice dropped to a whisper. "My lady, I saw Tiyron."

I knew it! She meant to betray me all along!

"Tiyron is dead, Larisa," Sunward said.

"I *saw* him," Larisa insisted. "I spoke to him."

Sunward rested a hand on her shoulder. "Larisa, I know Lumination shows you visions, but they are born from the desires of your heart, not the gods."

"It wasn't a vision," Larisa protested. "I saw him, I spoke to him, and he answered. During the testing."

"And what did he say to you?"

"He… he was angry at me." Larisa's eyes turned to the floor.

"As you thought he would be?" Sunward prompted.

Larisa reluctantly nodded, recognizing the direction of Sunward's probing.

"And did you see him afterwards among those who didn't succeed?"

"No." Larisa's voice was quiet.

Sunward squeezed the younger woman's shoulder. "I know you miss him still, but he's gone. The peace you crave can't come from others."

Larisa pressed an arm to her chest and closed her eyes. Though she didn't speak, Rykka saw her lips move. "I didn't imagine him."

Sunward released Larisa with a gentle push toward the door the new arrivals had taken. "See to the guests."

"Yes, lady." Larisa obeyed without further protest.

Sunward returned to her carriage and spoke quietly to someone still inside, too quietly for Rykka's ears. Rykka stayed where she was, hoping they left soon.

After a moment, a figure in a black suit and hooded coat stepped from the carriage, adjusting a featureless mask to cover his face. His stance proclaimed his distaste for the surroundings.

"Must all this business be conducted in such vile environs?" His bass voice carried easily across the room and his accent labeled him as upper nobility even more clearly than when Rykka heard him in the other factory, muffled by a wall.

"To reach these people, yes, it must," Sunward told him. "But if you truly don't want to see the results, we can leave now for a more palatable destination."

"Ugh. No, I have endured it this long. We can continue."

Sunward hooked her arm through his and led him out of the shipping room. Rykka listened for any more sounds or movement other than the shifting of the horses but heard nothing. As the colored lights faded, she stiffly rose from her crouch behind the wagon wheel.

This shipping room was larger than the previous factory, and it held the crates and supplies Rykka expected to find in an operational factory. Despite the complaints of the nobleman, the space was clean and tidy. Three sets of oversized statues of armored figures stood against the interior wall near the doorway Larisa had taken. Rykka eyed them. Their uniform design left her questioning whether they were simply decorative or if they served some purpose.

I haven't heard of Sunward having any interest or skill in artificing. And these don't look like traditional automatons. Could just be someone's poor taste in décor.

She strode quickly across the room. The horses were still hitched to the wagons and the drivers could return at any moment.

Rykka had nearly reached the doorway when she glimpsed movement from the corner of her eye and a metal hand grabbed for her. She flinched away, but the hand seized her sleeve. The other armored forms moved to surround her. As they closed around her, she ducked and jerked against the hold. The worn cloth of her sleeve ripped free, exposing her bare arm. Breath hissing between her teeth, she bolted for the exterior doors.

A fist slammed her in the side, throwing her across the room and driving the breath from her lungs. She hit the wood floor hard and rolled to her feet, panting. The armored forms moved far more quickly than anything of their bulk should. As they rushed toward her, Rykka scrambled up a pile of crates. The armor suits advanced without giving heed to the obstacle, tossing crates aside to reach her. She jumped to another stack, then another, searching for a window she could reach.

As her pursuers hurled aside the first of the crates in her current perch, she flung herself at the wall, straining to catch the bottom lip of the narrow window. Her fingers barely caught it, screaming in protest after the abuse they'd already suffered on the wagon ride.

Reyker please help me. Get me out of here!

It might have been only her imagination, but for an instant, it felt like a pair of steady hands cupped under her foot, boosting her onto the window ledge. She caught herself, panting rapidly as sweat plastered her hair. There were no footholds on the wall, nothing material to explain the support.

Thanks.

It was even less of a proper prayer than her first one, but if the gods were willing to help her, they had to already know what sort of person she was. She pushed the window open.

A white-hot burst of pain flashed across her left side. A spinning metal blade flew past, the edges stained red. Moisture ran down her side. Below, the other armored figures raised their arms to launch their own blades.

From the window, the dirt street was at least two stories below. She swung herself out the window as the armors released their blades. Spinning glints of metal flew past her.

Hope you don't mind helping me out one more time today, she prayed. Then she released the edge of the window and dropped.

Her body remembered how to move with the impact, how to roll and reduce the damage of hitting the ground. Her blood pounded in her ears and adrenalin surged through her veins. She didn't wait to see if the automatons or anyone else pursued her outside but took off running down the street until she could bolt into an alley.

When she didn't hear pursuit, she paused to gasp for air and take stock. The pain in her side was bad, and a glance showed the wound bleeding freely. She winced and pressed her elbow against it. Her ribs were bruised if not cracked from her flight across the room, and her right arm was completely exposed, the sleeve ripped and left in the hold of one of the armored sentries. A thin, humorless laugh rose in her throat.

Bleeding and battered, no problem, but gods forbid I should show exposed skin in public.

She cast about the alley for something to drape over her uncovered arm. She found a filthy, threadbare shawl with a faded geometric pattern tucked behind an empty barrel. It probably belonged to someone who lived here, but the resident was absent at the moment. Rykka grimaced, then grabbed the shawl and dropped a half-mark where it had been in apology. She wrapped the shawl over her shoulders and worked her way around the detritus to the main street.

She was still in an industrial area, but a better sector of the city than the previous site. The people on the street were better dressed and better groomed. Rather than just mobile carts, some eateries had actual storefronts. She even saw a small general store.

What factory was I in? Does it have a name? Who's the owner?

She looked down the street. Her vision swam and she wavered, steadying herself against a wall. Her eyes cleared and she picked out the building that seemed most likely to be the correct factory. It had been repainted in the recent past. An old emblem still lurked underneath, an indistinct shadow that couldn't be completely obscured by the image of a black bird that now adorned the front. The owner hadn't gotten around to replacing the carved maple front doors, though, and a stylized "Z" decorated them.

Rykka caught her breath and searched for a street name. By the time she reached an intersection, she struggled to keep focused. She did, at least, note the names of the intersecting streets: Rainwatch Way and Ivory Lane.

She tried to hail a carriage. The first three passed her without a pause. The fourth finally pulled to a halt, the driver eyeing her suspiciously.

"Where you headed?" he demanded in a Midcity accent.

Rykka gave him the address. His brow furrowed and he cocked his head to one side, silently asking if she was serious.

"That's gonna run you a mark and a half, and you pay the first mark upfront."

She pulled a mark from her purse and handed it to him. "I'll make it a second mark if you get there fast."

His eyebrows rose, and he looked her over more closely. "Get in, then."

She tried to hide a wince as she climbed into the carriage. She pulled the door shut and collapsed onto the bench. The carriage started moving. She closed her eyes and just breathed, pressing her arm tight against her bleeding side. The carriage jolted and bounced. She bit her lip to suppress a cry of pain.

Just breathe. Breathe through it. Gonna be fine. Be there in no time.

The carriage finally stopped. She straightened, checked that no blood had leaked onto the bench, and climbed out, gripping the edge of the carriage tightly to stay upright.

The driver eyed her with concern. "You aren't gonna topple over on me, are you? You look pretty pale."

Rykka pressed the promised mark into his hand. "Thanks for the ride."

"You sure this is where you want to be? You ain't exactly dressed for this part of town."

She gave him a thin smile. "Yeah, I'm sure."

Before he pressed further, she pushed away from the carriage and walked down the street.

This area was a far cry from the lavish estates such as De'seneth's, though still far better than someone in her state of dress should expect to be welcome. She moved down the street, checking the house numbers until she reached the one she sought. She squinted, trying to see more clearly before realizing it wasn't her sight that was failing, but the light, and dusk approached.

Blight, Dorne expected me back hours ago.

She walked to the townhouse door and knocked. A minute passed, then another, before she finally heard movement from within. A bolt turned and the door opened slightly.

"Hello?"

"Sorry to come calling without warning. Need a bit of help if you don't mind." She tried to sound unconcerned, but pain made her voice tight.

The elf within eyed her uncertainly. "Who are you?"

"Asp... Darkwood. Rykka. You healed my brother."

The door opened. Lamorage steadied her before she fell over, and he drew a sharp breath.

"Inside, now." He guided her to a wooden chair and shut the door. "What happened? How long ago? Were you stabbed?"

She gave him a thin smile. "Went poking where I wasn't wanted and found a little more than I expected. Thrown blade."

She flinched involuntarily when he touched her side. Lamorage pretended not to notice. "A thrown blade, you say? It must have been thrown with a great deal of force."

Her breath hissed between her teeth. "Automaton sentries."

"Automatons with orders to kill?" He stopped and stared at her. "You were trying to enter governmental facilities?"

"No, private owned as far as I know."

His frown deepened. "Automatons are restricted from lethal attacks. Disabling that protection violates at least a dozen laws."

"Maybe they just had really poor aim."

"I… doubt it." Warmth spread from Lamorage's hand into her side.

The pain of the wound eased, followed by the tightness in her chest from her abused ribs. She closed her eyes and drew a deep breath. "Blight… thanks."

"Better?" he asked.

"Yeah. She opened her eyes and straightened. "How much do I owe?"

Lamorage shook his head. "I don't charge people for the privilege of not bleeding out in my sitting room." He stepped back and studied her. "Excuse a rude question, but have I healed you before? That felt oddly familiar."

"It's been a while, but yeah, you have." She touched her side. It was still tender, but no longer bleeding.

"I suppose that could explain how you knew I am a healer. Though not how you know where I live. Or why you attempted to break into somewhere so heavily guarded." He watched her with distrust.

She let out a long breath. *Should have known this would be coming.* "You know my brother was tortured by Cemar. How involved do you want to become, Lamorage? How involved do you want to become again?"

He stiffened, eyes darting sharply to her face. "What's that supposed to mean?"

"It means that not all of Cemar's people and not all Cemar's plots are gone, and it means if you don't want to be drawn in further than you are, you don't want me to answer your questions."

Lamorage swallowed hard and looked at his hands.

When he didn't speak, Rykka stiffly climbed to her feet. "Don't suppose I could ask another favor?"

Lamorage gave a faint laugh. "You can certainly ask."

"Can you contact De'seneth?"

He blinked. "Which De'seneth? Alistar or Saskia?"

"Either, really. I'd rather not try to convince a taxi driver to take me up to that area of the city when I'm dressed like this, and it's late enough that going to the clinic would attract attention."

Lamorage looked her over again as if he'd forgotten the ragged state of her clothes and appearance. "I can do that."

When he stepped over to his desk, Rykka slipped a handful of marks onto the side table by her chair. Now that she was less preoccupied with not bleeding out, she could see the lingering air of wear around Lamorage's home. She'd noticed it when he came to heal Tiyron, but at the time had dismissed it as an effort to fit in better with the district around the clinic. She knew he had left Silverline Power, but from the look of things, whatever work he'd taken to replace it barely met his expenses.

I thought he'd immediately reject the idea of becoming involved in Cemar's plots, but maybe it's not as impossible as I thought. He certainly doesn't have much left to lose here.

CHAPTER 24

Alistar handed his coat and hat to Dorne as he entered the manor. "Sent a pot of tea up to my study in ten minutes. And send Darkwood when she's available."

"Darkwood went to the clinic this afternoon and hasn't returned yet, sir," Dorne told him.

"The clinic? All right. She should be back with Saskia, then, if not before." Alistar climbed the stairs to his rooms and dressed down for the evening.

He'd just gotten settled in the study when Dorne arrived with the tea tray. Alistar raised an eyebrow at his butler. Normally he'd send one of the staff on such a delivery rather than bring it himself.

"What's on your mind?" Alistar asked him.

"Darkwood let slip today that she was assigned her post by Captain As'enel." Dorne's expression was blankly professional.

Alistar highly doubted Rykka let anything 'slip' out, especially not something of that importance. "And you're concerned because I didn't tell you? Or about the accuracy of the claim?"

"Both, sir." Dorne poured Alistar a mug of tea, letting his professional mask fall and reveal his displeasure at the situation.

"Her claim is accurate, and you weren't informed because for her to maintain her cover, it was important that you didn't treat her like you would other members of the Rillwater staff. For her to perform her duties, her connection to Rillwater and the Family must remain a secret." Alistar looked Dorne in the eyes. "Is there any chance that others in the house overheard your conversation?"

Dorne considered. "I don't believe anyone overheard us, sir."

"But you're not certain."

"I didn't see or hear anyone nearby, sir, and I'm confident that if Darkwood had, she wouldn't have spoken as openly as she did."

"*Be* sure, Dorne. This cannot be allowed to spread."

Dorne bowed. "Yes sir." He withdrew, closing the door behind him.

Alistar let out a long, slow breath and sipped his tea. *Rykka wouldn't have told Dorne without good reason, but now he's one more person holding her secret. Loyal as he is, the more people know about Rykka's connections to the Family, the more chances for that knowledge to reach people who shouldn't have it.*

A speaking stone chimed gently, interrupting his thoughts. Alistar reflexively reached for the box where those for his family rested, but they weren't the source. He fumbled through his desk until he found the lit stone and activated it.

"Lamorage?"

"Evening, De'seneth. Sorry for the late call. Don't worry, it's not an emergency."

Alistar sank down into his chair. "All right... what's on your mind?"

"Darkwood's here at my place. If it's not too much to ask, could you send a carriage around to pick us up?"

Alistar stared at the stone, trying to make sense of Lamorage's statement in light of the conversation he'd just had with Dorne.

"I... have so many questions about those two sentences. But uh... sure, I can send the carriage down to pick you both up."

He could all but hear Lamorage's sudden flush in his voice. "She was injured! She came to me because she needed a healer. And she implied her injury was related to Cemar in some way."

"She said she was going to the clinic. Has something happened there?" Alistar pushed to his feet.

"No, no. She told me that she thought going to the clinic in her present state would attract attention."

Alistar heard movement in the background, then Rykka's raised voice. "I got sidetracked on my way to the clinic, got attacked, and needed a healer fast. Lamorage was closer."

That raised more questions than it answered, but they were questions Alistar wanted to ask face to face. "All right. I'll send the carriage to get you."

"Thank you, De'seneth," Lamorage said. "We'll see you soon."

Alistar deactivated the speaking stone and tucked it in his pocket in case Lamorage contacted him again. He stepped out of his study and summoned Dorne.

Night lay fully over the city by the time the carriage returned. Lamorage came into the sitting room, followed by a filthy figure in ragged clothes with a threadbare shawl draped over one shoulder that covered for the absence of a sleeve. Alistar didn't recognize her as Rykka until she raised her head and gave him and Saskia an apologetic grin.

Saskia looked her up and down. "Rykka, what in blight happened to you?"

"I was on my way down to the clinic to visit my brother, but I got a little sidetracked. Any chance I could change and wash up a bit before I completely stink up the house?"

"Be quick about it," Saskia told her.

Lamorage watched Rykka leave with a puzzled expression. "Does Darkwood… live here?"

Blood and sand, there's so much he doesn't know. Alistar nodded. "At the moment, yes. She's temporarily employed as Saskia's lady's maid. You said she was injured?"

Lamorage nodded slowly. "A deep gash on her side and several cracked ribs. She was bleeding badly when she reached my door."

What in blackened shoals were you doing, Rykka? Alistar pushed that question aside temporarily. "Make yourself comfortable. Would you like tea and refreshments?"

Before Lamorage could decline, a servant brought in trays with the tea service and fresh handpies from the kitchen. She poured tea for all of them and brought a plate of handpies to Lamorage. He'd eaten most of them by the time Rykka returned.

She'd washed away most of the grime and changed into a simple long-sleeved tunic and trousers. Her hands were scraped, and the nails trimmed short. The tips of her fingers looked raw.

Rykka eyed Lamorage for a moment before dropping into a chair. "Last chance to back out, Lamorage."

He let out a long breath. "I know. And I'm still here."

Rykka sighed softly. The servant brought her tea and food, then withdrew. Alistar waited until Rykka had a chance to sip her tea and eat a few bites of food before asking, "What happened?"

She wiped crumbs from her mouth with the back of her hand. "I was on my way to the clinic, like I said. Passed an alley, noticed a few people inside, and decided to eavesdrop. Realized it was Sunward, Larisa, and Merris."

Lamorage drew a sharp breath, paling.

Alistar pretended not to notice his friend's reaction. "Merris and Sunward, you're sure?"

"And Sunward's loyal drug addict, Larisa. I'm sure. Sunward

was giving instructions about something they were about to do. When they split up, I followed Sunward to the Deepwell factory district. She headed into a factory that appeared to not be in active use. Met her current lover there. I didn't see him, but I heard his voice. Upper nobility—high upper nobility. Evidently, she wanted him to watch whatever was taking place."

"What was taking place there?" Saskia asked. "And could you find this site again?"

"I can find it again, but I don't know how much help that will be. They gathered a bunch of Lower City and slums residents with the offer of a dose of a drug called Lumination. One dose per person, no option to refuse, with thugs to ensure no one tried to palm it or anything." She pulled a small capsule from her pocket and handed it to Saskia. "Don't know what's in it, but the people all acted very calm and compliant. Relaxed and not bothered by the extremely questionable situation once they'd taken the capsule."

Saskia quickly dropped the capsule into a small pouch. "How did you get this?"

"Uncomfortably. I tried to sneak around but got seen and pulled into the crowd. I had to wrap the capsule in a barrier to swallow it without being affected."

"But what was the goal? To make these people dependent on them for the drug?" Alistar asked.

Rykka shook her head. "From what I saw, they used it to find internal channelers. Somehow the drug either awakens the ability in those who have it or makes it more likely to manifest. Larisa demonstrated a 'test,' then the drugged candidates tried replicate it. Those who couldn't do it got sent off one way, those who succeeded were taken somewhere else with the promise of reward. They loaded those people into wagons and drove them to another factory. I managed to follow and get inside. When I tried to trail the successful candidates further into the factory, though, I was attacked by six automated suits of armor." She touched her side with a grimace. "Either they had a very lenient definition of 'subdue' or they were trying to kill me. I had to retreat."

"Automatons with permission to kill?" A chill ran through Alistar.

She nodded. "But I know where that factory is too and I can find it again. The automatons didn't chase me once I got outside, and I worked around to the front. There's a black bird painted on the front, but the doors have the letter 'Z' carved in them. It's on Rainwatch Lane. I didn't know if I was being followed, but I couldn't risk leading them to the clinic. Lamorage was relatively close, and I know he's trustworthy." She gulped a deep swallow of tea.

"Sunward is back in Lewarden," Lamorage said. "Is this true?"

Alistar nodded. "I haven't known it for long, but she is. And the Crown agents who have been trailing her all suffered convenient accidents or went missing in the past few days. Darkwood, this gathering you saw, would you say those running it were still sorting out the details on how to make it operate smoothly?"

"No, they were practiced. Anticipated most potential problems and accounted for them. They'd done this before."

Alistar massaged his forehead. So many things were happening now. "Are you willing to go back tonight? There's no telling when, or even if they're going to bring in more people. If we're going to find out what's happening to the channelers they collect, I don't know when we'll get another chance."

"Well, I know about the sentries now; I can watch for them," Rykka said slowly. "I want backup, though."

Alistar nodded firmly. "Absolutely. Also, I have a prototype of a device similar to a speaking stone that allows you to capture images and project them later. I'll send it with you to collect images of the sentries and anything else of significance."

Rykka frowned. "A prototype? This isn't some new Silver-line-confidential item that I'll be arrested if I'm found with it, is it?"

"No. It's a device the previous owners of this manor were working on at the time they went bankrupt. I visited the Zel'ens a few days ago." Alistar paused. "Was that... just yesterday? Blood and sand, so much has happened since then."

"Alistar, didn't the Ravencrest family buy the Zel'ens' factories? Some of them, at least?" Saskia asked.

"They did," he agreed slowly. "The Ravencrest family bought the factories, and Cemar and his group moved into the manor."

"And Lady Ravencrest stormed into the clinic demanding Seva," Saskia added. "Who escaped from a setup that sounds similar to what Rykka saw."

"What about Seva? What happened?" Rykka cut in.

Saskia briefly explained Seva's arrival at the clinic and first the thugs, then Lady Ravencrest attempting to reclaim him.

Rykka's expression was blank, but her eyes narrowed in anger. "So, we have Sunward, her noble lover, Ravencrest, and the crime lord Whitetooth, all connected." Her jaw tightened. "Seva witnessed a nobleman supplying Whitetooth with drugs. That could have been Sunward's lover. We need to identify him."

"I wouldn't know where to start on that. I can't even offer much about the Ravencrests; I only know the family in passing," Lamorage said. "Is there something I can do, De'seneth? Some way I can be useful? I don't know everything that's going on, but if it's connected to Cemar's plots, I want to help."

"Yes. There's actually a matter I was going to ask your help on," Alistar said. "You might know there are hidden rooms in the manor basement. We found a study—probably Sunward's. I haven't had any opportunity to go through what's in there or catalog the books within. Knowing what she studied might help us know what she's trying to do now."

Lamorage nodded. "I can do that."

"Before you commit, are you willing to stay here while you're working on the project? For your safety."

Lamorage nodded. "I'm willing. If you don't mind supplying a few toiletries, I don't need to get anything from my place."

"All right." Alistar rang for Dorne. The butler arrived promptly. "Lamorage is going to be assisting in the basement project. Grant him access to the lower study and prepare a guest room for him. And once you've show him to his room, send Soluthos down." He'd give Dorne more details later and ensure that Lamorage had clothes and the toiletries he needed.

"Of course, sir. Lord Lamorage, if you would follow me?" Dorne bowed and gestured for Lamorage to precede him.

Soluthos joined them several minutes later. "You called, sir?"

"Come in, sit down," Alistar told him. "Are you aware that the agents assigned to trail Sunward have all been disabled in one manner or another?"

Soluthos shifted uneasily. "I heard a rumor to that effect but hadn't confirmed it."

"Lady Syri told me this morning. There's a strong likelihood someone has the information to identify Crown agents, which may well include you," Alistar said. "However, if you're willing, I have a task for you."

"There is always a risk to what I do, sir. What's this task?"

"Rykka located a site where Sunward's working, possibly in conjunction with the Ravencrest family," Alistar said. "They've recruited internal channelers from the slums under false pretenses. She tried to infiltrate the site earlier today, but was stopped by automated sentries."

When Soluthos turned to Rykka, she said, "I think the people they took are still there, but I don't know for how long. Lord De'seneth recommended I make another attempt while we still have the chance to learn what they're doing with these people.

But given that the automatons tried to kill me, I want backup this time."

Soluthos straightened. "They have military automatons? To my knowledge, those remain in early prototype stages, and shouldn't be found anywhere other than a few select, isolated, very secure facilities."

"I couldn't tell you whether they were rogue prototypes or not. Just that they were fast, well-armed, and well-armored." Rykka drained her teacup. "Merris might also be there. I saw her talking to Sunward before the recruitment."

"How did they go about their recruitment?" Soluthos asked.

"The easy way. They offered free drugs. Ensures they know an easy way to motivate those they want, and usually means those who they take won't have many who will miss them." Rykka's voice was flat.

"Will anyone know you attempted to infiltrate the location?" Soluthos asked.

"They might know the sentries went after something. No one but the automatons saw me."

"I'd rather have more than just the two of you go," Alistar said. "Soluthos, do you think Dawncloud could join you, or find some other people to join you?"

"I'll ask, sir. I think she would join us if she's able, and she would know others who are trustworthy."

"Good. Set out as soon as you're ready."

Rykka grabbed the remaining handpies as she stood. "You'll need to give me the image capturing device. And if you have a spare set, it'd be nice to have a speaking stone in case I need to report in a hurry."

"Meet me in my study in a few minutes," Alistar told her.

She nodded and left the room. Soluthos followed her out.

Once only Alistar and Saskia remained, Saskia picked up the capsule that Rykka had brought. "So, this is Lumination."

"I know it's late, but if you want to head back to the clinic to start analyzing it, we can," Alistar said.

"I'd rather not go to the clinic tonight just in case Ravencrest or Sunward are keeping a watch on the place. If I were them, I know I would. Better not to give them reasons to be more suspicious." She considered the capsule, then looked at Alistar. "I'm worried about Rykka, and about sending her out again tonight."

"So am I," Alistar admitted. "Regardless of whether those sentries are stolen military prototypes or something else completely, they're trouble, and I'm not sure that she and Soluthos, and whoever Soluthos recruits, will be able to handle them or avoid them." He rose and paced around the sitting room. "I know the Crown's people are competent, but they aren't *my* people."

As he said the words, he recognized what he really wanted to do. Saskia smiled slightly, as if she'd been waiting for him to realize what she'd already figured out. He summoned Dorne. "Darkwood's about to head into a dangerous infiltration. She needs a good crew to back her up. Pick the best pair for the job."

Dorne didn't ask why. "Right away, sir."

Whatever Sunward is planning and whoever she's involved in her scheme, we're going to stop her.

CHAPTER 25

Rykka was keenly aware of the odd combination of Rillwater privateers and Crown agents who followed her down the street. She'd worried Alistar would insist on joining this mission himself. He was skilled at many things, but stealth wasn't one of them. Fortunately, he'd conceded that and instead sent two members of the Rillwater staff who had the needed light steps.

Even at this time of night, some factories remained active, and clumps of people moving between buildings weren't uncommon. All five members of their small infiltration crew wore plain clothes, worn and stained enough to not stand out among the factory workers. Windshadow had even swapped his red and gold eyepatch for a plain brown one.

Rykka stopped within sight of their target and turned to her companions, one hand resting on her belt purse as if they were discussing whether they could afford to step into a shop for a bite to eat.

"Three doors down, the factory on the left side of the street, with the black bird painted above the doors."

Investigator Dawncloud adjusted the cap that covered her

red hair, then checked a scrap of parchment. "A fabrication facility, currently owned by the Ravencrest family. Records are up to date. Ravencrests also own the factories to either side." She looked at the stylized raven on the building. "I do wonder why they only plastered this one with such an ostentatious display of ownership."

One of the two Rillwater staff with them, a squat man by the name of Colan with black hair and a scar down the side of his neck, tapped Rykka's shoulder. "Gonna ask the tea shack what they know about these factories."

Rykka nodded. "Do."

Colan sauntered to the tea vendor's stand and set down a half mark. "Something hot and strong, if you be so kind."

"Sure thing." The vendor yawned as he prepared the tea. "Don't get too many customers in the off periods. Shifts aren't out for a couple more hours. What brings you and your friends around?"

"Looking to see who's hiring and who's worth hiring on with," Colan answered. "How about those across the way?"

"Those? Ah, well, they used to have a good reputation for fair wages and fair conditions, but that's before Ravencrest got 'em. Now they're no better than the rest. Never even see workers going into the middle one, so I don't know if it's active or not."

Colan looked over to their target warehouse. "What, they plastered that giant bird all over it and aren't even using it?"

The vendor chuckled. "Right? Seems a waste, but what do I know about nobles? The other two factories stay busy enough. Might be hiring, but I'd recommend one of the Wavesong factories a couple blocks down. Heard decent things about them. Fewer injuries than most."

Colan gulped his tea down and set the mug on the tray. "Wavesong, huh? Thanks. Sounds like a place to start."

"Good luck. I'm sure you all can find something. Lots of

places adding more workers to prepare for the Exhibition." The tea vendor gave them all a polite nod.

Colan returned and said, "Seems as good a place to start as any, yeah?"

"Yeah," Rykka agreed. They walked until they were out of sight of the vendor and stepped into an alley.

Windshadow spoke quietly. "What's the plan, Darkwood? Do we go in the back?"

Rykka suppressed a shudder. "That's where I saw the automatons that tried to kill me, so I'd rather avoid it. I didn't have much chance to look for other entrances, though, and it seems like most of these places have at least one or two side entries."

"By law they need to," Dawncloud said. "We've had a few too many fires where people couldn't get out in time."

Rykka tried not to think about being trapped inside with the walls burning down around her. *Or worse, all those drugged people, blissfully unaware of the danger until much too late.* She swallowed hard. "Then let's hope Sunward doesn't consider that an acceptable method of destroying the evidence." She led the way through the alleys and back streets to their target factory.

The window she'd escaped through was still ajar. In the darkness, she couldn't see any bloodstains she might have left on the street. A few dull ghostlights offered sporadic illumination on the back street, and no lights at all graced the alleys. Rykka motioned to the window.

"That's how I got out. I assume those doors are locked."

Windshadow looked up, then at her. "Quite a drop."

"I noticed." Rykka moved into an alley along the side of the building, searching for doors. "Colan, check the other alley for an entrance."

Colan nodded to his companion, an elven woman who went by Cat and never spoke unless she had to. The two of them headed to the other alley.

Rykka tried to ignore the prickling at the back of her neck that came from having a pair of Crown agents flanking her. No matter how much she told herself they were allies, they were loyal to their lord first. And their lord had deemed her and her brother to be enemies.

Neither Windshadow nor Dawncloud asked questions as they moved through the shadows. They weren't as quiet as her, but Dawncloud, at least, had some practice in moving lightly. She also spotted the door first.

"Darkwood, can you open this? It's locked."

"Probably." Rykka followed Dawncloud's gesture to the door and crouched beside it. "Pretty serious lock on it." She slid her lockpicks into the keyhole and set to work.

It took longer than she liked to finally work the tumblers and release the lock. Rykka listened at the door but heard no sounds through the thick wood. She stepped back and found Colan's speaking stone.

"Found and opened a way on our side. You?"

"Found a spot. Cat's working on it," Colan answered.

"Get it open, then meet back on my side," Rykka told him.

"Aye, Cap."

Rykka smiled tightly at the honorific. She supposed she *was* in charge of this little mission. She certainly didn't want to cede that authority to Windshadow or Dawncloud, competent though they probably were.

"Did the others find anything?" Windshadow asked when Rykka tucked the stone back into her pocket.

"A door on their side as well. I told them to unlock it and come back here." She eyed the factory. "I'd rather know we have multiple exits if something goes bad inside."

Colan and Cat rejoined them several minutes later. Colan gave her a quick nod to say he'd done as she instructed. Rykka nodded in return and cautiously turned the knob and pushed the door open.

The hinges resisted but gave in with a weary groan. Rykka ushered everyone inside and pushed the door shut again. The air was dusty and still, a welcome relief from the stench of the alley, and the room nearly completely dark. When her eyes adjusted, Rykka saw a few thin shafts of weak light creeping under a door across the room. It gave just enough illumination to show crates piled around the room, though she couldn't tell how long they'd been here. They could easily have been here before the previous owners were forced to sell the factory.

Dawncloud moved behind one of the stacks of crates and whispered something. A faint glow of ghostlight bloomed in her hand. She closed her fist around it, letting only a little light leak between her fingers. She was careful to keep the stack of crates between herself and the door, to Rykka's approval. She joined the investigator and looked more closely at the crates. The markings on them were indistinct, but when Rykka leaned close and closed her eyes, she caught the faintest hint of salt water from the wood, mixed with touches of grease and metal.

"See any with clear markings?" she asked.

Dawncloud checked the nearest stacks and motioned Rykka to join her. "Here."

Rykka raised the image crystal De'seneth gave her and triggered it. Hopefully the light was strong enough for the image to be legible later.

"Do we open them?" Windshadow asked in a low voice.

"Not now. If we have time on the way out, we can do it then," Rykka decided. She waited until both Windshadow and Dawncloud moved away, then she eased open the lid of a crate, reached inside, and felt around. Her hand touched burlap and she pulled out a small pouch. She quickly stuffed it into a pocket, closed the lid, and followed them.

The storage room door wasn't locked. Colan eased it open and peered out before signaling the all-clear. The door opened onto the massive factory floor. Partitions divided the space into sections. Worn tracks in the stone floor showed the passage of heavy carts to move supplies from the storage room to the workers. A low, steady hum hung in the air, emanating from the far end of the floor and occasionally interspersed with clangs of metal. Glancing up, Rykka noticed a network of connected beams hanging on cables.

"What's all that?" she murmured, nodding at the beams.

The others' gazes followed her gesture, and Dawncloud answered. "It's for constructing large assemblies. The work in progress is hung from those beams and moved to different stations where each worker does their part."

"Large assemblies. You mean like if someone was building automatons?" Rykka asked warily.

Dawncloud grimaced. "Possibly."

The sound of footsteps silenced everyone. They ducked behind crates and pieces of equipment. A second set of footsteps approached the first at a rapid staccato. A sharp female voice spoke.

"That? *That* is what you send me to work with? I have a quota to meet to get this project ready for the Exhibition! How am I supposed to do that if the 'workers' you bring me are all unwashed addicts who don't know yellow from green?"

"They all possess the necessary qualification." The second female voice was clearly Sunward.

"The qualification for *your* part, perhaps. *I* need workers who are actually capable of working!"

Sunward sighed in annoyance, and the sounds of footsteps paused. "*You* came to *me* for assistance. If you don't like the assistance I provide, by all means, go back to trying to make this all work on your own."

A sound of frustration. "We're still missing shipments. We don't have time to rework or replace units that get mangled by idiots! Especially not after that incident the other day."

"That wasn't an incident, that was a spy," Sunward snapped.

"Who I trust you have moved to a location where they can't cause more difficulty."

An indignant sniff. "Of course."

Moved? But not killed? Why not?

Rykka edged around the boxes she'd used for shelter until she could see the two women in profile. Even as late as it was, Sunward hadn't changed out of the shapeless clothes she'd been wearing when Rykka saw her earlier. Her cosmetics couldn't completely conceal the dark shadows under her eyes or the weary slump of her shoulders. Rykka was reminded of her own long day and not enough sleep.

The other woman was an elf with waist-length black hair pulled back in a braid. She carried herself as if she wore the finest silkweave gown rather than the more practical, if no less embellished, embroidered tunic and trousers, with a pair of black mid-calf boots embroidered with an emblem matching the bird painted on the front of the warehouse. Her face was set in a perpetual scowl.

Sunward eyed her elven companion and laughed curtly. "At least I didn't manage to lose a street whore. Unlike you."

"He is not lost," the elven woman growled. "I know precisely where he is, and when it's time, we'll collect him. Until then he can stay hiding in his little hole."

Sunward smirked. "Of course. No problems at all there."

"If you don't have anything productive to offer, you can be on your way. I have work to do."

"You should use the new workers. I'm sure there are portions they can assemble without making things worse. They're all compliant—we've ensured that. And your current workers will only make more mistakes if they don't get enough rest, even with your healer countering the exhaustion."

"I know how to run my factories, Sunward!" the elf snapped. "If you want to do something *useful*, you could send your boys out to have a word with our supplier about holding up their side of the contract. Remind them what happens if they *don't* come through with the promised components. Now if you will excuse me, *I* have work to do." With a glare at Sunward, she spun on her heels and stormed across the factory floor.

Sunward shook her head and continued the direction she'd been going. Rykka eased back into hiding and waited for the sound of footsteps to fade from either direction. When it was quiet, the small band of infiltrators regathered.

"I heard Lady Ravencrest," Dawncloud said quietly. "Who was the other?"

"Lady Sunward," Rykka answered. "She headed that way, and Ravencrest went that way." She pointed as she spoke.

"Who you want us to follow?" Colan asked.

She almost told him to trail Ravencrest, but the conversation implied that Ravencrest was more likely to lead them to a better understanding of what this place was. The decision took longer than she wanted, but finally, fighting her desire to follow Cemar's lover herself, she said, "Follow Sunward. We'll tail Ravencrest."

"Aye, Cap."

"Be careful," Windshadow added. "She's already taken out several Crown agents."

Colan smirked. "Good thing we're not Crown agents, then." He nodded to Cat and they slipped away after Sunward.

Windshadow's jaw tightened and he let out a slow breath.

"I'm surprised you'd mention that," Rykka said quietly.

"Why? At least half the household staff knows whose service I'm in. Word gets around quickly, as you know. Especially when Merris called it out. And both Colan and Cat are on the night staff."

She hadn't been thinking about the fact that Windshadow had known the pair longer than she had. Rykka just nodded. "Merris might be here. I saw and heard her talking with Sunward earlier."

"You can confirm she's in league with Sunward?" Dawncloud asked.

"Yes." Rykka checked for any sentries or automatons and started in the direction Ravencrest had gone. "Are you two coming?"

The two Crown agents followed her around the edge of the factory floor, using looming equipment for cover. The steady hum in the air grew louder. A few voices spoke indistinct words muffled by the sounds of tools on metal.

Ravencrest implied she has people working all night, but why would they put up with this? Are they trapped? Who would put up with this if they had a choice? Are they worked too hard to think straight? That's a sure way to make mistakes.

After the relative stillness of the rest of the factory floor, Rykka was startled to peer around a crate and see a bustle of activity like a disturbed ant nest. Half-built metal torsos hung from the rails and workers clustered around them, bolting on plates section by section. An uneasy shiver ran down her spine.

They're building the automatons.

Further from her hiding place, another group of workers assembled what she guessed to be the internal workings of the automatons. Even from a distance, Rykka saw the weary droops of heads and shoulders. These people were exhausted.

One woman tried to work a pale blue crystal into its moorings. The crystal slipped from her grasp. She tried to catch it but missed.

Lady Ravencrest dove for the crystal, appearing from out of Rykka's field of view to snatch the fragile component before it shattered on the floor. The workers gaped.

Ravencrest rose and examined the crystal critically before dusting herself off. Her voice was chill and even. "You nearly cost every person on your team three days of work."

The worker swallowed hard. "I... I beg your pardon, Lady Ravencrest."

"Is that all you have to say for yourself?"

Others of her work group were looking at her, their expressions dark and angry. The woman shrank under their glowers. "I'm sorry. Someone should take my spot." She lifted a hand that trembled with exhaustion. "It... it won't stop shaking. I don't know why."

"We can't afford to lose any more crystals," Lady Ravencrest said sternly. Her gaze swept the rest of the group. "Whose hands are steady?"

The mood shifted from angry to uneasy. Several workers looked down to their own hands. After a moment, one of the men quietly said, "Mine are, lady."

"Swap stations. Don't let this happen again."

The workers complied, and assembly began once more. While Ravencrest's attention focused on the workers, and the workers focused intently on their tasks, Rykka grabbed the image crystal, pointed it toward the assemblies, and activated it to capture images of the work.

When Rykka pulled back into hiding, Windshadow whispered, "What are they making? What is all this?"

"They're building automatons like the ones that attacked me," Rykka whispered back. "And it sounds like they don't have as many of their components as they want. Not much in the way of spares, at least." She thought of the crates in the manor basement, then the many more stored in the warehouse in Rillwater.

"I don't like this," Dawncloud murmured. "Why have these ready for the Exhibition? Ravencrest couldn't intend to present and sell them openly there. But if she's planning to use the chaos of the Exhibition to deliver them to one or more buyers..." She looked toward Ravencrest, then scanned the rest of the factory floor. "We need to find her office."

Rykka looked at the workers once more. She didn't recognize any of them from the recruitment event. Where were they?

And why did Sunward want them, if not to help with the construction and assembly? Why internal channelers specifically?

Dawncloud and Windshadow worked their way to one of the doors from the factory floor. Rykka trailed them, the questions turning over in her thoughts.

She didn't hear any indication that they'd been noticed, and the door was unlocked. They entered a short hall that ended at a stairwell. The steps led to both the upper floor and the basement. Dawncloud nodded toward the ascending stairs and advanced.

She'd gone two steps up when a door slammed on the upper floor. Heavy steps clomped toward the stairs. Rykka hissed a curse, grabbed both Windshadow's and Dawncloud's sleeves and tugged them toward the stairs leading down. The heavy tread above covered the sounds of their hasty descent. They all listened at the bottom of the stairs, breaths held.

"Blight, woman, you know you can't work 'em forever. I can only heal so much." Weary exasperation filled the male voice. Rykka didn't think he was speaking directly to anyone; the tone was that of someone muttering complaints he wouldn't dare say to his employer's face.

The man didn't move on immediately, but paced around the hall, muttering. Rykka shifted uneasily, glanced to her companions, and nodded at the dimly lit passage before them. Going back upstairs was too risky right now, and waiting for the man to leave wasted time.

Windshadow dipped his head in agreement. Rykka took the lead.

Once the noise of the man's pacing faded, only the soft sounds of their steps intruded into the stillness of the passage. The passage was narrow and the ceiling low enough Rykka had to suppress the urge to duck as she walked. She paused to run a finger along the stone floor and found almost no dust. For all the silence and darkness, this area saw frequent traffic.

The passage wasn't long, and ended at three closed doors, one to the right, one to the left, and one straight ahead. She tested the knobs and found all three locked. Starting at the right, she listened at the door, then retrieved her lock picks and set to work. The complex lock took several tense minutes to trip.

"I'm going to be really annoyed if there's nothing in here," she muttered to Windshadow and Dawncloud. Before either responded, she pushed the door open.

At first look, the dark room appeared empty. The floor, however, showed patchy dark streaks on the stone as if something had been dragged. She stepped over them into the room.

Just as she started to crouch to look more closely, something large moved in the corner.

CHAPTER 26

Rykka snatched for her dagger, springing back. Her eyes searched the darkness for the source. A glint of metal caught her eye and ice ran through her veins. She backed out of the room, almost tripping over Windshadow.

"Darkwood, what's in there?" he demanded.

Metal shifted in the room as something moved and scraped against the wall. Rykka took another step away from the sound.

Dawncloud activated a handheld ghostlight orb and tossed it into the room. The pale illumination revealed a partially completed automaton with no visible weapons. It also lacked legs, though the gears and connection points were present for the limbs to be attached. The head jerkily tracked the ghostlight as it rolled across the floor. One arm reached out toward the light, but was stopped by the heavy chains that held it upright on the wall.

"Hematic perdition… why is it here?" Rykka whispered.

"Blight, that thing is huge," Windshadow said. "This is what attacked you, Darkwood?"

"Yeah. Except they had legs and blades."

Even without the lower appendages, the automaton was easily as tall as any of them. Its movements stuttered as if it operated under insufficient power. Rykka captured a rapid series of images of it with the crystal. It didn't respond to their whispers, but when Dawncloud crossed the threshold into the room, the automaton's attention swiveled immediately to her. Its massive hands reached toward her, straining against the chains.

"Stand down." Dawncloud raised her hand, palm out. A rune on her skin shimmered in the ghostlight.

The automaton stilled, as if the rune held significance to it, but when Dawncloud began to move again, it resumed its jerky efforts to reach her.

"What?" Windshadow hissed. "That should have put it into standby mode."

Rykka glanced at him questioningly, but he didn't elaborate. She asked in a whisper, "Sort of like how automatons shouldn't be able to try to kill people?"

His jaw tightened. "Very much like that."

"Stand down," Dawncloud repeated.

The automaton ignored her order completely, continuing to strain against the chains to grab for her.

Dawncloud kept out of its limited reach and grabbed the ghostlight. As soon as she retreated through the door, the automaton fell still again.

"It must be malfunctioning," Dawncloud said in a low voice. "It didn't obey verbal commands or hand signals."

"Doesn't explain why it's here," Rykka said. "Why leave it active at all? Why not disassemble it and reuse the parts? Ravencrest made quite a point about not having spares available."

Dawncloud and Windshadow both cast uneasy looks into the room, where the automaton hung inert once more. Neither offered an answer.

Why cripple and restrain it, yet still keep it active? Why not repair it if it's malfunctioning? What use is this thing to Sunward?

"I don't like the questions that raises," Windshadow finally said. "We could try to disable it, but doing so would leave unmistakable evidence of our intrusion."

"Still might be kinder to just kill it and put it out of its misery," Rykka said.

Windshadow shook his head. "Darkwood, it's an automaton. It feels neither pain nor misery. Destroying it adds too much risk."

Rykka pulled the door closed and relocked it with misgivings. Part of her wanted to disable the automaton before it could be unleashed for its purpose, whatever that might be. The rest of her wanted to bolt and never see another such monstrosity for the rest of her life. She tried to shake off the cold fear, but it clung to her like a relentless shark, and brought with it more thoughts.

It moved like a wounded creature. Like it was hurt. Why would it do that if it can't feel pain? I don't understand, and I don't like it.

The two Crown agents moved to the next door, then paused to look back at her expectantly. Rykka drew a steadying breath and joined them. "You sure you want me to open this?"

"Yes." Dawncloud was firm.

The second lock was just as complex as the first, but Rykka had a better sense of it the second time, and it yielded faster to her picks. She pushed the door open but stepped back to let Dawncloud enter first.

No sounds of movement rose from within the room.

Dawncloud triggered the ghostlight again to illuminate the space. The pale light showed rows of empty bunks. The beds had been slept in and most weren't made with any particular care. None appeared to be in use now. A brief search turned up only a few scattered belongings, nothing of value.

"Seems even when the workers are allowed to rest, they aren't allowed to leave," Dawncloud observed quietly.

"Is *that* legal?" Rykka asked. Even with the many ways the laws favored the nobles and property owners, this seemed like imprisonment and abduction.

"No, but if no one can get out to report it, and they are careful about selecting people without families to question their absence, some get away with it for a time. Clearly this area is overdue for unannounced inspections."

They closed the bunk room again. Rykka noted that the door required a key to unlock from either side. No sneaking off during rest time here.

The final door opened into a short hall. Rykka sniffed the air, catching a faint but lingering stink of the streets mixed with something syrupy sweet, familiar after the day's events.

"I think the people recruited today are here," she said quietly. She scanned the hall for more doors.

She saw only one at the end of the hall. Rykka caught fragments of sounds that finally resolved into snatches of a song as she approached.

"Is someone singing a lullaby?" Windshadow asked. "I'm not sure why, but that might be the most unsettling thing in this factory."

"It also means someone's awake and alert." Rykka approached warily. She pressed her ear to the wood and listened.

Someone walked on light feet around the room beyond, singing the lilting melody like a matron in an orphanage singing her charges to sleep. Rykka heard a few other sounds of shifting bodies, occasional indistinct murmurs.

"Shh, shh, rest now. We have a beautiful destiny before us. Rest. Sleep."

Larisa. What's her role in all this? What does she think she'll get out of all this? What keeps her loyal to Sunward? The drugs, or something else? What's this 'beautiful destiny' tripe?

Rykka stepped back from the door. In a whisper, she told Windshadow and Dawncloud, "I recognize the voice. One of Sunward's people. There are more people inside—probably today's recruits."

"We're here to gather information, not perform an extraction," Dawncloud said. "We need to find Ravencrest's office."

Rykka cast another look at the door but followed Dawncloud and Windshadow back down the hall. "Would you be saying that if we'd found a Crown spy imprisoned down here instead?"

"Yes. And a Crown spy, captured or not, would agree with me." Dawncloud headed for the stairs.

Rykka glanced to Windshadow, but he didn't appear to find Dawncloud's statement strange or off-putting. Pushing down her unease at the thought of leaving people in the hands of those who tortured Tiyron, Rykka trailed the two back to the stairs.

The man who had been pacing earlier no longer lingered. They climbed two flights of stairs to a far more comfortably appointed landing on the second floor. Rugs covered the floors and a pair of plush chairs for visitors faced a small table. Beyond that, a long runner spread down a wide hallway. This was the territory of nobles, where the common-born were not welcome.

"I'll keep watch," Rykka said.

Dawncloud raised an eyebrow at her. "And how will you send warning if someone's coming?"

"Darkwood has one of my speaking stones," Windshadow said. He gave Rykka a curious, slightly suspicious look. "I trust you know your business, Darkwood."

"And I trust you know yours," she retorted. "Go riffle through a noblewoman's personal effects."

Dawncloud scowled. "I'd prefer to riffle through her professional effects." She spun on her heels and strode down the hall. Windshadow followed.

Rykka moved partway down the stairs, listening for sounds of anyone coming from any direction as she untucked her shirt, tousled her hair a little, and adopted the swagger Tiyron could project even standing still. After long, silent minutes, she finally heard the sound she was waiting for: light footsteps padding up the hall below. She had to strain to catch the noise but had time to get into position before Larisa came up the stairs.

The human woman looked weary, but moved with the dreamy, fluid steps of one still under the effects of a drug. She steadied herself at the top of the stairs, then turned toward the door back to the factory floor, one hand trailing along the metal railing meant to prevent someone from falling into the stairwell. She passed the landing to the upper stairs. Rykka, arms crossed, leaned against the wall there, just slightly in shadow, watching her.

When Larisa didn't notice her, she spoke in Tiyron's voice. "What is all this really, Larisa?"

Larisa froze, breath catching in her throat. "You're not real. The lady said so." She didn't look at Rykka, keeping her eyes fixed on the door to the factory floor.

"The lady." Rykka snorted. "And you believe every lie that drips from her tongue, don't you?"

Larisa shivered. "She's been kind to me, Tiyron. You know she has. Everything she's done for me. I told you what she saved me from."

Blackened shoals, Tiyron, why did you hide this from me? "You think that gives her free rein to deceive you? To use you?"

"I'd be nothing without her and Cemar," Larisa whispered. "Worse than nothing. Those men who they saved me from..." She wrapped her arms tight around herself.

"You think that justifies this? Stealing people? Lying to them?"

"No! That's not… we're not… It's the only way! We have to force the change that the nobles won't accept. We have to *make* them accept it!" She turned her eyes to the floor, avoiding looking directly at Rykka. "You could help us again."

"Cemar and Sunward betrayed me, Larisa. And here you are, clinging to their shadows. Are you going to be Sunward's pet forever?"

"It's all I can do, Tiyron," she whispered, wringing her hands. "I can't slip around in the darkness like Merris to try to get back into the manor and recover what's there. I can't play at being a servant. This… this is what I can do. I can give her work what it requires."

Rykka's eyes narrowed. "What does it require, Larisa?"

She swallowed hard and finally looked at Rykka. Tears pooled in her eyes. "Everything." Before Rykka could speak, Larisa fled down the hall to the factory floor.

"Blight!" Rykka took a step after her, but stopped. Following was too risky. "Blight and rot."

She climbed back up the stairs to find Windshadow lingering near enough to hear, but positioned so he wouldn't be seen from below. Rykka gave him a long, silent look before finally saying, "What?"

"We found Ravencrest's office. Dawncloud is documenting everything she can, but we should make our exit soon. I was coming to retrieve you." He looked her up and down. "That woman called you Tiyron."

It wasn't a completely uncommon given name in the Lower City, though her brother had certainly raised its popularity. "She thought she was speaking to my brother. Or rather, hopefully, she thought she was speaking to a drug-induced hallucination of my brother." She strode past him.

"Your brother?" Windshadow repeated.

"Shocking though it may seem, I didn't spring fully formed out of the void, Windshadow. I do, in fact, have a family."

Rather than comment, Windshadow took the lead to Raven-crest's office. It was as opulent as the rest of the floor, from the plush rugs to the glass cabinet filled with bottles of imported wine worth hundreds of marks apiece. Papers rested in neat stacks on the desk with no indication they had been disturbed.

Rykka saw no one in the room until Windshadow whispered something. Dawncloud emerged from behind the wine cabinet and nodded to them both.

"The papers on the desk are complete lies. The real records are stored under the middle cushion of the settee. I noted what I could in the time I had," Dawncloud said.

Rykka lifted the indicated cushion and found a leather-bound ledger. She skimmed through it, scanning for mentions of Sunward or Cemar. Ravencrest used her own peculiar short-hand, complicating the task. Rykka made a sound of annoyance and finally used the image crystal to capture images of a sampling of pages whose dates loosely corresponded to times when an order might have been placed for a shipment of smug-gled goods. She could only estimate based on when Rillwater privateers intercepted those shipments, but Alistar had cautioned her that the crystal could only hold a limited number of images. She carefully returned the ledger to its place and set the cushion to rights.

Turning to Dawncloud, she asked, "Done here?"

"Yes."

They left the office and Dawncloud produced her own lock picks to close it once more. When the Crown agents moved as if to return to the stairs, Rykka shook her head and continued down the hall. They followed her. As she'd hoped, she found a second staircase at the end of the hall, a narrow, steep servants' access. To her great relief, no servants or staff were using it or the quarters below this late in the night. Or morning. Or what-ever time it was now. She'd long lost track.

A little more searching located a door to the outside. It

wasn't locked, and once Rykka oriented herself, she decided this was probably the door Colan had unlocked earlier. She tripped the latch after them and leaned against the grimy wall, exhausted. Larisa, Tiyron, and the recruits had to wait, much as she hated it.

"Let's go home."

CHAPTER 27

An hour before dawn, Dorne woke Alistar. "They've returned."

Alistar wiped sleep from his eyes and pulled on the clothes his butler offered in the shadowed bedroom. "Everyone? Any injuries?"

"All are accounted for and unharmed, sir."

He let out a long breath. "Good. Meet in the study."

"Of course, sir."

Dorne left and Alistar washed his face in an effort to summon his wits. Saskia's side of the bed was already empty. He didn't remember hearing her get up. He combed his hair and beard and made his way to the study.

Saskia offered him a steaming mug of tea. Alistar accepted gratefully and sank onto the settee beside her. "I hope you slept better than I did."

She smiled a little. "I doubt it. I've been up for a bit now."

He nodded understanding. When Saskia couldn't sleep, she preferred to get up and do something rather than lie about and hope elusive rest would arrive.

He drank his tea, letting the aroma and warmth draw him to

full consciousness once more. He'd shaken off most of the sleepy lethargy by the time footsteps announced the arrival of the infiltration team.

The long day and equally long night showed the most on Rykka. She flopped into a chair with no pretense at decorum. Dorne offered her tea, and she drained the cup in one gulp. While she refilled it, Soluthos and Investigator Dawncloud found seats. Colan and Cat trailed after them, Colan sat, but Cat declined chair and tea alike.

Once all were settled, Alistar looked them over, noting the dirt on clothes and the weariness in stances. "What did you find?"

After several seconds of silence as everyone waited for someone else to start, Investigator Dawncloud outlined their entry and exploration of the factory. The others contributed bits and pieces as she spoke. Rykka particularly recounted the conversation between Sunward and Ravencrest. When Dawncloud described the factory floor and the work taking place there, Alistar frowned.

"Production of automatons is regulated by the Crown. Do the Ravencrests hold the necessary permits to manufacture them? I thought they worked primarily in textiles."

"Oddly, they do hold the needed permits," Dawncloud said. "There were no records that they've made use of those permits, but they do hold them."

"So, while they supposedly can manufacture such things legally, any automatons they've produced have been in secret."

Dawncloud nodded in agreement. "In addition, their automatons also lack the required safeguards. Darkwood already discovered that they are able to attack with lethal force. They're also unresponsive to command phrases and instructions to stand down."

"You encountered some of them?" Alistar didn't see any indication they'd been in combat.

"We had an… interesting encounter." Dawncloud described a locked room with an operational but immobile automaton. "The commands I issued should have disabled it. Any automaton built in Calarand should respond to such instructions from someone of my rank. Somehow, that's been disabled. Which shouldn't be possible."

"If the components used in construction were supplied from outside Calarand, could this function be disabled that way?" Alistar asked her.

"Every single component would have to come from elsewhere," she answered. "And even then, we have accords with most other nations who are capable of manufacturing such components. No one wishes to be the first to break it by supplying war-ready automatons."

Rykka stirred from her weary slouch. "Why not? First to start gets the tactical advantage."

"First to start also gets the combined ire of every other member of the accord brought down on them in a unified assault," Dawncloud told her.

"If I were a member of such an accord, I'd ensure I had a force of the forbidden weapons constructed, but kept concealed, in the expectation that someone else will break the accord first," Alistar said.

"Are you suggesting Ravencrest's work is sanctioned by someone of authority in Calarand, sir?" Soluthos asked, shifting uneasily in his chair.

"Not yet, but we know that at least one nobleman is working closely with Sunward. We don't know whether his interests are aligned with Calarand or another power." Alistar sipped his tepid tea.

Cat snorted.

Alistar turned to her, one eyebrow raised.

"Don't know about *his* interests. Got an idea about Sunward's, though. Lady's pregnant."

Rykka jerked up straight in her seat. "She's *what?*"

"Are you certain?" Alistar asked.

Cat didn't indicate any offense at the question. "The lady is pregnant. More than halfway along."

"We didn't see or hear the nobleman," Colan said. "Not sure he was still at the factory. Darkwood had Cat and I follow Sunward when she and Ravencrest parted. Heard her talking with Merris." Colan's weather-worn face was grim. "Seems Merris has some access to the registry of channelers. Heard her sayin' she didn't find Windshadow's name on the list."

Soluthos grimaced. "I don't know who provided her that access, but no, she wouldn't find me there. I expect she was satisfied to confirm that I'm not actually a channeler."

Colan chuckled softly. "Rather think she hoped she *would* find you on the list. She was tellin' Sunward how they needed to be more careful with an unknown channeler at the manor. She also told Sunward that all the passages are still locked from inside. Assume she was talking about the basement."

"All the passages," Alistar repeated quietly. That confirmed his suspicion that the tunnel he and Saskia found wasn't the only concealed entrance. Still locked from inside—that sounded good on the surface, but...

"Colan," Saskia asked, "did Merris say that as if she expected to find any of them open?"

"It sounded more like she'd been hoping she might, but wasn't so much expecting to," Colan answered. "Didn't say enough to tell us one way or the other whether they still got an agent in the house."

Alistar glanced at Dorne, who answered with a curt nod of understanding. They needed to conduct another review of the house staff to definitively identify who worked for whom.

"Anything more from Merris? Did Sunward speak with anyone else?" Alistar asked Colan and Cat.

"Merris didn't stick around," Colan said. "Sunward sent her

off with a letter to someone—didn't catch a name. Mentioned another name, someone who was getting the new recruits settled downstairs."

"Larisa," Rykka said.

"Ya, that's the one. Merris didn't care much for that one if I read her right."

The name conjured an image in Alistar's mind—a human woman in her late teens who gazed at Cemar with the rapturous expression of an acolyte looking upon the face of her deity, rather than someone looking to a leader. He'd only talked with her once for any length of time, when he'd attended Cemar's gathering held in this very house. He remembered her clearly, though. He remembered all the details of that night far more clearly than he cared to.

"You know this woman, Darkwood," Soluthos said.

Rykka's mouth twisted in a tight smile. "Not as well as my brother did, apparently." She looked at Soluthos. "Like I told you earlier, that's who she thought I was. My brother."

Alistar looked at her in surprise, but she was focused on Soluthos.

Continuing, Rykka said, "Don't know if you noticed, but she was also fully in the midst of her Lumination experience. It didn't take a lot of effort to convince her that I was him. She saw who she wanted to see, and I tried to get some information out of her."

"Did you?" Alistar asked.

"It was disjointed. She claimed that whatever they're doing is intended to 'force the change the nobles won't accept,' which sounds a lot like Cemar's rhetoric. She also said she could 'give Sunward's work what it requires'."

"Which is...?" Alistar asked. A heavy weight sat in the pit of his stomach.

"According to her, 'everything'. Which is a meaningless

answer just vague enough to sound enigmatically ominous." Rykka turned her teacup around in her hands.

"That's the sort of answer you give if you don't expect to survive whatever you're doing," Dawncloud said. "That doesn't bode well for anyone else recruited into this conspiracy."

"Do you think you would be able to get anything more from her, Rykka?" Alistar asked.

"Not a whole lot. We'd likely have better luck if we could find the spy they captured. That's someone who might know more and be able to present it in a comprehensible manner." Rykka sighed heavily. "Don't know where they're holding the spy, though. We didn't find them in our search, but we didn't get into every dark corner."

"Earlier, I considered leading an unannounced inspection of the factory," Dawncloud said. "However, now I'm concerned that doing so would only catch Ravencrest, and alert the others involved to hide their tracks. And we could likely only make some of the lesser charges stick to Ravencrest unless we could prove she knowingly and intentionally avoided adding the safeguards to the automatons. She could almost certainly place the blame on someone under her, a sacrificial minion. We could disrupt the plan and the timeline, but lose the real goal."

"And bring you into their sights as a target," Saskia added.

"That's the least of my concerns," Dawncloud told her.

"These people kidnap, torture, and murder at the slightest provocation. It should be a concern," Saskia countered.

"We have a lot to consider, and you all need rest," Alistar said. "Investigator Dawncloud, would you like a room prepared? Or transportation home?"

"The offer of a room is generous, but I'll return to my own home." She rose stiffly. "I will accept a ride, though."

"Thank you for your help." Alistar stood, offering Saskia an arm. Soluthos followed immediately. Rykka heaved a sigh and pushed to her feet.

Everyone left the study. Rykka lingered back as the rest of the infiltration team descended the stairs. She handed Alistar the image stone.

"Hope you can use these." She rubbed her eyes. "Hematic perdition, I'm beat. And I still haven't talked to Tiyron."

"Rest first," Saskia ordered. "He'll still be at the clinic come afternoon. Although we should discuss bringing him to the manor. He's healed enough to do so."

"Oh, he'll hate that." Rykka yawned and headed to her room.

Alistar shook his head. "I wish I could go back to bed myself."

"You could," Saskia told him. "You won't, but you could."

Alistar shook his head. "Too much to do. The Exhibition is too close, an idiot prince thinks he can step into Prince Cero's position without any training or sense, and Lady Syri's trying to keep everything at Silverline functioning. And that's before we get into Sunward, Ravencrest, and their schemes." He let out a long breath. "I feel like it's been forever since I've even attended devotions."

Saskia smiled faintly. "It has been. I've been asked multiple times if you're ill when I've attended without you. But most have been understanding when I explained that you're involved in preparations for the Exhibition."

"It's ridiculous political posturing," Alistar said softly, glad they were alone and that only Rillwater staff attended this area of the manor. "Trying to prove to the surrounding nations that we're strong and imposing, that our king isn't a tired old man."

"Trying to convince other nations, or ourselves?" Saskia asked just as softly.

"I don't know. Maybe both. I'll come with you tonight to devotions."

She kissed him. "I look forward to it."

An hour later, Alistar sat in his office in Silverline Power. The building was quiet, most people taking advantage of the day of devotions to attend services to either the elven or the human gods. Historical records indicated that prior to their arrival in Calarand, humans hadn't set aside certain days or certain sites to their worship of the Reyker, but once they began integrating with the elven population, they'd adopted the practice. The gods themselves had never mandated a preference one way or the other—at least not through any reputable source.

A soft, persistent chime interrupted his thoughts. Alistar looked around for the source, startled. After a moment, he identified it as the speaking stone affixed to the corner of his desk, which connected to the front desk in the lobby. He activated it.

"De'seneth here."

"Senior Engineer De'seneth, this is Assistant Goldleaf," the front desk sprite said. "His Highness Prince Pietro just arrived at the Silverline offices and headed upstairs. He declined to state the reason for his visit, as is his right, of course. I'm contacting Lady Syri now, but if you are able, I would greatly appreciate it if you could ensure Prince Pietro has whatever assistance and guidance he needs until Lady Syri arrives."

He didn't swear into the speaking stone. Alistar drew a slow, deep breath, unclenched his fists, and answered. "Assistant Goldleaf, I would be *pleased* to make sure Prince Pietro has all the guidance he requires."

"Thank you, Senior Engineer."

I can't strangle him. He's the king's son. Alistar closed and locked his office behind him and set out in search of the wayward prince.

Fortunately, Prince Pietro hadn't gotten far in the brief time it took Assistant Goldleaf to contact Alistar. The prince had come up the stairs and passed the desks of most of the lower ranking engineers, but stopped, looking up and down a hall and seeming to debate which way to go. The bodyguard trailing after him saw Alistar first and cast him an apologetic nod of greeting. He wasn't the same Royal Guard who had accompanied Pietro on his previous visit.

"Your Highness, what brings you to Silverline on this day of devotions?" Alistar asked, striding to the pair.

Pietro started, recovered, and tried to regather his scattered dignity. "That's no concern of yours."

"As senior engineer present, I must beg to differ, Your Highness," Alistar said politely but firmly. "Many areas of this floor are restricted access for safety. I wouldn't wish you to accidentally enter somewhere that would put you at risk."

Pietro stiffened. "Are you *threatening* me?"

Alistar adopted a slightly insulted stance and tone. "Certainly not, Your Highness! I am reminding you, as you undoubtedly know, that we work with high concentrations of mahiy energy that can be very volatile if handled improperly." He addressed his words to the prince, but his gaze was on the bodyguard. The guard shifted uneasily.

"Your Highness, I think we should listen to him."

Pietro cast his guard an annoyed look but conceded. "Very well. I've come to see the experiments in progress that the technicians are working on."

"I don't believe any are being worked on today," Alistar began.

"That doesn't matter. Where are these experiments conducted?"

"Are there some of particular interest to you?" Alistar asked. "Depending on the field of study, they can be conducted in many different areas."

"Are you being intentionally difficult, or are you just slow?" Prince Pietro snapped. "Obviously I'm interested in my cousin's work, as it's clearly the most important. Why should I care what useless drabble others play with?"

The bodyguard winced and mouthed, "My apologies, sir," at

Alistar. Alistar wondered how the guard had suffered the misfortune of serving Pietro. He clearly wasn't accustomed to the prince's brusque, dismissive manner.

"How familiar are you with Lady Syri's work?" Alistar asked Pietro. *What are you after, and do you KNOW what you're asking about?*

Pietro waved a hand, dismissing the question. "I know enough. Take me there."

He considered refusing, but if he did, Pietro seemed liable to roam about on his own and potentially get somewhere he really shouldn't be. Alistar led the way down a hall toward the laboratories.

"I saw you before, didn't I?" Pietro asked. "Yesterday, wasn't it?"

"I believe so, Your Highness."

"I didn't catch your name then."

Alistar looked back to the prince. "Senior Engineer De'seneth, Fifth Class."

The prince's brow pinched. "De'seneth. I've heard that name before. Didn't you have something to do with that business with that uprising of the Successors a while back?"

"I had a part in preventing it, yes," Alistar agreed.

"There were some Silverline people involved in the uprising, as I recall."

"In the uprising?" Alistar asked. "Not to my knowledge. Unless you're referring to the employee who was blackmailed, then later murdered, by those who instigated the unrest."

Pietro paused as if he hadn't expected to be contradicted. "Perhaps I misremembered," he allowed finally.

"I'm sure." Alistar didn't say more, letting the silence hang as they walked.

Pietro broke it again. "Syri was working with an artifact recovered from that incident."

"Lady Syri is involved in many projects," Alistar said as they entered the hub of the laboratories. Halls branched off into the six wings. *What do you know about the crystal? What's your interest in it?*

"I'm not interested in what else she was working on. I'm interested in that. Take me there."

Alistar glanced to the directory and shook his head. "Your Highness, I'm afraid that particular lab is marked as a secure workspace. Only authorized personnel can enter."

"Senior engineer, I *order* you to take me into this laboratory."

"Only Prince Cero has the authority to override the restrictions of a secure workspace, Prince Pietro. Unless he has already granted you a key to enter that laboratory, you won't be able to enter. The only other way would be for Lady Syri to escort you." That was mostly true, omitting that Alistar also held a key and could, under dire need, serve as a substitute escort.

The prince's jaw clenched and his face flushed purple. "This is outrageous! You have no right, *senior engineer*, to deny me access to anywhere, *anywhere* in Lewarden!"

Alistar stood unmoved by the prince's anger. "Be that as it may, Your Highness, I also can't grant you access to a location that is inaccessible to me."

"Then why am I even talking to you?" Pietro snapped. "Get me someone who *can* give me access!"

"If you'd come on a day other than the day of devotion, that might be possible. Today, I'm afraid only Lady Syri might be able to grant you entry," Alistar said. *I hope she's on her way. I also hope Assistant Goldleaf is monitoring this conversation.* He wasn't completely sure the administrative sprites could monitor the entire complex, but they seemed constantly aware of everything going on within the Silverline Power headquarters at all times.

Pietro fumed, glaring at Alistar. "I know that crystal is in this building. I don't need *permission* from you, or Syri, or anyone else to find it."

Blood and sand! "To what end?" Alistar countered.

"No business of yours." Pietro's narrowed eyes never left Alistar.

"It's certainly business of *mine*, Pietro." Lady Syri entered, not from the hall Alistar and the prince had taken, but from one of the passages to the labs. A contingent of ten Royal Guards followed her. Though all the guards were armed and armored, they moved with almost no sound.

Pietro's mouth drew into a thin line. "Shouldn't you still be at devotions, cousin?"

"Shouldn't you?" she retorted. "Now I know you don't know the first thing about my work or what the artifact does. So, what exactly do you expect to do with it? Give it to your lover as a gift?"

"Don't be absurd!" Pietro floundered to reclaim control of the conversation. "If I had a lover, I would certainly give her a better gift than that."

"Good. Then unless you can give me a good reason to let you into the lab, you have no business here. Leave." Syri motioned to a trio of her guards, who strode up to the prince. "I see you seem to have misplaced your usual Royal Guard, cousin. In light of the recent attack on my father, I *must* insist you allow some of mine to see you safely home."

Pietro glowered first at her, then at Alistar. "You can't even begin to understand what you're toying with, Syri. You'll regret this."

Lady Syri said nothing until the sound of his footsteps faded from hearing. "Thank you for your help, Senior Engineer De'seneth. I came as quickly as we could."

"I'm glad you arrived when you did. I wasn't certain how much longer I could delay him." Alistar looked in the direction the prince had gone, then back to her. "Do you know how he knew about the crystal? He was aware that I recovered it from the Successors during Cemar's attempted coup."

"There was talk about it in the palace in the aftermath of that incident. I'm less certain how he knew it was here or that I've been working with it. And I have no wasting idea what he wants with it."

"Have you seen any new surges or other phenomenon from it?"

She nodded. "They're occurring more frequently now. I'm not sure the crystal should remain here at all. We discussed conducting some experiments with the flower at your manor. I think this an opportune time to do so. After that, I intend to move the flower to a secure location where any phenomenon or fluctuations are unlikely to cause harm to anyone."

"I have another engagement this evening, so I hope you weren't thinking of conducting those experiments today." In theory, he *could* miss devotions again, but he had promised Saskia, and he desperately missed the time of worship and community.

"Not today, no. I need to consult with my father first, and at this point, it can be a challenge to catch him when he is awake and alert. The healers are forcing him to sleep so he actually gets the rest he needs to heal. I hope to be ready by tomorrow, though."

Alistar nodded. "I can be ready tomorrow."

"All right. I realize that babysitting Pietro took you away from the work you actually came to do today, so I'll let you return to it."

"It was a worthwhile interruption." Alistar bowed and started out of the room. He stopped and looked back to her. "Does Prince Pietro have a lover?"

"He might. Some evidence points that way, but he denies it." Syri shrugged. "Why?"

"This is unofficial and not to be shared," he cautioned. It felt odd making such a statement to his superior both within Silverline Power and outside it. "I've received an unconfirmed report that Lady Sunward is pregnant."

Lady Syri stiffened. "She is... You've not confirmed this, though? No, of course not, you just said as much. Are you suggesting Pietro is involved with her?"

"I'm not making any accusations, Lady Syri, only looking at the possibilities. If he does have connection to her, it could explain his interest in and knowledge of the crystal."

Syri turned to her guards. "Find out. If Pietro has a lover, find out who, where, for how long, everything."

Alistar bowed and retreated back to his office, though the Exhibition and his complaints about the ever-shifting plans felt petty in comparison now.

We knew someone high in the nobility was involved, but could it really be that far up? Did Sunward somehow get her claws into a prince?

CHAPTER 28

Noontime sun flooded Rykka's room. She groaned, pulled the pillows over her head, and tried to find sleep again. When it didn't comply, she muttered several choice curses and resigned herself to waking.

When she came downstairs, dressed and almost ready to face a new day, the manor was relatively quiet. Rykka helped herself to the platter of meat and cheese in the kitchen. A little mental calculation confirmed this was a day of devotion, and most of the staff was probably attending a service or taking advantage of the chance to rest and handle personal errands.

She was nursing a cup of tea when footsteps announced someone else coming into the kitchen. She looked over her shoulder, expecting another member of the staff. Instead, she saw Alistar. He nodded to her and assembled his own lunch. Not until he finally sat down did he say anything.

"I hope you got enough rest, Darkwood."

"Enough to get through the day, as long as it doesn't run aground on shoals like yesterday," she said. Taking in his attire, she added, "You went to work?"

"Lots to do," he answered. "And just as well that I did. I had to handle a particularly entitled visitor." He spread jam on a thick slice of bread. "Would you recognize Sunward's lover if you saw him?"

"I doubt it," she admitted. "I haven't seen the fellow. If I heard him, I might be able to identify him. Seva might be able to pick him out; I don't know how good he is at that sort of thing. Why? Planning to line up noblemen so a couple street rats can try to pick out one of interest?"

"Not exactly, but I want you to keep your ears open."

She eyed him. "Do you know something new?"

"I don't know anything for certain. This isn't even a solid suspicion yet and I'm not ready to share it yet." He set his plate on the counter. "I'm going to services with Saskia tonight. You're welcome to attend if you want."

"I… thanks. I'd like to." She shouldn't have been so surprised, but it still caught her off guard when Rillwater natives both remembered and respected her devotion to the human gods rather than the elven ones. She'd experienced it on the *Conquest* as well; neither the human nor the elven sailors had expressed the disdain at her faith that she was accustomed to.

"Your brother can come as well, if he wants."

"I don't know if he would. I'll have to ask." And even if Tiyron decided it was time to reassess his tenuous relationship with the divine, Rykka wasn't so sure he'd be willing to attend a service with Alistar and Saskia.

"I'm heading to the clinic for the afternoon. Let me know when you're ready, unless you prefer to travel alone."

She gulped down the rest of her tea. "I'm ready."

It felt like forever since she'd last walked into the Coiled Dragon Clinic. She was almost surprised to see it unchanged since the previous visit.

She found Tiyron in his room, seated in a wheeled chair. He wore fewer bandages than last time and sat straight. His gaze snapped to the door when she opened it, and he only untensed a little when she entered.

"Rykka. Haven't seen you in a while." He touched a crystal on the armrest, and the chair turned to face him toward her.

"Been busy," she said. She hated feeling like she had to justify everything she did or didn't do.

"Well lucky me, so glad you could find a bit of spare time in your packed schedule."

Rykka fixed a cool gaze on him and said nothing.

The silence stretched until Tiyron finally rolled his eye and said, "I don't know what you think I'm responsible for, Rykka, but in case you hadn't noticed, I'm stuck here, in this stupid clinic with these human doctors, and I can't even begin to guess what you're mad about now."

"You never told me about Larisa."

He blinked. "Human girl, infatuated with Cemar, what about her? She was one of Cemar's lackeys. Should I have told you about every one of them? She hung off every word Cemar said like they came from the mouths of the gods."

"It wasn't an infatuation with *Cemar* I saw when she mistook me for you yesterday," Rykka snapped. *So typical. Dismissing her, dismissing me.* "Didn't she mean anything to you, Tiyron? Or was she just another tool?"

Tiyron stilled. His eye moved to her face. "You saw her? Where? What did she say?"

"She tried to tell me how glad she was to see you, that you weren't dead. I told her it was rather late to be expressing that *after* she betrayed you."

He braced against the arms of the chair, trying to stand. "Cemar betrayed me. Larisa had nothing to do with it!"

"She was Cemar's lapdog before and after he tortured and nearly murdered you, Tiyron. She might have had the excuse of ignorance for a while, but she was there when I first confronted Cemar. She heard everything—not just what I said, but what Cemar said in return. She knew what he did, and she still clung to her loyalty to him. And now that he's dead, she's become Sunward's lapdog instead."

"What? You saw her *with* Sunward?" He fell back into the chair. "Why would she stay?"

"Why would she leave the person who supplies her with drugs?" Rykka countered. "It was Ambrosia before, now it's Lumination. Sunward's using her to find other internal channelers from the Lower City."

"Hematic perdition. She said she wanted to stop. And I don't understand this 'internal channeler' crap. What's that even supposed to mean?"

"It means they don't draw power from the mahiy lines. There's some sort of internal source they can draw from. The sorts of things they can do seem distinct from what channelers do, and how they interact with that power is completely different from what I do when I channel. Did Larisa tell you anything about it?"

"She talked about rituals and awakenings, but most of it sounded like drug-induced hallucinations. She said they scared her sometimes, and claimed she wanted to get away from the drugs." He ran a trembling hand through his hair.

"Tiyron, why did you never tell me about Larisa?" Her voice was quiet.

He didn't look at her. "She may have read into my words, but I never made promises to her. I certainly didn't bed her, if *that's* what you're asking. She was a child. Barely seventeen at the most! I know she thought there was more between us than I was willing to give her, but I let her believe it. I didn't think you'd approve, and I didn't think you would run into her anywhere where she would expect you to acknowledge her." He twisted a fraying thread from his shirt around his fingers. "You said

Sunward is using her to find others with this... internal magic, whatever that is. How?"

He cares about Larisa. She means something to him. Blight it, Tiyron, you should have told me! "She helps recruit and identify them." She gave him a quick summary of the recruitment and Larisa's role in it. Tiyron listened, expression growing darker and harder. She almost glossed over the automatons attacking her, but he interrupted, demanding full details.

Once she'd described the attack and her escape, he said, "We broke into a lot of places that used automatons as sentries and guards, but even those that tried to stop us never tried to kill us."

"They shouldn't be able to. Any automaton built in Calarand or imported legally has to be restricted from killing. Even killing street rats. After I learned that, I checked a few schematics I had access to, and confirmed it. Their power supply automatically shuts off if they attempt to use lethal force."

"But these didn't stop," Tiyron said.

"Yeah. They kept right on attacking me."

"And you were injured." He looked her over carefully.

"I got out and caught a taxi to Lamorage's place. He patched me up." The concern in his eye reminded her that no matter how they might butt heads right now, Tiyron still worried about her.

He nodded slowly. "That's all you know about Larisa?"

"No. I went back to the factory, with backup. Lady Ravencrest owns the place, and she's got people building those automatons there."

His brow furrowed. "You said automatons built in this country have that... safeguard."

"It looks like she's importing all the parts, smuggling them into the country. She's on a deadline, too, and not everything arrived." A tight smile found her mouth. "Some of their smugglers got careless on the open seas."

Tiyron's eyebrows rose, then he frowned at her. "You mean Rillwater caught them."

"I'm crew on one of the ships that caught them. I *found* the cache of smuggled goods. Those components are safely in the keeping of the Admiral. Unless they planned for a lot of spare parts, Ravencrest will have trouble hitting her quota without cutting corners. Potentially a lot of corners."

"And Larisa?"

"I overheard Sunward and Ravencrest. Ravencrest was complaining about how the last group that arrived wasn't suitable as workers in the factory, which Sunward dismissed as not her problem." She saw his frown, but he exercised more patience than usual and waited for her to explain how this connected to his question. "We found the basement. In one of the rooms, we discovered an incomplete automaton in chains—for some reason active and restrained rather than disabled and salvaged for parts." The images of the machine still bothered her. Its chained arms reaching for them, but she wondered whether it sought to attack, or if it was reaching out in a plea for help.

Tiyron looked confused at that description but nodded for her to continue.

"The recruits were held in another room down there. I heard Larisa in there, telling everyone they were here for a great purpose. I caught her alone later, without my companions. She thought I was your ghost."

"My ghost? The first time, you made it sound like she thought I was alive."

"She did, the first time. Then she told Sunward she'd seen you, and Sunward told her that she had to be hallucinating from the drugs. And Larisa believed Sunward over her own eyes and ears. So, I had to be your ghost, haunting her."

"What did you say, Rykka?" Tiyron leaned forward in the chair, eye intent.

"I questioned what she was doing. She claimed she owes Sunward her devotion for what she and Cemar saved Larisa from. I'm guessing you know what that means?"

He winced and nodded slightly. "I know."

"She spoke of the things she isn't able to do for Sunward and the plan, whatever it is, then said she can only give Sunward 'what her work requires.' When I pressed as to what was required, she said... 'Everything.'" She tried to say that word the way Larisa said it, with an unbearable weight of pain, despair, and loss.

"Everything... But if you give everything, what's left?" Tiyron whispered.

"She ran off when she said it, and I couldn't follow her safely."

"We have to find her." Tiyron touched the crystal and the chair rolled forward. "If I can talk to her, I can convince her... Rykka, if she says Sunward's plan requires her to give everything, she means *everything*. Especially if she said it... like you just did." He let out a breath. "Blight. Where is she?" The question was almost a plea.

"I've only seen her in Sunward's company or close by her. I'm sorry."

"Then we have to stop Sunward before this plan goes into action." He braced against the arms of the chair again and forced himself to his feet.

Rykka grabbed him. He steadied himself against her, sucking in deep breaths. "I have to get stronger. Can't keep sitting around."

She braced him. This was the time to ask. The time to convince him that he needed the alliances she'd made. "Tiyron, are you willing to work with us to stop Sunward? With De'seneth and his people? Even with agents of the Crown?"

He tensed and drew another long breath. "If… if we must, I will. But only for this, nothing more."

"And are you willing to help us figure out how to access Cemar's hidden passages in the basement of the manor he used?"

He cocked his head slightly at her. "You have access to it?"

She laughed softly. "Oh yes. Yes, we have access to it. It belongs to the De'seneths. We have all the access we need."

"I know my way around it. I'll… help." He glanced around the room. "You'll have to get me there, of course."

She nodded. "I'll make it happen."

He rested his head on her shoulder. "She doesn't deserve this, Rykka. Larisa doesn't deserve any of this. Not after everything she's suffered—the men her parents sold her to, then Cemar, Sunward. She deserves to be happy. Blight, it's enough to make me ask your gods for help."

"I'm going to devotions tonight. You can come if you want," she offered. Tiyron had never been particularly faithful, but perhaps the Reyker could give him guidance she couldn't.

He raised his head and finally nodded. "Better the Reyker than the sadistic taskmasters we're 'supposed' to bow to. Couldn't hurt. Maybe they'll even listen, for once."

"They listened enough to help me bring you back," Rykka told him. "Maybe they'll be willing to listen again."

The ride to Night's Eve Sanctuary was only moderately awkward. Tiyron glowered periodically at Alistar and Saskia but didn't say anything beyond what he had to. Passive hostility the best Rykka could ask of him, and it was an improvement over aggressive hostility.

The carriage navigated the busy midcity streets and entered the courtyard. While the sharp angles and looming architecture of elven houses of worship reflected the strict, unyielding nature of the Tenets and the Path, the human sanctuary was softer, offering welcome. Even though Night's Eve stood at least four stories tall, it didn't dominate the surroundings or demand fealty.

Rykka helped Tiyron out of the carriage and into his chair as Alistar and Saskia made their way inside. Even though she trusted they would welcome the elves, Rykka didn't want to draw more attention than necessary. She and Tiyron drew some curious looks from the human worshipers. For a moment she drew herself up taller, ready to argue their right to enter to anyone who challenged them.

No one did, though. They entered the sanctuary and received the same warm greeting as every other worshiper. Rykka had been in Night's Eve Sanctuary twice before—once when she attended devotions with Alistar, and once when she attended his wedding. She made her way to the benches at the back of the sanctuary. Elven followers of the human pantheon were uncommon and tended to try not to attract undue attention.

The elves already there shifted and made room for her and Tiyron. The closest to them, an older man, said, "Don't think I've seen you here before."

"I'm recently returned to Lewarden," Rykka answered. "And my brother's been unable attend until recently."

"Ah? Well, I've been attending devotions here for near on thirty years, if you have any questions."

Rykka held back a wry smile. Devotions on the *Conquest* hadn't carried the same posturing, but there, no one needed to impress anyone else with the length of their faith. "We were introduced to the Reyker as youths by a human street evangelist in a part of the city not nearly as nice as this."

"A street evangelist?" The older man's eyebrows rose. "Haven't heard of many of them, even in the lower districts."

Tiyron snorted. "For good reason. The guards might have been useless at catching thieves or enforcing the law, but gods forbid that someone suggest that we might not be forever locked into the roles of our birth. The guards wouldn't tolerate *that*. It might give us *ideas*."

The older elf grimaced. "Ran him out, did they?"

"Something like that." Rykka didn't know whether the human who'd preached near her parents' home had survived the beating the guards had dealt him. "They thought they were teaching us to hold to our parents' faith. The lesson I learned was that this was something they wanted to hide from us. And I wanted to know what they were afraid of us finding."

And that's a lesson I've never forgotten.

CHAPTER 29

After devotions, Alistar and Saskia made their way back to the carriage. Rykka and Tiyron waited for them in the vehicle.

Tiyron had spoken little since they picked him up at the clinic. He looked out the carriage window as they rode toward the manor. "How did *you* end up with Cemar's hideout?"

"It was part of my reward for stopping Cemar and Sok'lof. Additionally, a point that's become relevant in recent weeks, the Crown pays all the taxes on the estate."

Tiyron raised an eyebrow. "Well, *that* certainly sounds convenient, though I don't know why it would matter more now than it has before."

"It matters more now because someone, possibly someone connected with Sunward, attempted to oust me from the place by means of the same tactic they used on the original owners: a claim of unpaid and improperly paid taxes."

He saw Tiyron's interest piqued in spite of the elf's projected boredom. "Never heard about previous owners."

"They also owned the factories that Ravencrest obtained during the bankruptcy," Alistar added.

Tiyron frowned. "How... convenient."

When they reached the manor, Saskia took charge of Tiyron and the necessary arrangements for his room and care. Alistar headed for the stairs. Dorne intercepted him on the first step and handed him a sealed missive of heavy parchment.

"This arrived for you while you were out, sir."

Blood and sand, what now? "Thank you." Alistar turned it over in his hands, examining the seal. His breath caught in his throat.

An upraised sword wreathed in flame. The royal family's crest, and it's not the Silver Prince's variant.

He hurried to his study, broke the seal, and unfolded the parchment. The sheet alone cost more than a laborer earned in five days' work. An elegant script that could only be achieved by a scribe of the royal court proclaimed, "Senior Engineer Lord Alistar De'seneth, your presence is required by His Royal Highness Crown Prince Filipp Feyblade, Lord of Paran, regarding critical updates to His Royal Highness's Grand Exhibition. His Royal Highness will expect you at the ninth hour of the morning of the seventh day of the fourth month within his chambers in the royal palace."

Alistar read it twice. "Tomorrow. Crown Prince Filipp expects me to drop everything and show up at the palace tomorrow." He combed his fingers through his beard. "Blackened shoals, Lady Syri was hoping to begin experiments here tomorrow." For a moment, he considered, then as quickly rejected, the option of Lady Syri conducting her experiments without him and Rykka assisting instead. "Blight." He opened the study door and leaned out into the hall. "Dorne, I need a runner to take a message to Lady Syri."

After the missive was on its way, Alistar leaned back in his chair with a heavy sigh. *Pietro today, Filipp tomorrow. What happens next week? A personal summons from King Suelton?*

He picked up a gear he'd been using as a paperweight, turning it over in his hand as he thought. After a moment, he found his father's speaking stone and activated it.

Several minutes passed before the soft blue pulse of the stone became a steady emerald glow. His father's deep voice spoke from the stone. "Ah, Alistar. Good to hear from you. All is well?"

"I'm well enough. And you?" he asked, offering the familiar coded phrases.

"Pretty well. Your mother was preparing to retire for the evening, but she's still about."

"Good. I'd like to catch you both up on things here."

A few sounds of movement and a muffled voice drifted from the stone before Alistar heard his mother speak. "I'm here, Alistar. What news? Have you had any luck determining the purpose of those bits and pieces we collected from the smugglers?"

"Evidence points toward them being components intended for use in the construction of contraband automatons." Alistar briefly outlined their findings, especially those of the last few days. "Ravencrest is working under a strict deadline, and our acquisition of those crates jeopardizes that goal."

"Automatons built to kill," his mother said quietly. "You know, we have tales of such things. Old, old tales from Heiset."

Alistar drew a sharp breath. Little was known of the homeland that the humans had fled generations ago. The people who had reached Calarand through a series of portals had retained no precise memories of Heiset except the name of the land and the knowledge that they fled from terrible disaster. Some stories remained, though, inscribed in the books and relics the refugees brought with them. But Alistar couldn't remember any that spoke of automatons. "We do? I don't recall any such tales."

"I might not have told them to you or your siblings. By the time you were old enough for such grim legends, you'd outgrown an interest in bedtime stories. My parents have the original books tucked away somewhere."

"Could you find them and send me a copy?" Alistar asked. "I don't know if they'll have any connection to this, but if they do, or if they inspired someone in Lewarden to pursue the idea, it might help."

"Of course."

"I'll be checking in on Roddek later. Anything you want passed on to him?" Father asked

"Tell him to be careful."

His parents both chuckled. "We will. And he'll listen about as well as he always does. That's why backup is en route."

Alistar smiled, not without misgivings. "All right. Good night. I have to prepare for tomorrow. Apparently, I've been summoned by Crown Prince Filipp to discuss the Exhibition personally."

CHAPTER 30

Alistar arrived at Silverline Power shortly after seven in the morning, long before most engineers came in. He wore one of the tailored suits he'd commissioned for the Silver Prince's Winter Ball, sea blue and oak brown in the De'seneth family colors.

He wasn't the first person to arrive for the morning. In addition to Assistant Tempest, Lady Syri and her Royal Guards waited in the lobby. Most of them were only passingly familiar faces to Alistar, but one of the Guards caught his eye, and Alistar smiled. The elven woman was several inches taller than him with short-cropped brown hair and a stern expression that softened slightly when she met his gaze.

"Lady Syri, good morning." Alistar bowed.

"Good morning, Lord De'seneth. Thank you for arriving so early."

"Of course." Alistar also nodded to the guard. "Star, it's a pleasure to see you again." He'd worked with her brother Dahr more than with Star during his investigation and its eventual revelation of Cemar, but Star had shown herself as strong and reliable as her brother, and she carried on Dahr's legacy.

"Always good to see you well, Lord De'seneth," Star responded.

"I'm sending Star with you to the palace. Given all the uncertainties and the attacks that have taken place, you should have a guard," Lady Syri said.

"I admit the royal palace isn't the first place I would expect to be in danger of physical attack. I appreciate the escort," Alistar said.

Lady Syri motioned for him to follow her upstairs. "Let's go to your office."

Once inside, she said, "I don't know the full details of what's been going on with the Exhibition. Do you know why Filipp wants to talk to you?"

"Not for sure, but if I had to guess, he's hoping Prince Cero's injuries and convalescence will give him an opportunity to force through the changes he wants. Changes that, quite frankly, we don't have the infrastructure to support while maintaining power to the rest of Lewarden. In Prince Cero's absence, are you designated as his backup in matters regarding the Exhibition?"

Lady Syri shook her head. "One of the first instructions he gave when he was awake and lucid is that all such approvals remain under him, not to be delegated to anyone else."

"That's reassuring," Alistar said. Not that he didn't think Syri fully capable of rejecting changes to the Exhibition's requirements, but if Prince Filipp gave her as little respect as Prince Pietro, she could face immense pressure to bend to the demands.

"You were told to be there by nine, correct? You should arrive at the palace gates by eight. That should give you enough time, with Star's help, to navigate through whatever security steps you need to go through."

Alistar checked his pocket watch and nodded. "It'll take me only a few minutes to collect the copies of the documents I want to bring in case I need to explain why Prince Filipp's expectations are not realistic. Hopefully, I won't have to."

"You probably will," Lady Syri said. "Once Filipp gets an idea stuck in his head, he doesn't release it easily. His wife, Naiya, was good at tempering him, but since her murder, he's fallen back to his old habits. Lean on my father's authority if he won't listen to reason."

"I will." It didn't reassure him about the meeting he was about to have, and Alistar was all the more glad to know he had Star guarding him.

Marble walls set with abstract murals ringed the Feyblade Palace. Spires soared above the walls, reaching toward the sky. Periodically, sections of intricate iron latticework interrupted the marble, allowing a view of the palace proper. Emerald-capped arches topped doors and window frames. White columns ran up the walls, framing the multitudes of windows. Topiary shaped like animals large and small posed around the grounds, as if a menagerie roamed freely about the palace.

Alistar's carriage stopped at the front gates. Alistar presented Crown Prince Filipp's missive as proof of his invitation. The guards took their time about verifying it. After a quarter of an hour, Alistar turned to Star.

"Lady Syri wasn't exaggerating about the time I would need to enter the palace."

"If they dally more than another minute, I'll have words with them," she replied. "They've had more than enough time to confirm its validity, and this begins to feel more like an intentional delay."

"You think someone doesn't want me to meet with Prince Filipp?"

"Perhaps. Or perhaps the order to delay you came from the

prince himself, so he can berate you for arriving late, putting you at a greater disadvantage."

"I'd hope His Highness wouldn't employ such a petty tactic. I'd expect that more from his brother."

"I regret to say that Prince Pietro did learn from somewhere," Star said. She opened the carriage door and stepped out.

Alistar heard her speaking to someone, but he couldn't pick out the words, only her firmly pointed tone. A moment passed. Star climbed back into the carriage. The gates opened, and the carriage continued onto the palace grounds.

He looked to Star, one eyebrow raised in question.

"I simply reminded them that the Silver Prince would be displeased with excessive delays to a senior engineer of your status who has been called to meet with the crown prince on Silverline matters." Star settled comfortably on the seat, a satisfied smile tugging at the corners of her mouth.

"I do appreciate your timely reminder to them." Alistar glance to his pocket watch, reassuring himself that they still had a comfortable cushion.

They were met at the front door by another assembly of guards. They checked both Alistar and his document case for anything suspicious. Alistar kept a careful watch that none of his documents went missing. Once again, Star ensured the matter went smoothly and without excessive delay, and they passed through the heavy oak doors.

Alistar had entered the palace only once before, in the aftermath of Cemar's attempted coup, and that visit hadn't brought him any further than the opulent entry room. The royal crest was not only inlayed into the floor but could also be found within the patterns on vases, paintings, and statuary around the entry room.

A member of the staff greeted him with a bow. "Senior Engineer Lord De'seneth, please follow me to His Royal Highness's audience chamber."

"Thank you." Alistar and Star followed the woman through the labyrinthine halls to what Alistar presumed to be Crown Prince Filipp's wing of the palace. The audience chamber was a comfortable room with thick, plush green carpet, sky blue walls, and three ceiling-to-floor tapestries depicting scenes of the foundation of Calarand as told in *The Feyblade Ascension*. The clock on the mantle showed the time as ten minutes to nine.

That clock is set at least five minutes fast. Blight, I wish Star wasn't right about the prince employing petty games to gain an advantage over his guests.

At the staff member's invitation, Alistar settled in one of the high-backed chairs. Star remained standing at attention.

When the clock showed five minutes to nine, the door at the far end of the audience chamber opened and Crown Prince Filipp swept into the room with a flourish of his long, violet coat. Alistar rose immediately and bowed. As he straightened, he caught the slightest glint of annoyance in the prince's eyes, but he couldn't be certain it was because Prince Filipp had hoped to arrive before Alistar.

The elf stood half a foot taller than Alistar, golden brown hair drawn back in a braid. He was a few years over one hundred, but his features bore many similarities to Prince Pietro's. His voice was deeper and stronger, though. "Senior Engineer De'seneth, I assume."

"I am, Your Highness."

Prince Filipp waited a moment, as if expecting Alistar to ask why he'd been summoned. When Alistar said nothing, the prince said, "Thank you for your timely response to my message."

"I would have answered it earlier, Your Highness, but I was at devotions yesterday." Alistar made his tone politely apologetic.

"Of course. Sit, please. Hilde, refreshments."

Alistar sat again. A servant brought him tea and petite

pastries filled with jam. The tea was sweeter than he preferred, but he sipped it with a nod of thanks.

"I understand, De'seneth, that you are responsible for ensuring my Grand Exhibition has all the magic it requires to operate. Yet my most recent updates have not been implemented, and I have even heard it said that you refuse to accommodate these new requirements. Explain yourself."

"Your Highness, when I designed the initial specifications, based on the approved estimates provided by yourself and the rest of the Exhibition council, I allowed for a generous margin to accommodate changes or increases in demand. However, the changes made to date have not only consumed the entire margin I budgeted, but also required an additional twenty percent more magic. Much as it might seem, the power from the mahiy lines is not limitless, and there is little more we can add without causing other sections of Lewarden to lose access to the lines."

The prince sniffed, dismissive. "Let the Lower City manage without."

The heat of anger boiled in Alistar's gut. He drew a deep breath and spoke. "Your Highness, we cannot draw magic for the Exhibition from the Lower City. To serve the needs of the Exhibition, we would have to divert energy from the Middle City industrial zones and from the Upper City."

"And why, exactly, is *that*?" Prince Filipp demanded.

Alistar pulled a rolled document from his bag. "If I might have somewhere to lay this out?"

Prince Filipp gestured impatiently. Several servants quickly cleared a table. Alistar spread out the map of Lewarden. The mahiy line networks spread across it in intricate, colorful webs. Alistar indicated a particularly heavy cluster of blue, green, and amber.

"The Exhibition site is here, and these lines feed magic to it.

With the load as it is now, without the most recent changes you submitted, this arm of the network is at capacity, which is already a tenuous situation." He indicated the violet lines that supplied the Upper City, the palace, and the houses of the nobles. "We could divert a small amount from these lines during periods of high demand at the Exhibition with only a little impact on the rest of the network, but over an extended period, the residents of the Upper City would notice the degradation in quality." He indicated another set of blue lines around the industrial area. "These lines are also compatible, but this area is a high-demand district and the loss of quality in service would be noticeable quickly."

"Why do you ignore these?" Prince Filipp demanded, jabbing a long finger at the orange and red lines of the Lower City and the slums. His rings caught the light, casting splinters of color across the parchment. "They extend as close to the Exhibition site as the rest."

"To maintain a balance of magic across the city, Your Highness, different sections of the web of mahiy lines are powered by local generators. The strains of kurowa flowers in each site are carefully planned and bred to the Silver Prince's specifications. As a result, not all sections of the network operate on the same harmonics. The colors on this map are intended to aid an engineer in knowing what sections are and are not compatible. Introducing the red or orange into the network around the Exhibition will destabilize that entire network. Rather than having less magic than you would like, you would have no magic at all, and it would take months to correct and restabilize that section."

"Absurd," Prince Filipp scoffed.

"Your Highness, are you familiar with the Tailors' Wall?" Alistar indicated a section of the map that appeared oddly devoid of color.

"Yes…" The Prince eyed him, then the location on the map. He frowned. "The lines are black in that section."

"Yes. That area was an early test site where Prince Cero experimented with theories. Unfortunately, that is the site where he came to understand the effects of improperly harmonized mahiy lines. Though Silverline has been working to restore the lines to their proper operation for thirty years, it still remains problematic, and remains isolated from the rest of the mahiy lines." Alistar met the prince's gaze steadily. "This is why we cannot draw excess magic from the Middle City, Lower City, or the slums without developing filters we do not have time to create, test, and implement."

Prince Filipp glared at the map. "And why have you not increased the capacity of the lines that *do* safely feed the Exhibition, *Senior Engineer?*"

"Given the expected duration of the Exhibition, we are planning an additional generator to supply the site," Alistar told him. "However, it's not a fast process, nor an inexpensive one."

The prince sneered. "I'm sure it seems 'expensive' to *you.*"

"To construct and commission a medium sized generator, such as the Exhibition would require, easily ranges in cost from eight hundred to nine hundred thousand marks," Alistar told him. "And the process requires a full year under ideal circumstances."

The prince stopped, blinked, and let comprehension of those numbers work through his mind. After a long moment, he folded his arms and fixed a cool gaze on Alistar. "What, then, do you propose, Senior Engineer De'seneth?"

"I propose, Your Highness, that unless there is deep symbolic significance to having forty-two dancing automatons in the central ring of the stage, the number could remain at thirty and the spectators will be none the wiser. And if you *do* require their number to be forty-two, I propose we reduce the number of spotlights from eight to five, which will still cast more than enough light while offsetting the increased demand for the automatons."

"Forty-two dancing automatons, De'seneth. No less than that." His jaw tightened. "Very well. Reduce the spotlights to accommodate them. My daughter *will* have her dancing dolls."

Alistar's irritation softened. *This is his tribute to his murdered wife and daughter. Of course he wants everything exactly as he envisions it.*

"Which other of the recent changes are non-negotiable?"

He saw the prince on the verge of saying "All of them." Prince Filipp caught himself, drew a deep breath, and motioned to Alistar. "Follow me."

Alistar heard Star collect his map of Lewarden before she joined them. The prince strode from the audience chamber into the inner portion of his wing—the more personal, private section. Without offering an explanation to Alistar, Prince Filipp climbed a staircase, moved down the hall, and entered a room. Alistar followed and saw a child's bedroom, pristine and preserved. A room fit for a princess. A glass door led onto a balcony, and it held the only imperfection to the room—a small greasy handprint streaked across one of the lower panes. The assassins, it was said, had come in through the princess's bedroom, and she had been their first victim.

Star stepped over to the balcony door. Prince Filipp ignored her, instead picking up a musical carousel with miniature figures posed as dancers. The prince looked at the toy in silence for a long minute.

"This is my vision of the core of the Exhibition, De'seneth. I will bring Nessa's dream to life and display it to all who come. I will bring the world to my daughter, and I will show my daughter to the world. This I will not give up, and I expect you to ensure that it happens."

Alistar inclined his head in a small nod.

"Very well, Your Highness." He glanced to Star, who seemed to find something of particular interest in the balcony door. "I will endeavor to keep that in mind as I make adjustments."

"Good." Prince Filipp set the toy down abruptly. "You are dismissed."

CHAPTER 31

Alistar looked out the carriage window, thoughts wandering in all directions as he considered how to fit Prince Filipp's vision of the central stage of the Exhibition within the constraints of the mahiy lines. Across from him, Star scribbled notes on a pad.

"Did you take note of the balcony doors, sir?" she asked.

Alistar turned to her, frowning. "What about them?"

"They are woven with an enchantment that prevents anyone but a handful of select individuals from unlocking them."

"I assume that would be the bare minimum protection on entry points into the royal palace," he said.

"It is," she agreed. "And that protection remains intact. If the assassins had interrupted it or otherwise disabled it, temporarily or permanently, the enchantment would have shown signs of the tampering, for those who know how to detect such things."

"The assassins... I'm sorry, my mind was on the Exhibition. You were looking for something regarding the assassination attempt on Prince Filipp?"

"Yes. In the wake of the attempt on Prince Cero, Lady Syri

has assigned some of us to look into certain details regarding the attack on Prince Filipp and his family. However, as the subject is understandably sensitive, we must be circumspect about our efforts. This was the first time I've had any access to Princess Nessa's room."

"Does Lady Syri doubt the work of the investigators who originally looked for the breach in the palace's defenses?" Alistar asked.

"She found the report's conclusions to be unsatisfactory in addressing her questions. And having confirmed that the enchantments are still whole and undisturbed, I share her concerns."

"Are you sure the enchantments weren't repaired or recreated after the attack?" he asked.

Star nodded firmly. "That too leaves traces. The balcony door was unlocked by someone with the permission and access to do so." And the list of people with that access was certain to be very short.

"Could the princess herself have done so, intentionally or accidentally?"

"Only if her life was already in danger. A child her age would not be trusted to use such access wisely."

"But you believe someone unlocked the door, allowing the assassins an entry point. And that those who conducted the first inspection missed this?" Alistar cocked his head at her.

"The report was written to imply that the assassins forced entry, but vague enough to not state so outright," Star said.

Alistar frowned. "Would they have concealed that from Prince Filipp?"

"It's possible. Doing so would be difficult, but a skilled wordsmith could convince a grieving man to accept that the blame lies entirely on an outside power rather than someone closer and more accessible. If the investigators believed the breach was entirely accidental, with no malicious intent, they may have chosen that route."

"Or if there were other political considerations in play?" Alistar asked.

"There are always other political considerations in play, sir," Star said. "Was your meeting with Prince Filipp useful?"

"It was. And hopefully it was useful to him as well. I understand his desire to honor his family, but some of the things he wants are simply not possible." He watched Star. "This investigation you're working on—do you suspect someone particular? Do you think it *was* a careless mistake?"

"I believe the balcony door was unlocked intentionally and for the purpose of allowing the assassins an entry point. I have several potential suspects but must confirm more before I am willing to put names to them."

Who would have the most to gain from the deaths of Prince Filipp and his family? Prince Pietro, though what I've seen so far of his attempts to scheme and claim power don't do much to convince me that he could enact such a plot. Who else? Guards whose loyalty lie somewhere other than the Crown, perhaps. But anyone with access to the crown prince's personal residence ought to be above corruption. On the other hand, the far reach of Cemar's schemes is evidence that just because someone seems like they should be above corruption doesn't mean they really are. He had people not only in Silverline, but even in the Royal Guard.

The carriage brought them back to Silverline Power shortly before eleven in the morning. Assistant Tempest called Alistar over as he crossed the lobby.

"Lady Syri wants to see you once you're settled. She should be free now, but she has meetings for the majority of the afternoon."

"Thank you." Alistar headed upstairs. He stopped by his office long enough to drop off the documents he'd brought, then he made his way to Prince Cero's office.

The guards admitted him immediately. Lady Syri sat at her father's desk, paperwork spread out before her. She looked up with obvious relief when he entered. "Senior Engineer De'seneth, thank you for coming."

"Of course. Is there a problem?"

"Other than wondering how my father tolerates the ridiculous amount of inane questions and mind-numbing legal babble in every document crossing his desk, no, no problems beyond those you're already familiar with. How did your meeting with Prince Filipp go?"

"I think he and I reached some level of balance," Alistar answered. He outlined the changes required and the prince's reasons behind them. "I explained why it wasn't possible to direct more power from other areas of the city to the Exhibition, and why we could not simply erect another generator overnight."

She massaged her forehead. "Do none of them listen? Prince Pietro thought he could push that sort of new construction through as well. He seemed to think it just needed someone willing to 'overrule the bureaucracy' to add another generator, rather than a delicate process of integrating a new source of mahiy lines into the existing network."

"Prince Pietro intended to create a generator for the Exhibition? Or did he think to put it somewhere else?"

"The Exhibition, as far as I understand. He's taken some interest in the planning, and Filipp has let him do a few things. Still, he wasn't able to circumvent reality enough to will a new generator into existence."

"If only an earnest belief that it's possible was, in fact, the only thing required to expand the mahiy line network," Alistar said. "Our jobs would be far easier."

Lady Syri chuckled softly. "True enough. Unfortunately, I have no free time today, but tomorrow I want to resume our experiments with the crystal, if you have no objections."

"None, unless I receive another summons I can't ignore."

"Good. Expect me at ten in the morning. Now, I need to prepare for my afternoon meetings, so I will speak with you tomorrow."

"Thank you." Alistar bowed and took his leave.

He arrived home wondering what sort of chaos to expect from Tiyron's first day in the manor. Nothing was on fire, at least—a good start. When Alistar entered the manor, he heard Rykka and Tiyron speaking, and the tone sounded conversational rather than antagonistic.

He followed the sound and found them in the sitting room. Tiyron sat in the wheeled chair, leaning forward to examine an image that Rykka projected from the capture stone onto a table. One of Rykka's ears flicked toward Alistar, acknowledging his presence as he quietly closed the door behind him, but she didn't interrupt her conversation.

"You can see the size," she told Tiyron. "Just compare it to the worker. They could practically crawl inside one. The principles of energy conversion mean a crystal that size can't contain enough energy to operate an automaton of this size. It might hold an emergency reserve, but more likely it serves as a concentrator and converter between the actual power source and the automaton."

"Hmm." Tiyron cocked his head, examining the image. "But they can't take power from the mahiy lines, or they'd have those safeguards against killing. No way around that?"

Rykka shook her head. "Calarand is the only place that makes reliable transformers to draw from the mahiy lines. Some other countries make imitations, but their quality is... well, about like the difference between a glass of wine in the

Upper City or a glass of wine in Dockside. You know which one's more likely to be watered down vinegar."

Tiyron snorted softly, amused. "Right. But that only tells us what the power source *isn't*."

"I know," Rykka sighed. One finger tapped the side of the image capture crystal as she thought, and the image projected on the table changed with each touch.

"Wait, stop. What's that?" Tiyron cut in.

Rykka looked down at the image, then looked up and turned to Alistar. "De'seneth, what is this?"

Tiyron stiffened and glanced over his shoulder, giving Alistar a scowl.

Alistar joined them. "Oh, that's a schematic of a mining suit the previous owners of this manor were working on." He frowned for a moment. "Ravencrests bought their factories and whatever prototypes the Zel'ens didn't manage to sneak out. The prototype of this suit was among those Ravencrests acquired. However, they hadn't figured out how to provide it with reliable power either. Mines don't exactly have mahiy line networks." He looked over the squat, bulky suit in the schematic again. "It doesn't resemble the images of the automatons you took."

"No, but they might have lifted some elements from it," Rykka said thoughtfully. "The Zel'ens schematic still had the problem of power. So whatever role these automatons play, that's the big question Ravencrest had to solve." She looked back to Alistar. "I want to take another look at those crates of components, if you don't mind. Now that I've seen the automatons, I hope to get a better sense of what components we actually have downstairs."

Alistar nodded, satisfied. "The crates are in the workroom. They'll be shut up tomorrow, though. Lady Syri is coming to conduct a few experiments and see if we can trigger some of the other doors in the basement to open."

"They won't do much unless you have the frost's breath crystal," Tiyron said.

"Eight jagged petals, about this large?" Alistar indicated size with his hands.

Tiyron's eye narrowed, and he nodded.

"Sok'lof was using it to convince the Successors that he was a messenger of Rechmal. I removed it from his keeping. And yes, Lady Syri will be bringing it with her tomorrow."

"Who is this lady?" Tiyron asked suspiciously.

"She's Prince Cero's daughter, acting head of Silverline Power while he recovers. She's been leading the study of the crystal. What do you know of it?"

"Not much more than you'll get from a storybook," Tiyron said. "Supposedly a lost relic of your people, once given to a mighty hero by the god of magic. Contains the pure essence of the frost's breath plant that's sacred to Rechmal. Sunward claimed it had come from her birth mother. I always assumed she stole it, and when I pressed her a little about it, she spun a tale of how it should have been left behind when the humans left their homeland, but one of her ancestors smuggled it through the portal. How firm a believer in the human myths are you, De'seneth?"

"It depends on the myths, though I'm not familiar with any that involve the crystal. I'll look into that when I have a chance. I already have one myth to study when I receive a copy of it. You might be interested in it as well, Rykka."

"Oh?" She raised an eyebrow.

"My mother mentioned it when I told her about the automatons. Seems there's a tale that includes automatons that can kill. She's going to send me a copy."

"That's terrifying, De'seneth," Rykka told him. "Do humans actually have myths, or did you collect the worst fears of other lands around and write stories about them to scare off the neighbors?"

"Hard to say now," Alistar said. "The myths are what we have left, and records show that early after our arrival in Calarand, some officials tried to wipe them out as well."

A knock on the door interrupted the conversation. Alistar opened it, and Dorne bowed. "Sir, when you have time, Lamorage wants to speak to you."

"Thank you. Is he in the lower library?"

"He is."

"Good. I'll go talk to him shortly." Alistar nodded to Rykka and Tiyron. "Excuse my interruption. I'll leave you to your discussion."

Tiyron frowned. "Lamorage is here? I thought he lived elsewhere in Lewarden."

"He does," Rykka said. "He's helping with a few things here right now."

Alistar left the sitting room, closing the door after him, and followed Dorne. They'd found the concealed latch that opened the door into the hidden study, so no longer needed a ladder to access the room. Alistar descended into the basement. Several minutes later, he reached the study.

Lamorage sat on the edge of the desk, books spread out around him on the desk and floor alike. Dust coated his clothes and brown hair, but he didn't seem concerned by it. Books lay in stacks on the floor around the bookshelves, and several shelves were bare or nearly so.

"How are things going, Lamorage?" Alistar asked.

Lamorage barely glanced up. "De'seneth, there is *so* much here. It's a treasure trove of knowledge! A lot of magic engineering theory, though some of it is rather questionable, starting from very atypical premises."

Alistar looked at the book open in his lap, noting that the woodblock images on the page didn't look much like engineering. "Anything else of interest?"

Lamorage didn't appear embarrassed to be found reading

the tome. "I've been focusing on the other texts to determine if they have any connection to the rest. The layout of this library implies that everything is where it is for a reason, and that even tomes without obvious connection are somehow related. This one is a collection of legends and myths. It's a mix of elven and human stories—quite rare, actually. Unfortunately some of the pages are missing and I haven't found them yet. Loose stitching."

Alistar smiled. "Any about magical crystal flowers or killer automatons?"

Lamorage froze, staring at Alistar. "What? How did you know? That's… why I asked to speak to you."

An uneasy chill crept down Alistar's spine. "I… intended it to be a joke. You *did* find something about one or both of those?"

"Both. But not everything. Like I said, pages are missing." Lamorage gestured at the book. "But along the margins on earlier pages of the tale, someone jotted cryptic notes." He flipped back several pages and offered the tome to Alistar.

He took it and peered at the writing along the margin, the script so small he could barely read it. Calling the words cryptic was generous—without context, he couldn't begin to guess the meaning behind "glow? Stable source."

"Do you know what the notes refer to?" he asked Lamorage.

"Not yet. I only found this book today. I hope the missing pages are on the shelf or in the desk." Lamorage smiled slightly. "For one, I want to know how the tale ends. Because of course it's the conclusion that's missing."

Alistar scanned the text to see if he recognized the story. His gaze fell on a description of a powerful wizard calling to life an army of warriors made of stone and steel, binding them to his command. Of course, the story offered no explanation for how the wizard could wield such power or what source he drew from.

"This is the third time in two days that I've encountered

mention of human legends in connection with Sunward or Cemar," Alistar said. "It's starting to feel less than entirely coincidental." His throat was dry, and he tried to conceal his unease with an attempt at humor.

Lamorage frowned. "You also mentioned a crystal flower, right?"

Alistar nodded. The crystal's existence wasn't common knowledge outside Silverline, and even within, had been restricted and confidential information. Even while still employed at Silverline, Lamorage had not had the position or rank to know about it. "Do any of the stories mention something like that?"

"It plays a role in this one. Supposedly, Rechmal first revealed himself to humans when he manifested before a great warrior and gifted him with a crystal formed like a flower with eight petals that radiated magic. And when the god of magic appeared, the first frost's breath flowers sprouted and bloomed around his feet. There were notes around that scene as well, but I couldn't make any sense of them. Still, maybe having all these mentions at once means the god of magic is trying to communicate something to you?" Lamorage shrugged. "Is that something the Reyker do?"

"They have multiple ways of communicating to mortals," Alistar said slowly. *But if Rechmal has a direct hand in all this, what does it mean? What message am I meant to understand?*

He looked at the book once more, flipping forward to the point where the story cut off, the final pages absent. Fallen out, or intentionally removed? He ran a finger down the center but didn't find any jagged scraps to hint of pages ripped out. Just an absence that left only questions.

"I don't know for certain, but this might be the story my mother referenced when I spoke with her yesterday. She's going to make a copy and send it to me. If it's the same, we can fill in some of the blanks this copy leaves."

Lamorage nodded. "This was the book that stood out the most as an oddity among the technical texts. Everything else has been magic theory and as many studies of the mahiy lines and related research as can be acquired without being a Silverline employee." He gave Alistar a thin smile. "At least I haven't come across any actual confidential documents yet. I know I wasn't the only Silverline employee they got their claws into."

Alistar looked over the piles of books, nodding slowly. "Speaking of Silverline and… potentially confidential materials, tomorrow, Lady Syri is coming to the manor to conduct some experiments, see if we can't unlock access to some more areas of Cemar's lair."

Lamorage blinked. "Lady Syri? Coming here? I suppose I would be better making myself scarce during her visit, then."

"Actually, if she doesn't object, I'd be glad to have you present. You and I both know it wasn't a lack of skill or understanding of magic that led you to resign."

Lamorage winced slightly and looked at the books on the desk. "I don't know how much help I can be. But if Lady Syri is willing to accept my attendance, and you think it will be useful, I'm willing to try."

CHAPTER 32

Rykka was returning from the kitchen, where she'd convinced the cooks to let Tiyron assist with prep work, when she nearly ran into Windshadow. She jumped back to avoid a collision as the footman stumbled and caught himself.

"Blight! Apologies, Darkwood. You were on my blind side and you walk like a skulking thief."

"Only when I'm not trying to be quiet. When I am, I make much less noise," she said.

"Oh, I'm aware. I was with you in that factory," Windshadow reminded her.

"What's the rush?"

"Do you know where Lord De'seneth is?"

"I think he's talking to Lamorage right now." She indicated the basement with a slight tilt of her head.

Windshadow let out a sigh "Hopefully he'll be done soon. It's not urgent, but important." He started walking toward the ballroom.

She walked with him. "Some new revelation?"

"Maybe. I don't know if it will be useful or not." His eye

swept the hall in search of others near, then he looked to her and made a small hand gesture.

Rykka frowned and raised an eyebrow, expression quizzical.

An expression of annoyance flashed briefly across his face. He mouthed, "It means 'can we be heard?'"

She paused a moment to straighten a wall hanging and scan the hall. "Clear. And some time, we ought to exchange signs and signals so we both know what the other means."

He sighed again but didn't dismiss the idea. "I hope you at least know the standard signals."

"Standard for who, Windshadow? The military? I was never involved. I know the signs and signals we used on the streets, but everyone develops their own private codes. In any case, no one's eavesdropping on us just yet, so, what's wrong?"

"I learned something about the architect of this manor that Lord De'seneth might find useful." He studied Rykka. "You lived on the streets of Lewarden?"

"Didn't have enough marks to bribe an orphanage into taking me in," Rykka said blandly. As a child, she'd sometimes dreamed of getting into one of the Lower City orphanages. She couldn't imagine they'd be worse than living in her parents' house as an unplanned and unwanted second child. Stories she'd later heard out of some of the orphanages were terrible, but they still sounded better than life at home had been. If Tiyron hadn't taken her with him when he ran away, she didn't know what she would have done, except that it might have resulted in patricide.

Windshadow digested that for a long moment. When he spoke, his voice was quiet and sincere. "I'm sorry."

She'd expected dismissal or scorn but didn't find any in his words. She eyed him with distrust for the apparent sympathy. "Why?"

"Several members of my squad came from Lower City

orphanages. I know some of the abuses they endured there. For that to seem like an improvement over your situation growing up, I can only imagine how terrible it must have been."

"Not a sentiment I usually encounter from those of better birth."

"We didn't have room for class distinctions in my squad. We couldn't afford it with what we were doing. And my blood is no more noble than yours."

She wanted to laugh, but Windshadow radiated sincerity, and she couldn't bring herself to mock that. "If more people shared that sentiment, Windshadow, Cemar would never have found the support to build his attempted coup."

"Perhaps not. Or perhaps he would have found different support for it."

She considered, then shook her head. "Sunward would have found different support. Cemar believed his own propaganda. Not so much that he wouldn't bend the principles when it suited him, but he convinced himself that everything he did was working toward his ideal." She hated giving the bastard any credit, but he had believed in the world he wanted to build.

They neared the ballroom. Rykka heard a murmur of voices.

"I think De'seneth and Lamorage have returned. Also, if you hadn't heard, Lady Syri is planning to come over here tomorrow."

Windshadow started. "I… had not heard. Thanks."

Alistar and Lamorage stood near one of the concealed doors in the ballroom, talking in low voices. Alistar glanced toward Rykka and Windshadow, said something to Lamorage, and excused himself. Lamorage followed his gaze, nodded in greeting, and walked toward the dining room door.

"What brings the two of you here?" Alistar asked, striding to them.

"I've been looking into some matters as you requested, sir,"

Windshadow said. "My research turned up interesting details about Lorne Ashfall, the architect of this manor."

With a wave, Alistar invited them both to follow him. He unlocked the concealed door and let them into a small study. Closing the door behind them, Alistar said, "Tell me."

"Ashfall, while not part of Cemar's innermost circles, was undeniably involved in the cabal. He wasn't arrested in the initial sweep of Cemar's followers but was caught in the following months. A number of blueprints were seized from his home, and I was able to view them. They included one that appears to be of this manor, with passages underneath far vaster than what you've found thus far. The blueprints also showed what appeared to be the flow of magic through the manor, though I wasn't able to make sense of how it worked."

"I need a copy," Alistar said immediately.

Windshadow sighed. "I could access them by virtue of my rank, sir, but they are stored among highly confidential documents. I'm not certain even Prince Cero's permission would be enough to grant you access. It might require an allowance from King Suelton or Prince Filipp for you to see them. Likewise, I wasn't permitted to make any sort of sketch or copy."

Rykka tilted her head to one side. "Why would house blueprints be *so* confidential that they require a writ from the king to see them? Especially when someone is, in fact, living in that very house?"

"All Ashfall's blueprints were secured in the vault," Windshadow said. "They had previously been held in less secure storage, but evidently were transferred into the vault at Prince Filipp's instructions. No one I asked knew the reason why."

An idea played though Rykka's thoughts. At first, she dismissed it, then she remembered that this was Windshadow, not Dahr, and that Alistar's footman might not be so rigidly rulebound as the Royal Guard.

"Can you return to the vault without raising suspicions?"

Alistar cast her a curious look, then turned his gaze back to Windshadow.

"Certainly. But I cannot bring someone else with me, nor can I bring quill or parchment to make notes."

"Do they let you take, say, a speaking stone with you?" she asked.

"They do, but the vault is shielded, and the stone would not be able to communicate with anyone outside."

Alistar started to smile, catching onto her idea.

"How willing are you to... go around rules in this sort of situation?" Rykka asked.

Windshadow's eyebrows rose. "Stealing documents from the vault would be a capital offense even for me, Darkwood."

"That's actually not where I was going with this," she said quickly. "I'm thinking of ways to stay within the letter of the law, if not the spirit."

"I'm listening."

She took the image--capture stone from her pocket. "With Lord De'seneth's permission, of course, you could use this."

Alistar nodded. "Exactly. And I should talk to the Zel'ens about creating more of them. This stone is proving its worth. Although they also need to develop a means of transferring images into another storage device, or into another medium."

Windshadow took the stone cautiously. "I saw you use this several times during our investigation of the factory, Darkwood, but I didn't know the purpose. What is it, exactly?"

"A prototype device loaned to me by the Zel'ens," Alistar answered. "When activated one way, it captures an image, and when activated another, it projects the images it's captured. If you can take it with you into the vault and capture an image of those blueprints, we might get an idea how much we have and have not discovered about this place." He held out a hand for the stone.

Windshadow handed it to him. Alistar gave a quick demonstration of how to operate it, which Windshadow watched with obvious interest.

"This device has so many possibilities," he murmured. "Think how investigators could make use of it! They could preserve images of the scene of a crime to study later, even after others have potentially contaminated the site."

"The scandal rags could start including pictures of nobles in compromising positions," Rykka added under her breath.

Alistar's soft chuckle indicated that he heard her. "There are many potential uses for it, certainly. At the moment, though, let's focus on this one. Windshadow, are you willing to attempt to capture images of the appropriate documents?"

"I am."

"If I ask how it is you have access to the vault, will you tell me?" Rykka asked.

Windshadow shrugged, smiling slightly. "I had to be granted access. Otherwise, I'd be unable to look after the things I'm responsible for putting there."

The things he... who is Windshadow? And if he has the skills that statement implies, why is he... here?

If Alistar wondered the same things, his stance didn't betray it. "It shouldn't be a problem for you to return there tomorrow, then. Be careful, though." He handed the stone to Windshadow.

"I will, sir. Is there anything else you'd like me to research while I'm there?"

Alistar shook his head. "Not unless you happen to find out who had the authority to leave Princess Nessa's balcony door unlocked on the night of the assassination."

"Access to that information has been kept restricted since the completion of the investigation," Windshadow said, pursing his lips in thought. "I'll check with Investigator Dawncloud, though. She might know or might know who to talk to."

Alistar straightened slightly, the tilt of his head expressing surprise. "If you learn anything, let me know."

Windshadow nodded, not asking why Alistar wanted to know any more than Alistar was volunteering the information. He dipped a bow and strode out of the ballroom. Rykka turned to leave as well, but Alistar spoke her name.

She turned. "Yes?"

"Would you talk with your brother tonight about whether he'd be willing to assist in matters tomorrow? I'm sure he'll be reluctant to help anyone associated with Silverline, much less the Silver Prince's daughter. Or me."

"Oh. Well. I'll try. He does like the chance to show off. Maybe a chance to show up both of you would appeal to him." It would also make Tiyron insufferable, but Alistar had plenty of practice dealing with that. Rykka herself had been insufferable plenty of times when she'd been coerced into working with Alistar the first time.

"Well, I suppose I'm asking for it," Alistar said with a wry smile. "Thanks."

Tiyron wheeled his chair around and glared at her. "You want me to do *what*?"

"Show off in front of De'seneth and the Silver Prince's daughter."

"And by show off, you really mean help them get deeper into the lair." He folded his arms.

Rykka sighed. "Unless you know a way to get around needing the crystal to open the doors, it's the only way we're going to get further in. I don't know what Cemar left there, but Sunward wants to get her hands on it. Whatever she wants, I don't want her to have it."

Tiyron's jaw tightened. "I don't know what's still down there." She saw him twisting the hem of his shirt around his fingers. She'd thought he was angry, but that was a sign of unease, even fear. "Not all Cemar's secrets need to be found."

"If you assist De'seneth, you'll have opportunity to make sure they aren't."

"You really want *me* to help the Silver Prick and his lackeys?"

Rykka closed her eyes a moment and shook her head. "No, Tiyron, I want you to help *me*."

"How does this help you? If *you* want to go poking around down there, I'll help you find a way in. But how does letting *him* down there help *you*?"

"I don't have the same knowledge or resources De'seneth does. He can do things with whatever we find there. He can get other people to do things with what we find. He can make the right people uncomfortable and uneasy, so they make stupid mistakes. He can move among the nobles like we can move though the slums, knowing who to poke, who to leave alone, and which ears to whisper in. And while he's doing that with the nobles, you and I can focus on Whitetooth, the drugs he's dealing, and find out more about the noble who supplies them to him."

"Hematic perdition. I nearly forgot about him. Did you hear that the Ravencrest noblewoman came to the clinic looking for Seva?"

"Yeah, I heard. And Lady De'seneth told her off."

"That was fun to watch, honestly. Did you know that some of Whitetooth's thugs came looking for him first?"

Rykka shook her head, a chill running down her spine. "What happened?"

"A couple heavies came in and scared the boy at the front desk, but they got run off by the local thugs. Seems Whitetooth's influence hasn't spread that far yet, even if he does post his whores on the streets around there."

"The local thugs don't deal in whores. I checked." Rykka drummed her fingers on her arm. "That seems to confirm that

Whitetooth and Ravencrest are connected. But so far, I've only heard of activity from the Lady Ravencrest. Not even sure if there *is* a Lord Ravencrest."

Tiyron raised an eyebrow. "What difference would that make?"

"Whitetooth gets his drugs from a nobleman, according to Seva." She considered, frowning. "Unlikely to be Ravencrest anyway. The family's low nobility, and the man Seva saw was high nobility."

Tiyron growled in the back of his throat. "Meaning we'll have to go through De'seneth to reach the nobleman if we don't want to swing on the gallows."

She nodded. "Depending on just *how* high in the nobility this goes, De'seneth might even need to go through the Silver Prince. Or if that's not enough, Admiral As'enel. But if this mess runs that high, we need an alliance with De'seneth for our own protection."

"Don't you already have one?" Tiyron countered.

"I do. You don't."

His jaw tightened. Fists clenched and unclenched. "Fine. I'll help De'seneth poke about Cemar's lair and avoid the traps I know about. But only for as long as necessary to untangle this scheme and end Cemar's plot, however Sunward intends to pervert it."

It was less than she'd hoped for and more than she'd expected. "Thanks, Tiyron." She turned to leave.

"Rykka."

She turned back. "Yeah?"

"After everything we fought for, why did you choose... this?" He gestured at the house around them.

"Because we were fighting the wrong battle, Tiyron. It took me losing everything to realize it. Even if we'd somehow won, the slums and the Lower City wouldn't be any better off than they were when we started. People would still freeze. Children would still starve. People like Doctor Tan'shyo and Doctor De'seneth do more for them than we ever could. Being here might mean working with the people we used to call enemies, and it might not grant us the fame and glory the Masked Thief earned, but it might actually make a difference in a few lives beyond our own."

She waited a moment, but Tiyron didn't respond. Once again, Rykka turned and left.

CHAPTER 33

When Alistar came downstairs in the morning to prepare for Lady Syri's arrival, Tiyron was waiting for him, arms folded and a scowl fixed in place. Alistar finished buttoning his suit jacket. "I would ask what I've done today to earn that look, but since I just got up, I don't think I've had time to do anything yet."

Tiyron didn't blink. "Why does she trust you?"

"Your sister?"

"Of course."

"Come with me into the sitting room," Alistar said, gesturing in that direction.

Tiyron didn't move. "Why?"

Alistar cocked his head at the elf and spoke in a low voice. "Half the servants in this house are spies for my father, who I haven't told about you. Another quarter, at least, are spies for other houses. The remainder are just trying to get by wherever and however they can. How many of them do you want listening to this conversation?"

Tiyron didn't answer, but he did guide his chair toward the sitting room. Alistar closed the door behind them and settled into a plush chair. Tiyron navigated his wheeled chair to face him, closer than protocol deemed polite.

"Rykka trusts me because I've proven to her that I'm worthy of trust," Alistar said.

Tiyron's lip curled. "Because she was useful to you when you were hunting Cemar, and because you didn't hand her over to the Silver Prince when you were done."

"For the majority of our time working together, I believed she was you, and it was only an injury she received from Cemar that revealed her to be someone else. I didn't expose her deception—it remained known only to me, Saskia, and Doctor Tan'shyo."

Tiyron looked on the verge of asking why the other two would know but reached the logical answer before the question escaped.

Alistar continued. "When she dropped the ceiling of Prince Cero's ballroom on Cemar, I couldn't be certain whether her barrier would hold against the weight of stone, but I hoped it would protect her. I reported Tiyron Onyxflame to be dead. At the time, I believed *that* to be a true statement."

Tiyron shifted uncomfortably in his chair.

"I didn't provide any statement about the existence or potential survival of Rykka Onyxflame, and I didn't attempt to find her after she sent a token indication that she lived. I felt I owed her that. She'd earned her freedom, and that was the bargain I'd made with her when I recruited her."

"You *didn't* look for her? Then why's she here now?" Tiyron demanded.

"Unbeknownst to me, she signed on with the Rillwater fleet. Ended up assigned to my younger brother's ship. When Saskia and I were last visiting, the admiral wanted my opinion on some goods recovered from some smugglers' ships. The most recent take was claimed by my brother's ship, and he brought Rykka with him to report on their findings. Things got awkward for a bit when I had to explain how I knew her and some details about her previous identity. My brother was rather furious about it all. If I hadn't spoken in Rykka's favor, she could have faced severe consequences."

"For not telling her secrets?" Tiyron asked.

"It's a bit more complex than that. Rillwater captains have expectations that if something from a crewmember's past is liable to cause an issue in one port or another, they should inform the captain rather than letting it come as a surprise later. And in Roddek's opinion, the fact that Rykka had some history with me, his older brother, fell into that category. He didn't like being surprised, especially not in front of the admiral. After discussing the matter, we decided it best to temporarily transfer Rykka to my household. Her knowledge and skills are quite useful for what I'm working on, and it gives Roddek time to cool off."

"I still don't see why she trusts you."

"She trusts that I won't hold the less legal aspects of her life against her. She trusts that I won't hand her over to the authorities. And now, she trusts that I will give a fair and honest assessment of her work to both Admiral and Captain As'enel. I trust her to help me and to want to end Sunward's plots. It's not just a matter of her trusting me, Tiyron. We trust each other. You don't have to trust me. But I hope you trust her."

He wasn't sure what answer Tiyron had wanted, or what he'd expected. The elf's face was a mask. "I'll help you find Cemar's secrets, but that's as far as I'll go, and I'm only doing this because you let the Silver Prince run off with the crystal."

"Are there any other ways you know of to open the secret passages in the basement?" Alistar asked. "I bring up the question because not long ago, we had a door open for no discernable reason, and also, the crystal itself has been radiating pulses of energy in response to an unknown source. Our theory is that Sunward is causing it to activate."

"I don't know a wasted thing about *how* it works," Tiyron snapped. "Rykka liked all the theory and formulas and whatever." He waved a dismissive hand. "I know *what* works. Figure out the how yourself." After a pause, he asked, "Were you talking when whatever it was opened?"

Alistar frowned, thinking back. "Rykka and I were talking at the time, yes. I don't recall the details. Why?"

"Could have been something you said. Cemar did love to talk about himself, and he loved to have other people talk about him too. Say his name enough times and, well," Tiyron chuckled softly, "sometimes, something happens."

"As much as that should surprise me, somehow it doesn't. We probably mentioned his name a few times. I'm not inclined, however, to wander about the basement chanting it just to see if anything happens."

Tiyron actually laughed. "Oh, but you could. The keyword is just his name, regardless of what profanities you attach to it."

"I'll keep that in mind."

Lady Syri and her entourage arrived promptly at ten in the morning. Alistar met them in the ballroom near the basement entrance. She'd brought ten guards, including Star. Five took positions around the basement entrance.

"Welcome to my home once again, Lady Syri. Do you need anything before we head downstairs?" Alistar asked.

"I don't believe so." Her gaze shifted from Alistar to a point over his shoulder, and she frowned.

Alistar didn't turn, but motioned for Lamorage, Tiyron, and Rykka to approach. "Before we begin, with your leave, I'd like to expand our available experts."

"I'm only familiar with one of them," Lady Syri said

cautiously. "I did not expect to encounter you here, Lord Lamorage."

Lamorage bowed, his gaze not meeting hers. "Lord De'seneth invited me to help him catalogue some of the books and documents he's found here, Lady Syri."

"I've heard little news of you since you left Silverline," she said. "You're still interested in engineering?"

Lamorage cleared his throat. "My departure from Silverline Power was not due to any loss of interest in engineering on my part. Rather, I was firmly encouraged to seek other pursuits when my unwilling participation in Cemar's plots became known."

Her eyes narrowed, but Alistar couldn't read her thoughts from the expression. He ached to tell her that Lamorage had been blackmailed, and how he'd both tried to warn Alistar and tried to break away from Cemar, but this was not the time for it.

After a long moment, Lady Syri asked, "Are you currently in Lord De'seneth's employ, then?"

"I am."

"Very well. As he is willing to vouch for you, I don't object. And the others?"

Rykka spoke. "Rykka, milady. Lady Saskia's maid and assistant artificer. This is my brother, Ty Darkwood."

"And your... qualifications?" Lady Syri asked dubiously.

"We hired Rykka as Merris's replacement and also to offer her expertise on the remnants and incomplete constructs and devices we've found thus far in the manor," Alistar said.

"I didn't know there had been enough to justify hiring assistance." Lady Syri turned to Tiyron.

He gazed back at her, expression cold as ice. "I'm here because I've spent more time than the rest of you combined in the areas you're trying to reach."

Several of the guards shifted, hands resting on weapons. Lady Syri's jaw tightened. "Explain yourself."

Tiyron gestured at himself, lip curling slightly. "I thought it obvious. I got on Cemar's bad side. But if you *really* want, I can start going into details about my experience."

A long, uncomfortable silence fell. Lady Syri finally broke it by turning back to Alistar.

"We shouldn't waste the time we have, Lord De'seneth. If you would?"

"Of course." Alistar opened the basement door.

Star entered first with another guard, then Lady Syri. Lamorage followed after a momentary hesitation. The guards shot each other glances when Rykka and Tiyron entered but didn't move to stop either of them.

Alistar had seen Tiyron's chair navigate stairs several times. The prototype was capable of handling most terrain while keeping the occupant comfortable and stable. Alistar followed Tiyron, and three guards brought up the rear, leaving the remainder to watch the entrance.

At the bottom of the stairs, Lady Syri watched Tiyron curiously as the chair readjusted to flat ground. "An interesting device. Is this your creation, Rykka?"

"Much as I'd love to claim it, no," Rykka answered. "An acquaintance of Doctor De'seneth provided it."

"It seems quite versatile in its design. I hope they make more." Lady Syri didn't press further.

Alistar led the way to the room with the crystals on pedestals, ghostlights springing to life before him. The four smoky crystals remained unchanged and dark in their corners. Lady Syri strode to the marble table in the center of the room and drew a locked wooden box from her satchel. Star handed her the key, and Syri withdrew the crystal flower. Looking at it now, Alistar saw more clearly than ever the resemblance to a frost's breath blossom. He also noticed that it vibrated slightly when Lady Syri set it on the table, and continued to do so after she set up a metal stand and rested the crystal in it.

Tiyron looked around the room, then at the crystal flower. "So, what door are you trying to open? The study? The laboratory? Sleeping quarters?"

"Can all the doors be open at the same time, or is there a limit, and one must be closed before another opens?" Alistar asked.

"You can only open one at a time, but you don't have to close doors behind you, no. Just don't try hitting all the crystals at the same time."

Lady Syri raised an inquisitive eyebrow. "What door does that open?"

He gestured down, voice icy. "That opens the trap door under our feet and drops us into the torture room."

"I'd prefer to avoid falling anywhere today," Alistar said. "So, how about the laboratory, then?" The study was tempting, but it might be another entrance to the study he already had Lamorage working on.

Tiyron smirked, a small twitch of his lips. "Well, let's see. Since you have the fancy flower, shouldn't be too hard. Activate north first, then east, then west, then deactivate north." He looked at Alistar expectantly.

"What activates them?" Rykka cut in. "Touching them, or something else?"

He looked momentarily annoyed, as if he'd hoped to let them fumble about a while first. "Put a hand on it until it glows to activate a crystal. Tapping or pulsing them is different."

That's at least three potential states for each crystal, and four crystals. That's not endless possible combinations, but a lot more than I was anticipating. Add the possibility that some options trigger traps, and Cemar could hide secrets very well down here.

Rykka followed Tiyron's directions, activating and deactivating crystals in order. Soft humming filled the room until she deactivated the north crystal. When the light blinked out from that stone, the others went dark as well. The room fell silent. Eyes turned to Tiyron. He ignored them. A long moment passed before the sound of a click broke the stillness. A panel on the south wall opened.

Alistar stepped toward it, but Lady Syri's Royal Guards reached the door first. He waited impatiently while they checked for hazards and traps, then entered the room.

The large room was equal parts workshop and laboratory. A lingering odor of sulfur and ammonium clung to the air, enough to make his nose wrinkle but not enough to make his eyes sting or water. An assortment of equipment and tools lay on the long wooden tables, lightly coated with dust. Alistar looked them over curiously.

"They were well supplied," he said. "No second-hand scavenged equipment here. I wonder if some of it came from Ravencrest's buyout of the Zel'en factories."

Lady Syri turned sharply to him. "Ravencrest is involved? In what way?"

He assumed Soluthos had updated Prince Cero on their findings, but that information had evidently not reached Lady Syri yet. Alistar gave her a high-level overview, leaving the details of how some information was obtained intentionally vague. She listened, expression unreadable.

"Some of this may be difficult to verify," Lady Syri finally said.

"Investigator Dawncloud had a part in collecting it. She may be able to assist in that area," Alistar told her.

Lady Syri's shoulders visibly relaxed at the news that someone legally permitted to spy on others had been involved. "Very good." One of her guards scribbled a note on a pad and tucked it in a pocket.

Tiyron settled himself to one side, not joining the inspection of the laboratory. Rykka frowned suspiciously at a large cloth-draped shape in one corner. Lamorage examined a shelf of glass bottles. Alistar joined him and saw that each bottle was neatly and carefully labeled with the name of a chemical.

"They were well supplied indeed," Alistar murmured.

"With the right combinations, they could have crafted deadly explosives," Lamorage responded grimly.

"Hey. Someone take a look at this thing," Rykka called.

One of the guards approached the shrouded shape she indicated and pulled off the drape, then sprang back with a startled curse, hand dropping to the hilt of his blade.

Alistar recognized the shape from the Zel'en schematics, but they didn't do the mining suit's bulk justice. A form of brass, leather, and wood, it stood close to six and a half feet tall. Pipes and hoses ran between the shoulders and the body. The head was a translucent dome with no neck. Combined with the over-wide shoulders and body, it looked squat, and only the presence of Rykka and the guard near it gave him enough scale to realize it wasn't as short as it looked from across the room.

"*That's* new," Tiyron said, eyeing the suit.

When the suit didn't move, Rykka cautiously approached it. She opened a latch on the chest, and a large panel swung open. "Large enough for a person to get inside. Damned heavy, though. Not much room to move around, either. There are a bunch of levers. It's clearly intended to use a power source of some sort."

"The mahiy lines," Lady Syri said.

Rykka stepped back and closed the chest panel. She shook her head. "Not if this is a mining suit prototype, which I assume based on the tools on the hands. They wouldn't have reliable access to the mahiy lines. Power source has to be internal, and strong enough to keep this thing moving, digging, and smashing through stone."

"Why is it here, though?" Lamorage asked. "Why not in Ravencrest's factory? For that matter, how did they get it in here?"

"Tapped into the house's power core, maybe," Tiyron said thoughtfully. Eyes turned to him once again. This time, he smirked, an expression Alistar recognized instantly. He'd seen it on Rykka's face frequently during their previous investigation. "Oh, that's right, I bet none of you know about that, do you?"

"I've known this manor isn't connected to the mahiy line network," Alistar said. "I assume the power source is somewhere in the basement."

Tiyron's smirk grew.

"Would you show me how to reach it?" Alistar asked him.

The smirk became a satisfied grin. Rather than returning to the room with the chiming crystals, Tiyron directed his chair to the shelf of chemicals. He reached under the second shelf from the bottom, feeling around until something clicked. The shelf slid to the left at his push, rocking bottles with a force that made Alistar flinch. Tiyron moved the chair into the dark doorway, casting a look over his shoulder at Alistar.

"Come on. You're going to love this, Silverline Senior Engineer."

CHAPTER 34

Alistar glanced over his shoulder. Only Lamorage and Star followed him and Tiyron through the concealed door. Ghostlights sprang to life down the stone hall. The ceiling was low enough that the elves ducked slightly as they walked, though their heads probably wouldn't quite brush the ceiling.

At the dark end of the hall, where the ghostlights hadn't yet illuminated, Alistar saw a pale blue glow. Tiyron headed toward it confidently.

"Was Cemar the sort to leave traps in places like this?" Alistar asked.

"Other places, sure. Not in here. He didn't want to risk any damage to it."

To what? The question lurked on Alistar's tongue, but he bit it back. Tiyron slowed, as if daring Alistar to rush past him and be the first into the chamber ahead. The thought tempted him. Ever since he'd moved into the manor, he'd searched for the source of the magic that powered it, using every tool at his disposal, but all he'd been able to determine was that the source was hidden somewhere in the basement.

They turned a corner and the chamber opened before them.

Polished marble tiles paved the floor. In the center of the room, they curved gently down to form a wide, shallow bowl. Water filled the bottom quarter of the bowl. Floating in the water was the source of the light in the room. Alistar drew a slow, deep breath. The air wasn't humid, but he did catch the faintest hints of the odor of frost's breath. He wasn't sure if the fragrance was his imagination, or if it truly emanated from the plant in the water.

He slowly stepped closer, crouching just before the water touched his shoes. He could barely see the net of roots extending from the plant into the water—they, like the rest of the plant, were formed of pale blue crystal, almost white. The edges of the leaves were jagged, as the petals of its flowers would be when they bloomed. Buds grew on several stalks, not yet open. Alistar leaned cautiously closer, looking over the plant without touching it. It was larger than a normal frost's breath plant, nearly two feet wide.

Large enough to produce the crystal flower we've been studying.

Looking over the buds, he saw a stem that had been cut. A shiver of unease crept down his spine. Standing, he turned to Tiyron. "This is the power source?"

"This is it," Tiyron said.

Lamorage entered, trailing Star. He took in the room, then the crystal plant in the water. Lamorage's eyes went wide. "Moonless night… Is that…" He grabbed the notebook from the pouch on his belt, flipping rapidly through the pages.

"Lamorage?" Alistar asked.

"She had notes about this! In the storybook, Sunward made notes! It was about the translation." He scanned a page, one finger running down the paper. "Right, yes… okay. She didn't have much in the margin, mostly a reference to something else she'd written elsewhere, which I haven't found yet. But it was a note that in the dialect of Heiset the story was originally written in, the words for 'flower' and 'seed' are very similar, with the implication that it might not have been a crystal frost's breath *flower* Rechmal gave to the hero, but a crystal frost's breath *seed*." Lamorage slowly approached, eyes on the plant.

"What do you know about it?" Alistar demanded of Tiyron.

"Not a lot," he admitted. "Supposedly, Sunward planted it in the pool. Don't know if it was already growing when she did, but I assume so. The thing doesn't grow fast. The flower you have back up above was the only full bloom she knew of, and I can say the buds haven't changed much since I was here last." He frowned, moving around the plant to look at it from all sides. "Except that there's one fewer of them."

"You mean another blossomed? We might have another crystal flower somewhere in the city?" Alistar cursed.

"Nah, I just told you it doesn't grow that fast. But someone— probably Sunward—picked one of the more mature buds." Tiyron leaned toward the plant, then settled back in his chair.

"Are you knowledgeable in horticulture?" Star asked.

"Am I what?" He looked at her dubiously.

"Horticulture. The growing and tending of plants."

Tiyron snorted. "Sure, that's definitely something I've spent *so* much time learning."

"I doubt horticulture would be much help with this plant," Lamorage said. "I don't think even Silverline botanists would know how to tend to a living crystal that might have been given to mortals by a god."

"I wonder what would happen if we brought the crystal flower in here?" Alistar mused.

"I wouldn't," Tiyron said. "Don't know the details, but Cemar and Sunward were both adamant that the flower shouldn't be brought into this room. They talked about energy feeding energy and a risk of feedback."

"How close is too close?" Lamorage asked warily.

"I never saw anyone bring it closer than the laboratory, but they would carry the flower around in there without concern," Tiyron said.

The elf's openness surprised Alistar. He'd expected to need to pry answers from Tiyron and accept the sarcasm and snark that naturally accompanied such answers. At the moment, though, Tiyron seemed in the mood to share with minimal prompting.

"Do you think it safe for Lady Syri to enter, Lord De'seneth?" Star asked.

"I think 'safe' is relative, Star. But I would like her opinion on this," Alistar answered.

Star nodded curtly and strode up the hall.

"Lamorage, did the myth tell you anything about why the Reyker gave the crystal to the hero, or what it could do?" Alistar asked. He turned to Tiyron. "Or do you know anything more about it?"

"Just the part about it being smuggled out of Heiset and carried through the portal in secret," Tiyron said. "If Sunward knew why it had to be taken in secret, she didn't share that detail. If you humans were running from something, hardly makes sense to leave your gods-given sacred relic behind, unless it was the reason you had to run away in the first place."

"Well, in the tale, the hero called on the crystal's power to destroy the army of animated golems," Lamorage said. "At least, I assume that was the conclusion. He called on the crystal's power, and the golems shattered, but the rest of the pages were missing. Perhaps the act of using it had some additional, dangerous effects."

If this is the same artifact, why would our ancestors want to leave it behind? Alistar gazed at the plant as if it might whisper the answer to him.

Star returned followed by Lady Syri and Rykka. Rykka's eyes swept the room, settled on the crystal flower, and grew wide in shock. "What in hematic perdition is *that*?"

"Evidently, the power source of my home," Alistar answered.

"Right. Of course. That's perfectly normal. Everyone's got one in their basement."

"The Successors said the crystal flower was a gift from the god of magic," Lady Syri said quietly. "They said nothing about this."

"I doubt the Successors knew anything about it," Alistar said. "I don't imagine Cemar and Sunward trusted the knowledge of this plant to many."

She nodded, though her gaze moved briefly to Tiyron, silently questioning how he'd known of it.

To distract Lady Syri, Alistar pointed out both of the broken stems. "We don't know much about this plant's growth cycle, but if we can assume that our flower was the first harvested from it, the second one is probably not a mature flower."

"*Can* we assume that?" Lady Syri asked.

"We can be reasonably confident," Alistar said. "We certainly heard about the effects of the one that we have. If another like it were present in Lewarden, I think we would have heard."

"You don't think yours was the second bloom, and the first could have been taken some time before?" Rykka asked.

Lady Syri reached into the water, feeling the delicate web of roots. "Unlikely. It appears that this plant grew here for most of its life. So, barring the possibility that this entire chamber was secretly transported into this location and the rest of the house built around it, the plant's little older than the house. Frost's breath plants mature slowly." She withdrew her hand and shook droplets of water off.

Her statement startled Alistar for a moment. He reminded himself that as heir to Silverline Power, she certainly had to understand botany as well as engineering.

Lady Syri drew tools from her bag. Alistar immediately moved to assist her, recognizing instruments for monitoring and measuring magical output and wavelengths. They set up around the edge of the pool.

"If you have more readers, we should also monitor the flower," Alistar said. "We should know if having them in proximity causes a reaction."

"Agreed." Lady Syri looked around the room. "Star, I must discuss some Silverline matters with Senior Engineer De'seneth. Escort Rykka and her brother back to the laboratory."

Rykka raised a questioning eyebrow at Alistar. He nodded. She grimaced slightly but complied. Tiyron scowled fiercely at both Alistar and Lady Syri but followed Rykka. Star took the rear, ensuring neither stayed close enough to overhear.

Lamorage hesitated. "Should I leave as well?"

Lady Syri waved a hand. "No need as long as you can abide by the confidentiality agreement you made when you joined Silverline Power."

"Of course, Lady Syri," he said quickly.

"Good." She turned her attention to Alistar. "You just reminded me of something. You recall, I'm sure, that I told you of the strange reading and phenomena we witnessed in recent months while studying the crystal flower. You observed some unexpected opening of passages here in your manor, and we hypothesized that an outside influence might be the catalyst for the reactions."

Alistar nodded slowly. "I recall."

"If there is an immature flower in Lewarden, we must consider that it might be the source."

"I think we all suspect Sunward to possess such a flower," Alistar said. "If the Crown agents who tailed her kept detailed reports of her location, I'd recommend someone study those carefully to see how near she was to Silverline when you observed the phenomena with the flower."

Lamorage cleared his throat. "If you can determine the energy patterns put off by this plant and the flower, both when they are near each other and when they aren't, you might also be able to use that pattern to locate the other flower."

Lady Syri nodded. "It would be even better if we could activate the flower as Sok'lof could."

Lamorage's brow furrowed. "You haven't been able to reproduce the 'miracles' he worked with it?"

"Not as of yet," she admitted. "And my team and I have been testing and studying it since De'seneth provided it to us. We have, however, suspended that work until my father returns to full capacity."

Lamorage nodded slowly and helped set up the monitors around the pool. Once the task was done, Lady Syri returned to the laboratory. Lamorage lingered at the doorway. Alistar waited for him.

When Lady Syri was out of earshot, Lamorage whispered, "Can you convince her to leave the crystal flower with you?"

"Probably…" Alistar said slowly. "Why?"

"I have an idea. A theory, really. It's easier to test it if the flower is here rather than at Silverline."

"Alright." Alistar considered pressing for more information, but decided he would know soon enough.

They rejoined the others in the laboratory, and the group returned to the room where the crystal flower still awaited. Alistar, Lamorage, and Lady Syri arranged another series of monitors around it.

As they did, Alistar spoke. "We should give the monitors at least a full day with the plant and flower in this relative proximity to ensure we have solid readings. I trust you won't object to leaving it here, Lady Syri."

"As I said, my own work with it has been temporarily suspended. I do trust you will keep it secure," she said, and though she didn't look directly at Rykka or Tiyron, the implication was clear.

"I certainly will," Alistar said. "I'll also make use of it to open other chambers as we're able."

"Report anything else of interest that you discover," she told him. She started to say more, but a chime interrupted. Lady Syri pulled a speaking stone from her pocket. It glowed with a vibrant emerald light when she activated it. "Yes?"

"Lady Syri, you wished me to remind you that you have a meeting in an hour." The voice was that of one of the administrative sprites, though Alistar couldn't tell which one specifically.

"Yes, thank you." She inactivated the stone and returned it to its pouch. "De'seneth, I must take my leave."

"Of course, Lady Syri." Given that she was still covering for Prince Cero's duties, she'd probably dedicated more time than she necessarily could afford to coming to the manor. Alistar wondered if some of her willingness to leave the crystal flower in his care stemmed from a need to remove the temptation of studying it further.

The entire group returned to the ballroom. Lady Syri did watch Tiyron's chair navigate the stairs with open interest, though she didn't make any further comments about it. Alistar closed and locked the door after everyone. Within a relatively quick quarter of an hour, Lady Syri and her guards took their leave.

Once the house quieted, Alistar signaled Lamorage to come with him. He tried to be subtle about returning to the ballroom and the door to the basement, but despite the effort, Rykka silently invited herself along. Alistar eyed her but let her join them.

Once they were back in the basement with the door closed behind them, Alistar asked, "What's your theory, Lamorage?"

Lamorage ran a hand through his brown hair and smiled uncertainly. "Assuming the crystal is the one from human myths, my theory is that to tap into its greatest potential, the one trying to use it must be human."

Alistar blinked, coming to a halt. "That's… possible. But Lady Syri had a full team of technicians working with it. That should have…"

Lamorage cleared his throat uncomfortably. "Lady Syri and Prince Cero are better than many elves among the upper Lewarden nobility, but they still tend to… associate more with those they are familiar with. I worked a few times with Lady Syri in her role as Technician Feyblade. The team she worked with did consist of members from lower social circles, but I honestly don't remember seeing any humans among them. I acknowledge that I've been gone from Silverline for over a year now, but I don't think it's outside the realm of possibility that few, if any, humans aside from you have had any contact with the crystal, De'seneth."

"Blood and sand." Alistar shook his head.

"Cemar's rhetoric about equality got people's attention for a reason," Rykka said in a low voice.

Alistar's thoughts whirled. Without responding to Rykka, he walked into the room of crystals. The flower rested innocuously on the table, except for the motes of light like distant stars flickering within its eight jagged petals.

Sok'lof used this to convince people he was a prophet and that the gods granted him the ability to work miracles. He demonstrated that by using the crystal to give the people of the Hollows light and heat after Cemar drained the magic from their mahiy lines. Other stories claimed he could move objects with nothing more than a wave of his hand.

"Lamorage, would you keep an eye on the monitor? See if any readings change."

"Of course."

"I don't know how to make this work," Alistar warned. "Did you ever see Sok'lof or the others use it?"

"No. I only saw it once, and it was attached to a staff," Lamorage said.

"It was," Alistar agreed. "I rather ruined the staff when I removed the crystal, much to Sok'lof's distress. If 'raging fury' could be called distress." He rested his hand on the table beside the crystal. The flickering glints of light seemed to draw toward it, though they didn't react to Lamorage's equally close presence on the other side of the table.

"So, what are you going to do?" Rykka asked.

Alistar looked past her to the door into the laboratory. "Just going to try closing that door." He imagined the door sliding shut.

Nothing happened.

He shifted his stance and his hand touched one of the petals. A quick, sharp bite of pain hit his hand, as if he'd shuffled his feet across a heavy carpet, then touched a doorknob.

Moving silently on its track, the laboratory door slid closed.

Alistar's breath caught. "Blood and sand…"

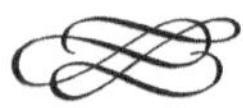

CHAPTER 35

Saskia settled her protective glasses in place and pulled on a pair of gloves. The dose of Lumination that Rykka had recovered rested in a sample jar, a small, innocuous crimson pill.

Just what are you, exactly? What are you made of? Why is Sunward invested in using you to find people with one particular, peculiar ability?

Ambrosia had come in several forms she knew of—powder that could be added to drinks or small shards of crystal similar to rock candy that could be ingested. She didn't know if Lumination likewise took other forms, but after discussion with her father, they'd agreed the best place to start was with crushing the pill and analyzing the powder. Saskia took a clean mortar and pestle and set to work.

She scraped a sample of powdered Lumination onto a glass tray and moved to the magnification scope. The device was well outside the clinic's budget—especially one as well-made as this one. It had been a gift from Alistar's parents, along with a lot of other expensive laboratory and medical equipment "salvaged" from a ship. They'd told her the owner had been engaged in numerous questionable experiments and that the equipment would be better served in her hands, then deftly changed the subject when she'd tried to inquire as to exactly what sort of activities took place on the ship.

The Lumination powder didn't have the same crystalline structure that had marked Ambrosia or its toxic counterpart Elixir. That was reassuring. She dreaded the thought of another outbreak like Rat's Disease.

"What *are* you, then?" she murmured, leaning back from the scope and selecting a bottle from the shelf. Now came the challenge: analyzing this drug.

An hour later, her father checked in on her. "How fares the battle, Saskia?"

"I'm not sure, to be honest." Saskia pulled off her gloves and glasses, rolling her shoulders. "It's definitely not the same drug as Ambrosia and doesn't release magic in the way the other drug did."

"It doesn't release magic at all, or it doesn't release magic the same way that Ambrosia did?" her father asked.

"I'm not sure, and I feel like if I could be certain, I'd be closer to understanding it. The evidence we've collected implies that Lumination targets internal channelers rather than traditional channelers, but we know so little about the phenomenon that is internal channeling that I don't know how to calibrate the instruments to detect it."

Doctor Tan'shyo nodded thoughtfully. "May I?"

"Of course."

He repeated many of the same tests as Saskia. When he finished, they compared results. Doctor Tan'shyo frowned thoughtfully. "It is unusually hard to pin down, as you said. Perhaps if we knew someone who could channel in this way, they might be able to give us more insights, but I'm not sure how we would even go about finding one."

Saskia started to nod in agreement, then stopped. "Seva. He

took refuge here after being subjected to a test like the one Rykka described. And Ravencrest pursued him because he succeeded in that test."

Her father's face lit up. "Indeed! If he's willing to assist us, at least."

"Only one way to know." Saskia headed for the stairs to the upper floor.

For the past four days, Seva had quietly stayed in the upper apartment, sleeping or otherwise occupying himself. Saskia didn't think he could read, but he'd spent some time drawing and sketching. It clearly wasn't his strongest skill, but he was far from the worst artist she'd seen.

She knocked lightly on the door before opening it. "It's Doctor De'seneth."

He didn't answer, but she entered regardless. A rough pile of drawings lay on the dining room table. Seva peered around the kitchen doorway, then relaxed when he saw her. "Good morning, doctor."

"Good morning. I hope you're well today." Saskia nodded to him with a warm smile.

He answered with a quick nod, causing pale blond hair to flop into his eyes. "I was getting food," he answered hesitantly, as if expecting to be chided.

"Of course. Do, by all means. I'll send Kir to fetch any staples you need here, so please tell any of us if you are lacking anything."

The thin elf looked at his hands. "Has... the noblewoman sent anybody else for me?"

"She hasn't, and neither has Whitetooth." Saskia sat at the table.

Seva sat across from her immediately. "I don't wanna bring trouble here."

"You haven't," she told him. "And if you are willing, you might be able to help us."

Uncertainty crossed his face. "I'm nothin' special. Dunno what I could do."

"You succeeded in a test that was given to you, didn't you?"

Seva shifted uncomfortably and nodded. "Whitetooth made everyone take Lumination and try to complete this puzzle... thing. Most couldn't make anything happen. I dunno how they were trying to make it work. I watched the girl who showed it to us, and I... reached inside, like she did." One hand rose to press against his chest. "With Lumination, I just saw how it all went together. Didn't mean to actually do it, but it's like seeing *how* it worked made it happen. Then I got pulled off to another room an' heard Whitetooth's thugs saying he was gonna sell my debt to a noblewoman. I heard about some factory where nobody ever leaves. Didn't wanna end up there. Slipped the thugs and made a run for it."

Saskia cocked her head. "You said you reached inside. Have you always been able to? Did someone teach you?" Traditional channeling usually manifested close to puberty, though sometimes external stressors could cause it to become active earlier.

He considered. "Dunno. Didn't need to reach inside 'til 'Lixir. Then I had to learn how to reach inside and tell the good parts from the bad parts. Could use the good parts to burn out the bad parts."

He could use the condensed magic in the drug to burn out the toxic dross. He could use Elixir without succumbing to Rat's Disease. How? Is that why some people never suffered Rat's Disease?

Saskia nodded slowly as she processed that revelation. "Do you have to do the same thing with Lumination?"

Seva shook his head. "Lumination's different. Not made of the same stuff and doesn't have the bad parts."

"'Lixir was made from magic stolen from the mahiy lines. I know Lumination isn't the same, but how does it feel when you reach inside when you take Lumination? Is it easier to do than with 'Lixir?"

Seva fidgeted with the hem of his shirt. "Yes… no… When I took 'Lixir, it was easier to reach inside and find that… place. I *could* use it when I took 'Lixir, but when I took Lumination, I *had* to use it. I couldn't *not* use it."

"Have you taken Lumination often?" she asked.

"A couple times. Whitetooth gave everyone doses along with food and bed and all that, but usually I hadda give mine to someone else 'less I wanted to get hit."

"Can you still reach inside to that ability without the drug?"

He nodded. "It's always there. Just stronger with Lumination."

Saskia let out a breath. "Do you know that Elixir was the cause of Rat's Disease?"

"I heard that. Not…really sure if I believe it, you know."

"Rat's Disease is what happened to the people who didn't have the ability to reach in and separate the good parts of it from the bad parts, so the toxic elements built up until their bodies couldn't take any more."

Seva absorbed that silently for several moments. "It didn't… make everyone able to do that?"

Saskia shook her head. "I don't know why, though I suppose it's as much of a mystery as why some people can channel from the mahiy lines and others can't."

Fear washed across his face. "It's not like that!"

She made a gesture of appeasement. "It's not. There are no regulations or registrations for your ability. There's nothing illegal about you being able to do this."

Seva wasn't completely reassured, but he calmed a little. "Are you… wantin' to learn 'bout it?"

"Eventually, I'd like to. But right now, I'm more concerned with understanding why someone, or a group of someones, is trying to collect people like you who have this ability. My guess is that they're also the ones creating Lumination and are using it to find the people they're looking for."

"I don't know who makes it or anything like that. Just know what I told Rykka—real rich elf nobleman brought some to Whitetooth. Whitetooth bowed and scraped, and the noble had this air like he was gonna burn his clothes as soon as he got outta the slums." He paused. "I still got the gloves he tossed out after he left. You... want them?"

"If I could borrow them from you," Saskia answered. *He has something that belonged to the person who delivered the drugs? Could that give us some way to identify this nobleman? And if there are any residues of Lumination in the cloth... I have to analyze them.*

Seva pulled a tightly balled wad of black cloth from his pocket. "You can borrow 'em. They still smell nice, even despite me carrying 'em around."

Saskia frowned slightly as she took the cloth from him. She caught the scent of cologne. "There are certainly ways to imbue cloth with an ability to repel odors the wearer dislikes, but it's expensive. Most nobles wouldn't bother on a pair of gloves, especially not gloves they discarded."

Seva shrugged slightly. "He was rich."

"Apparently. You're welcome to come downstairs while I run an analysis. The clinic's quiet today. After you've gotten food, of course. I realize I interrupted you."

"Thank you. I'll... come down in a little."

Saskia nodded and withdrew, giving him space once again. Returning to the laboratory, she laid the gloves out on a counter, examining the dark fabric. She didn't know the cologne, but the scent invoked a sense of refinement and wealth. The cloth was fine silkweave tailored for the hands that had worn the gloves. She noted several spots where the cloth was oddly stretched and deformed, though she wasn't certain what caused it.

A little while later, she heard soft steps on the stairs. Saskia stepped out of the laboratory to invite Seva to join her. The elf cast nervous looks around the clinic halls and seemed relieved to join her inside a room with no windows.

He sniffed the air as Saskia closed the door. "It smells like Lumination in here."

"I received a sample of the drug and have been trying to analyze it, determine its origins and what it's made of," she explained.

"It's made of the stuff I feel when I reach inside," he responded.

"Maybe so, but I want to know what that *is*, or at least how someone captured that power and infused it into a drug."

"An' you think those gloves are gonna help with that?" he asked curiously.

"They might. Do you know why these areas are stretched?" She indicated the odd lumps.

Seva nodded. "He were wearing rings under 'em, even though they weren't meant fer that."

"Rings? Could you tell any signets?"

Seva frowned, staring at the gloves. Saskia waited, trying to read his expression.

He raised one hand. A soft purple light glowed at his fingertips, then, before Saskia's eyes, the gloves took shape as if invisible hands slid into them.

This isn't something I've seen a traditional channeler do. What can Seva and those like him with this ability do? Can their abilities mimic those of traditional channelers, or are they something entirely different?

"You're able to do that, Seva?"

He nodded. "It's a trick I figured out—make my clothes look like they're on a body with more... body than I got. Most people think a scrawny whore is prob'ly a sick whore. Anyway, this is even easier, 'cause the gloves already know how they're supposed to fit, so it's just makin' 'em act like those hands are in 'em."

As if it was just that simple. Saskia nodded, running her hand over the lumps that would have been rings. Her fingers could distinguish ridges her eyes couldn't, but not well enough to understand the image. "If you don't mind keeping them like this for a little while, I'll see if I can get rubbings of the rings."

"Tha's easy," Seva agreed. "It's easy to keep 'em in the shape they want to be."

She grabbed sheets of thin paper and made rubbings of the rings, capturing as many details as possible. The cloth didn't retain as much precision and clarity as she could have wished, and at a glance, she couldn't tell what signets they might represent. "Thank you, Seva. You can let that go now."

The gloves remained as they were. She turned to Seva. He stood in the center of the room, eyes closed, swaying slightly and breathing deeply. A shiver of concern and apprehension ran down her spine.

How much Lumination is in the air? I don't smell anything unusual other than the cologne on the gloves—is that preventing me from smelling the drug? Is it affecting me?

She put a hand on his shoulder. "Seva, you can release the magic you're channeling into the gloves."

His eyes opened slightly and his mouth curled in a contented smile. "Okay."

Nothing changed with the gloves.

"Seva, release the magic you're channeling into the gloves."

Phrasing it as an order proved effective, though he still had the smile and half-lidded eyes. "Okay." The glimmer of purple light at his fingertips faded, and the gloves deflated on the countertop.

"How do you feel? What do you feel?" Saskia asked.

He drew another deep breath, eyes sinking closed again. "Feels nice, like I'm in a flower, an' it's wrapped around me soft an' close."

"In... a flower?" she repeated. It was such an odd description, she could only wonder what inspired it. "Why a flower?"

"Feels like petals," Seva said confidently. "An' smells like flowers."

She sniffed the air, trying to find any floral scents, but none caught her nose.

Seva continued. "White flower. The petals look like they'd bite, but they're soft. White flowers an' water cold as ice."

She stopped. The words sounded so familiar, she could almost place them, but the thought was too fleeting, slipping away like mist as soon as she tried to focus on it. Saskia gently steered Seva to the door.

"I think we've done enough work today. Go back upstairs and rest."

He was placidly compliant, letting her guide him down the hall and up the stairs to the apartment. Inside, he walked to the table, sat down, and grabbed paper and a charcoal stick to start drawing. Saskia waited a few minutes, but he seemed content, and didn't show any signs of physical or mental distress. She headed back downstairs.

She found her father in the surgery, cleaning and organizing the tools of their trade. He looked over when she entered, and his expression immediately grew concerned. "Saskia, what's wrong?"

She sank down on a chair and related everything she'd observed and her conversations with Seva.

"If Lumination is powerful enough to affect him just by being in a room that presumably had particles of the drug in the air, am I being affected as well? I don't feel different, but when Cemar and his people slipped Alistar a dose of Ambrosia, he didn't realize it either until Rykka pointed it out to him."

"If it is affecting you, it's certainly not doing so to the degree that it's affected Seva," Doctor Tan'shyo assured her. He checked her temperature and pulse as he spoke. "You theorized that

Lumination is being created to identify those with abilities like Seva's. It could be designed to affect them more quickly and more intensely."

"The thing he said about feeling like he was wrapped in a flower… something about it's scratching at my memories, but I can't pin it down." She heaved a frustrated sigh.

"Do you remember exactly what he said that bothered you?" her father asked.

"White flowers and water cold as ice," she repeated.

"Hmm." Her father's brow furrowed. He shook his head. "It doesn't spark anything for me, I'm afraid." He squeezed her shoulder. "Why don't you head home and rest on it? I'll keep an eye on Seva. Maybe Alistar or someone else at your manor can help you identify the images on those rubbings you took."

Saskia kissed him on the cheek. "Thank you. But let me know if anything changes."

He chuckled softly. "Don't worry, I will. I'll see you tomorrow unless something comes up before then."

CHAPTER 36

Dorne greeted Saskia at the door. "Welcome home, Lady De'seneth. Lord De'seneth is down in the basement at the moment."

"Still?" Saskia asked. "Is Lady Syri here as well?"

Dorne shook his head. "Lady Feyblade departed before midday. Would you like me to send someone to let Lord De'seneth know you're home?"

"No, thank you. I'll go down and join him."

Dorne nodded and walked with her to the ballroom. Two of the Rillwater staff stood guard at the door into the basement. Both nodded politely to Saskia as she passed them and descended the stairs.

She knew the area where Alistar had planned to experiment, and walked toward the room with the four crystals. As she approached, she caught a scent in the air. Saskia paused a moment, trying to place it. It was familiar, and it reminded her of her earlier work in the laboratory at the clinic.

It's not the smell of chemicals, though. What other smell I have noticed there? Is this... floral? How odd.

Hearing voices, she called, "Alistar, I'm home."

"Saskia?" he called back. "We're down here."

The sound of his voice came from the direction of the room with the crystals. As she neared it, she shivered, noticing a dip in the temperature she hadn't experienced on previous visits. Perhaps they'd opened more doors, and doing so had caused a shift in the overall temperature down here.

The table in the crystals room was covered with equipment that she knew related to Alistar's engineering work, though she didn't know what any of it did, exactly. A new door stood open. She followed the path into a laboratory, where she found Alistar, Lamorage, and Rykka. Alistar carried a frost's breath flower the size of his hand, its jagged petals strangely stiff and translucent. It caught the light and she realized it was made of crystal.

That must be the crystal Alistar took from Sok'lof. Is it safe to handle bare-handed?

Alistar set the crystal down on a table and swept over to her, catching her in an embrace. "You're home early."

She yelped in surprise. "Slee's Breath, Alistar, have you been dunking your hands in ice water?"

He looked amused but confused. "No? Why?"

"Well, they're certainly chilled enough. Maybe it's just because it's colder down here."

Rykka cocked her head. "Now that you mention it, it is chilly. I hadn't noticed earlier."

"I assume you've been busy, then?" Saskia asked.

Alistar's face lit up. "Yes! It's incredible, Saskia. So many things we never knew were down here!" His eyes glittered with excitement.

Saskia saw a similar gleam on the faces of Rykka and Lamorage, though not as intense as Alistar. The elusive but familiar scent hung around Alistar. "Obviously you found this room. What else?"

"Watch this." Alistar picked up the crystal flower. "See that prototype mining suit over there?"

She followed his gaze to the hulking automaton across the room. "Yes. One of the Zel'ens' prototypes?"

"Probably. They built it but couldn't find a power source strong enough to let a worker move around in it." Alistar pointed at the suit, then curled his finger in a beckoning gesture.

With a heavy rattle of metal plates, the suit clanged five steps toward Alistar. He raised his hand in a stop motion, and it stilled. Saskia gasped in surprise, and saw a hint of steam from her breath in the cold air.

"Alistar, what…?" She caught a stronger whiff of the scent, as if Alistar's actions caused its release.

Her husband grinned like a boy opening birthday gifts. "After Lady Syri left, Lamorage had a theory about why her team couldn't make the crystal do anything. We've been testing it, and all the evidence supports it so far."

"And that is?" she prompted.

"It's a human artifact, Saskia! A gift given by Rechmal to a human hero before our people left Heiset. It has to be used by a human."

That made sense, to a point. "But should you be using it like this? Carrying what could be a sacred relic in your bare hands?"

"Why not? The taboo on uncovered skin is elven in origin, not human," Alistar responded.

"Because you're handling an unknown artifact of uncertain origins without protecting yourself," she told him flatly. "And every time you use it, the room gets colder."

"It's not unknown origin!" Alistar protested. "You haven't seen the most important part yet." He set the crystal flower back down on a table. "This way!"

She followed him past a shelf of bottled chemicals, down the hall, into a room illuminated by pale blue light. She took in the marble tile floor as a peripheral only, her gaze arrested by the frost's breath plant blooming in the pool at the center. Saskia drew a sharp breath. It wasn't as cold as the laboratory, and the scent wasn't as strong, but unbidden, Seva's words came back to her.

It smells like Lumination in here.

Feels nice, like I'm inna flower, an' it's wrapped around me soft an' close. White flower. The petals look like they'd bite, but they're soft. White flowers an' water cold as ice.

Saskia slowly turned to Alistar. "What… is this?"

"It's the source of the power in the manor," Alistar said. "The crystal flower was cut from it, and it appears that someone also took a less mature bloom." He directed her attention to the two cut stems. "My guess is Sunward has the other."

Saskia stood in silence for a long moment, trying to make sense of anything she was seeing. "Alistar, what *is* this? How is it here, and how long has it been here?"

"We think it could be an artifact given to our people by Rechmal long before we came through the portal into Calarand. Lamorage found a portion of the story in one of Sunward's books in the library." Alistar outlined as much of the tale as he knew. "I don't yet know what Sunward intended to do with it. I'd wager a ship this is the reason Merris was trying to gain access to the basement, though."

"And the reason for the tax issue that was 'discovered'," Saskia said. "An attempt to get us out of the manor by whatever means possible." She twisted a lock of hair around her finger. "Other than moving the mining suit, what experiments have you done?"

"Opening and closing doors. Seeing what other objects I could move or manipulate." He motioned at devices around the edge of the pool. "Lady Syri and I set up monitoring equipment to study the energy readings from the plant and the flower. By tomorrow we should have more data."

Saskia crouched for a better view of the plant. "You said this is the power source for the manor, but how does it provide the power? There are no mahiy lines to feed whatever energy this produces into the devices in the manor and on the grounds."

Alistar frowned at her. "I'm not sure. Hadn't given it much thought yet, to be honest." His gaze moved from the plant to the rest of the room. "Channels in the stone, perhaps. Marble isn't a good conductor, but if it has other elements in it like iron, those could carry magic from this room to other areas."

"Is there much loose magic in this room?" she asked. "Do your monitors record that?"

"Hmm." Alistar began to check the devices. "No, there doesn't seem to be. The levels seem normal." He stopped abruptly. "That can't be right."

"What's wrong?" Saskia asked, unease running down her spine. She couldn't shake the sense that something was off.

"It must be misconfigured. One monitor reads levels you wouldn't see unless you were measuring the output of an actual mahiy line." Alistar checked the monitor carefully. "If that were the case, everyone in the manor would be suffering the effects of overexposure…" He picked it up. "Oh. Now it's reading at expected levels."

That's not reassuring, Alistar. Saskia bit back the words. Then she noticed a small damp spot beside the monitor. "Was one of its sensors in the water?"

"Maybe. I didn't check." He set the monitor back down, considered, and dipped one of the sensors into the water.

Saskia didn't need to be an engineer to understand the sharp spike in the line displayed on the monitor. Alistar pulled the sensor out of the water, and the reading dropped again. He tested it another time, then moved to another monitor and repeated the experiment.

As he did, Saskia checked her pockets and found an empty sample jar she'd tucked away. Using tongs, she dipped it in the water, avoiding touching it bare-handed.

"The waveform differs from those of mahiy lines," Alistar

observed thoughtfully. "Why does it channel the energy into the water, though?"

"I don't know, but I'll run tests on this." Saskia held the bottle carefully.

"Right, good," Alistar said, distracted.

She caught his arm and led him back to the laboratory. "We should see if we get the same results if we put the bloom in water."

Alistar blinked. "Saskia, it's crystal. It doesn't need water."

"Maybe it does, but we just haven't noticed the effects on it yet," she countered. "And how accurate will the readings you're collecting be if you keep playing with it?"

Alistar had immediately moved toward the crystal flower when they returned to the laboratory. He paused, stopping just short of picking it up. "I suppose that collecting readings was why Lady Syri left it here." He sighed. "I could learn so much more by *using* it."

Rykka, who had been waiting with Lamorage, cleared her throat. "De'seneth, wasn't the story that Sunward's ancestors had to take this plant, or the seed this plant grew from, through the portal in secret, and they were supposed to leave it behind? If that's actually true, should you be playing with it?"

Alistar raised an eyebrow at her. "I thought you wanted to see what it could do."

"I… do," Rykka admitted. "But maybe… in small doses."

"We don't have a lot of time." Alistar looked from her to Saskia. "Being overly cautious won't reveal Sunward's intentions."

Saskia rested a hand on his shoulder. "We'll put the flower in water overnight and see what readings you get from the water in the morning. All right?"

Alistar sighed and picked up the flower. "Fine." He strode toward the room with the four crystals. Following him, Saskia noticed the light within the flower shifting and moving, throwing shadows on the walls to either side of Alistar. She caught movement from the corner of her eye and saw the light layer of dust on the floor sweeping to the corners of the hall without being touched. Alistar was smiling again when he set the flower into the nest of sensors on the central table. The sensors' glows shifted from orange to green once the flower rested back in its place. Alistar pulled on his gloves and nodded in satisfaction.

Saskia linked her arm with Alistar's and walked him back upstairs, making sure Rykka and Lamorage followed. Alistar let himself be guided out of the basement, though he seemed mildly exasperated by Saskia's concern.

Alistar turned toward the kitchen. "All right, let's get some water and see where this experiment takes us."

Saskia kept hold of his arm. "Before you do, Alistar, would you indulge me in one thing?" She was uneasy asking this, and unsure whether she hoped her tentative theory would be proven or disproven.

Alistar looked at her curiously. "All right. What is it?"

Even his response, agreeing before asking what she intended, bothered her. "I want to examine you to see if what you were doing affected you physically."

He raised an eyebrow, but shrugged and let her lead him out of the ballroom and upstairs. Saskia trusted the Rillwater staff to ensure the basement was properly closed and guarded.

In their suite, Alistar asked, "What's bothering you?"

Saskia let out a long breath. "The way you acted when you were holding the flower. That's what's bothering me." She held up her hand, pointer finger raised. "Follow my finger with your eyes."

He tracked it without problem. "I didn't feel any ill effects. I don't know what you mean about how I was acting. I was conducting experiments to test our theory."

"How did you feel? What did you feel when you held it?"

His expression relaxed and he smiled contentedly. "At first it felt like the bit of a shock you get when you touch someone after shuffling your feet on a carpet on a dry day. But that faded, and afterwards, I felt like I was reaching into a deep, deep well and pulling up fresh, cold water. As much as I could want and more. Not endless, probably, but more than one man could ever want. It felt like it wanted to be used." He raised his hand as if he still cupped the flower.

Saskia caught his hand and gently tugged off his glove. Blisters puckered his palm. Alistar looked down at his hand in surprise. He pulled off his other glove and compared his palms. Only one was blistered, but the other was red and irritated, as if he'd suffered a minor burn on it.

Alistar stared at his blistered left hand. "This… it didn't burn. I don't know how this happened. It doesn't hurt."

"It doesn't hurt *yet*," Saskia corrected. "Because you're still under the effects of it."

"The effects of what? The flower?" He shook his head. "I don't see how that's possible."

She was quiet for a moment, then asked, "When you used it, did you feel like it was… wrapping around you?" She hoped, even expected that he would scoff at the idea.

Alistar cocked his head. "I suppose it did, in a way. Why?"

"That's how Seva described the experience of taking Lumination," she said quietly. She didn't like the theory she'd begun to form. "Father and I were testing the sample of the drug earlier. We didn't learn much from that, but I also spoke with Seva about it and its effects."

"You think Lumination is connected to the flower? And that using the flower has had similar effects on me?" He was dubious.

"I hope not. But I'm worried. If the tale is true, our ancestors *wanted* to leave this artifact behind when they abandoned the land of Heiset. Why would they give up something so powerful, unless the cost of the power was higher than they were willing to pay?" She caught Alistar's blistered hand in her own. "You were sweeping dust, moving a mining suit, opening and closing doors. We don't know what it could do to you if you push further."

His fingers curled, and he winced as the pain finally pierced through. "I don't know why our ancestors would have wanted to leave it, if they really did. But whether they did or not, it's here now, and we have to understand it. We can't wait. We don't have time. The Exhibition is looming too close."

"We don't know that Sunward is going to make her move then," Saskia said.

"She is," Alistar said firmly. "If we can't stop it, the Exhibition is when her plans will come to fruition. I *know* it."

"*How* do you know?"

He shook his head. "I *know* it, Saskia. Does it matter how?"

"Yes."

He chose not to hear her. "If you want to put the crystal flower in water, we should do that soon." Alistar pulled on his gloves and strode out of the room.

CHAPTER 37

There's nothing wrong with understanding how the flower works and what it can do! Alistar stormed down the stairs. We don't have time to dally and fuss, and I'm fine. His stinging hand belied the thought, but he ignored it. We just figured out how to use the flower, and now everyone has second thoughts and wants to stop? This is ridiculous!

On his way to the ballroom, he flagged down a passing servant. "Get me a bowl of water."

She blinked. "Of… course, milord. How large of a bowl?"

He held his hands apart to indicate a circumference a little larger than that of the crystal flower. "About this size, half full."

"Right away, milord!" She scurried off toward the kitchen.

Alistar continued to the ballroom. The girl was prompt, arriving with the bowl before he grew too impatient.

"Exactly what I needed. Thank you."

She curtsied quickly to him, gave him the bowl, and hurried off to whatever task he'd interrupted. The guards opened the door and let Alistar back into the basement with his bowl.

I really don't know what this is supposed to prove, or why Saskia's so insistent. Although admittedly, it IS strange that the main plant is releasing magic into the pool rather than the air. How does that transfer into the manor house? There must be some mechanism for extracting it from the water. Or maybe I was right, and there are conductive channels in the floor. If that's the case, the entire manor had to be built with that in mind, meaning Cemar, Sunward, and the architect planned to oust the Zel'ens from the start.

Caught up in his thoughts, he entered the room with the crystals and set the bowl on the central table. When he lifted the flower from its nest of sensors, he felt the urge to use it again. Alistar watched the glimmers of light within the petals flicker toward the spots where his gloved hands made contact. It would take so little effort to draw them out again.

Tomorrow. I can wait until tomorrow. After this experiment.

He set the flower in the bowl. As he removed his hands, the glimmers lingered a moment, then pulled to the center of the flower. Gathering at the short stem, their concentration created a glow that grew brighter and brighter. Alistar stepped back with the sudden worry that something might shatter.

He heard a faint crack of crystal. As if an obstacle had been removed, the glints of light poured from the stem into the water, dimming instantly. Alistar waited, watching. The water glowed briefly, but the light faded quickly.

He let out a long breath, surprised to discover he was shaking. Alistar caught himself against the table, then hissed in pain as his burned hand objected.

"Are you all right?" Saskia asked

Alistar turned sharply to see her standing in the doorway, watching him with concern. "Saskia. I didn't hear you come in. I'm all right. It just… stings." He shook his hand as if he could toss off the discomfort.

"I didn't mean to startle you. I thought you'd heard me come down after you."

"I was distracted, sorry." Alistar straightened slowly. "Did you see how the motes drew to the water?"

Saskia frowned. "Motes?"

"There are motes of light in the flower." Alistar looked at the flower and amended, "There *were* motes of light in the flower. They'd congregate around my hands when I touched it, and more when I was using it. When I set the flower in the water, they all drew down through the stem into the water. Did you hear the crack?"

"I heard something. Did the flower... crack?" Saskia cautiously stepped closer.

Alistar shook his head. "No, not that I can see. But perhaps like a cut flower, the end of the stem sealed itself, and the motes had to remove the blockage to reach the water." He rubbed his palm. "Do you have a salve or something I can use for my hands?"

"Of course." She sounded relieved at the question. Alistar wasn't sure why. "They're hurting more now?"

He nodded. "Stinging and itching, mostly." He looked at the flower again. The glow in the water was barely perceptible. "The flower should be fine for now."

"The main plant has been fine in its pool for however many years it's been there. I'm sure the flower will be fine here overnight," Saskia said with a small smile.

They returned to the main floor together. Saskia went upstairs for her medicine bag. Alistar started to follow, but Dorne caught his attention.

"Sir, a package arrived for you from Rillwater."

"A package?" Alistar wracked his memory for anything about a package from his family.

"Yes, sir. I brought it to your study."

"Thank you, Dorne." With a nod, Alistar headed upstairs, letting Saskia know he would be in his study on the way.

On his study desk, he found a compact package wrapped in oiled leather. The tag simply addressed it to him, but he recognized his mother's handwriting.

The book! I nearly forgot. It was only a couple days ago that we talked about it, though. Mother must have gotten it immediately.

He cut the cords binding it closed and unwrapped the leather. Inside he found a captain's logbook. His brow furrowed and he opened the cover. A folded letter was tucked into the inside cover pocket. The logbook itself was filled with neat, precise script in a hand he didn't recognize. It took him only a moment to realize that they weren't log entries, but a story had been scribed into the book.

In the Age of the Blood Wars, before Rechmal gifted his magic to our people, many who sought powers beyond their reach turned to dark, corrupted paths to find it. Such were the days of necromancers and soulbinders. In the darkest days, the soulbinder Kajal claimed the lands from the Western Sea to the Plains of Emerald.

Alistar didn't know either location, and without context, could only assume the statement implied a large and valuable area. The following description of conquered cities and strongholds confirmed his guess. What caught his attention most, though, was mention of Kajal's army consisting almost entirely of stone and metal golems powered by the trapped souls of his victims, bound to obey him.

He shivered. *I'm glad this story doesn't give any details about how Kajal gained his powers or used them. Even if this is myth, I wouldn't want anyone taking ideas to follow his path.*

As was the nature of such tales, a hero arose to challenge Kajal. The story described him as a valiant warrior, proven in battle and unmatched in skill, but when it came to the first instance of his identity, his name was blacked out. Alistar frowned at the page. Glancing to the next page, he saw another blacked out square obscuring the name. *Odd. Clearly deliberate. I wonder if Lamorage's copy has the same thing. He didn't mention it.*

The hero's first confrontation with Kajal ended poorly. Despite his skill, the nameless hero was unprepared for the power the soulbinder wielded and the might of his golems.

Badly wounded, the hero fled, pursued by the relentless, tireless constructs.

Deep within the Pale Mountains, exhausted and wounded, he stumbled upon a valley sheltered from the snow and stinging wind. Within, he found a shrine. Though the god was unknown to him, he prostrated himself before the shrine and pleaded for aid.

A voice whispered in his ear, soft and sourceless. "Will you pledge to me your wealth?"

"If you will give me victory over Kajal, I will give you all my wealth, my lands, everything I possess."

"Will you pledge to me your life?"

"My life and the lives of those who serve me," he answered.

"Will you pledge to me your faith?"

"For Kajal's destruction, I will pledge you my faith."

The wind swirled around him. "And why, human, are you so free to offer not only your own self, but that of all who follow you, to a god whose name you do not even know?"

Only then did he realize the god's test was not a demand for blind submission. "The Soulbinder's hold on these lands crushes all who defy him. His golems stalk me even now. If I fall to them, I will be bound as they are, and he will use me to destroy all who stood at my side, as he's done with every conquest. I do not know who you are or what name to call you, Great One, but clearly, there are or have been those who thought you worthy of their devotion, and I see no signs that the blood of men has been shed upon this altar."

The wind grew chill. "I do not ask the blood of men, nor of any other. I ask loyalty and honesty of those who invoke my name. I am Rechmal."

The hero stood. "Lord Rechmal, all that you ask, I pledge to you. These lands and these people suffer, and alone, we lack the strength to defeat Kajal. Please grant me your favor."

Alistar looked up when he heard footsteps. Saskia came in with a jar of salve. She cast a curious look at the pages on his desk.

"The story that Mother mentioned last time we spoke. She sent a copy."

"Ah. Does it have any clues about the flower?"

"Not yet, but it does have a powerful 'soulbinder' who created murderous constructs to subjugate the land. The hero is appealing to Rechmal for a boon."

He pulled off his gloves and kept reading while Saskia applied the salve. The scene that followed was similar to the one Lamorage described in the book he found. Rechmal manifested before the hero, and around his feet, the first frost's breath flowers bloomed. The god held a crystal flower in one hand. To Alistar's surprise, however, the god did not offer the crystal to the hero. The story described radiance shining from the crystal, and Rechmal formed the light into a blade, promising that it could cut through even stone, and that if given the proper components, it could consume Kajal's protective magics, rendering him vulnerable.

The hero stood in awe of Rechmal's gift, but he saw also that the crystal held greater power yet, and he lusted for more. And so it was that when Rechmal put the blade in his hand, the hero also saw a single crystal seed fall from the flower to the ground.

Once the god departed, the hero let the sword fall and searched the ground frantically for the fallen seed. He found it nestled among the living flowers. Only once it was safely hidden did he collect the sword.

Alistar stopped. "*That* wasn't in the copy Lamorage found."

"What wasn't?" Saskia asked.

"In this version, Rechmal gave the hero a magical weapon to fight the soulbinder. The god was carrying a crystal frost's breath, but he didn't give it to the hero. He got a seed of the flower when one fell to the ground, not because it was given to him."

"You mean he... essentially stole it from Rechmal?" Saskia asked.

"That's the implication." Alistar flexed his fingers, feeling the sting starting to fade. "Thanks."

Saskia looked over his shoulder at the text. "'But great was his folly, for Rechmal knew his thirst for power, and the seed had not fallen by accident, for the god still tested his new devotee. Thinking he had deceived the god, the hero set himself to completing the sword's magic so he might overcome Kajal's protections.' Well, if Rechmal set a trap to trip up his new champion, that seems a bit unfair."

"I'm not sure..." Alistar's brow furrowed. "It reads to me more like Rechmal had doubts about this hero. You missed the part where said hero offered to pledge his fortune, the lives of both himself and anyone in his service, and his devotion to a god he knew nothing about—not even a name. Desperate, sure, but this was a time when all manner of powerful beings, evil as well as good, could masquerade as divine."

"Still..." Saskia frowned. "Also, why is the hero's name blacked out?"

"I'm not sure," Alistar told her. "Still hoping for an explanation of that. This version also seems longer than Lamorage's. I'm guessing because the hero has to do something with the sword before he can face Kajal."

He skimmed through the next section, where the hero single-handedly defeated an ancient dragon. When he drove the sword through its heart, the blade captured the dragon's greed and wove it into its own spellwork. Thus empowered, the hero challenged Kajal once more.

Kajal's army of golems stood between him and the soulbinder. The hero tested the strength of his newly empowered blade. It sliced through stone and metal like parchment, and with every cut, the constructs bled.

Alistar stopped, reading the words again.

With each swing, the bound constructs fell, blood spilling from their wounds. He advanced toward Kajal's throne. Behind him, the bodies of the soulbinder's enslaved constructs transformed, in death restored to their own forms.

Alistar shuddered. The idea of someone's soul being trapped in a construct was horrifying enough. The idea of their own bodies being warped into the constructs that trapped them was far worse. If it troubled the hero, though, the tale gave no clues. It described the battle between the hero and Kajal, making it clear that even with Rechmal's gift, the fight wasn't easily won. When Kajal finally fell, the hero offered thanks and praise to Rechmal, and claimed Kajal's conquered lands as his own.

His valor freed us from the soulbinder's grasp, and under his rule, we thrived. He was called the greatest of the kings. And in time, as worship of Rechmal and the rest of the Reyker spread like the frost's breath flowers across the land, he convinced himself that Rechmal had gifted him the seed he stole. That it was his due reward. That the power hidden within it belonged to him and his descendants.

Thus it was that our savior sowed the seed of our doom.

For his valor and his victory, his deeds will never be forgotten. For his greed and the doom he brought upon us, his name will never be remembered.

Alistar stared at the closing lines in silence for a long moment. Finally, he said quietly, "Saskia, is it just me, or do those lines make it sound like this nameless king's use of the crystal seed is somehow responsible for the destruction of Heiset?" His voice was steady and calm as he fought to keep a sharp spike of fear under control.

"Um." She rested her hand on his shoulder. "They do... seem to imply that. I take it Lamorage's version didn't include this bit?"

"Oh, his copy was missing the end, so I have no idea if it did or not, but since it claimed the seed, or flower, *was* Rechmal's gift to the hero, I imagine not. So, what does it mean? What does it mean about..." He gestured toward the floor. "About what's growing under our feet?" He shoved to his feet and paced. "Why are the stories different, and are either of them right?"

"Is there a way to know which one's older?" Saskia asked.

He combed his fingers through his beard. "I don't know if Lamorage's book gives any information on the age or origins of that version. As for this one, I can ask Mother." He returned to the desk and found her speaking stone. A glance at the clock confirmed that it wasn't yet the hour for dinner. He activated it.

A little time passed. Alistar began pacing impatiently again until finally the stone's glow shifted colors. His mother's voice carried through the stone. "Alistar. What news?"

"Saskia and I are well here," he responded. "And you?"

"Your father and I are well also."

"Your package arrived today. Thank you."

"Ah, good. I hope you found something useful in it."

He hesitated, then asked, "Where did that story come from? How old is it?"

"Well, obviously the exact age is hard to say, but we can be fairly sure that the Blood Wars referenced at the start was the time before the Dynasty, and the Dynasty probably lasted between five to six hundred years before it gave way to the Oligarchy. Of course, the Oligarchy lasted only a decade until the situation, whatever the situation was, in Heiset became untenable and our people escaped through the portals and ended up in Calarand." She paused a moment. "Well, some of us ended up in Calarand. There are theories that some sections of the populous ended up elsewhere. But regardless, that's the best estimate I can give you as to the age of the story."

"But do you know how old this *version* of it is?" Alistar asked. "Another book we found in the depths of the manor seemed to be the same overall story, but with some important differences."

"The book it came from belongs to my father and came with the family through the portal," she answered. He pictured her cocking her head to one side as he heard the note of curiosity in her voice. "What sorts of differences?"

"Rechmal's gift, primarily. In this version, the god gave the hero a sword, and let the seed fall as a... test, I guess? In the other version, Rechmal gave the crystal flower to the hero."

He heard the crash of a chair falling backwards as Mother sprang to her feet. "That's a blasphemous lie!"

Alistar and Saskia both jumped at the outburst. In the background, Alistar heard his father say something, tone surprised.

His mother spoke again, furious. "Because he *stole* it! That power was never meant for mortals! Do you think Rechmal would *give* any human that power?"

Alistar cleared his throat. "The story was vague about just what powers were held in the seed."

"As it should be!"

"Mother, please, what else do you know about this seed?"

She let out a heavy breath. "After he established his throne, the thief planted it, and once it sprouted, he made it the symbol of his reign. His house used the frost's breath flower as their emblem from then on. It's thought that none of his line passed through the portal, fortunately. If they had, they would have tried to bring something of the plant with them."

Alistar shifted uneasily, glancing at Saskia. "But what does the plant *do*?"

"Most of that knowledge is lost, Alistar. The best I can tell you is that it gave great power to one who could harness it, and that power grew addictive. It also came with progressively greater cost. Perhaps my father could tell you more. But why the interest in the plant? I thought you were interested in the idea of constructs that could kill."

Alistar rubbed his tender palm. "I was interested in those, yes. But the plant has become a more immediate concern."

"Why?" she asked cautiously.

"Because..." He hesitated a long moment. "Because at least

one seed *was* smuggled through the portal, planted, and allowed to grow. And today, I found it. In the basement of my manor."

A long silence. Then, "What?"

"There's a crystal frost's breath plant growing in a pool of water in my basement."

Only a few times in his life had Alistar heard his mother swear so fervently and at such length. Finally, she paused, drawing a deep breath. "Are you certain of this, Alistar?"

"I am."

"I can confirm it," Saskia added. "But we don't yet know what danger it might pose—to us, to Lewarden, to anyone."

Another slow exhale. "You said it's in water? That's good. Water blocks and diffuses most of its power. Does it have any blooms?"

"Water diffuses its power?" Alistar repeated. "And none of the blooms currently on the plant are fully grown yet. There's one full bloom—I have possession of it right now, but during the coup attempt, Sok'lof used it to convince the Successors that he was a powerful priest, maybe even a prophet. Based on the state of the stems, we assume another flower has been taken, though it's probably not a mature bloom. We suspect Sunward has it."

"Your flower is in water as well?"

"It is now. It hasn't been until today, though," Alistar told her.

Another, shorter burst of profanity. "Don't take it out of the water again. Make sure it's a *lot* of water. And don't discard the water if you need to change it out. *Definitely* do not pour it into the yard or the sewers."

"Mother, what *is* this plant? How do you know so much about it?"

"I don't know nearly enough about it, just what my father taught me. Blood and sand, I need to talk to him. He'll know more. But I can tell you that plant holds more potential for destruction than any artifact Calarand has ever produced.

Blackened shoals, how did anyone smuggle a seed through the portal. And *why?* *Why* would they bring a piece of the very thing that destroyed Heiset? "

Alistar stared at the stone. "It did… what?" He thought again of the last lines of the story she'd sent. "You mean that this plant, growing within my house, holds the potential to destroy nations?" *I was opening doors and moving a mining suit with that flower. I was PLAYING with the artifact that destroyed our homeland?* The thought was both baffling and horrifying.

Silence again, then his mother quietly answered, one word. "Yes."

CHAPTER 38

The long silence was broken not by Alistar or his mother, but by Admiral As'enel. "Now, I don't mean to question this tale, but I can't say it's one I've heard you tell before. Might be the most details I've heard anyone tell about Heiset history. More than most anyone even knows about Heiset history, what with our ancestors forgetting so much when they went through the portal."

Alistar wished he could see his parents. He could only imagine what expressions might be on his mother's face, though he could picture his father's easy smile to accompany the deceptively casual tone.

His mother sighed. "It never came up before, and until today, I had no reason to think it ever would. You're right, it's a lot more than most know about our history. I know it from my parents, and they learned it from my father's parents."

"But *how* did they know it?" Alistar cut in.

Another sigh. "Someone had to remember enough to watch for signs that the disaster we fled found a way of following us, and the best candidate to carry that knowledge was a member of the family charged with containing the source of the destruction. It's the legacy of the De'seneth family."

"But you didn't pass this on to your children?" Saskia asked.

"The duties went to my older sister and her family. In theory, at least. Apparently, Rechmal has other ideas." Her voice was dry.

Alistar smiled tightly. "So it seems."

"I'll speak with my parents. Neither of them cares much for travel anymore, but for this, they might make the trip to Lewarden."

"All right. I should be able to convince Lady Syri to leave the cut flower here for a while." Alistar considered the logistics and how to frame that request.

"Lady Syri?" his mother repeated. "How is the Silver Prince connected to it?"

Alistar blinked, then realized he hadn't explained enough about how they'd discovered the flower. "It's been in Silverline keeping for the last year and a few months. We first encountered it when Baron Sok'lof used it to convince the Successors that he was a prophet of Rechmal. Lady Syri had been leading a team to study it. We only brought it to the manor to test some theories and find out if it could open the sealed basement doors."

"And it's been unshielded, in the city, the whole time." She cursed. "Under no circumstances should you take it out of the water, Alistar. Do you understand?"

"I can't say I understand the *reason*," he admitted. "But I can keep it in water."

"Water draws the more dangerous effects and blocks them. But if it's already been out this long... Have you heard any rumors of strange phenomena? Unconventional magic? Previously undocumented abilities?"

Saskia spoke, her voice quiet. "Internal channeling. People

who demonstrate abilities different from a channeler, and who draw from a source that's not the mahiy lines."

"Yes, anything like that," Alistar's mother said.

Alistar cleared his throat. "Um, yes, that's… happening now. The first time I heard about it was during Cemar's attempted coup. At least one of his devotees had this ability, and he implied that others did as well."

"You've seen it?" she demanded. "Personally?"

"Yes."

Saskia spoke. "From a conversation I had with an elf with this ability, I suspect that some of those who survived Rat's Disease, or never succumbed to it despite constant use of Elixir, had the ability. He described it as being able to 'see' the 'good' and the 'bad' parts of the drug after ingesting it, and being able to use the good parts to burn out the bad so it wouldn't kill him."

"And is keeping the plant and flower in water the only means of containing them?" Alistar asked.

"The only one available to you," his mother answered. "Once, those charged with containing the plant used the champion's sword. Its ability to absorb magic was the most effective way of containing it. However, the blade was stolen, and is either still in Heiset, or it was carried through a different portal. I don't know anything more about it."

Alistar grimaced and nodded. "It's more than I knew before. Thank you."

"I'm just glad you asked for a copy of the story. If I'd known about the plant, I'd have sent it to you far sooner. But I never told you the tales, and that fault is mine."

His father spoke again. "Well, Alistar, it sounds as if we'll be visiting you this time. Expect us within the week. And perhaps we can stay for this Exhibition I keep hearing about!"

Before Alistar could respond, he noticed another speaking stone pulsing with the low light that indicated someone trying to make contact. Roddek's stone. He nudged Saskia and nodded at Roddek's speaking stone.

She motioned for him to answer it as she said, "You're welcome to stay as long as you're able. My father would be delighted to see you as well."

Alistar took Roddek's stone and stepped to the far corner of the room to activate it. "Alistar here," he said quietly.

Roddek spoke in an urgent, breathless whisper. "I hope it's a good time to talk, because you need to hear this."

"Hear what? Are you hurt? What's wrong?"

"Not hurt. Close call, not hurt." Roddek panted, then spoke again. "Okay, don't think any of them saw me. Heh."

Alistar heard an echo of distant shouts from Roddek's stone. "Are you sure?"

A tight laugh. "Oh, well, that would be the distraction, you see. So I *could* get back out of the pirate encampment." A soft grunt, some shifting, and Roddek spoke again. "We've been watching the pirates, like Father told us. Was pretty dull until today, when a couple guys showed up. They've had scouts coming and going the whole time, but these new guys aren't pirates. They're messengers. We spotted them before they got to the entrance, so we also saw where they stashed their gear before going in."

"What sort of gear would they have been stashing?" Alistar asked. "And messengers from who and where?"

"They stashed anything with an emblem. Weren't close enough to identify the markings when they were changing, but I sent someone to have a look after they were gone. Pirates seemed to recognize them, or they gave some identifying signal. Pirates weren't *happy* to see them but didn't seem surprised either. The captain came out to the messengers personally."

"Do you know the captain's name or his ship?" Alistar asked.

"The messengers hailed him as Captain Seaspray," Roddek answered. "This was the first time I saw him actually come out to the edge of the camp. Usually scouts and the like go to him instead. From the way the messengers spoke, they considered him coming to them as their due, like he owed it to them."

"Can't imagine the captain was pleased," Alistar said. "Who did they say sent them?"

"They didn't, at least not out there. Just said they'd come to ensure that deliveries were on time. The captain led them into the encampment, and no one looked happy." He heard the smirk in Roddek's voice. "Decided I needed to listen in on their chat."

"Roddek, are you *in* the pirate camp?"

"Not anymore," Roddek said quickly. "And the distraction shouldn't raise suspicion—we took advantage of their carelessness."

"You're not there now, but you did get in? Did you hear their conversation?" Sometimes, trying to get information from Roddek was like wrestling an octopus.

"Oh! Yes, I snuck in after them. Didn't hear much until they got inside, but none of them said much until then either. Once they were inside, the messengers started making a fuss about missing shipments, and contracts, and due dates."

"I'm sure they were quite upset about that," Alistar murmured.

"The part that worries me, though, is one of the messengers told the captain that failure to meet his obligations would make their lord question his interest in 'giving the rule of our seas to you' and that 'perhaps Rillwater will remain.'" Roddek's voice dropped low and anxious. "Alistar, no Lewarden noble could promise *that*, could they? The *king* gave us that charge."

"I know one who might think he could," Alistar said darkly, thinking of Prince Pietro's assertions that he could run Silverline Power by his word alone. "But legally, that's for the king to say. And a pirate should know that." *Or do Prince Pietro's ambitions stretch toward the throne?* A knot of anger simmered in his gut. "They're idiots if they think we'd stand by and let them."

"I don't think they do expect us to," Roddek said tightly. "I think they expect much the opposite."

Is someone trying *to start a civil war? Or are they just idiots?* Alistar bit back an angry growl. "How about the messengers' gear? What did they have?"

Sounds of movement, a soft clattering of rocks. "Heading over there now."

Alistar heard a brief conversation between Roddek and his first mate, then more movement. Then Roddek sucked in a sharp breath and started cursing softly and fervently.

"What is it? Roddek, what is it?" Alistar hissed.

Roddek gulped audibly. "Alistar, you know more noble houses of Calarand than I do. Please, *please* tell me that the emblem of a fiery sword is used by *someone* other than the Crown?"

Alistar dropped into the closest chair, feeling like the air had been driven from his lungs. Fighting to keep his voice steady, he asked, "Is there a crown around the hilt?"

"No, no crown." Roddek sounded desperately hopeful.

"Well, it's not King Suelton's emblem, then," Alistar said. He wracked his mind for the small differences between Prince Pietro's emblem and Crown Prince Filipp's. He'd know them apart if he saw them, but trying to conjure images of them in his mind was like trying to remember a dream. "What color is..." The flame? No, the flame was always the same color. "The hilt? Or the decorations on it?"

"Uh... Blue? Yeah, blue," Roddek said.

Alistar's free hand clenched. He couldn't remember, was that Pietro's or Filipp's color?

In the background, Roddek's first mate spoke. "It's green on the other coat, though."

Alistar stilled, breath catching in his throat. "They're different?"

"It looks like it. And both are crisp, not like one's more faded out than the other. Why? What does that mean?"

"That means… Oh, that could mean something very, very bad." His chest was tight and his heart hammered. "Roddek, I need you and your crew to do something for me."

"All right. What is it?" Roddek asked uneasily.

"When those messengers leave the pirates, I need you to ambush them. Don't kill them—take them alive. But *do not* let them return to Lewarden. And don't let *anyone* know they've been taken."

"Not even… Father?" Roddek asked.

Alistar shook himself. "Tell Father. Yes, tell him about this, tell him what I've told you to do. But no one outside your crew and the Family."

"All right. Yes sir."

The stone went dark. Alistar exhaled and closed his eyes. His hands were shaking.

Green hilt and blue hilt. Doesn't matter which one belongs to which prince now, not if they're both represented. Are these messengers acting independently? On someone else's orders? Or are both princes involved?

CHAPTER 39

Saskia rested a hand on Alistar's shoulder. He started from his thoughts and turned to her. "Are things arranged for my family to come calling?" he asked. She'd returned his mother's speaking stone to its cradle, now inactive.

"On their end, at least. We still have to take care of the preparations on our side." Saskia paused, then lowered her voice. "Did you just tell Roddek to abduct someone?"

"Two someones. Who might be in the service of the royal house." Somehow the words came out without the raging wash of conflicting emotions that tore through his thoughts.

"What?"

"They have some sort of arrangement with the pirates and aren't pleased with the delays in receiving their goods."

"Who is 'they'? The royal family, or these two individuals?" Saskia asked uneasily.

"I'm not sure. The envoys could be acting without authorization, but... I don't think that's the case. In the gear Roddek found, one carried the emblem of Prince Pietro, and the other, that of Prince Filipp."

Saskia paled. "Both princes?"

Alistar nodded, grim. "These envoys spoke to the pirate captain, wanting to know about shipments that haven't arrived yet. Roddek said they implied that the envoys, or those they represented, have promised these pirates control of the seas in the place of Rillwater."

Saskia shook her head. "Alistar, let's be sensible. What reason would our princes have to ally with the woman who tried to overthrow the Crown?"

Alistar glanced at the door and around the room, confirming that they were still alone and none of the speaking stones had been left active. "Prince Pietro is ambitious, selfish, and overly confident in his abilities. Ever since the assassination attempt on Prince Cero, Pietro has repeatedly attempted to take charge of Silverline Power and to undermine Lady Syri while the Silver Prince has been recovering. Not only that, he knows about the crystal flower and that Lady Syri's studying it. He's tried to gain access to it at least once, probably more. He's intent on getting hold of it and on getting some form of control within Silverline Power."

"Does he have any technical training? Skills as an engineer?" Saskia asked.

"None I know of. Certainly none he's demonstrated in the conversations I've had with him." Alistar grimaced.

"So, his interest in the flower has you suspicious of him," Saskia said.

"That and some suspicions Lady Syri has implied," Alistar told her. He considered briefly how much he should share, but right now, he desperately wanted and needed his wife's level head and her perspective. And perhaps something he said could give her insights into the goings-on in the Lower City. "She thinks he might have instigated the assassination attempt on Prince Cero."

Saskia drew a sharp, startled breath. "What?"

"I think she also suspects he might have been involved in the assassination attempt on Prince Filipp as well," he said quietly. The words felt dangerous to utter aloud, even in the security of their own home. "Lady Syri sent Star with me when Prince Filipp summoned me, and she spent the time examining the rooms, especially the princess's rooms. There were very few people who could have unlocked her balcony door."

Saskia sank down in a chair. "But his own brother? His niece? If that's the case, why would he and Prince Filipp be working together with Sunward? And what evidence is there that the crown prince is involved?"

"I can only assume someone's concealed any suspicious evidence from Prince Filipp, and Pietro is now either looking at Silverline Power as a secondary prize, or he plans to stab his brother in the back once they've secured their ambitions. As for Prince Filipp..." He thought of the haughty, proud man he'd met. "He's waited a long time for the throne, and King Suelton has given up very little power or authority even in his advanced years." Which was an entirely different problem, given the king's age and, some believed, declining mental acuity. "Prince Filipp signed the order for back taxes on the manor. At the time, I assumed he'd simply taken someone else at their word and signed the document without knowledge of the details. But if it was a ploy that he knowingly took part in..."

"That's..." Saskia trailed off. "But why would they work with Sunward, if they *are* working with her? What can she offer them that they don't already have?"

"Automatons that can kill."

"But kill who?" Saskia asked. "Who do they want to attack?"

"I don't know!" Alistar snapped in frustration. "Their father? Rillwater? Another country? Anyone who disagrees with them?"

"I don't know either," Saskia said. "That's why I don't want to leap to conclusions."

"If you have some evidence to support one conclusion or the other, I'd be glad to hear it," Alistar told her.

She started to answer, then paused, brow furrowing. "I don't know if it will help, but maybe." She quickly outlined her conversations with Seva, then explained their experiment with the discarded gloves.

Alistar frowned as she described Seva's responses when he came into the laboratory after Saskia's attempts to analyze the drug, Lumination. "He didn't respond to requests, only orders?"

"Once he was using his abilities, yes. Before then, he was distracted, but responsive. I didn't think there would have been enough Lumination in the air to affect him, but he seemed quite sensitive to it. Terrible as it sounds, I wish we had more samples of the drug to better judge how he responds to it. However, I brought the matter up because of the rubbings." She carefully unfolded several sheets of thin paper and spread them on the side table.

Alistar leaned over the arm of his chair to study them. The shapes weren't as crisp and distinct as they might have hoped, but far better than they could expect under the circumstances. Alistar tried not to mentally superimpose the shape of the royal crest, wracking his memory for other noble crests that used a straight central shaft with some sort of oval shape around the base.

A knock on the study door interrupted those thoughts. He started and pushed to his feet. "Yes?"

Dorne spoke from the other side. "Sir, Guard Star Riverblade wishes to speak with you."

Alistar and Saskia looked to each other in surprise. Saskia folded the rubbings again as Alistar said, "Of course. I'll be down in a moment."

"She requested that, if possible, she speak to you and Lady De'seneth in private. If you don't object, I'll show her up."

"I… see. Certainly, show her up," Alistar said.

Once Dorne's footsteps faded, Saskia spoke softly. "Why would Star come here?"

"She was here earlier with Lady Syri. Maybe Lady Syri sent her with a message she didn't want to send by speaking stone?" Alistar paced around the study, listening for approaching steps.

When he heard them, he paused and straightened his shirt and coat. A moment later, Dorne knocked again and announced, "Guard Star Riverblade to see you, sir."

"Send her in, please," Alistar answered.

The door opened and Star entered. Her uniform was clean and pressed, her hair pulled back in a tight tail. She bowed to Alistar and Saskia.

"Lord De'seneth, Lady De'seneth, thank you."

"Of course. What can we do for you this afternoon?" Alistar asked as Dorne pulled the door closed again.

Star waited a moment for Dorne to leave before answering. "Lord De'seneth, this might be asking a great deal of you and your house, but I'm here to request you to keep the crystal flower, and not return it to the Silverline Power headquarters."

Alistar blinked, taken aback. "I can do that, of course, but why? And does Lady Syri know you're asking this? Did she send you?"

"Lady Syri did not," Star answered. "Prince Cero did."

"Has he recovered enough to return to Silverline Power?" Alistar asked, hopes rising. If the Silver Prince had returned, his injuries weren't as bad as had been implied.

"I'm afraid not," Star answered, dashing those hopes. "But I have spoken with him about the matter and about matters at Silverline Power."

"Did something new happen?" Saskia asked. "Please sit and make yourself comfortable."

Star accepted the offered chair with a nod of thanks. "Shortly after we returned to Silverline Power, Prince Pietro paid another visit."

"Again? Does he think Lady Syri's going to change her mind if he persists long enough?" Alistar shook his head.

"He seems to have begun to grasp the idea that she's not swayed by his words. This time, he bypassed Lady Syri and instead headed to her laboratory and testing chambers. Fortunately, other technicians took note and immediately escorted him away from restricted areas, despite his objections and insistence that he be granted entry."

Alistar growled in frustration. "I *told* him those areas are dangerous the *first* time he tried to get in there."

"Hopefully the lesson will take this time. Lady Syri was informed promptly, and confronted him in the workrooms," Star said.

Alistar frowned. "The workrooms? Where the majority of the technicians work?"

"The very same," she agreed. Though her tone was mild and calm, Alistar recognized the formality as a front to conceal her own thoughts about the children of the royal house having a public spat in front of so many witnesses.

"I take it she wasn't pleased with his intrusion," Alistar said.

Star seemed to struggle with how to respond while remaining appropriately respectful.

Saskia gave her a reassuring smile. "You don't have to be formal here, Star. Neither Alistar nor I will spread tales."

Star let out a long breath, shoulders sagging. "Lady Syri's been jittery and restless since we left here, though she denied it when I mentioned it. When Prince Pietro showed up and made another play for her work, she finally had a target for all that energy, and she unleashed on him. He didn't expect it, but he reciprocated quickly enough. Took the guards to intervene and hustle him out of the building. The other technicians were too shocked to do anything, and I know Prince Cero sent people to talk to them and make sure nothing too scandalous leaves the premises." Star shook her head. "Never seen Lady Syri lose her cool like that."

Saskia glanced to Alistar, then back to Star. "This shift in her behavior happened after she left here? Did you notice any sign of it before then? While she was here?"

"Not that I noticed," Star said.

"Did she interact with the flower, or the main plant, while she was here?" Saskia asked.

"Lamorage didn't suggest I attempt to use the flower until after Lady Syri departed," Alistar said. He thought back to their examination of the plant. A chill ran down his spine and his breath caught a moment. "She did dip her hand in the water to examine the roots of the plant."

Star looked between them, questions in her eyes.

"The crystal frost's breath plant in the basement produces, on its own, more magic than a generator," Alistar said. "The water absorbs the majority of it, and acts as a shield to prevent that magic from running rampant and poisoning everyone here. But it means that water is also saturated with magic."

Star's brow furrowed. "Frost's breath flowers aren't known to produce magic. I only know of the kurowa flowers doing so."

"The common variety produces miniscule amounts, nothing as strong as the kurowa. But it produces enough for Prince Cero to experiment with integrating them into the mahiy lines. However, the crystal flower is an artifact of Heiset that, if certain legends are to be believed, once belonged to Rechmal, god of magic." He didn't add that it might have been the artifact that destroyed Heiset. Much as he respected Star, anything he told her could reach Prince Cero's ears, and Alistar wasn't ready to spread that tale yet, if ever.

"I haven't analyzed the water yet," Saskia added. "However, if Lady Sunward does in fact possess one of the flowers, and the magic within it is even half as potent as what's found in the pool, she could intend to weaponize it. Or she might repeat her previous tactics. Have you heard of the drug Lumination?"

"Mentions of it," Star said. "Unlike Ambrosia, it hasn't found its way out of the Lower City yet. You think Lady Sunward is using her flower, or byproducts of that flower, to craft Lumination?"

"I'm not dismissing the possibility," Saskia told her. "And Lady Syri's contact with the water could have inflicted a similar effect on her. Most recipients of Lumination that I've heard of tend toward overly calm and compliant, but there are always some people who react differently to drugs."

"Members of the Royal Family are protected against forces that would influence them toward compliance," Star said. "I hadn't thought about that protection, but the lady's increased agitation does match the expected response to an attempted influence." She shifted in her chair and toyed with the tassel on her dagger sheath. "You have the flower and the plant as contained as you're able?"

"We do," Alistar said. "And we're conducting what research we can into their origins."

"Good. After Prince Pietro's departure, I spoke with the Silver Prince. Given Prince Pietro's persistence, Prince Cero decided it best that the crystal flower remain in your keeping for the time being. That's acceptable to you?"

"It is," Alistar said. "Does anyone else in Silverline Power know Lady Syri was bringing it here? The other technicians on her team?"

"No. Only Prince Cero, Lady Syri, and the Royal Guards who accompanied her know she brought it here. As far as anyone else in Silverline knows, the flower is currently sealed in a vault until experiments and studies on it can resume." Star's eyes narrowed. "If the knowledge of it reaches other ears, the source lies within your house."

"I understand," Alistar told her. "I trust those who came into the basement with us." Which was a stretch when it came to Tiyron, but he trusted that the elf wouldn't be chatting with nobles, and certainly not with Sunward. "We'll keep it safe."

Star nodded and stood to leave.

Alistar rose as well. "Star, one more question, if you don't mind."

"Yes sir?"

"With the things you saw in Crown Prince Filipp's suite, and in his daughter's room, do you believe Pietro orchestrated the assassination attempt?"

She froze, drawing a sharp breath. "Sir, that's not something I can speak about at this time."

"And possibly the attack on Prince Cero as well?"

"The evidence is… not conclusive enough to level accusations at any individual," Star said. But her head moved in a subtle nod.

"Of course. I ask your pardon for prying."

Star bowed to both Alistar and Saskia and took her leave.

CHAPTER 40

Rykka found her brother in his room. He'd been given space in the guest quarters on the ground floor rather than the servants' quarters. The larger rooms offered him more space to maneuver the chair, and the better amenities improved his disposition, though the difference might not have been evident to anyone else.

She knocked on the partially open door and walked in. Late afternoon sun bathed the room in light, brightening the space far more than it would one of the cramped rooms in the servants' quarters. Tiyron was standing, leaning against the chair, and gripping one armrest for support. He looked worn and tired, shadows under his eyes. He nodded to her. "Hey."

"You're getting steadier," she said.

He snorted. "If you say so. I'm sick of sitting in this thing."

She nodded. "At least it can manage stairs."

"Would be pretty useless for getting around most houses if it couldn't." He slowly moved around the chair, each step placed with care, until he stood in front of her. "The young woman who was here today, Lady Syri. She's the Silver Prince's daughter?"

"Yeah. I met her a couple times while we were stopping Cemar, but I was using a different identity then."

Tiyron's eyebrows rose. "Expected her to be older. Expected her to be more stuck up, too."

"I suppose. Thinking of being down there, though, did you ever see Sunward or any of the others using the crystal?"

He waved a hand dismissively, though quickly resumed his firm grip on the chair. "A few parlor tricks, nothing spectacular. Sok'lof kept experimenting with ways to attach it to a staff while still being able to activate it."

"Did you notice any strange behaviors from them or anyone else when someone did use it?" Time to think had made her realize that Saskia's point had been valid. Alistar had been acting odd—and she and Lamorage had followed right after him without a second thought.

Tiyron frowned at her. "Strange how?"

"Did you ever find yourself wondering why you'd said or done something afterwards? Like you were under the influence of some mild narcotic?"

He started to deny the possibility, but stopped again, frowning deeper. "Nothing major. Larisa tended to hang around a lot when they were doing anything with the crystal, though. She seemed to have a sense for when they were using it. I suppose there were some times that she seemed more drugged than usual afterwards. You must have noticed something today?"

She sighed. "I didn't at the time. Looking back now, though, it feels like my thoughts weren't as clear as they should have been."

"All right," Tiyron said slowly. "If that's the case, what's it tell us and what can we do about it?"

"Sunward likes using drugs to control people. She could be taking what she learned from Ambrosia to make a second attempt." Rykka wasn't satisfied with that answer. Something was missing, but she couldn't capture it.

His brow furrowed in thought as he lowered himself back into the chair. "Seems to have a different goal, though. You said she's giving out samples and then testing people. What's she doing with those she collects? Taking them to this factory and then… putting them to work? She could just nab any random bunch off the street for that. Why does she want *these* people?"

"I don't know!" Rykka threw her hands up in frustration. "I don't know enough about what internal channelers can do to know how she might use them. And she didn't have them all working. A bunch were just locked up in a room in the basement." She frowned. "And there was also that partially functional automaton that was restrained for some reason."

"Experiments?" Tiyron suggested. "Using it for a test subject? You're the one who's good at making devices and that sort of thing."

"I need to go back there." Rykka shifted her weight back and forth in an attempt to resist the urge to pace.

"Well, that's a terrible idea," Tiyron said, voice flat.

Her head jerked up in surprise at him. "What?"

"First time in, you almost got killed, Rykka. You got in and out the second time *and* ran into Larisa. She's seen you a couple times now. She's an addict, but she's not so stupid that seeing a supposedly dead man snooping around three times in a couple days isn't suspicious. You want her to really try to convince Sunward that she's not hallucinating?"

Rykka's jaw tightened. "I *know* I can find out more about what's going on if I get in there. Especially if I get in there without Crown agents on my heels."

Tiyron nudged the chair forward until he was unavoidably in her space. "I will be *damned* if I let you go off and get captured, tortured, or killed and leave me *here*, with *these* people." He grabbed her wrist, voice dropping low. "I won't lose you."

The intensity of his voice stopped any glib response. Her shoulders slumped. "How else are we going to know what she's doing? If we wait too long, the Crown agents are going to raid the warehouse and take everything off to their own warehouses. Probably take all the people too, because what's the problem if some slums dwellers just never reappear? I'm sure someone would love to have a bunch of identified internal channelers to study."

Tiyron released her wrist. "While I can't believe I'm suggesting this, you seem to have connections with these agents. Could find out when the raid is and see if you can get yourself in with them."

It wasn't ideal at all, but he had a point. She let out a long, heavy sigh. "I hate that idea almost as much as you do. But I can find out the plan. I know who to lean on for information."

After she left her brother's room, Rykka tracked down Windshadow. She found him in his room in the midst of his official responsibilities as Alistar's footman, which reminded her that she had quite a list of things she hadn't done for Saskia, and some of the maids had begun gossiping. Fortunately, either Windshadow or Dorne had let slip a rumor that her "real" job was to be Saskia's bodyguard rather than a true lady's maid, and the gossip reflected that.

His door stood slightly ajar and opened silently at a gentle push. A window let in the afternoon light, and one pane was tilted open to let in the spring air and scents of recently cut grass.

"Have a moment?" Rykka asked.

Windshadow bit back a curse, and she knew she'd startled him once again. He set aside the suit coat he'd been mending and stood. "I can make one. What can I do for you?"

She closed the door behind her and approached so they

could speak quietly. "Investigator Dawncloud was considering an unannounced inspection of Lady Ravencrest's factory. When is that happening? I want to be there when it does."

"Oh." He glanced around the room and closed the window-pane before answering. "She wanted it to have happened already, but someone higher up the chain of command is blocking approval. She's not sure who or why. I've devoted most of my available time to the tasks Lord De'seneth already assigned me, and I've had little opportunity to find out more from my contacts. What I have learned, though, points toward the involvement of someone quite high ranking."

A chill ran down Rykka's spine. "Is Dawncloud's name attached to the request? I don't know who Sunward's lover in the nobility is, but they have enough standing to have protected her so far. Dawncloud could be in danger."

"She's often in danger. It's the nature of her job."

Rykka waved a hand dismissively. "Different sort of danger. Just tell her not to push, all right?"

Windshadow raised an eyebrow. "You assume I'm in frequent contact with her."

Rykka rolled her eyes. "Windshadow, the two of you have cute pet names for each other. Of course I assume you're in frequent contact."

He flushed.

"I don't need or want to know about your relationship, to be clear. I also don't want someone you care about to get mysteriously reassigned to somewhere that gets her killed."

Windshadow collected himself quickly. "She shouldn't be. She made the request for a number of warehouses on that street, multiple owners, to avoid the appearance of targeting Ravencrest in particular. The rest were approved; only Raven-crest's factories were denied."

Her eyebrows rose. "And no one thought that would sound suspicious?"

Windshadow gave her a long, bland look. "Suspicious? No, most would think it meant that Ravencrest paid better bribes to the officials."

As soon as he said it, that answer was obvious. Of course factory owners regularly bribed officials to overlook various infractions. "Right. Reyker forbid that nobles follow the laws. So, when will she be conducting the surprise inspections of the rest of the factories?"

"You still want to take part?"

"I want to know when it's happening so I can perform an unapproved and unofficial inspection."

"That's the answer you're *not* supposed to tell me, you know," Windshadow said. "And I don't know exactly when the inspections will take place. Dawncloud isn't one to respect the protection bought by bribes, so she's been pushing for an answer about why Ravencrest is exempt. And no one who knows her reputation would be surprised by that. Maybe she can get the permission pushed through."

"We don't have time to wait on a maybe. I have to know why Sunward and Ravencrest want those people and how they intend to use them."

"And you think that justifies flouting the laws?"

Rykka cast him a sidelong look. "I guarantee you don't want me to answer that."

"Which begs the question of why you're telling me any of this."

She drew a breath and let it out slowly. "Because whether I like it or not, I need backup."

Windshadow shook his head. "We got away with it the first time. We're not getting away with skulking into that warehouse against direct orders."

She ground her teeth in frustration.

"I know you don't like it, Darkwood, but I can't and won't help you break into that warehouse again. You want to help the people of the slums, find another way."

"How many layers of approval would Dawncloud need to conduct a raid in the Lower City?" Rykka asked, voice tight.

Windshadow frowned, eying her curiously. "If she could give a good reason, her superior could approve one."

"How about going after a rising crime lord for dealing in illegal substances, indentured servitude, and…" She considered for a moment what sorts of crimes might actually matter to the nobility. "Tax evasion."

Windshadow smothered a startled laugh. "And who is this proposed target?"

"His name's Whitetooth. He's been around a while, but recently started to gain power. He dealt in Elixir in the past, now he's cornered the market on a new drug. He's gotten powerful enough to attack other dealers with impunity and without retaliation. And I'm certain he's not been giving the Crown its cut of his illicit earnings."

"How do you know about this Whitetooth?"

"You remember scolding me about having a meal with a young man of ill repute? He was my contact."

Windshadow straightened. "Was? Was he discovered?"

"Not for his connection to me. However, for reasons I can only speculate about, Whitetooth allowed Lady Ravencrest to conduct the same test I witnessed Sunward doing, drugging people to check for a specific ability. My contact managed to escape, narrowly, and found a safe place to hide, but has had to give up his connections to Whitetooth."

"But he's not dead, at least." Windshadow nodded slowly. Then his brow furrowed in thought. "If he had to escape, though, did he demonstrate the ability they were looking for?"

"He did," Rykka acknowledged, not without reservations. "Evidently, Ravencrest was buying the debts of those who passed the test from Whitetooth." She'd been meaning to talk to Seva, but hadn't gone back to the clinic since Tiyron moved into the manor.

Windshadow's expression darkened. "Indentured servitude. Your contact isn't the only one of Whitetooth's people trapped in that situation, I assume." He didn't wait for her to confirm. "How do you see yourself being involved if Dawncloud were to conduct this raid?"

"Well, I doubt she'd let me come along."

"You could present yourself as a local contact." Windshadow's expression pinched, as if he couldn't believe what he was saying. "I'm sure you're... skilled enough that such a persona couldn't be connected to this house or your work here."

Rykka nodded thoughtfully. "I know for certain that another drug dealer confronted Whitetooth, and he had his thugs beat her and toss her out. Of course, any new persona wouldn't say they *were* acting on behalf of the Lady of Nightbane, but they also wouldn't say that they *weren't*."

"I'll speak to Dawncloud, see what she can do—and when. She'll appreciate a lead that she *can* pursue. I expect it'll happen soon."

"The less time the rats have to scurry into their holes, the better." Rykka brushed back her hair. *I can't believe I'm knowingly sending agents of the Crown to raid a Lower City crime lord. Feels wrong. Feels like we should be handling it ourselves. That's what Tiyron would say. But... am I still one of them? Being in the Lower City and the slums feels like being home, but yet, even then, it's almost like I'm stopping in to visit, not returning to a place where I belong.*

It doesn't feel the way being on a ship and being part of Captain Roddek's crew feels.

While that unexpected and uncomfortable thought lingered, a knock on Windshadow's door interrupted further conversation. They both started and Rykka cursed herself for not hearing approaching footsteps. She sidled out of immediate line of sight. No need to advertise her presence, whether the person on the other side was someone who posed a threat or just a nosy servant looking for rumors to spread.

Windshadow opened the door. "Dorne. What can I do for you? Does Lord De'seneth need me?" He glanced toward the silver bell on his wall as if wondering whether he missed its chime.

"Lord and Lady De'seneth request your presence," the butler answered. "And yours as well, Darkwood."

She *had* asked Dorne where Windshadow was earlier, but even still, she was startled to be called out. "Right now?"

She couldn't see Dorne's expression from her angle, but she was confident he didn't do anything as undignified as visible roll his eyes at her question. "As soon as possible, yes."

"Right. Well, I suppose I'm ready now, so, sure. Let's see what new disaster awaits us."

Windshadow shot her a disapproving glower. She unapologetically walked past him and out of the room.

CHAPTER 41

Dorne led them to Alistar's study. Bookshelves lined one wall, and the room always smelled of leather and a hint of pipe smoke, although neither Alistar nor Saskia indulged in that habit, as far as Rykka knew. Maybe it had been a vice of the previous owners. The mood in the room was serious.

Dorne closed the door after them. Once the sound of his footsteps faded, Alistar spoke. "Rykka, when you followed Sunward and found the recruitment meeting, you also heard Sunward and a man, correct?"

She nodded. "Sunward's lover, yes."

"Would you recognize his voice if you heard it again?"

Her eyebrows rose. "I think so. Do you have something in mind?"

"The start of an idea. Still working out how to set it up." Alistar turned to Windshadow. "Soluthos, were you able to capture images of the blueprints in the vault?"

"I was, sir." Windshadow handed the image stone to Alistar. "And I confirmed that the instructions to move them into the vault originated from Prince Filipp personally."

Alistar nodded thoughtfully. Looking at him now, Rykka

could see the difference from earlier when he'd been using the flower. He was focused now, fully present, no longer distracted by mysteries only he could see. Or at least not as distracted by them. She wasn't sure how long the effect lasted.

"Why would Prince Filipp care about the blueprints to this house?" Rykka asked.

She'd directed the question to Alistar, but Windshadow answered. "I'm not sure. I understand that Prince Cero spoke quite firmly with him after the Crown Prince signed his name to the documents authorizing the tax issue. It could be that is when he learned the history and significance of the property, and ordered the blueprints locked away for security purposes."

Rykka watched Alistar while Windshadow spoke. Alistar was good at maintaining a neutral expression, but even so, she didn't think he agreed with Windshadow's theory.

She offered another. "Or he moved them as petty revenge for getting chewed out by his uncle."

"I suppose that's… possible," Windshadow allowed. "No reason was given for his instructions."

"Whatever the reason, I'm glad you're able to access them, Soluthos," Alistar said. "Thanks to today's experiments, we have access to more areas than before, but not everything yet. These images will help."

"Of course, sir." Windshadow bowed.

How does Alistar convince people like Windshadow or Dahr, loyal lackeys of the Crown, to do things that skirt or outright ignore the spirit of the law, even if not the letter of it? How does he convince them that doing what he asks is necessary and aligned with their duties to crown and country? Blight, how did he convince me *of the same?*

The answer came as quickly as the question had. Even on land, with no ship and no captain's title, Alistar carried himself as master of his vessel, with an unconscious assumption that his will was law.

Saskia spoke. "While you're both here, I'd like you to take a look at these rubbings. I'm hoping to identify the sigil." She motioned to several sheets of thin paper on the desk. "I know it belongs to one of the noble houses."

Rykka and Windshadow both moved to examine the small rubbings. One thought came immediately to Rykka's mind, but she didn't say it, instead glancing to Windshadow.

"The shapes and style resemble that of His Highness, King Suelton," Windshadow said. "It lacks the lightning bolt of Prince Cero, unless the rubbing failed to capture that detail." He studied the images thoughtfully, head tilting to the side as if to get another angle. "Although if the upper shaft is a tree trunk, and the oval represented a hill, it might be the Pineridge crest. I apologize, Lady De'seneth. The image is quite small and not crisp enough for me to say with confidence."

"The royal crest is what came to my mind," Rykka added.

Saskia nodded. "Thank you. Unfortunately, the source wasn't as detailed as I would have liked either."

"You can return to your regular duties, Soluthos," Alistar said.

"I need to speak with you about several matters, Rykka," Saskia said.

Windshadow left. Rykka waited, not sure if she was about to be berated for her inadequacies as a lady's maid, or if she was about to become privy to information Alistar and Saskia weren't ready to share with Windshadow.

Her answer came quickly. Saskia gestured at the rubbings. "With Seva's help, I made the rubbings from the gloves he retrieved after the nobleman visited Whitetooth."

Rykka looked at the small, ring-sized images again. "So presumably not the royal crest, then."

Alistar and Saskia exchanged a look.

Rykka stood straighter, looking from one to the other. "It's *not* the royal crest, right?"

"It's not the king's crest," Alistar said. "It might be one of the princes', though." He summarized Captain Roddek's findings in the wake of the emissaries' visit to the pirate hideout.

Rykka listened in stunned silence. When she finally found her voice, she whispered, "Hematic perdition. The crown prince might be anxious to take the throne already, but the king's old enough he shouldn't have to wait *that* much longer."

Alistar winced. "Inappropriate, but not inaccurate."

"Don't worry, I won't say it in front of Windshadow. But why conspire against his father *now*? Why didn't he make an attempt at the throne years ago?"

"He didn't have Sunward whispering in his ear years ago," Saskia said.

Alistar shook his head. "No, it's not just that. He had a family. That's where his focus was. Now he's lost them."

Rykka didn't know much about either prince, but Alistar's words slid another element into place. "He's lost his family, and he blames his father for not protecting them."

Alistar straightened, sucking in a sharp breath. "Motive."

"And he's planning to make his move at the Grand Exhibition," Saskia said. "That's the direction this all points, doesn't it? And all the additions he keeps making to the Exhibition infrastructure could reflect adjustments in his plans."

"I don't know anything about that side of things, but Ravencrest did say her deadline was the Exhibition," Rykka said. Her brow furrowed. "If the princes are involved, that explains why Investigator Dawncloud can't get permission to do an inspection on Ravencrest's warehouses. But it could make a raid on the drug dealer Whitetooth's lair more interesting." *If we get really lucky, Whitetooth's noble supplier will be visiting at the time of the raid. Lord Rechmal, if you can make that happen, I'd appreciate it.*

Not her most reverent prayer, but neither was it her least reverent one.

"Investigator Dawncloud is going after Whitetooth? It's about time someone did! When?" Saskia asked.

"Soon, hopefully. Windshadow should be suggesting it to her now."

"Ah, so it's your idea."

Rykka shrugged. "He told me she wasn't having any luck getting the permissions to raid Ravencrest's warehouse. Whitetooth seems a good alternative."

Alistar nodded. "Keep us informed."

Thus dismissed, she walked to her room. She'd just reached the door when Windshadow hurried over.

"Dawncloud's superior is as frustrated with the blocks as she is, and when she proposed the raid on Whitetooth, he approved it immediately. You can join them, but you only have an hour to get ready," he told her in a hushed, hurried voice.

"An hour? Where do I meet her?"

"An hour to prepare so you have time to reach the meeting point," he clarified. "Dawncloud wants you to meet her and her team behind Lady De'seneth's clinic."

"I'll be there." She paused. "Are you coming too?"

He shook his head. "Not this time. Good luck."

After considerable debate about her persona for this raid, Rykka settled on an adaptation of one she and Tyrion had used in the past, the main difference being that this iteration was female rather than male. Dressed in a worn set of day laborer's brown shirt and trousers, she lurked in the shadows of the alley behind the clinic, mentally practicing her accent until she had the Mudgulch dialect firmly in mind. She didn't want to adopt a full slums accent, but Mudgulch was widely recognized as a district on the ill-defined border of Lower City and slums.

By the time Investigator Ilithela Dawncloud and her team arrived, Rykka was confident in her presentation. She wasn't trying to hide, and Dawncloud's sharp eyes found her quickly.

The investigator's sharp features pinched in a frown and her expression didn't show any recognition. Good.

"Yeh must be thems I's told to meet," Rykka said in greeting.

The rest of Dawncloud's crew, just shy of a dozen, turned quickly toward her voice with varying degrees of surprise. Dawncloud answered. "We are. What do we call you?"

"Yeh kin call me Ash," Rykka told her. "An' yeh?"

Dawncloud studied her, and Rykka could almost read the question in the woman's thoughts as she searched for clues that "Ash" was Rykka. "You can call me Pyre," she said finally. The name suited her red hair—and possibly her temperament after being denied her prime target of Ravencrest's warehouse. "Don't worry about what to call the others."

Rykka tilted her head in a nod. "Fair 'nuf. Yeh waitin' fer anyone else, or we ready?"

"Everyone's here," Dawncloud said. "Let's go."

Briefly, Rykka worried that Dawncloud expected her to act as their "local guide," but the investigator took the lead through the narrow streets. The sky was edging toward dusk, and the air had a crisp bite that did nothing to dispel the stink of the residents and the wastes they dumped into the gutters. The further up in society one lived, the more measures were in place to counter the stink and clear away the waste, but here, only the most basic disease-mitigation efforts operated. The slums didn't even get that much. Rykka longed for a deep breath of fresh salt air and the roll of a deck under her feet.

Dawncloud motioned Rykka up to walk beside her. Leaning close, she spoke softly. "You're not the person I expected to see. Give me some proof that you're an ally."

Dawncloud wasn't stupid, and she hadn't lived this long as an investigator by taking everyone at face value. Rykka answered equally quietly, dropping her accent. "I know that when it's just the two of you, Windshadow calls you 'Ilith' and you call him 'Sol.' Does that help?"

Dawncloud's eyes narrowed as she analyzed both that shockingly private detail and the voice that spoke it. "Darkwood."

"Yes."

"You're quite adept at appearing to be someone other than yourself."

"When I need to be. And right now, I need to *not* be Lady De'seneth's personal maid. Though I'm sure the scandal rags would love the idea. The family's good at staying out of their notice, and I'm not going to be the one to change that." She fell back into her accent. "Places like this, yeh do whatcha gotta iffin yeh gonna make it. And right now, we gotta take care of Whitetooth. Yeah?"

Dawncloud was silent for a long moment, then she nodded. "Yeah."

The team proved adept at stealth and at maneuvering through the maze of alleys and streets. Rykka knew they kept one eye on her. She didn't blame them—she was keeping an eye on them as well. They avoided anyone else moving around, which became harder as they approached what she assumed was Whitetooth's lair. Without stealth, she guessed the walk would take around half an hour, maybe a little more, but at their pace, it was closer to an hour.

Dawncloud gestured to a shabby apartment building. It had been built to house ten families, so probably actually contained closer to twenty. Two thugs stood near the front entrance, and five more lingered in the area, pretending to be doing anything other than standing guard.

"Whitetooth uses this as his base of operations," Dawncloud said. "Word is he prefers to conduct most business after dark, once he's sent his people out to work."

The door opened and a clump of six whores, four female, two male, shuffled out, shivering in their thin clothes. As they headed down the street, one of the guards trailed discreetly after them. Rykka wondered if the man's purpose was to protect the whores or to ensure none of them tried to run away like Seva had.

Two of Dawncloud's people peeled off to circle around the building. Another two moved around the perimeter.

Rykka looked to Dawncloud. "What's the plan?"

"We wait. I allowed for time to deal with any troubles we encountered on the way, so we're early."

"And what we waitin' for?" Rykka pressed.

"We're waiting for fewer bystanders to be caught in this raid. We're not here to chase down prostitutes and loan rats. I'd rather as many of them be gone as possible."

It was a sound plan and a reasonable decision. Rykka hated it. They were here, now, and Whitetooth was inside, possibly meeting with a nobleman right now.

Not just any nobleman. Possibly meeting with a prince right now. If he's there, I can't let him escape. She took a deep breath, which her nose regretted immediately. *Dawncloud's right, though. The more people in there, the more likely my theoretical target will get away.*

She leaned against a building and watched more clusters of people leave. Most looked scared when they left the building, sometimes casting nervous glances over their shoulders. Once out in the open, the fear receded, even with guards following them into the night.

Four groups of prostitutes left before Dawncloud signaled her people. "It's time. Teams at the back and side entrances are in place. Don't have anyone covering the sewers or the rooftops, so we need to cut Whitetooth off before he reaches either." She looked to Rykka. "Do you know which he's more likely to take?"

She slipped back into her chosen accent. "If 'e's alone, could be either. If 'e's got a guest, the roof." It was pure speculation, but she couldn't imagine a prince willingly stepping foot in the sewers.

Dawncloud nodded. At another signal from her, they advanced. To Rykka's relief, Dawncloud didn't attempt a frontal assault as she'd seen too many stupid Crown agents do, expecting their presence to be enough to cow organized criminals. Instead, they entered an adjacent and apparently unoccupied building. Briefly, Rykka wondered why they hadn't moved in here earlier, but a look around revealed evidence that Whitetooth's thugs used the building as a sentry post, and if the food debris was any indication, a place to take a break away from their boss's gaze.

"You arranged all this in a couple hours? I'm impressed," Rykka murmured, ducking low to avoid a window.

"We've had eyes on Whitetooth for a while. Just needed a solid lead to justify a raid. You gave me that."

She shrugged uncomfortably. If she'd thought she could take Sunward or her minions without involving the Crown, she'd never have suggested this raid.

Dawncloud left one of her people to keep watch. The rest of them climbed the stairs to the roof. Rykka balanced easily on the slick slate tiles. Without waiting for instructions or approval from Dawncloud, she took several steps back for a running start and sprang across the gap onto the roof of Whitetooth's lair. She thought she heard Dawncloud curse at her, but Rykka was already moving to the door on this roof. Not surprisingly, it was locked. A good lock, too. By the time Dawncloud and her people got across, Rykka was at work.

The tumblers aligned, finally. She eased the door open a crack, stopping it when she felt slight resistance. Sliding her fingers into the gap, she carefully felt up and down until she felt a taut wire. "Prob'ly an alarm," she said quietly. "Lessee what I kin do."

"Doesn't want people sneaking in," Dawncloud said.

Rykka snorted. "More like don't want people sneaking out an' runnin' off." She jiggled the wire gently, trying to determine how the alarm was triggered. There was just enough give that she decided it was probably connected to a device that would sound if the pin was dislodged. Easier to reset if it was triggered.

Also easier to disable.

She gripped the wire between two fingers. With her other hand, she slid a slim blade into the gap and cut the wire below her fingers. Keeping the upper portion of the wire between her fingers, she pushed the door open.

No alarm sounded. No trap erupted in her face. Rykka let out a breath and cautiously eased the tension on the wire. When nothing changed, she nodded.

"We's in." She stepped into the shadows of the attic, trusting Dawncloud and her people to follow.

CHAPTER 42

She expected the attic to smell musty and disused. Instead, the still air held a faintly spicy odor like a lingering memory of strong seasonings that had been stored in a location for a long time. The floor was clean, and no cobwebs hung in the rafters. Light was dim, but once her eyes adjusted, it was enough to see by.

Enough to see the cages at the far end of the attic.

They appeared to all be empty, but their presence told her plenty about how Whitetooth punished his people. No wonder they'd rather work the streets than stay here. And no wonder he supplied them with drugs. If he didn't, more would take their chances and run.

Despite the shabby exterior appearance of the building, the floors only creaked a little as Dawncloud and her people followed Rykka. Rykka strained her ears but didn't hear any indication that their entry had drawn notice. She found descending stairs and listened again. Her heart pounded, and she had to take a moment and several deep breaths before she trusted that she really didn't hear anyone below.

Blight it, why am I so nervous now? I've broken into more places than I can count, and into the homes of people with more power than Whitetooth could dream of.

"What's that odor?" one of Dawncloud's people asked softly. "Is it the drug Whitetooth's dealing?"

"Dunno," Rykka responded. She didn't remember any similar smells when she attended the recruitment, but it could be another form of Lumination. But would Whitetooth want the drug to suffuse the air so heavily that even he would be affected by it?

She ghosted down the stairs, coming to the upper residential floor. Looking down the hall, the first thing she noticed was that most of the doorways lacked doors. She cautiously peered around the frame into the first room. The space had been constructed to serve as an apartment for a single family, but now it was closer to barracks, beds shoved together and crowded into the space. Even a Rillwater privateer ship offered more personal space and privacy than this. Removing the doors from the rooms was another indignity over the rest. The thought of not even having privacy to dress sent a shudder down her spine.

Sounds of shifting and movement from a doorway stopped Rykka. She raised a hand to halt the others and waited. When the sound came again, she identified the location and approached the doorway.

A look inside the dark room showed a space similar to the rest, but a tumble of small forms occupied several beds and a mat on the floor. She stepped back and whispered to Dawncloud. "Children sleepin' in there. Probably beggars during the day."

"Blight," Dawncloud cursed softly. "Don't have anyone to keep an eye on them. And no doors to keep them shut in. Hopefully their first reaction to fighting will be to hide."

Rykka eyed the doorway. "Aye kin keep 'em from commin' inna the hall. Won't stop 'em from trying a window, though."

Dawncloud frowned for a moment, then seemed to remember how Rykka had protected Windshadow from Merris's attack. "I don't want them running into the fight and I don't want Whitetooth's thugs using them as shields. Do it."

Rykka's senses reached up to the mahiy lines and she pulled magic into herself. The energy flowed through the ceiling to her in thin purple threads.

She knew how the magic of the mahiy lines felt, and before she left for Rillwater, it had always felt the same no matter where in the city she was, from the slums to the grounds of the Royal Palace. Here, though, it felt off. She tried to analyze the difference in the brief moments she handled it. The power responded as it always had, no changes in its behavior. She couldn't put a name to the oddity.

A localized problem? Has Whitetooth done something that altered the mahiy lines? I need to tell Alistar when we're done here.

Despite the odd flavor to the magic, she wove it into a transparent barrier across the doorway that would stop anyone from entering or leaving for as long as she maintained it. She fed enough magic into the barrier to sustain it for several hours without her direct attention, as long as no one devoted a concerted effort into breaking through. If any of the children woke as she set the barrier or when the team softly passed the doorway, they kept quiet.

At the next set of stairs, Rykka heard a few muffled voices. Signaling the rest of the team to remain at the top of the stairs, she descended and moved closer.

"Ugh. How long they gonna keep talking? What's there to say 'cept 'Here's your goods, now pay me'?" The speaker had a raspy voice, deep for a woman.

"Why? You got something better to do?" retorted a male voice.

The woman sighed. "No. Just don't like when we got strangers around. That guy makes me nervous."

"Pah. You worry too much. 'Member, Boss used that incense stuff that makes people on edge so he can get that guy to leave sooner," the man said.

"Doesn't seem to be helping get that guy gone faster. Think he started arguing with the boss. But maybe that stuff's bugging me too."

"It is," the man agreed. "So, we gonna play or not?"

A creak of wood as someone thumped into a chair. The woman said, "Yeah, just deal the cards already."

Rykka crept back upstairs. "At least two guards below. They said Whitetooth's got a visitor, too. Guessing Whitetooth's on the ground floor, not this one."

"It's time, then." Dawncloud nodded firmly and activated a speaking stone. "In position. Move in five."

Her team began to move down the stairs. Dawncloud turned to Rykka. "If I tell you to stick close, will you?"

Rykka paused until the rest had passed them. "I'll tell you that I will."

Dawncloud drew a deep breath and let it out. "Just don't get in the way."

Rykka followed her back downstairs. Dawncloud's people disabled the two guards efficiently and quietly. A sweep of the floor found quarters for the guards but no additional people.

They came down the final staircase to the ground floor, Rykka tense and expecting a fight. Unlike the upper floors, she heard multiple sounds of people moving around, talking and laughing. Thinking of the mostly empty guard quarters, she realized one of the flaws to Dawncloud's timing. This was the overlapping time for the shifts of guards, and they seemed to use it for socializing.

She didn't know who was spotted, except that it was neither her nor Dawncloud, but a startled shout rose from one of the rooms. "Intrud—"

It cut off abruptly, but not fast enough to escape notice.

Heavyset men and women burst out of rooms, hastily grabbing weapons and looking about wildly.

Dawncloud and her people didn't hesitate. They were already armed and ready for a fight. Most carried blunt weapons as a nod toward intent to disable and arrest rather than kill, though Rykka knew as well as anyone that a solid crack to the skull could kill just as easily as a blade to the chest. She hung back, letting them engage the thugs.

As soon as Whitetooth's people were occupied, she darted through the fray, dodging a clumsy swing and rushing past the fight. She had no time to waste.

"It's the Crown!" someone yelled. "We're being raided!"

There was no way the crime boss and his visitor hadn't been alerted now. Rykka bolted through the entry chamber, past more combatants, to a door out of place amid this squalor. The gilding was chipped and peeling at the edges, and the carvings in the wood weren't the work of a master, but compared to the rest of the building, it proclaimed that the space beyond it belonged to someone superior to the rest.

The door wasn't locked, but an elven man waited in the room beyond, blade at the ready. Though he wore no uniform, he was cleaner, better dressed, and better trained than Whitetooth's thugs. Seeing Rykka, he demanded, "Identify yourself and state your business here."

"Like I told th' others, you kin call me Ash, pretty boy," Rykka responded. "Need ta talk ta th' boss. Bit 'o a hurry, ya'know." She jerked her head in the direction of the fighting.

The "pretty boy" comment flustered him for a moment, but he kept his wits, and kept his blade pointed at her. "You'll have to wait. He's busy."

She huffed in annoyance, stepping closer. "Sorry, pretty boy. Not feeling real patient right now."

Either he saw the knife in her hand or he interpreted her approach as potentially hostile. He stabbed at her in a precise, rapid thrust. Rykka flung up a buckler-like barrier, deflecting the blade harmlessly aside before it found flesh. In his momentary confusion, she lashed out with her blade, opening a long gash on his arm.

I could wear him down, as long as I can deflect his attacks, but every moment I'm occupied here, Whitetooth and his guest have more time to escape. Hematic perdition!

"Pyre!" she yelled, using the code name Dawncloud had provided. She didn't bother adding any further information. No reason to tell their enemies *why* she was calling out.

The man stabbed at her again. She deflected a second time. His eyes narrowed and his mouth tightened in a thin line. She didn't like the look in his eyes—not anger, but calculation, as if he'd already figured out her means of defense and was reworking his strategies to account for it.

She slashed at him, but he pulled out of her reach and retaliated with a series of rapid thrusts and cuts. She had to expand the size of her barrier to stop them, and the force behind each strike weakened the barrier rapidly. She pulled more power from the mahiy lines, though the abnormality in the magic made her skin crawl, and maneuvered so her opponent's back faced the door to the hall.

The man's gaze flickered just slightly toward the threads of violet flowing down to her. "Well, at least you're not one of the freaks."

"Th' freaks?" she repeated.

"The ones who claim their magic's 'inside' them. Unnatural freaks." He sneered in disdain.

Behind him, Dawncloud appeared in the doorway. The man started to turn, hearing her. Rykka lunged at him, forcing his attention back on her. Dawncloud recognized an opportunity when she saw one. Her club slammed into his back, knocking the breath from him. He dropped to the floor, gasping.

"Got this?" Rykka asked Dawncloud.

"Go."

Leaving Dawncloud to handle the man, Rykka opened the next door and rushed deeper into Whitetooth's lair. She took peripheral notice of the gaudy flaunting of wealth displayed in artwork and furniture. There was nothing tasteful about Whitetooth's décor, no attempts at a coherent theme.

She stopped to listen at the next door. A male voice, low and raspy, cursed. Another male voice responded, the second deeper and thick with the refined accent of high nobility.

"Are your people not equipped to handle such... inconveniences?"

Rykka tried to compare the voice to her memory of Sunward's lover. The dialect and diction were similar, but the voice wasn't the same. *Blight. Is this the prince? Did he send an underling here instead? Wouldn't blame him.*

The raspy voice became a snarl. "They shouldn't *have* to! *You're* supposed to make sure nothin' like this happens 'ere! I was promised protection."

"I authorized nothing of this! Are you *certain* your people didn't mistake some local... rival for an official raid?"

"If Redtail says it's Crown agents, it's Crown agents," Raspy snapped. Wood creaked as a door opened. "After you."

The noble made a sound of revulsion. "In *there*?"

I can't let them leave! Rykka slammed the door open and burst into the room, ducking low and dodging to one side in anticipation of something being thrown at her. She heard the thunk of metal striking wood as a dagger slammed into the door frame to her left.

The two elven men within could hardly be more different. Raspy—presumably Whitetooth— reached for another dagger. At least four sheaths adorned his belt. He had a long, narrow face like a weasel and a lanky build. Greasy dark brown hair was pulled back in a short braid. His eyes were sharp and calculating. For an elf, he was short, an unfortunate fate that likely contributed to his want for power and respect. He stood beside an open trap door, a bag strapped over one shoulder.

The other man stood a full head and shoulders taller than Whitetooth. Ringlets of golden-brown hair framed his angular features. His coat was black, with red accents on the high collar and sleeves, embroidered with gold. He wore a matching pair of red gloves with black and gold trim. As Seva once mentioned, lumps on his fingers indicated that he wore his rings under the gloves. Rykka didn't recognize him, but she recognized the air of superiority he carried. He was as out of place here as Seva would be in the royal court.

Whitetooth flung another dagger at Rykka and sprang through the trap door. She jerked aside, and the blade only grazed her. The elven nobleman's head jerked toward Whitetooth, but he hesitated to follow through that dark portal into the sewers. Escape won over decorum. He ran for the trap door.

He tried to, at least. Rykka shoved magic between him and the exit. He got three steps before slamming hard into an invisible barrier. He staggered, reeling. Rykka seized the opportunity to weave her barrier into a solid pillar with the nobleman inside. Pulling once more on the mahiy lines, she anchored the pillar to the floor and ceiling, then rapidly manipulated it further. As the nobleman opened his mouth with an expression of outrage, she prevented sound from passing through the barrier, in or out. No longer threads, but streams of magic flowed down to her as the barrier consumed more power.

Hematic perdition, I could hang for imprisoning a nobleman. Can't let anyone see him. Dawncloud might let it go, but I don't trust her people.

The next alteration was even more taxing. She forced it to bend light in such a way that the barrier grew opaque, then reflective. Rykka sucked in deep gulps of air and leaned heavily against the wall. The nobleman beat against the walls—she felt the blows against the barrier—but he didn't have any weapon but his fists.

Dawncloud rushed into the room, gaze sweeping the space and falling on the trap door, then on Rykka. "Are you injured? You're bleeding."

"It's nothing," she panted. Rykka gestured at the trap door. "Whitetooth, that way. Getting away." With an effort, she slowed her draw from the mahiy lines to a trickle, not wanting the questions the steady flow would bring, since Dawncloud didn't seem to have noticed the visual distortion that marked her barrier pillar.

Dawncloud put her fingers to her lips and blew an ear-piercing whistle. Rykka winced, both because of the sound and because of the running footsteps that answered it. She wanted Dawncloud chasing Whitetooth, not calling more people into the room while she struggled to keep the barrier intact and unnoticed. Every instinct screamed against revealing the trapped nobleman.

Three members of Dawncloud's team, a bit worse for wear, rushed in. Dawncloud gestured to the trap door, and they jumped down after Whitetooth. Dawncloud, however, didn't follow, but turned her attention back to Rykka.

"What happened? You're hurt."

"I'm fine," she insisted through gritted teeth. As much as she tried to resist, she needed to pull more magic from the lines. As the flow gained strength, she caught her breath and straightened. "I'm fine."

Dawncloud's eyes narrowed. "What are you hiding?"

"Hematic perdition, you don't give up, do you? Just... fine, close the door." *This is a bad idea. I don't know if I can trust her.*

Dawncloud pushed the door shut, watching Rykka closely. Rykka laughed faintly. "You're looking the wrong way." She gestured toward the pillar.

Dawncloud frowned and followed the motion. It took her a

moment to realize the source of the distortion in the air. "What is this?"

"Not what. Who." Rykka focused, carefully manipulating the barrier yet again until they could see inside, though the nobleman couldn't see out.

He was still slamming against the barrier, alternating between beating on it with his fists and flinging himself bodily against it. His handsome features were distorted not only with anger, but now with fear as well as he struggled against his cramped, unyielding prison.

Dawncloud drew a sharp breath, her eyes going wide. She looked back to the closed door, then to Rykka. "What have you done?"

"I've stopped Whitetooth's guest from leaving."

"You realize who... you know who he is, don't you?"

"Should I?" Rykka asked far more casually than she felt. Her pulse raced. *This isn't just a lackey, is it?*

"That is Prince Pietro Feyblade! Yes, you blighted well should know who he is!"

"Hematic perdition, Investigator, I barely know what the king looks like!" she snapped. "It's not like *this* is a place where people like *him* just drop in for a casual chat and tea."

Dawncloud stopped, took a deep breath, and collected herself. "This is... the implications of this... Can he see us?"

"He can't see or hear anything through the barrier," Rykka said, glad for a question with a simple answer.

"Why would Prince Pietro be here?" Dawncloud shook her head. "You're certain he and Whitetooth were meeting?"

"I certainly didn't bring him with me," Rykka retorted. "What are the chances that guy you handled in the other room was a Royal Guard?"

Dawncloud shifted uncomfortably. "He... is. I assumed he had gone rogue."

"One of his guards?" Rykka gestured at the trapped prince.

"I'll have to confirm that," Dawncloud said. She rubbed her eyes. "I have to report this. Have to bring him in." She trailed off, contemplating the enormity of arresting the son of the king.

"You don't, though," Rykka said quietly.

Dawncloud's gaze snapped to her. "Yes, I *do*. My duty--"

"Is to protect Lewarden, Calarand, and the Crown, right?" Rykka interrupted. She just hoped Dawncloud was smart enough to understand. She jabbed a finger at Prince Pietro. "If *he* is tied to Whitetooth, Ravencrest, and Sunward, you can't allow his capture to be known. Not until we have irrefutable proof that he's involved. Without that, he'll be walking free tomorrow morning, your reputation will be destroyed by the afternoon, and you'll be hunted if not already dead, Investigator Dawncloud. Do you think the king will believe his son is a criminal? Do you think he will *care*, as long as he can pay people to make the accusation disappear?"

Dawncloud's hands clenched. "You... I absolutely hate that you're right. Do you have an alternative?"

"There are cages upstairs. But getting him up there would be difficult. I could reshape the barrier into a ball and roll him to another location." She looked around. "Any large crates you could justify packing out of here?"

"We'll be collecting evidence now that the guards have been disabled. I could probably justify calling a carriage for you and loading cargo onto it as well. The question remains exactly *where* you intend to take *the king's son*." Dawncloud's narrow eyes fixed sharply on her.

Rykka let out a heavy breath. "I think the only place I *can* take him is Lord De'seneth's manor."

Alistar's going to kill me.

CHAPTER 43

Even with the arguments she made, Rykka was astonished that Investigator Dawncloud, loyal servant of the Crown, agreed to send Prince Pietro with Rykka to the De'seneth estate. Possibly she was counting on Windshadow being there to ensure nothing too unacceptable happened to the prince. Or perhaps she recognized that she didn't have anywhere else to hold the prince that wouldn't immediately come to the attention of those with more power and political authority than herself.

Whatever her reasons, she helped Rykka find a crate large enough to hold a man. Rykka altered the shape and size of her barrier to make it fit within the crate, much to Prince Pietro's distress. When the top of the barrier pressed down, forcing him to sit, he tried to brace against it. Rykka saw the fear of being crushed in his eyes.

His alarm didn't relent when they pushed the barrier into the crate and closed up the side wall. He couldn't see or hear anything they did, but he could feel that he was being moved.

"Where do you want the carriage I call to take you?" Dawncloud asked.

Rykka gave her the address of a rarely used warehouse in the Middle City, a location that wasn't near the clinic, the manor, or any hideout she still used. "I'll get a ride home from there."

Dawncloud's expression and stance said she wasn't happy about any of this, but she nodded slowly. "Very well. Keep me informed."

"I'll do my best. Let me know if you catch Whitetooth. And... be kind to the whores and the like who work for him. Most of them are just poor people caught in a bad spot."

Dawncloud's expression softened a little. "I know."

Not until she was in the carriage headed toward the warehouse did the impact of her actions start to catch up with her. It began with a trembling in her hands that she couldn't stop. Then shivers down her spine.

I just imprisoned and abducted a blighted PRINCE! And now I'm going to take him to De'seneth's house? And I expect him to accept that? This is insane. I can't...

She sucked in deep breaths and pulled her legs up against her chest, squeezing her eyes shut while she shook. When the sharpest edges of panic eased, she uncurled, glad to be alone in the carriage.

"I need a plan," she whispered to no one. "Something I can present to Alistar to look like I know what I'm doing. Telling him 'I accidentally abducted the prince, sorry, and he's your problem now' isn't going to be enough."

She reached out to the mahiy lines to maintain her barrier and let out a relieved sigh. The weird taint was gone, and the magic felt normal once more. Another thing she needed to tell Alistar.

Peeking out the carriage window, she watched the city pass. This late at night, most buildings were dark except for the occasional tavern, game house, or theater. The ghostlights illuminating the streets cast pale light, bathing the stones in silver. The carriage rumbled on, drawing curious looks from those few people skulking along the streets.

Noticing them, Rykka decided she'd rather not linger in an abandoned warehouse in the middle of the night longer than she needed to. She checked her belt pouch and found her bag of speaking stones. Alistar was almost certainly asleep by now. Dorne likely was as well, but he was a better choice to arrange her transportation, and managing the household was his job. She selected the butler's blue-green stone and activated it.

She only had to wait a few minutes for him to answer. His voice, while curt, didn't betray any indication that she'd woken him. "Darkwood. What do you need?"

"A ride home. I need a carriage to pick me up from the last warehouse on Dustwall Street."

"The one next to the automaton factory that burned down? Very well. Anything else?"

"I'm bringing back a crate for Lord De'seneth. It will need to go into the basement. Should only be handled by people you trust completely."

"Understood. The carriage will be on its way shortly."

"Good. Hopefully it'll get there not long after I do."

"Only one question, Darkwood. How sensitive is the package you're bringing?"

She gave the question a long thought, mentally running though the answers to find the best one. "Blood and sand and blackened shoals, Dorne."

Long silence on the other end, then he said, "Lord De'seneth will meet you when you arrive."

She grimaced, but there was no other logical response to the code she'd used. "Thank you, Dorne."

The stone went dark. She let out a long breath and leaned back against the seat. *Blight, I'm tired. If I didn't have to keep the barrier, I'd go to sleep right here. But I can't risk it. The barrier goes down, and Prince Pietro can see, hear, and be heard. And a few determined kicks would be all it took to break out of the crate. Blight, what do I tell Alistar?*

She closed her eyes. *What would Tiyron do? He'd find a way to make Pietro think someone other than us took him. The prince suspected Whitetooth was wrong about Crown agents enacting the raid and thought Whitetooth's Lower City rivals were responsible. We can play on that. Maybe we even...* She swallowed hard. *Maybe we even imprison him in the place where Cemar kept Tiyron captive. If Pietro thinks we don't know who he is and we question him about Whitetooth, we might get something useful from him. If he thinks we don't know who he is, would he believe us if we threaten violence?*

She wasn't sure Alistar would approve, and she was certain Windshadow wouldn't. Tiyron would, though.

The carriage finally drew to a halt. The driver didn't ask if she was sure this was where she wanted to stop, any more than he asked what was in the crate Rykka helped him unload. They set the crate in the shadows around the corner of the warehouse, then the driver returned to his vehicle, nodded once to her, and drove on.

Rykka looked at the crate, sighed, and sat down on top of it. "You are a royal pain in my ass, you know."

The movement of the crate had roused the prince, and he was beating against the barrier again, but the blows felt sluggish. Perhaps he was as exhausted as she was.

"How long do you figure before someone notices you're missing? I wonder, are they going to keep it quiet, or raise a public fuss? Who's going to get the blame for it?"

The prince banged a few more times, then lapsed back into whatever else he did.

Blight, what if he has speaking stones with him? I don't think my barrier blocks that.

Trepidation ran through her. Rykka carefully pulled the side of the crate up to check on the prince. There wasn't much light, but he appeared to be slumped against one wall, cradling one hand against his chest. She didn't see the glow of an active speaking stone, though he could have already used one.

There wasn't anything she could do about it now, though. She closed the crate again and listened for the approach of a carriage. The chirps of crickets broke the silence. The warehouse stood at the end of a row of factories and storehouses. Past it was a large, empty patch of land that was being reclaimed by weeds. A couple years ago, it had been the site of a factory that built horse-type automatons to draw carriages.

Something had gone wrong and the entire place burned to the ground. The owners had deflected blame toward Silverline Power rather than admit their own negligence caused the fire. The Silverline investigation pushed the blame firmly back where it belonged. Even though Rykka had no love for the Silver Prince or his company, she had even less for nobles who risked the lives of their lower-class workers to save a few marks.

The crickets trailed off when a carriage rumbled across the cobblestones. Rykka turned toward the sound, ready to duck out of sight if she couldn't identify the vehicle.

She relaxed, recognizing the manor's general-use carriage. The driver was a stocky human woman from Rillwater. She stopped the carriage, casting a suspicious look around before she spotted Rykka.

"Oy, Darkwood, you coulda picked a nicer spot to have your package delivered," she greeted.

"I coulda," she agreed. "But what fun is that?"

They hauled the crate onto the carriage luggage rack and strapped it on. Rykka climbed inside and flopped down on the hard wooden bench. It was harder to convince herself to stay awake and maintain the barrier. She hadn't kept one this large active for this long in longer than she could remember.

Constantly channeling magic from the mahiy lines through her body took a toll.

The ride back to the manor passed in a blur punctuated by surges of sharp panic when she caught herself dozing. The barrier held despite her momentary lapses.

When the carriage stopped, Dorne opened the door and offered her a hand out. Rykka was too tired to object. She put her hand in his and climbed out unsteadily. "Thanks."

"Lord De'seneth is mostly awake. Your brother, unfortunately, is also awake, and Lord De'seneth allowed him to accompany him to the basement."

Rykka let out a heavy breath and nodded. "Okay." She looked up to the sky. "What time is it?"

"It is very early in the morning, Darkwood. So early, even the kitchen staff hasn't roused to start the day. So, unless you want them asking curious questions about your nocturnal activities…"

"No, let's go." Rykka straightened. Members of the staff loaded the crate onto their shoulders, and she followed them inside and down the basement steps.

Alistar and Tiyron waited in an empty storeroom. Tense silence hung between the two men. Both nodded to Rykka as she entered, but they all waited until everyone left before speaking.

When they were alone, Rykka sighed wearily and leaned against the crate. "Brought you a present, De'seneth. Not sure you're going to like it." She turned to Tiyron. "Before I open this, swear on our blood that you won't say a word to anyone else about this."

Tiyron stiffened in the chair. "Are you serious?"

She fixed her gaze on him and didn't blink, didn't look away, didn't speak.

"Hematic perdition," Tiyron groaned. "I swear it, Rykka. On our blood."

"I'm liking this gift less already, and we haven't even opened it yet," Alistar said.

"You know we went after Whitetooth tonight, right?"

Alistar nodded.

"I thought if we were lucky, maybe his fancy noble supplier would be there. If not, I hoped we'd get some Lumination."

"I would hope if you were bringing Lumination, you'd bring a smaller amount than… this." Alistar gestured at the crate.

"Oh, no, blight, this is not Lumination!" she said quickly. She briefly described finding Whitetooth and a nobleman on the verge of escape and trapping the nobleman in a barrier.

Alistar's attention fixed on her as she spoke. When she finished, he asked, "Do you know who the noble is?"

This was the part where everything could fall apart. She released the latches on the crate and let the sides fall away, revealing the barrier within. Prince Pietro hunched in a corner once again. Dark-ringed eyes stared ahead blankly. His brown ringlets, once neatly styled, stuck to his sweat-streaked brow. He still cradled his hand. She wondered if he'd actually injured himself beating against the walls.

"He can't see or hear out, nor can he be heard," she said quickly.

Alistar stared at the figure inside the barrier, then turned his gaze to Rykka. "What did you do?" His voice was hard, a captain interrogating a crew member who'd done something indescribably stupid.

She desperately wished for a pebble or something to roll between her fingers. Taking a deep breath, she answered. "I inadvertently abducted Prince Pietro, sir."

Tiyron had been studying the man, smirking at the prisoner's predicament, but his head jerked up at Rykka's words. His mouth opened, but no sound came out. His single wide eye darted from her to the prince.

"Investigator Dawncloud knows about him. No one else on

her team does," Rykka continued. "Initially she wanted to arrest him and bring him in for questioning. I convinced her that wasn't the best course of action."

"And you thought bringing him here *was* the best course?" Alistar asked.

"The best? No, but it was better than the other options."

Tiyron interrupted. "This is a prince? You're sure?"

"This is most certainly Prince Pietro," Alistar said, voice flat.

"Then what in perdition was he doing with *Whitetooth*? He couldn't have been *that* desperate for a whore."

"An excellent question," Alistar said. "Conveniently, the best person to answer is right there." He gestured at the prince.

"I think we'll have better luck getting answers if he doesn't know who we are," Rykka said. "He thought the raid was initiated by one of Whitetooth's rivals, thought Whitetooth was certain it was the Crown. The only person the prince saw was me."

Alistar frowned thoughtfully. "You have an idea?"

She cast an uncomfortable glance at her brother. "We all know that Cemar kept Tiyron captive. There must be places in this basement where someone could be confined."

Tiyron stiffened but jerked his head in agreement.

"If the prince thinks we don't know who he really is, he's more likely to believe we'd be willing to do him harm to get answers," Rykka continued. "And if we focus our questions on his dealings with Whitetooth initially, he'll have good reason to think we're Lower City rivals of Whitetooth."

"You are *not* conducting treason by torturing the prince in my house, however much of an insufferable ass he might be!" Alistar interrupted sharply.

"I mean *threaten* to do so, not actually do so," she said quickly.

"Don't let him sleep. He won't have the wits left to lie after a day or two of that," Tiyron said.

"Sleep deprivation is considered torture in many places," Alistar told him with a glower.

"Many places, but Calarand isn't one of them," Tiyron countered. "*His* father said it was acceptable." He nodded at Prince Pietro.

Alistar took a deep breath and let it out slowly. "Blood and sand, this is madness." He rubbed his eyes. "Utter madness."

Quietly, Rykka said, "And it's someone we know is involved, who might know what's really going on. And who no one knows is missing yet."

"I know. Blight it, I know." He turned to Tiyron. "How do we access Cemar's dungeon?"

The holding cells, as Tiyron referred to them, were a half-dozen cages tall enough for a man to stand in without hitting his head, but not wide enough for one to lie down comfortably. The room was dimly lit, chilly, and musty.

Four Rillwater staff members helped move the crate, closed up once again, and Dorne accompanied them, supervising the activity. He and Alistar had both changed from their manor clothes to workman's shirt and trousers, and at Rykka's suggestion, everyone wore masks to conceal their faces. The entire process took longer than she liked, and she leaned wearily against the wall, waiting once again as final preparations were confirmed.

Tiyron leaned against the wall beside her, having left the chair out of sight. "Rykka, how long have you been channeling that barrier?"

She gestured vaguely. "Since the raid, I guess."

"How long's it been since you channeled for this long?" he pressed.

"This long? I dunno, never? Probably never. Why?"

"You need to stop. You're not looking good." His expression pinched in worry.

"Tell them to hurry up, then."

Tiyron turned to the others. "De'seneth! You better be ready."

Alistar cast him a long-suffering look. "We're almost ready."

"No, you better be ready *now*, before my sister burns herself dry."

Alistar stiffened, looked at Rykka, and nodded. "We're ready. Drop the barrier."

She was surprised to find it was difficult to drop. She closed her eyes and focused on the magic she was conducting through herself into the barrier. It didn't want to stop. There was more magic, endless magic in the mahiy lines, ready, eager, just waiting to pour into her creation.

Tiyron jostled her shoulder roughly. "Rykka, let go of it."

His words, his presence gave her focus. She forced the floodgates to close. The last flickers of magic sparked to the barrier, then it collapsed.

Prince Pietro, half-conscious, suddenly had no wall to slouch against. He fell to the floor with a startled sound, blinking and shaking his head as sight and sound abruptly returned to him. Before he recovered, two of the Rillwater staff grabbed his arms and pulled him to his feet. While they kept firm hold on him, the others stripped the prince's overcoat, jacket, and vest, then his belt and gloves. Rykka didn't see any rings on his fingers, and guessed he'd concealed them somewhere in his clothes.

"Unhand me, ruffians!" Pietro demanded, struggling against the firm grips on his arms. "How dare you—mmmmphh." His cries were cut short by Alistar shoving a thick rag in his mouth.

"You're not impressing anyone," Alistar said. His attempt at a Dockside accent sounded more like a caricature of one, but the prince probably wouldn't know the difference.

Pietro was shoved into a cage. Someone reached through the bars and caught his arms, pulled them behind him and outside the bars. Another of the men bound Pietro's wrists together. The prince struggled, but he was exhausted and outnumbered. His hands were bruised and raw. He'd been cradling one of them earlier, but Rykka couldn't tell if he'd broken anything.

"We gonna question 'im now?" asked the man who'd trapped Pietro's arms.

Pietro stilled, eyes darting around the assembled figures. Alistar looked him up and down. "Nah, not yet. It'd be rude not to let our guest here get settled and comfortable." His eyes never left Pietro's as he spoke.

His tone sent a shiver down Rykka's spine. She didn't blame the imprisoned prince for shuddering and looking away. The quiet, self-assured menace in Alistar's voice could have convinced a pirate fleet to surrender on the spot.

Two men settled on stools to keep watch on Pietro. Alistar turned and strode from the room, Rykka and Tiyron fell in after him, leaving the prince to contemplate his fate.

CHAPTER 44

If not for the pressing needs of his work on the Exhibition, Alistar would have stayed home for the day. Instead, he was sitting at his desk, looking over the diagrams one more time and trying hard not to think about the kraken-sized problem in his basement.

Logically speaking, Rykka couldn't have brought Prince Pietro anywhere else once she realized who she'd caught. Less logically speaking, not even Family connections would save Alistar or his household if anyone discovered the prince, and he wished she'd taken him anywhere else.

Alistar doodled idle patterns on the margins of his notepad, gazing at the map spread out over his desk. If his calculations were correct, and if Prince Filipp didn't try to force yet another change, this setup should provide the Exhibition with the magic it needed, with a margin of error not as generous as he would like, but enough.

If Sunward is in league with the princes and they're making their move at the Exhibition, what purpose will all this serve? How do they intend to use it? I can't let them abuse and pervert everything we've worked for.

Alistar focused on the diagrams again, and carefully sketched in additional disconnect points throughout the Exhibition, giving them the ability to cut off individual sections, as well as the entire Exhibition, from the mahiy network.

He leaned back and stretched, wincing slightly at the creaks and pops from tense muscles. Alistar pushed to his feet and rolled up the map. Tucking it under his arm, he left his office and strode down the hall toward Prince Cero's office. A low hum of distant, muffled voices filled the air, not enough to be distracting, but a comfortable reassurance that Silverline Power was operating business as usual. As much as Alistar enjoyed the privacy and prestige of his office, he did miss the casual interactions with his fellow engineers.

As he approached the Silver Prince's office, he noticed additional guards at the door, several of whom he recognized as Prince Cero's personal guards. He nodded to them and asked, "Is His Highness in today?"

"He is, Senior Engineer. Do you have an appointment?"

Alistar shook his head. "I don't, but if he or Lady Syri is available, I need to update them on the status of the Exhibition."

One of the guards spoke quietly into a speaking stone. After a moment, she nodded and opened the office door. "They will see you, Senior Engineer."

Prince Cero's office always smelled like stepping outside into a summer garden. Plants, both flowering and not, spread across stands, tables, and the walls. Alistar bowed to the two elven occupants of the room. He straightened and got his first look at the Silver Prince since the assassination attempt five days ago.

The prince's silver hair was pulled back in a short braid. A fresh scar ran along his hairline and vanished across his scalp. He sat straight and tall in his chair, but Alistar had to convince himself that Prince Cero wasn't actually slumping. His right arm rested in a sling. His face was thin and dark rings marked the skin around his eyes. Still, his gaze was sharp and keen on Alistar.

"Good morning, De'seneth. Syri and I were debating making a wager on whether our first visitor of the day would be you or if my nephew would make a nuisance of himself first."

Lady Syri, standing at her father's side, rolled her eyes. "There was no wager to be made. Senior Engineer De'seneth arrives promptly half an hour before the majority of the employees. Pietro doesn't get out of bed until a good three hours later."

Alistar chuckled awkwardly. "Your Highness, it's good to see you. I didn't know you would be in today."

Prince Cero waved dismissively with his free hand. "The healers may fuss, but I have work to do. And, from what Syri has told me, I have a nephew who needs to be firmly put in his place."

Alistar grimaced slightly, thinking of a holding cage in his basement. Rather than say anything about the wayward Prince Pietro, he said, "Lady Syri has dealt with him well in the interactions I witnessed. However, sir, I came to provide my report on the plans for the Grand Exhibition."

Prince Cero gestured for him to present the map. Alistar unrolled it across the massive desk. Briefly outlined the current scope of the project, including the most recent adjustments and additions. Prince Cero's attention was drawn to the disconnects Alistar had added.

"You don't think these are redundant, De'seneth?"

"Given the scope and publicity of the event, sir, I prefer to err on the side of caution. With additional disconnects, we can limit the effects if, for some reason, we need to cut or redirect power in an area."

"Are you expecting problems?" The Silver Prince's eyebrow rose.

"I expect that with the crowds, especially with foreigners

unfamiliar with the mahiy lines, someone will try to do something stupid, sir."

"Unfortunately, I can't argue with that assessment," Prince Cero acknowledged. "And what of the changes in the lighting around the central stage?"

"A concession Prince Filipp made in order to add to the number of dancing automatons," Alistar explained.

"Dancing dolls." Prince Cero shook his head. "Very well, if that is what he wishes to prioritize, so be it." He continued to study the map. "The rest seems in order. You calculated the energy requirements?"

Alistar offered another sheet of parchment. "Based on both the estimated average usage and the full potential."

Lady Syri took the sheet from him and reviewed it before giving it to her father. "Have you learned anything more regarding the crystal flower?"

She had been studying and experimenting on the crystal for the last year without success. Alistar was reluctant to tell her that the key to activating it had been both obvious and inaccessible to her. Instead, he offered a different truth. "I found references to a similar artifact in surviving fragments of Heiset myths. If it is the same artifact, then the tales indicate that it came from Rechmal, the human god of magic."

Prince Cero frowned. "How reliable are these tales?"

"As reliable as any," Alistar answered. "There were some discrepancies between the myths, and not all the context is clear, but I intend to act cautiously while working with the crystal."

"Do you believe you can keep it secure?" Prince Cero asked.

"I believe it's more secure where it is than it will be most other places."

His confidence satisfied the Silver Prince. "Very good, senior engineer. Teams will begin these additions to the Exhibition immediately. Do you need anything else, or have any other reports?"

"Not at the moment, sir."

"If you wish to spend the rest of the day conducting tests on the crystal, you are free to do so."

"I'll make certain the rest of my projects are in order, then do so." Alistar dipped a bow to Prince Cero. "Thank you, Your Highness."

He returned to his office to double-check the status of his other projects and assure himself that he hadn't missed any deadlines. With that confirmed, he made his way to the break room to catch up on the gossip and rumors. Prince Pietro's repeated visits featured in many, with wild speculation about what his goal was. When he was asked, Alistar denied any knowledge beyond what his fellow engineers already knew, though he clarified a few events he'd witnessed. From the tone of the comments, Alistar concluded that no one knew Prince Cero was here today.

By early afternoon, he was home once more. After Alistar changed to clothes more suitable for home wear, Soluthos found him.

"Good afternoon, sir. Do you have a moment?"

"I do." Alistar gestured for Soluthos to close the door behind him. "What's on your mind?"

"Investigator Dawncloud told me about the raid she conducted on the Lower City criminal Whitetooth."

"I'm guessing she also told you that Rykka returned here with a package," Alistar said.

Soluthos shifted uneasily. "She did, and she told me of the contents of that package."

"Honestly, I'd hope she would. As a servant of the Crown, you're the most sensible person for her to tell. Although if you're going to make any argument for why he should be released or turned over to some other authorities, we're going to have a problem."

"Investigator Dawncloud explained her reasons for allowing Darkwood to bring him here. I don't like them, and I don't like having him here, but I accept her logic."

Alistar gave a strained laugh. "Believe me, I don't like having him here either. But the circumstantial evidence points to him being involved with Sunward and her plots. We *can't* let him go until we know how involved he is."

"How do you intend to go about learning that, sir?" Soluthos asked.

"Rykka suggested we give him the impression that he's been captured by rivals of Whitetooth who don't know who he is. Question him about his connections to Whitetooth and see if he incriminates himself. And I was reminded that sleep deprivation is an acceptable interrogation method. By now it's been at least a day since he slept, assuming he didn't catch a midday nap yesterday. Would you be considered a reliable witness if he says something incriminating, Soluthos?"

"I would," Soluthos acknowledged. "You want me to witness his interrogation?"

"Of course. For multiple reasons, one of which is your duty to the Crown and responsibility to watch over the safety of the royal family. You will, however, need to dress down. And I'd prefer you stay out of his sight."

Soluthos inclined his head in understanding. "When do you intend to do this, sir?"

"Not yet. I have a few things to take care of first. Two hours."

"Yes sir."

Alistar didn't invite anyone else to join him in questioning Prince Pietro. He and Soluthos descended through the basement to the room with the cages. Alistar pulled his mask up to cover nose and mouth before he entered.

Prince Pietro sat hunched in his cage, chin resting on his knees and eyes half open. Brin, one of his guards, jabbed him in the side with her cudgel.

"Look lively and mind your tongue. The boss's here."

Pietro lifted his head slowly, turning toward the sound of Alistar's steps. His eyes were sunken and heavy. He'd managed to work out the gag at some point—Alistar hadn't bothered to tie it in place, just stuffed the thick rag into his mouth.

"Release me." Pietro tried to give the words force, make them intimidating and threatening, but his mouth was parched, and the demand came out scratchy and hoarse.

Alistar strolled to the cage, studying the occupant. "And why would I want to do that?" His accent felt like a parody of Lower City residents, but it was also the accent most often adopted in the theater to identify a character as low class.

Pietro shifted and sat up straighter, settling into a cross-legged position. "Do you know who I am?"

"You're the upper-class patsy who Whitetooth swindled into working with him," Alistar said dismissively. "The one he abandoned when he ran off."

Anger flashed in Pietro's eyes. He pulled against the rope binding his hands to the cage bars. "I am Prince Pietro Feyblade, Heir Secondary to the throne of Calarand, you ignorant bastard!"

Alistar laughed. "The prince? Right, sure you are, 'Your Highness'. And I'm heir to the fleets of Rillwater."

Pietro sputtered angrily. "You... you dare *mock* me?"

Alistar stepped closer and leaned against the cage, looking down at Pietro. "Just how stupid do you think I am, patsy? You expect me to believe that a *prince* would ever step foot in the slums? Or deign to speak to Whitetooth?" He sneered. "Pretty sure if a prince wanted a whore that bad, he'd send someone to fetch one for him."

"A *whore*?" Pietro burst in disgust. "I would never touch one of Whitetooth's filthy, diseased, half-dressed streetwalkers!" He still pulled against his bonds, to no effect. In response to Alistar looming over him, he pushed to his feet. Alistar watched him eyeing the distance between them and concluding that he couldn't kick far enough to reach Alistar.

"Oh? What *did* bring you to him, 'Your Highness'?"

Pietro's jaw tightened. His eyes darted around the room as if someone might appear from the air to free him. "I had business with him."

Alistar caught Brin's eye. She jabbed Pietro in the side with her cudgel. The prince staggered, coughing and gasping profanities.

"What sort of business did you have with Whitetooth?" Alistar asked, voice cool.

"No concern of—" Pietro began. Brin jabbed him again. He doubled over, gasping for breath.

"Oh, but you see, your business with Whitetooth is very much my concern, 'Your Highness'." He made sure to infuse the title with every drop of scorn and sarcasm he could muster. "So, I ask you again: what sort of business did you have with Whitetooth?"

Pietro lifted his head and spat at Alistar.

Alistar gave him a dark smile. "There's a thin line, patsy, between being entertaining and being annoying. Push too far onto the side of annoying, and you might find yourself back in a box, blind and deaf. But next time, it'll just be around your head. You won't know when the next blow's coming. You won't know what questions you're failing to answer. You won't see anything but darkness, and you won't hear anything but your own panic."

The prince flinched back as Alistar spoke, pressing his back against the bars. His breathing was quick, and his eyes betrayed fear. He didn't speak.

Alistar continued. "Or you can answer my questions, and maybe I'll see fit to give you a drink. Maybe even food, if I *really* like the answer."

It was a very large stick and a very small carrot to dangle before the prince. Pietro licked his lips. "Water first."

Eddie, Brin's partner guard, gave Alistar a questioning look. Alistar nodded. Eddie splashed a couple swallows of water into a cup and brought it to the prince's mouth. Pietro gulped it down, straining to capture every drop. Eddie pulled the cup away. Pietro looked to Alistar. "More."

Alistar folded his arms. "Earn it."

He saw the protests rising on the prince's lips. Alistar held his gaze, not blinking.

Pietro gritted his teeth. "You have no right to do this! You have no right to keep me here! Release me!"

Alistar shook his head. "Poor choice, 'Your Highness'." He looked to Brin and Eddie. "Don't let him nod off."

He turned on his heels and walked out of the room.

"Wait."

He didn't pause.

"Wait!"

He didn't look back or dignify Pietro's cry with a response.

"Wait, damn you! Come back! I command you!"

"You command?" Alistar looked over his shoulder. "You think you can give me commands? Look around. Do you know where you are? Do you know who you've made your enemies by allying with Whitetooth?"

Pietro didn't answer.

"Whatever authority you think you can claim, it has no power here. No one knows where you are. No one knows you're in my hold. I wonder if your servants will worry over your absence or rejoice in it and enjoy their day free of your presence. It doesn't matter, because regardless of anyone's feelings, no one will look for *you* to be *here*. So, enjoy the amenities I offer you, or don't. It makes no difference."

"You'll pay for this! You'll see!"

Alistar didn't dignify his shout with a response. He turned around and continued walking away.

Soluthos joined him. Once they couldn't hear the prince yelling, he said, "Was that what you expected?"

"Yes, mostly. I didn't expect him to be cooperative on the first round."

Soluthos cleared his throat uncomfortably. "The threats you made… do you intend to follow through on them?"

"I'm not going to let him starve or die of thirst, but I'll let him get uncomfortable. As for leaving him blind and deaf, even if I did want to carry that out, Rykka needs to recover first."

"Was she injured? Dawncloud didn't mention that," Soluthos asked in concern.

"She kept the barrier around our guest for much of the night, and it was quite taxing."

Soluthos winced. "I can only imagine."

Both men changed back into their normal clothes before leaving the basement. Alistar headed up to his study, trailed by Soluthos. Before they reached it, Alistar saw Rykka in the hall, leaning against a wall. Her hair was an unbrushed tangle, her clothes rumpled as if she'd slept in them, and she seemed to be staring at nothing. She turned to him, blinked, and looked momentarily confused.

"Oh, there you are, De'seneth. Was looking for you."

Alistar approached. "You should be resting."

She waved a hand dismissively. "I'm fine."

"No, you're exhausted." Alistar turned. "Soluthos, would you get her water and something to eat?"

"Of course, sir." Soluthos nodded and hurried downstairs.

Alistar guided Rykka into his study and into a chair. "Why were you looking for me?"

She plopped into the chair. "Guess I am tired. Sorry. Oh, right, was gonna tell you about the magic feeling weird by Whitetooth's lair."

Alistar straightened. "What do you mean? Weird how?"

She searched for a word. "Like… sticky and thick. It *worked* the same, but it was like… like when you eat some food you know and like, and it tastes and smells the same, but the texture just isn't right. You know what I mean?"

"I understand the analogy," Alistar assured her. "Where did you feel this? Just around Whitetooth's lair?"

"That's where I started channeling. The magic felt normal by the time we got to the Middle City. Thought I should let you know in case he or Sunward have been messing with that stuff."

Alistar nodded. "Thanks. I'll see what I can find. Even if no one's tampered with the lines, maybe one of the generators is out of specifications, and no one's prioritized it because of the work on the Exhibition."

A knock announced Soluthos's arrival with a tray. He set it in Rykka's lap. She didn't seem to notice it, but it only took a moment before she was popping cubes of cheese and hard sausage in her mouth. When she'd cleared the plate and drunk the pitcher of water Soluthos brought, Alistar directed her back to her room with orders to get more sleep. To his knowledge, that was the most effective recovery method for a channeler who strained their abilities too far.

I hope that's all this is, and that this "strangeness" in the mahiy lines hasn't had some ill effect on her.

Once he was alone in his study, Alistar studied a map of the mahiy lines, identifying generators that could be affecting the magic in the Lower City and slums. *Whitetooth, Prince Pietro, Lady Sunward, and now this aberration in the magic. How are they connected? What is Sunward trying to do?*

CHAPTER 45

When Rykka woke, she wasn't alone in her room. She could sense the soft sounds of movements that weren't her own. Her eyes opened to slits, searching for the intruder.

She relaxed when she saw Tiyron sitting nearby. A book sat open in his lap, and he frowned down at the pages. Her door was closed and no one else appeared to be in the room.

Bone-deep weariness still clung to her, but the muzzy haze from channeling too much for too long had relented. She let out a long breath. Tiyron looked up from the book.

"Anything interesting?" she asked him, gesturing at the book.

"Your friend De'seneth has strong opinions about writers who can't get what he considers 'basic facts' right about sailing." He held up the book and she saw it was a two-chip novel. The cover was illustrated with an image of a sailor leaping from a ship's mast, cutlass drawn, swinging at the toothy maw of a kraken. "His annotations are at least as entertaining as the story. You've been out for most of the day. Dinner's on the nightstand."

She sat up slowly, wincing as muscles complained. "I think I got up earlier?"

"You did. Had something to say to De'seneth, apparently. Windshadow tracked me down and strongly suggested I keep an eye on you in case you decided to get up before you really woke up again."

"And you listened to him? I thought I was awake, now I'm not sure."

"Very funny. He was telling me that you needed my attention. Of course I listened."

She sat up and took the dinner tray. The soup was lukewarm, but edible, and she was hungry. "Any news on the guest?"

Tiyron gave her a dubious look. "You think they would tell me if there was?"

"At least that means no one else knows he's here. I'm sure none of us could miss the chaos if his presence was discovered."

Tiyron glanced at the closed door and leaned close. "Do you really believe that flapdoodle is a prince?"

"Well, I'd never seen him before, but people who have are certain that he's the younger prince, and that's not something any of them are likely to lie about. Or at least, they aren't likely to lie that he *is* the prince if he *isn't*."

"Then what in the gods' piss pot was he doing with Whitetooth?"

"If he's the same nobleman Seva saw, he was delivering Sunward's drugs. And how she got the gods-damned *prince* to run around as her errand boy, I have no idea." She combed her fingers through her hair. "I need to get dressed so we can find out what De'seneth's gotten out of him so far."

Tiyron closed his book, slid it into a pocket on the side of his chair, and maneuvered out of her room. She knew he didn't like using the chair, but he was rapidly growing skilled in manipulating it.

She dressed, then collected her dinner tray and joined Tiyron in the hallway. The first stop was downstairs in the kitchen, where a maid took her tray with a quick nod of thanks.

They only got a few steps down the narrow servants' corridors before Windshadow found them.

"Darkwood, good to see you've recovered," he greeted her. To Tiyron, he simply gave a nod of acknowledgement.

"Yes, I'm fine now. Anything I should know about while I was unavailable?"

"A few things," he said with a look that clearly said they weren't things he was going to say in the frequently trafficked hall.

She gestured for him to lead the way. Windshadow strode down the hall and exited near the ballroom. He stepped into a small sitting room. Rykka and Tiyron followed. Windshadow looked askance at Tiyron.

"My brother is going to hear about what's happened one way or another. If not now, from you, then later, from me," Rykka said.

Windshadow gave Tiyron a disapproving scowl. "Fine. Lord De'seneth spoke to the guest earlier, with little useful results. You spoke to Lord De'seneth earlier, in case you don't remember."

"I vaguely remember. My brother mentioned it as well. Any news of Whitetooth?"

"Unfortunately, they weren't able to capture him. However, they did apprehend most of his crew, and Dawncloud specifically wanted me to tell you that his whores and their children are safe and under protective custody. She also sends her thanks for your initial suggestion that the raid be classified as an investigation into tax evasion."

Rykka's eyebrows rose. "It was more of a joke than anything, but I'm glad it apparently helped."

"More than any of us knew before the raid. There's a certain hierarchy of criminal activities, and different levels of permission needed to investigate them. For an accusation of tax evasion, permission to investigate can be granted by Dawncloud's superior. An accusation like trafficking of prostitutes, illegal drug sales, bribery, blackmail, or the like requires approval from several levels higher. And it seems that those bureaucrats at the higher levels were informed that no such raids should be approved on Whitetooth's lair. However, that message was not passed down so far as her superior, conveniently. When he was questioned about why he granted approval for this activity, he claimed that the events that took place were not a raid at all, but an investigation into tax evasion."

Rykka snorted. "And they accepted that Dawncloud needed that many people to investigate tax fraud?"

"In *that* part of town?" Windshadow countered. "A Crown tax collector travels with at *least* that many guards in areas like that."

"They'd better," Tiyron muttered. "So, who decided Whitetooth was untouchable?"

"I don't know," Windshadow admitted.

"I have a pretty good idea," Rykka said. Both men looked to her. "Whitetooth told his visitor 'you were supposed to make sure this didn't happen.'"

"That's much further up the hierarchy than I was hoping, but I admit I'm not surprised." Windshadow walked to the window and looked over the grounds.

"So, did you come this way because it was the first convenient room where we could talk, or because you're heading into the basement?" Rykka asked. "And is De'seneth down there?"

"He intended to pay a visit this evening," Windshadow acknowledged. "He didn't say if he wanted you to join him."

It felt like an invitation. Did she want to witness the prince's interrogation? She wanted to know what he knew, and what he would tell them, and much as she trusted Alistar, he didn't focus on the same things she did.

"Well, De'seneth's perfectly able to tell me to leave if he doesn't want me there. Let's go."

A little while later, Rykka and Tiyron stood with Windshadow just outside the prince's prison, dressed in coarse clothes and wearing masks to obscure their features. Alistar hadn't objected when she and her brother came in with Windshadow, though he'd clearly considered telling Tiyron to leave.

Alistar settled his mask in place and strode confidently into the room. The prison was brightly lit. Rykka, Tiyron, and Windshadow could easily see him from where they stood, but compared to the prison, they stood in shadow. If he looked toward them, the prince might see shapes, but not details to identify them. Prince Pietro was slumped in the cage, head drooping. The Rillwater guards sat closer to the bars now. The prince flinched when one stood, lifting his head with an effort. The guard hit his club against the metal bars. Pietro cringed, gritting his teeth at the sound rang through the room.

"Still awake," he hissed through his teeth.

"Better be. Got a visitor."

Pietro turned dark-ringed eyes to the doorway, saw Alistar, and muttered something that was probably profane.

"I trust you've used your time to think about your situation," Alistar said, moving closer.

"You'll hang for this!"

Alistar laughed. "That's hardly incentive to release you. Care to try again?"

Pietro's mouth tightened in a thin line. He said nothing.

"I know you've been working with Whitetooth. I know what he gets out of the deal. But what drives some pampered prick to turn to someone like him?"

"A lowborn like you could never understand my goals."

"Because no one could possibly guess you want power and prestige?" Alistar snorted. "Really, Your Highness?"

Rykka was startled to hear him address the prince by title, but more so by the scorn he said it with.

"I *am* Prince Pietro, you filthy gutter lover!"

"Of course you are. Working with Whitetooth. Coming down to the Lower City without an escort. Very princely. So, what princely reward did you get from him?"

"*My* reward wasn't from *him*," Pietro snapped. "Whitetooth was nothing more than an unsavory necessity."

"A necessity, was he? Why?" Alistar tilted his head inquisitively.

Rykka held her breath. *Will he answer? Give us something useful here! I already regret bringing you here. At least make it worth my effort.*

"It was easy to get him what he wanted. We had the tools he needed to gain power, and the further he spread our goods, the more he furthered our goal." Pietro glared at Alistar as he spoke.

Alistar looked at one of the guards. "Give him water."

The guard reached through the bars and held a cup to Pietro's lips. The prince gulped the water greedily.

"What did you give Whitetooth?" Alistar asked. He walked around the cage and picked up the water jug, his gaze never leaving Pietro.

"Something he couldn't get anywhere else, and something no one else could obtain."

"Drugs?" Alistar asked.

Pietro glanced aside, shoulders rising in a small shrug.

Alistar leaned against the cage. "Someone who claims to be a prince, supplying illegal drugs to a dealer in the Lower City and the slums?"

Pietro spat. "What difference does it make? They barely even count as peasants." He said the word as if he couldn't think of anything lower.

Alistar cocked his head. "And who is it you think the royal family are supposed to serve?"

"*People*, not peasants!"

Rykka's hand twitched. She fought the urge to slug the self-righteous barnacle in the mouth.

Alistar, however, only laughed. "People like Whitetooth?"

Pietro hesitated. Rykka could hope he was questioning his dismissal of every person in the kingdom not of noble blood, but doubted he was capable of such introspection. He could, however, sense that he was being herded into a verbal trap. "Whitetooth is… a convenient tool."

"But not a person?" Alistar asked.

Pietro shifted uneasily.

"How do you intend to use those who, in your words, aren't really people?" Alistar pressed.

"They're going to work, and finally earn their keep," Pietro growled. "Unlike the rest of you."

Rykka frowned, not just because of the prince's arrogant dismissal of those outside the nobility. The people Sunward collected had been brought to Ravencrest's secret factory, that was true, but she clearly recalled the argument between Sunward and Ravencrest. Ravencrest dismissed the new arrivals as useless for assembly work, while Sunward plainly had another use in mind for them—one that didn't further Ravencrest's efforts to assemble the murderous automatons.

She glanced at Windshadow, wondering if he asked the same question. He met her gaze, but his expression was questioning, silently asking her what was wrong.

Rykka leaned close. "What work are they supposed to be doing? Ravencrest complained that the new recruits were no use to her."

"Work, is it?" Alistar asked the prince. "So, you have to come down out of your high and mighty estate, make a deal with Whitetooth, and supply him with drugs, all so you can deign to employ a handful of people… oh, I'm sorry, peasants? Seems a bit excessive, don't you think?"

"We have particular needs!" Pietro snapped. "We require certain qualities to these peasants."

"And you turned to *Whitetooth* to find them?" Alistar chuckled. "You know he's scamming you."

"He wouldn't dare! He has no way to. Those he sends meet the required criteria."

Alistar leaned against the bars of the cage. "And how many of those who meet these criteria does he keep? How many does he *not* send once he's found them?"

"He doesn't have the means of testing them himself. He can't hide them once they've been found."

"But he can let them 'slip away' from his thugs." Alistar smiled like a shark toward a sailor cast overboard. "Don't tell me he's never 'lost' anyone."

"That's someone else's problem," Pietro said stiffly.

"Ah, of course. It's always someone else's problem when things go wrong." Alistar turned to the guards. "Give him another drink. Tell me, Your Highness, have you ever tried this drug you've been supplying to Whitetooth? Have *you* ever been tested?"

Pietro stiffened indignantly. "The ability is only found in the slums, sometimes in the Lower City."

Is that true? But why would it only appear there? How can he be sure?

As if he'd heard her thoughts, Alistar asked, "Is it really only found there, or do you just not bother looking for it among the people who have loud enough voices to make their objections known? Maybe we should see what you're capable of."

Pietro shifted and gave the cup of water an uneasy look. "You don't know how they're tested, or for what ability."

"Don't I?" Alistar countered. "I know you're collecting those who can channel without using the mahiy lines, and you're collecting them from the people who won't be missed. Isn't that right?"

The prince's eyes grew wide. "How do you know... I... I don't know what you're talking about."

"And just what sort of 'work' are you trying to extract from such people?" Alistar pressed.

Pietro pulled frantically against his bonds. "I don't know! Something to do with automatons. I don't know!"

"Don't you? Is that 'someone else's problem' as well?"

"Yes! It is! Go ask them yourself if you care so much about the blighted answer!"

"It would be my pleasure," Alistar said with a sharkish smile. "Who do I ask?"

A wave of fear washed over the prince's features, as if he only now realized what he'd said. He shook his head in rapid, silent refusal.

"Your lover, perhaps?" Alistar continued. "Or what about your brother?"

Pietro stared wild-eyed at Alistar. "Who are you?"

Alistar just chuckled, folding his arms across his chest. "Or maybe someone else is handling that aspect of this plan? The others involved haven't done much of a job of protecting you, have they? Were they planning to sacrifice you all along?"

"No! They wouldn't!"

"And yet, here you are."

Windshadow listened intently, and from the corner of her eye, Rykka saw his frown deepening. She gave him an inquisitive look, sensing that something in the conversation troubled him.

Windshadow leaned close to Rykka and answered her silent question.

"This line of questioning implies Prince Filipp could also be involved. I know of no evidence to support such suspicion."

Right, Alistar's always waited until Windshadow's out of earshot before talking about anything indicating that the princes are involved. "We don't know who is or isn't involved," she said.

"Who better to reveal that if not him?" She nodded toward Pietro.

Windshadow didn't look reassured. "But why should the question even come up?"

"Because De'seneth is thorough," Rykka said. "Very thorough."

Windshadow accepted that but didn't look happy about it. Rykka kept her gaze on their captive.

I wonder if you'll be willing to sell out your brother to save your own hide. What about Sunward? Ravencrest? Do you still think you're dealing with one of Whitetooth's rivals, or do you start to suspect you're in the hands of someone far more dangerous, Prince Pietro?

CHAPTER 46

The house was still and quiet in the early hours of the morning. Saskia sat on the balcony, cup of tea steaming in her lap, watching the sun rise. On the grounds, tiny birds hopped about, pecking at the grass. A squirrel scolded them from one of the trees for imagined slights.

She sipped her tea, enjoying the quiet. Enjoying a few minutes to pretend the world was as peaceful as it seemed right here, now, in this moment, because all too soon, there would be no avoiding reality.

A soft knock on the door frame drew her attention. "Lady De'seneth?"

Saskia turned and nodded. "Hello Rykka. Come, join me. Would you care for tea?"

"I'm pretty sure that's not proper for a lady's maid, but sure, please." Rykka settled into the second chair on the balcony.

"I'm going to the clinic this morning. You're welcome to come if you like."

She assumed Rykka would decline, but the elf surprised her. Rykka scooped generous spoonfuls of sugar into her tea. "I will.

With things as they are, I want to keep an eye open for problems around there. When do we go?"

"After breakfast." Saskia sipped her tea, enjoying the comfortable warmth. She watched the elven woman out of the corner of her eye. "How are you doing, Rykka?"

"Um… what? What do you mean?"

"I mean, how are you doing?" Saskia repeated. "Being back in Lewarden. Being here. Being involved in the current events. Being reunited with your brother. A lot's happened in the last half a month. How are you doing?"

Rykka was quiet for a time. She stirred her tea, looking into the depths of the cup. "I don't know. I haven't thought about it much. Haven't had time to."

"Haven't wanted to?" Saskia asked gently.

Rykka shrugged, not looking up from her tea. "Maybe. I just… want to get through this. Deal with Sunward. Deal with whatever plot she's running. Then I can try to convince Captain Roddek to let me sail with the *Conquest* again."

"Roddek's not the only captain in the fleet," Saskia reminded her. "And you'll have a chance to demonstrate to the Captain and the Admiral that you're worth keeping on."

Rykka cast a sidelong look at her. "Oh?"

"They're coming for a visit, potentially with the patriarchs of the De'seneth family. I expect them to arrive in two days."

Rykka swallowed hard. "Oh. Is the reason anything I can ask?"

"The Captain's parents know something more about what's down in the basement. They might know more about how best to safeguard it." She didn't elaborate—she'd already said more than she wanted most of the staff to know.

"All right. I appreciate the warning." Rykka finished her tea. "Thank you, Lady De'seneth. I should get to my tasks." She set the cup on the tray and retreated back inside.

And she never answered my question. Slippery. Saskia continued to sip her tea, looking over the grounds. *Well, I can only do so much. I just hope she'll let me help her when she needs it.*

After breakfast, Saskia and Rykka took the carriage down to the clinic. Rykka kept her gaze studiously out the window. Saskia assumed she was primarily working to avoid conversation, but she noticed the shift in Rykka's stance as they neared the clinic.

"Is something wrong?" Saskia asked.

"We're near the alley where I overheard Sunward, Merris, and Larisa plotting. Doubt they'd meet in the same place regularly, but I can always hope."

"This close to the clinic?" Saskia shifted uneasily on the bench.

Rykka shrugged. "Whitetooth had whores in the area, and some of Ravencrest's factories are close. I don't know if she owns the warehouse where the recruitment was happening, but I wouldn't be surprised."

Saskia looked out her own window. "I still find it hard to believe that Merris is in league with Sunward. She and I didn't see eye to eye on many things, but plotting against the Crown is far beyond what I imagined."

"So, what sorts of things did you disagree on?" Rykka asked.

"Mostly on the proper role of a noblewoman," Saskia answered. "She really didn't like that I was a doctor, or that I continued to work after I was wed. And she especially didn't like that I worked in *this* part of the city. At least those were the arguments she raised most often. Maybe the truth is she didn't like that I didn't take her into my confidence, and that I expected her to help around the manor and she didn't have free reign to poke around the basement. She probably thought she finally had the chance when Alistar and I traveled to Rillwater."

"I assume Dorne kept a watch for anyone trying to get down there while you were gone," Rykka said. "He's a smart one."

Saskia nodded. "He'd dismissed Merris by the time we returned to Lewarden. At the time, I was relieved. Now I wish I had gotten a better sense of who she was allied with."

"I'm sure she would have lied," Rykka said. "Could have sent us off on a wild cat chase."

"True," Saskia allowed. She still wondered what signs she missed and overlooked.

Rykka continued. "If Merris's attack on Windshadow was any indication, she's good at deception, and she's good at trying to kill people. Those aren't skills she picked up after getting dismissed as your maid."

Saskia's mouth tightened in a thin line, and she nodded.

The carriage ride back to the clinic was uneventful. Saskia had a small notebook in which she was writing—probably some sort of doctor's notations. Rykka watched the city streets pass and wondered when she'd last felt the sense of wonder that something as simple as a carriage ride could inspire in those like Seva who could never dream of attaining such a luxury.

The first time I sailed out of harbor on the Conquest, that's when.

She closed her eyes and tried to recall the smell of the sea and the ship—not just the salt in the air, but the timbers of the ship, the smell of canvas as the sails unfurled. The sounds of creaking ropes, flapping fabric, of sailors calling instructions or bawdy jokes. With a pang, she realized just how much she missed being there, and how much she had not missed the city in which she'd been born and raised.

The stink of Lewarden's lower districts pulled her from the memories. Stifling a sigh, she looked out the window again. They were nearing the clinic once more. Her gaze swept the alleys out of habit rather than from an expectation of seeing anything noteworthy. She didn't think Sunward would make a habit of meeting her underlings in the same alley.

Unless she has someone watching the clinic. Would she keep an eye on Saskia? I'd think Alistar would be the better one to follow, although once he's inside Silverline walls, they can't do much to see what he's doing. It might be useful for Sunward to know when both of them are out of the house. Blight, I'm glad Seva covered up before leaving the clinic.

"Sunward might have someone spying on the clinic," she said aloud.

Saskia looked up from her notes. "That's certainly possible. It would make sense for her to keep track of the people who currently reside in her old lair. I don't know whether she realizes that Alistar is the Lord As'enel who she and Cemar tried to ensnare. If she does, she had even more reason to keep watch on us."

"You already thought about this, then."

"Honestly, no, I hadn't considered it. But you're right that it's a reasonable precaution for her to take, assuming she has the people to do so. I assume she has plenty at her disposal, but we don't know that for sure. Her well-positioned followers can only provide so much aid without drawing notice. She might not have as many loyal underlings as she would like. At least not ones who are also capable of effectively spying."

"Huh. And if she used any of Whitetooth's people, she's lost that source."

Saskia nodded. "The more of her allies we remove from play, the fewer resources she has available."

"And here I assumed that of the two of you, Alistar was more likely to be the schemer."

Saskia smiled. "A common misconception. He grew up at sea. I grew up here, following my father around as he made house calls." She gestured toward the neighborhoods around them.

"Huh. I just assumed you grew up somewhere Middle City." Rykka realized how little she knew about Saskia's background. "What about your mother?"

"She served in the military and fell in battle when I was quite young. So, Father took me with him a lot as I got old enough." She was quiet for a moment before adding, "The payout from her pension gave Father the funds he needed to make the first payments on the permanent clinic building."

"How'd you meet Alistar, then?" Rykka asked curiously.

Saskia smiled fondly. "He was new to the city, just getting settled as an engineer. He'd gone out for drinks with some others in a dive somewhere, probably Dockside, and made the mistake of getting something to eat there as well."

"Oh. Oh no." Rykka winced sympathetically.

"Evidently none of his drinking buddies thought to warn him, because yes, he did. Sick as a dog. A local took pity and brought him to the clinic. Not the first time we had some misplaced nobleman in the place, but he was one of the few to return after he recovered to pay for his treatment."

Rykka nodded with a small smile. He'd probably never considered *not* doing so, unlike the nobility of Lewarden, who either would try to put the entire incident out of mind or convince themselves that the honor of treating someone as magnificent as themselves was payment enough. "Ever do house calls to collect payment?"

Saskia chuckled. "Sometimes, I wish we did. But really, we don't make many house calls anymore. They're reserved for special circumstances."

"Like what?"

"Low nobility elven patients, for one." Saskia saw Rykka's shocked expression. "We don't have many, but there are times when someone suffers an ailment that doesn't respond to healing magic. In those situations, I usually make the house call, because, as a lady myself, I could, presumably, be calling for purely social reasons, and they can maintain their social status. It does mean I sometimes need to pay real social visits here and there." She looked thoughtful. "I haven't made any since we returned from Rillwater. The invitations are probably piling up."

Rykka shifted uncomfortably. "Is that one of those things your maid is supposed to manage for you?"

"It can be. I'm not worried about it right now. Why?"

Rykka sighed. "Oh, just one more example of how I'm not doing my job."

Saskia's eyebrows rose. "Not doing your job? You've spied on Sunward, tracked her to a lair, and confirmed her connections to both Lumination and to Ravencrest. You took White-tooth out of play, at least for now, helped his people, and captured Pietro. How is that *not* doing your job? Because you're too busy to playact at being a maid I don't actually need? Of any of the roles you've been playing here, that is by far the least important."

Rykka sat back, frowning. "It's the role we agreed I was to play, originally."

Saskia nodded but shrugged. "And was the role of Lord Aspendark one you played exactly as originally presented? Or did you and Alistar alter and adjust it to fit you better?"

"We made adjustments," Rykka admitted.

"And we've done so here as well. Other members of the staff know that your role as my maid is a cover, and most believe your actual role is to be my bodyguard. Merris attacking Soluthos actually helped a lot on that front."

"It helped convince people you needed guarding," Rykka said. *Including you.*

"True enough."

The carriage drew to a stop and the driver opened the door

for them. Before she got out, Saskia looked to Rykka. "I assume you'll be going out the back door to look for any spies?"

Rykka nodded. "That was my plan."

"Good." Saskia handed her a speaking stone. "I've been meaning to give this to you. Let me know what you find."

Rykka pocketed the stone and followed Saskia out of the carriage and into the clinic. As Saskia spoke with Kir, Rykka headed into the back. No matter how many times she came here, entering the clinic never failed to send an uncomfortable shiver down her spine. Saskia probably assumed her fear of doctors grew from her fear of discovery while she was posing as her brother. She was wrong. That fear had been born when she was still in her teens, the first time she and Tiyron ventured to one of the slum's chop-docs who'd set up shop in a grungy alley. Tiyron had been worried about a nasty cut Rykka got, and not even all their pooled chips totaled enough for a real healer to even look at either of them.

The chop-doc, a wiry human man with a persistent twitch and abnormally long fingers had been treating another patient when they found him. Rykka had watched in horrified fascination as the chop-doc declared the only reliable treatment for his current patient's infected hand was amputation. She'd seen how his eyes gleamed with eager delight at the prospect, and she'd smelled the stink of decaying flesh from previous operations.

She'd pulled away from her brother and fled, but the whimpers of pain from the unlucky patient, then his scream, had haunted her nightmares for years.

Rykka stopped in the hall, closing her eyes and breathing deeply. The clinic smelled of cleaning solutions and pungent chemicals, but not of blood or rotting flesh. She'd yet to hear either Saskia or Doctor Tan'shyo mention amputations. She *knew* this was a place of healing and medicine, but she still had to steel herself every time she crossed the threshold.

It was a relief to slip out the back door and be outside again.

She moved quietly down the alley to the main street. Standing in the shadows of the alley mouth, Rykka studied the surrounding buildings. She already knew the back door was all but invisible from any distance, and none of the buildings had windows overlooking that alley. In theory, someone could watch from the roof, but there were no good angles, and the shadows were thick enough that even elven eyes would struggle to pick out details of anyone leaving the clinic by that route. The front door made a far more tempting target.

Those two buildings offer good views, but the best observation posts are also easy to see from the street. Sunward wouldn't want her spy to be noticed or recognized. She continued to scan the street. *A little further away sacrifices clarity but increases the chances of avoiding notice. What about...* Her eyes continued to rove, and she let out a heavy breath. *I'm overthinking this. If Tiyron and I had to keep an eye on this place, where would we set up?*

Her gaze found a building further down the block. The windows on the first floor were boarded up, and some effort had been made to do so on the second floor, but whoever was responsible for it had given up by the third floor. The windows that faced the street offered an acceptable view of the clinic, and if someone had a spyglass, they could track who came and went, and when.

Rykka moved back into the alley and followed it several blocks north before exiting onto the main street. No one on the street paid her notice as she crossed the street to the same side as her targeted building and walked back toward the clinic. When she reached her target, Rykka turned into another alley and began searching for an entry point.

Even knowing what clues to look for, she almost missed the narrow entrance. Whoever used the building had been careful to cover up the telltale scrapes where opening and closing the door would leave tracks in the dirt and debris that littered the alley. Rykka eased the door open far enough to squeeze inside and pulled it back nearly closed, as she'd found it.

As expected, the first floor was filled with trash and evidence that people had, at various times, lived in squalor until forced to leave. She moved carefully to where she expected the stairs to be and found the collapsed ruin of rotting boards that remained of them.

Hematic perdition. Now what? Climb? She peered up into the shadows. *Certainly discourages anyone from poking around too far.*

It took longer than she liked to find the rope hanging down a long, narrow shaft against one wall. She couldn't tell what it was anchored to, but it was stable and held her weight. The shaft gave her the means to brace herself on the climb, but as she started, Rykka realized that she didn't need the assistance, and despite the height, a stationary shaft was easier than scrambling up the mast of the *Conquest* while waves tossed the ship.

Leaves and weather-worn scraps of parchment scattered the floorboards around unboarded windows, stirred by the gentle spring breeze. Rykka stepped lightly over and around them, moving toward the windows that faced the clinic. Here, finally, someone had taken a few steps to make the space more comfortable. She found a compact brazier and kettle tucked in a nook, and a blanket tucked in another. She ran her fingers over the blanket. The cloth was some sort of silkweave blend, nothing that anyone living in this area could afford. For a blanket this warm, locals would have to stoop to wool. Growing up in Lewarden, Rykka had always known wool to be the cloth of the poor, just as mutton was their meat. She'd never realized wool's utility until joining the fleet, and she'd never completely shed her reflexive aversion to it.

She froze and crouched low when she heard a voice. Rykka held her breath, straining to hear. The voice spoke again, a muffled sound. She released a silent sigh of relief as the tone indicated that the speaker was continuing an existing conversation, not informing Rykka that she'd been discovered.

Moving at a crawl, she advanced toward the sound. The voice was female, pitched low. Rykka saw a figure perched on a stool to one side of a window, positioned where she could look out. The glare of light from outside obscured her features, but she held something in one hand raised close to her face.

"No, no sign of him. Doctor De'seneth and her new maid arrived a little while ago."

The other voice was harder to hear, more muffled, but Rykka caught enough words to fill in the rest. "I *need* you to find Pietro, Merris. Find who has him. Find if he's dead or alive."

That's Sunward. The muffling probably means she's communicating through a speaking stone.

Merris sighed in exasperation. "Yeah, I know. Are you sure you really *want* him back, though?"

"Yes." Sunward's voice left no room for argument. "Alive. And when you find him, find a way to free him. Get him to one of the hideouts."

"What if he isn't alive?" Merris countered.

"Then retrieve his body. He'll be useful one way or another."

"Fine." Merris's displeasure dripped from the word.

"If I don't need him in the end, I'll let you slit his throat, or eliminate him however you prefer, afterwards."

"It would save plenty of time and aggravation to not wait that long."

"Merris."

"I know, I know. Keep him alive until he's more useful as a corpse."

"And just as importantly, find out what he's said to whoever has him."

"You going to send someone else to watch here? Even if Doctor De'seneth knows something, I'm confident she's not keeping him at the clinic."

"Yes. When your shift is over tonight, hand everything over to the night shift. Someone else will take your place in the morning."

Blight, this is organized. I don't like not knowing how much they know about us. Do they know about Tiyron? She shook her head. *No, Sunward couldn't know that. If she did, she'd be trying to eliminate us before we come for revenge.* She eyed the silhouetted figure by the window. *I don't like having you sniffing at our heels, Merris. I don't suppose you're careless enough to accidentally fall out that window, are you?*

Merris lowered her hand and leaned back against the wall with a muttered curse. "Can't wait to be done with this farce."

On that, at least, you and I agree. Rykka quietly withdrew, keenly listening for any indication that she'd been spotted or heard.

She returned to the clinic through the back door and found Saskia and Doctor Tan'shyo taking a tea break. Doctor Tan'shyo poured another mug of tea and offered it to her. Rykka accepted, sipped it, and added a generous spoonful of sugar.

"What did you find?" Saskia asked.

If she was asking the question now, Rykka assumed she didn't mind her father hearing the answer. "Right now, Merris is watching the clinic. Sunward has her looking for White-tooth's accomplice." She wasn't sure she should be announcing Prince Pietro's identity.

"Our houseguest?" Saskia asked.

Rykka nodded. "Yeah, that one. Seems Merris thought he might be here but decided that was unlikely. She'll be looking other places, and Sunward will have other people watching the clinic. But she'll still have people watching the clinic. And Merris might try to sneak into the manor again."

"Lady Sunward is aggravatingly persistent," Doctor Tan'shyo said. "As is Merris. I can speak with our contracted protection about evicting uninvited spies."

Saskia shook her head. "For now, I'd prefer they not know we're aware of them. Rykka, do you think Sunward knows we were involved in Whitetooth's fall?"

"My impression is that Merris was checking potential leads, not that she specifically thought you were involved. She's aware that I'm your new maid, but she also sounded quite dismissive of me when speaking to Sunward." Rykka shrugged. "So there seem to be some advantages to being terrible at this job."

Saskia chuckled softly and finished her tea. "I'm going to spend the rest of the day here, but you should return to the manor and make sure Dorne and Soluthos are aware of the situation. I'll contact you if I need anything."

She wasn't completely comfortable with the idea, but Rykka nodded. "Until later, then." Relieved that she didn't have to spend any longer at the clinic, she gulped the last of her tea, savoring the excessive sweetness, then made her way out to the carriage.

CHAPTER 47

For as close as they were to the Exhibition, Alistar's day had been remarkably uneventful. He hadn't been interrupted with any emergencies. The reports from the teams implementing the updates around the Exhibition grounds didn't introduce any new reefs to scuttle their schedule. He wasn't sure why the absence of trouble unsettled him.

He assembled his progress report for Prince Cero, left his office, and started down the hall. He'd gotten less than a dozen steps when Senior Engineer Sandbraid, an elf twice his age, who Alistar had never seen act with anything less than perfect decorum, hurried out of his own office and narrowly avoided colliding with Alistar.

"Blood and sand! I'm sorry," Alistar apologized quickly.

"Ah, my fault, my fault, pardon me, De'seneth," Sandbraid said quickly. "Couldn't let the opportunity slip by, though, you know. You're on your way there as well, I assume?"

"I was on my way--"

Sandbraid just nodded and strode up the hall in the direction of the lobby. "Of course! Even we don't get many opportunities to see the Crown Prince apologize in public!"

Alistar blinked, then his curiosity got the better of him, and he followed Sandbraid. "Did someone inform you of this?"

"Assistant Bellsong sent me a message. She's quite kind, and knows I have a fondness for witnessing the foibles of the Crown when I can."

"Oh?" Alistar hadn't thought Sandbraid the sort to chase after royal scandals. "Did you hear any of the interactions between Lady Syri and Prince Pietro?"

"Not as many as I wished, but I caught parts and pieces of several." Sandbraid looked back at Alistar, his eyes lighting. "You were present for at least one, weren't you?"

Alistar nodded. "I was, though I can't discuss their conversations, you understand."

Sandbraid's expression grew even more excited when he caught Alistar's use of the plural. "Of course, of course, I understand. But if you were to think of something you could share, I would of course be extremely grateful."

They reached the overlook to the lobby below and stopped at the railing. Looking down, Alistar saw Crown Prince Filipp standing near the reception desk with three Royal Guards. Prince Cero strode down the stairs, standing tall and straight as if he'd never suffered a life-threatening assassination attempt. His arm wasn't even in a sling.

"Good afternoon, nephew. What brings you here today?" the Silver Prince greeted politely, but not warmly.

"Uncle, it's good to see you looking so well," Prince Filipp responded. "I know you're busy, so I'll avoid taking longer than necessary." As he spoke, he looked past Prince Cero as if judging how much of an audience he had. Apparently satisfied, he continued. "It's come to my attention that in your absence, my brother... made a bit of a nuisance of himself."

Alistar frowned. Prince Filipp obviously wanted other people to hear, or he would have gone directly to Prince Cero's office—or even spoken to him outside of Silverline Power, in a more private family setting. Although given Prince Cero's obsession with his work, his office was a more likely place to find him.

"He did and has evidently made himself scarce since my return." Prince Cero gazed at his nephew, waiting.

"Yes. I came to offer my apologies for my brother's behavior and to assure you that he won't be continuing to bother you. I have sent him to take care of some Exhibition-related tasks for me. Those tasks have, for the time being, taken him out of Lewarden. He should not cause you any further distress."

Both Prince Cero and Prince Filipp ignored the murmurs of surprise that rose around the lobby and from the overlooks. Alistar just stared at the crown prince, mind racing.

Do you know what he's been doing? Are you covering for his absence because you know he's been taken by someone, or because you don't know what happened and are hiding the fact that he's missing?

"I see," Prince Cero said. "I trust, then, that with his assistance in these tasks you've given him, we will not be seeing any additional changes to the already approved and agreed upon plans for the infrastructure of the Exhibition."

That got a slight grimace from Prince Filipp, then a tight smile. "Certainly not. I wouldn't want to cause any delays that might get in the way of your work."

"I'm pleased to hear that." Prince Cero's expression was unchanged. "As crews are already working at the site, any changes at this point would be very difficult to accommodate."

"So I have been informed." The crown prince bowed to his uncle. "I'll take no more of your time, then. Don't let me keep you from your work."

The words sent an uneasy chill down Alistar's spine, though he couldn't say why. Not the words. How Prince Filipp said them, the air he projected felt almost malicious. Alistar glanced at Senior Engineer Sandbraid, but the elf didn't appear to notice anything concerning about the interaction.

Prince Filipp and his Guards took their leave. Prince Cero strode to the front desk and spoke with Assistant Bellsong. The rest of the employees gradually dispersed back to their duties.

"Did it live up to your expectations?" Alistar asked Sandbraid.

"It's quite the potential for gossip, perhaps even scandal," Sandbraid said in obvious delight. "I shall be surprised if we see Prince Pietro in public for some time. If he's embarrassed his family enough that the crown prince has sent him away and has to publicly apologize, his behavior has been truly outrageous. Someone with a great deal of influence must have complained."

"Like the Silver Prince or Lady Syri?" Alistar asked.

Sandbraid shook his head. "Someone outside the Royal Family. Someone with enough power to make the Crown decide it would be better to temporarily exile the problem son to another province for a while."

Filipp's laying the foundation to discredit Pietro. Protecting himself in case Pietro reveals too much to someone?

It was obvious that Prince Cero didn't intend to return to his office anytime soon. Alistar walked back to his own, setting his report aside to deliver later. Alone with his thoughts for a time, he drummed his fingers on his desk as he tried to mentally arrange pieces of the puzzle that was Sunward's scheme. His gaze moved to the framed map of Lewarden, its various districts demarcated in a manner starker and more definitive than reality. Colored lines represented the mahiy lines and indicated which lines could safely merge with others, and which were too out of synchronization with each other to blend. The maps were updated periodically as new developments were tested, new lines added or removed, or other changes were implemented.

After several minutes trying to place an undefined sense of disquiet, he pulled an older map from the bottom drawer of his desk and unrolled it, comparing it to the newer one. Even between the two, one only a year older than the other, the difference between the mahiy lines that fed the slums and the Lower City and those that provided power to the nobility grew pronounced. Certainly, the poor districts were most often the testing grounds for new techniques and new strains of kurowa flowers, but a year ago, if he'd really had to, Alistar could have rerouted enough power from the Lower City into the Middle City, and the Middle City to the Factory District to keep operations going in an emergency. To do the same now would require drawing power from the Noble District instead, or creating an extremely complicated, roundabout path through the Middle City in the highly likely circumstances that a request to remove magic from the Noble District was rejected.

But what's changed? Why are the slums and Lower City so far out of synchronization with the rest of Lewarden? And why has it been allowed to continue?

As a senior engineer, Alistar had access to more information than those of lower rank. He looked through the records of the previous year's projects until he finally found a report from Botany that referred to an ongoing project in one of the Lower City generators, indicating that the cross-breeding continued to be successful and showed good results. He read the full report, hoping for more information. It wasn't until the conclusion that the author finally stated what crossbreeding they meant. Not, as Alistar first assumed, different strains of kurowa flower, but a crossbreed of kurowa flowers with frost's breath, one of Prince Cero's experiments into methods of increasing magic generation.

Crossbreeding the native kurowa with frost's breath. That's a piece of Silverline-confidential research that was leaked to Cemar and his people. Baron Sok'lof used it to incite the Inheritors to riot, capitalizing on their rejection of anything elven and calling it a corruption of Rechmal's sacred flower.

His gaze moved back to the map on the wall. He located the

generator mentioned in the botanist's report and found it, part of a ring of Lower City generators toward the heart of the unsynchronized lines.

Whitetooth's lair lay within that area as well. Coiled Dragon Clinic stood outside it, although at the current rate of expansion, it wouldn't stay that way for more than a couple years.

Every internal channeler we know of comes from the Lower City or the slums.

Every internal channeler we know of comes from an area where the magic of the frost's breath flower has been mixed with that of the kurowa.

Every one of them we know of has manifested that power after this experiment began.

It's not Sunward who's creating internal channelers. It's us.

He sat down heavily and shook his head. *I don't know this for sure. I could be seeing false connections. Incorrect inferences. But given the legend around the crystal flower and the effects it evidently can cause, I worry what we could be creating with these experiments.*

He abruptly stood and walked out of his office, locking the door behind him. If his fears were founded, he needed guidance he wouldn't find within the walls of Silverline Power.

Night's Eve Sanctuary was neither the largest nor the finest of Lewarden's sanctuaries dedicated to the Reyker, the pantheon worshiped by humans. It was, however, the one where Alistar felt the most at home.

Today was not a Day of Devotion, and the sanctuary was mostly empty. He sat on one of the benches toward the back. His eyes moved to a carving along one of the stone pillars—an image of the frost's breath flower, sacred to Rechmal, god of magic.

Lord Rechmal, please do not judge us too harshly for errors committed in ignorance. Whatever the reason was that our ancestors left their history behind when they walked through the portal, it appears we may not have safeguarded everything they entrusted to us. But the people who are likely to suffer the most are those with the least ability to stop what's being done. Please protect them from those who would do them harm.

He sat, gazing at the carving, for some time, letting his thoughts find quiet and peace. Eventually he rose and walked outside to his carriage.

"Where to, sir?" his driver asked.

Alistar opened the carriage door and considered. The responsible answer would be to return to Silverline Power, but it didn't feel like the right one. "Home."

When he arrived at the manor, Alistar saw Rykka, Soluthos, and Dorne gathered in conference outside. Rykka appeared particularly animated in her gestures, and the men listened intently. Soluthos invited Alistar to join them with a wave.

"Has something happened?" Alistar asked.

"Not yet," Rykka answered. "And we're trying to keep it that way."

"So you're discussing the matter on the front lawn?"

"Harder for someone to sneak close enough to overhear," she answered. Her gaze swept the area to confirm her own statement. "Sunward has people spying on who comes and goes to the clinic. I located the site and caught part of a conversation between Merris and Sunward. Sunward ordered Merris to find Whitetooth's noble ally, dead or alive, and bring him to one of their safehouses until they need him. I don't know if she'll try to come here, but if she does, we need to be prepared."

"I see."

"Sunward also said that if they end up not needing him, Merris can slit his throat."

Soluthos stiffened, fists clenching.

"I… see. Let's move this conversation downstairs."

All three nodded and followed him inside. Not a subtle way of conducting business, but any servants who'd noticed the trio outside likely already suspected secrets were being discussed.

Down in the basement, where Alistar felt more comfortable saying Pietro's name openly, he said, "This will probably hit the scandal rags by tonight, but Crown Prince Filipp staged a public apology in the Silverline Power lobby today, ostensibly to apologize for Pietro's behavior while the Silver Prince was convalescing. He stated that he personally had given Pietro busywork that will keep him out of Lewarden for an indeterminate period of time. While there are undoubtedly people looking for Prince Pietro, there is currently no one *officially* searching for him because he's not *officially* missing."

Rykka frowned. "Seems to imply a scandal that the Crown wants to keep quiet. Interesting choice of a cover story."

Soluthos glanced at her. "Prince Pietro and Crown Prince Filipp are not close, and Prince Filipp has more than once expressed annoyance at Prince Pietro's antics. He may well assume that his brother's disappearance is connected to some scandal that hasn't been discovered yet."

Dorne snorted. "Or he's in on the whole thing and is perfectly happy to have his potential rival out of the way."

Alistar hadn't discussed his suspicions with Dorne, but his butler was a smart man, and he kept his ears open to the whispers around the manor. "His public statement doesn't prove anything one way or another about his possible involvement. I did get a sense before he left that Crown Prince Filipp was displeased with Prince Cero over something. The source wasn't clear, though."

"Huh. So, sounds like there's only one person in the house

who can tell us whether or not Filipp's involved in the plot," Rykka said.

Alistar nodded. "Soluthos, Rykka, listen in. Dorne, I trust the rest of the manor into your care."

"Of course, sir." Dorne headed back upstairs.

Alistar dressed down, put on his mask, and entered Prince Pietro's prison. The prince sat hunched and miserable, head drooping. At Alistar's approach, his head jerked up. His face was heavily lined and his eyes dark with bags. Alistar looked to the prince's guards first.

"Has he been minding his manners?"

"Aye, sir. And as you told us, when he can't keep his eyes open any more, we've let him close them for half a candlemark."

Pietro shivered. His breathing was ragged. He turned exhausted eyes to Alistar. "Please... let me sleep..." His voice rasped in his throat.

"Give him water," Alistar ordered.

Pietro gulped down the liquid when it was put to his lips. When it was gone, he focused on Alistar again. "What do you want?"

"Tell me, Your Highness, how exactly did someone like you have any contact with someone like Whitetooth? Why would you even speak to him? Why not send someone else? Why you personally?"

Pietro swallowed hard. "We didn't trust anyone else with the task."

"Is that so?" Alistar cocked his head to one side. "Or is it that your allies insisted you had to be involved so they could be sure they had something to hold over you if you became a liability?"

Pietro shifted uncomfortably. "That's... no. Wasn't to create a hold over me."

Alistar's eyes narrowed. "Is it because they already have one? You had to follow their instructions, or they would reveal your secret?"

The prince shifted again, not meeting Alistar's eyes and not speaking.

"How terribly inconvenient for you."

Pietro glared at him. "You're no better. Trying to pry out something you can use, blackmail me. Think you can make a scandal out of it. You want marks? A favor to demand at your whim?"

Alistar leaned against the cage, looking down at Pietro. "I want to know about your brother. What's his role? Is he as close with Sunward as you are?"

"My brother? Why do you care about him? He didn't have any dealings with Whitetooth." Pietro blinked, brow furrowing. "I didn't say anything about Sunward."

Alistar chuckled. "You think that means I don't know about her? She set you up to take the fall if Whitetooth ever went down. She has her personal assassin hunting for you." He leaned closer. "And your brother claims you're working on a project for him to explain your sudden absence."

Pietro stared at him. Alistar saw realization slowly work through the fog of exhaustion. He saw the moment when Pietro realized that his captor knew exactly who he was. Pietro's breath hitched, then quickened. He looked up at Alistar. "Who are you?"

"I told you who I am," Alistar said. "Or have you forgotten?"

"You mocked me! I told you my name, and you mocked me!"

Alistar only raised an eyebrow and waited. "And what did I tell you?"

"You said if I was Prince Pietro, you were the heir... to the fleets... of Rill..." The prince's voice trailed off as color drained from his face.

"Good. I'd hate to think you'd forgotten."

"But why... What are you doing *here*?"

Alistar raised an eyebrow. "Do you think we wouldn't follow

the trail of those pirates you have trying to smuggle in the components for your automatons?"

The prince stared up at him and finally remembered that he should keep his mouth shut if he didn't want to incriminate himself further.

"How long have you known Sunward?"

"A year or so."

"Did she approach you, or did you seek her out?"

"Mutual acquaintance."

"Did you know her part in the plot to overthrow your family before or after you became lovers?" Their relationship was speculation, but Alistar knew Sunward used her charms with skill.

"I..." Pietro hesitated again, then pressed his lips together and refused to answer.

He wasn't denying it. Alistar pressed harder. "Perhaps that's what drew you to her, hmm? The idea of securing a better place for yourself by removing the... obstacles standing in your way." His eyes narrowed. "Obstacles like your brother and his family."

Pietro's eyes grew wide as saucers. He shook his head rapidly.

Please tell me that Syri's suspicion is wrong. Tell me you weren't involved in the assassination of your niece and your brother's wife.

"I didn't want Nessa to be harmed." Pietro's voice shook with those soft words.

Strings of profanities fit for any Dockside tavern ran through Alistar's mind. His voice was cold and hard. "How do you manage to say a lie that pathetically false? You didn't want your niece harmed? Your assassins came in through *her room.*"

Pietro looked up at Alistar desperately. "She wasn't supposed to be there. I spent months convincing Filipp to let her go on holiday with her friend—a family loyal to the Crown. He'd finally agreed. They should have left. I didn't..." He swallowed hard and his eyes dropped to the floor. "I didn't know he'd changed his mind and kept her in Lewarden until after... when word of the deaths..." His breath came in short, ragged gasps. His legs pulled up against his chest, and he pulled at his bonds as if he wanted to wrap his arms around them. He was shaking. "I didn't know. She wasn't supposed to be there. I didn't want... I didn't want Nessa to be killed!"

The prince's confession hung in the still air. Pietro squeezed his eyes shut and pressed his face against his knees. Alistar let several long moments pass before he spoke. "And this is what Sunward has on you. The reason you follow her instructions when she sends you to deliver her drugs to Whitetooth like an errand boy. Because all she has to do is tell Filipp that you sent the assassins."

"Yes."

"Did you know she had his ear as well, when you set your plan in motion?"

"I... wondered but didn't know for certain. But she helped me plan the attack. I thought... she wouldn't do that if she was his mistress." Pietro didn't lift his head, and his words were slightly muffled.

Alistar frowned in thought. *Where exactly was Prince Filipp on the night of the assassination attempt? Could it be that he wasn't in his suite because he was visiting a lover?*

And if that lover was Sunward, and she helped Pietro plan the attack, she would know when to ensure Filipp wasn't there. Perhaps she even took steps to ensure that Filipp didn't let Princess Nessa leave on holiday. Clearing the path for her own child to be the heir.

"I've told you what you wanted to know, As'enel," Pietro whispered, lifting his head slightly. "Please, let me sleep."

"Why is Sunward collecting people who can channel without the mahiy lines? What does she plan to do with them?"

"She never told me."

"And the automatons? What do you know of them?"

"Smuggled the parts in from other countries. Needs them done by the Exhibition. Ravencrest is building them."

"And you promised the pirates that if they could smuggle in the goods, you would replace the fleets of Rillwater with them. Which is a promise you don't have the slightest idea *how* to fulfill. The pirates are getting more and more panicked about losing some of those shipments to us. Looks like they won't make their deadline. What happens if they aren't able to hold up their end?"

"Execution, probably," Pietro answered. "Maybe Rillwater kills them."

"Well, at least you understand that much." He shook his head. "What does Sunward intend to do with the automatons? Why the Exhibition?"

Pietro bit his lip.

Alistar spoke in a low, dangerous voice. "What is she planning to do? What has she promised to you and your brother?"

"The throne." Pietro swallowed hard. "We all know King Suelton's barely fit to rule, but as long as he's alive, no one else can take the throne."

Alistar's face hardened. "She intends regicide, and you intended to help her murder your father. And what would you have done if you succeeded? Make another attempt on your brother's life?"

"We... he and I agreed that... she should decide which of us she would wed. Whichever of us she chose... would take the throne."

Alistar scoffed. "And you expected that to *work*? Would you have accepted it if she chose Filipp?"

Pietro didn't answer.

"If you believed any of her promises, then I sincerely hope Sunward would not have been stupid enough to choose you." Alistar stepped back from the cage. Pietro's guards watched silently, faces grim. He spoke to them. "Next time he passes out, don't wake him."

Nods answered him. Pietro let his head droop again. Alistar strode out of the room, past the dumbstruck Soluthos and Rykka, without another word.

He almost reached the basement stairs before another question nagged at him enough to stop him. "Blood and sand."

He spun on his heels and marched back to the prison. Soluthos and Rykka scrambled out of his way.

"De'seneth? What's wrong?" Rykka asked.

"I need to ask him about something else," Alistar said.

"What, there's more treason we haven't covered yet?" she asked.

Alistar snorted. "There's a lot of depth left to plum in that topic. We're barely under the surface."

Soluthos's expression was grim. "Even with my testimony, convincing anyone of Prince Pietro's confession will be... difficult."

"Right now, I'm honestly more concerned with preventing Sunward and Filipp from assassinating the king," Alistar said tightly.

When Alistar returned to the prison, Pietro's head jerked up, and fear flashed through his eyes. The prince had been slumped, falling rapidly toward sleep, but the alarm at Alistar's return banished sleep, temporarily, at least. Alistar strode to the cage and stared down at the prince.

"Why did you attempt to assassinate Prince Cero?"

Pietro's eyes grew wide. "What? No, I didn't."

"Oh? So the resemblance between the attacks is coincidental?"

"I don't know what you mean!" Pietro insisted desperately.

"You wanted to take control of Silverline Power," Alistar said, eyes narrow. "You tried to insert yourself into control both before and after the attack on the Silver Prince. Why *wouldn't* you attempt to remove an obstacle to that goal?"

"I would have convinced him and Syri with enough time! I didn't wish harm to either of them!"

Are you really that blind to your own incompetence? You think either Prince Cero or Lady Syri would trust you with the Silver Prince's legacy?

"You say that, but by the same logic, you had the most, potentially, to gain by removing Prince Cero," Alistar said. "If not you, then who?"

"I don't know." Pietro's exhausted gaze begged Alistar to believe him. "Maybe Filipp? He was furious after Prince Cero humiliated him in the middle of the tax office."

Alistar's eyebrows rose. "Oh? Do continue."

Pietro swallowed, considered his words, then apparently decided he had little to lose. "There's a manor house that Sunward used to use. I guess she still has things hidden there, but now someone else lives in it. Filipp cooked up some sort of tax violation on the house to try to push out the new residents without checking whether that violation applied. Turns out the Crown covers the taxes on the property by some arrangement Prince Cero made. When he found out about it, he showed up at the tax offices personally and berated Filipp in front of everyone there. Filipp was furious about it."

He has no idea he's in that very manor or that I'm the noble they tried to steal the manor from. "So, did Filipp attempt to assassinate Prince Cero as revenge for humiliating him, or because the Silver Prince denied Sunward access to the manor in question?"

"Both, I suppose. I don't know who else would try, unless Sunward set it up herself. She... doesn't like Prince Cero."

Alistar nodded slowly. "And what do you know about the flower?"

Pietro shifted uncomfortably, looking nervous. "The flower? What... about it?"

Alistar fixed a hard gaze on him. "Do you insist on playing games, Your Highness? Shall I keep prying until you answer, or will you simply tell me, so I will leave and you can pass out?"

"I don't know much about it. Just… a crystal flower. Supposedly Syri has one as well that she's been experimenting with, but I never got to see it. Sunward uses the water the flower grows in to make Lumination."

You DO know something of how the drug is made. But if it's created with the magic-infused water from the flower, what effects is it having on the bodies of those who use it? We barely know what Ambrosia and Elixir did to people. "And you provided that drug to Whitetooth, who spread it through the slums."

Pietro just nodded. "Don't know where she got the flower. Don't know how she knew the water would make a drug." His eyes sank half shut. "Done now?" His words were slurring again.

"For now." Alistar turned and walked away for the second time this day.

Pietro didn't say anything after him, only let out a heavy, relieved sigh.

Soluthos and Rykka joined Alistar again once they were well out of earshot of the prince's prison. Soluthos spoke first.

"Sir, what do you want to do? We can't just take accusations of treason against the Crown Prince to His Majesty and expect them to be accepted. Especially not given the… nature of the circumstances under which Prince Pietro confessed."

"No, we can't," Alistar agreed. His lips pressed together in a thin frown. "Blackened shoals, I need to know more about those automatons. I need to know why Sunward is collecting internal channelers." *I need to know what Lumination is actually doing to people. I need to know if the addition of frost's breath to the mahiy lines in the slums created internal channelers. I need answers.*

"Ravencrest's factory," Rykka said. "That's where they're building the automatons. That's where they took the internal channelers. That's where we need to look."

Soluthos shook his head. "Nothing you find there can be used as evidence for as long as the injunction against investigating the Ravencrest factories stands."

"Even if it's been put in place by someone we know is trying to cover his own blighted tracks?" she countered.

Soluthos sighed. "Yes."

She looked to Alistar. He shook his head slightly. Her jaw tightened as she restrained further argument. "Fine. So how do *you* suggest we answer these questions, Windshadow?"

At that, Soluthos grimaced. "Lure them into a trap? Present an opportunity too good to pass up? If they can be forced to reveal some of their hand, we could convince someone to overrule the obstructions to Ravencrest's factories as well as whatever others we haven't discovered yet."

Alistar climbed the stairs out of the basement, wondering how they could bait such a trap with anything less than King Suelton himself. He heard the other two come up after him.

"Don't do anything stupid, either of you," he said quietly. "I'll be in my study if anyone needs me."

He spent the next hour documenting everything Prince Pietro had confessed or admitted into a journal while it was still fresh in his memory. He locked the journal in a concealed compartment in his desk chair. The desk itself held several hidden drawers and compartments as well, but the desk was the obvious place to look for such things. The chair was a trick his father had taught Alistar and his siblings.

Thinking of his family, Alistar found Roddek's speaking stone. He hadn't heard anything from his brother since he instructed him to capture the envoys who visited the pirates two days ago. He activated the stone.

The stone pulsed silently, waiting for an answer from its mate. Alistar waited.

And waited.

And waited.

He might not be paying attention to the stone. Or he's in the middle of something and can't answer. I'm sure he's all right. He let out a heavy breath. *Reyker, please let Roddek be safe.*

"Blight! Sorry! I'm here, I'm here!" Roddek's rushed voice suddenly poured from the stone, out of breath.

Alistar let out the breath he'd been holding. "Are you all right? Can you talk now?"

"Uh, yeah, pretty much okay. It's been… uh… busy."

"'Pretty much okay' and 'all right' aren't the same thing," Alistar said.

"No, but I can always hope you won't notice." He could all but see Roddek's innocent grin.

"Roddek, are you well?" Alistar asked slowly.

Another pause, then Roddek let out a long breath and responded with the appropriate code phrase. "Well enough at the moment. You?"

"Well enough," Alistar replied. "What happened? Where are you now?"

Roddek's voice grew hushed. "We were going to nab those envoys as soon as they were away from the pirates. Trouble was, right when we were ready to grab them, the pirates sprang their ambush."

Alistar stiffened. "The pirates knew you were there? Is your ship safe? Your crew?"

"I thought they were after us at first too, but no. They waited until the envoys reported to their superiors that they were on their way back, then tried to grab them."

"The pirates attacked the messengers sent by their… business partners?" Alistar asked in confusion.

"From what I could tell, yes. The pirates attacked, the envoys had just enough time to panic, then we attacked—because we initially assumed the pirates were coming for us. Unfortunately, we weren't able to stop a few pirates from running back to the cove for help. One of the envoys made a break for the road, but we snatched the other and ran for *Conquest*. He didn't protest much when he realized the pirates were after him and might not have capture in mind."

"Are the pirates pursuing you now?" Alistar couldn't imagine pirates as organized and motivated as this group would give up easily, especially knowing they'd been discovered.

"Not anymore!" announced a cheerful, singsong, and decidedly female voice. "Hi Alistar. Guess who got to come save our little brother's hide?"

"Cheska?" he burst, surprised.

"Yeah…" Roddek sighed. "Her timing was perfect, no argument, but she's *never* going to stop crowing about it."

"*And* my crew scooped up that runaway envoy before he scuttled off too far," Cheska added. "Though mine's been less cooperative than Roddek's, so he's slightly ahead of me on that side."

"The pirates," Alistar prompted. "I'm sure they didn't give up just because you arrived, Cheska."

"No," she acknowledged. "I doubt they've given up. But we made a mess of the harbor cave entrance, and they'll have to clear out the rocks before they can get their ships out. Gives us time to get some distance."

Roddek spoke. "Despite her saying like she swooped in just in the nick of time, Cheska did arrive before we went after the envoys, and let me know she was there. Our parents sent her to back me up. We shouldn't stick around here, though. We can head for home, but if you need to talk to these envoys, we could sail up the river to Lewarden instead."

"Come to Lewarden." The answer felt right. "Our parents are already on their way because of another discovery on my end.

Might as well have the whole family. Who knows, maybe you can stay for the Exhibition."

A moment of silence from the other end of the stone. "The Admiral and the Captain are heading to Lewarden?" Roddek asked. "Alistar, what's going *on* over there?"

"It's a long story. I'll tell you when you get here."

"In all seriousness, Alistar, are you all right?" Cheska asked, dropping her playful, joking tone.

"Yeah. There's a lot going on, and some aspects have an unsettling potential connection to Heiset myths—specifically, myths about events that contributed to the calamity that caused our ancestors to flee."

Another long silence, then Cheska said, "Alistar, sometimes I wish you *did* joke about things like that, because then I could try to convince myself that's what you're doing now. But you don't, so… blood and sand."

Alistar smiled wryly. "That's the part that's bringing our parents here. Evidently, our grandfather knows more than most people about these myths. And if either of you knew that and never told me, I'm going to be cross with you."

"Well, I certainly didn't know that," Roddek said. "Cheska?"

"Nope. I only ever asked Grandfather for stories about his adventures as a captain."

"Didn't we all," Alistar agreed. "Get here as fast as you can. And keep those envoys aboard your ships. Don't tell them you're bound for Lewarden. Get what you can from them—especially who they work for and why they were treating with pirates. And… be careful, please."

Both his siblings made sounds of agreement, then the stone went dark.

CHAPTER 48

Step. Step. Step. Each movement ached, but the ache was an improvement over stabbing pain and agony. Tiyron continued his deliberate path back and forth in his room, trying to work out the stiffness after Lamorage's most recent healing.

Afternoon sun flowed through his window. He paused to lean against the sill and look outside at vast stretch of green outside. Nothing like the dirty window he'd peered through as a youth, where any glimpse of green was moss growing on the wall of the next house over, so close that if he reached out the window, he could peel it away. He'd done that sometimes, when he was desperately hungry and willing to test whether or not the moss was edible. He could still recall the bitter taste.

The only other building in sight was the groundskeeper's cottage. Even it was larger than the home—if he could call it that—where he and Rykka grew up. For all he knew, their parents still lived in that hovel in the slums where no one could imagine having a vast expanse of ground dedicated simply to grass and trees, most of which couldn't even be eaten.

Someone knocked on his door. He turned quickly, judging

the distance to his wheeled chair and how quickly he could reach it. "Who is it?"

"Me," Rykka answered.

His shoulders relaxed. "Come in."

She entered, closing the door behind her. "You're up. How are you doing?"

"Lamorage came by earlier today, so I'm stiff. What's new with the royal pain in the ass?"

"He cracked." Rykka related De'seneth's interrogation and the prince's confessions.

Tiyron leaned against the windowsill, taking in everything she told him. When she finished, he spoke slowly. "So, let me get this straight. Both princes are tired of waiting for their dad to finally kick off and Cemar's old lover is playing them both. Not only that, she got your downstairs guest to try and assassinate his brother, and that didn't go as he wanted because his brother conveniently wasn't home at the time, but his family was. Sounds like she arranged things so the wife and kid died, clearing out obstacles for her."

Rykka cocked her head to the side. "You think Sunward set the assassination attempt up to fail?"

Tiyron shook his head. "I think she'd call it a success for getting rid of the people *she* wanted removed. You've heard how she became the sole heir of her adopted family, right?"

Rykka's frown said that she hadn't. "Did she have siblings?"

"I poked around her past a little after I met her, trying to figure out why she made my skin crawl. Her father served with Lord Sunward in the army. He saved Lord Sunward's life a time or two. When the girl's parents died, Lord Sunward adopted her, and supposedly she became good friends with the Sunward's daughter, who was close to her age. The family also had an older son and a younger one. From what I could tell, the youngest one's death probably was an accident—toddling around and fell into a pond. I have my doubts about how the other two died."

Rykka's frown deepened. "She was a child herself, though. You think she could have murdered other children? Especially ones who were supposedly her friends?"

Tiyron looked his sister in the eyes. "Yes. I do think she could have killed them and been conniving enough to deflect suspicions when she did. Just like I think she would have murdered Cemar and pinned the blame on Sok'lof if doing so would have furthered her goals."

Rykka sat down on the edge of the writing desk. "What do you think she'll do to Larisa?"

"Hematic perdition, I don't know, Rykka! Use her in some way until she's used the girl up. You know more about machines and automatons than I do."

Rykka stiffened. "Automatons?"

"You said that's what they were building in that factory. And it's where they took the people they collected. I assume the two are related." He waved a hand in the air. "The automatons need power to work, right? And these internal channelers, in all the tests you described, could channel their power into objects, right? Make them glow or float or things like that."

Rykka nodded slowly.

"So have them channel that power into the automatons to charge up their parts and pistons and crystals. Have them drain themselves to give Sunward her war machines." He swallowed. "Larisa would do it if Sunward told her to."

He could see the girl in his mind's eye—waifish, too thin, with intense eyes and a desperate need to believe in something or someone. She'd wanted more from Tiyron that he would give her then, but he'd tried to help her understand that she didn't *need* it, that she had worth in herself, not just in what she could give to someone else.

Maybe I still can.

Rykka's thoughts evidently moved in a different direction than his. "If the channelers can direct their power into the automatons, it's no wonder Sunward needs so many of them, and doesn't care what other skills they have. The energy they would need for the automatons, though…"

"A lot?" he asked.

She grabbed a pen, found paper in the desk, and started jotting down calculations. "A lot. No matter how much they optimize the automatons, they have to replace all the energy the machines would normally draw from the mahiy lines. I don't know how much an internal channeler can produce, so these estimates have a serious gap in that area, but even so…"

"It's possible, though?" Tiyron asked.

She nodded slowly. "Possible. If you don't care whether the people drain themselves dry."

"Sunward doesn't." His leg wavered and he sagged a moment, catching himself against the window. Tiyron grimaced and straightened again. "Wish I'd realized that a lot earlier. But she's good at making people doubt themselves, too."

Rykka nodded. She looked at her equations again, then turned her gaze to Tiyron. "The answers are in Ravencrest's factory. I've tried convincing De'seneth and Windshadow that we need to go back, but they're stuck on the idea that because they can't get any official approval to go, they can't report things we find there to authorities."

"The place where automatons tried to kill you." Tiyron's eye narrowed.

"Yeah. The place where those automatons are built. The place where they keep all the channelers they collect."

"The place where, if you're found, the guards or the automatons will murder you without a second glance," Tiyron finished.

One of Rykka's eyebrows rose. "And that's different from three quarters of the jobs we used to pull how, exactly?"

His jaw tightened. She waited. Finally, Tiyron answered. "Because I'm not planning this one."

Her expression darkened. "Because you're not planning it or because I am?"

His brow furrowed. "I'm not sure what you mean. Your plans are usually almost as good as mine."

For some reason, she looked more angry rather than less. "What a sincere, heartfelt compliment."

"Yes?" He wasn't sure if she was being deliberately confusing. "What?"

"It just amazes me that I never realized how much of a self-centered ass you can be, Tiyron."

"Excuse me?" He straightened, affronted. "I haven't changed, Rykka."

She gazed at him in silence for a moment, then said, "No, you haven't."

He made a sound of frustration. "What is it, then? If you're frustrated about De'seneth and Windshadow blocking your access to that factory, then fine, we'll get in there ourselves. Murderous automatons or not, you've been there before. I'm sure you can plot the best way to get inside and where we need to be. We'll find out what we need to stop Sunward and depose a couple princes and be done with this. Once we're done here, we can find some new hideouts, start rebuilding connections and contacts, and—"

"And what, Tiyron?" she cut in. "Slink back to Lower City? Fight pointless battles with Silverline Power? Go back to what you were doing before Cemar?"

"Well, I'm not staying *here*. And you haven't told me what hideouts you've established yet, or what contacts aside from Seva."

"Contacts? Oh, you mean, say, both De'seneths, Lamorage, Windshadow, Dorne, Investigator Dawncloud, and Doctor Tan'shyo?"

"I said contacts, not nobles and royal lackeys!"

Rykka stepped closer, getting in his face. "Yet as contacts, any one of them has done more for me than a dozen men like Whitetooth and his kind. You wouldn't be awake now without them. You certainly wouldn't be mobile without them. We wouldn't know Sunward was planning *anything* without them."

His hands clenched. "They're *nobles*, Rykka," he hissed between gritted teeth. "They'll toss us aside as soon as they're done with us. We need to prepare for the future. For *after* this. We need to reestablish ourselves. Tiyron Onyxflame might officially be dead, but there's no reason we can't build a new legend. It'll be harder for you to pass as me without a lot of work, so we have to think about that."

"No."

He blinked, frowning at his sister. "No what?"

"I'm not going to pretend to be you, Tiyron."

"We can make it work," he argued. "Need to make an eyepatch part of our new signature look." He flexed his left hand. "Gloves, too. I'm sure someone can figure out how to make prosthetics for my fingers."

"Tiyron!" she interrupted sharply. "I'm not going to pretend to be you any longer."

He shook his head. "You know the sorts of people we deal with in Lower City and the slums. It takes a lot for most of them to respect a woman." *Why is she being so difficult about this? It's the best way to reestablish us. Why would she* want *to fight off every leering crime lord? This is how we've always done it.*

"I'm not staying in Lewarden, Tiyron!"

He blinked, staring at her. *She didn't say that, did she? I misheard her. I must have.* "Hematic perdition, Rykka, where else would you *be?*"

"On the *Conquest*, with the rest of Captain Roddek's crew. Blood and sand, Tiyron, did you *forget* that I told you I joined the Rillwater privateers?"

"While you were looking for a way to restore me, sure." He shrugged. "I signed on with that Narnan ship briefly to get a part you needed for the device you were building. It's a useful means to an end, even if being a sailor is miserable. Don't know why anyone would do it longer than they had to."

"Because they enjoy it," Rykka answered sharply. "Because when I sailed on that ship, I felt like I'd finally found a place where I belonged."

Tiyron started to laugh, but the sound died away when she didn't join. "Rykka, what are you talking about? You belong with me, working side by side to attain our dreams."

Her expression grew hard again. "No, Tiyron. They're *your* dreams, not *our* dreams, and my place in them has always been as your shadow. Hematic perdition, can't you *see*?! I always had to be you. Act like you, talk like you, think like you. And then, suddenly, you were gone.

"I kept playing the part until Cemar was dead, but when I brought the ceiling down on Cemar and myself, I left your shadow in the rubble. De'seneth told the Silver Prick that Tiyron Onyxflame was dead, and from then on, I couldn't be you. I had to be... me. And it took me a blighted long time to figure out who in perdition that person was. Who I am. And here's the thing. I'm not you."

He shook his head. Nothing she was saying made sense. "Of course you're not me. But we always worked together. We had the same goal. We have a legend to achieve, Rykka!"

She stepped back, shaking her head. "For once in your life, would you just *listen* to me? Yes, I did believe in what we were trying to do. But it was always *your* dream, Tiyron, just like it was always *you* who claimed the notoriety. Yours is the name people know. You never asked what I wanted. You simply decided that I had to want the same things as you. Then I spent two years without you, and I realized that I wanted something else for myself. I wanted to be someone other than the 'backup' Tiyron Onyxflame."

"And you found that on a Rillwater privateer ship?" Tiyron asked dubiously.

"Yeah. I did. And that's where I'm going back to once everything is done here. I don't expect you to come with me. It's not your dream and it's not what you want."

"Don't... you can't." The idea was incomprehensible. Rykka had always been his partner. Hearing her talk of leaving made no more sense than if his own arm had declared an intent to detach itself. "I need you."

"I've lived my life by what you need, Tiyron. But it's time I look at what *I* need, and what I need, I can't get in Lewarden."

He couldn't find any words, just a hollow numbness that crept from his chest through his body. Rykka waited for him to speak. When he didn't, finally, she turned and walked out of the room.

When the door closed behind her, he sank to the floor, staring after her.

But... why?

CHAPTER 49

Alistar walked through the Silverline Power lobby toward the stairs, giving a wave of greeting to Assistant Goldleaf at the front desk. She returned his greeting and said, "His Highness asked after you yesterday afternoon, Senior Engineer. He was expecting some reports from you."

Alistar guiltily recalled the reports he'd left on his desk when he left early. "I apologize. I needed to take care of something in the early afternoon, and it took longer than I anticipated. I'll bring my reports to him as soon as he's in."

Assistant Goldleaf nodded in approval, her pearlescent wings folding against her back. "He will appreciate it."

Back in his office, Alistar looked once more at the map of Lewarden and the lines from the slums. *How did I not notice the growing lack of synchronization? The maps are refreshed every couple of months—I suppose that contributed.* Then, with a stab of guilt, he murmured, "Or maybe I just don't pay attention to the slums or the Lower City unless I need something from them."

Shortly after nine in the morning, he collected his reports and one of his older maps of the mahiy lines across Lewarden—not the oldest, but old enough that the change could be seen—

and made his way to Prince Cero's office. The guards at the door announced him and ushered him inside.

The Silver Prince sat at his desk, though from the looks of the documents scattered about and the full, steaming mug of tea, he'd only just gotten settled. "De'seneth. I expected your reports yesterday." He fixed a disapproving gaze on Alistar.

"I apologize, Your Highness. I intended to do so, but Crown Prince Filipp's arrival complicated matters, and I didn't think the reports critical enough to interrupt you immediately after his departure. Regrettably, something came up after that, and I was unable to bring the reports to you yesterday." He set the documents on Prince Cero's desk.

The prince took them with a curt nod and scanned the documents.

"Your Highness, there's another matter I need to discu—"

"Later, De'seneth," the Silver Prince said in a tone that left no room for argument. "I have a meeting to prepare for."

Alistar drew a breath to protest, but let it out slowly. "Very well, sir." Map still tucked under his arm, he left the prince's office.

Bloody shoals, what now? This can't wait. He ran fingers through his beard. After a moment of thought, he turned to the guards at Prince Cero's door. "Do you know where Lady Syri can be found at the moment?"

"I believe she's currently in her laboratory, Senior Engineer."

"Thanks." Alistar strode in the direction of the laboratories. He wasn't sure what Lady Syri might be working on, since the crystal flower remained in his basement, but she undoubtedly had other projects as well.

He was surprised to find her working alone in the laboratory, accompanied only by Star. Lady Syri didn't look up from the piece of equipment she was adjusting until Star said, "Good morning, Senior Engineer De'seneth."

"Good morning, Star. I hope things are well here?"

Lady Syri straightened and brushed her hair from her eyes. "Senior Engineer. Can I help you?"

Alistar's mouth twisted in a wry smile. "I hope so."

At his tone, Lady Syri immediately glanced at the laboratory door. Star checked that it was closed and twisted the bolt to lock it.

"What's wrong?" Syri asked.

"I was hoping to speak to Prince Cero about this when I delivered my reports this morning, but evidently, he's very busy. I have a theory about internal channelers."

Syri's full attention fixed on him. "Please, go on."

Alistar looked around the laboratory. "Do you have... ah, there it is." He rolled out his map on a table under the more recent map of mahiy lines that hung on the laboratory wall. "In an appalling lack of attention on my part, I only noticed how much synchronization between the slums and Lower City has drifted from the rest of Lewarden while I was trying to accommodate Crown Prince Filipp's increasing demands for power to the Exhibition. But if you compare the current map to this one, from nine months ago, the change is evident."

Syri frowned at the maps, studying them intently. "All right, I see the difference. And it is concerning. But why do you think it's related to internal channelers?"

Alistar tapped a spot on the older map where the desynchronization was noticeable. "I found some reports about the Stonecarver Generator. It appears to be one of the first areas where this desynchronization became noticeable. It's also the first generator where Silverline Power experimented with adding a strain of frost's breath flowers into the existing kurowa beds." He paused a moment, and Syri nodded for him to continue. "This area of the slums has also been identified as the home of some of the internal channelers who were arrested at my manor when it was still being used as Cemar's base of operations."

"All right." Syri nodded thoughtfully.

Alistar gestured at the current map of Lewarden's mahiy lines. "All the internal channelers we know of, and all those who Sunward had recruited with drugs and promises, have come from areas affected by the change in synchronization. And all these areas share a common trait: the addition of frost's breath to the generators."

Syri looked at him sharply. "Are you suggesting that the frost's breath is creating internal channelers, De'seneth?"

"I'm suggesting the effects are not coincidental." Alistar let out a heavy breath. "I'm suggesting that Prince Cero doesn't understand all the possible effects of mixing the magic of a non-native species with that of the kurowa."

"And you do? I wasn't aware that you were also an expert in botany, Senior Engineer," she retorted tartly.

"I'm not," Alistar acknowledged. "Nor am I an expert in human mythology. However, I do know that the frost's breath is sacred to Rechmal, god of magic, and that our myths say he gifted the plant to humans. I know the crystal flower and the plant it came from are a far more powerful form of frost's breath, and the flower defied your attempts to study it, while sometimes producing an energy you couldn't define or explain."

Lady Syri shifted uncomfortably at that reminder.

"I also know Lady Sunward intends to use the magic it produces, the flower she possesses, and all the internal channelers she can collect in her plan to seize control of Lewarden, and that by continuing this experiment, we are furthering her goals."

That cut past Lady Syri's defensive indignation. She sat down, her gaze on Alistar. "How can you be sure? What have you learned about her plans?"

"She's manipulating matters at a much higher level than I thought." Alistar paused, then turned to Star. "Star, I know your sworn duty is to protect the Crown and the Royal Family. For the safety of King Suelton, Prince Cero, and Lady Syri alike, I must ask for your word that nothing I'm about to say leaves this room."

Both Lady Syri's eyebrows flew to her hairline. Star's stoic expression didn't change. She held Alistar's gaze for long moments before answering. "Lord As'enel, if revealing this information to others will endanger those I've sworn to protect, you have my word that I will hold it in confidence." Her deliberate use of his patronym warned him that she didn't like the idea.

Alistar didn't break gazes with her. "And what do your oaths demand if you must defend against some of those who you've sworn to protect in order to keep the rest safe?"

"Pietro," Syri hissed.

Alistar waited for Star's response.

"My oath is to my king first," Star said. "Will holding this knowledge in confidence protect King Suelton?"

"It will. As well as others."

Star nodded slowly. "You have my word that I will not share the information you reveal here."

"Thank you." Alistar sat on the edge of a stone table. "Sunward has people working with her in all levels of society. In the slums and Lower City, she used a criminal leader by the name of Whitetooth to spread the drug Lumination through the populace and to help her reveal the internal channelers. In the Factory District, she's working with Lady Ravencrest, who acquired the factories that formerly belonged to the Zel'en family, the original owners of my manor. She's taking the internal channelers there, presumably until she needs them. Ravencrest is using some of them as workers, building automatons." His jaw tightened. "Automatons built from components smuggled into Calarand by pirates and capable of lethal attacks."

"*What?*" Syri demanded, surging to her feet.

"They can't build as many as they initially intended. The

Rillwater fleet captured at least three smuggling ships, but I don't know how many more slipped in through other paths. Automatons guarding the factory almost killed one of my people who snuck inside. There's no doubt they were aiming killing blows."

"Blight," Syri cursed. "The political implications... The treaties that would be broken if any other country discovered we had automatons with lethal capabilities... We would be at war within a year."

"How does Sunward intend to use these automatons?" Star asked.

"She plans to use them at the Exhibition. I believe she intends to station them throughout the Exhibition grounds, disguised as elements of the presentation."

"That'll be difficult," Syri said. "Filipp has every detail mapped and planned to the minutia."

A knot of dread grew in Alistar's gut. "And Crown Prince Filipp's been adding automatons all around the Exhibition. He insists that each and every one is absolutely necessary."

"Precisely! He would notice if anyone changed or added automatons without his approval," Syri said.

Alistar searched for a better phrasing without outright stating his accusation. Star spoke quietly. "My lady, I believe Lord As'enel is implying that these automatons *are* being added with Prince Filipp's knowledge and approval."

Syri looked from Star to Alistar. Her voice was low and chill. "To what end, exactly?"

"To remove the obstacle that stands between Crown Prince Filipp and the throne of Calarand," Alistar said. The words hung heavy in the silent room.

Syri finally spoke. "You're accusing Filipp, Crown Prince, Heir to the Throne of Calarand, and a cousin who has been like a brother to me, of treason."

"I wish that I was not, Lady Syri." He didn't know how close she and Filipp were, but every tense line in Syri's body warned that she wouldn't be easily convinced. "Gods know I wish I had another answer."

"And where does Pietro fit in this scheme? Or do you claim that he's uninvolved and innocent?" she demanded.

That startled a laugh from Alistar. "Innocent? Certainly not. Sunward is playing both princes. They're vying for her affections while she uses them for her goals. But at the moment, Prince Pietro is not an active player."

Star cocked her head at him. Her expression was a mask, and he couldn't guess how much she believed. "How certain are you of that, Lord As'enel? Can you base it on more than just Prince Filipp's claim that he has sent his brother on other errands?"

Alistar raised an eyebrow at her. "Do you already know that Prince Pietro has been missing for three… going on four days now?"

Star simply nodded.

"Missing?" interrupted Syri. "How? When? Where were his guards? You knew this, Star?"

"I did, my lady, but the information remains strictly confidential. I would ask how you know it, Lord As'enel, but I find myself… hesitant to learn the answer."

"He's alive and he's not harmed," Alistar told her. "And at the moment, he's safer than he would be if Sunward knew where to find him. She has her personal assassin searching for him as we speak."

"And you… *do* know where Pietro is?" Syri asked cautiously.

"Yes. More importantly, though, is where he *was* when he disappeared."

"And that was…?"

Strangely, the topic of Prince Pietro's capture and abduction felt safer to discuss than Prince Filipp's involvement. "In the Lower City, with a single guard, delivering a fresh batch of Lumination to the criminal leader I mentioned earlier, Whitetooth. A group of Crown agents investigating Whitetooth for tax evasion interrupted their meeting. One of my people, who knew of Whitetooth's connection to Lady Ravencrest, if not directly to Sunward, accompanied the agents and was instrumental in preventing Prince Pietro's escape—though didn't know his identity until later."

"I haven't heard of this raid," Star said, frowning.

"Not a raid," Alistar corrected, remembering things Soluthos told him. "An investigation. A raid would have required a higher level of approval, and, we learned after the fact, a raid wouldn't have been approved because someone in high authority had placed a blanket denial to any raids on Whitetooth. Just the way they have placed one on raids on Lady Ravencrest's factories. And also, I assume, why the architect's blueprints of my manor were moved into the vault, where very few can access them." Alistar sat back, grimacing as the facts circled back to Pietro's brother. "Those orders came from Crown Prince Filipp."

Syri cursed in a decidedly unladylike manner.

Star was quiet for a long time before speaking. "You say both Prince Filipp and Prince Pietro are working with Lady Sunward. Are both aware of the other's involvement? Relations between them are often less than harmonious."

"Prince Pietro is certainly aware of his brother's involvement, and implied that she's unofficially Prince Filipp's mistress, as well as having a similar relationship with Prince Pietro."

"His *mistress*?" Syri snapped. "Filipp loved his wife! Still loves her! I won't hear her memory dishonored by such a foul accusation. Even if he *did* take a lover or mistress, why would he take one *known* to be wanted for treason?"

"I don't know. That's a question only he could answer," Alistar said. "I assume that Filipp is aware of Pietro's involvement with her as well, though I don't know how much he knows. I also know Sunward is following one of Cemar's strategies and ensuring she has sufficient blackmail material on her 'allies' to keep them under her control."

"Oh? Blackmail such as Pietro attempting to assassinate my father?" Syri demanded.

"Surprisingly, I don't think *that* assassination attempt actually was Pietro's doing," Alistar told her.

"Why, because he denied responsibility?"

He wasn't sure whether to be relieved or concerned that she didn't question how he was able to question Pietro or where he was. "Given that he'd already confessed to more than enough to convict him by that point, I believe he was sincere in his denial of responsibility," Alistar told her. He paused. He could tell her more, but she was already resistant to the idea of Filipp's involvement. Pushing further could cause her to reject everything he said. He knew how far he could go with Prince Cero, but he wasn't as sure with Lady Syri.

She watched him closely, her jaw tight. "There's more, isn't there?"

"Yes," Alistar told her. "I know what I've already told you has been difficult to hear, and even more so to accept."

She drew a deep breath. "Lord As'enel, do you know who tried to kill my father?"

"I know who Pietro believes was responsible. Pietro thought he could step into what he thought was a gap in power at Silverline, but he didn't have any personal grudge against your father. On the other hand, Filipp has recently had at least two conflicts with Prince Cero. The first involved the continuing changes Filipp kept making to the already approved specifications for the Exhibition. That one Prince Cero handled privately. However, Filipp signed the order to attempt to publically embarrass me and force me out of my manor under the pretext of unpaid taxes. In response, your father humiliated him in front of the entire tax office of the Ministry of the Treasury, while also making it clear that tactic wouldn't work to return control of the estate to Sunward. Although I don't believe Prince Cero knew of Sunward's possible involvement." He paused. "Is your father aware that I've been looking into Sunward's activities?"

"Not unless you've told him," Syri said, voice tight.

Alistar remembered the sense of apprehension he'd felt the previous day when Prince Filipp bid farewell to his uncle, the unidentified undertone of malice he'd felt. *I'll take no more of your time, he said. As if he'd already attempted to take far more of Prince Cero's time than he had a right to.*

Syri's hands clenched. "I can believe that Pietro is stupid enough to be enchanted by Sunward, but Filipp? What could she possibly give him that he wants badly enough to try to kill his own uncle? Or, if your implications are correct, his *father?*"

"Sunward's pregnant," Alistar said simply.

Syri stiffened, drawing a sharp breath.

He could have continued—told her how Sunward had manipulated Pietro's assassination attempt to ensure Filipp's daughter lay in the assassins' path—but he let the statement stand.

"If His Majesty is the target, and the Exhibition is the site where they intend to strike, can we lure them into moving early?" Star asked, directing the conversation away from dangerous theories. "Lord As'enel, you're the most familiar with the current state of the Exhibition grounds. Are they fit to be toured yet?"

He caught the thread of her thought. "Not yet, but if a royal visit were to be placed on the schedule, they would quickly become ready. I don't know if Ravencrest's automatons are complete yet, but if Sunward and Filipp are worried about who has Pietro, and what he might tell them, they'd be smart to seize an opportunity."

"And if they do not?" Syri asked.

"Then we have a peaceful tour of the Exhibition grounds,

and no one tries to kill anyone," Alistar said. "I would be *very* happy to be proven wrong."

Her eyes were dark. Her mouth pressed into a thin line. "Very well. I'll suggest the idea to my father and see what comes of it." She looked to Star. "*Nothing* we discussed here leaves this room."

Star just nodded. "As you will, Lady Syri."

Mid-afternoon, someone knocked on Alistar's office door. He looked up, startled, and called, "Enter."

Star opened the door and stepped inside alone. "Good day, Senior Engineer. Lady Syri is meeting with Lord Cero and doesn't require my services at the moment. I wondered if I could have a few moments of your time."

"Of course." Alistar gestured at a chair.

She shook her head. "Could we speak in the laboratory?"

His brow wrinkled in confusion for a moment before he understood. Much like her brother, Star could interpret her orders very literally when it was convenient to do so. "Of course."

They returned to the empty laboratory. Star closed and locked the door. Alistar leaned against a table. "What's on your mind?"

"A question I didn't want to bring up in Lady Syri's presence. When you spoke of the assassination attempt on Prince Cero, you said Prince Pietro wasn't responsible for *that* attack."

Alistar nodded. "He admitted to the attempt on Prince Filipp." He outlined everything Pietro told him—the unplanned change that had put Filipp's daughter directly in the assassins' path, the way Sunward used the attack as blackmail to keep Pietro under her control. He added his own theory that Sunward had manipulated Filipp as well to ensure that Nessa's planned vacation was cancelled, and Filipp's own unexpected absence from his suite when the attack occurred.

Star listened, nodding slowly. "Lady Syri is more willing to believe Prince Pietro is involved than Prince Filipp. Do you have proof of Prince Filipp's actions aside from Prince Pietro's confession?"

"Circumstantial evidence. However, more should arrive soon. The rest of my family are en route to Lewarden and if they aren't here tonight, they'll arrive tomorrow. Star, I don't suppose you know any legal way to get around Prince Filipp's block on investigations of Ravencrest's factory?"

She pursed her lips but shook her head. "None that does not involve direct intervention by King Suelton. And unfortunately, I believe His Majesty would simply ask Prince Filipp why the restriction was placed, which would alert him that we sought access."

"I was afraid of that," Alistar sighed.

She cocked her head at him. "Is the lack of permission such a deterrent, sir?"

"It does complicate things," he told her.

"Certainly," she agreed. "But, unofficially speaking, of course, I hope the complication won't become an insurmountable obstacle."

Despite himself, Alistar chuckled softly. "Understood. Unofficially speaking, of course. Thank you, Star."

"No. Thank *you*, sir."

CHAPTER 50

The remainder of the day passed without incident. Alistar and Saskia were dressing for the evening when Dorne knocked at the master suite door and announced, "Milord, milady, a carriage from Rillwater just turned into the drive."

Alistar's heart soared, knowing it had to be his family. "Tell the kitchen we have guests. We'll be down momentarily."

"Of course, sir."

He hurriedly buttoned his shirt and pulled on an evening jacket. By the time he and Saskia came downstairs, Dorne was escorting Admiral and Captain As'enel into the foyer while the house staff unloaded trunks from the carriage and carried them to the guest rooms. Both wore comfortable, sturdy traveling clothes that barely hinted at their station. Mother's pale hair was pulled back in an elaborate braid down her back, and somehow, she'd convinced Father to let her braid his salt and pepper beard as well.

"Welcome!" Alistar embraced his parents. "I hope your travels were pleasant."

"Not as nice as taking a ship," Mother said. "But uneventful, and I suppose that's something to respect." She turned to Saskia. "You're looking radiant as ever, dear."

Saskia smiled warmly. "You flatter me. I take it your parents weren't able to make the trip?"

"Unfortunately, no," Mother said. "My mother finds the dry climate of Lewarden bad for her lungs, and my father didn't want to leave her alone while we were gone and my sister is at sea. But he sends his best."

A stab of disappointment ran through Alistar. He'd hoped to ask directly about the myths about the flower. Mother met his gaze and added, "We spoke about it quite a while, and I have a speaking stone if you need to speak to him directly."

He nodded understanding. "Alright."

Alistar and Saskia gave a brief tour of the ground floor of the manor and walked their guests to their rooms. His parents had visited for the wedding, but Alistar and Saskia had drastically redecorated since then. They kept the conversation polite and innocuous all the way through dinner, discussing the journey from Rillwater, the Exhibition and Alistar's work in designing the needed infrastructure, and staying far away from talk of treason, crystal flowers, and human myths. Only once night had fallen, the day staff had retired for the evening, and the family gathered in Alistar's private study did the subject turn to the reason for the visit.

Father leaned back in his chair, a goblet of wine in hand. "So, Alistar, Saskia, catch us up on what's happened since we left home."

Alistar let out a long breath. "There's been... a lot. I assume you spoke with Grandfather about the flower and the internal channelers."

Mother nodded. "Of course. Though I couldn't tell him much about these internal channelers."

Alistar briefly summarized events since his return from Rillwater. He considered glossing over Tiyron's return, but it was too important to conceal, even if it was another secret Rykka had been holding to herself. He didn't linger on it and continued the narrative. When he described the discovery of the crystal frost's breath in his basement, Mother leaned forward, listening intently.

When he reached the point where the raid on Whitetooth's lair came in, Saskia called Rykka in. Mother's sharp gaze studied Rykka carefully, and the elven woman shifted uneasily under the scrutiny.

"As we discussed in Rillwater, Darkwood's officially working in the manor under the guise of my lady's maid," Saskia said. "But she's been the most helpful working in the Lower City and in uncovering Sunward and Ravencrest's work there."

"I'm catching everyone up on recent events," Alistar said. "Thought it best to have the tale of your raid on Whitetooth's lair directly from you. Have a seat."

Rykka nodded and sat. Saskia offered her wine, which she declined, and tea, which she accepted. She added a generous spoonful of sugar, sipped, and drew on the confident air of a notorious Lewarden criminal. "So, you want to know about the raid... oh, sorry, the tax evasion investigation on Whitetooth?"

"Please," Alistar said.

She spun the tale with a bard's artistry without distracting from the gravity of the situation. Everyone's interest piqued when she described reaching Whitetooth's chambers and finding a nobleman in the midst of a business deal. Father and Mother both leaned closer as Rykka described capturing the nobleman as Whitetooth escaped. When she revealed his identity, a collective sharp breath filled the room.

"Where is he now?" Father asked. All humor was gone from his eyes. "Given that we haven't heard news of this on the road, his treachery must not be common knowledge."

"Pietro's in a holding cell in the basement," Alistar told him. "And his involvement is known to only a handful of people. Neither King Suelton nor Prince Cero is among them."

"Interesting choice," Mother said, not disapproving.

"It took a few days, but he decided to cooperate and tell me what he knows about Sunward's plans." Alistar grimaced. "Unfortunately, his confessions have added further complications."

Father's eyebrows rose. "Further complications? What, is the other prince involved as well?"

"Yes. And they intend to murder their father."

"Bloody shoals! You're certain?"

Alistar nodded grimly. "Ravencrest is building automatons that can kill. It seems likely they intend to incorporate them into the Exhibition. And then there's the matter of the internal channelers Sunward is collecting. I don't know what role they play yet."

"Internal channelers can infuse objects with their power," Rykka said. "Tiyron suggested their purpose is to infuse the automatons with enough magic to operate."

Chills ran through Alistar. Channelers could overuse their abilities, even burn themselves out if they extended themselves too far and never be able to channel again. *But what happens to someone whose source of power is within them? Their own bodies? Do they die? Or is there something worse?*

In the thoughtful silence, Alistar debated. Knowledge of the Silver Prince's experiments with frost's breath was confidential, not even known to many Silverline Power employees. Sharing it broke confidence. Not sharing it risked concealing vital information from those who knew more about the plant and its origins than he did.

"I have a theory, so far unproven, about why this ability has only appeared in the slums and the Lower City and may contribute to Lumination's growing influence. You know that greenhouses around the city generate the mahiy lines that produce the magic we use."

Nods answered.

"In some greenhouses in the poor areas, strains of frost's breath have been added to the beds. The effects are gradual, but they've taken root and are changing the mahiy lines."

Rykka frowned. "Is that why the magic felt strange when we were after Whitetooth?"

"Probably," Alistar said. "More than that, I think the magic of the frost's breath may be creating internal channelers."

His parents looked at each other. Alistar hoped Mother might refute his theory, explain that it was impossible, but her expression warned him not to place any wagers on that hope.

"What you describe does resemble abilities alluded to in myths of the Heiset Kingdom." Mother turned her goblet in her hand. "And, unfortunately, Darkwood's theory that their powers might be used to power automatons or golems also holds merit. Such people were often enslaved and used by those in power. It's said that many of the wonders of the ancients were created by harnessing their ability to infuse artifacts."

"What happened to those people? They must have had limits on how much they could use their abilities," Alistar pressed.

"I don't know, I'm afraid. If we had details, they were lost when we passed through the portal." Mother frowned. "As the crystal flower should have been. Do you know how it came here?"

"Sunward claimed her family smuggled a seed through the portal," Rykka said. "If that's true, either they only planted it within the last few years, or it was significantly easier to transport when it was smaller. How fast is it supposed to grow, and how large does it get?" Her focus was clearly on the information; she'd forgotten her earlier unease at being the focus of attention.

"All good questions, Darkwood—none of which I can answer, unfortunately. What little my family retained was intended to be used to prevent the tragedy from repeating, not to give us enough information to follow our predecessors' misguided steps."

"Are there ways of draining the flower's magic?" Saskia asked. "Magic saturates its pool to the point that even touching the water causes unpredictable effects on people."

"There was," Mother answered. "The champion who originally gained Rechmal's blessing—and stole the flower's seed—imbued a sword with the essence of a dragon, and that sword was capable of consuming magic. However, the blade was stolen long ago and lost to us. I don't know whether it remains in Heiset, or if it was brought through another portal into another land. We've long speculated that those who came to Calarand weren't the only humans to flee Heiset. But as far as I know, the champion's sword is lost."

Essence of a dragon. Devours magic. Lost in another land. Alistar's spine stiffened as if someone had poured ice water down his back. His eyes darted to Rykka, but her face was a mask.

Alistar swallowed, throat suddenly dry. "And this sword could absorb the magic from the flower? Could there be too much for it to drain?"

"It was described as 'endlessly hungering'," Mother told him.

Blood and sand. Has Rechmal been preparing this the whole time? It can't all be coincidence. "I… think I know where it is."

"The Silver Prince's vault, I suppose," Rykka muttered.

"No. In mine." Alistar sipped his wine.

"You have what, exactly?" Father asked in a mild tone that Alistar knew heralded trouble if the answer didn't satisfy.

"Before we met, Darkwood acquired a rare artifact from another country that she used in the construction of a device. Said device was later altered and abused by Cemar and his people to drain power from the mahiy lines so they could create

Ambrosia. When we disabled it, Darkwood entrusted me with the artifact. Given its nature, I chose to conceal its existence and keep it safe." Alistar met his father's gaze. "From everyone." He turned to Mother. "It's not a sword, but a cylinder of amber-colored crystal etched with runes. When I acquired it, it was stored in a case specifically designed to contain it, and I've not removed it from the case."

"The thieves, or their descendants, certainly could have modified the artifact's form," she said slowly. "Can you retrieve it? We should test it. Also, I want to see the flower."

Alistar nodded. "Of course. I'll retrieve the artifact while you get settled, and then I'll show you to the basement."

Alistar turned the dull metal tube over in his hands. A layer of dust coated it, and the smell brought to mind the crack of stone and shudder of the floor when Rykka brought the ceiling of Prince Cero's ballroom down on Cemar. His fingers traced over the runes on the tube. He'd never been able to translate them, and given Rykka's warning that its discovery could cause an international incident, he'd not involved anyone else in his attempts to learn their meanings.

"This is it." He offered the tube to Mother.

She gingerly took it. Like Alistar, she ran her fingers over the runes, then shook her head. "I don't recognize these. Perhaps it's the language of whatever land last held it. Do you know it, Darkwood?"

"I'm afraid not. I didn't retrieve it personally."

Father frowned at the tube. "The style looks familiar, but I can't place it right now."

Light glowed dimly around the ballroom. Outside, night blanketed Lewarden. A handful of the night staff, all from Rill-water, stood watch around the room. They visibly restrained themselves from saluting Alistar's parents. Alistar led the way into the depths of the manor.

In the room with the four crystals that controlled access to the various wings of the basement, the crystal flower that had been the focus of Lady Syri's study still rested in its oversized vase. Seeing it, Mother stopped cold. Alistar gently guided her out of the doorway to allow Father, Saskia, and Rykka to enter as well.

Mother slowly approached the flower. "Blood and sand. I hoped... I hoped you were wrong." Her shoulders slumped heavily. "The bloom isn't fully mature. That's a small blessing, at least. Not mature enough to produce seeds."

"Are you sure?" Alistar asked. The idea of Sunward harvesting seeds from the plant raised a fear he'd never considered before.

"Yes. Absolutely."

"This was the most mature bloom," Rykka said. "Another was harvested from the plant, but it wasn't as large. Can they continue to mature once they've been cut from the main plant?"

"Under the right conditions, yes, but very slowly," Mother answered. "This one, for example, would take decades to mature in ideal conditions, and I'm not confident it could produce a viable seed."

"Good. Then Sunward won't be getting a seed from her bloom either." Alistar stood across from Mother, studying the flower. Lingering this close to it again, he longed to pluck it from the water and experiment again.

"Assuming she doesn't have any more seeds," Father added grimly.

"Smuggling one seed through the portal would have been a monumental risk," Mother said. "Trying to take a second would have been all but impossible."

"How do you know so much about the portal and what

could or could not have been taken through?" Alistar asked. "I've never heard any of this before."

"None of it's familiar to me either," Saskia said.

"And under other circumstances, you never would hear it," Mother said. "My ancestor created the portal that let us escape Heiset before the destruction claimed everyone. She preserved enough knowledge that if a fragment of the threat slipped past her, someone could stop it." She eyed the flower with deep distrust. "Unfortunately, her caution appears to have been justified."

"What do we do about it, then?" Saskia asked. "I understood from the myth we read that the crystal flower is sacred to Rechmal. If it could or should be destroyed, someone must have tried already."

"No, not destroyed. The cut flowers will have to be allowed to mature and any seeds they produce must be harvested from them. For the full plant, if the power it produces isn't being harnessed, it must be syphoned periodically." Mother gestured to the metal tube. "Alistar, show me to the plant."

He pulled himself away from the flower and did as instructed. His parents spoke in low voices, but Alistar couldn't pick out the words. Everyone fell silent when they reached the oversized crystal frost's breath plant.

To break the stillness, Alistar indicated the threads through the walls. "The manor was constructed with channels to draw magic from the pool and use it to power the estate. The original owners didn't know about this. Their architect was part of Cemar's cabal, and he used the owner's funds to construct the ideal lair for the cabal. The manor was completed about six years ago. That's as much as I can offer as an estimate of the plant's age."

"Sadly, the knowledge passed on to me didn't include details about the size of the plant," Mother said. "The dimensions of the pool do seem correct, though." She pulled on a pair of leather gloves and unscrewed the metal tube.

Rykka made a small sound of protest, and all eyes turned to her. "I was warned that it should remain in the tube when used. When activated, it draws all magic toward the core, but as long as the core is sealed within the tube, it can't absorb the power. Supposedly the core houses the spirit of an ancient, very angry dragon, and if it absorbs enough magic, it could break free."

"Hmm." Mother carefully tipped the amber cylinder into her hand and examined it. "If this used to be the sword, it has absorbed far more power than this pool holds without the dragon regaining its form or freedom. And if the magic in this pool builds unchecked, a raging dragon will be a better fate for Lewarden. Simply extracting it from the pool won't help anyone unless it is contained. This artifact is the only means we have at the moment of dealing with this."

"It also gets scalding hot when activated," Rykka said.

"That *is* good to know," Mother said. "Alistar, do you have tongs or something similar?"

"I'm sure there's something in the laboratory." He excused himself and scoured the laboratory until he found several sets of tongs of various lengths.

Mother took the longest set and clamped the artifact into them. She lowered it into the water. "What's the activation word?"

"Dragonbane." When Alistar said the word, the runes on the artifact illuminated, pale blue on amber.

All other lights in the room snuffed out.

"Dragonbane!" Alistar said again quickly.

The glow of the runes faded, leaving the chamber entirely dark. Alistar stood unmoving, acutely aware that he didn't know this space nearly well enough to navigate it without light.

After a moment, Father cleared his throat. "It appears that

we neglected to consider a detail of draining the magic from the source of power for the manor."

"It… does seem that way," Mother agreed.

"Hematic perdition," Rykka sighed. Alistar heard movement from the direction of her voice, and he wondered if her elven eyes could pick out some source of light too faint for humans. Instead, he heard a rasp of metal and saw a sparkle of light. "Am I the only one who keeps a sparkflint on me?" A moment later, a small flame cast enough light that Alistar could orient himself.

"It won't last long," Rykka warned. "I don't have much to feed it."

"It helps," Alistar said.

With the aid of Rykka's small flame, they found their way back to the laboratory, through it, and back to the passage to the room of crystals. The fire burned out, but a gentle glow emanated from the crystal flower, giving just enough light to navigate.

Is the whole manor dark now? How long will it take for the plant to generate enough magic to operate as normal?

Blight, I never realized just how dark it could be down here.

In the dim light of the flower, Alistar looked to Mother. "Is that what the stories said the sword could do?"

She still carried the artifact with the tongs. "It was described as less abrupt and more controllable." Her mouth twisted in a reluctant admission. "Darkwood, I shouldn't have dismissed your earlier warning."

"It *can* be directed and controlled," Rykka said. "That was the purpose of the device I built, which Cemar stole and misused."

"Would you return it to the metal case, please?" Alistar asked.

"Of course." Mother complied and handed the metal tube back to him. It was warm to the touch, but not scalding.

Alistar tucked it into his belt. "Darkwood, I might need your expertise to craft another extraction device. Hopefully with a safe way of storing the magic, if this needs to be done periodically. I'd rather not lose all lights in the house every time."

Saskia peered into the passage toward the stairs. "I'm not certain, but there might be a little light coming back."

Alistar looked as well, but the only light he saw was as likely to be a trick of his eyes as actual illumination. He checked his pocket watch. "I should have marked the time when we started to time how long it takes for the light to return."

Saskia chuckled and leaned against him. "Spoken like an engineer."

No one expressed great hurry to leave the room while the heavy darkness remained. Looking into it, a pang of guilt stabbed Alistar.

I hope Lamorage is already asleep. I hope his lightstone wasn't affected by this. It should draw from the mahiy lines, not from the house. It's probably still glowing. Lamorage feared the dark for good reason—monstrous creatures that roamed the mountains of his birth hunted in darkness. Light drove them away, but light could be a precious resource during their long, cold winters.

His gaze moved back to the crystal flower. *I wonder if it is strong enough to supply the manor with power. If I directed its magic, could I activate the lights again?*

Saskia gripped his arm. In a whisper, she said, "Don't."

He bit back a protest and let her guide him to sit against a wall.

Half an hour passed quietly as they made themselves as comfortable as possible in the room. Alistar stirred from the edge of a doze to realize that the ghostlights in the basement shed enough illumination to make the halls navigable. He climbed stiffly to his feet, and his movement roused everyone else.

Rykka rolled her shoulders. "Was that as long as it felt?"

"Approximately three quarters of an hour since everything went dark," Alistar told her.

"That's a no, then. Rather not do that again if I have the option. Though I'd wager it was worse for your involuntary houseguest."

Alistar cursed sharply. "I need to check on his guards. Saskia, would you show my parents upstairs?"

"I'll come with you," Father said.

Alistar nodded and led Father through the passages that led to Prince Pietro's holding cell. He didn't try to soften his steps, reasoning that the guards were likely to be more wary of someone sneaking through the dark toward them. He added a particular staccato to his stride to signal that he was a friend.

A figure stood at the side of the doorway, warily watching the shadows. The light was still too dim to see their features clearly. Alistar's hand fell to his side for his belt knife. The figure tapped a pattern on the stone wall with the pommel of their weapon. Alistar paused and tapped the answer on the wall nearest him.

He heard an exhale of relief. "Sir?"

"It's me," Alistar answered. "And the Admiral."

A sharper, startled breath, and the guard straightened.

"We came to check on you. Any changes in the situation here?"

"Other than everything suddenly going dark? Well, we've been hearing some scuttling and scratching sounds. Not sure if they're rats or something else. Lit a couple candles we had on hand. The prisoner kinda panicked for a bit but wore himself out pretty quick." She paused and spoke quietly. "What happened, sir?"

"The lights went out as an unexpected side effect of an experiment I was conducting," Alistar said. "I apologize for the strain it's put on you."

"Well, feel better knowing it was your doing and not someone outside trying to get in."

Alistar nodded, but the skin prickled on the back of his neck. *What if someone tried to get into the manor while we did this?* "I'll send a few more people down to back you up and bring in some lanterns."

"Appreciate it, sir."

Alistar looked past her into the room. Prince Pietro remained a hunched form inside the cage, while the second guard kept close watch on him. Nothing appeared out of place.

"Keep your eyes and ears open," Alistar told both guards.

"Yes sir!"

CHAPTER 51

By breakfast, the manor was all but back to normal, though Rykka heard the cooks grumbling about the ovens taking longer to heat, the maids complaining about how long the water had taken to warm when they drew baths, and other small inconveniences. She caught whispers about how everything went dark in the night, but no one seemed to want to talk about it or speculate on the cause. She didn't understand why until one of the scullery boys said, "Least it's not winter this time."

"Hush!" ordered the girl beside him. "Don't bring that dark luck on this house. Don't you dare!"

The idea that naming a misfortune could manifest it wasn't exactly part of the doctrines of the Tenets and the Path, the elven religion, but it could be inferred from some readings. Adherents among the poor had enough misfortune in their lives that they avoided any risk of drawing more.

Hard to believe I forgot about that. It really has been that long since I lived in the slums.

Usually, Alistar was the first down for breakfast. Today, Admiral As'enel was the first to arrive in the dining room. "Good morning, Darkwood," he said.

"Good morning, sir." She glanced around quickly to ensure the only ears nearby were Rillwater. "And given relative stations, you should really be calling me Rykka."

"Well, that's one way to aim for a promotion—going straight for claiming a captainship." He chuckled and waved a hand to dismiss her immediate apologies. "It's the local nomenclature, I know. I'll just have to adapt to the capital's backwards way of doing things." He poured himself a mug of tea. "It sounds like you've been an aid to Alistar and Saskia."

"I do my best, sir," she said slowly.

"Good. Alistar's word holds a lot of weight with his siblings."

"I can understand why," she said. "It was my good fortune that the Silver Prince assigned him to the investigation that led to Cemar. I doubt I'd be here if I'd been forced to work with someone else."

"And your brother? Does he share your sentiment?"

Rykka shook her head. "Not yet."

"A pity. We could certainly use two with your skill set. If he comes around, or is open to some… freelance work, point him my way."

She blinked. "I don't think he's interested in leaving Lewarden."

"Even better. I could use more agents here. Especially in the less refined areas of the city."

"I'll see if he's interested, but no promises."

"No rush," Admiral As'enel said, waving a hand in casual dismissal of the subject.

I think he'd rescind that offer if he'd met Tiyron. Blight, though, what's Tiyron going to do when I'm gone?

Asking herself that question, it finally hit her that when she left Lewarden, whether she returned to Rillwater or not, she would be leaving Tiyron.

I kept searching for a way to bring him back and never thought about what would happen after that. I never wanted to think about after that. Somehow, I just expected him to have changed with me, and now that he's still the same person he's always been, I don't know what to do about it.

Alistar entered the dining room and nodded to both of them. "Morning, Father. Good morning, Rykka. Are you up early, or very late?"

She snorted a laugh. Alistar knew quite well her dislike of mornings. "Early, unfortunately. I wanted to check the status around the house."

"Anything I should be concerned about?" Alistar asked.

She shook her head. "People are unnerved by the loss of power last night, and some are comparing it to the outages Cemar caused, but that's it so far. They aren't sure exactly what happened."

"I hoped it was late enough that not many people would be awake, but I should never underestimate what the staff will notice," Alistar said.

"Just wait until you're a father and can start underestimating what your children will notice," Admiral As'enel chuckled. "Speaking of which, have you heard from Roddek?"

"I have. He and Cheska had a narrow scrape with the pirates but appear to have gotten out cleanly. I asked them to sail for Lewarden. They have an interesting cargo to deliver that hopefully will corroborate my guest's claims. They ought to be arriving today or tomorrow."

Captain Roddek will be here. Tightness settled in Rykka's chest. *Will he allow me to prove myself? Will he take me back into the crew?*

Breakfast trays were brought to the table. Rykka had already eaten with the rest of the staff, and poured herself another mug of tea while the men ate. After they finished, Alistar said, "Will you join me in my study?"

The admiral nodded and stood.

Alistar looked to Rykka. "You're welcome to join us."

She'd assumed Alistar wanted to speak to his father privately and started. "Thanks."

They climbed the stairs to Alistar's study and, at Alistar's invitation, settled in the comfortable chairs.

"What's your plan?" Admiral As'enel asked.

"I haven't told Prince Cero about Pietro or Filipp, but I have told his daughter, Lady Syri, and one of her guards, Star. You remember her, Rykka?"

"Dahr's sister, yeah. I remember her. So, she knows where Pietro is?"

"She knows that I know where he is," Alistar said. "Lady Syri readily accepts that Pietro is involved with Sunward, but she wasn't ready to believe Filipp is also involved. I didn't tell her Pietro was responsible for the assassination attempt that killed Filipp's family. Unfortunately, doing so would have detracted from my argument that both brothers are involved. I did speak with Star about it in private."

"Oh yes, now I remember why I avoid getting involved in capital politics. All the murder," Admiral As'enel muttered. "Patricide, matricide, fratricide, sororicide... It's a wonder anyone survives."

"So how do we prove it?" Rykka asked.

Alistar sighed. "We set a trap and bait it with everything they want."

The admiral's eyebrows rose. He leaned forward in interest.

"A tour of the Exhibition grounds for Prince Filipp and King Suelton," Alistar explained.

"Ravencrest wasn't confident they would have all the automatons ready by the Exhibition. They're certainly not all going to be done before then," Rykka said.

"Exactly. The fewer murderous automatons they have available, the better," Alistar said.

"But will they take the bait without them?" Admiral As'enel asked.

"If they're worried about who Pietro is talking to and what he's saying, they'll take it." Rykka pursed her lips in thought. "At least, I would, in their position. Do you think they know how much we know?"

"No one on Sunward's side should be aware that I'm connected to any investigation into her activities. I am known to be the senior engineer on the Exhibition, so my attendance at any tour of the site would make sense. We don't have a date yet; Lady Syri was going to propose the idea to Prince Cero."

"Is she going to tell him *why* she's proposing it?" Rykka asked.

"I have no idea," Alistar said. "That's between them. But that's the plan, so far. When Roddek and Cheska arrive with the envoys, it might change, depending on how willing the envoys are to talk."

Envoys? I haven't heard about this before. It sounds like I'll find out soon, though.

"I also have extremely unofficial encouragement from Star to investigate Ravencrest's factory further," Alistar added. "Whenever the tour of the Exhibition site happens could be a good opportunity."

"Hmm." The admiral stroked his beard. "That might not be soon enough to help the people who we assume will be providing power to the automatons."

"I know," Alistar admitted. "I'm counting on the whole process of designing and building these automatons being far more complex than a simple assassination, even that of a king, would require. They must have more plans for these automatons, thus will want to preserve their power sources." He said it as if the words left a foul taste in his mouth.

"Don't get the sense she cares about these people," Admiral As'enel said.

"She doesn't," Rykka agreed. "But she does care about managing her resources, and she's already scoured the slums and Lower City for people. If they die, she doesn't have anyone to replace them." *I hope. Hematic perdition, I hate this idea.*

"And you think these people will be kept at the factory?" Admiral As'enel asked.

"The first time they're used to power the automatons, probably. That's where the automatons are. After that, though, she could take them anywhere," Rykka said, thinking what she would do in Sunward's position.

"Will you take charge of the factory infiltration, Rykka?" Alistar asked.

"Of course. I assumed you wanted me to."

"I do, but you have the option of declining. I'm confident I can extract permission to invite my family to join us on the tour, but I doubt I can bring more people than that, so think about who you want to take with you."

She just nodded, deciding not to reveal that she'd already been planning how to get back to the factory and get in alone.

Admiral As'enel and Alistar discussed a few details of the tour of the Exhibition, and Alistar sketched out a map of the site. Rykka peered at it curiously. For all the talk, she hadn't gotten a good sense of the scope of the project. Rumors claimed that Prince Filipp spared no expense on the project, but she hadn't realized the Exhibition could be a small town in and of itself.

What are they going to do with it when the Exhibition ends? Tear it all down again? Use it for something else? Some of those structures could be repurposed, I suppose, but walking through it when it doesn't have crowds must feel like walking through a fairy tale—the sort where naughty children get devoured by monsters.

Before that unnerving thought took a firmer hold, Rykka distracted herself. "Are you planning to check on your downstairs guest this morning?"

"Not this morning," Alistar answered. "After work, probably. I'll let you know when I'm ready to visit him." He checked his pocket watch and sighed. "Speaking of work, though, I need to get ready for the day."

The impromptu conference ended. Alistar departed for Silverline Power. Saskia assumed the role of hostess to Alistar's parents. Rykka helped around the house, occupying herself with a dozen tasks that didn't bring her near the areas where Tiyron tended to be.

Mid-afternoon, while she was straightening books in the library, she heard the roll of wheels on the floorboards. Tiyron spoke. "I heard you've been in the house today. Thought I'd... have run into you before now."

She didn't look away from the shelf. "It's a large house."

"Large enough to avoid someone if you want, I guess." He grunted with effort, and she heard a shuffle of footsteps. "You're mad at me."

Her jaw tightened. "I'm frustrated at you." She turned to face him.

He stood beside the chair, holding onto the table for support. "Fine. Frustrated, then. Which from here still looks a lot like mad."

This wasn't the place to have a conversation like this, but it was where they were. Rykka let out a heavy breath, walked to him, and pulled on the mahiy lines to weave a cloudy barrier around them that wouldn't allow their voices to escape its confines. "Yes, frustrated. I know that for you, it hasn't even been a month since you were Cemar's prisoner, but for me, it's been two years, Tiyron. Two years that have changed me. So yes, it's frustrating when you keep trying to force me back to who I was rather than trying to see who I *am*."

His grip tightened slightly on the table. "So why'd you bring me back?"

"Because you're my brother and I love you!" she snapped. "Because I don't want you dead. I just wish you would at least *consider* that I might know what I'm talking about!"

"What's wrong with the way things were? You were happy with it then!"

I didn't know any better then. "And that means I should be satisfied with it forever?" She held up a hand to forestall the response she saw in his eyes. "It doesn't make a difference. Things aren't the way they were before, and I can't change that any more than I could find an artifact to restore you whole and fully healed."

He involuntarily glanced at the stump of his missing fingers, then back to her. When he spoke, his voice was quiet. "Did you do that? Look for one?"

"Yeah. I thought I told you that before."

"I think you did. It's why you signed onto the Rillwater fleet, right?"

She nodded. After a moment of hesitation, she said, "I tried to build a device that could heal you."

He straightened. "What? I thought that was impossible. You told me no one ever made one that worked. What happened? Did it work?"

She sighed and looked at the book in her hands. "I don't know if I could have made it work. I had to scavenge parts that weren't tagged by Silverline, and I missed one. It's how I got caught and arrested."

Tiyron swore softly.

"I shattered the device before they nabbed me and haven't tried to build another."

"You could," Tiyron said. He was quiet a moment, then said, "You have a head for those things. If I hadn't been sure they'd take you away from me and toss me out on my ear, I'd have tried getting you into one of the fancy academies." He looked away. "But I didn't want to lose you. So I never told you."

Academy. The thought made her pulse quicken. She made her voice steady. "Don't know what they could have taught me that I didn't learn just as well on my own. Besides, I'd never try to do things they say are impossible if I let them fill my head with all their nonsense." She leaned against the table. "Gonna tell you something you don't really want to hear."

His mouth twisted in a wry smile. "Something other than everything else you've said?"

She smiled slightly in return. "Guess you'll have to decide that yourself. When I was working with De'seneth to figure out who was draining the mahiy lines and how, we met a couple street kids. Humans. The boy was… nine, maybe. The girl was maybe six. She saw Cemar and his people, and one of them gave her what she thought was candy."

"It wasn't candy," Tiyron said.

"It wasn't. It was the toxic dross from Ambrosia. She ate a piece, and it triggered her ability to channel." She closed her eyes, remembering the little girl cradling her burned hands, tears cutting tracks down her dirty cheeks. "She could channel fire. A six-year-old channeling fire."

Tiyron paled.

"Her brother didn't want us to come near them. Didn't trust us. He reminded me of you. He was terrified we'd take his sister away and he'd never see her again. De'seneth could have left them there. He could have just taken the girl. Instead, he arranged for them both to be taken to an academy. He promised them they wouldn't be separated, and when we got to the place, he demanded the headmistress honor the promise he'd made to those kids. All I could think at the time was 'Where would you and I have ended up if someone had done that for us?' I don't envy those kids—poor girl is too young for that burden—but I was jealous. And I realized that De'seneth saw his actions as the only acceptable path. He'd never considered that they didn't have to be his problem. I thought that kind of noble only existed in fables—someone who doesn't have to debate between the most expeditious actions, the cheapest ones, or the right ones, and actually has the resources to do something."

"And he had the authority to make the headmistress comply for longer than it took him to walk out the door?" Tiyron asked dubiously.

"At that point? He had the Silver Prick's blessings to employ any resources he wanted in his investigation. He flashed the prince's insignia in her face. She wasn't stupid enough to argue with that."

"If he had that authority, why'd you have to fake your… our death? I've heard enough whispers to know Onyxflame is officially listed as dead. Didn't trust him to give you the pardon he promised?"

"Didn't trust the Silver Prick to let it happen unchallenged." She sighed, then smiled. "Especially not after I dropped the ceiling of his ballroom on Cemar's head."

"You did what?"

Rykka briefly described the final encounter with Cemar in Prince Cero's own home, all the way through her battle with Cemar, crushing him between two barriers, and destroying the ballroom in the process. By the end, Tiyron actually smiled.

"Better than I could have done," he said. "Did De'seneth know you got out?"

"He probably suspected. And he knew for sure a few months later when I dropped in on his wedding. I'd promised I'd bring the ugliest gift to the event. Succeeded, but there was some stiff competition, to be honest."

Tiyron shook his head and eased himself back into the chair. Rykka let the barrier fall and continued shelving books.

Several minutes passed in silence before footsteps approached and she heard Windshadow. "Darkwood, are you in here… ah."

"Something wrong?" she asked.

"Lord De'seneth requests your presence." He looked at Tiyron, jaw tightening. "He requests yours as well."

Tiyron's eyebrows rose. "Mine? Really?"

"Where are we meeting?" Rykka asked, though she was as curious about Tiyron's inclusion as he was.

"Lord De'seneth's study."

Windshadow walked with them to Alistar's study. Inside, Alistar and Saskia, Admiral and Captain As'enel, and Lamorage had already gathered. Dorne brought in platters with an assortment of tea, wine, and finger foods, then assumed a post beside the door.

Alistar nodded to Rykka, Tiyron, and Windshadow and gestured for them to make themselves comfortable. "Good, everyone's here. For those who don't know, Lady Syri and I discussed setting up a tour of the Exhibition grounds for the royal family as bait to lure Lady Sunward and her allies into acting, reasoning that they'd be more inclined to move quickly when one of their important members is missing and possibly captured."

Nods answered him, though Tiyron simply cocked his head curiously.

"She brought the suggestion to Prince Cero, without explaining the motive behind it, and he's arranged the tour. It's taking place the day after tomorrow."

"That soon?" Saskia asked in surprise. "Will the Exhibition site be ready by then?"

"Prince Cero believes it will be," Alistar said. "Even if it means crews working day and night to make it happen. Prince Filipp, evidently, is quite keen on the idea."

"I think I'll regret asking this, but if the tour is for the royal family, how do you expect Lady Sunward to hear of it or bring her allies in?" Lamorage asked.

Rykka winced internally. *Blood and sand. Alistar hasn't told him yet. He probably doesn't know about Pietro either.*

"Evidence points toward both Prince Filipp and Prince Pietro making alliances with Sunward," Alistar said. "Prince

Pietro is, according to the official sources, currently on an assignment outside of Lewarden."

Lamorage shifted uneasily. "But he's not really?"

"He's not. But for now, he's out of play for Sunward's schemes. However, because Prince Filipp agreed to the proposed time for the tour, we should assume that the automatons are being charged and moved into place. King Suelton will, of course, have Royal Guards accompanying him, but we can't give them advanced warning, or their oaths would require them to insist he not attend."

"But Star knows," Rykka interjected. "You don't think her oaths require the same?"

Alistar smiled wryly. "Much like her late brother, Star is very good at following the law to the letter, and no further, when she needs to."

"The day after tomorrow," Captain As'enel mused. "Roddek and Cheska should be here by then, yes?"

"They should," Alistar agreed. "I thought they might arrive today. I'll check in with them tonight if I haven't heard. Rykka, we might need your help to ensure that the guests they're bringing don't have a clear sense of where they are, if you're recovered enough."

She nodded. "Don't worry, I can channel."

"Good. Soluthos, if I can arrange for you to accompany me to the Exhibition tour, will you?"

"Of course, sir," Windshadow said immediately, sitting to attention.

"While we're there, Rykka, have you made the arrangements you need?"

"Not yet. I'll take care of them."

"What about me?" Lamorage asked. "I don't see the Silver Prince approving a disgraced former engineer to join this tour."

"Unfortunately," Alistar said. "But I'm going to ask that you keep a watch on the manor. Sunward wants back into here very badly, and she might send someone to try to gain access while we're all elsewhere."

"I… all right. I can do that."

"Good. That's the plan, then. Any questions?" He looked around the room and nodded when no one spoke. "Then I bid everyone a good evening."

CHAPTER 52

Only family remained in the study. Alistar took Roddek's speaking stone out of the case and activated it. "Hopefully it doesn't take as long for him to answer as last time."

"He wasn't prompt last time?" Mother asked, displeased.

"He prioritized avoiding pirates," Alistar explained. "I thought the delay reasonable once he told me that."

The stone's color shifted and Roddek's voice spoke from it. "Hey Alistar. Is all well on your end?"

"Oh, we have a little family gathering over here at the moment—me, Saskia, Dad, and Mom. And you? Are you well?"

"Just Cheska and me here. No major problems in our travels so far."

"Will you arrive tonight?" Alistar asked.

Cheska answered. "If we push, we could get in tonight, but Roddek and I decided to target tomorrow morning instead. If we just had one ship, it would just raise a few eyebrows, but two Rillwater ships arriving in port in the middle of the night will raise questions that arriving in daylight won't bring."

"Unless you *want* us to draw attention?" Roddek asked.

"I'd rather you not," Alistar said. "Much as I'd love to make some people really nervous, this isn't the right time."

"Any more trouble from the pirates?" Father asked.

Alistar was sure he heard both his siblings straighten to attention. Cheska answered. "We blocked most of their ships in the harbor, but those on patrol pursued us upriver until it got too difficult for them to navigate. Our ships took a few scrapes and scuffs, and some of the crew as well, but no serious damage."

"And your passengers?" Alistar asked.

Roddek answered. "My fellow's been chatty, but he works pretty hard to avoid saying anything of substance about why he was meeting with pirates or who he works for. He's also promised a substantial reward if we take him back to Lewarden. Seems pretty nervous that we might be heading to Rillwater instead."

"Mine just likes to make demands, and gets more and more upset that I'm ignoring them," Cheska said with a sigh. "Alistar, Roddek showed me the envoys' stowed gear. The symbols look unpleasantly similar to the royal crest."

"Based on the descriptions Roddek gave me, those crests belong to Prince Filipp and Prince Pietro," Alistar said.

Long silence from the other end. Roddek finally broke it. "So… what are the chances they stole the crests to impersonate servants of the princes?"

"I'm sorry to say, unlikely," Alistar answered. "Both princes are working with Sunward. I intended to tell you once you got here."

"Blood and sand…"

"If you can, learn who works for which prince." Alistar considered. "Oh, a little news you can share with them. Officially, Prince Pietro is taking care of some undefined Exhibition-related tasks outside Lewarden, and he hasn't been seen in the city in a few days."

"I'm not sure whether I'm more concerned with that news, or with the way you sound very pleased about it, Alistar," Cheska said.

"Unlike the two of you, Alistar doesn't brag. So if he sounds pleased about it, you should definitely be more concerned about that," Mother said.

"That's a good point," Cheska said. "So will you tell us, Alistar, or let us guess?"

"Darkwood caught Pietro while he was delivering drugs to a Lower City criminal boss. He's alive, but he's no longer an available element for Sunward."

"Darkwood, huh?" Roddek's tone grew cooler.

"Yes. She's been invaluable in exposing Sunward's plans." Alistar understood his brother's response, but Roddek needed to hear that Rykka was an asset, not a liability. "We wouldn't know half of what we do without her."

Roddek answered with a noncommittal grunt.

"I might send her down to the docks when you arrive—her barriers will make it easier to move the envoys without them knowing where they are," Alistar added.

"Shouldn't be necessary," Cheska said. "We'll drug them before we make port. They can sleep it off on the ride to your place."

"As long as they aren't out too long. We have a narrow window. The day after tomorrow, the royal family will be taking a private tour of the Exhibition grounds. Unless Sunward and Prince Filipp surprise me greatly, they'll take that opportunity to try to murder King Suelton and Prince Cero with minimal witnesses."

Roddek cursed softly. "Blackened shoals... in two days? Is the Exhibition even ready?"

"There's a lot of detail work still to complete, and the mahiy lines aren't stabilized there yet, but as long as no one strays too far from the guide, it's ready enough."

"If the mahiy lines aren't stable, what happens if someone needs to draw on them?" Saskia asked, concern pinching her brows.

"Channelers shouldn't have problems, but devices that draw on the mahiy lines might not work correctly," Alistar told her. "Even ones with minimal power requirements like speaking stones could be affected."

"So we might not have reliable communications. Good to know," Father said.

"Do you think Sunward and the prince will need the mahiy lines to be functional to assassinate the king?" Cheska asked.

"No, unfortunately," Alistar said. "I told you I saw connections to Heiset myths. Sunward's found a way to tap into a power other than the mahiy lines, at the cost of people."

Mother interjected. "I don't know how much is 'too much' or how the use of the power Sunward wields drew calamity to Heiset, but the risks of it taking root here are too great. She can't be allowed to succeed."

"That... sounds like details better discussed in person," Cheska said. "Expect us first thing in the morning, Alistar."

"We'll see you then. If you need anything, let us know."

Roddek and Cheska made port shortly after dawn. When they assured Alistar that they didn't need aid with transporting the envoys, he sent the carriage to pick them up, sans Rykka. Knowing it would be at least an hour before they finished all the docking paperwork, he allowed himself leisure to dress, drink some tea, and read the morning broadsheet. Nothing particularly caught his attention—predictions regarding attendance at the Exhibition, theories about what new inventions might be unveiled there, a few discussions about upcoming expansions in the factory district, and repetitions of the perpetual fears of war with Narnan or another nation. No mentions of Prince Pietro's absence, strange occurrences in the Lower City, or other hints of Sunward's activities.

The front door opened and Roddek cheerfully asked, "What are the chances we got here before everyone's up?"

Cheska snorted. "Slim. The only one who might not be up yet is Mother, and if you don't keep it down, she'll remind you why no one wakes her before she's good and ready to be awake."

Alistar strode out of the sitting room to greet his siblings. Both wore their captain's dress uniforms of crimson and navy. Roddek's golden brown hair was pulled back in a braid, while Cheska had cut her black locks short. Both were far more tan than Alistar from days on the open water. Roddek was still grinning when he turned to his elder brother.

"Well, I was pretty sure you'd be up when we got here. Good to see you, Alistar! Blood and sand, it hasn't even been a month since you were home to visit."

Alistar embraced Roddek. "Good to see you again too." He turned to Cheska. "It's been too long since I last saw you, though! Welcome to my home. Neither of you have been here since the wedding, have you?"

Both shook their heads.

"Well, let's get you breakfast. Come on. Dorne will take care of your luggage and everything else." *Mainly, he can discretely ensure the envoys are taken to comfortable but secure quarters.*

The rest of the family joined breakfast. Alistar quickly steered the conversation away from any sensitive topics, though it took his siblings several minutes to realize he didn't want to discuss secrets at the table. He didn't blame them. If they'd been in Rillwater, all the staff would be trustworthy, loyal to the Family and the fleet. Here, though, no such guarantee existed.

After breakfast, the family took a walk around the manor grounds, coming to a storage building intended for the groundskeeper's use. Within, Dorne had overseen the furnishing of several rooms into a sort of makeshift suite. A guard kept watch outside the suite.

"Unless Roddek or Cheska disagree, I think you'd be the best to lead this conversation, Admiral," Alistar told his father.

"I'd be delighted to," Father said with a sharkish smile. He opened the door and strode inside.

Two groggy elven men sat at the table with mugs of tea in front of them. Both turned quickly when the door opened, confusion filling their expressions. "Who are...?" one started to say.

"Admiral As'enel," Father said. He folded his thick arms across his chest. "I hear you've been promising my fleet to pirates. And don't pretend you don't know what I'm talking about."

The two men looked at each other, then at the admiral. A long, awkward pause stretched as they considered how to respond.

Finally, the one who hadn't spoken said, "Regardless of the reason we were in that... situation, I personally am thankful your privateers happened to be in the area and came to our assistance. Although we had, admittedly, engaged in certain conversations with those brigands, our negotiations broke down."

"Negotiations with pirates often do," Father said. "What were you trying to get from them? Some sort of goods not commonly available in Calarand?"

The one started to speak. His companion glared at him, and he bit back his words. Father waited, one eyebrow raised. When neither elf spoke, he said, "Strange. I didn't think any of the stories that get told about me praised my great patience."

Nervous shifting. "Your pardon, Admiral, but we were sent on a delicate and classified task in service of the Crown."

"Yes, yes, of course. Now, which of you works for which prince?"

Both sputtered protests that no one believed. Father cut them off. "We found the gear you stowed outside the pirates' hideout. Answer the question." Though he still smiled, his voice was laced with steel.

Long hesitation, then the more talkative of the two said, "I have the honor of representing His Highness, Prince Pietro."

"Making your friend here Filipp's underling, then." Father looked at the other elf.

After a moment, the elf nodded in tight-lipped silence.

"Negotiating for contraband with pirates on behalf of the princes. Not a good look for any of you. And you realize, I'm sure, the princes will deny any connection to you, should they be asked. So, what exactly were you after?"

"Why should we answer?" asked the sullen one. "You've already decided we must be guilty of something, no matter that we acted in the service of the Crown."

"You might convince me you *were* acting in the interests of the Crown, and not against it." Admiral As'enel's eyes were narrow. No hint of humor touched his face. "Otherwise, I'll infer from what I already know that you're willing and knowing participants in treason against the king."

"Treason?" demanded Pietro's servant. "There's no treason to obeying the directions of my prince!"

Filipp's servant, the sullen one, was quiet, color leeching from his face. "If there is treason in the instructions I was given, I do not know of it."

"But…" Father prompted.

"But the smugglers were to deliver components not available in Calarand."

"Not available, or not permitted?"

"I'm… not certain, Admiral."

"Do you know the name Celyn Sunward?"

Filipp's man frowned in thought. Pietro's man shifted uncomfortably. Father's gaze focused on Pietro's man. The elf shifted again, looking away and finally mumbling, "I might have heard it somewhere."

"Perhaps your prince mentioned her?" Father suggested.

Filipp's man still frowned, but asked, "Was she involved in the attempted coup? Two winters ago? I recall hearing that name or a similar one."

"Or you heard Prince Filipp talking about his mistress," Pietro's man said, not entirely under his breath.

"What were you instructed to promise the pirates if they delivered the goods your masters want?" Father asked.

The abrupt change of subject caught both elves by surprise. "We were to offer them the right to freely…" Filipp's man trailed off, finally realizing the danger to answering that question to this audience.

"The right to freely operate in Calarand waters? Regardless of Rillwater?" Father's eyes narrowed. "Or is Rillwater the prize your masters thought to offer?"

Both swallowed hard. "I… do not know the specifics of Prince Filipp's intentions, Admiral."

"I should hope your prince wouldn't be stupid enough to destroy an alliance that has served us all well for generations just to get a few baubles and build some wind-up toys," Father said coldly. "But I suppose you wouldn't know anything about that."

Neither elf spoke.

He waited a long moment, then snorted. "Ignorant lackeys. I *do* hope you enjoy your stay. It will undoubtedly be longer than you'd like." He strode out of the room, slamming the door firmly behind him. The guard locked it and resumed her post.

Father didn't speak for several minutes as they continued to walk around the grounds. His jaw was tight and his breathing tightly controlled. Finally, he growled, "Arrogant ratbags."

"The ones you just spoke to, or their masters?" Mother asked.

"Both! And if they think we'll quietly cede the seas to bilge-water crawlers like those pirates, they've forgotten why the Crown forged a treaty with us in the first place."

Sometime during the walk, Rykka had joined them. Roddek noticed her shortly after Alistar did. He cast her a dubious look but didn't protest once he confirmed that Alistar was aware of her and not objecting.

"We could discuss the matter with one of the people who gave those instructions," Alistar offered. He checked his pocket watch and cursed softly. "After I return from Silverline. I need to prepare for the tour tomorrow."

"Tonight," Father agreed.

The day was a whirlwind of rapid, on-the-fly adjustments to plans interrupted all too many times by technicians and lower-ranking engineers who needed someone to reassure them that the decisions they already knew to be the best options were, in fact, the correct choices. During one of the multiple meetings Prince Cero called him into, Alistar managed to slip in the request that he be allowed to bring his family on the tour.

Prince Cero started to agree automatically, then paused, looking at Alistar closely. "Please define how many members of your family we are discussing, Senior Engineer."

"My parents and my siblings have come for a visit," Alistar told him without batting an eye, as if it were the most normal thing in the world for Admiral As'enel to make an unannounced trip to Lewarden.

Prince Cero's eye twitched. Alistar saw him mentally weighing the ramifications of allowing the most powerful privateers in Rillwater to accompany the tour against the ramifications of insulting those same privateers by refusing to allow them to do so.

"Your parents. *And* your siblings." His eye twitched again. "I will hold you responsible for their behavior, Senior Engineer."

"Of course, Your Highness," Alistar agreed. "They are all quite interested to see the project that has occupied me for so long."

"I suppose it is… allowable, with your voucher of their behavior," Prince Cero said.

"I assure you, Your Highness, my family is perfectly aware of the difference between raiding a pirate ship and touring an upcoming national festival," Alistar said, stiffly polite.

"Very well. I will ensure the arrangements are made for their attendance. You are dismissed, De'seneth."

After dinner, the family, along with Soluthos and Rykka, gathered in the ballroom and entered the concealed passage into the basement. Neither Roddek nor Cheska had seen it before, though they'd heard of it from Alistar. They looked around curiously as they followed Alistar, occasionally commenting on details.

When Alistar entered Prince Pietro's prison, he had everyone else wait within hearing but out of sight, as in previous visits. Four guards stood on watch. The nearest approached Alistar.

"He's been quiet for the most part. Everyone's been jumpy since the lights all went out a couple nights ago. Could be nerves, but sometimes it sounds like there's something moving in the passages. We've looked and haven't seen anything, but it happens just enough to keep us on edge."

Alistar nodded. "Thank you." *When we checked on the guards after the draining, they mentioned strange sounds too. Did something find a way inside during that time? Were there protections I didn't know about that kept them out before?*

Pietro roused when Alistar approached. Some of the heavy lines of exhaustion had eased and his eyes weren't as heavily shadowed. He watched Alistar in tight-lipped, wary silence.

"You're looking rested, Your Highness," Alistar greeted.

"What do you want?"

"The envoys you and your brother sent to talk to the pirates almost got themselves killed. Seems the pirates didn't care for the threats they made. Or maybe they decided the reward you promised wasn't worth the risks you expected them to take."

Pietro straightened a little, wincing as stiff muscles protested. "'Almost' got themselves killed? They are... still alive?"

"No thanks to you or your brother. They're safe, for the moment."

Pietro looked away. "You removed them from the pirates' reach."

"Not personally, but yes, they're in Rillwater custody. Now, why would you and Filipp go promising pirates that they could claim our place?"

"Filipp said Rillwater was too unpredictable. That we couldn't be sure the privateers would stay loyal to the Crown. And Sunward's had dealings with them, said they were too much of a threat to leave in place."

Alistar snorted. "She's had 'dealings' with us? You mean she's had dealings with *me*. Did you know she offered to marry me the first time we met? While standing beside her lover at the time."

Pietro leaned forward, trying to look more closely at Alistar, though the mask Alistar wore obscured the lower half of his face. "She said she met a man who claimed to be an As'enel, but she didn't believe him."

"Yet it was enough for her to decide that we need to be eliminated? Replaced with worthless pirates who can't even smuggle contraband past us?" Alistar shook his head.

"Enough for her to deem you a threat."

Alistar folded his arms and studied the prince. "And what do you think? Was she correct?"

Pietro was quiet for a time before he finally said, "I think you're very dangerous to have as an enemy."

"Well, at least you've learned something. I'd suggest you think about that long and hard, Your Highness. For your own sake."

CHAPTER 53

"Rykka, a moment," Alistar said as she turned down the hall toward Tiyron's room.

She turned quickly. "Yes?"

He stepped closer and spoke in a low voice. "Would you ask your brother if he knows of other entrances to the basement, aside from those within the house? Our guest's watchers have heard unexpected noises since we drained the pool. I'm concerned something might have found a way inside."

She read the unspoken "or someone" in his eyes. Rykka nodded. "Sure, I'll ask him."

"Thanks."

"Is the tour tomorrow in the morning or afternoon?"

"Morning, at ten," Alistar answered. "Do you have what you need?"

"I have enough," she said.

He accepted the non-answer and went upstairs.

She knocked on Tiyron's door. "It's me. Can I come in?"

"Still up, so, sure."

She found her brother sitting on his bed, leaning against the wall and looking out the window. He'd opened one of the panes and a breeze stirred the air. Without turning, he asked, "So, what's the news?"

"Depends. Are we clear out there?" She nodded at the window.

"Wouldn't ask if we weren't." Still, he did close the window-pane, then pulled the curtains shut.

"The tour's tomorrow."

"And all the De'seneths are going, right. I was there for that conversation."

Irritation stabbed her before she realized Tiyron wasn't being intentionally insulting but making an honest mistake. "As'enels," she corrected quietly. "All the As'enels are going. Alistar uses his matronym, De'seneth, in Lewarden, but he and all his family are As'enels."

"What?" Tiyron stared at her, eye wide.

"Alistar's father is *that* Admiral As'enel."

"Hematic perdition, Rykka…" He massaged his forehead. "All right, so the leaders of all the privateers of Rillwater are attending the Silver Prince's private party to catch the crown prince committing treason. Sounds like a fun time. Can't wait to see how the scandal rags spin this."

She chuckled softly. "Right? Let's hope they never find out about Pietro, though." She let out a long breath. "Alistar asked if you knew the locations of any entrances to the basement from outside the manor."

"You're on first name basis with him now?" Tiyron's eyebrows rose.

"Not as far as he knows," she retorted. "Just want to be clear as to which De'seneth or As'enel I'm talking about."

"Sure you are." He smirked. "But yeah, I know a couple outside entrances. They're hidden, of course, and have crystals on the inside to open them."

A chill of apprehension ran down her spine. "What if the manor no longer had the magic from the crystal to power it?

Would the doors stay locked, or unlocked?"

"Damned if I know, Rykka. You think someone got in?"

"Maybe. I know one of Sunward's people, a woman named Merris, is looking for Pietro at Sunward's orders. She's tried to get into the manor before."

Tiyron cursed softly. "I'll show you where they are, but I need rest first."

The delay rankled, but she could see he was drooping. "The skulking hour, then?" If she was honest, she could use some rest as well.

"The skulking hour," he agreed.

An hour after midnight, Rykka tapped her knuckles on Tiyron's door. It swung open. She stepped back, and he steered the chair into the hall. She'd never noticed how quietly it moved. He'd taken time to apply a blackener to any reflective surfaces. Rykka gave his work a look over and nodded in approval. Neither of them spoke as they moved through the still and silent manor.

Leaving through a servants' door, they moved outside. Tiyron took a moment to orient himself, then another moment just to look at the sky.

"I remember when we could see the stars, not these damned glowing purple cords," he muttered.

"Yeah. And you complained about it then, because it meant the Silver Prick hadn't yet deigned to provide magic to the slums," Rykka said.

Tiyron snorted a soft laugh. "All right, true, I guess."

He led the way across the manicured grounds toward the far back, where a wall of cut stone stopped careless walkers from tumbling down a rocky slope.

"Past this wall?" she asked.

"Yeah. There's a door concealed along here..." He moved his

chair along the wall, stopped, and pressed at several stones, first lightly, then more forcefully. He growled angrily, glaring at the wall.

"What's wrong?"

"It's here! It should be here." He hit the stones again.

"Well unless it's activated by blood, that's not helping. What are the signs of the right spot?"

He drew an angry breath and let it out. "It's…" He paused, looking up the wall. With another small growl, he moved a pace to the right and pressed on a stone. It sank under his hand with a click that sounded far too loud for the night.

"It's right here." He pushed the concealed door open and peered into the darkness. "Time to find out how sturdy this thing really is."

She didn't understand what he meant until he rolled the chair through the doorway to the slope. "Hematic perdition, don't be a lunatic!" She raced after him, closing the concealed door behind her.

Despite the ominous sounds of rocks sliding and wheels skidding, she found her brother intact at the bottom, still seated in the chair. She scowled at him. "You're insane."

"I'm testing the capabilities of this chair. Come on. You want to check the entrances or not?"

"Where's the closest one?"

Though the chair proved capable of both surviving and navigating the rocky terrain, it didn't move quickly over it. Rykka constantly had to slow her pace to not leave Tiyron behind. She didn't see the first entrance they reached until Tiyron told her specifically what to look for. The door didn't budge when she checked it. In the dark, she couldn't tell if the ground held any signs of visitors before them.

They moved on to the next. Rykka marveled to realize the extent of the tunnels. "How did the original owners not realize their architect was making all this under their noses?"

"Same way any con artist does, probably. It's always 'a few more expenses' and the project is 'a little delayed.' Show enough visible progress that they're too invested to cancel and lose everything they've put in."

A familiar game, one they'd played before, but never at this scale. *Would we have tried something so brazen? Could we have pulled it off if we did?*

The door, when they finally found it, was locked, as the first one had been. No tracks in evidence, either.

"How many more?" she asked Tiyron.

"One I know for sure, another I suspect."

It was late enough that some of the kitchen staff had undoubtedly roused to start breakfast preparations. The sky was still dark, and the quiet night was sometimes broken by the call of an owl or, less often, the chirps of a small, night-hunting wyvern. Tiyron kept moving around the base of the slope, wincing sometimes when the chair jolted over particularly rough patches. Rykka tried to guess where they were in relation to the manor, but she couldn't see it from here, nor tell any other clues from the landscape.

Tiyron stopped, looking at the cliff, then away into the darkness. "Ground's smoother here. Someone could probably get a cart along it. Check the wall, see if you find anything."

"This is the one you're not sure about?" She picked her way up to the slope and searched for the signs Tiyron had shown her at the last two.

"Yeah." His voice was quiet. "I couldn't see much of it, but I know they didn't carry me far before we were outside and they threw me in the cart."

When Cemar and his men dumped Tiyron in a ditch and left him to die.

She searched for a door all along the rock face for at least half an hour before Tiyron quietly said, "It's not there, is it?"

"I'm not finding it. Doesn't mean it's not there," she told him.

"Let's keep going, find the next one and check it. Don't want to linger here."

They reached the final spot as the first hints of dawn colored the sky. Rykka started toward the spot Tiyron indicated, then stopped with a hissed curse.

"What is it?" Tiyron immediately pitched his voice just above a whisper and hunched lower in the chair.

"Something… someone slipped over here recently. Left a long scuff." She looked up, then scrambled up the low embankment to the cliff face. At the top of the slope leading to it, the lip had crumbled. She studied it, frowning. "I think it was someone leaving, not someone entering."

"Can you find the door there?"

She checked. "Yeah. And… it's shut but not latched." *This isn't good. Hematic perdition, who got inside and what did they do?*

Tiyron cursed and looked around quickly. "Gotta be a way I can get up there." He moved further along until he could maneuver the chair up to where she waited without destroying the tracks.

Rykka apprehensively opened the door and stepped inside. The hallway looked like any other in the basement—long, dark, smelling of dust, though none marred the stone floor. She saw no tracks and no hints as to where in the basement they were. The hall continued straight for a while before curving to the left before ending in another concealed door. Like the exterior door, it was closed but not locked. She gave Tiyron a questioning look. He shrugged in answer. She cautiously opened the door.

They entered a room she didn't recognize, but that appeared to be intended for storage space, judging by the shelves built into the walls. In addition to the door at their backs, three others stood closed. Tiyron looked around and his shoulders relaxed.

"I know where we are now," he told her.

"If someone got in here, is there anywhere they couldn't reach?"

"Depends how many other doors are already open, and if they know the triggers for any that aren't. Might have a hard time getting into the manor itself."

"Could they get to the holding cages?" She had an uneasy suspicion.

"Yeah." He pointed to one of the exits. "Take that one."

Another blank hall, another concealed door, and they were in a passage she recognized as the one they took to reach Pietro. Rykka hurried her steps. A sharp, metallic smell hit her nose. She cursed and sprinted.

No guard stopped her at the doorway. Inside, four members of the Rillwater staff sprawled in chairs or on the ground, their blood staining the clothes and stones around them. Prince Pietro's cage was empty.

While Rykka looked around in horror, Tiyron eased out of his chair and inspected the bodies.

"Not more than an hour dead," he said. "Only a couple drew weapons. Whoever attacked was fast and good."

"Merris," Rykka said quietly. *I could have sailed with any of these men. Instead, I don't even know their names.*

"Don't know the name, but if this is her work, I'd rather not meet her." Tiyron stood slowly. "You okay, Rykka?"

"No," she told him. "Sunward's assassin got in here, murdered four Rillwater privateers, and took the prince. If she'd chosen to, she could have killed even more people. No, I'm definitely not okay." Her wits caught up with her, and she searched her pocket for a speaking stone. Finding Dorne's, she activated it.

Tense seconds stretched by until he answered. "Darkwood. What is it?"

"Are you well?" she asked, voice tight.

"Well enough. You?"

"My brother and I," she said, unable to force herself to say she was "well" even as a code word at the moment. "Find whoever of the family is awake and bring them down to the basement guest room."

"What happened?" Dorne demanded, voice low and urgent.

"Merris found a way in. The guards are... dead and the guest is gone."

A burst of profanity worthy of any privateer issued from the stone. "When?"

"Within the last two hours." *Blood and sand, if we'd moved faster in our search, we could have run into her. I don't know if that'd be better or worse.*

She heard the sound of Dorne walking quickly. "Any trail? How's your tracking?"

"We can track," Tiyron said.

"Give me ten minutes; I'll have someone down to accompany you. Find her." The last was said with icy anger.

Rykka and Tiyron learned what they could from the scene without disturbing the bodies of the fallen guards. It was far from the first encounter Rykka had with bodies, or with murders, but it felt different in a way she struggled to define. It felt... personal, even though she'd only known these guards in passing, and even though Merris knew nothing about Rykka.

Sometime longer than five minutes, but less than ten, Rykka heard footsteps running down the stone hall. She was wincing even before her conscious mind identified the footfalls. *Blackened shoals, of course he'd be the first one up. Couldn't have been Alistar, or literally any other member of the family.*

Captain Roddek skidded to a halt in the doorway. "Blood and sand! Darkwood, what happened?"

"Sunward's assassin found an unlocked door and snuck inside, found Pietro, murdered his guards, and ran off with him. My best assumption, at least. We didn't see her."

Captain Roddek stopped, looked at her, and frowned. "I thought Merris was the name of Saskia's maid."

"She was. Got dismissed for trying to sneak down into the basement through the main entrance."

Roddek's eyebrows rose. "She got dismissed so she... turned to murder?"

"More like playing at being a maid was her backup plan when murder was too much hassle," Tiyron put in.

"She got in by this path." Rykka led the way back through the concealed doors and blank passages to the exterior door. She pointed out the slide. "If I had to guess, Pietro left that mark, not Merris."

"Huh." Captain Roddek crouched to look more closely. "Maybe. You said she rescued him?"

"No, I said she took him. From what I know, she doesn't like Pietro, and if Sunward hadn't given her specific instructions to bring him alive, he'd be another body in that room."

"Makes more sense. Looks like there are some bits of rope on a few rocks, so he's probably still bound." Captain Roddek straightened and looked at Rykka and Tiyron. His jaw tightened for a moment.

Rykka jumped down to the ground. "Tiyron, you should—"

"Not staying here, Rykka," he said flatly. He navigated the chair back the same way he'd gotten up the slope and rolled up into Captain Roddek's space. His good eye fixed on Roddek. "Got a problem with that?"

Roddek folded his arms across his chest. "So *many* problems I can't decide where to start." He shot a look at Rykka, then back to Tiyron. "You're surprisingly active for a dead man."

Hematic perdition. I hoped Alistar had already explained Tiyron.

"Can I explain *later*, Captain?" Rykka said. "Merris has a significant start on us." She wanted to argue with Tiyron, but he was as stubborn as she was, especially in front of a stranger. Even more so when he had something to prove. And knowing that Captain Roddek hadn't forgiven her for hiding her past while on his ship, it would be nothing short of a miracle if they found Merris and Pietro without anyone killing anyone. Without waiting for either man to respond, she followed the uneven trail into the undergrowth.

Either Pietro was intentionally trying to leave signs of his passage, or he was too exhausted to care if he left tracks. If he had any sense of survival, he'd realize he didn't want to stay under Merris's hold. Merris had to know Pietro's path could be followed, but she couldn't do much to conceal it. Rykka guessed she was trying for speed rather than stealth.

She's probably told Sunward that she has him. Unless, of course, she's still holding the option of murdering him in reserve. No, probably not. Sunward would want to know as soon as Pietro's been secured so she doesn't have to worry about who he's talking to.

Tiyron and Captain Roddek followed her without speaking. When they finally emerged from the overgrown area back to maintained streets, Rykka swore. Indents in the dirt showed where a carriage had been parked, and the torn and uprooted grass indicated that at least one horse had grazed for a while.

Roddek watched her. "Ideas, Darkwood?"

"I can track an unknown carriage about as well as you can track a ship you've never seen with no stated destination, Captain," she growled. "Unless someone left a convenient hint, I can only guess."

"How about this for 'convenient hint'?" Tiyron asked. "At least I assume it means something, and someone made the effort to really dig the toe of his boot in to make the mark."

Rykka and Roddek both spun toward him. The mark Tiyron indicated was on the edge of the grass, where it might not have been noticed by someone preparing a carriage. Two straight lines with a slash connecting them.

"A glyph?" Roddek asked, frowning.

Rykka frowned as well and started to walk around it to

search for other clues. She glanced at it again, from another angle, and straightened. "It's the letter Z." The letter Z, like the one that adorned the doors of a factory now owned by Lady Ravencrest.

She wouldn't have taken him there, would she? We know that's where they're working. But... but we didn't get caught. Larisa saw me, but Merris doesn't know. Hematic perdition, Prince Pietro, thank the gods you're not quite as stupid as I thought.

"I know where they're going."

CHAPTER 54

Alistar swallowed bile. Beside him, Father rested a hand on his shoulder as they both gazed around the room.

"I'm sorry, Alistar," Father said quietly.

"It looks like they didn't even know what happened. Didn't have time to react," Alistar said. "Merris knew all of them. Blood and sand, she worked in this house long enough to know the rest of the staff." *And she murdered these men before they could respond. She couldn't have hesitated at all.*

"Takes a cold heart to do that," Father said. "She must have hidden it from you and Saskia well."

Alistar nodded, jaw tight. "The guards all mentioned strange noises since we drained the pool. I didn't want to believe someone got into the tunnels then." *And now four of my people are dead.*

Father's grip on his shoulder tightened in a comforting squeeze. "We all wonder what we should have done differently when we lose some of our own, Alistar. You did what you could with what you knew."

Alistar let out a heavy breath and turned to Dorne, who

waited behind them. "Please see to them. I want to send them home, to be buried with their families."

"Of course, sir."

He had yet to see Roddek, Rykka, or even Tiyron, which implied that all three, gods only knew why, had found some trail to follow. He cursed himself for not having informed Dorne of the tension between Rykka and his brother, and he cursed Roddek for being the first person downstairs.

Alistar and Father moved out of the way of the others Dorne had called in. As they somberly walked back toward the stairs, Alistar said, "Of course she'd act today. I can't even help in searching for her."

"She's not stupid," Father said. "If she were, she wouldn't have fooled you and Saskia for as long as she did."

Roddek's speaking stone chimed. Alistar grabbed it and activated it. "Did you find anything? Where are you?"

"She had a carriage waiting at... where the blackened shoals are we, Darkwood?" Roddek said.

Rykka spoke. "We're south of the estate at Wender Street. Merris's companion has slightly higher survival instincts than I expected and left both a trail and a hint as to their destination."

"You know where they're going? Where?" Alistar asked urgently. Then he added, "It's the Admiral and I here."

"Captain Roddek, me, and my brother here," Rykka said. "The prince drew a 'Z' in the dirt. I believe she's taking him to Ravencrest's factory. Also doesn't look like he cares for his new situation, which says a lot if he thinks tied up in a cage in an unknown location is better than Merris."

"And you got there from the manor?"

"Yes." Rykka described the location of the concealed door. "We didn't lock it when we left, so at the moment, it's still accessible."

"I'll ensure it doesn't stay that way. What's your plan?"

Alistar asked. "Head to the factory?" It made sense Merris would take him to the factory. It was a central hub for Sunward's activities. With Prince Filipp's restrictions in place, that location was safe from official raids or inspections, and it undoubtedly had areas that could be used to confine Pietro.

"Yeah. Can you spare me a ride there before you head to the Exhibition?"

"I'm going too," Roddek said. "Sorry Alistar; you'll have to handle the Exhibition without me."

"All right. Then the two of you—"

"Three," interrupted Tiyron. "I'm not staying here."

Alistar's jaw tightened, and he could only imagine the expressions on Roddek's and Rykka's faces. "I'll send a carriage, and you can sort things out however you need to." *I can't begin to guess what in Slee's name Tiyron thinks he can do skulking around that factory.* "Be careful. Could be a trap."

"We will," Roddek promised, grimly serious.

Before they left the basement, Alistar stopped and leaned heavily against the wall. "I need to be at my best for the tour of the Exhibition. Blood and sand, Merris knew this would throw everyone in disarray. She could have waited until we left for the tour, and it would have taken most of the day before anyone discovered what she'd done. She could have gotten out with no pursuit close enough to track her."

"Unless she was worried we'd bring Pietro to the Exhibition with us as evidence," Father said. "I considered suggesting doing so. My point being, we're not the only ones worrying about what's going to happen today and thinking about all the elements outside our control."

"Bring Pietro with us... the chaos that would bring." Alistar shook his head. "I wouldn't trust him to keep his mouth shut, though."

"Cero knows you caught him, doesn't he?" Father asked.

Alistar shook his head. "I don't think he knows I've looked

into Sunward's involvement at all. He didn't tell me she was in Lewarden. Lady Syri did. I haven't told either of them about the components you claimed from the smugglers, either. And I certainly haven't told Prince Cero that I think one of his nephews tried to murder him."

"Hmm. Can I assume you haven't told him this tour is meant to be a trap, either?"

"You can assume that," Alistar said.

"Ah. Well, that promises to make today very interesting indeed."

As much as he wanted to remain in the manor and scour every dusty corner of the basement for more access points, Alistar made himself go to Silverline Power early. Several messages awaited him in varying degrees of urgency and panic from the crews working at the Exhibition site, and a first-year technician waited anxiously in the lobby to rush his answers to those at the site.

Rather than go up to his office, Alistar reviewed the messages immediately, writing answers to the more straightforward questions before focusing on the more complex issues. "How long have you been waiting?" he asked the technician.

"About an hour, Senior Engineer," she said.

He nodded and handed her his responses. "Take those out to the site and return or send someone else back. By the time you return, I should have the rest of these ready." He flipped through the remaining questions and held up a hand to stop her. "Actually, for these three, the best resolution at the moment is to not present this area during the tour." He marked the questions appropriately and added them to her stack. "I'll take care of the rest of these."

"Yessir!" She bobbed her head in a nod and scurried outside.

Alistar let out a breath and turned to the front desk. "Good morning, Assistant Torrent. I hope your morning has been pleasant."

"Good morning, Senior Engineer. For this hour, the morning's been quite busy, though that's not a surprise, given the day's schedule," she answered.

"Do you know how many we expect to attend? I spoke with Prince Cero about inviting my family to join the tour, but if you have a complete list of those expected, I'd appreciate a chance to see it."

"Certainly, Senior Engineer. I'll have that ready by the time you've completed the needed review and research to answer the remaining questions from the site."

Alistar smiled faintly and accepted the dismissal. He hurried up to his office and set to work.

Half an hour later, he returned to the lobby with hastily written instructions to address the difficulties described in the messages. The technician hadn't returned yet, but he expected she'd arrive soon.

Assistant Torrent nodded to him. "I have the list of guests here."

"Thank you." Alistar took the offered document and looked it over. In addition to his family and Soluthos, Prince Cero, Lady Syri, and their respective Royal Guards were listed—five for Lady Syri, a full ten for the Silver Prince. Then came King Suelton, with another ten Royal Guard, and Crown Prince Filipp, his aide, listed as Snowdale, and a mere five Guards, like Syri.

Will Sunward be there? If she is, they were smart enough not to list her name. Maybe she's this Snowdale? If so, they really should have used a human surname for her. But even so, would she take the risk of being recognized? They couldn't have masked her as one of the workers, could they? She'd never pass for a Silverline employee, but maybe one of the general laborers? She has *to be there. They* have *to make their move now. We've baited the trap. We've set out the opportunity they need.*

Unless she decides this is her opportunity to reclaim the flower, and she leaves the assassination to Filipp.

Without explaining his thoughts to Assistant Torrent, Alistar raced back to the relative privacy of his office and activated his father's speaking stone.

The Admiral answered promptly. "Problems?"

"Has the entrance Darkwood mentioned been closed yet?"

"It has, and I've sent some people to scour the passages for any other rats that snuck in."

Alistar let out a breath of relief. He should have thought to do that, but he felt like he was running a footrace and tripping over his own boots while everyone else charged past.

"Sunward might try to get the flower while we're all at the Exhibition, and she might know how to unlock the doors from outside."

"And we can't risk hobbling ourselves at the tour by leaving more of us here to guard it," Father said. "Lamorage is staying, though. I'll make sure he knows what's happened and that he needs to be on guard at the flower."

"I was trying to keep him *out* of danger," Alistar said.

"I know, but don't insult him by rejecting the aid he has to offer, Alistar. Let him help you."

This morning, men died because they helped me.

"Tell him to be careful," Alistar said finally.

"I will. We'll see you soon."

Gods, I hope I'm wrong about this.

He collected himself and returned to the lobby. The technician had returned and was collecting Alistar's answers from Assistant Torrent. She looked relieved when Alistar came down the stairs.

"How are things looking at the site?" he asked.

"Everyone's nervous. It's a lot to be ready for His Majesty to see it."

Alistar gave her a sympathetic smile. "And you didn't get much time to make it happen. Everyone's doing amazing work. Thank you. Anything unexpected or giving you problems aside from the questions you brought?"

"His Highness sent some automatons he wanted placed in specific spots, but he said they didn't need to have mahiy lines routed to them. We figured he wanted to have the look, even if they aren't ready to perform yet."

He hoped his face didn't reflect his flurry of emotions. *Of course he's not worried about the mahiy lines. The automatons don't need them.* "I certainly hope he doesn't expect power for them. We don't have time to reroute anything at this point. Now, get those back to your team. Is there anything else you need, or I can do to help you?"

"I don't think so, sir. Thank you!"

Alistar watched her go with a stab of guilt. Whatever happened during the tour, workers all through the Exhibition site would be present, possibly in danger. He couldn't warn them, at the risk of anything reaching the wrong ears, and he didn't know who among them might work for Sunward or Filipp. He also had little doubt that either would sacrifice underlings without a second thought.

And Filipp has brought in the automatons.

"Is something bothering you, Senior Engineer?" Assistant Tempest asked, and he realized he'd been staring into nothing.

He shook himself out of it. "Ah, sorry, thinking about what today could bring. I'm going to be in my office if you, or anyone else, needs me."

At his desk, he reviewed the planned route through the Exhibition once again, making sure they avoided the areas where the crews were still having issues. The central stage, at least, wasn't showing any signs of problems yet. He kept

Roddek's speaking stone close at hand, but it remained inactive. He fought the urge to activate it himself, knowing he could interrupt their infiltration by doing so.

No additional crisis materialized that required his attention. Time crawled by until finally he could justify going back to the manor to prepare and collect the rest of the family.

Gods, please watch over all of us. And please, let this work.

CHAPTER 55

Travel to Ravencrest's factory was tense, but quiet. As much as Rykka wanted to demand Tiyron explain why he insisted on accompanying them, she didn't want to give him reason to antagonize Captain Roddek. And she didn't actually need Tiyron to say anything to know he didn't trust Roddek with her safety.

At least Tiyron's chair had been easy to manage—easier than she expected. When not occupied, it compacted and took up no more space than a piece of luggage might. Tiyron had rather smugly enjoyed her surprise at that.

Captain Roddek broke the stillness as the carriage turned toward the factory district. "What do you know of this place, Darkwood? And what does the letter 'Z' have to do with it?"

"The letter is carved into the front doors of the factory. It was owned by the Zel'en family, who also owned the manor before Cemar and his allies arranged for them to go bankrupt. Cemar began using the manor as his base of operations, and the Ravencrest family bought the factory, along with a lot of other stuff. Ravencrest is working with Sunward now and has been secretly building automatons in this factory." She briefly recounted her previous visits to the site.

Roddek listened intently, frowning, until the carriage stopped. Rykka checked out the window and saw that, as she'd requested, they were parked on a narrow side street.

The driver opened the door and nodded to them all. "We're a quarter mile or so from the factory you mentioned. Can't tell if the alley there runs all the way to it, but it should get you close." His face was grim. "If you find Merris, make her pay."

"We will," Rykka promised.

He lifted Tiyron's chair out and unfolded it. Tiyron climbed carefully out and sat again. Rykka thought he was intentionally underplaying his ability to walk in front of Roddek. The ploy was effective enough that Roddek cast her a questioning look, silently asking if it was really wise to allow Tiyron to join them.

In response, she mouthed, "He can do more than he lets on."

Roddek nodded in understanding, though he didn't look reassured. She didn't blame him.

The carriage departed and Rykka led the way through the alley. When they neared the Ravencrest factory, she slowed. A nondescript carriage stood near the back entrance. She approached cautiously, seeing no driver. Peering in a window, she didn't see anyone within. The doors didn't open when she tested them. The horse turned to watch her and nickered. Its lead was tied to a ring in the wall.

"Did she leave you out here like this?" Rykka asked. "Not very nice of her." It did imply that Merris didn't intend to remain here, though.

"This door?" Roddek asked, nodding at the nearest door.

She shook her head. "Follow me."

She circled around to the side door she'd entered when she infiltrated the building with Windshadow and Dawncloud. It was still unlocked. Inside, the space she remembered being packed with crates was nearly empty. She crossed the storage room and peered out to the factory floor.

Last time, the space had been filled with a hum of activity, people moving about, machines in operation. Now, everything was silent and still. Looking around, it might not have seen activity in months if not for the scrapes on the floor and the lack of dust on the heavy clothes draped over equipment.

Roddek leaned close and whispered, "Are you sure we're in the right place?"

"I'm sure," she whispered back, but the eerie absence of life made her question herself.

A distant crash echoed through the cavernous space, and all three of them jumped, heads snapping toward the sound. Rykka didn't see any source, every sense alert as she moved closer, slinking behind the shelter of bulky equipment. She reached the hall that led to the offices and the downstairs without seeing any indication of the source of the noise. When she turned to signal Tiyron and Roddek to join her, she found they had silently followed a little distance behind her as backup.

Though the hall was no less empty, it didn't inspire the same unease that the cavernous, echoing factory floor did. Rykka raised a hand to signal a halt, closed her eyes, and listened.

"Downstairs," she whispered. "That's where they kept the collected channelers." She looked at Tiyron. "Larisa might be there."

He swallowed and nodded.

"Merris might be there as well," Roddek said, hand resting on the hilt of his cutlass.

Rykka stopped again at the top of the stairs before slowly moving down, testing each step before putting her full weight on it. She stopped, shaking her head. "Tiyron, there's no way you can take your chair down quietly."

He hissed a curse.

Roddek looked up and down the hall and opened a side door. "A closet. We can conceal it in here if you go on foot."

Tiyron hissed another curse but pushed himself upright. "Fine."

Roddek helped Tiyron down the stairs. The ground floor had been well lit, but only a few ghostlights illuminated the basement hall. As they stood in the shadows, letting their eyes adjust, Rykka heard a muffled sound, like someone trying to speak through a gag, and sounds of movement. She pressed herself against the wall, breath catching.

"Guard the prince. Shouldn't be hard—that's your job, anyway, isn't it?" Merris said.

The muffled voice made alarmed sounds of protest. No one else responded.

A door closed. Footsteps moved further down the hall, away from them.

Is she checking on the channelers? If they're still here, someone should be checking on them, right? Sunward wouldn't leave them to starve after all this time collecting them, would she?

"The internal channelers were kept in a room at the end of the hall," she said softly to her companions. "I don't know if there's another exit from that room. Two other rooms down there. Last time, one had bunks, the other a semi-functional automaton with no legs."

"And now there's someone else who's in charge of guarding Pietro, presumably," Roddek said, scanning the shadows. "How well can you see down here?"

"Well enough to get around," Rykka said. "You?"

"Barely." He grimaced. "Let's find the prince."

Rykka strained to hear any hint of Merris, but she didn't even hear the other woman's footsteps anymore. She advanced slowly. If Merris returned or anyone else arrived, they didn't have anywhere to hide.

All three doors stood closed. The automaton had been in the

one to the right, and the channelers in the center. Rykka put her ear to the center door and heard nothing. She checked the left door, again only hearing silence.

Hematic perdition, don't tell me that half-broken automaton is Pietro's guard.

When she listened at the right door, she heard faint sounds of movement. Rykka closed her eyes and silently cursed.

"Watch the other doors," she whispered.

The door was locked, of course. She crouched and set to work picking the lock. It was as aggravating and complex as before.

She finally aligned the tumblers, and the latch clicked audibly. Roddek stepped closer to edge the door open.

Rykka sensed a subtle shift in the air. She sprang to her feet and spun around as Tiyron hissed, "Rat."

"Don't move."

Merris stood behind Tiyron, a knife at his neck. Her eyes darted over Roddek and moved to Rykka. Her lip curled in scorn. "You're the rasher who replaced me."

Rykka's eyes narrowed. Merris was too fast and her blade too close for her to throw a barrier between Tiyron and the knife. "Maybe I am, but at least I haven't failed at my job as miserably as you did."

Merris snorted. "Is that your best?"

"Not even close. She's going easy on you," Tiyron said with no indication that he felt any concern for his current state.

That startled Merris enough to shift her gaze to him. "What?"

He chuckled. "I said she's going easy on you, darling. She's nicer than I am." Tiyron grinned. "Don't tell me you don't remember me."

His evident lack of fear for his own life and his overconfident arrogance threw Merris off balance enough that she didn't immediately stab him. "I don't remember every filthy rat I happen across."

Beside Rykka, Roddek stood tense, hand hanging just over the hilt of his saber. She could tell he'd made the same calculations as her, and knew he wasn't fast enough to stop Merris from killing Tiyron.

Tiyron tutted. "No need to be rude just because I flirted more with Larisa than I did with you. Don't tell me you're still upset about that, Malice? Oh, wait, you go by 'Merris' now, don't you?"

Merris sucked in a sharp breath. "Who are you?"

His voice dropped to a hateful hiss. "Someone you should know better than to let this close to you, Malice." His clenched right hand jabbed behind him.

Merris gasped and staggered. Tiyron jerked away from her as her blade cut a thin line across his throat. Her gaze moved to his face and her eyes grew wide. "No. Tiyron? You're dead!"

His face twisted in a manic grin as he lunged at her. "You think *that* would stop me? You carved out my *eye!*" In his right hand, he clutched a surgical scalpel.

Rykka took a step forward, not sure if she wanted to stop him or aid him. Merris blocked Tiyron's stab, recovering from her shock all too quickly. She sprang back and drew a second blade. She stood between them and the stairs, her own escape route open, theirs blocked.

Roddek reached into his inner coat pocket. Rykka glimpsed a small orb in his hand. He squeezed it hard and flung it at the ground behind Tiyron. Rykka closed her eyes and turned away as blazing light burst in the hall.

Merris snapped a curse. Roddek rushed past Rykka. She thought he was going to attack Merris, but he dodged past her blind slashes to get behind her. Merris turned, following the sound of his heavy steps.

Rykka raised a hand to shield her eyes from the light. She

saw Merris slash at Roddek with one blade, then stab with the other. The knife hit but didn't penetrate the thick leather jerkin Roddek wore under his coat, though he grunted at the impact and fell back a step.

Tiyron rammed the scalpel into her back. Merris gasped and started to turn. Roddek grabbed her arms, trying to twist the blades from her grasp. Tiyron stabbed her again, then again. Rykka stepped closer, ready to throw a barrier if Merris broke free.

The scalpel struck again. Merris sagged with a wheezing gasp.

Tiyron leaned close to her. "I told you I wouldn't forget."

"Tiyron," Rykka said.

He shook his head. "She won't tell us anything. And if she did, she'd lie."

"Then for the gods' sake, be quick about it," Roddek ordered. He twisted one of the knives out of Merris's weakening grasp and held it hilt-first to Tiyron. "And use something a little more civilized."

Merris sneered and tried to spit at both of them.

Tiyron gripped the knife in a trembling hand. For a moment, he looked like he was trying to summon some witty final words to Merris. His jaw tightened and he stabbed her twice in the kidney.

Roddek forced the other knife out of her hand as her strength failed. He glanced around. "Darkwood, check the other rooms. Rather not leave her in the hall."

The left door wasn't locked, and the room held the same empty bunks she remembered from last time. "In here."

Merris was fighting to stay conscious, but she lost that battle when Roddek and Rykka dragged her across the stone floor into the room. Rykka searched the other woman, finding two more daggers, a garrote, and a length of tightly woven rope. She used that to bind Merris's hands behind her back.

"She'll probably bleed out, but I don't want to chance it," she said softly to Roddek.

He just nodded, casting an uneasy look toward Tiyron.

Tiyron crouched on the floor, breathing heavily. He didn't look at either of them, staring at the bloody knife in his trembling hands.

Rykka crouched beside him. "Tiyron."

"She was one of them. One of his torturers. I remember her laughing."

"I didn't know. I'm sorry. If I had, I'd have killed her earlier, consequences be damned."

He shook his head. "I told her I'd kill her. She laughed then. Not laughing now." His grip tightened on the knife. "Not laughing now."

A door opened. Rykka's head snapped up.

Roddek, standing in the doorway into the center room, made a gesture of apology. "Checking in here." He stepped inside, and Rykka realized he was offering them a modicum of privacy.

"Can I have the knife?" she asked Tiyron.

He held it to her without question or hesitation. He would never relinquish a weapon so easily to anyone else. She wiped the blood from the blade with a handkerchief and slid it into an empty sheath taken from Merris. Then, without a word, she wrapped her arms around her brother. He leaned into her, and she held him as he shook.

After several moments, he collected himself, pulling together the fragments of his mask of arrogance. Rykka helped him stand, but she didn't return the knife. He didn't ask for it, either.

"Anything in there, Captain?" Rykka asked.

From beyond the center door, Roddek answered. "No one in here now, but there definitely were people in here recently." He stepped into the doorway, paused a moment, and decided he wouldn't be intruding by returning.

"The channelers were there." Her throat tightened. *Where are they? What did Sunward do?*

Tiyron gripped her arm, fingers digging in tightly. "Larisa?" His eye turned to Roddek. "There's *no one* there? You're *certain*?"

"I'm certain. I searched the whole room. No other exits, no cubbies someone could hide in."

"Then it's time for the useless bleating sheep of a prince to give some real answers," Tiyron growled, eyes turning to the door Rykka had unlocked.

Rykka swallowed hard and cautiously opened it.

Roddek's light orb still blazed, casting illumination into the dark room. In one corner, Prince Pietro, bound and gagged, hunched against the wall. He turned away from the light, wincing. At the opposite wall, Rykka saw the automaton. Its head turned toward the door, tracking movement. It looked the same as the last time she'd seen it, chained to the wall and lacking legs. When Rykka stepped into the room, the automaton strained against the chains. Stone groaned, and she realized that while the chains might hold, the wall into which they were anchored might not.

"Hey, calm down," she told it quickly, tasting fear in the back of her throat. "You listened when Merris told you what to do, right? Will you listen to me too?"

Pietro tried to speak through the gag. Rykka edged closer to him.

As soon as she did, the automaton's efforts to break free redoubled. Rykka turned back to it. "Hematic perdition, I'm here to *help* him, not harm him. She told you to guard him, right? Don't tell me you think *this* is a place where a damned *prince* should be!"

The automaton stilled, head focused on her. It felt like it was listening to her, though she could only guess how much it understood.

"I'm going to remove his gag. Okay with you?"

The automaton didn't respond.

Keeping one eye on it, Rykka moved to Pietro. She gave him a hard look. "Don't make me regret this."

He swallowed hard.

She teased loose the tight knots and pulled the coarse cloth from his mouth.

"Who are you?" he rasped.

"Doesn't matter right now. You know something about that thing that we need to know?" She nodded at the automaton. "Like why it obeyed Merris?"

Pietro's gaze shifted to the automaton, then back to Rykka. "Don't know."

Her eyes narrowed. "Are you *sure* about that?"

He flinched. "I don't know. Please, let me go."

From the doorway, Tiyron laughed. "Then why'd she say it was this one's job to protect you? Sounded like she meant that's its job regardless of whether she ordered it or not. Is that really how little you're worth to Sunward?"

"That's not what that meant!" Pietro protested. "She meant…" He trailed off.

"No, Prince Pietro, please continue. She meant what, exactly?" Rykka asked.

Another long pause. Without looking at any of them, Pietro said, "Let me walk."

Rykka gave him a long, dubious look before untying the rope around his ankles. He tried to stand, but his bound wrists hindered his efforts. Rykka caught his elbow and lifted him to his feet. Pietro staggered unsteadily to the automaton. It didn't move to stop him or attack him. Its head tracked Rykka as she followed him.

Pietro tugged at the ropes binding his wrists but didn't ask her to release them. "Open this panel. There's a hidden latch at the base of the neck, left shoulder."

Rykka's eyes narrowed. "If this thing attacks me…"

"It won't. I'm too close. Too much risk of hitting me."

Her breath caught for a moment. *He intentionally placed himself there, in its way. Why? How is he so certain it won't attack?*

Despite her misgivings, Rykka reached toward the spot Pietro indicated. It even seemed as if the automaton leaned forward slightly, granting her a better angle. As if it too wanted her to see whatever secret it held. She was aware of Tiyron and Roddek flanking her and Pietro. Someone had moved the light orb into the room.

Her fingers brushed over the smooth, cool metal until they found a narrow indentation. Within, shielded from accidental hits, she felt a latch. Hooking her finger into the loop, she pulled until it yielded. The automaton's chest panel released with a click and the massive machine seemed to sigh as it deactivated.

Wary, Rykka pried the panel open. She expected the gears and pistons that moved the automaton. She expected everything to connect to a central power source.

She did not expect to see a person curled in the automaton's chest cavity.

The figure appeared to be unconscious or asleep. Leather straps secured their arms and legs against the walls of the cavity. Wires and tubes were strapped all over their body. A mask covered their mouth, connected to a tube that she guessed provided food and water. At the top of the cavity, a glowing crystal rested in a metal cage. Rykka recognized it as the same size and shape as those she'd seen Ravencrest's workers installing into an automaton.

Pietro hissed in pain when Roddek grabbed him roughly. "What is this?" he demanded of the prince.

"This is… a Crown spy sent to watch Lady Sunward," Pietro answered. "They discovered this one could do the… unnatural channeling, so they used her to test the theory rather than killing her."

"Test the theory," Rykka repeated in a low, dangerous voice.

"You mean that inside each automaton, there's a *person*?" Her stomach twisted and bile rose in her throat. "A person who's being drained to power the automaton. Is that it? That's why Sunward's been collecting them?"

"They're not—," Pietro started.

"I swear to the gods, if you say they're not people, I will punch you in the mouth, Prince Pietro," Rykka warned.

His mouth snapped shut and his eyes darted to the automaton as if hoping it would suddenly reanimate and protect him.

"How does the automaton follow orders if the person within is unconscious?" Roddek cut in.

"Not unconscious," Pietro said. "Drugged. Lumination. The crystal focuses their ability and ensures they obey, to a point. They couldn't make this one act against the Crown. That's what Merris meant about its… job."

Rykka struggled to find the words to express her fury. She caught a glimpse of movement to her side, then heard the sound of a fist connecting. Pietro doubled over, coughing and gasping, held upright by Roddek's unyielding grip on his arm. Tiyron loomed over the prince, fists clenched.

"You disgusting waste of air. You mock and spit on one of your own people? She's *loyal* to you and your useless bloodline, and you *mock* her for it." Tiyron's voice was cold rage. "And you dare act like any of you *deserve* devotion. If this is what you think of your own people, no wonder you can't imagine that anyone else matters."

Pietro fought for breath. He clearly thought about responding, then just as clearly thought better of it.

Rykka untangled the Crown agent from the restraints, wires, and tubes and awkwardly lifted her out of the automaton. She was a gaunt human with dirty brown hair. Rykka laid her on the floor and lightly slapped her face, hoping to rouse some sort of response.

Glazed brown eyes opened partially without focusing. The woman turned toward the sound of Prince Pietro's coughing and her face screwed in an expression of concern, as if she knew something was wrong, and that she should respond, but she wasn't certain how.

"Take it easy," Rykka told her. "He'll be fine. Do you hear me?"

"Ex...hib...i..." The woman's hoarse voice rasped in her throat.

The Exhibition. The other automatons must be there. We were right; Sunward and Filipp are going to try to kill the king. Rykka turned. "Captain, let them know at the Exhibition! Tell them about the automatons!"

Roddek's head jerked in a nod. He released his grip on Pietro, who crumpled to the floor, and rushed into the hall.

Rykka searched her pockets and found Dorne's speaking stone.

He answered moments after she activated it, his normally steady voice more worried than she'd ever heard before. "Darkwood, report."

"We found him and someone else. Need a carriage to meet us at the back of the factory; not worried about stealth right now."

"And the threat?" Dorne demanded.

"Handled. Is Windshadow still at the manor?"

"No. He accompanied Lord De'seneth and his family to the tour of the site."

She cursed. "Do you have a way of contacting the investigator he hangs out with? You know who I mean." She didn't want to say Dawncloud's name in front of Pietro.

"I'll find out. You want her to meet you there?"

"No, at the manor. It's urgent."

"On it. Carriage is on the way back."

Roddek cursed in the hall and stepped back into the doorway. "No one's answering. Alistar said some areas of the Exhibition grounds don't have reliable power, and speaking stones might not work. They must be there."

"Or something's interfering with the stones," Tiyron said. "They wouldn't want anyone calling for help, would they?" He directed the last more at Pietro than the rest of them.

Pietro had caught his wind and looked at them all in confusion. "Exhibition hasn't started, has it?"

"A select group has been given the opportunity to tour the site before everything's complete," Rykka said. "Namely, your brother and your father."

He understood. By the paling of his face, he understood very well.

Rykka dragged him to his feet. "Captain, would you help her?" She nodded at the drugged Crown agent.

Roddek picked up the woman and carried her into the hall. Rykka pulled Pietro with her after him. Tiyron followed, lagging slightly behind. Rykka hauled Pietro up the stairs and left him under Roddek's watch, then hurried down to help her brother.

Tiyron gripped her arm hard, breathing heavily. "Rykka, the other channelers. Larisa. They're all inside those… things."

"I know," she whispered. "And Sunward's controlling them. Using them to murder the king."

"Have to stop them. Whatever happens, they'll hang for treason."

She swallowed hard and nodded. "Tiyron, I need you to do something. I need you to take that woman and the prince back to the manor and make sure no one gets to either of them. You can trust Dorne and anyone he trusts on the staff, but you *must* get them there, so Captain Roddek and I can get to the Exhibition. We can take Merris's cart if you'll wait for the carriage."

His jaw tightened. Tiyron nodded. "Find them, Rykka. Save them. Save… her, please."

CHAPTER 56

Alistar didn't know if he should be more relieved or worried that Lady Sunward wasn't visibly part of Prince Filipp's retinue. Prince Filipp, King Suelton, and their respective guards and attendants slowly walked the planned route through the Exhibition site, politely listening to their guides pointing out matters of interest. At the moment, Prince Filipp was asking clarifying questions about the arrangement of the colored lights that would display on the opposite wall. Alistar suppressed a groan, remembering how many changes he'd made to the mahiy line architecture to accommodate the addition of those lights.

The first hour of the tour had been uneventful. Aside from Prince Cero's occasional suspicious glances at Admiral As'enel, no one acted as if the event were anything other than what it appeared. While they were paused, Alistar took the opportunity to step away from his spot near Lady Syri to check the runes carved into one of the stone pillars. The etching looked rough to his eye. He ran a finger over it and confirmed that the edges hadn't been properly polished. He pulled a notepad from his pocket and scribbled a quick note.

Alistar's father slipped up beside him and rested a hand on

his shoulder. "Quite the impressive work here. Looking forward to seeing it when it's all alight."

"So am I," Alistar said. He gestured toward the sky. "The entire area will be covered with a dome of magic—keep everything temperate, sheltered from weather and sun, and of course serve as a display surface for art, images, announcements, and a reminder to everyone that Calarand controls magic."

"Ah. And that's why you've had to juggle so much to make sure everything has power." Father nodded thoughtfully. "I did wonder what could be consuming so much power that you couldn't make everyone happy." He gestured toward the tiered structures all around the site. "And those?"

"On this end of the grounds, those will have exhibits, both from Calarand and from other lands. Further east, they'll be filled with vendors," Alistar explained.

Father nodded thoughtfully.

People began moving again. Alistar excused himself to return to his expected position in the tour. He still hadn't heard from Roddek or Rykka, and worry lurked like a shadow in the back of his mind. To refocus, he turned his attention to their most important guest.

Prince Pietro's grievances with his father had painted King Suelton as a doddering old man with fading wits and declining health. The king's health might not be as strong as it had been in his youth, but he walked steadily, if slowly, only occasionally pausing to steady himself against one of his aides. His eyes were keen and bright as he looked about the Exhibition.

"Filipp, this will be a wondrous legacy you're building," he told his son. "And an honor to those you lost."

Filipp's jaw tightened for a moment as his eyes narrowed, but he kept his composure. "Thank you. I am certain it will never be forgotten." He turned to Prince Cero. "Uncle, shall we move on to the main stage in the Crown Pavilion? I had several specific requirements for that area and want to be sure they were done correctly."

"Of course," Prince Cero agreed. "It is the center point of the Exhibition."

The main stage, as Prince Cero said, was both the conceptual and physical center of the Exhibition. Tiered rows of benches encircled it, capable of seating thousands, and even the worst spots still commanded a breathtaking view of the circular stage.

Alistar's pulse quickened when he saw the automatons positioned around the stage. Some stood posed like dancers, while others stood still and silent as statues or pillars. Exotic flowering plants spilled long trailing vines over the edges of the stage, filling the air with fragrance. Like a moment frozen in time, nothing upon the platform moved.

Filipp strode to the stairs and sprang up onto the stage. Initially, Alistar thought he was doing as he'd said, checking that all his requests and requirements had been fulfilled. The prince's guards stood at attention while the rest of the guests milled around the base of the stage, examining the intricately detailed panels and paintings that could only be appreciated up close. Alistar glanced at his family and noticed that, despite the casualness of their stances, they'd positioned themselves so they had a view of the entire stage. Saskia stayed close to Alistar. Soluthos positioned himself near Prince Cero. Mother placed herself close enough to King Suelton to react to any threats against him.

Filipp climbed to the elevated throne at the center of the platform, followed by the reedy elf who Alistar assumed was his aide. Filipp rotated the throne in a full circle, nodding in satisfaction. A person seated on the throne could face any direction they wished. Alistar watched him, tension crawling up his spine. Others shifted and glanced around uncertainly, sensing that something momentous loomed.

Filipp sat on the throne, turning to face King Suelton. "What do you think, Father? Does it suit me?"

"It always has, Filipp," King Suelton answered.

Filipp's jaw tightened. "There should be another chair beside mine. One where my daughter could see everything, where I could show her all the wonders and delights that I brought to her feet."

To Alistar's right, Lady Syri inhaled sharply, sensing something in his words. "Filipp, what are you doing?"

He barely glanced at her. His fingers moved over the arm of the throne as he manipulated something no one could see from the ground. "Claiming what's mine."

Alistar expected the automatons on the stage to spring to life. Instead, the carved panels around the base of the stage fell open and a dozen automatons surged out.

Rykka had warned they were fast, but their speed caught Alistar off guard. One suddenly loomed over him, more than a foot taller than him. He narrowly dodged aside as a massive metal fist swung at his head.

Chaos erupted on all sides. The Royal Guards rushed to protect King Suelton and Prince Cero, shouting commands that the automatons ignored. Two guards climbed onto the stage and ran to Prince Filipp. Of all the guards, they seemed the least flustered and made no attempt to deactivate the automatons.

"They won't respond to the codes, and they *will* kill!" Alistar shouted, drawing his cutlass. "Protect the king!"

Putting aside any concerns about how such automatons could exist or how Alistar knew about them, the guards obeyed. Aside from the pair on the stage, Filipp's guards shook off their confusion and joined the rest of the Royal Guards. Filipp's face twisted in anger as he glared at Alistar. Though he couldn't hear what the prince said, Alistar was sure he saw the words "How dare you" on Filipp's lips.

"Who dares?" King Suelton demanded. "What are these… things? Stop them at once!"

"They aren't responding, Your Majesty!" a guard answered. "We must get you clear!"

Wait. Is she one of Filipp's guards? Can she be trusted?

"Captain! High ground!" Alistar called to his mother.

Her head jerked in understanding. She barked orders at the guards and the king alike. "Into the stands! Stay close. More of them may wait beyond the stage."

"Saskia, go with them, please."

Saskia's jaw tightened but she nodded and joined Captain As'enel.

Alistar couldn't give them much more attention as a pair of automatons took interest in him. One carried a length of metal pipe like a club, while the other's arms ended in blades. Both rushed toward him.

He ducked under the blade arm and twisted around to awkwardly deflect the pipe with his cutlass. The strength of the blow vibrated through the blade and up his arm, numbing his fingers.

Someone rushed up behind the blade-hand automaton and leapt onto its back. Alistar saw Cheska's distinctive burgundy coat billow behind her as she scrambled up to the automaton's head. "Thanks for distracting it!" she called.

"You're crazy, and you're welcome," he answered.

"Roddek better be working hard to top this!" She jammed a knife into the automaton's neck seam, trying to pry it open.

The automaton reached for her, awkwardly trying to slash over its back. The club-wielder remained focused on Alistar, preventing him from going to Cheska's aid. As he dodged its swings, Alistar noticed that it had speed and strength, but no particular skill with the weapon. Admittedly, it wouldn't need expertise to smash his ribs if its blows connected.

Cheska seemed to have limited success with her dagger, and

her automaton was determined to get her off its back. With a curse, she dropped to the ground and rolled to her feet as the automaton slammed its blade arm into its own back, leaving a dent in the metal.

"You won't leave here!" Filipp shouted. "This is *my* throne, *my* inheritance, *my* ascension! And these are *my* warriors, who won't fail me the way yours did, Father. These won't allow harm to come to my child."

"Filipp! What are you saying?" King Suelton demanded. He was in the stands now, out of the immediate reach of the automatons.

"It sounds as if your son is saying he intends to murder us all right here and now," Prince Cero answered, his voice cold and calm. Alistar glanced toward the Silver Prince but couldn't tell from his expression whether this was a revelation or a confirmation of an existing suspicion.

"You know who killed Nessa!" Filipp screamed. "You know and you hid them from me!"

Alistar's gaze flickered to King Suelton in time to see the king flinch and look aside, an expression of guilt darting across his face.

Blood and sand, he does *know. It makes sense; someone had to have put the pieces together then actively prevented Filipp from doing so. But the king himself?*

Alistar ducked under the automaton's swing and dodged behind it. "And who convinced you to pull Nessa back from the holiday she should have been taking when the attack happened?" he yelled at the stage. "Who convinced you, if not the very person whose child had the most to gain if the elder, legitimate child was eliminated?"

Filipp surged to his feet. "How *dare* you?!" He jabbed a finger at Alistar. "Kill him!"

Both the club-wielder and the blade-armed automatons rushed at Alistar, but with no coordination between them.

Alistar scrambled behind Blade-Arm, and the other automaton's metal beam slammed into Blade-Arm, knocking it off balance. Alistar threw himself against Blade-Arm, wincing as pain shot through his shoulder at the impact. Despite the significant height and weight difference, Alistar's blow proved enough to send Blade-Arm crashing to the ground. Club continued to attack Alistar, paying no heed to Blade-Arm. It didn't even step over the fallen automaton, but stepped on it, caving Blade-Arm's chest in with one heavy tread. Blade-Arm thrashed, trying to rise, for several seconds more before falling still.

"Two starboard side!" Cheska warned.

Alistar looked to the advancing pair and cursed. Everyone else was engaged in their own battles, and the Royal Guards, though skilled, would be overwhelmed if more automatons emerged from beneath the stage. A clump of guards stood around King Suelton in the stands, out of the immediate fighting, watching with growing fear.

"Knock them off their feet!" Admiral As'enel's order bellowed across the amphitheater with enough force and authority that even Filipp's pair of guards straightened and gripped their weapons as if about to obey.

One of the automatons advancing toward him stuttered to a stop at the admiral's bellow. Its limbs twitched, then it swung its weapon at the legs of its fellow, sending the unsuspecting automaton crashing to the ground.

Alistar pointed at the one still twitching. "Cheska, try to disable that one before it remembers that it's supposed to be attacking me."

She dashed over and scrambled up its back to make another attempt to pry into the inner workings. Alistar ran past the downed one. The club-wielder still pursued him, and like before, it paid no heed to the plight of its fellow. It didn't step on the chest this time but crushed one of the fallen automaton's legs under its heavy treads.

I never thought playing Keep Away as a child would be a survival skill.

Captain As'enel's shout of warning came a moment too late. Pain slashed across Alistar's side. He staggered, pressing a hand to the spot, and felt blood. Club thundered toward him, weapon pulled back for another swing.

Alistar retreated as fast as he dared, each step a sharp stab of pain. On the stage, Filipp shouted orders at the automatons, cursing at them for not having killed everyone already. On every side, guards fought to hold back the relentless tide. Metal creaked and groaned as some of the automatons reached the stands and began to ascend the stairs.

Alistar tripped over a fallen Royal Guard and hit the ground hard. He tried to roll back onto his feet, but the pain in his side took his breath away.

Rechmal, please don't let me die here.

Club staggered, its charge slowing momentarily as something hit it from behind.

"Alistar, get up!" Cheska yelled at him.

"Trying," he managed between gritted teeth, far too quietly for her to hear.

Strong hands lifted him to his feet. "You should get to safety, sir," Star said in his ear, steadying him.

Protests formed on his lips but didn't emerge. The automaton that had been chasing him was now entirely focused on ridding itself of Cheska, who clung to its back. Alistar's eyes moved to a fallen automaton with a crushed chest. He sucked in a sharp breath. Gripping Star's arm tightly, he said, "Am I hallucinating, or is that automaton bleeding?"

"What?" Her gaze followed his, then she was pulling him with her to the fallen machine.

Alistar pressed his arm against his bleeding side. The color that stained his clothes looked far too similar to the liquid he saw seeping from the seams of the automaton's chest plate. Star dropped to a crouch and tried to pry open the plate. It resisted, and she pulled harder. Metal groaned and finally gave way.

Alistar choked on bile and a sound of horror at the grisly scene Star revealed. *A person. There's a person inside the automaton. One of the channelers Sunward collected? But why? How? Why didn't the automatons have a way of storing magic channeled into them? Couldn't they have done that?* His gaze flickered around the inside of the automaton, trying not to focus on the gore. There was no way to be sure without moving the body, but he didn't see anything that resembled an energy reservoir or storage device. With growing horror, he looked up to the rest of the automatons mindlessly following their orders.

"They used people as the power source," he whispered. "There's someone inside each automaton."

He tried to stand, but a wave of darkness washed over his vision for a moment, leaving him lightheaded. Star steadied him quickly. "If they are willing traitors to the crown, they should be glad if they receive a quick death here." She started moving him toward the stands.

"They aren't in control," Alistar said. "If they were, the automatons would coordinate, use strategy, not blindly obey instructions. They wouldn't walk over the bodies of their own. They're victims."

"A swift death now might still be kinder to them," Star said quietly. Raising her voice, she called, "Lady Saskia, your husband needs aid."

Saskia rushed to him carrying the doctor's kit she'd brought in her handbag. Alistar steadied himself, realizing he wasn't the only injured person who'd withdrawn to the stands, and Saskia had been tending to the wounded as best she could under the circumstances.

Her smile was as tight as her voice as she checked the long slash that skimmed his lowest ribs across his side. "You're supposed to *not* stand in the path of the flying blades."

He gripped her arm. "The channelers are trapped inside the automatons, Saskia. Sunward didn't use them to charge the automatons; she's using them as the power source right now."

Color drained from her face. "What?"

Alistar just nodded grimly and started to get to his feet.

Saskia stopped him with a hand on his shoulder, pushing him back down. "You can't help them if you're bleeding. Hold still and I'll be done faster."

He didn't argue, though he wanted to. Every moment, more blood was spilled while Filipp watched from above, showing no sympathy for either the guards who fell or the commoners trapped inside the machines.

"I don't know how to stop them," he whispered.

"None of my speaking stones are working," Saskia told him. "Prince Filipp must have a means of blocking them so no one calls in aid. Do you have any way of drawing the power from those channelers? Can the mahiy lines draw it from them somehow?"

"Maybe. Blood and sand, I wish I'd brought the dragonbane shard." He wished he'd even thought about bringing it. "There must be something."

Saskia finished bandaging him. Before he stood up, she pulled him close and kissed him. "Be careful, Alistar."

"I will," he promised. As he hurried down the steps, another injured guard stumbled into Saskia's care.

He counted ten automatons engaged in battle on the ground and three in the stands, fighting King Suelton's guards. Captain As'enel shouted orders, constantly maneuvering to block the automatons from reaching the king. On the ground, Admiral As'enel had taken charge of one group of guards, and Soluthos and Prince Cero commanded another. Star had returned to Lady Syri, who stood beside her father. He didn't see Cheska immediately, but the automaton that had been chasing him lay face-down on the ground.

Filipp stood. "Incompetent! I told you to *kill them!*"

Alistar's side still burned and each step sent a throb of pain through the injury. "Maybe your new warriors aren't as traitorous as you, Prince Filipp."

Filipp glared at him. "They don't have *opinions*, they have *orders!*"

"Do you even know *what* they are?" Alistar countered, moving toward Prince Cero's group. "Or do you just not care that your own subjects were deceived and compelled? That they are caged inside those machines?"

"Peasants have no purpose but to fulfill the wishes of their betters," Filipp snapped.

Beside Filipp, his aide shifted uncomfortably, gaze shifting to the automatons.

Prince Cero's guards drew Alistar into their midst, and he found himself next to the Silver Prince. Despite the situation, Prince Cero's voice was calm and cool. "Expound please, Senior Engineer De'seneth. Our subjects are inside these abominations?"

Alistar didn't know if his theory was correct, but he didn't have time to qualify his explanation. "Internal channelers. Sunward has been collecting them from the slums and Lower City with promises of a new drug. She's found a way to harness their magic and force them to channel it into the automatons. However, she either didn't bother or didn't have time to create an internal power storage system for the automatons. Instead, she put the channelers themselves inside the automatons to act as the power source. I don't believe they're there willingly or that they have any knowledge of how they're being used. They're not traitors by choice. If we can manipulate the mahiy lines in some way to interfere with their abilities, we might be able to disable the automatons."

"Would have to be something that could be changed rapidly," Lady Syri said. She didn't project the same confidence as her father. "Do you have ideas? They aren't drawing from the mahiy lines, so are you suggesting we amplify the lines high enough that they project ambient interference?"

Alistar thought quickly, recalling the map in his office. "Cut the connection to the Middle City and pull exclusively from the Upper City and the noble districts. Change the line harmonization to one that doesn't draw from any lines where frost's breath has been integrated."

Prince Cero's frown deepened. "I should very much like to know the reason behind this theory, as well as how you acquired such knowledge of these channelers and of Sunward's involvement. And why I was not made aware of the same." He turned to Syri. "Go. Attempt De'seneth's proposal."

She nodded to both of them and broke from the group at a sprint, Star and another guard accompanying her.

"Soluthos, go with Lady Syri. Your Highness, I'll be glad to explain once the king's life's not in danger," Alistar said, drawing his cutlass.

"No, De'seneth, I fully expect you to provide a full dissertation, complete with handouts, right now," Prince Cero said, deadpan.

"Ah. I must apologize, then, for leaving the handouts in my office," Alistar said. "I had a few other things on my mind. Like taking steps to ensure this ambush didn't go as smoothly as your nephew intended."

"I knew there was some reason for your entire family to be here," the Silver Prince said under his breath.

Movement from the pavilion entrance caught Alistar's eye. He turned and saw Rykka sprint in. He didn't see Roddek with her and worry spiked. She ran toward him, though he was sure he saw her grimace at the sight of Prince Cero. When the guards shifted to block her, Alistar said, "She's one of mine."

They let her into their defensive ring. She paused a moment to catch her breath. "Roddek's with Windshadow and Syri. Said she wanted our cart to get across the Exhibition. Merris is dealt with. Guest is safe and with my brother, back to the manor."

"Understood." Pietro under the watch of Tiyron wasn't what Alistar considered "safe," but saying so in front of Prince Cero would tell him far more than Alistar wanted to reveal.

"There's more. Channelers are trapped inside the automatons."

"We just found that out," Alistar told her, and his voice betrayed his horror at the discovery.

She glanced around the battle and winced at how he must have learned. "We found a missing Crown agent trapped in a semi-functional one. Drugged, couldn't tell us much except that something was happening here."

"You found a Crown agent?" Prince Cero demanded. "Who? Where?"

"Don't know her name. She wasn't fit to say anything, really. Sent her with my brother to De'seneth's manor. Do know a way to disable the automatons thanks to her. Have to get at the back of their necks, though." She touched her left shoulder. "Indent around here has a release for the chest plate. Open it and they disable."

"Go tell the admiral," Alistar told her. "And tell Cheska! She's been climbing all over these things."

Rykka nodded quickly and dashed toward Admiral As'enel.

Roddek and Rykka are both alive. Thank the gods. And they found Pietro.

"You heard her," Prince Cero said. "Disable those automatons!"

While some of the prince's guards kept the automatons' attention, Alistar and others scrambled onto the automatons' backs. The smooth metal was harder to hold onto than a wooden mast, and Alistar's injured side screamed at him. He was certain he was bleeding through Saskia's careful bandaging.

The automaton attempted to throw him off as he scrabbled

to keep his grip. As he sought a better hold, his fingers found an indent on the shoulder. Inside it, he felt a ring that yielded when he pulled on it.

The automaton under him suddenly fell slack. The sudden stop caused him to lose his grip and he slid to the ground, knocking his breath from him when he landed. He braced for an attack, but none came.

Filipp screamed in wordless fury. He tore something from his belt and raised his hand to throw it.

His aide lunged, grabbing his arm and attempting to wrest the object from his grasp. The two men guarding Filipp spun to attack the aide as the crown prince cursed and fought against his aide. Filipp's guards stabbed at the aide, but their blades skidded off an unseen barrier. Alistar looked for Rykka and saw her gazing intently at the platform, threads of purple light flowing to her from the mahiy lines overhead.

The aide's eyes were wide with panic. He ripped the object from Filipp's hands and stumbled back against the barrier. Filipp snarled and tried to grab it, only to discover that the barrier had shrunk to enclose only the terrified aide.

The light from the mahiy lines pulsed brighter. Rykka's gaze snapped up toward them, then to Alistar, silently asking if he knew what was happening. He raised his hand and signed the Rillwater signal that indicated "part of the plan." He wondered what the rapid changes to the magic felt like to her while channeling.

With a loud crash, one of the automatons trying to reach King Suelton fell back, then through the stands, smashing into the ground. The stands trembled alarmingly, and more so when the automaton stood up and began smashing the supports around it.

Alistar started toward it, but stumbled, pressing a hand to his side. He felt blood leaking into his clothes again. The sound of his mother shouting orders seemed to come from a great distance. Someone caught his arm and steadied him, but he wasn't expecting to hear Prince Cero's voice in his ear.

"One, if not both, of your parents would undoubtedly hold me personally responsible if you were to fall here, De'seneth. In addition, I'd have to train another engineer to handle your duties, and I've yet to see any of the more junior engineers display sufficient skill."

Alistar tried not to laugh. "Apologies, Your Highness. I'd hate for my death to inconvenience you."

"As you should. And it would. See to it that you don't, and let those not already injured deal with that."

Filipp and his guards still tried to break through the barrier, Filipp screaming profanities and vile threats. Above them, the glow of the mahiy lines intensified until Alistar couldn't look at them directly. Long exposure to such intensity caused harm to living beings, but Alistar hoped it would only take a burst to disrupt the internal channelers.

If it works at all.

"Rykka! Flare coming!" he yelled, hoping she would understand and stop drawing from the lines before the magic reached its peak energy.

"Hematic perdition, *what* are you doing?" she yelled back.

He clapped a hand over his eyes as a burst of violet light flashed from the mahiy lines. Voices shouted and screamed in alarm and pain. Metal crashed against metal or against ground.

Then everything fell silent.

CHAPTER 57

Alistar blinked away afterimages, head spinning. All around, the automatons stood unmoving, limbs slack. Dazed guards cast looks around, searching for an enemy that for the moment no longer threatened them.

It worked. Thank the gods, it worked.

"You! What did you do?" Filipp jabbed a finger at Alistar.

The prince's pair of guards sprang off the stage and rushed at Alistar, blades raised to cut him down. From the corners of his eyes, Alistar saw movement from either side of him. One cutlass and one military saber intercepted the attacks before he could raise his own blade. Cheska was on his left, Soluthos on his right. Alistar let out a breath of relief.

"Thanks."

"I gotta stay ahead of Roddek!" Cheska told him with an impish grin, never taking her eyes off the guard. "Now you, fellow, you should be asking yourself if you really want to be part of the prince's failed insurrection."

"Insurrection?" scoffed the man. "His Highness *is* the heir."

"Who you just left unguarded," Soluthos observed mildly.

Both guards glanced back to Prince Filipp at that, a careless, if understandable, mistake. Their first mistake, though, had been leaving Filipp without a guard in the first place.

Admiral As'enel stood before the crown prince, his blade leveled at Filipp's neck.

"I'll ask you nicely once to stand down, boy. Decline, and I'll ask less nicely."

Filipp's jaw tightened. Hands clenched, he growled, "You dare?"

"You threatened my son. I take that personally."

Slowly, bitterly, Prince Filipp held out empty hands in a gesture of surrender. On the ground, his guards lowered their weapons. The prince's aide remained huddled behind the throne, making no attempt to escape.

Soluthos disarmed Filipp's men while Prince Cero's guards rushed onto the stage to secure Filipp. Cheska caught Alistar's arm and pulled him toward the stands.

"You're really pale. Are you hurt?"

"Yeah. Saskia patched me up a little, but I'm pretty lightheaded," Alistar admitted, leaning against her. "Need to disable the automatons, though. Don't know how long until they recover from the burst."

"Darkwood's on it," Cheska assured him. "I know Roddek's upset at her over something or another, but from what I saw here, he'd be stupid not to have her in his crew. And if he's *that* stubborn about it, I'll take Darkwood in my crew any day."

"I'd give her a place here if she wanted to stay," Alistar said. "But she doesn't. Glad she'll have a spot in the fleet regardless." His vision was dark around the edges. "Need to sit."

She eased him to the ground. Moments later, Saskia was at his side, peeling up his shirt and applying pressure to the wound. Alistar focused on breathing and staying conscious.

He looked up when steps approached. Prince Cero stood over him, expression difficult to read. "I've called for a healer.

They should arrive soon—I impressed on them the need for haste."

"Thank you," Saskia said.

"I suspect the thanks should be going toward you rather than from you," Prince Cero said. "As I suspect the degree to which your family was prepared for this event is not coincidental, De'seneth."

"Very As'enel of me," Alistar murmured.

Before the Silver Prince responded, King Suelton and his guards reached the ground nearby, escorted by Captain As'enel. Alistar's mother strode quickly to him, and though she didn't speak it, he sensed her concern. Alistar tried to stand, and Saskia helped him to his feet to face the king.

Every one of King Suelton's hundred and eighty years hung heavy on his face. The white-haired monarch wearily approached Prince Cero and gripped his brother's arm. "Are you injured?" he asked.

"No," Prince Cero assured him. "You appear to have come through unscathed."

"Thanks to Lady... Captain As'enel, yes." King Suelton nodded to the captain. His shoulders sank when he looked to the stage. "I never thought Filipp capable of this. I would have *given* him the throne. I wanted to surprise him. Ever since he announced this Exhibition, I intended to step down, pass the crown to him then. To let this be his coronation celebration as well as his Exhibition." He closed his eyes. "I'm so *tired* of it all, Cero. So tired, and I couldn't even see my own son plotting my demise. I wanted to see him crowned and seated on the throne, not hanging on a gibbet. I have no other heir."

Pain stripped away Alistar's restraints against speaking his mind. "I'm glad you're at least not suggesting that Pietro could take the throne, Your Majesty."

King Suelton looked at Alistar in surprise, as if he hadn't

realized Alistar was there, but his face didn't hold the same scandalized shock as everyone else's.

Alistar continued. "Filipp was right. You do know who was responsible for the assassination attempt that killed his wife and daughter."

"As, it seems, do you," King Suelton said. "You must be the As'enel heir. The one who already preserved our throne once. Did Cero put you on the scent again?"

"Not to my knowledge," the Silver Prince said, frowning.

"I was looking into what originally appeared to be a separate matter at Lady Syri's request, sire," Alistar said.

"And what matter would that be?" Prince Cero cut in.

Alistar turned to him. "Lady Sunward. Who, it turned out, maneuvered her way to the point that she had both princes as her lovers and at her beck and call."

Heavy silence fell over his listeners.

After a long moment, Prince Cero spoke. "You implied that she had a part in the assassination of Filipp's family."

"Yes, I believe she did." Alistar's gaze was on King Suelton. "But she's not the person who put it in motion. And knowing how thoroughly the evidence was covered up, it makes sense that you would know, Your Majesty. Who else would have the authority to keep that knowledge out of Filipp's hands?"

"Then how is it you know?" King Suelton asked.

"Pietro told me."

Soluthos cleared his throat. "I witnessed Prince Pietro's confession and corroborate this account."

"You know where Pietro is?" King Suelton asked.

Alistar nodded. "I do, Your Highness. He's as safe as he can be at the moment."

"Sunward's not here, Alistar," Captain As'enel said.

He cursed at the reminder. "Cheska, grab Roddek and Darkwood. Get to the manor as fast as possible."

Cheska ran off without so much as an apology to the royals. He saw her speak to Rykka briefly, then dash on to find Roddek.

"Are speaking stones working?" Alistar asked. "Tell Dorne too." He noticed that Rykka had moved close enough that she could probably hear at least some of their conversation.

"They're working," Prince Cero said. "And I don't know why that damned healer hasn't arrived yet."

Healer... "The channelers in the automatons. The healer should check them as well. I don't know how the burst affected them."

Prince Cero eyed him. "They've committed treason, De'seneth."

He shook his head. "They're not there willingly." He was confident of that. He'd seen the cramped interior. He'd seen the restraints that held the channelers in place. "They were drugged and forced to serve as a power source. Doubt they had much, if any, control."

"Those people are victims," Captain As'enel said firmly. "Sunward manipulated and abused them."

Prince Cero didn't look convinced. "So far, none have been found conscious, though it appears most are alive, aside from those who were killed during the ambush." His gaze sharpened on Alistar. "Perhaps once the healer has tended to you, you can explain more about the nature of this... situation and how we found ourselves in it."

"I'm sure Lady Syri can speak to it as well," Alistar said. It likely wouldn't deflect all the Silver Prince's ire off himself, but Lady Syri could fill in many details for her father. "Your pardon, Your Majesty, Your Highness, but I think I need to... sit..."

Saskia eased him back to sit on the bare dirt. Moments later, an elf in healer's robes rushed into the amphitheater under the escort of two guards. Prince Cero directed the man to Alistar first. Upon seeing the vicious slash across Alistar's side, the healer made a sound of distress and set to work immediately. Alistar's attention faded from the discussions happening around him as numbness and warmth flooded through him.

CHAPTER 58

One criminal, one drugged agent of the Crown, and one treasonous prince. If it were a chapter in a Masked Thief pulp novel, Tiyron would engage in witty repartee with the prince, deftly maneuvering through arguments, counterarguments, effortless exposing flaws in the prince's logic until the royal had no choice but to sullenly concede.

In reality, there was no conversation, witty or otherwise, just sullen silence. Prince Pietro's hands were still bound behind his back. The one time the prince had started to speak, Tiyron threatened to remove his own sock and use it as a gag. The carriage window curtains were drawn shut so Pietro couldn't see where they were or where they might be going, and he wisely hadn't asked.

"Is that woman dead?" Pietro's question broke the silence.

"Which woman?" Tiyron countered. "Your guard here? Clearly not."

"Obviously not her." Pietro's jaw tightened, as if he were trying to resist admitting something. Tiyron waited, one eyebrow raised slightly. "Merris. Is she dead?"

"Oh, so you *do* know the name of someone outside your station. How scandalous. Yes. She is."

Pietro looked slightly reassured, despite his situation. Tiyron couldn't bring himself to mock the prince's fear. He knew what Merris could do too. He had nightmares about her torturing him.

Rykka and Roddek probably hadn't reached the Exhibition yet. Tiyron wondered whether the fight had already begun there.

The carriage rounded a corner, and the sounds of other people and vehicles faded as they moved away from the higher traffic areas. Some minutes later, they finally stopped. Pietro shifted uneasily, glancing at the door as if he expected to be manhandled and thrown to the ground.

Tiyron stood. The confined space of the carriage gave him enough surfaces to brace again without looking obvious. "I'm blindfolding you now."

Pietro drew breath to protest, looked Tiyron in the eye, and left the words unsaid. He submitted to Tiyron wrapping a strip of cloth over his eyes and around his head. Tiyron lifted the edge of the curtain and looked out the window.

The carriage driver caught the movement and nodded to him. Tiyron opened the curtain further. They were parked on one side of the manor near a servants' entrance. The butler, Dorne, stood beside the door with a handful of the staff. All De'seneth's people, presumably. Tiyron opened the carriage door and climbed out. The driver had his chair already set up and waiting. Tiyron eased himself into it, appreciating the comfort after the hard carriage seat.

"He's in there, blindfolded," Tiyron told Dorne. "Along with a woman we found there. Don't know her name. Better get a healer to check her over."

"Lord Lamorage is here," Dorne said. He walked to Tiyron and leaned close. "Lord De'seneth warned that Sunward might attempt to infiltrate the manor while everyone else is occupied with the tour. If you choose to go into the depths of the manor unescorted, I won't stop you."

Tiyron nodded curtly. "You got this?" He nodded toward the carriage.

Dorne nodded. "I've got this. Also, another Crown agent is on her way. Investigator Dawncloud. She was with Darkwood when they found him." He nodded at the carriage.

Tiyron entered the manor. Inside, it was quiet, even when he passed the perimeter set by the Rillwater staff. He thought back through his time spent with Cemar and his followers, searching for any faces that matched people he'd seen here who might still work for Sunward. None came immediately to mind. Maybe she'd assumed Merris could handle things herself and hadn't had time or opportunity to get someone else in after Merris got the boot.

Or she'd recruited more people and was using them instead of underlings he knew.

With no particular hurry, he swung by the kitchen to grab a small meal, then entered the ballroom.

So strange to see it empty. How many events did I attend here? How many evenings did Cemar spend on the balcony with me, trying to convince me to join his cause?

He didn't like thinking about that. The pain of betrayal cut too deep. He directed his chair to the concealed door and down the stairs, past guards who acknowledged but didn't stop him.

If Sunward comes, where will she go? She wouldn't come in the front doors—probably through one of the secret entrances, and possibly not one I know about. Merris might have unlocked other entrances while she was here.

So, would Sunward head for the flower first? She'd want to ensure no one could interrupt her and that even if she couldn't force everyone upstairs to leave, no one else could get into the basement. He rubbed his forehead in thought. *Cemar said something about ways to seal the basement. Not from the room with the flower, though. He mentioned a specific channel to... where? I remember joking that he'd know if Sunward were mad at him, because she could lock him out.*

Her study. That's where he said it was.

With a touch, he sent the chair racing down the hall, navigating by memory. He'd always preferred the side routes rather than opening the direct path with the crystal chimes. Some of the concealed doors were still closed, but he remembered the locations of the latches as if he'd used them yesterday.

Or a month ago, not... two years. Hematic perdition, how could I have been in a timestop that long? Those trinkets were meant to be novelties, used for pranks or distractions. How did it survive... how did I survive two years? Maybe there really is something to Rykka's human gods. Because it certainly wasn't the doing of the elven ones.

The door slid open. He came to the end of the hall, a solid panel of wood in front of him. Tiyron ran his hand over it until he found a raised bolt. He worked the plug free and peered into the room.

Lamorage scribbled notes as he pushed back from the desk, starting to stand. The healer muttered, "Be right there, be right there, just need to get this down before I forget..." A speaking stone lay on the desk, but it was dark and inactive, leading Tiyron to conclude he was talking to himself rather than Dorne. He dropped the pen into the inkwell and scooped the speaking stone into his pocket, starting toward the door. Tiyron waited for him to leave before opening the door in the bookshelf.

Lamorage jerked to a sudden stop at the doorway, spine stiffening. Tiyron leaned as far as he could, but from the spy hole, he couldn't see what had stopped the healer. Lamorage stepped back once, then again, and a third time. "How did you get here?"

"How did *I* get into a house I designed, into the study *I* configured specifically for my personal use? I knew you weren't all that bright, Lamorage, but do you really need to ask?" A woman stepped into Tiyron's field of view. A bun contained most of her golden brown hair. An expression of contempt painted her high-boned face. She wore gray trousers and a loose-fit shirt with long sleeves.

"How did you get inside?" Lamorage reached toward his pocket.

"Hands where I can see them, Lamorage. Someone left a door open for me. I should ask what you are doing in my study. Looking for something?"

Lamorage didn't answer—a tactic Tiyron approved of, since his assessment of the man so far didn't incline him to think the healer was a good liar.

Sunward held a hand crossbow, currently pointed at Lamorage. He held his hands open at his sides, backing into the center of the room at her instruction. Sunward strode to the desk and looked over the papers. She raised an eyebrow at Lamorage. "Have you taken an interest in human mythology now?"

"As much as you did," Lamorage said. "Why are you here? What do you want?"

Her eyes narrowed. "I want what's mine. My family's legacy." Her lips curled in a smile that never reached her eyes. "I know what you want, though. You want that sweet release, that surge of euphoria and power. You want something no one but me can give you." She took a pouch from her pocket and tossed it on the floor between them. "It's called Lumination."

Lamorage drew a sharp breath. "I don't want your drugs."

She laughed. "Don't you? As if you don't search and scrape for every sliver of Ambrosia you can find. You loved it. You craved the escape from your failures. And look at you now— playing lapdog to a new master. Go ahead. Take the pouch. Escape again."

Lamorage's hands trembled. "No, I—"

Tiyron didn't open the bookshelf, but he projected his voice to disguise the source, and he pitched it lower in imitation of

Cemar. "Come now, dearest, trying to shove drugs down some-one's throat already? You just got here."

Lamorage flinched with a choked gasp. Sunward's gaze darted around the room.

"What? How?"

"You don't think death would stop me, do you?"

Lamorage edged back, and Tiyron could see his eyes wide with panic. The healer tripped over a stack of books and fell to the floor.

"Death stops pretty much everyone, so you're not Cemar." Sunward continued to scan the room. She took a step toward the bookcase that separated Tiyron from her. "Leaving the far more interesting question as to who you *are*."

Tiyron threw himself out of the chair onto the floor a heart-beat before a crossbow bolt slammed through the bookshelf and imbedded itself into the back of his chair. He made himself stand and spoke again, still pitching his voice similar to Cemar's. "Hmm, good guess, but not good enough. But if I'm not your 'beloved', who could I possibly be?"

He heard her rush to the bookcase, and pressed himself against the wall where he would have the most shadows. He searched for the scalpel he'd stolen from the clinic, only to remember that he'd relinquished it and the knife to Rykka.

"It doesn't matter who you are—I'll let the gods sort *that* out," Sunward snarled. The bookcase began to slide open. Light fell on his chair and the bolt in it. "What in—"

Sunward started to step into the passage. Tiyron knew how the tunnels carried sound. He knew how to pitch his voice to echo until it came from all directions and no direction at all. And he had long ago perfected a deep, mocking laugh. The sound of it filled the hall. Sunward jerked back with a gasp. Before he could congratulate himself, though, she shoved the bookcase open the rest of the way and leveled her handheld crossbow at him.

Her eyes narrowed and her brow pinched in puzzlement. "Who are you?"

Tiyron leaned against the wall in a casual pose. "Really, Celyn? I can understand Merris not recognizing me at first, but you?" He tsked. "After all those nights your lover spent trying to woo me?"

When he spoke in his own voice, he saw recognition glint in her eyes, but she shook her head. "No. I don't know what corpse-eating face-stealer you are, but Tiyron is dead."

"Everyone wants to think that," he sighed. "Can't accept that Cemar did a piss-poor job of it, despite seeing how all the rest of his plans fell apart?"

"Get in here where I can see you," she ordered.

Tiyron shrugged and entered the study, walking slowly to keep himself from limping. Lamorage blinked when he saw Tiyron, but the healer didn't say anything. Tiyron pretended not to notice that Lamorage's hand had been in the pocket with the speaking stone.

Tiyron found another wall to lean against, though he was careful to keep his hands where Sunward could see them, not wanting to try dodging another crossbow bolt.

"What's your game?" he asked Sunward. "Trying to continue Cemar's plot? Or aiming for something more interesting?"

"Cemar's plot failed. I have my own. But the goal is still the throne of Calarand."

He nodded thoughtfully. "Might as well aim high if you're going to try, right? What about all that gibberish you were talking before about human mythology? You aren't still trying to make that be something, are you? I mean, sure, it worked on the Successors, but they're a bunch of raving fanatics anyway."

"Gibberish?" she snapped, glaring at him. "You think my family's legacy is *gibberish*, Tiyron? You've seen Rechmal's gift! You *know* it's real!

Good to know that's still a fast way to rile her up.

"Sure, a big plant that puts out a lot of magic. We already have those, and I don't hear people claiming that *our* flowers came personally from some god." He waved a dismissive hand.

I hope Lamorage actually alerted someone. I can probably keep her talking for a while—she loves the sound of her own voice almost as much as Cemar did—but it won't do us any good unless someone else is coming to deal with her. I'm not fast enough or strong enough to take her yet.

She made a sound of annoyance. "You're as frustrating as ever. And what are you even doing here?"

"I heard this place had a new owner who didn't know its secrets. I figured I'd see what might be tucked away here or there. Wasn't able to get in until recently, though." The lie came easily. "I also heard you got run out of town. Didn't expect to see you here."

He watched her eyes, saw her assessment shift, saw her suspicions relent slightly. She didn't know he had any connection to the current residents of the manor. But then her eyes narrowed again. "You were at the gathering we invited the supposed As'enel heir to. You *helped* him."

What gathering? Ah, blight, must be something Rykka didn't mention. But if Sunward was there, Cemar were there. His mouth tightened in a thin, angry line. "After what Cemar did to me, I didn't care if that man was the Narnan crown prince. I was taking away Cemar's new toy."

"*You* ruined Cemar's plans."

"Cemar ruined his own plans when he betrayed me."

A shadow moved in the study doorway, slinking into the room behind Sunward's back.

"I don't trust you, Tiyron," Sunward said. "And why did you bring up Merris? Why not Larisa instead? She's the one who claimed to have seen you."

His breath hitched. *Larisa.* "You're drugging her again, aren't you?"

"Larisa begged me for something to replace Ambrosia. Just like this one craves it." She nodded toward Lamorage.

Lamorage's hands clenched in fists. "I don't want or need your drugs."

She ignored him and picked the bag up from the floor. "Care to give this a try, Tiyron? A new drug called Lumination. It'll take away your pain."

Tiyron's eyes narrowed.

Sunward laughed. "Yes, I can see you're in pain, and that chair in the hall is evidence enough."

"And you think you can make me another addled minion like Larisa?" he countered.

Her gaze and voice grew chill. She raised the crossbow to point at his chest. "You can take Lumination, or I can kill you now."

The shadow sprang into motion, becoming an auburn-haired elven woman in dark clothing. She rushed Sunward, throwing a pouch that burst in a thick cloud of white powder. Tiyron shoved himself toward the passage that had been concealed by the bookcase, but his legs finally reached their limits and his right knee buckled when he put his weight on it. He fell to the floor with a heavy grunt.

He heard the crossbow release but didn't feel any sharp bursts of pain, nor did he hear any cries of pain to indicate it found another target. The obscuring cloud gradually settled. He saw the auburn-haired woman holding Sunward in an armlock with the crossbow pointed toward an upper corner of the study. Sunward cursed and tried to break free.

"By order of His Majesty King Suelton, surrender," Auburn-Hair said.

"King Suelton is dead," Sunward scoffed. "And King Filipp will most certainly order my release."

"Oh, are you talking about Filipp's ambush at the Exhibition grounds? With the automatons you had Ravencrest building?" Tiyron asked, rolling onto his back and sitting up.

Her gaze snapped toward him in shock.

He continued. "Because that's going to fail, if it hasn't already."

"How do you— *Why* would *you* interfere?"

Tiyron snorted. "Even the senile old codger would be a better ruler than *you*."

Auburn-Hair gave him a pointedly disapproving look. "If you're done insulting your monarch, give me a hand."

Tiyron turned to Lamorage. "You'd better handle that part. I'm just gonna sit here for a while."

Lamorage cast him a concerned look, but Tiyron waved it off. Sunward tried to break free again as Lamorage twisted the crossbow from her grip. "This isn't done, Tiyron."

"Pretty sure it is," he told her. With a gesture at the manor, he said, "They know the princes are dancing on your puppet strings. They know about the automatons, they know about Lumination, they know about the channelers inside the automatons, they know about the flowers." He smirked. "They even know that *your* version of the myth is wrong, and that the nameless champion you admire so much actually stole the seed, and it wasn't gifted to him at all."

"That's a *lie!*" she screamed. "A blasphemous *lie!*"

"You think that champion stuffed his own people into automatons like you did? Or did you get that idea from the necromancer he fought?"

She shrieked like an enraged siren. Lamorage winced as he assisted Auburn-Hair in restraining Sunward and binding her hands. Sunward's seething glare never left Tiyron until she was dragged out of the room.

Tiyron sighed heavily and leaned against the closest wall. In solitude, he finally allowed himself to squeeze his eye shut and suck in short, sharp gasps of air. Every bone in his body hurt, but that pain was secondary to the stabbing torment of betrayal.

She knew what Cemar did to me. She didn't care. Don't even know why I expected something different from a woman who murdered her adopted siblings, but... I did. I expected the alliance we made to MATTER! He gritted his teeth. *Instead they imprisoned and tortured me.*

Footsteps approached rapidly. He raised his head and opened his eye. Rykka rushed in. Dirt and blood streaked her face and clothes, and she was breathing heavily as she scrambled to his side. Behind her, Roddek followed, looking less worse for wear than Rykka.

"Are you hurt?" she asked. "Lamorage said Sunward had a crossbow."

He let out a breath. "Just aching. Tired. She missed me. Chair's in the hall behind me."

Roddek pulled the chair into the study, grimacing at the bolt jutting through the back. He snapped the bolt and freed the two halves from the cushion.

"Exhibition?" Tiyron asked.

"Filipp's in custody and the automatons are disabled. De'seneth won't let the channelers be executed without some kind of trial." She paused a moment. "All the channelers I saw were unconscious, but I did see Larisa. She's still alive."

Hematic perdition, I don't want to have to thank De'seneth for anything. But if he can use whatever sway he has to protect Larisa and the other channelers, then he'll have earned it.

Roddek lifted Tiyron into the chair without asking, and Tiyron was too tired to do more than glare at the privateer over it. "Why'd you come here?" Tiyron asked.

Roddek spoke. "My brother's orders. Sunward wasn't at the Exhibition, so the next best guess was she'd come here to attempt to reclaim the manor."

"Little late," Tiyron muttered.

"Ran into a complication we had to address when one of the staff tried to knife Pietro. Sorry," Rykka said. "Roddek's sister Cheska is making sure everything's settled upstairs with regards to that situation. Pietro's not injured. The staff member seems to have been one of Sunward's people who kept their head down until now."

"Who was the woman who arrested Sunward?"

"Investigator Dawncloud. She's not bad, for a Crown agent."

Tiyron directed his chair toward the main study entrance. Rykka and Roddek followed him out, down the hall, and up the stairs back into the study on the ground floor. As his chair crested the steps, Tiyron heard Lamorage.

"Yes, she's most certainly pregnant, somewhere just past six months, though she hardly shows. And no, I can't tell who the father is, except that he's an elf."

"Blight and rot," Dawncloud cursed. "That complicates things. Are you *certain* you can't tell who the father is?"

Tiyron considered both of them. "Problem?"

"Our recent arrestee might be carrying the heir to the throne, so, yes," Dawncloud said bluntly. "And that problem is that we don't *know* if she is."

Tiyron snorted. "And you had to get stuck with an honest healer, right?" He turned to Lamorage, whose brow knit in confusion. "Just say the kid's Filipp's."

"But I can't be sure—" Lamorage began.

"Just *say* it, Lamorage. Sunward is pregnant with Crown Prince Filipp's bastard. Problem resolved. Right?" He shot a look at Dawncloud.

"As long as we have more than one *reliable* witness to his statement, yes."

Lamorage looked distinctly uncomfortable with the lie. "But I cannot be sure! I *do not know* who the child's father is."

Rykka and Roddek had come up the stairs after him, and both listened without interrupting. Tiyron leaned forward in his chair. "The king is how old now? He's not going to spawn another kid. The Silver Prick isn't much younger. Either one could keel over any day. The Silver Prick at least *has* an heir. You want to see how fast the nobles go for blood if the king dies with no clear successor?"

Lamorage swallowed hard. "Lady... Lady Sunward is pregnant with... with Crown Prince Filipp's child," he managed hesitantly.

"There you go. The healer said it, and you witnessed it."

"To be accepted, we still require a second reliable witness," Dawncloud reminded him.

Tiyron jerked his thumb toward Roddek. "Is an As'enel good enough?"

Roddek cleared his throat and bowed. "Captain Roddek As'enel of Rillwater."

Dawncloud's lips quirked in a smile. "If the rumors I've heard of your family are accurate, I wouldn't want to be the person who said the word of an As'enel *wasn't* good enough. Are you willing to swear testimony that you bore witness to this statement of paternity?"

"Yes, I am," Roddek said without hesitation.

"Thank you." Dawncloud turned to Lamorage. "And my thanks to you as well. If you will excuse me, I have a report to make."

CHAPTER 59

Arms still bound behind his back but no longer blindfolded, Prince Pietro sat in a plain wooden chair, eyes fixed on the floor, refusing to look at anyone. Alistar had seen him glance up when people entered the room, but the heavy, sad expression on King Suelton's face and the hard one that Prince Cero bore had told the prince more than enough. No argument he could make would absolve him. So instead, he chose silence, staring at the stone floor of the cellar where he'd been confined.

Alistar was glad Pietro was here rather than in a cage in the basement. He'd easily explained the cellar when Dorne had told him about one of Sunward's followers attacking Pietro. A cage wasn't so easily excused.

"Pietro," King Suelton said.

Pietro's jaw tightened, but he didn't respond otherwise.

"Pietro. Look at me."

Pietro let out a heavy breath. "Why?"

"Because your king told you to, boy," Prince Cero said.

Pietro finally raised his head. His eyes were ringed with dark shadows. His hair was unbound and filthy, his clothes rumpled and unwashed. "There. Happy now?" He didn't sound as sullen as Alistar expected, rather, resigned and exhausted.

"No," King Suelton said quietly. "There's no joy to losing my children."

"What do you want me to do, Father? Throw myself at your feet and beg? Should I be wracked with guilt? Proclaim myself changed? Contrite? What difference does it make now?"

"How long was this going on?" Prince Cero demanded.

"Depends what you mean," Pietro sighed heavily. "The automatons? The drugs? Sunward? Assassination plots? Which part, Uncle?"

"What came first?" Prince Cero watched him with cold, hard eyes.

"Sunward, about a year ago. An acquaintance introduced us."

"Just to you, or to Filipp as well?" Alistar asked.

"I don't know how she met him. Didn't ask, neither of them offered."

King Suelton spoke, his voice shaky. "Were you planning to assassinate him before then?"

Pietro's jaw tightened. "No. Hadn't seriously considered it." He looked back at the floor for a moment, then lifted his head almost defiantly. "Does it make things any *better* that I didn't want Nessa harmed? That I only intended to murder my brother and his wife, not my niece as well?"

Alistar spoke. "Sunward was involved with both Prince Filipp and Prince Pietro at that point. I suspect she purposely convinced Filipp not to allow his daughter to leave on her holiday to ensure Nessa *was* in the path of the assassins. I also suspect, though haven't confirmed, that Filipp was with her that night, ensuring that he wasn't present when the attack happened."

"It was a while after that when she told us about the automatons," Pietro said. "Don't know where she got the idea, but she couldn't get the materials without assistance. Then it... grew from there."

"There are very good *reasons* that automatons are not allowed to kill," Prince Cero growled. "To say nothing of a dozen treaties that would be broken."

"Did you know how the machines were powered?" King Suelton asked.

Pietro nodded.

"Those are *our people*, Pietro!"

"They're rabble from the slums."

"You think that justifies using them as something less than animals?"

Pietro said nothing.

King Suelton turned and walked toward the cellar door. Prince Cero cast Pietro a hard look and followed. Pietro glanced at Alistar uneasily, as if expecting a beating. Alistar met his gaze, held it, then broke it, leaving after the monarch. He closed and locked the door behind him, leaving Pietro alone in the dim light of the cellar.

The Royal Guards swept around King Suelton and Prince Cero protectively. At Alistar's invitation, the group moved to the sitting room. Rillwater staff brought refreshments, then withdrew.

"Has my nephew been here the whole time he's been missing?" Prince Cero demanded.

"Most of it," Alistar said. "One of my people assisted Investigator Dawncloud in raiding the lair of a Lower City criminal and drug dealer by the name of Whitetooth. They interrupted a meeting between Whitetooth and the nobleman who supplied him with drugs. Upon capturing the nobleman, they discovered he was Prince Pietro."

"Why wasn't this reported?"

"Because at that time, it was the only evidence we had. Neither my agent nor Investigator Dawncloud has the authority or reputation to survive accusing one of the king's sons of conspiracy and possible treason. Keeping him here, where I could prevent him from assisting Sunward further, was the best option I had, Your Highness."

"Though it pains me to say, Lord As'enel, you have done a great service to Calarand," King Suelton said. "I fear my line may never be able to repay the debts we owe to your family. Like my father before me, I seem able only to indebt us further. If there is any boon you would ask of us, speak it."

Other debts? What other debts? And what happened that the previous king also owed us a debt?

"There are several things I must ask, but they're boons for Lewarden, not myself. The first, Your Majesty, is that the channelers who were forced to power the automatons not be treated as traitors, but as victims. I ask that they receive the best care possible until they have recovered. Assuming they do wake again." No one knew how the mahiy surge might have affected or damaged them, and so far, none of the internal channelers from the Exhibition had gained consciousness.

"Very well," King Suelton agreed. "What else do you ask?"

Alistar turned to Prince Cero. The Silver Prince's icy anger had not thawed in the hours since the ambush at the Exhibition. "Your Highness, Silverline Power needs to cease all experiments with frost's breath immediately."

Prince Cero's spine stiffened instantly. "Your success in defending against usurpers does not give you leave to dictate my policy and research, De'seneth."

"I'm not speaking as Senior Engineer De'seneth, sir. I'm speaking as Alistar As'enel, heir to the fleets of Rillwater and heir to truths guarded by my family." Alistar met the Silver Prince's gaze steadily. "The maps of Lewarden's mahiy lines show significant changes between the slums and Lower City, where frost's breath has been integrated, and the areas of the city where it hasn't been introduced. Internal channelers have all come from those areas, and we have no record of people manifesting this ability before you began this experiment. That is not coincidence, Your Highness, and if the research team you have assigned to study frost's breath had even one human moderately knowledgeable in the Reyker or Heiset mythology, they would tell you it's dangerous to toy with gifts bestowed by the gods."

He knew from rumor that originally, the research team had included one such human. She had not just been removed from the project, she'd been dismissed from Silverline Power for her objections.

The vein in Prince Cero's forehead pulsed angrily. He kept his voice forcibly stiff and even. "We will… examine your concerns, Senior Engineer."

"Good. Please do so thoroughly." He refused to back down even in the face of his employer's anger. "Have you taken Lady Ravencrest into custody?"

One of the Royal Guards answered that question. "Yes sir, and her factories are currently being investigated. So far, we've only found evidence of unauthorized automaton creation in one of them."

There was more he wanted to know, but some questions didn't have answers, and other answers shouldn't be given.

"Will you be taking Prince Pietro back to the palace?"

"Yes, I… believe we should," King Suelton said. "I will not impose him upon you any longer."

"Soluthos Windshadow witnessed his confessions, as well as myself," Alistar added. *In case he tries to deny anything once he has his wits about him.*

"Very well. We will collect my nephew and take our leave, De'seneth." Prince Cero rose and offered King Suelton an arm to stand. With little flourish, the royals departed.

Rykka stood on the ballroom balcony. The last time she'd been on it, she'd been dragging Alistar away from Cemar and into a winter night. Today she was watching a string of carriages with the royal crest move up the drive and back onto the street, leaving the manor and taking the king, the Silver Prince, and Pietro away.

"Slee's Breath, I never thought I'd be *stopping* coups and attempts to kill the king. Hematic perdition…"

"Darkwood."

She looked over her shoulder. "Captain Roddek."

"Mind if I join you?"

"I don't mind." She nodded at the spacious balcony.

Roddek walked to the railing and leaned against it, looking over the grounds. The last of the carriages rolled out the gates, and he let out a sigh.

"Blood and sand, I'm glad they're finally gone. And I thought pirates could be pompous."

She raised an eyebrow at him. "Not very diplomatic, Captain."

"Father and Alistar handle land-based diplomacy. It's not for me. I'd rather be on a ship." He turned toward her. "Which is what I want to talk to you about."

She braced herself. "I'd rather be on a ship myself."

"Are you sure?" Roddek asked. "You know Lewarden well. You know where to look for trouble and what type of trouble is worth pursuing. You could be a lot of help to Alistar here."

"Captain, I truly hope Alistar doesn't *have* to deal with this sort of trouble again. Yeah, I know Lewarden, and I *know* I don't want to stay in the city." She met his gaze. "My skills are just as useful for a privateer as they are for a thief."

"I was prepared to hold everything you didn't tell me against you. But blackened shoals, you are damned good at what you do. I'm stubborn, but I'm not stupid enough to ignore everything you've done. I've heard… probably not everything, but everything Alistar and Saskia know about your work here. I'm willing to offer you a place on my *Conquest*. But," he held up a finger, "you won't be coming back at the same rank."

"I don't think my rank can get much lower than it was, unless you're demoting me to deck swab."

"You can decide for yourself whether it's a demotion or not. It's not a rank we normally have aboard a ship; more often found on the land-side hierarchy."

Rykka shifted uncertainly. "And... what rank is that, Captain?"

Roddek grinned. "Spymaster, of course."

She blinked. "What?"

"I'll take you back on my ship, and your rank will be Spymaster."

"But what would my duties be?" Her thoughts were spinning too fast to pin any others down.

"Same as any other sailor, most of the time. Until a situation requires your specialized skills." He grew more serious. "Darkwood, I mean it. You're not a bad sailor—need more experience, probably never going to be the best, but decent. But spy work, you are *very* good at. So, that's my offer. What do you say? Or if you need time to think about—"

"Yes. I say yes."

Roddek smiled and held out a hand to her. "Good. Welcome back aboard, Spymaster."

She clasped his hand. "Thank you, Captain." She felt a weight lift from her shoulders. *I'm going home.*

CHAPTER 60

Rarely did a royal wedding take place hastily. Even more rarely did one occur without pomp and festivities.

Rarer still was the royal wedding that took place with neither the bride nor the groom present.

"By my authority as sovereign of the nation of Calarand, blessed by the gods, faithful adherent to the Tenets and the Path, I, King Suelton Feyblade, tenth ruler upon the throne of Lewarden, declare the union of my eldest son, Filipp Feyblade, to Celyn Sunward, sole remaining heir of the Sunward family, in marriage." King Suelton read the declaration firmly and without emotion, gaze fixed on the pane of stained glass set high in the back wall of the Royal Family's private chapel. "Let their union bind them for the rest of their days." He lowered the scroll and stiffly turned away from the light. His fist clenched around the parchment and his lips moved in words to which he did not give voice. "And may those days not be long."

No applause filled the room, no cheers rang out, only grim silence.

Wind stirred the chapel chimes, clattering them together in dissonant cacophony. Alistar's eyes darted up to them, then returned to the aged monarch who stood, shoulders slumped and head bowed, before the altar.

After a long moment, Prince Cero rose and walked to his brother.

"Come, Suelton. There's work yet to be done."

"Yes. Yes, I know." King Suelton allowed himself to be led out of the chapel.

Only a handful of people attended the ceremony, and anyone witnessing them leaving the chapel might think they'd attended a funeral rather than a wedding. Alistar passed the new bride's adoptive parents, who sat stiffly at the back under the watch of the Royal Guard. They'd been put under house arrest since the ambush at the Exhibition—only two days so far, but their every move came under intense scrutiny. Even the most politically inept could conclude the Sunward family had come under royal disfavor.

Filipp, Pietro, and Sunward all resided in discomfort in separate cells in the dungeon. News of the princes' treason had not spread far yet.

"De'seneth, walk with us," Prince Cero ordered.

"Of course, Your Highness." Alistar approached, and the Royal Guards parted to allow him close to the royals. He hadn't expected to be summoned to witness the marriage by proxy that would legitimize Sunward's child, and now that it was complete, he wasn't sure what else Prince Cero wanted.

They walked through a wrought iron gate into an inner garden of the palace. Prince Cero spoke.

"We've been discussing the fates of the conspirators. Once the child is born, Filipp and Sunward will be executed. However, though Pietro took part in the conspiracy, and despite his attempt to assassinate his brother, he did not take part in the attack at the Exhibition. Because of that, His Majesty decided to grant Pietro some small measure of clemency."

Though the Silver Prince's expression and voice were steady, his eyes told Alistar he did not agree with the king's decision. "What manner of clemency?" Alistar asked.

"Exile," King Suelton said softly, voice trembling. "Upon pain of execution should he ever return to Calarand."

You both know the only reason he wasn't right there with Filipp is because he was my captive. "Have you decided where to send him?"

"Rillwater," Prince Cero said.

"What?" Alistar made no effort to stop the startled exclamation.

"To Rillwater," Prince Cero repeated. "With an escort who will accompany him from there, and whatever small supplies he's granted. We request simply that Admiral As'enel see Pietro safely to a destination of the admiral's choice."

Alistar blinked as the implications set in. "I... see. Do you *want* to know where he ends up?"

"I think it better that I do not," King Suelton answered. "We have people who will keep track of him, ensure he's not attempting to return or to undermine the kingdom from a distance. Beyond that, I want only to know that he lives."

"I'll speak to the admiral about it. How soon do you want this to happen?"

"Before the Exhibition. I don't want any visitors getting ideas about trying to release him," Prince Cero said. "Those envoys you delivered revealed that the princes were also attempting to make deals with pirates, and the Exhibition is bound to draw some such unsavory patrons."

"Your Highness, you know the admiral is at my home right now. Why don't you speak to him yourself?"

For the first time all day, the ghost of a smile found King Suelton's mouth. "Yes, brother, why don't you?"

Prince Cero scowled and didn't answer.

The king continued. "I'm sure it has nothing to do with having to acknowledge to him that you made an error."

"No, it does not," Prince Cero said tartly. "I simply thought it more expedient for De'seneth to pass the message to him, as he's already here."

"I will speak to the admiral, of course, but he'll still need to meet with you to discuss logistical details and payment," Alistar said.

Prince Cero's scowl deepened, but he didn't argue. "Of course. Thank you, De'seneth. That's all."

"Darkwood. A moment, if I may."

Rykka spun, startled to hear the voice of Investigator Dawncloud on the manor grounds. "I'm sorry, I didn't know you were here. What is it?"

With a wave, Dawncloud invited Rykka to walk with her. They strode down a garden path until they were far enough to speak privately.

"I owe you a great deal for your help during this investigation, and there's little I can do right now to repay it. There is one thing, however. When you first began working for the De'seneths, Windshadow asked me to look into you."

Rykka cocked her head curiously. "Didn't find much, I imagine."

"Not about Darkwood, certainly. I didn't bother looking up the ridiculous name you gave when we raided Whitetooth."

"So, are you here to ask who I am, or...?"

"No need. The surname was clearly fake. But then your brother arrived."

Tension crept up Rykka's spine.

"There've been a number of Tiyrons born in the Lower City. A number of Rykkas as well, but I only found one entry in the registry of a brother and sister within the right age range. Tiyron and Rykka Onyxflame."

Her pulse raced. "And?"

"And officially, Tiyron Onyxflame is dead, and Rykka Onyxflame is so little known that she's practically invisible. Does De'seneth know the truth?"

"Officially, Tiyron Onyxflame worked with Alistar De'seneth to uncover the plot and stop Cemar and his cabal. Officially, Tiyron Onyxflame died by dropping the ceiling of the Silver Prince's ballroom on himself and Cemar."

"So I read," Dawncloud agreed.

"At that time, my brother was held in stasis, moments from death because of Cemar's tortures, and had been for months. And at that time, De'seneth both knew my identity and that I can create barriers." She could endanger Alistar by admitting that, but Dawncloud had proven reasonable so far, and willing and able to look past the strict limits of the law when necessary.

"Well, it is certainly an interesting fluke that you and your brother share names with a notorious criminal, Darkwood. Despite that, thank you. You might not have acted for king and country, but you preserved them in the process. And if we have occasion to work together again, I welcome your expertise."

"I don't know that we will. I'm returning to the Rillwater fleet. But thanks."

Dawncloud nodded, then frowned slightly. "What is it the privateers say as a blessing? Storms take you? Always sounded more like a curse to me."

"That's because it's the shortened version," Rykka told her. "The full version is 'Seas guide your rudder, and may the storms ever take you home.' Storms take you as well, Dawncloud."

And for some of us, the storms are *home.*

EPILOGUE

EXCERPTED FROM THE FEYBLADE ASCENSION, THIRD EDITION

On the first day of the Grand Exhibition, His Royal Majesty King Suelton Feyblade opened the event with the announcement of the birth of his granddaughter and heir, Princess Yanina.

On the second day, while throngs of thousands celebrated the newborn princess, King Suelton attended the execution of his eldest son, the former crown prince Filipp Feyblade, and Filipp's wife, Celyn Sunward.

King Suelton never made another appearance at the Grand Exhibition.

ABOUT THE AUTHOR

Sanan Kolva is a technical editor by day, and writer of fantasy the rest of the time. She is the author of The Silverline Chronicles, the epic fantasy series The Chosen of the Spears, and the post apocalyptic fantasy Ghost and Guardian. Her short fiction appears in a number of anthologies. When not writing, she enjoys baking, leather working, battling the forces of evil in various video games, and appeasing her feline overlords. She can be found at https://sanankolva.com.

If you enjoy this book, please tell someone else who might like it or leave a review on your preferred platform.

9 789898 689520 8